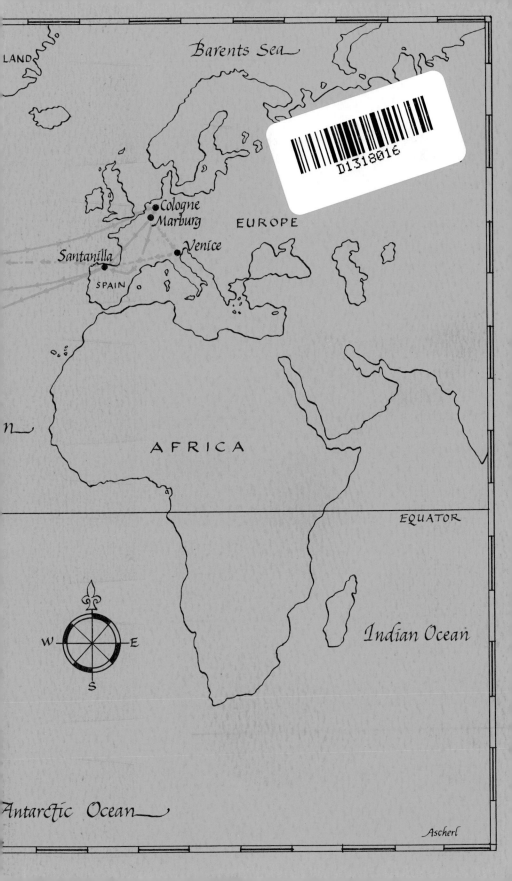

The Marburg Chronicles

OTHER BOOKS BY ALFRED COPPEL

The Burning Mountain
The Apocalypse Brigade
The Hastings Conspiracy
The Dragon
Thirty-four East
The Landlocked Man

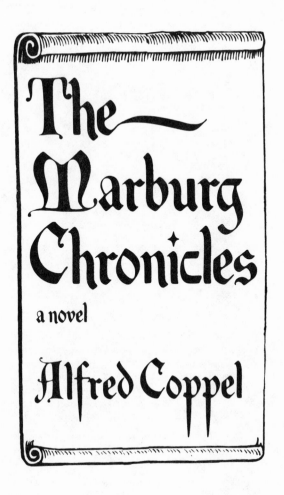

The Marburg Chronicles

a novel

Alfred Coppel

A William Abrahams Book
E. P. DUTTON

Published in the United States by
E. P. Dutton, Inc. 2 Park Avenue, New York, N.Y. 10016
"A William Abrahams Book"

Library of Congress Cataloging in Publication Data
Coppel, Alfred
The Marburg chronicles
"A William Abrahams book."
I. Title
PS3553.064M3   1985   813'.54   85-1604

ISBN: 0-525-24309-7

Published simultaneously in Canada by
Fitzhenry and Whiteside Ltd.

DESIGNED BY MARK O'CONNOR

COBE

10 9 8 7 6 5 4 3 2 1
First Edition

For Elisabeth and Jessamyn,
who for twenty years
said that I should write this book.
And for Billy Abrahams—
who said the time is now.

"Las Parcas nos mandan . . . the Fates command us."

—*Old Spanish proverb*

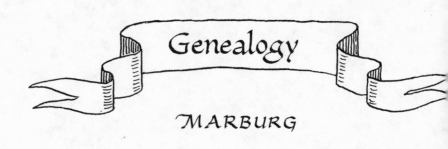

Genealogy

MARBURG

Isaac Marburg
b. 1799

Sarai Leyden —— m. 1841 —— Micah Marburg —————— m
b. 1816   b. 1815

5 Stillborn children   Cecilia Mar
                                                        b. 1864

Julia Marini —— m. 1872 —— Aaron Marburg
b. 1848   b. 1843

Marina Marburg   Miguel Marburg   Caridad Marburg   Alex Marbi
b. 1873   b. 1876 d. 1877   b. 1879   b. 1881

Maria-Elena Alvarez —— m
b. 1863

Marianna Marb
b. 1881

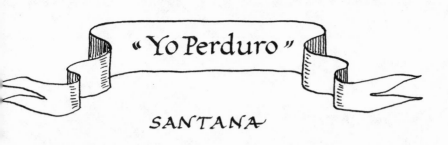

"Yo Perduro"

SANTANA

Alvaro Santana —— m.1830 —María Isabella Borjas
b. 1801   b. 1810

| go Santana | Alfonso Santana | Alfredo & Guillermo Santana |
| b. 1836 | b. 1839 | (died in infancy) |

—— Adriana Santana
b. 1840

Julio Santana — m.1882 —Soledad Segre
b. 1837   b. 1839

o Marburg — m.1888 —Ana-María Gomez
b.1861   b. 1861

| Marburg | Esteban Marburg | Miguel Marburg |
| 888 | b. 1889 | b. 1891 |

| antana | Clara Santana | Caridad Santana | Milagro Santana |
| 871 | b. 1872 | b. 1875 | b. 1890 |

ONE

1860

Mounted on a cobby gray gelding, one of the least desirable beasts from the Hacienda Santanilla herd, old Lopez clattered through the outskirts of Santander in the predawn dark. A letter had arrived for Don Miguel from his brother in Germany, and Lopez, as senior servant remaining in the townhouse, had selected himself to carry it the twenty kilometers to Santanilla.

Though it was already November, the province of Old Castile baked daily in the heat carried from Africa by the *khamsin.* The oppressive morning darkness promised another scorching day. Lopez's wife Amalia was certain he had decided to ride to Santanilla himself in order to escape Mass in the sweltering church in Santander. She was right. Lopez was a Castilian, born on Santanilla, the Santana hacienda in the foothills of the Sierra Cantabrica. He had never reconciled himself to living in the town. He disliked it most in late fall, when the south wind blew and Santander stewed in its sweat and harbor stinks. He had accepted the post at the Santana townhouse because El Patron, Don Alvaro, wished it. Lopez, like all the Santanilla *peones,* had spent his lifetime doing what El Patron wished.

The cobblestones gave way to the unpaved surface of a country road. Poplar trees, planted before Lopez was born, lined the road, tall presences against the pale stars. There was barely a hint of dawn in the eastern sky, but the wind was rising, smelling of warm earth and dry grasses.

The gelding was an unwilling nag and Lopez urged him into a sullen canter. If possible, he wished to arrive at Santanilla before Mass so that he could deliver his letter and be gone before he found himself trapped into enduring one of Father Sebastio's droning homilies in the family chapel. Don Alvaro's wife, Doña Maria, tiny tyrant that she was, insisted that all the household servants attend Mass whenever they happened to be on the estate on a Sunday. If he could escape that, Lopez thought, he could return in a leisurely manner by way of Liencres or La Horca Francesa and stop for a sherry or a glass of *aguardiente,* the local, fiery brandy. In the course of a long life, Lopez had developed loitering to a fine art, and since Doña Adriana had married Don Miguel Marburg, even the household servants had a bit of pocket money to spend. Amalia would berate him if he arrived home at dusk, but that was something to which Lopez had long ago become accustomed. Don Miguel and Doña Adriana were staying at Santanilla until her baby was born, and the townhouse was, for a time, the domain of the servants.

Old Lopez was still undecided about Doña Adriana's marriage to Don Miguel. The servants and tenants on the hacienda gossiped about it endlessly, but after a year and a half they had still come to no conclusion. Don Miguel Marburg was the factor, agent, and representative of the Marburg Bank for all Spain, and therefore a man of consequence. Lopez, who like many of the Santana family retainers could neither read nor write, envisioned the Marburg Bank as a feudal fortress filled with money on the banks of some distant German river. He did not know what a bank did or how it did it, but in some mysterious way the Marburg Bank had refurbished the fortunes of Santanilla and its dependents. The female Santanilleñas said that he was a gloriously handsome man, and that it was no wonder the only daughter of Don Alvaro and Doña Maria had fallen in love with him. Lopez grudgingly agreed that he was handsome—in a foreign way. He was a fair man to work for, though lacking the warmth, Lopez thought, of the Spanish character. He had renewed and improved the Santana townhouse in Santander and he treated his young wife with respect and generosity.

All of these things, weighed in the balance, stood in Don Miguel's favor.

Against him, other things had to be thrown onto the scales.

He was a foreigner, a Hessian (which Lopez now knew was a sort of German). He was a widower with a son almost as old as Doña Adriana. He was a poor horseman. And, most unfortunately, he was a *Marrano,* a Jew converted to Catholicism. Amalia found it romantic that he had accepted the True Faith in order to marry Doña Adriana.

That was as may be, thought Lopez, but didn't the Church teach that the Jews were a perfidious race who had killed Christ? Of course, it was for Don Alvaro Santana, El Patron of Santanilla, to judge the propriety of marrying his only legitimate female child to Don Miguel Marburg, but the Santanilleños and the people of the district worried the situation like sheepdogs gnawing at a succulent bone. It was to be expected. Such a thing had not happened in living memory.

The sky had changed from dusty blue to gray when Lopez left the main road and turned toward the foothills of the Sierra Cantabrica. The poplar trees and the planted fields were left behind as the sulky gelding and his rider followed the narrow road into the eroded hills above the narrow coastal plain. Behind them lay the sea and the villages clustered about the bay of Santander. Ahead lay a rolling emptiness of meager grasslands and dry creekbeds. The haciendas in this part of the province were vast, but the land was poor, suitable only to running sheep. The Santanas ran flocks on their holding, but the greatest effort was expended on the horse herd that grazed on the upland meadows of the Cantabrica. The horses had never been able to subsist on the natural grasses; the land was too poor for that. But Don Alvaro persisted, supplementing the sparse feed with oat hay and alfalfa bought from the small-holders of the marginally more fertile coastal shelf.

As the first sliver of sun climbed above the horizon, Lopez stopped to drink a mouthful of wine from the leather *bota* slung at his saddle-bow. Two hours of riding had brought him little more than halfway from Santander to Santanilla. Some small distance ahead of him stood the rock cairn that marked the northernmost boundary of the hacienda. He had a full hour's ride still to the main gate. As far as the eye could see, the brown land lay in folds, bare of topsoil and burned by the long summer's sun to an almost desert sterility. A few scrub oaks struggled to survive on the flanks of the dry watercourses that were filled only by the flash floods of winter.

The old man swallowed the thin wine and replaced the *bota* on his saddle. The rising sun already burned his grizzled face. The day would be warm, though perhaps not so windy as yesterday, he thought.

He shifted his bony buttocks on the saddle and drew the dry air into his lungs. This was far better than the town. He hated living in Santander, but El Patron had assigned him to Doña Adriana's household, and there he would remain until El Patron or death released him. All the servants at the townhouse were from families living on Santanilla. Lopez did not hold with the townsmen's practice of hiring strangers.

He kicked the gelding into motion and passed the rock cairn. A spike bearing a wrought iron S rose from the stones. The moment he had passed the marker, Lopez felt at home.

From far to the north, on the edge of the sea, he could hear the wail of a train whistle. He did not turn to look. Lopez did not approve of the new railroad connecting Santander with Bilbao and Gijón. If God had meant for men to travel at thirty kilometers an hour, He would have given them longer legs or made swifter horses. Nothing good came into the district on iron rails that carried hissing, clattering steam trains, or into the harbor of Santander in noisome, smoke-belching ships with ugly wheels, like those found at millponds, on their rusty iron sides. Young Aaron Marburg, Don Miguel's son, had once told Lopez that it was now possible to travel all the way across Spain, from Santander to Seville, on the railroad and that this vast journey could be accomplished in less than seven days. If the young gentleman said it, it must be true. But Lopez, who had never in his life traveled outside these dry hills, found it difficult to believe. Still, Don Miguel and his son had come to Santanilla from Germany, to Lopez a place as distant as the moon, so Don Aaron must know whereof he spoke.

The boy was personable, Lopez thought, though suffering like his father the fault of not being Spanish. For the last six months he had been living at the *hacienda* acting as treasurer and bursar for the estate. Doña Adriana's brothers, nasty young brutes that they were, treated him badly. All the servants said so. But then, they treated everyone badly. It was their privilege, as principal heirs to Santanilla.

The sun grew hotter as it climbed into a white, empty sky. Over the next range of hills the black buzzards called *zopilotes* circled. That meant a sheep was down. This long season of heat, stretching into November, had been hard on the animals on the haciendas that ringed Santander in a great arc. Altamira had lost two dozen head of cattle. Miraflores, to the west, had borne even heavier losses. By contrast, Santanilla had done well. Perhaps the coming of the Jews had been a secret blessing. Father Sebastio said that Our Lord Jesus had been born a Jew—though Lopez found this hard to believe.

From the gate of Santanilla, a Roman arch of whitewashed mud brick from which hung another wrought iron S, Lopez could see the dusty red-tiled roofs of the great house, a sprawling single-story structure of thirty rooms and more, and the scattered outbuildings: barns, barracks for the seasonal herdsmen, woolshacks, stables, and kitchens. Sited near the main house, known as La Casa, but on slightly higher ground, stood El Patron's mysterious observatory. Lopez had never been inside this strange building with the movable panels on the roof. Amalia said that El Patron cast horoscopes there, though Lopez found this as hard to believe as Aaron's tale about crossing Spain in seven days. But whatever El Patron did in that odd building, and even though it had to do with looking at the stars, Lopez was certain that it was nothing forbidden by Mother Church. Don Alvaro was a religious man.

The small stone church where Father Sebastio, the Santana's chaplain, celebrated the Mass, stood in a fold of ground invisible from the gate.

Lopez looked at the height of the sun and sighed. The gelding had not served him well. The family and the servants would be in church and he would be expected to join them. Unless he could manage to delay longer.

He slouched in the saddle and let the horse set his own pace, stopping from time to time to crop of the sparse roadside grasses. Lopez gave himself the last of the wine in the *bota*. If he could not stop at La Horca on the return journey, he could at least replenish the *bota* from the kitchens.

Another half hour, he estimated, would bring him to the church. If he could stretch that to forty minutes, he could still manage to miss Father Sebastio's tedious homily.

That was not the best solution, but it would have to do.

"Orate pro nobis nunc et in hora mortis nostrae."

Adriana Ana-Maria de Marburg y Santana listened to the old priest with somnolent inattention. It was suffocatingly hot in the church. Candle flames and the press of human bodies raised the temperature already elevated by the burning sun on the tiled roof.

The child in her womb stirred and she placed a hand on her belly, fascinated by the activity of the new life within her. It would be a son. That was a foregone conclusion. All the Santana women's firstborn

8

were males. She half-closed her eyes and made an effort to concentrate on the Mass. It was useless. Her attention wandered. Behind her she could hear the soft shuffling of the servants. On her right sat Doña Maria, her back like a ramrod wrapped in black taffeta, her thin white hands holding her rosary. Miguel had once asked how it was possible that the tiny, dark Doña Maria could have produced such a daughter as Adriana. And El Patron, angry with his wife, as he often was, had said: "The same way night produces day." Adriana was slender as her mother, but there the resemblance ended. Doña Maria was dark, with black eyes and hair like jet. Adriana was all silver and gold, like the sunlight.

She glanced at Miguel, sitting beside her. She often wondered what he, as a *converso,* actually felt for the Mass. One could not know from his expression. His long, handsome face was composed.

Adriana could not look at her husband without feeling pleasure. Their marriage was her personal triumph. With an assist from her father, of course; she was willing to concede that.

She had first seen Miguel—his name had been Micah then—as she stepped into the bright Venetian sunshine of the Piazza San Marco. Was it only three years ago?

She had emerged from the basilica with Doña Maria and Felicia, her maid. Her father, Don Alvaro, had materialized out of the throng of people in the square, and with him had been this tall, handsome man, the banker El Patron had come to Venice to see. Micah Marburg.

Doña Maria had been cold to him because he was a Jew.

But Adriana, barely seventeen then, had decided that very day that she would have him. It did not matter to her that he was a widower, that he had a son near to her own age, or that he was not of her faith. The upbringing Adriana Santana had received from her father (despite all her mother's objections and complaints) contrived, in that single day, to change her life forever.

She had changed Micah Marburg's life even more.

She considered that fact as she sat beside her husband in the dim stone church where her ancestors had worshipped for two hundred years.

She had taken a Jew and turned him into a Catholic, a Hessian banker and transformed him into a passionate husband and lover. But it had not been easy. The quarrels with her mother had been bitter, and her father's consent had come hard, despite his liberalism.

Don Alvaro had an innate prejudice against Germans. He was fond of quoting the Holy Roman Emperor, Charles V, who said: "I

9

speak Spanish to God, Italian to women, French to men, and German to my horse."

In the sweltering heat of the small church she smiled enigmatically as she remembered a freezing winter night not long after the family's return from their eventful sojourn in Venice.

Adriana had spent most of a gusty, cold afternoon in a long and stubborn argument with Doña Maria, who had been aghast at her announcement that she intended to marry Micah Marburg. Don Alvaro had retreated to the privacy of the observatory and there he had remained, having his *cena* brought to him by one of the *mozos,* who returned with the message that El Patron did not wish to be disturbed.

Adriana had retired in a fury. Doña Maria's objections to Micah Marburg as a possible son-in-law had been stated with embellishments that had aroused Adriana to a combative rage.

But Adriana was her father's daughter, Spanish to her fingertips. She was young, aroused, determined, and in fighting trim. She already had a developed instinct for seizing the initiative at the critical moment in any conflict.

She lay sleepless in her great bed, measuring the obstacles she must overcome before Micah Marburg could become her husband. There was the matter of religion. That posed no great problem. Micah, besotted with this young Spanish beauty, was scarcely a Jew at all. He had promised willingly to embrace the Church. There was the question of his age. Adriana had swiftly decided to overlook it. After all, it was common practice in her world for girls barely past puberty to marry mature men. Nor did it concern her that Micah had a son but three years her junior. That was a matter of no consequence. She would charm young Aaron once she had what she wanted and could take the time to win him. Her mother's objections were purely and simply instinctive prejudice. Doña Maria was a reactionary both by breeding and by natural inclination. She had the ability to infuriate, but not to command Adriana's obedience. Don Alvaro had not raised his favorite child to be overborne, even by a daughter of the aristocratic Borjas.

The key to success, Adriana thought, staring wide-eyed at the shadowed beams across the ceiling of her room, was Don Alvaro's agreement. She had put his liberalism to a severe test by informing him that she intended to marry this German banker, and he, manlike, had decided to avoid making a decision in the hope that she might change her mind.

You should know me better than that, Papa, she thought. You, of all people. Allowing Doña Maria to rant against the match was pure subterfuge. The decision would be made by father and daughter. As it should be, Adriana thought. And the moment is now.

She threw back the heavy quilts that covered her and swung her bare feet to the icy tiled floor. She struck a *cerillo* and lighted the oil lamp on her bedstand. The flame flickered in the drafts. In the next room Felicia slept on her pallet, snoring slightly. It irritated Adriana that Feli should be sleeping so soundly while she had lain awake and restless. She considered waking her but decided against it.

She found her dressing gown in the great carved wardrobe and put it over her nightdress. Over that she threw a sheepskin coat she sometimes used while riding. In the light from the lamp she could see her reflection in the pier glass. Her hair hung to her waist, her face was pale. She looked distrait. As she should, she thought. Good. The hour of decision was upon the only two Santanas who counted in this matter.

She took the lamp and stepped out into the open gallery. The wind almost extinguished the light, but she guarded it with a hand. The shrubs and trees in the patio garden lashed the whitewashed stones. The sky was stark and crystal-clear, with the winter constellations bright in the moonless night. El Patron, she thought firmly, would soon be brought back to earth from his contemplation of the heavenly bodies.

She walked swiftly through the gallery and onto the stone path leading to the observatory. Her feet were nearly frozen. In her preoccupation she had forgotten to put on shoes. Well, let it be so.

The roof panels on the observatory were open and through a narrow window she could see the tiny red light of the altar lamp her father used to safeguard his night vision.

She marched to the door and pushed it ajar without knocking. Her father sat at the telescope, a huge shape in the darkness. The frigid wind rustled the papers and open books scattered about on the worktables.

"It's Ana, Papa," she said.

Don Alvaro sighed and sat back. "I have been expecting you, *hija*. Close the door."

He came to her and took the lamp. "You are like ice," he said. He guided her to a chair and from a chest took a heavy woolen blanket. "Wrap this around you." When she had done as he bade her, he asked ruefully, "Did you quarrel all through dinner?"

"We did," Adriana said.

"Don't blame La Patrona, *hija*. She doesn't mean half of what she says."

"I don't blame Mama, Patron," Adriana said firmly. "I blame you."

In the red light Adriana could not see her father's face clearly, but she knew him well enough to know that he was frowning. "That is unfair, Ana," he said. "We want what is best for you."

"I can understand Mama," Adriana said. "Everything she knows she was taught by the sisters of St. Theresa. The Borjas family is still living in the fifteenth century. But you, Papa, you know better. Why haven't you spoken for me?"

Adriana could hear the discomfort in his tone: the conflict that always seemed to arise when a liberal was brought face to face with the consequences of the ideas he claimed to believe. She said, "Haven't you always taught me that a man should be judged by how he lives rather than by what he was born?"

"As you grow older, Ana, you may find that it becomes more and more difficult to be certain about that," Don Alvaro said. "And in this particular case it may be that you have not given enough thought to the problems you are creating for yourself."

"You make it sound as though I were still a child, Patron," Adriana said. "I am not."

"I want only your happiness, daughter," Don Alvaro said.

"I love him, Papa."

"I do not trouble myself that he is a Jew, Ana. *Marranos* are part of our history—"

"I love him, Papa," she said again.

"He is twice your age, Ana."

"Aren't you listening to me, Papa? I *love* him."

"He is a German, Ana. Life would be hard for him here."

"Don't tell me again how Charles V spoke German only to his horse, Papa."

It was the right thing to say. When he spoke again she could hear the amusement in his voice and she knew that her battle was won, that he intended all along that she should have her man.

"I like Micah, daughter. I hope you didn't tell him about the Emperor Charles. Germans are not known for their sense of humor."

"Well, Papa," Adriana said. "I won't tell him if you do not." She shivered and said, "It is freezing in here."

Don Alvaro went to a table and poured a glass of *aguardiente* for her. "If this is going to be a long discussion, you had better drink this."

"There is really no need for a long discussion," Adriana said. But she took the glass and sipped at the fiery brandy.

"It is arranged, Papa," she said. "Micah will become agent for his bank in Spain. He is already taking religious instruction. But it must be settled among *us*. I want your blessing."

12

"You *will* make me face the dragon."

"Mama is a very small dragon," Adriana said.

"What have I done?" Don Alvaro murmured. "I have created a new kind of woman. I think you frighten me a little, *hija.*"

Adriana stood and settled into his lap with her brow on his cheek. "God created me, Papa. You simply taught me to think for myself. And the only woman on earth who frightens you is Mama. And she not enough to matter."

A small smile played over her lips now in the sweltering church as she remembered that late-night talk.

Father Sebastio stumbled on through the liturgy in his badly pronounced Latin until he reached a final, rusty "Amen." Miguel glanced questioningly at Adriana, concerned for her comfort. She shook her head to reassure him and fingered her rosary. We pray to the Virgin, she thought, because God is a male and needs to be gentled. Only a woman can do that.

Aaron Marburg watched as the Spanish "cousins," impatient to go whoring, made the sign of the cross and jostled one another to get to the altar rail to take Communion.

His father knelt beside them.

A Hessian Jew, Aaron thought. Shoulder to shoulder with the ancient enemy. How very strange life had become for the Marburgs in the last two years.

Adriana walked by him, the heavy silk of her dress rustling, her body swollen with Micah Marburg's child. My half-brother-to-be, Aaron thought. No one at Santanilla even considered the possibility that it might be a girl.

The heat in the hacienda's chapel was oppressive. Even stone walls two feet thick failed to blunt the dagger of the Spanish sun. The stained-glass window above the altar burned with color. Beneath it, an insipid plaster Christ hung nailed to a gilded cross, painted blood on His hands, feet, side, and brows. The image had soft auburn hair and blue eyes lifted to Heaven in banal forgiveness. If He ever really lived, Aaron thought, He most certainly had not looked like *that.* At his feet, according to Father Sebastio's rustic dogma, ghostly Roman legionnaires, damned for all eternity, cast invisible dice for His garments. Aaron stared at the gentile face and thought: "Tell them You are a Jew, Yeshua bar Joseph."

Don Alvaro Santana looked at Aaron with his customary bafflement as he lumbered by. It troubled him that Aaron still refused to partake of the Body and Blood of Our Lord.

The patriarch of Santanilla was a large man, thick through the chest, ruddy and balding, with deep-set black eyes. At his side Doña Maria, a funereal doll in black, showed her displeasure by keeping her stiff, narrow back turned toward the son of her son-in-law.

The household servants trooped behind the family to accept their salvation in order of precedence. One of the kitchen girls smiled shyly at Aaron. He hoped that Adriana had not seen. It disquieted him when Adriana—Ana, the family called her—chaffed him about how attractive the younger *criadas* found him. Lately he had been obsessed by thoughts of Adriana. Her pregnancy made him uneasy.

Incense and candles filled the church with the odor of holiness— Adriana, laughing, called it that. Her bright presence was the only thing that made his compulsory attendance at the Mass bearable.

Micah followed his young wife from the Communion rail toward the door, beyond which the white sunlight burned like a furnace.

Aaron looked defiantly at his father. Micah met his gaze and frowned. The quarrel was already old between them. But Ana gave Aaron a generous smile. Accustomed to having her way in all things, Adriana Marburg was convinced that Aaron would eventually, as his father had done, accept baptism. At her command Father Sebastio spent hours upon hours instructing Aaron in the true religion. But Aaron remained unconverted.

In moments of introspection, Aaron found his reluctance difficult to explain. The Marburgs had never been observant Jews. Micah and his brother and partner Isaac had always been secular men. Their interests were centered on business rather than on religion, on the bank they had founded in the Hessian town from which their branch of the family took its name.

Yet on the day the Bishop of Liencres had sprinkled the holy water on Micah's head and changed his name to Miguel, Aaron had felt a surprising stab of humiliation. His German tutors had taught him about the Spanish *Marranos.* Some, they said, had been sincere. Some had dissembled. But all had been threatened with the fire. Until his father had become a *converso,* those Jews had been only a historical curiosity to Aaron. But as the water dampened Micah's dark head, Aaron had heard within himself an echo of the cries of lamentation uttered by those ancient Sephardim forced by the Inquisition to convert or burn.

Obduracy became a matter of inward, personal honor. He attended the Mass because he must, and because Adriana wished it. But he refused to become a Catholic, embarrassing his father, irritating

14

Doña Maria, puzzling Don Alvaro, and providing his stepmother with a sense of mission.

Until he was fourteen, Aaron Marburg had lived in a large, gloomy house on the banks of the Lahn. He was educated to become a banker. He was physically and psychologically attuned to German life: disciplined, orderly, and certain. He was accustomed to living on the green land of the Hessian plain, to seasonal changes, to *civilization*. All of that changed when his father accepted the task of representing the Marburg Bank in Spain. And it had vanished irretrievably when Micah Marburg became Don Miguel Marburg in order to wed the daughter of the hacendado of Santanilla.

Aaron now found himself transplanted into a harsh landscape surrounded by new relations, only one of whom, Adriana, seemed to care what became of him.

Her three brothers, Santiago, Julio, and Alfonso, despised him—a sentiment he heartily reciprocated. The brothers Santana were arrogant louts, half-educated spendthrifts who wasted Don Alvaro's money and amused themselves by mistreating women, gambling, and bullying anyone who permitted them to do so. Adriana, loyal to her family though she was, almost certainly shared Aaron's opinion of her brothers.

Adriana had once, while riding, caught Julio in the act of forcing one of the herdsmen's daughters. Furious, she had laid her riding crop across her brother's bare buttocks to such effect that he still bore the scars. Aaron had seen them.

Aaron now watched the brothers make their sketchy genuflections and rush out into the blaze of morning. Doña Maria would expect them to take the Sunday midday meal with the family, but by the time she left the church on Don Alvaro's arm, they would have mounted their horses and escaped. The remainder of the family would pay for their defection. Doña Maria more than made up in temper what she lacked in size.

Aaron, last to leave, acknowledged a surly greeting from Father Sebastio. The priest had received his religious education in a Dominican country seminary and many of his notions of Catholic dogma were sketchy. But Spanish priests were better known for discipline than for learning. When Father Sebastio looked at Aaron Marburg he saw a young man destined to burn in hell unless he accepted baptism. Sebastio took this as a personal affront. He had spent most of his life as chaplain to the Santanas. Aaron was a Santana by marriage, and in all the years of Sebastio's tenure at Santanilla, no Santana had ever died unbaptized. He did not intend to blemish that record now.

Outside the church the sun was brutal. The oaks and cypresses cast hard black shadows. Grooms held the horses hitched to El Patron's French landau and Micah's American buggy. Adriana, seated in the buggy next to her maid, Felicia, watched as her brothers mounted their horses and cantered off in the direction of Liencres.

Old Lopez, the townhouse *mozo,* had appeared and was speaking to Micah and Don Alvaro while Doña Maria sat impatiently in the landau.

The appearance of Lopez must mean that a letter had arrived in Santander for Don Miguel. This set Adriana's inquisitive mind to work immediately. She had an active interest in all that her husband did. It still seemed to shock him whenever she displayed it: traditionally, the intricacies of banking and finance were not for women. But he told her, at first only to humor her; then, impressed by her understanding, because he valued her opinions.

Adriana was now twenty years old, half her husband's age. She had pale, clear skin that never reddened in the sun, hair the color of ripening wheat, and sea blue eyes (a legacy from some roving Vandal ancestor, Miguel said).

Even as a child she had been the talk of the district. To begin, she was the daughter of a liberal—or what passed for a liberal in royalist, Catholic Spain. All of Don Alvaro José Esteban Santana y Avila's children had been reared indulgently, with much personal freedom. His sons had taken El Patron's modern notions for license, running wild and ignoring the educational opportunities he offered them. Doña Maria, who loved her husband but thought him a dangerous radical, had tried to prevent his experimenting on Adriana. She failed utterly. Don Alvaro was not a man who gave up easily.

He delighted in Adriana's quick intelligence and high spirits. At the age of seven, when a girl of her class would have been given to the sisters of some convent to train, Don Alvaro undertook his daughter's education himself. To the amazed dismay of the local gentry, who knew that women's concerns should be limited to religion and childbearing, Adriana Santana y Borjas had been tutored in languages (she now spoke French, German, and English in addition to her native Spanish), in mathematics, science, history, and—of all subjects most subversive to the female mind—politics.

Ever annoyed at having her daughter effectively stolen from her

16

and reared in this outlandish way, Doña Maria, a daughter of the aristocratic Borjas family of Liencres (and a convinced reactionary) often berated her husband with remarks such as, "And you see, you wicked man, where all this liberality and education has brought her. To marriage with a Jew." Doña Maria Isabella de Santana y Borjas had accepted Miguel Marburg as a Catholic because Holy Church said that she must. But she saw no reason to be gracious about it.

Alvaro Santana had ridden out with General Baldomero Espartero in the Carlist War, fighting to drive the Bourbon Pretender, Don Carlos, across the Pyrenees into France.

The campaign had made Espartero a hero. Isabella II's mother, the Regent Cristina, had given him the grandiloquent title of Duke of Victory. But soon Iberian fractiousness had begun again to disturb the peace, and the hero (in the name of law and order) became the oppressor.

Alvaro, along with other liberals among the gentry, had turned against him, driving the great Duke to follow Don Carlos into French exile. And when, in the natural turmoil and chronic reversal of Spanish politics, Espartero was forgiven his excesses and recalled by the Regent to form still another government of military men with General O'Donnell, Alvaro Santana found himself among the outs and plagued with an endless succession of fines, lawsuits, quarrels, and persecutions. The wealth of the Santana family, once considerable, was now reduced to the three thousand hectares of Santanilla itself, the livestock on the hacienda, and an ancient (and legally tangled) royal land grant in California no living member of the family had ever seen or expected to see, now that Alta California had been stolen by the Americans.

Micah Marburg had come into the lives of the Santanas as money-lender and savior. By an act of will, Adriana had seen to it that he remained as a *converso* and son-in-law to the hacendado of Santanilla.

The wedding, which had taken place in the very stone church outside which Adriana now waited for her husband, had been the most gossiped about event of the season. The local gentry had been scandalized, but they had attended *en masse,* cowed by the Santanas' exalted social position and hoping, perhaps, to find that Adriana's new husband was unworthy of her. Adriana, angelic in virginal white, had surveyed the assembly with enormous satisfaction as their hopes were dashed. Miguel Marburg was easily the handsomest man in the district, and so obviously in love with his young bride that Adriana's peers wept with envy.

Detractors of Don Alvaro muttered that he had sold his daughter to the Jews for money. Only one had ever made the mistake of saying it in his presence. El Patron had broken a silver-headed cane over the unfortunate man's head.

The accusation was, in fact, totally untrue. Don Alvaro Santana was an often angry, impulsive, violent, and overbearing man, but his liberalism was as genuine as his love for his daughter. Once the shock of Adriana's choice had worn off, he had accepted Micah Marburg willingly as a son-in-law. He swiftly came to believe that his daughter's choice had been his. Certainly Miguel was more intelligent and energetic than any of the eligible young *machos* of the district. Given her upbringing, Don Alvaro thought proudly, what could be more natural than for Adriana to love an educated, cosmopolitan man rather than some callow, arrogant hacendado's son. That Micah Marburg's bank held mortgages on Santanilla was a matter for the local gossips. Don Alvaro dismissed it as unimportant.

Adriana, shaded by the buggy's hood, watched her husband and father with affection as they stood in the road, deep in conversation. Young Aaron had emerged from the church and stood near the older men, listening but not joining the discussion.

It troubled Adriana that Miguel was so resentful of his son's recalcitrance in the matter of baptism. She was fond of Aaron—a young man who closely resembled his father and who was growing into an appealing manhood. Before her pregnancy began to restrict her activities, Adriana often rode with Aaron. He had a talent for horsemanship that delighted her, and a quick intelligence that accommodated itself easily to her own. The girls of the district were beginning to notice her stepson, and well they might, she thought possessively. Except for his fairer skin, light eyes, and coppery hair, he was a younger version of her beloved Miguel.

El Patron had grown as fond of Aaron as she was herself. Her father, Adriana thought, could be an intimidating man, but recently, since Aaron had come to work at Santanilla, the boy's reserve had been diminishing under the rough regard of the hacendado.

Adriana knew that her brothers resented the troubles Don Alvaro had brought upon the Santanas with his political activities—activities she never failed to defend. Privately, she was saddened that he had been forced into a kind of unwilling retirement. But one did not ever completely retire so active a mind as Don Alvaro's. Warned by the authorities that further political activity might finish the Santanas, he had turned to science. He had an observatory built adjacent to La Casa, equipping it with the first (and possibly the only) Fraunhofer telescope in Spain—an eight-inch refractor driven by an ingenious clockwork of his own devising. He ignored Doña Maria's complaints about the expense involved, and to the observatory and the contemplation of the stars he would retreat whenever her temper tantrums drove him from their bedroom.

He shared his enjoyment of astronomy with Adriana as he had shared most of his enthusiasms. "Only you, Ana, of all the family, have the intelligence to know that the universe is in ferment—that things must always change," he often told her. Progress and change obsessed him. Adriana suspected that he had acquiesced in her marriage because it represented change. Spain exasperated him with its determination to cling to the past. "History has always beckoned to our country," he once told her. "Why do we persist in looking away? Many of the grandest families in Spain have the blood of *Marranos* in their veins. This is nothing to be ashamed of, Ana. It is progress." He liked to say—though to her alone—that Spaniards had an inborn taste for political anarchy, bloody revolution, personal tragedy, and death. "Jews, on the other hand," he said, "are survivors, the products of two thousand years of breeding for cleverness. An infusion of *Marranía* may be the salvation of the Santanas." It did not distress Don Alvaro one bit that he would soon have a grandson who was half *Marrano*.

Adriana felt a lusty kick in her belly that made her catch her breath.

"Doña Ana, what is it?" Felicia, a plump Asturian girl, fanned Adriana nervously. "You should not have to sit here in the heat while the *señores* argue."

"They are not arguing, Feli. Be still," Adriana said.

"Doña Ana, they are arguing about the American visitor. I am certain of it."

"Don't *you* argue with me, Feli. And stop fussing. I am perfectly comfortable."

Aaron was watching her. He left his father and Don Alvaro and walked to the buggy. "Are you all right, Ana?"

Adriana was aware that Miguel's first wife, whose name had been Sarai, had tried repeatedly to bear him a second son. There had been five miscarriages, and the last had killed her. Aaron had been only nine when she died, but he had been in the house to hear the poor woman's screaming. Now anything relating to pregnancy tended to make him uneasy. He looked up at his stepmother with touching concern. It was at such times he most resembled a child, Adriana thought, rather than a young man only three years younger than she.

"Should you be out in the sun like this?" he asked.

"That is what I asked her, Don Aaron," Felicia said self-righteously. "Heat is very bad for the baby."

"Be quiet, Feli," Adriana said. "And don't you begin, *hijito*. Castileñas thrive on the sun. We are born to it. Come sit with me until your father comes." She patted the seat beside her and Aaron climbed into the buggy.

"Did the Mass move you?" Adriana asked. "Or was it bad again today?" She knew how very irksome he found his required attendance at Sunday Mass.

"I am getting used to it," Aaron said noncommittally.

"Open your heart," Adriana advised. "Father Sebastio will help you."

"Sebastio is always angry with me," Aaron said grimly. "He thinks me stubborn."

Adriana's laughter was clear as birdsong. "Where could he get such an idea?"

Aaron managed a grudging smile. "Where, indeed?"

"El Patron says he should take a stick to you. That's the way *he* was taught religion."

Aaron considered that statement as having been made only half in jest. Perhaps that was the only way he would ever absorb sufficient holiness to please the Santanas. Even the Jewishness he was born to had never really taken hold of him—though that was as much his father's doing as his own. When the Marburgs lived in Germany, Micah had been one of the most assimilated in the Jewish community. He had always found Mosaic laws and customs oppressive. Aaron had not been bar-mitzvahed because at the appointed time Micah had been embroiled in some petty quarrel with the Chief Rabbi of Hessen. Many of the more orthodox Jews in Marburg am Lahn said that it was Micah's refusal to be observant rather than her inability to bear a second living child that had killed Sarai Marburg. So religion was not something Aaron enjoyed discussing, even with Adriana.

Adriana sensed his discomfort and changed the subject. "Mama will be furious. She wanted the boys at home this afternoon."

Aaron noted that Adriana always spoke of the hacienda as home, despite the fact that she and Micah had been living in the Santander townhouse for more than a year. She was here now only because it was an unbreakable tradition among the Santanas that children of the family be born on the estate. Santanas were born and were buried at Santanilla, and nowhere else.

"They always go to La Horca Francesa on Sundays," Aaron said. He approved. Anything that separated him from the Santana brothers he regarded as pleasurable.

"But we are having a visitor today. Mama always thinks the entire family should be on hand to receive guests." Adriana smiled. "In case the guest is an enemy."

"This guest is just a horse-buyer," Aaron said.

"I know. Feli heard El Patron and Mama arguing about him this morning."

Felicia smiled primly to show her satisfaction at being vindicated in her snooping.

"Papa and Miguel will want you to translate," Adriana said. A major part of Aaron's education to be an international banker had been languages. He had the gift of learning them easily. He spoke English well, though with an American accent acquired from practicing with Simon Pauley, the American consul in Santander.

Adriana could have been pressed into service as a translator, and might have been had she not been under Doña Maria's strict injunction to lie down for two hours each afternoon.

"Who is this American visitor, Ana?" Aaron asked.

Adriana suppressed a sigh of impatience with her husband. Miguel should really make a greater effort to keep Aaron informed. The boy was doing a fine job of acting as bursar for the estate, and it would cost Miguel nothing to acknowledge it and take Aaron into his confidence, at least in matters that concerned Santanilla's finances.

"His name is Langhorne Chase. He wishes to buy horses. A great many of them," she said. "For the government of the state of South Carolina."

Aaron's interest quickened. Anything about the United States intrigued him. At Simon Pauley's he read the American newspapers, and from the consul he knew that an election had taken place in America and that a country lawyer named Abraham Lincoln was to be president. The slave states, said Pauley, were furious because Republican Lincoln opposed slavery. The state of South Carolina—Mr. Chase's state—was known to be drafting an Ordinance of Secession.

Both Aaron and Adriana had studied the American quarrel over slavery intently. The United States was the only modern nation that tolerated it, and many Americans were resolved to end it. Simon Pauley was one of them, an Abolitionist.

In private discussion, Aaron and Adriana had puzzled over the peculiarly American concept of "states' rights." In Spain the provinces were administrative units, nothing more. Any sovereignty they might claim had been abolished long ago. Yet in America the several states apparently had the legal right to separate themselves from the central government should they feel themselves aggrieved. "Like unruly children," Adriana had remarked disapprovingly.

Aaron had asked Simon Pauley to explain all this, but the consul, a hawk-beaked, six-foot-three-inch Yankee from Massachusetts, had grown so angry and agitated about "those rebellious traitors who threaten the Union" that he swiftly outran Aaron's command of English.

Now one of those "rebellious traitors" was coming to Santanilla.

Adriana said, "Papa did not wish to entertain Señor Chase. He forbade Mama to ask him to stay for *cena.*" Adriana knew that Aaron would find the omission significant. Spanish hospitality could be extravagant, but it was also carefully graded. Miguel wanted El Patron to sell Mr. Chase the horses he came to buy. But El Patron, true to his liberal convictions, did not wish to do so. Doña Maria disapproved of El Patron's disapproval. It was more liberal politics, and the hacendada loathed liberal politics.

Felicia, who had been fairly trembling with desire to enter the conversation, could restrain herself no longer. "It was a terrible quarrel, Don Aaron. I could not help overhearing. El Patron said that he saw no reason to entertain a man who kept slaves, and Doña Maria said that his own ancestors, may the Lord bless and keep them, had kept slaves themselves in the New World, and then El Patron grew very angry and said that the *encomedia* was not the same thing at all, and—"

"*Ya basta,* Feli," Adriana said. "Enough now."

Felicia, her dark face damp with sweat and gleaming in the bright sun, said reproachfully, "It was only what I heard, Doña Ana. Señor Chase must be one of those men of whom you told us."

The servants of the estate were, most of them, illiterate, and Adriana felt it her duty to read to the female house staff. Her most recent offering had been *La Cabina del Tío Thomás,* by the American lady novelist Harriet Beecher Stowe. Felicia had been deeply moved.

"We shall see, Feli," Adriana said. To Aaron she said, "Do we really need money so much?"

"Ana," Aaron said, "we always need money at Santanilla."

"Then your Uncle Isaac should send us more," Adriana said firmly.

Aaron smothered a sigh. Adriana knew four languages and could do calculus, but she would never understand what it meant to have Santanilla mortgaged to the limit. Don Alvaro had been a rich man when he galloped off to do battle with the Carlists, but even he did not truly understand that his gallantry had impoverished him. No Santana seemed able to grasp what this really meant.

The last of the servants who had been at Mass with the family straggled up the slope toward La Casa, bowing as they passed the hacendado and hacendada. Don Miguel still stood in earnest conversation with Don Alvaro. About the sale of the horses, Aaron felt certain.

He turned his attention back to Adriana. When she said that Castileñas throve on the sun, she spoke no more than the simple truth. In the brilliant light her hair gleamed like pale gold, her skin looked cool to the touch. When he had first arrived at Santanilla he had been overwhelmed by the prospect of spending his life in this new place surrounded by these odd Spaniards. He had seen Adriana as the young woman his father had chosen to replace his sad, remote mother. He had been aloof and resentful.

But no one could be near Adriana Marburg and remain hostile. She was a child of light as his mother had been a child of darkness. To see Adriana's hair blowing in the wind, to hear the lilt of her laughter, to feel the warmth of her personality was a joy. She welcomed the exile and made a boy feel like a man. His father, Aaron thought, was the most fortunate man alive.

"Keep yourself available after *almuerzo*. El Patron and I will have need of you."

Aaron became aware that his father stood beside the buggy speaking in that managerial manner that he always used when addressing his son. Don Alvaro and Doña Maria were away in the landau behind the English thoroughbreds trotting smartly up the hill toward the hacienda.

A groom stood behind Micah with Aaron's mare, a delicately made half-Arab allotted him by Don Alvaro. Aaron, more pleased than he could say, had named her Estrella for the white star on her broad forehead. She was tossing and backing away from Micah. She sensed the older man's uneasiness around her kind, and she resented it. Aaron scrambled down from the buggy and quieted her. Adriana watched with amusement. She was aware that it gave Aaron pleasure that he was at ease with horses while his father was not. Rivalry between father and son was to be expected, Adriana thought, with a wisdom greater than her years. There were times, such as now, when she felt far, far older than Aaron.

He was a sweet boy, she thought, and one who must take his small triumphs where he could. It could not be an easy thing to be the son of Miguel Marburg, growing up in his considerable shadow.

She regarded her husband with genuine satisfaction. He might be a Jew born a thousand Roman miles from this harsh country, but he looked more the Spanish caballero than any man on Santanilla, not even excepting El Patron. He was tall and slender, with an elegance of carriage worthy of a matador. His dark broadcloth suit fit him to perfection, the narrow trousers showing off the length of his legs, the spotless linen accenting his olive skin, dark brown eyes, and black hair. She had fallen in love with him that first day in the Piazza San Marco —mainly for his looks, she was quite willing to concede that. After all, she had been little more than a child then. But he had not disappointed her. His intelligence and intensity suited her perfectly. What wonders could not one expect from his child under her heart? But she *did* wish that he could be kinder to Aaron, who would, one day soon now, be a lovely man in his own right.

She watched them together now, father and son, dark hair and copper. She smiled remembering that Aaron was certain that he was a throwback to some Celt who had insinuated himself into the Marburg line while the tribe was wandering from Roman Palestine to German Hessen.

Miguel climbed into the buggy and said, "La Patrona is displeased with your brothers, Ana. She wanted them here this afternoon."

"*Caray,*" Adriana said. "What use would they be?"

"None at all," Miguel said. His opinion of Don Alvaro's sons was very low. He picked up the reins and spoke again to Aaron. "I have had a letter from Isaac. See me in the office directly after lunch. Before the American arrives."

"Aaron and I have been discussing the American," Adriana said.

"Have you, indeed?"

She smiled innocently. She enjoyed her position between father and son. To heavily chaperoned Spanish matrons, flirtatiousness was a way of life.

"How many horses does Mr. Chase want to buy, Papa?" Aaron asked.

"He will tell us," Miguel said.

Adriana, frowning at her husband's tone, said, "He is after cavalry horses. To fight against Señor Lincoln. It is not right, Miguel."

"Politics, Ana, does not mix with business," Miguel said. *"Almuerzo* at two, Aaron." He flicked the reins across the horse's back and without a backward glance left his son standing in the roadway before the old stone church.

Aaron mounted Estrella but did not move out immediately. He sat in the saddle, looking thoughtfully after the buggy. The occupants were all in black. Black broadcloth on his father, black cambric on Felicia, black silk on Adriana. Only his stepmother's bright hair caught the light.

He still felt the chill of his father's manner. The religious disagreement was a part of it. He had embarrassed his father with his unexpected intransigence. But the estrangement went deeper still. It came close to jealousy. Micah Marburg resented his son's friendship with Doña Ana. Aaron was certain of it.

Aaron nudged the mare with his boot heels and she ambled away from the church, past the stark stones of the plot where the Santanas' servants had been buried for a hundred and fifty years, past the garish mausoleum with its family coat of arms weathered almost to smoothness, in which the hacendado's ancestors lay in their crypts, still wedded to this harsh and unforgiving land. On the lintel above the bronze door could be read the Santana family motto: *Yo perduro*—I endure. Whichever king had given them that knew them well, Aaron thought.

There were two infant sons in the crypts: Alfredo, who had died of diphtheria at the age of four, and Guillermo, who had lived only a single day. But they were Santanas, and their small bones lay with those of their grandparents, Don Alejandro and Doña Elvira Santana.

How very different from the Santanas were the Marburgs, Aaron thought as he rode past the churchyard. The Santanas clove to the past —even Don Alvaro, who thought himself modern. The Marburgs (at least Aaron's branch of the family) seemed to take joy in rootlessness.

The Hessian cousins, without exception, thought Aaron and his father overly arrogant and proud. Cousin Rachel Silber, whom Aaron remembered now only as a fat, unpleasant girl with enormous breasts and a dark moustache, liked to say that when the Jews of Hessen were required to buy their surnames a few short generations ago, the Micah Marburgs were so filled with *chutzpah* that they wasted a large sum of money to buy for themselves the name of the town in which they had settled—"like *goyische* noblemen." That, thought Aaron grimly, from

Rachel, whose family was so filled with smarmy humility that they had taken the name of the *second* most precious metal.

It was incredible to Aaron that his father and uncle, to seal a family alliance, had once thought of betrothing him to Rachel. They had actually spoken to the matchmaker of Marburg about it.

But matchmakers and the eastern *shtetl* from which the original Marburgs had come were parts of a fading past. Micah Marburg, with his conversion and marriage, had put the generations of the Diaspora behind him. And despite Aaron's stubborn refusal to accept the Church, he had been carried along, separated from his past and launched into an uncertain future.

He drew a breath of the hot wind and urged Estrella up the sloping path past La Casa and toward the ridge of the hills beyond. When he reached the crest he reined in and sat looking out across Santanilla toward the distant sea.

The red-tiled roofs of the hacienda seemed to glow in the high sunlight. Aaron wondered if the Santanilleños realized that the buildings in which they spent most of their lives were arranged in the manner of an ancient Roman villa, with the wings of the house enclosing a walled garden and the barns and woolshacks disposed about the main structure so as to make the hacienda defendable if attacked. Probably Don Alvaro knew this, and possibly Ana, but no one else.

Aaron looked beyond the hacienda, across the low ranges of hills falling away to the coast, barely visible in the heat haze. To the west lay Asturias, to the east Navarre. To the north the mist covered the Mar Cantabrica, the great sound other Europeans called the Bay of Biscay.

Only fifty years ago the English navy and the fleets of revolutionary France had contested those waters, the British trying desperately to put the Napoleonic genie back into the bottle. The battle had spilled over onto this land, the very ground on which Estrella stood had been bloodied in the Peninsular War. Santanilla itself had served as a field headquarters for the Duke of Wellington. Don Alvaro remembered him.

The histories said that England and her allies, which sometimes had included Spain, had won that war. Perhaps they had: Napoleon (the real Napoleon, not that vain and foolish man in Paris who now called himself emperor) was thirty-nine years dead, poisoned by his jailers on St. Helena, so the rumors went. Yet there was revolution everywhere. In Italy, Garibaldi and his Red Shirts were molding a new nation. There were uprising of anarchists in Austria, France, Russia. Republicans (to Don Alvaro's not-so-secret delight) were demonstrating in Andalusia, peasants were demanding land reform in Extremadura. Only three years ago the Sepoys had revolted against the British in India. There was revolution in Mexico and threats of war in the United States. The globe was in ferment. Important things are happening, Aaron thought with sudden defiance. I will not stay in this limbo forever. The thought of leaving, of never seeing his stepmother again, gave him a thrill of delicious grief.

The wind ruffled the mare's long mane. Aaron stripped off his coat and let the hot air cool the sweat on his lean torso. He stood in the stirrups and surveyed the scene around him like a man about to depart on a long journey.

War and conquerors had leached the life from Old Castile. Romans, Vandals, Goths, Moors, Frenchmen, and Englishmen had all ruled here in their time. The original inhabitants, the dark Iberians, remained. They were the *peones,* the *campesinos.* They had occupied this peninsula since time began, and when everyone else had gone they would still be here, scratching a living from the rocky soil.

He was filled with an awareness of the vastness of time and the persistence of the human species. But this is someone else's land, he thought, not mine.

He flicked Estrella gently with the reins and let her pick her own way back down the track toward Santanilla.

2

Alfonso Santana's current mistress
was a sixteen-year-old former servant girl named Concepción Paredes.
And though he was not more than ordinarily superstitious, he wondered if her name were prophetic. Concha (as she was familiarly called)
was pregnant.

As it happened, Alfonso had not chosen Concha. His brother
Santiago had seduced her and passed her on to him. At the time of the
exchange, Alfonso had been grateful to his elder brother. Though
handsome—as were all the Santanas—Alfonso was not very successful
with women. Even servant girls.

At the age of twenty-two, Alfonso had accomplished little in life.
He was not as clever as his sister Adriana, nor as dashing as his brother
Julio (who had devoted himself to acquiring the skills and manners of
a country caballero), nor as shrewd as his eldest brother Santiago. He
was afraid of his father (who thought him stupid), and of his mother

(who thought him a buffoon). Adriana's intelligence and education made it impossible for him to communicate with her. His only hope for approval lay in doing what his brothers—particularly Santiago—told him to do. For as long as he could remember he had been doing exactly that.

Alfonso was not a perceptive young man, but some animal instinct had warned him long ago that there was a streak of gratuitous cruelty in Santiago. He had bullied Alfonso since childhood, contemptuous of his slow wits and his clownish desire to please. But Santiago, for all of his meanness, remained the surrogate for the terrifying and unpredictable figure of El Patron.

When Santiago presented him with Concha, Alfonso had been inordinately pleased. The girl was sixteen, darkly pretty, still buxom with baby fat, and as lustful as anyone could wish. She was short (which pleased Alfonso, who had not inherited his father's inches), with sturdy arms and legs and breasts like melons. In addition to these graces, she had the hocks and intelligence of a mare. Alfonso tended to think of women in rancher's terms, and the last thing he would have wished for was a woman cleverer than he.

Santiago had taken Concha from the household of Simon Pauley, the American consul, where she had been placed by her family, *peones* on Altamira, a hacienda near Santanilla. Señor Pauley, a puritanical Protestant, irritated many people in the district with his habit of engaging house servants and attempting to educate—and convert—them. He was a man constantly dismayed by the Spanish capacity for cloaking sexual license in papist prudery.

Santiago had seen the girl when she was fifteen and a virgin. He had dazzled her with a display of horsemanship and a few cheap presents, and set her up in a house on the outskirts of Liencres. He saw to it that her family learned of her disgrace, knowing that they would direct their anger not at her Spanish seducer but at the Protestant foreigner who had turned her head with the idea that she might become something more than she was born.

Santiago tired swiftly of Concha. Another woman caught his attention, and rather than support two mistresses (which he could not afford to do), he passed the girl on to Alfonso—sold her to him, actually, for the price of a silver-mounted saddle he fancied.

Alfonso had made an unaccustomed effort to make Concha happy. He had bought her more of the gaudy trifles Santiago said she liked, he had given her money to send to her family (who had, of course, disowned her), and he had indulged her in all the lusty sexual tricks she had learned to enjoy while she belonged to Santiago.

But now the stupid cow was pregnant, and Alfonso was angry and concerned.

He sat naked, sprawled in a chair near the half-shuttered window, puffing sullenly on a thin black cigar.

A blade of sun passed through the gap in the shutters, divided by the shadow of the *reja,* the wrought-iron bars fixed to the window casements. The shaft of light slashed through the dimness directly across the large, rumpled bed that was the room's most prominent feature. It made Concha's dusky hide glisten where it was still moist with sweat, his and hers.

The girl had large, well-shaped buttocks. At the top of the crease, a delicate fan of fine black hair spread out over the base of her spine. Another pattern of the same silky black pelt fanned downward across her shoulders from the nape of her neck. Her shoulders were narrow, but muscled and strong. Her calves, thighs, and back were substantial and well-defined. She had the body of one meant to re-main close to the soil, to stoop and work the earth with her blunt-fingered hands. In fact, Alfonso thought, she always seemed to smell of Spanish dirt. She was pure Celtiberian, a bloodline stretching back through time to an age when the land was populated only with these stocky, dark folk, long before even the Romans came. Alfonso did not think of this, of course, because he knew nothing of it, nor did he care. All that he knew of Concepción was that she was a *peon,* one of the people who existed to break the soil, harvest the corps, care for the animals, and provide men like himself with sex. As he regarded her through layers of blue cigar smoke, he felt his penis rising, hard-ening. It was those damned great buttocks and that delicate feather-ing of her hair that aroused him.

"Concha."

The girl continued to sob.

"Conchita."

She did not stop weeping, but she rolled onto her side and stared at him with great, dark, wet, accusing eyes.

"Conchita," he said again. "Forgive me. I should not have struck you."

There was a bruise forming on her cheek and another on her breast. He had completely lost his temper when she had told him she was with child. He had hit her with clenched fists.

"It was a shock to me, that's all. We make love, and then you calmly inform me that you are *embarazada.* I lost my temper."

30

The skin of her breasts was marked by the rumpled bedding. Her nipples were erect in their large purplish areolas. Her pubis was thickly pelted and the hair extended upward in a line over her belly to the deeply indented navel. Her smothered sobbing made her abdomen jerk and contract in spasms that to Alfonso were indistinguishable from her normally violent orgasms.

He was still very angry, though he tried to dissemble. His penis stood fully erect, and he felt an urge to strike her again. Santiago always said that there was some cruelty in all sexual desire.

He crushed the cigar in a tray and went to the bed and sat beside her. He put a hand on her injured breast and squeezed. She moaned and rolled away.

He caught her by a handful of dark, damp, tangled hair. "I said I lost my temper. Now, *forgive me, chiquita.*"

"It was my fault, *Patron*" she said in a constricted voice. Whenever he frightened her, she always called him Patron. She knew that it pleased him. It had pleased his brother Santiago as well. She lifted her arms to pull him down onto her belly, but he gave her head a little shake and pulled her face into his lap.

He relaxed his hold on her hair as she took his penis into her mouth. She sucked and rolled her mouth and tongued him for a time until he caught her face and lifted her head back onto the bolster. She regarded him with hollow, cavernous eyes, vulnerable as a wild animal in a steel-jawed trap.

He spread her thighs wide and mounted her, driving into her with all his strength and weight. She was burning hot, slick with sexual juices. Her eyes rolled back to show the whites and she wrapped her heavy legs around him, moaning without shame.

"*Puta,*" he muttered, pumping breathlessly. "*Puta descuidada—*" Careless whore. What now, he wondered? El Patron would be displeased. He would shout and call Alfonso stupid. It wasn't just his father's disapproval Alfonso feared. Children got on the wrong side of the blanket were common enough. It was that having vented his annoyance, Don Alvaro would then proceed to make arrangements to care for Concha and her child. He would handle it all with swift efficiency. There were, after all, plenty of his own bastards scattered about the district, all with their own little nest eggs. He would arrange the same for Concha's bastard. With Alfonso's money. With funds taken from his share of Santanilla. That was the way these things were done. Always.

Trembling with rut and anger, Alfonso grabbed Concha's broad buttocks and pulled her against him as he climaxed. He pushed her away and sat on his haunches, regarding her with disgust. Thick-bodied *peon*. She could easily cost him half his patrimony. Particularly if she bore a son. El Patron doted on male children, even if they were peasant bastards.

No, by Saint Mary, Mother of God, he was doubly damned if Alfonso Santana was going to allow his father to beggar him just because a slut was careless. There was little enough left to go around now that the Jews had come to Santanilla.

Santiago would know what to do. Santiago *always* knew.

He left the bed, and without another look at the girl, began to dress.

By midday the regular Sunday gathering of the local *bravos* was well underway at La Cantina de la Horca Francesa. The tavern, typical of rural Spain, consisted of a two-story half-timbered building in a grove of sparse poplar trees some five kilometers from the town of Liencres.

Flanking the main building, an optimistic *cantinero,* gone for years, had built two single-story wings intended to house travelers journeying between Santander and Gijón along the coastal road. But the construction of a railroad had reduced road traffic almost to the vanishing point, and La Horca Francesa had fallen on bad times.

The inn had been bought by a family of half-gypsies and given over to a purely local clientele. In this mode it prospered; La Horca was the only place within a hundred kilometers where the sons of the local gentry could gather to get drunk, fight, see flamenco dancers, gamble, and enjoy such other pleasures as their affluence and inclinations might permit.

The current *cantinero,* a burly gypsy known simply as El Gallo, had cultivated his clients carefully. After fifty years of wandering the roads of Spain he knew exactly what the sons of the gentry required in a gathering place. First there must be a certain exclusivity. This was not to suggest that the passing *campesino* with a few coppers to spend on a glass of cheap wine was unwelcome. But the local *peones* did their drinking in the east wing of the tavern, or in the open in the rammed earth yard between the tavern and the stables. Second, facilities must be immediately available to any *caballero* who happened to be between mistresses or chanced to arrive at La Horca without one. For this purpose, El Gallo had divided the west wing into cribs and rented them at a nominal percentage to the dozen or so prostitutes who made a chancy living in Liencres under the uncertain protection of the Guardia Civil. And finally, regardless of how rowdy or illegal the behavior of La Horca's favored patrons, there must be no scandal. In order to assure this, El Gallo and his family opted for the simple device of giving the local captain of the Guardia a share in the profits (this share being known in Spanish slang as *la mordida*—the bite), and, of course, enjoyment of all the services of the place without charge.

La Cantina de la Horca Francesa was by no means unique. Rural inns and taverns all over Spain and Spanish America were run on exactly this well-oiled system. The rigidity of Spanish morals, the oppressive nature of any government the Spanish managed to contrive, and the narrow-eyed supervision of everyday life by the Church made such establishments as La Horca more than inevitable—it made them necessary.

The name of the inn, the Canteen of the French Gallows, was not the fiction of El Gallo and his inventive family. The main building had, in fact, been a French billet during the Peninsular War, and a feature of the forecourt had been a high gibbet upon which many Spanish partisans had twitched their last moments away under the appreciative eyes of a squadron of French Dragoon Guards. In the *sala,* the large public room on the ground floor, there was a hempen halter preserved under glass, though this was generally known to be an example of El Gallo's entrepreneurship—he being convinced that there was a taste for the macabre in everyone.

On this late autumn Sunday, La Horca was even more festive than usual. El Gallo had engaged a troupe of gypsy dancers and was entertaining three members of a traveling *quadrilla* of bullfighters.

The *toreros* had performed at the Brave Festival the previous afternoon in Santander. It had been an indifferent display, with sorry bulls, one of which had managed to gore the single *novillero* of the *quadrilla* in the thigh. The boy, no more than nineteen years old, now sat in the seat of honor in the *sala,* his leg propped on a stool, his thigh heavily bandaged, trying with El Gallo's brandy to kill the tetanus infection working in his blood. The *quadrilla's* matador, a second-rater past his prime, had gone on to Bilbao, leaving the *novillero* in El Gallo's care. Two of the *picadores,* cadaverous men as gaunt as the crow-bait horses they rode in action, had been detailed to remain with the injured *torero* until he should mend or become so ill recovery was unlikely.

The boy, who called himself El Moréz, after his native village south of Madrid, had been given an ear by the judges at Santander. This would never have happened in the ring of any large city, where ears and tails were granted only for outstanding performances, but the Santandeños' civic pride had been humbled by the poor quality of the bulls their contractor had provided, and they wished to reward the boy's bravery and endurance despite his lack of style.

33

It had taken him five attempts to place the sword as he lurched about the ring with a deep *cornada* four inches from his genitals, and his slippers filled with blood. But he had managed it finally, and they had granted him an ear, his first. He had it with him now, on the table, black hair matted with dried blood. Sweating and lightheaded with fever, he regaled his listeners, between performances by the dancers, with descriptions of how he was forced to discard his slippers to maintain his footing in the sand. Two of the prettier local whores sat with him, petting and kissing him and keeping his glass filled. El Gallo believed in honoring the brave.

The *caballeros* filling the *sala* all knew they were very probably drinking with a dead man. Horn wounds killed sometimes at once, sometimes by infection. Because of this they deferred to El Moréz as they would not have done had he been whole. Many of them fought the bulls in the Portuguese manner, on horseback with a lance, as bulls had been fought by gentlemen on the Iberian Peninsula since the Middle Ages. Some of them had been gored; all had lost expensive horses in the game. Because of this, and because like all Spaniards they placed a high value on public bravery, they listened intently to the injured *torero*.

Presently El Morez stopped talking and looked drunkenly, expectantly, about the room. His listeners and their women applauded him with clapping and cries of "Olé, Morez! Olé!"

He sank back in his chair, grinning foolishly, his face sickly white. A guitar player took up a Moorish refrain, and others joined in. One of the *gitanas* began to dance around the bullfighter's table, whirring a tambourine and whining the minor-key melody in her throat. The boy watched her with half-focused eyes.

Santiago Santana, sitting at a table with his woman, Marta Ordoñez, and his brother Julio, said over his brandy, "I give him three weeks, no more. It's a pity. I hear he really did well. No artistry, but plenty of *cojónes.*"

Señora Ordoñez flushed at his language, but said nothing about it. She had learned not to criticize Santiago Santana.

Julio, whose current mistress had not yet arrived at La Horca, showed Marta his dazzling smile and said, "You haven't touched your Jerez, Martita."

"Let be," Santiago said. "She never drinks much." He regarded the woman amusedly. "She doesn't approve of drunkenness, do you, Martita?"

Marta Ordoñez mechanically lifted her glass, wet her lips with sherry, put the glass down again.

34

"Now you will have to tell the priest at confession," Santiago said ironically.

"I will, Patron," she said.

Santiago Santana seldom kept a mistress very long, but he had had Marta Ordoñez for almost a year now. Her melancholy intrigued him still.

She was older than he; thirty-two was what she admitted to, but she could even be older. She had appeared in Liencres three years ago, claiming to be a widow, though Santiago doubted it.

She had spent two of those three years trying to eke out a living as a seamstress, doing the odd job for the local gentlewomen. But since every upper-class household had plenty of girls trained to do such work, Marta Ordoñez lived at the edge of starvation. Santiago had first seen her, unchaperoned, on a blustery, rainy day in the plaza of Liencres, hurrying through the empty square wrapped in a wet shawl and shivering in the wind.

He had approached her at once, and within a month's time she had agreed to become his mistress.

It was not that she was so physically attractive, though she had a certain sombre beauty. It was that Santiago Santana had a poacher's instinct for picking off the wounded bird.

Marta was a bargain. She was passive to the point of lethargy, but Santiago was a cold young man who preferred obedience to passion. She asked for very little: only that he give her a small sum of money each month, which he was willing to do, since the amount for a year was less than he might lose during an evening of cards with his friends. He soon discovered that she sent this money to the sisters of a contemplative order in Valladolid, where there was a daughter undergoing religious instruction. Santiago sometimes toyed with the notion of going to Valladolid and having a look at this younger version of Marta Ordoñez, but nothing ever came of it. The nuns of a cloistered order were unlikely to trot the girl out like a filly for his inspection. Yet the knowledge of the girl's existence gave Santiago a hold over Marta, and from time to time, when the mood was upon him, he would threaten her with a journey to Valladolid. Her reaction was so uncharacteristically emotional, even violent, that he wondered what there was in her past besides a daughter—almost certainly a bastard—that she would go to such lengths to keep hidden.

Capitán Luis Torres of the Guardia Civil and two of his troopers appeared in the *sala,* to be warmly met by El Gallo. Torres, a corpulent man in his fifties, was as well tolerated in the district as any policeman was ever likely to be. He had been passed over for further promotion, and it was generally understood that unless he committed some really gross impropriety, he would remain comandante of the small police garrison at Liencres until he retired or died.

Torres in turn knew that the regard of people among whom one worked and lived was more valuable now than the good opinion of faceless bureaucrats in far-off Madrid. He therefore enforced the law with a delicate discretion, acknowledging human frailty and never expecting the impossible. Over time he had become a silent partner in several local business ventures, including La Horca. He was a reasonably wealthy man.

It was the captain who arrived, year in and year out, at Santanilla with writs and liens. He genuinely regretted this duty, because he admired Don Alvaro. El Patron of Santanilla was the region's most famous soldier, even though he had so often found himself on the wrong side.

Torres claimed that he himself was from a family with an ancient military tradition. When drunk, he bragged that his forebears had fought for Spain when the Tercios were the scourge of Europe. But everyone knew that the Torres were a family of sheepherders in the Sierra Cantabrica, hardy, honest folk, but of no military or social significance.

Most of the local gentry regarded Torres as a harmless parvenu. But Santiago Santana found his pretensions contemptible, and he lost no opportunity to greet the policeman in the most elaborately military manner, as though he were a *generalisimo* of the army. Torres knew this was done to humiliate him, but he had enough wit to swallow his resentment and hide his injured pride. The Santanas were large landowners and Don Alvaro was an important man. But his son should know better than to ridicule the district police commander. The Santanas had, after all, come down in the world, had they not? Hadn't Santiago's own sister married a Hebrew?

One day Santiago Santana's grinning insults would be repaid. What Capitán Torres wanted most to do to Santiago was to relieve him of Marta Ordoñez. The captain, eighteen years a widower, had at one time seriously considered offering Señora Ordoñez his hand and name in marriage. But he had been too slow off the mark and Santiago Santana had scooped her up. Naturally now any possibility of marriage was out of the question, but Torres still wanted her. Though no longer chaste, she was still mysterious, still darkly beautiful, still desirable. It would be a triumph to steal her from Santana's bed.

36

Torres dismissed his troopers and walked around the *sala,* returning greetings from El Gallo's patrons. He spoke briefly to the by-now-very-drunk guest of honor, the *torero.* He admired his bull's ear and caressed the bottoms of the young whores who attended him. He nodded distantly to the two *picadores* (who were socially a cut below the apprentice *matador*) and waved to the musicians. They responded to his policeman's uniform as gypsies always did, by scowling. But they struck chords from their instruments to show it was nothing personal.

The amenities performed, the captain marched to the table, made a stiffly correct military bow to the brothers, and lifted Marta Ordoñez's hand to his lips. He felt her flinch, but he gripped her hand firmly and tongued it as he kissed it, hoping that she would respond to his secret signal. She did not. She fears Santiago's jealousy, he thought.

If Santiago was indeed jealous, he gave no sign of it. He greeted Torres in his customary manner, calling him comandante and inquiring, with an insolent grin, after the state of crime in Liencres.

"Lawbreaking does not prosper in Liencres," Torres said woodenly.

"That does ease my mind, Comandante," Santiago said. "The Guardia is our shepherd."

Julio, the younger Santana sprig, giggled at his brother's thrust. He lifted his glass in a toast. "Spain's glory," he said.

Torres, his face flushed, stood hoping that no one else had heard the reference to his family's true occupation. Marta had, of course, but she was too refined, Torres thought, to show any emotion.

Then he realized that, standing here, he looked as though he were waiting like some supplicant to be offered a place at the Santanas' table. He clicked his spurs together and bowed to Marta Ordoñez. *"Su servidor, señora,"* he said with all the dignity he could muster, and moved on, seething.

Santiago looked at Marta and smiled. Julio shook his head, grinning.

The musicians began the first of a familiar series of *jotas.* The dancers rapped their heels on the floor, and the *sala* erupted into shouts and applause. This—and what was almost certain to follow—was what the people had come to La Cantina de la Horca Francesa to see.

$\mathfrak{3}$

Langhorne Chase, the American from South Carolina, was not what Aaron had expected. Influenced by the opinions of Consul Simon Pauley, Aaron had imagined that Mr. Chase would arrive enveloped in the smell of sulphur and brimstone.

But surprisingly, Mr. Chase exuded an air of joviality and friendship. He appeared to assume that these landed Spaniards he was visiting would automatically understand his concerns and sympathize with his intentions.

He was a portly man, of middle height, with a fine head of gray-streaked hair. He was tanned, well barbered, and elegantly dressed in a gray broadcloth suit, English boots, and an Italian silk waistcoat. He had arrived from Santander in a two-seat sulky of exquisite construction, drawn by a single Arab-thoroughbred cross that the groom awaiting him in the forecourt of La Casa had immediately identified as having been purchased from Don Eugenio Morelos, the patron of neighboring Miraflores.

With Mr. Chase had come a black man (the first Negro Aaron had ever seen), as elegantly outfitted as Mr. Chase himself, immensely tall, six and a half feet at least, and thin as a stick. This, Aaron learned, was Randolph, Mr. Chase's body-servant, without whom the South Carolinian never traveled.

It took Aaron some moments to realize, as he examined Randolph through the open window of the library, that he was actually looking at a slave. It had never occurred to him before that a slave owner might take a slave into a country where slavery was not legal. Simon Pauley had said that no Southerner dared do such a thing because the slave would inevitably bolt.

But it was plain to see that the fastidiously liveried Randolph, watching over his master's trap and gelding, had no such intention. It was also obvious that the tall black man regarded the grooms and other servants at Santanilla as rough creatures, scarcely worthy of his attention.

Mr. Chase spoke Spanish reasonably well, though with a most peculiar accent that from time to time created confusion. When this happened, he would smile charmingly, repeat the statement in English, and wait courteously for Aaron's translation.

He explained that no, Spanish was not generally spoken in his part of the country, which lay along the Atlantic seacoast. He had learned his Spanish from an old servant of his mother's, whose "mammy" (Aaron surmised that this meant either the servant's own mother or simply some other elderly female retainer) had been a nursemaid in a family of Louisiana *criollos*. Most Creoles, Mr. Chase said, were of French descent, but many were Spaniards.

This occasioned some polite discussion, either through Aaron or sometimes directly, between El Patron and Mr. Chase, as they searched for common acquaintances—of which, as it turned out, there were none.

With Micah, or Don Miguel as he called him, Mr. Chase was voluble and easy. He knew the German states well, though not, unfortunately, Hessen. He thought Berlin architecturally the equal of Paris and culturally the French capital's superior.

He had only recently come to Santander, he said, from Vienna, where he had indulged his two passions. He had attended the Spanish Riding School to see the Lippizaner stallions, and he had met Franz von Suppé at the premiere performance of *Das Pensionat*. He was, he admitted agreeably, addicted to the trivial in music. The new operettas suited him well.

By the time Langhorne Chase had been at Santanilla for two hours,

Aaron had to admit that he found the American interesting and friendly and not at all what he had been expecting.

Mr. Chase seemed to know instinctively that business was not conducted apace in Spain, that amenity must be layered on amenity before anything so crass as buying and selling was discussed.

But eventually, after a second decanter of El Patron's best Jerez had been broached, Mr. Langhorne Chase came to the point of his visit.

"You will have heard," he said, "of the dangerous political situation in my country. A party of upstarts has elected—" Here he spread his hands, almost like a Spaniard, to express his doubts about the legality of what was taking place in America. "—has elected a president who has sworn to destroy the Southern states."

"I did not know that Mr. Lincoln had any such intentions," Don Alvaro said, nodding to Aaron to translate.

For the first time, the expression of easy joviality left Langhorne Chase's face. His pale eyes glittered with real hatred. "Lincoln," he said. "*Abraham* Lincoln. A man with no popular support, Don Alvaro. The kindest thing that is written of him is that he is a baboon, a grinning clown."

He sipped at his sherry and drew a deep breath. "I should not allow my personal feelings to influence calm judgment, but we Carolinians are an emotional people, very like yourselves, Don Alvaro. We value love of our land, tradition, dignity, and honor. The man who will move into the White House next March prizes none of these things, none. That is why the legislature of the sovereign state of South Carolina has passed an Ordinance of Secession."

After a silent family meal and an hour before Mr. Chase and his servant had appeared at Santanilla, Aaron and his father had gone over the hacienda's accounts. Micah had wished to determine, within a few hundred pesetas, what Mr. Chase should be asked to pay for the animals he wished to buy.

Micah had shown Aaron the letter brought from Santander by old Lopez. Isaac Marburg, always alert to financial rumors, had written a general caution to guide his brother in conducting the business of the bank.

While not referring specifically to the business affairs of Santanilla, Isaac wrote concerning the possible effects of the troubles in America.

If you, as agent and representative of the bank, are approached by any American regarding loans or other credit transactions, you must limit

40

*disbursements to sums less than ten thousand Hessian marks. Furthermore,
if the bank must stand guarantor for any commercial transactions with
Americans, be extremely cautious. Paper currency and letters of credit
backed by American assets must be refused. Demand payment in gold.*

The admonishment and the demand for bullion was not simply a
Jewish banker's quirk, Aaron knew. Isaac Marburg was a hard, astute
money man. He had indulged his younger brother in financing Santanilla out of family loyalty. But he had no such reason to indulge the
citizens of a nation seemingly intent on plunging into civil war. Micah
wanted desperately to make Santanilla solvent, but he dare not ignore
his brother's warning.

"Aaron," Micah said, "translate this carefully. There must be no
mistakes." He addressed himself to Langhorne Chase in his guttural
Spanish. "I have no wish to be impertinent, Señor Chase, but before
we go further in this matter of the horses you wish to buy, I must ask
you if they are for your personal use or for some other."

"That has not yet been decided, Don Miguel," Chase said after
listening to Aaron.

"Again, Aaron," Micah said. "I have received information that
your state is mobilizing its militia, Señor Chase. Is it at all possible that
the horses will be used for some military purpose?"

"All things are possible, Don Miguel."

"I have been told," Micah said, "that Mr. Lincoln has said that he
is determined to preserve the American Union even if it means using
force."

Langhorne Chase's voice lost some of its softness. "Never, sir.
Yankees have a penchant for making threats, but in a battle they would
run from us. The Baboon knows it."

"They did not run when they occupied Mexico City in 'forty-
seven," Don Alvaro said grimly. "When they departed they walked,
and took half of Mexico with them."

Chase listened to Aaron's translation of El Patron's remarks, and
then said, "That army was officered by Southerners, Don Alvaro. I
understand that your family suffered a loss when California was taken,
and I am sorry for it. But that is war, sir."

El Patron's black eyes gleamed angrily and he said, "The losses of
the Santanas are a private affair, Señor Chase."

"Forgive me, sir. I had no wish to offend."

"Very well, let that go," Don Alvaro said. "What troubles me is
your easy estimate of American military ability. You are dangerously

41

near to civil war, Señor Chase. Now that is something I have experienced. No war is more savage than one that pits brother against brother." It was the old anti-Carlist soldier speaking, not the hard-up horsebreeder. Aaron felt a surge of admiration for El Patron.

"You have been a soldier, Don Alvaro, and I have not," Langhorne Chase said. "But our quarrel with the United States is bitter and it *will be* resolved. If they will let us go in peace, amen. But if they will not, we will fight them. Honor demands it, sir. If—*when*—war comes, my country will not find me reticent."

It was plain to Aaron that Langhorne Chase was looking forward to war. The elegant Southerner seemed to think of it as a grand adventure. That was not the picture of war Don Alvaro had given Aaron. El Patron's stories were filled with blood and dying and men living rough in the snows of the Pyrenees.

"You puzzle me, Señor Chase," El Patron said. "What is this country of which you speak? You are an American, are you not?"

"I am, sir. But first I am a South Carolinian," Chase declared with feeling.

Don Alvaro seemed to study one of the dark portraits on the whitewashed wall. A ray of afternoon sun illuminated a bearded face under an iron morion. It was the face of Don Bernardo Diaz y Santana, who had gone to the new world with Francisco Pizarro and never returned.

Don Alvaro spoke almost wearily. "And gentlemen such as yourself, Señor Chase, who are residents of, say, Alabama or Virginia, do they feel as you do?"

"Be assured that they do, sir," Mr. Chase responded.

"Once again, Señor Chase, permit me to ask. Which country will not find you and those other gentlemen reticent?"

"The Confederate States of America, Don Alvaro," Langhorne Chase said proudly.

"I am an amateur geographer, Señor," Don Alvaro said, "But until this moment I have heard of no such country."

"Few have, sir. But many will. And soon."

"I see," Don Alvaro said. "News reaches us slowly here." He regarded his visitor steadily. "And do the *campesinos* of South Carolina and Alabama and Virginia feel as you do?"

"We have no peasants, Don Alvaro," Mr. Chase said. "But our small farmers and our working class are as Southern as we."

"And your slaves?"

"I hope that you have not been influenced by what has been said and written of us, Don Alvaro. Our slaves are loyal. Why should they not be?"

"Why indeed?" murmured El Patron thoughtfully. "I ask, however, because to us slavery seems a peculiar institution."

"It suits us, sir," Chase said stiffly.

Don Alvaro turned to Micah as though he had made his decision and wished only, out of innate courtesy, to give his son-in-law an opportunity to do the same. Aaron wondered if Micah sensed this as strongly as he, Aaron, did.

Micah said, "Assuming for the moment, Señor Chase, that we are able to come to mutual agreement about the animals you wish to buy—" He waited impatiently for his son to translate and then continued, "—how would you be prepared to offer payment?"

Langhorne Chase's eyebrows arched. "How? I don't quite understand you, sir."

Micah said, "Did you translate correctly, Aaron?"

Aaron rephrased the question, knowing perfectly well that the visitor's *amour propre* was causing the difficulty, and not his understanding. "What my father wishes to know, Mr. Chase, is the form in which payment for the horses would be made."

"Why, in a note of hand issued by the government of the sovereign state of South Carolina, sir."

When Aaron had explained that to his father, there was a frowning moment of silence. Then Micah said, "We could not accept payment in that form, Señor Chase."

"Damn, sir!" the Carolinian exclaimed. "We haven't even been asked to inspect the stock, or state how many animals we require, and already our method of payment is being questioned. I find that mean spirited, sir. I had not expected such treatment at Santanilla." The well-barbered cheeks had grown flushed with quick anger.

Aaron began to translate, but his father silenced him with a gesture. "I understood him well enough," Micah said. "Now explain to him that he may inspect the herd and select one hundred head which he may buy at one hundred fifty pesetas each. Payment to be made in gold when the horses are delivered to the quay at Santander."

Aaron, who by now had begun to conclude that Mr. Langhorne Chase was less engaging than he had earlier seemed to be, translated precisely.

"Damn it, boy!" Chase exploded. "In *gold?* Ten thousand five hundred pesetas? That's close to eight thousand dollars, sir. Gold is out of the question." He contained himself with some effort. "Ask Don

Miguel if he will accept my *personal* note. Go ahead, boy, ask him."

Before Aaron could relay this angry offer to his father, Don Alvaro spoke. "With regret, Señor Chase, no."

Aaron was shocked by the abrupt finality of El Patron's refusal. Spanish gentlemen seldom spoke so directly, except to their social inferiors.

Langhorne Chase was nonplussed. "You astonish me, sir. You do astonish me." A man accustomed to indulging his anger, he let it build, fueled with a mixture of injured pride, surprise, and Anglo-Saxon feelings of superiority. "I see now, sir, that there was never any intention here to deal with me fairly." As he grew more choleric, the sirs in his speech grew more frequent and more contemptuously accented. "Is it possible, sir, that you have merely been milking me for information, sir?"

"What does he say?" Don Alvaro asked, frowning.

Aaron translated.

Don Alvaro said ominously, "Tell him that we have listened to his offer and refused it."

Chase required no translation. Red-faced, he plunged ahead with his accusations. "I was received with courtesy at Miraflores, sir. But I was warned that things might be different here, sir. I see that is the case. You are friends with that Yankee Simon Pauley, and this is his doing, I have no doubt. That swinish Boston Jew has maligned me and my cause, sir. A Hebrew trick—"

Aaron felt as though he had been slapped. The sudden surge of his own anger almost frightened him. With no thought for the possible consequences, he said quickly, "I will not translate what you have just said, Mr. Chase. El Patron is an expert with sword and pistol and if I were to tell him, he would call you out and kill you." He paused to take a trembling breath and then added firmly, "For your information, Mr. Chase sir, Mr. Pauley is not Jewish. But my father, Don Miguel Marburg, and I are. Go away now. You are no longer welcome here."

Langhorne Chase's mouth opened but no words emerged. His face looked purple. For a moment Aaron feared he was about to have some sort of seizure.

Micah Marburg looked startled. The exchange had far exceeded his meager English.

Chase had bounced to his feet. With obvious difficulty he managed a sketch of an angry bow to Don Alvaro and marched swiftly across the library, slammed open the door to the garden, and moved like a stick man to the courtyard, where his slave and sulky awaited him.

Micah said, "Aaron! What's happening?"

"He insulted us, Papa," Aaron said, his anger collapsing under the weight of his own appallingly bad manners toward a guest of the house.

In the courtyard, Langhorne Chase climbed to the seat of his sulky and snapped angrily at the frightened Randolph, who scrambled up beside his master. Chase snatched the reins from the surprised groom, sawed at the little Arab gelding's mouth, and slashed him across the rump with his whip. The slender horse kicked furiously at the sulky, breaking the dashboard to splinters, and then sprang into a gallop down the dusty road toward the distant gate of Santanilla. Aaron watched, wide-eyed.

"*Aaron,*" Micah shouted. "*What did you say to that man?*"

"I—" Aaron swallowed, began again. "He called Mr. Pauley a swinish Hebrew, Papa," he said miserably.

Micah Marburg stared at Don Alvaro.

Aaron looked intently at the tiled floor. There was no help for it. He had to go on. "I told him that El Patron knew how to use a sword and pistol."

"You said *what?*"

Aaron felt as though he were falling into a bottomless pit, but what must be said must be said. "I told him that if I translated what he had said, El Patron would challenge him." Aaron tried to dampen the dryness in his throat and failed. "Then he went away."

"He went away? *He went away?* Is that how it seemed to you? He just went away?" Micah Marburg's eyes were red with anger. For a moment, Aaron thought his father might strike him.

"I—I'm sorry, Papa. I didn't think—"

"You most certainly did not think. You never think before—" Micah checked himself with what Aaron could see was an enormous effort. "Go to your room, Aaron. Stay there until I send for you. And when I do, you will have something better by way of explanation for your fantastic behavior." Micah was speaking in German, his voice trembling with fury.

"Wait," Don Alvaro said as Aaron turned to go. To Micah he said, "Miguel, I want to speak to the boy."

Micah looked angrily from Aaron to Don Alvaro.

"It will be better if I speak to him alone, Miguel," Don Alvaro said.

Micah seemed about to protest and then thought better of it. "*Con permiso, Patron,*" he said, and left the room.

Aaron looked, stricken, at Don Alvaro Santana's large face. The deeply set eyes were like those of a bird of prey. Slowly, very slowly, El Patron's great yellow teeth showed in what could only be, Aaron thought wonderingly, a smile. El Patron was actually laughing.

"You told Señor Chase more than that, I think," Don Alvaro said. "I understand English better than your father does, Aaron."

Aaron lowered his eyes and shifted his weight uneasily. "Yes, Patron," he said.

Don Alvaro lumbered to his feet and Aaron suddenly found himself engulfed in an *abrazo* of Herculean proportions.

"Macho," Don Alvaro said approvingly. "You did well, boy."

Aaron was embarrassed to realize that his eyes were brimming with tears of relief.

Don Alvaro held his shoulders in a strong, warm grip. "You surprised me, *nieto,*" he said, "but you make me proud."

Aaron found it difficult to believe his ears. El Patron had actually called him "grandson."

"Patron, I—"

"Did you really think I would have killed him?" Don Alvaro asked.

"I don't know, Patron."

"Nor do I. But let us believe that I would have done. Twenty years ago, it would have been certain."

Soberly now, Don Alvaro studied Aaron's pallid face and teary eyes. "It has not been easy for you, *nieto,* coming here to a strange country and new people."

"No, Patron," Aaron said warily.

"Don't worry. I am not going to plague you with the question of religion. I sometimes behave impatiently, Aaron, though not often, because it is not my true nature. Well, never mind about that. In other circumstances we might argue the matter of you and the Church and arrive at some accommodation."

Aaron could not conceive of any argument with Don Alvaro that would not be resolved on his terms, but decided that he had indulged in enough frankness for one afternoon.

"Your father is very angry," Don Alvaro said. "As he has every right to be," he added, softening the judgment with a smile. "Miguel wanted very much to sell that fool the horses he came to buy."

"We do need the money, Patron," Aaron said grudgingly.

"I am sure we do," Don Alvaro said. "But you were provoked, and you chose honor rather than money. Not that your father disregards honor. You must not believe that. It is that his view is broader than yours. Or mine," he added. "You behaved like a Spaniard, Aaron. Do you realize that?"

"No, Patron."

"You don't think of yourself as a Spaniard."

"No, Patron. I don't."

"Well, that is understandable. We have done little enough to make you feel at home here." He took a leather cigar case from his waistcoat, extracted a thin cheroot, and clipped it with tiny gold scissors from his watch chain. For a moment Aaron thought he was going to offer a cigar. When he appeared to think better of it, Aaron was silently grateful. Don Alvaro's cheroots were poisonous. Doña Maria claimed that they were imported from hell.

"I spoke without thinking, Patron," Aaron said. "I should not have done that."

Don Alvaro filled the air with bitter blue smoke. It swirled in whirling patterns through the shaft of sunlight from the garden. "Well, you will have to make your peace with your father. It may not be easy. But you will endure." He regarded the young man speculatively. "You seem to have grown up while no one was looking. Your father may think it too soon. But all fathers think that. It is the way of the world. Do you understand me?"

"I think so, Patron." Aaron hesitated and then said, tentatively but with complete honesty, "But I am sorry about the American's money."

Don Alvaro laughed and said, "I hear your father in you now. Well, to tell you the truth I am sorry, too. But there it is. *Las Parcas nos mandan.*" The Fates command us. The Spanish, Aaron thought, were strangely fatalistic for so devout a people. There was a pagan strain in them. That was a very Jewish judgment, Aaron told himself.

"He won't return, will he," Aaron said.

"The elegant Señor Chase? No. Do not trouble yourself about it. The man is a fool. I knew many like him in the war. All brass and silk banners and noise, like the people in those operettas he says he enjoys. He will find real battle quite different from what he imagines, if it should ever come to him. Black blood and swordcuts filled with maggots are not glorious. Forget him. He is of no consequence."

"Yes, Patron. I will try."

"You could call me *abuelo,* Aaron. It would please me."

Aaron wondered if he could ever think of this often intimidating man as "grandfather."

"Con permiso, abuelo," he said diffidently.

"Now go speak with your father." Don Alvaro patted Aaron's

cheek with a large, oddly gentle hand. "Come to the observatory tonight. I will show you some important things."

Aaron had been in El Patron's observatory before, but never by specific invitation. He had never been allowed to look through the gleaming brass tube at the night sky.

"And Aaron."

"*Abuelo?*"

"Your father has had a shock this afternoon. Deal gently with him."

Long before Alfonso Santana's lathered horse brought him within sight of La Horca Francesa, the sounds of music and shouting reached him, borne by the wind.

As he trotted his mount into the earthen courtyard of the *cantina,* he caught the rich redolence of mingled odors: *paella* cooking, uncollected refuse, the stink of the stables. El Gallo and his people were not a fastidious lot.

The customary crowd of peasants who did their drinking in the yard were gathered around the windows of the *sala,* the nearer folk clinging to the wrought-iron *rejas* so as not to be forced from their favored places by others pressing to see inside.

Alfonso had to catch one of the *mozos* by the scruff of the collar to make him take his sweating horse. This added to the young man's agitation. He had been brooding about Concha's inconvenient pregnancy all the way from Liencres, and he allowed himself to release some of his anger by striking the groom across the back with his riding crop and shouting at him to rub the horse down properly or receive more of the same later. El Gallo's servants were taken from the dregs of the peasantry, men and women without families grateful for the shelter and the pittance paid them by the *cantinero*.

Alfonso pushed open the plank door to the *sala* and was engulfed in noise. Four guitar players were improvising variations on a gypsy *jota*. A dark girl in flounced skirt and tight, sweat-soaked bodice was executing a *zapatada*, her heels clacking on the floor like Gatling guns while the rest of her body writhed in sensuous rhythm with the music. The heat in the large, low-ceilinged room was oppressive; the air smelled of food, wine, and damp bodies.

The girl was dancing round and round a dazed young man whose shoulders were draped with the stiffly brocaded jacket of a cheap suit of lights. His thigh was tightly bandaged, his leg extended and cradled in the lap of one of the local whores. Alfonso recognized the bullfighter as the *novillero* who had put on such a ludicrous performance yesterday in Santander.

Near the *torero* sat Capitán Torres of the Guardia Civil, his uniform coat unbuttoned at the throat, his plump face flushed with wine. Two more of El Gallo's girls sat with him, keeping his glass filled.

Alfonso looked through the cigar smoke. Santiago and Julio were at their customary table. Marta Ordoñez sat with them. Alfonso had never understood what it was about the woman that appealed to Santiago. Alfonso thought her too old, too thin, and too solemn. She seldom spoke to him and he could not recall ever having seen her laugh or even smile.

He made his way across the crowded room and threw himself into a chair at his brothers' table. With the excess of drama to which he was addicted, Alfonso helped himself to a long draught of brandy from the bottle on the table.

Santiago snapped his fingers for a *mozo*. When the man appeared, he said, "Bring the *caballero* a glass. And me a fresh bottle of *aguardiente*."

Julio grinned at Santiago and said, "Baby brother seems upset. What do you suppose La Yegua has done now?" He frequently referred to Concha as "the Mare," a habit Alfonso resented primarily because the epithet was so clearly suitable.

"Shut your mouth, Julio," Alfonso said. "Go away. I want to speak with Santiago alone."

Marta Ordoñez started to rise. Santiago caught her wrist and held her in her place. "Stay," he said. He studied Alfonso thoughtfully. The younger man's agitation was genuine, though he was such a fool it was impossible to know whether or not something was actually amiss. Alfonso was, in the local idiom, *scandaloso,* given to making a great fuss about every little thing. To Julio, Santiago said, "Go watch the dancers."

Julio Santana hesitated, frowning. Santiago had a way of issuing commands that affected others like the screech of a knife blade on glass. But it was not in Julio's makeup to challenge Santiago. He stood, picked up his glass, and stalked off to join the crowd around the injured bullfighter.

Santiago looked calmly at Alfonso. "Well?"

"I would rather speak with you alone," Alfonso said.

"Señora Ordoñez is the soul of discretion. Isn't that so, Martita?"

"If you say so, Patron," the woman murmured.

"I do say so." Santiago smiled. "The señora can give us the woman's perspective on your problem, Alfonso. We don't pay enough attention to the opinions of women."

The *mozo* appeared with a glass and the fresh bottle of brandy. Alfonso waited uncomfortably until he had opened the bottle, wiped the table, and departed. He looked uneasily from Santiago to Marta Ordoñez. He did not understand the odd relationship between his brother and Marta. It was too complex and shadowy. In any case, he preferred not to think about it now. He had more than enough on his plate at the moment. He had left Concha still in bed, bawling like a calf at his "desertion," as she called it.

"May I assume that Julio was right?" Santiago said. "There is trouble with Concha?"

Alfonso nodded. He poured a glass of *aguardiente,* filling it to the brim.

"Getting drunk is not going to solve a problem," Santiago said.

Alfonso drank the brandy with a touch of defiance.

Santiago laughed. "Let me guess, baby brother. You have been careless."

"I? No, by God, not *I!*"

"Not you? Then who? Some stranger? The mayor of Liencres? The Holy Ghost?"

"Santiago," Alfonso protested. "This is no laughing matter. The cow is pregnant. What am I to do?"

"Poor Concha," Marta Ordoñez whispered.

"Under ordinary circumstances, señora," Santiago said, "you

51

would be right to say 'poor Concha.' But the circumstances are not ordinary. Because the Santanas are not ordinary. We are the sons of Don Quixote, the last knight in all Spain." He looked across the table at his brother. "That's what is bothering you, isn't it, baby brother?"

"For Christ's sake, Santiago. Stop calling me that."

Santiago ignored the outburst. To Marta Ordoñez he said, "Why is Alfonso so distressed, you may ask. What is a pregnancy on the wrong side of the blanket between friends? It is common enough, as you undoubtedly have good cause to know."

Marta closed her eyes. "How cruel you are, Santiago," she said in a low voice.

"Not at all, señora. I am only explaining my baby brother's dilemma. You see, when the Last Cavalier hears of Concha's condition, he will arrange for her to bear the bastard and raise it—if not in luxury, then at least in comfort. That is El Patron's way. There are several bastards of both sexes living within a hundred kilometers of where we sit—and all of them at Santana expense." Santiago grinned at his brother. "Don Quixote will be proud of you, Alfonso. He has always said you can do nothing right. Now you have proved him wrong." To Marta he said, "The difficulty is that the lord of Santanilla can no longer afford such chivalrous gestures. His politics have beggared the estate and put us at the mercy of the Jews. The cost of keeping Concha and her bastard will have to come from our inheritance. That is why, now that his *cojónes* have borne fruit, my idiot baby brother comes to me for help. True, Alfonso?"

"Santiago, in God's name—" Alfonso protested.

"In God's name what, *hermanito?* Have I stated the case clearly?"

"Yes. I suppose so."

"You suppose? Why is it that the only time you are certain of anything is when you have an erection or a skinful of liquor? Julio will have to know. He has the right."

Alfonso nodded glumly. He looked at Santiago and said, "But not Ana. Please, not Ana."

"That will depend on whether or not we can contrive to get your *cojónes* out of the snare. We will have to think very carefully."

"Have you an idea, Santiago?"

"Not yet, baby brother. You have only just given me the wonderful news, after all."

"But Papa won't have to know."

"Not right away. Perhaps not at all. We will have to consider. How far along is she?"

"Two months. Maybe three. The cow is so *descuidada*—"

"We won't argue that point. When I gave Concha to you I warned you she was not clever. Only willing." Santiago looked at Marta Ordoñez. "This conversation does not shock you, I hope, señora."

"I am not easily shocked, Santiago," Marta said softly.

"How gratifying," Santiago said. "Then tell me. Have you anything to suggest?"

"I don't understand you, Patron," Marta replied.

"Oh, I think you do, *querida*. Is there a midwife in Liencres or Santander who could relieve Concha of her little packet?"

Marta Ordoñez regarded the young man with genuine horror. In Catholic Spain, abortion was not only a mortal sin, it was a capital crime.

"That shocks you, does it? I guessed it might." He was beginning to have serious second thoughts about Marta Ordoñez's history, about what she had done—about what she had *been*—before arriving alone and destitute in Liencres.

"Well, there is time. Concha won't begin to swell for a month or two," Santiago said.

A sudden commotion in the center of the smoky *sala* interrupted further discussion. Santiago and Alfonso stood to see what the source of the disturbance might be. It was their brother Julio, engaged in a heated argument with Elvira Ubeda, the gypsy girl with whom he had recently been sleeping.

The girl had a plain face, but the body (as Julio liked to boast) of a Venus. She was a distant cousin of El Gallo and had some reputation as a dancer, all of which made her too independent for Julio's taste. She was the only local girl willing to perform the *jota desnuda,* and she was prepared to do it now. She was wrapped in a large shawl, black with red roses. A high comb held her long hair piled on her head, and there were red shoes on her feet. She was flanked by the two gaunt *picadores* attending the wounded matador. Both were very drunk and urging her to get on with her performance. Julio was furious. He had warned her that now she was his mistress, such exhibitions were to cease. Obviously, she had ignored his prohibition. The *jota desnuda* invariably earned her a shower of coins, and she had no intention of sacrificing her income to Julio Santana's jealousy.

"Julio is making a fool of himself," Santiago said, "We had better take a hand." The brothers left Marta Ordoñez at the table and pushed their way into the crowd around Julio and Elvira Ubeda. The occupants of the room were on their feet, clapping and shouting encouragement to the dancer.

"I told you there would be no more of this," Julio shouted heatedly at the girl. "I forbid it!"

"I do not need your permission to dance," the girl said haughtily. "I am an artist."

"Artist? You are a whore!" Julio Santana was red-faced and sweating. He caught her by the shoulders and had to be restrained by the two picadores, who were grinning drunkenly but still with good humor.

Elvira pulled away from Julio, the shawl slipping from her shoulders to expose a breast momentarily. This elicited a roar of appreciation and shouts of *Olé Elvira!* from the onlookers.

"Whore! *Puta! Ramera desgraciada!*" Julio struggled in the grasp of the cadaverous bullfighters, wild-eyed with anger. Santiago and Alfonso intervened. Santiago said in a low voice, "Control yourself, idiot. You are making a spectacle."

Julio rounded on his brothers. "You knew about this. You knew—!"

"Of course we knew," Santiago said, grinning. With Alfonso's help he forced Julio into a chair and shouted, "Someone bring this jealous lover an *aguardiente!*"

The guitar players began strumming their premonitory chords, calling for the unruly crowd to clear a space for "*la gitana hermosa, Elvira Ubeda!*"

Santiago held Julio tightly in his chair and hissed in his ear, "Now sit still and stop acting like a fool."

Julio looked wildly at his elder brother. He was consumed with jealousy, humiliation, and fury. The woman was *his,* and she was going to dance naked before every lecherous bravo in the district. He was angry enough to kill, but he stopped struggling and glared at his brothers. The bastards would pay for this. They had known what Elvira intended all along. He would never forgive them.

He could see the faces of the peasants pressing against the *rejas.* Elvira began with a slow *zapatada* as the music started. The whore, the filthy whore!

Santiago whispered, "She has been doing this for years, you stupid man. Do you think she would stop just because you took her to bed?"

Julio looked at his elder brother with hatred.

Alfonso was already captivated by the dance. He watched the swirling of the shawl and the glimpses of naked flesh avidly.

The men formed a tight circle around Elvira as the tempo of the *jota* increased and she stamped her heels on the worn floor. Capitán

Torres, delighted by Julio Santana's jealous humiliation, had pushed to the edge of the floor and was clapping his thick hands in rhythm to the music, which was becoming faster and more abandoned with each variation by the *guitarristas.*

Elvira's face had begun to shine with sweat. She danced with her eyes half-closed, opening and closing the shawl to give the viewers flashing glimpses of her breasts, belly, and thighs. Julio watched in agonized fury.

The speed of the dance increased and with it, the excitement of the audience. The circle of rapt faces surrounded the dancer, the rhythmic clapping was a counterpoint to the sounds made by the wooden heels of her red satin shoes. She had begun to grunt and wail with each explosive movement of the *jota.* There were calls of *Olé gitana!* and *Now, Elvira!*

With a swirling movement, like that of a *torero* performing a *verónica* with his cape, Elvira wrapped the shawl about her waist, baring herself to the hips. The *sala* exploded with sound. She spun on her heels, the shawl whirling free. Then, with a shout, she released it to fall over the reeling matador seated at the edge of the cleared circle.

Elvira scowled, eyes closed now, arms raised above her head, fingers snapping. Each time her heels struck the floor her thighs, buttocks, and breasts quivered. Her arched back drew the flesh tight across her ribs, raised her out-thrust breasts, flattened her naked belly. Sweat ran down her flanks from the hairy patches under her arms. Her entire body gleamed with perspiration, and as she whirled she snatched the comb from her hair and flung it to the crowd in a gesture of contempt. Her long tresses brushed the faces of the nearest onlookers, the muscles in her calves and thighs were sculpted by the tension of her prancing, posturing body.

The wounded *novillero* lurched forward out of the grasp of the whores who supported him and sprawled on the floor, clutching at Elvira's legs. The whores wrestled him back into his chair where he lolled, his bandage reddening but totally ignored.

Elvira completed one more circuit of the dancing floor in a spinning *zapatada* that set her naked belly to trembling. She caressed herself ecstatically and then collapsed into a crouching position, head down, arms crossed against her body in sudden modesty. El Gallo pushed through the crowd and draped her with the shawl as coins clattered and rolled about her and the room exploded into cheering.

"There," Santiago said in Julio's ear. "Was that so terrible, brother?" He tossed a silver *real* onto the dance floor as he spoke.

Julio wrenched free of his brothers and lurched to his feet. "I will never forget this," he said in a choked voice. "Never!" He took a handful of coins from his pocket and flung them at Elvira with all his strength. Then he pushed his way through the laughing, applauding crowd to the door.

Many days later, a *peon* lucky enough to have been near the *reja* told old Lopez, the head *mozo* of the Santana townhouse, that he had missed the event of the season at La Horca.

To assuage his disappointment and chagrin, old Lopez punished the slow gelding he had ridden to Santanilla that Sunday by withholding the beast's grain for a week.

The three bright stars were misted by a softly glowing veil, and within that veil a dark cloud floated mysteriously. Aaron could not remember ever having seen anything so strangely beautiful. The only sound in the darkened observatory was the slow ticking of the telescope's clockwork.

The stars were diamond bright, more piercingly brilliant than he could have imagined. Seen though the heat still rising from the eastern hills magnified by the telescope, they seemed to whirl with constant motion. This, Don Alvaro had explained, was an illusion caused by the motion of the air.

"What you are seeing, *nieto,*" Don Alvaro said quietly, "is the Great Nebula in the sword of Orion, El Casador. No one knows for certain what it is, but some believe it is a place where stars are born."

The night of space, seen through the long Fraunhofer, was deep black. It was like a field of velvet on which gems had been carelessly spilled. Aaron was aware of distance, of enormous, almost unthinkable emptiness. "Is it very far away, *abuelo?*" he asked, unwilling to take his eye from the tiny aperture of the ocular.

"Hundreds of millions of kilometers," Don Alvaro said. "Perhaps millions of millions. No one is certain. It is far beyond the orbit of Neptune, the planet farthest from the sun. The light you are seeing tonight left the nebula before Christ was born."

Reluctantly, Aaron sat back in the observer's chair. He had been unconsciously resisting the need to blink his eyes and they burned with the effort.

In the tiny, red-glassed candle flame fixed to the base of the telescope, he could see El Patron as a looming, shadowy figure.

"What do you think of it, *nieto?*" Don Alvaro asked. "How does it make you feel?"

"Very small," Aaron said. "Unimportant."

The older man laughed. Light flared as he struck a match and puffed alight one of his cheroots. The tip glowed in the darkness after the match died. "Yes, that is the first reaction. It never completely leaves one. I have it myself, often." He paused, and as his hand moved, the red tip of the cigar described an arc in the dark. "But with time, and thought—" Another pause. Aaron realized that Don Alvaro was seeking to express things of which he seldom spoke. "Not unimportant, Aaron. Never unimportant. Consider the possibility—and a possibility is all that it is, of course—that we are the only living things in all that immensity." The red tip rose toward the open panel in the roof of the observatory, a strip of the night sky that showed a faint dusting of stars. "Think what that might mean. Consider the responsibility. Think what, if that is so, we owe to God. And to ourselves, Aaron, to each other."

Aaron found himself drawn back to the telescope. The three bright stars of what Don Alvaro had told him was called the Trapezium were brilliant in the misty nebulosity. Aaron tried hard to imagine the distances involved and found it impossible.

"A man needs something to give him perspective, *nieto,*" Don Alvaro said. "For me it is this place. I am not a true scientist. I discovered astronomy late in life, and I indulge myself in it because it gives me—serenity. Only Ana, of all my family, has any idea of what I mean by that. Do you, Aaron?"

"I think so, Patron," Aaron said. "Is it a way of standing back and looking at—" Words seemed inadequate to the concept in his mind. "Well, at the way we live?"

"Bravo, *nieto.* I wasn't wrong about you. There are more than pesetas and Hessian marks in that head of yours." Aaron could hear the amusement in the older man's voice. "Have you already discovered the need for a private place from which to look at our foolish world? How old are you, sixteen?"

"Seventeen. Almost eighteen."

"Ah. That old. Then, I can speak to you as man to man."

"I know how young I am, Patron," Aaron said reproachfully.

"I am not teasing you, *nieto*. I mean what I say. This afternoon you proved that you are not ashamed of who you are or what you are. I don't suggest that it was wise. Wisdom comes hard, and seldom early in life. But I am sure you have had a conversation about this afternoon with your father. You don't need a lecture from me. Nor do I want you to think that your father is wrong. He is not. But what is right for him may not be so for you. You may be just beginning to understand this." Don Alvaro inhaled deeply from his cigar, making the fiery tip brighten enough so that Aaron could actually see the rugged outlines of his face, limned in shadow. "I hope, Aaron, that you and Miguel do not reach a parting. It happens often enough. Sons and fathers grow apart."

Aaron heard genuine regret in Don Alvaro's voice. For the first time since arriving at Santanilla he realized that Don Alvaro was a man deeply disappointed in his own sons. It struck Aaron as a sad thing to know.

Don Alvaro sighed heavily. "When I was born, Aaron, Napoleon Buonaparte was still First Consul of France. Did you realize that? In America, President Thomas Jefferson bought the Louisiana Territory. Did you know that the American states of Massachusetts and Connecticut threatened to secede from the Union because Jefferson acted without consent of the Senate? Simon Pauley told me that. I found it fascinating. Everything the Americans do is fascinating. They may become the greatest people in history, or the most foolish. But think how the world has changed in my lifetime, *nieto!* Is it any wonder one must look at the stars to see something constant and immutable?"

"I should like to go to America one day," Aaron said, moving away from the telescope. The darkness made it easier, somehow, to speak freely to El Patron.

"I would not recommend it soon," Don Alvaro said dryly. "The Langhorne Chases and the Simon Pauleys will be at one another's throats before spring."

"You went to war, Patron," Aaron said.

"Yes, and see what it has brought upon the Santanas."

"You did what you believed was honorable, sir," Aaron said.

59

"I am going to assume that when you say that, you do not mean what Señor Chase would mean," Don Alvaro said.

"You are not like Señor Chase, Patron," Aaron said with feeling.

Don Alvaro laughed in the darkness. "I trust not, *nieto.* But there was a time—ah, well, let that go. I told you wisdom comes late if it comes at all. It has come very late to me. I do not think I would have ridden out against Prince Carlos if I had known then what I know now. What did we accomplish, after all? We talked very grandly about freedom, but what we gave Spain is a dynasty of *generalisimos.* The Bourbons, all of them, are a wasted lot. They cannot rule properly. If we had all supported the Republicans, things might have been very different. But the *peones* have a saying: *Si mi tía tenía cojónes sería mi tío.* If my aunt had testicles she would have been my uncle. Peasant wisdom. When I was a young man we were all too grand to think so simply and directly. Well, you see how one's thoughts wander under the influence of the stars, *nieto.*"

Aaron was struck by a sudden thought. "Does Father Sebastio ever come here, Patron?"

By Don Alvaro's tone Aaron could tell that the question amused him. "Do I sense a clever and devious Semitic mind at work behind that question? Why do you ask, *nieto?*"

"It is hard to think of the *padre* as a man of science," Aaron said carefully.

"In other countries priests can be men of science and remain priests, Aaron, but not in Spain," Don Alvaro said. "Father Sebastio is no Jesuit. He is a Dominican. The Dominicans have ruled the Church in Spain since the Inquisition. I once brought Sebastio here and showed him what Galileo showed the world—the moons of Jupiter. Sebastio is not an educated man. Dominicans place more value on faith than on learning. Do you know what he did? He crossed himself and said that if God had meant for men to see such things, he would have made our eyes like this." Don Alvaro touched the brass tube of the Fraunhofer. "But before you laugh at him, *nieto,* think of the faith that sustains him. He *knows* what is right in the sight of God and His Son. He will *always* know. A simple man, yes, but filled to the brim with simple truths. I would not select him to school you in astronomy, Aaron, but in matters of the Faith, he is unassailable."

Aaron remained silent for a moment. He felt curiously unsettled, as though the religious recalcitrance he had felt all these months were suddenly petty and ungenerous. *"Abuelo,"* he said slowly, "would it please you very much if I were baptized?"

"You know the answer to that, *nieto,*" Don Alvaro said heavily. "But conversion must come from conviction—from the soul. It is not a garment we put on to please others."

Aaron absorbed the gentle rebuff and considered the big man sitting nearby in the darkness. Don Alvaro seemed curiously naive. Micah Marburg had felt no sincere conviction before partaking of the Blood and the Body. He had simply done what he must do to marry Adriana and take up his new, gentile's life. To Micah there was nothing whatever dishonorable about conversion on those terms. Yet Don Alvaro, because his own faith was so staunch, could believe that Don Miguel Marburg's Catholicism was as genuine as his own. Such ingenuousness in one so worldly as El Patron of Santanilla was a thing to be pitied—even loved. Aaron wished that he could express this adequately, but he could not. Don Alvaro would be offended.

The older man put a hand on Aaron's knee and shook it. "Do not despair, *nieto.* Faith comes, or it does not. It is in the hands of God. Surely your rabbis told you this?"

"I have spoken very little with rabbis, Patron. Papa was always quarreling with them."

Don Alvaro laughed. "You keep active a family tradition, then, Aaron, quarreling with *our* rabbi, Sebastio."

Aaron and Don Alvaro laughed together at the thought of the fiercely militant Dominican as rabbi.

They sat for a time in companionable silence. The only sound in the observatory was the soft ticking of the telescope clockwork.

Aaron found himself wondering why he had never experienced a moment such as this with his father. For as long as he could remember, Micah and Isaac had treated Aaron as a kind of conditional adult, someone to be trained as a future business associate, never simply and warmly as a son or nephew. Why, they had even considered marrying him to loathsome cousin Rachel in order to consolidate an intrafamily alliance with the Silbers.

Aaron could not imagine Don Alvaro, dynast though he was, doing such a thing to Santiago, Julio, or Alfonso.

Aaron felt a furry brushing against his leg and heard a peremptory mew. Adriana's great tomcat, El Cid, leaped into his lap and began to purr.

If only, Aaron thought, Ana were here in the cozy darkness with her father and stepson instead of in her bed with her husband, one could be content.

1861

In early December, the weather broke violently. The hot African winds were suddenly replaced by gales blowing across Old Castile from the Bay of Biscay. There were cold rains and flash floods in the eroded hills behind Santanilla. Electrical storms flickered like witchfire across the ridges of the Cordillera Cantabrica. Snow fell in the high passes and some stock, both horses and sheep, were lost.

On the third day of January, with a hard freeze in the air and ice glittering on the ground, Adriana Marburg was delivered of a son at La Casa de Santanilla. For a first confinement, the birth was relatively easy. The first labor pain struck at one in the morning. Adriana, as tradition demanded, was attended by her mother Doña Maria, her maid Felicia, a medical doctor from Santander, and the family chaplain Father Sebastio. By noon the child—to be baptized Roberto Alvaro de Avila Marburg y Santana—lay washed and in his mother's arms. A wet nurse stood by to suckle him at each indication of hunger. Roberto was robust, fair skinned, born with a shock of pale hair. He swiftly enchanted the women of Santanilla, from Doña Maria to the wives and daughters of the herdsmen and tenants on the estate (who were permitted to parade through Doña Adriana's rooms to admire the new man-child).

The birth at Santanilla was duly noted in *La Gaceta de Santander,* together with the intended date of the baptismal Mass.

The same issue of *La Gaceta* announced, on a back page, the death of the promising *novillero* El Morez, at the age of nineteen years, of a mortified *cornada* received in the arena of Santander. The journalist failed to mention that El Morez had been given an ear on the day of his goring.

To Aaron, the arrival of his half-brother Roberto was both a revelation and a stunning shock.

All through the course of Adriana's pregnancy he had been concerned for her welfare and solicitous of her comfort. He had dealt with the event as an adult, without giving serious thought to the effect the new baby would have on his relationship with Adriana and his father and the rest of the household. Aaron had experienced the fears that had accompanied his mother's several pregnancies, and he had imagined that once the birth took place safely, his quite natural uneasiness would vanish and life would assume a familial normality.

The first problem arising was that he was totally unprepared for the joyous turmoil the birth ignited among those very members of the household Aaron cared most about: Adriana, of course, his father, and Don Alvaro. From the moment of Roberto's arrival he became the center of all attention and future planning. The change in Micah Marburg was astonishing to Aaron. He had always regarded his father as a man unable to express affection, and over time he had learned to accept this. There were, after all, people who loved sincerely enough but who were constitutionally incapable of bestowing upon the objects of their love those attentions that came easily to warmer personalities.

But suddenly this accommodation became invalid. Micah lavished affection on the baby, bestowing on the pretty child a doting concern Aaron had never known.

It was to be expected that Ana would devote much attention to the baby, Aaron realized. To have done otherwise would have been unnatural. Yet it came as a surprise to Aaron that his stepmother now seemed to have no time or inclination for anything else. When Aaron visited her, the long and intimate conversations he yearned for simply did not take place. Young Roberto Marburg, blond, blue-eyed, and lusty, dominated Adriana's every waking moment. It did not make matters easier for Aaron that motherhood had given his stepmother's girlish beauty a serene maturity that raised an impenetrable barrier around her.

Don Alvaro was enchanted by the first legitimate grandson of his own blood, and even Doña Maria softened her coldness toward Micah in many small but telling ways.

There were no more quiet meetings in the observatory with Don Alvaro. In fact, the observatory was abandoned in preference for hours spent admiring the new son of the household.

The shock for Aaron came when he realized, with a clarity he would not before have imagined possible, that he was jealous of his new sibling.

The realization humiliated him. He was, after all, a man. How was it possible, then, to regard the beautiful, gurgling infant in the bassinet as a rival? And yet it was unequivocally so. Within days of the birth Aaron found himself comparing the joyous warmth and affection surrounding young Roberto with the memory of his own childhood. His father seemed a totally different man, a loving parent filled with such pride that one might even imagine that Roberto was his firstborn, or even his *only* child. Don Alvaro's behavior was not very different. It was impossible not to see that El Patron regarded his favorite child's new son as the promised heir to Santanilla.

In his newly discovered affection for Don Alvaro, Aaron had only just begun to feel less lonely at Santanilla. With the appearance of the baby, this burgeoning relationship fell on lean times. Aaron found himself spending more time with Simon Pauley in Santander, and, perhaps not so strangely, in the company of "the cousins."

He had not learned to like the Santana brothers, and there was no sign that they had suddenly developed any regard for him, but the birth of young Roberto appeared to have forged a tenuous—and wary—bond among the four young men at Santanilla. On more than one occasion Aaron accompanied them on their Sunday visits to La Horca and a few other drinking places in the district.

Aaron found to his dismay that he had no head whatever for liquor and that his original disapproval of the entertainments favored by Santiago, Julio, and Alfonso remained intact. Aaron was by nature fastidious, and the licentiousness of the Spanish rural gentry did not appeal to him. Yet he had reached an age to be stirred by the open sexuality of the women who frequented the taverns and *cantinas*. He avoided contact with the local whores, despite the urgings of Adriana's brothers, because he could not imagine himself coming into her company fresh from a prostitute's crib. This earned him some contemptuous chiding from Julio and Alfonso, but strangely, Santiago took his side. "Not all men," he said in his supercilious way, "are forever at the mercy of their baser instincts."

Aaron had the distinct impression that Santiago was laughing at him, but he was unable to say exactly why he thought so.

Santiago, in fact, seemed to have decided that he would make a companion of Aaron. Clearly, he sensed Aaron's feelings of exclusion at Santanilla, and indicated in many small ways that he shared them. He made repeated little jokes about the way in which the arrival of Adriana's son had turned the household into "a royal nursery." Aaron was secretly ashamed to listen to such talk, and doubly shamed by his own similar feelings.

It was ironic that Micah, when he took the time to speak with Aaron at all, mentioned indifferently that he was glad to see that he and Adriana's brothers seemed to be getting on well together at last.

Unable to have the companionship he wanted, Aaron accepted the companionship he was offered. He met Santiago's sad-eyed mistress, Marta Ordoñez, a woman who chilled him with her introspective melancholy, and Alfonso's simple, thick-bodied Concha. Julio was between mistresses, having had, as he said, a disagreement with one of the dancers at La Horca that had caused him to discard her.

Aaron sensed that the attention paid him by the cousins and their cronies was not true friendship, but he allowed it to continue because he had nothing better to take its place. It shamed him that he had no nobler antidote for the envy that poisoned him each he saw his father, Adriana, and Don Alvaro smiling over the beautiful child in the heirloom bassinet of the Santanas.

On the day of Los Santos Reyes, gifts were exchanged to celebrate the Christmas season. The following week the local gentry gathered in the stone church at Hacienda Santanilla to celebrate Mass and to watch Father Sebastio administer to young Roberto the sacrament of baptism. Doña Maria had been disgruntled because Don Alvaro had not invited her relative, the Bishop of Liencres, to conduct the rites. But El Patron had been adamant. He insisted that Robert Alvaro Avila Marburg y Santana be sprinkled with the holy water by the family chaplain who had given the sacrament to all of the Santana children. Father Sebastio had pretended to take it simply as his due, but to Aaron it was apparent that he was swollen with a most unchurchly and very Spanish pride.

Don Patricio Avila and his wife Doña Alicia, cousins of the Santanas, stood as godparents to young Roberto, making for him the proper responses as Father Sebastio cleansed him of original sin and welcomed him into the Communion of Christ. They also undertook to stand, if need be, in loco parentis, should Roberto Marburg find himself orphaned or in need of their assistance.

Aaron watched these ceremonies distantly, from the back of the church. He had heard more than once of the remarks passed by the Avilas and their many children concerning the unfortunate marriage Adriana Santana had made with a converted Jew. But for the New Year's season and the time of celebration of Roberto's baptism, all of these tensions and disapprovals were forgotten. The servants and tenants on the estate declared that the new baby was so fair, so blond, and so beautiful that he was clearly a sign of God's grace bestowed upon Doña Adriana, absolving her completely of any blame for having married a new Catholic.

Simon Pauley stood, an angular black shadow against the tall window of his study, his hands clasped behind his back and under the tails of his long and rather shabby frock coat. He had completed his usual comments about the unsettled weather, which had turned once again so that a cold rain beat against the windows and rattled the door.

Aaron always found this room in the consul's house fascinating. It contained a disorderly array of books and papers—among which, amazingly, Pauley could always and unerringly find whatever it was he was seeking—an American flag on a wooden staff, old maps framed on the walls, a huge globe of the world, a rack containing six muskets and a cutlass Captain Pauley had used during his time as the master of a tea clipper, several ship's lanterns of brightly polished brass, a mariner's chronometer in an oiled hardwood case, several African masks (taken, Pauley said, from the captains of slavers he had run down and boarded with a militant Abolitionist's disregard for the law of the sea), and stacks upon stacks of European and American periodicals, most of them years old and yellowing. These last articles were saved for the modern European history he one day planned to write.

Simon Pauley had been American consul in Santander for five years, a tenure that was now coming to an end. "We shall not be able to practice your English and my Spanish much longer," he told Aaron. "I have been offered a commission in the navy and I intend to take it up."

Aaron, who was fond of the hawk-nosed Yankee, had received this piece of information glumly. It seemed consistent with everything that had been happening to him recently.

"I could not in conscience remain here, young Marburg," Pauley said, still at the window watching the weather. "Not at this time."

"Will there be war in America, Mr. Pauley?" Aaron asked.

"There is already war, though no one has called it that yet," Pauley said. "South Carolina has gone. The other slave states will go soon, and the Union will fight them. Rebellion cannot be allowed to prosper," he added sternly. "Discipline, young Marburg. Discipline is what makes nations great. The South will be punished."

Aaron could think of no answer to make to so categorical a statement, particularly when it was delivered with such firmness and conviction. Yet the idea of discipline through war was disturbing. It brought to memory some of the gruesome descriptions of battle Aaron had heard from Don Alvaro.

"I watched you at the christening, Aaron," Simon Pauley said, looking down his long hawk's beak. "You seemed to hold yourself aloof."

Aaron was only marginally certain that he understood the meaning of the English word, but he remembered well enough how he had felt as all the attention of the Santanas and their neighbors centered on young Roberto. Once again, his jealousy shamed him, but he could not deny it. It rested in a knot in the pit of his stomach.

Simon Pauley, for all his tendentiousness, was a sensitive man. "Santanilla is not the world," he said. "Nor is Spain. Or Europe, for that matter. Great events are unfolding in my country. Great wrongs will be righted. There will always be work for brave young men in America. You might think about that."

"I have thought about it," Aaron murmured.

Simon Pauley left the window and seated himself, like a great dark bird, behind his littered desk. "Have you, now?" he said. "That is interesting. I thought you were betrothed, as one might say, to the Marburg Bank."

"It is what I have been trained to do ever since I was a small boy," Aaron said.

"But?"

Aaron shrugged. "Sometimes I think I want to do something else."

"But you are not certain what that something else may be," Pauley said understandingly.

"No, sir."

"You remind me of myself. You might find it hard to credit, but I was seventeen once."

"Almost twenty."

"Yes, well. When I was a young man, my father sent me off to Harvard College to become a minister of the gospel. But I hadn't the calling. I left university on my own—oh, there was a terrible to-do about it, you may be sure—and went to sea on one of my uncle's ships. I was a great disappointment to my father, who was himself a minister. But I wanted to see more of the world than Cambridge and Boston. And I did so, I most certainly did so. I became an officer of the Consular Service only after that hunger was satisfied. I like to think that my father, who went to his reward while I was still at sea, has forgiven me and is proud of the service I have done—and will now do—for my country."

"Will Mr. Lincoln give you a ship of war to command, Mr. Pauley?"

"Who can say? Whatever I am called upon to do in the navy, I will do willingly. All true Americans must put aside their personal lives now and help to save the glorious Union."

Aaron was bemused to hear in Simon Pauley's speech an overtone of similar things said that day last November by Mr. Chase at Santanilla.

Pauley found and extracted a letter from the turmoil on his desk. "This is a letter from an old friend of mine, Aaron. From General John Charles Frémont. A great man, known to Americans as 'the Pathfinder' for his explorations in the West. Have you heard of him?"

"No, sir," Aaron said.

Pauley was plainly disappointed that the fame of the Pathfinder had not reached Santanilla. "Well, no matter. General Frémont is largely responsible for bringing the state of California into the Union. A man of great ability and resource." He placed a pair of pince-nez on his great nose and studied the paper, which was covered with lines in a small, meticulous hand. "He writes: 'I shall prevail upon Mr. Lincoln to offer me command of the armies of the Union. I do not say this vaingloriously, but in the sincere conviction that there is no one better suited to the task than am I.' " Pauley removed the glasses and nodded approvingly. "No false modesty there, young Marburg. General Frémont is a man who knows his true worth. He has asked me to see if there are Spanish gentlemen with military experience who would be willing to join his staff. There could be a place for a young man such as yourself, I have no doubt."

The idea of becoming a soldier in a foreign army struck Aaron as

70

ludicrous, but he was inordinately pleased that Simon Pauley, a man he admired, would even entertain such a notion.

"I have no military experience sir. None at all." Honesty forced him to say it, even as he imagined himself dressed in something like the hussar's finery that hung in El Patron's great wardrobe.

"Nor much of any other kind, I'll warrant," the Consul said laughing. "No, I did not expect you to have been a soldier, my young friend. But your excellent training at the hands of Don Miguel and your uncle in Marburg might make you valuable as a financial officer or quarter-master."

"I don't think my father would approve, Mr. Pauley," Aaron said. His momentary flash of imaginary glory as a soldier did not extend to keeping regimental accounts or handing out boots and blankets.

"No, I don't suppose he would, Aaron," Pauley agreed. "It was only a passing thought."

On the long ride back to Santanilla through the pelting rain, Aaron reviewed his conversation with the American. He would be sorry to see Simon Pauley leave Santander. Though years older and given to a certain pomposity in his manner, the consul had been a good friend to him. Soon, Aaron thought darkly, he, Aaron Marburg, would be the only true foreigner living in the district. Simon Pauley was going off to a distant war, and Aaron would miss him.

$\mathcal{7}$

Adriana, wrapped in fine wool against the cold as she sat before the fire in her day room, regarded her new son with a mixture of curiosity and affection.

The baby was making wet noises as he suckled Tomasa's swollen breast. Her own child, a dark-skinned girl two weeks older than Roberto, lay kicking contentedly in a large reed basket on the hearth. Tomasa Gomez, wife of Raoul, a herdsman, had been given the privilege of naming her baby Ana-Maria after Doña Adriana when she had been selected to become wet nurse.

There was considerably more advantage to the selection than merely good food and special care. When Doña Maria had determined that Tomasa had sufficient milk for both her own infant and Adriana's, the woman and her husband had been moved from their herdsman's cottage into the main house. Raoul Gomez was given work in the stables as a groom; it would no longer be necessary for him to spend days and weeks on the range with the sheep. His stipend was increased, and it was understood that Ana-Maria would become young Roberto's godchild. This was far more than a religious formality. It meant that for as long as she lived, Ana-Maria Gomez would have a claim on Roberto Marburg. It would be his responsibility to see to it than she was never in need, and when in time she came to be married it would be his duty to assure himself that it was a suitable marriage and one that would benefit his godchild. Until Roberto was grown, his parents would undertake to fulfill these obligations, but he and he alone would bear the weight of them.

Nor did the relationship stop there. Tomasa Gomez, presently eighteen years old, was now his *nana.* It was her task to tend him, indulge his wishes, deal with his aches and pains, comfort him, and serve him in every way possible. She became his surrogate mother and, in many subtle ways, his servant for life. In return he would be expected to provide for her and, if need be, make a home for her in her old age.

It pleased Adriana that Tomasa was a near relative to her own *nana,* Eusebia Gomez, who had unfortunately died, with Adriana's own godchild, in the smallpox epidemic of 1856.

Adriana endured the discomfort of having her breasts bound to inhibit lactation just as she endured the enforced inactivity traditionally prescribed for young mothers by the French-trained Doctor Martinez of Santander. She was expected to play the invalid for at least thirty days from the time of Roberto's delivery, and though her good health and her natural restlessness made it difficult, her training at the hands of Doña Maria made it possible.

Doña Maria Santana believed that childbirth was a severe ordeal designed by a wrathful God to punish women for quite possibly having enjoyed the sinful behavior that caused their pregnancy.

Small, dark, and driven by an unadmitted (but very real) desire to dominate all around her, Doña Maria conducted the domestic affairs of Santanilla with the zeal of a Dominican inquisitor. She had been a great beauty when she married Don Alvaro in a ceremony that very nearly bankrupted her land-poor father. Possessed of enormous energy and passion, she had received a harsh and cruelly inhibiting education at the hands of the Sisters of Santa Teresa at Avila. Twenty-nine years of marriage to Alvaro Santana had severely tested the strength both of her character and her training. She loved him still as passionately as ever, but she had not approved of him when they were first wed, and she did not approve of him now. She believed that God had punished her for her carnal desires. She had lost two children in infancy and her living sons were dissolute and, in Alfonso's case, stupid. She had concentrated all of her attention on Adriana, only to have that wicked man, her husband, corrupt the girl with new and radical ideas.

Alvaro had outdone himself in perversity when he had approved of Adriana's marriage to a converted Jew. Doña Maria had spent many hours on her knees in the chapel seeking some divine intervention to prevent the wedding. But it had inexorably taken place, in the same way that everything Alvaro contrived took place. Even Father Sebastio and Maria's cousin, Carlos Borjas, the Bishop of Liencres, had sanctioned it.

Despite her prejudice and her inner conviction that Adriana could have done far better, Doña Maria had begun to respect Miguel Marburg. Grudgingly she admitted (to herself alone, and occasionally to Father Sebastio in the confessional) that Miguel Marburg had certain qualities she admired in a man. And, thanks be to Mary Virgin, he didn't *look* like a Jew. Aaron Marburg she simply dismissed as unimportant to the Santanas.

The seduction of Maria Isabella de Santana y Borjas was very nearly completed by the birth of her first grandson. The blond, blue-eyed, happy baby captured her heart. She resolved that he would be all that her sons were not, and that he would be nothing at all like her unruly, dangerous, and quixotic husband. She was determined that Roberto Marburg y Santana would be a man she could love without pain or risk. Her grandson would be a caballero. She would see to it.

The selection of Tomasa Gomez to be his *nana* was only the first of many decisions Doña Maria intended to make for young Roberto.

Adriana had lost interest in watching Tomasa feed the baby and had returned to reading her book when Doña Maria appeared in the sitting room.

It struck Adriana, not for the first time, that her mother never simply walked into a room. She came through the door rustling, like an army in taffeta, always prepared to do battle.

Instantly Doña Maria went to the chair where Tomasa sat holding the baby and cuffed the girl for having allowed Roberto's tiny feet to become uncovered in the chilly room.

"Be more attentive, girl," she said sharply. "I lost Alfredo because a *criada* was careless in winter."

Adriana knew perfectly well that her brother Alfredo had died of diphtheria in the middle of summer. Everyone at Santanilla had heard the story many times.

Roberto stopped feeding and gurgled happily. Doña Maria took him from Tomasa and carried him to his bassinet, whispering gently to him. Tomasa sighed and took up Ana-Maria, giving her a full breast. Ana-Maria was a placid baby, fat and healthy, with eyes like buttons of jet.

Doña Maria settled before the fire. Even in the deep, chintz-covered chair, she sat straight as a spear, a fragile Dresden figurine all in black. The hacendada always wore black. It accentuated the pale delicacy of her complexion, which was never exposed to the sun. Spanish women of Doña Maria's class prized fair skin above all other attributes of beauty.

"Ana," Doña Maria said, "El Patron and I have talked about it and we wish that you would stay at Santanilla for another month." Adriana and Miguel planned to return to the townhouse within the week. The duties demanded by family tradition had all been fulfilled.

"I'm sorry, Mama," Adriana said, "But Miguel must return. Isaac must not think he is neglecting his work."

Tomasa Gomez followed the conversation with lively interest. She had lived all her life on the hacienda, and the prospect of now living in Santander was exciting. Raoul Gomez was less enthusiastic, wondering what he would do as a groom in a household that kept only three horses.

"There would be no need for Miguel to stay," Doña Maria said.

"Our plans are made, Mama," Adriana said. One could never retreat an inch in dealings with her mother. To do so was swiftly to be overrun.

"Very well," Doña Maria said stiffly. "I warned Alvaro that you would not stay longer, that you would take the baby and leave."

"Mama," Adriana said chidingly.

"No. I quite understand. You have your lives to lead, your fiestas to attend, your friends to see."

Adriana fixed her mother with a gaze as flinty as her own. "I am happy you understand, Mama."

Doña Maria sighed theatrically. She had never really learned to refine that sigh, thought Adriana. But then, it had to be difficult for one with so much steel in her personality to assume the character of the long-suffering, acquiescent parent.

"We promise to bring Roberto to see you often," she offered.

"Oh, often, you say." Doña Maria held a handkerchief of fine lawn edged with lace. Adriana half-expected to see her lift it to wipe her dry eyes. But she did not.

"I give you my promise, Mama," Adriana said.

"You must be generous with him, Ana," Doña Maria said. "He is our first grandchild." Her wistful tone took on an edge. "At least he is the first we can acknowledge, your brothers being what they are."

"Miguel and I have discussed it, Mama. We agree that Roberto must spend time here at Santanilla."

"Your father has already selected a pony for him," Doña Maria said. "He is making lists of tutors."

"He is barely a month old," Adriana said. "I think he is safe from Papa's ponies and tutors for a while."

"Yes, you can smile, *hija*. But I have lived with Alvaro Santana for almost thirty years. I have had to deal with revolutions and lawsuits and telescopes. I know how beguiling he can be when he chooses, how he can steal a child's heart—"

Adriana, having heard this diatribe begin many times, moved to forestall it. She leaned forward and took her mother's hand.

Doña Maria snatched her hands away. "Do not patronize me, Adriana," she said.

"Forgive me, Mama."

Doña Maria shivered and drew her shawl around her. "It is freezing in this room. It is too cold for the baby."

Adriana, who preferred this room in her suite to all the others, told Tomasa to call a *mozo* to build up the fire.

The rain beat against the thick panes in the glass doors that opened out onto the inner patio garden. It was a cold room, with a scatter of rugs on the blue-tiled floor and bare walls of whitewashed stone. But all of La Casa was cold in winter. The rambling design of the great house, the glazed floors, and the long overhangs outside were intended to keep the house cool in the blazing summers. Winters at Santanilla were to be endured.

"Where is Aaron?" Doña Maria asked. "I haven't seen him for days." From her tone she made it clear that she was simply making conversation. She didn't care where Aaron might be or what he might be doing.

The question, empty though it was, set Adriana to thinking about her stepson. It was true that he was seldom seen about Santanilla these days. Since the birth of the baby, in fact. She wondered vaguely if he were avoiding her for some strange adolescent reason.

"Don Aaron has been going out with Don Santiago and his brothers," Tomasa volunteered.

"Have you been spying on them, then?" Doña Maria asked coldly.

It seemed to her that servants were more outspoken now than they used to be. When she was a girl in the Borjas house, servants spoke only when addressed by their betters.

"*Ay,* no, Doña Maria," Tomasa said, her plain face flushed with confusion. She swiftly busied herself with wrapping Ana-Maria in her blanket and buttoning the bodice of her dress. Doña Maria noted with faint disgust that her nipples had leaked milk through the fabric. Ah, servants were not what they were years ago. Not at all. She forgot the wet nurse and turned to her daughter.

"I am pleased to see that Aaron is not simply loitering around you, as he has done in the past," she said.

"Aaron is a good boy, Mama," Adriana said firmly.

"Well, certainly a clever one," Doña Maria said, "But then, they are good at being clever."

Adriana suppressed a retort. It did no good whatever to quarrel with her mother over Aaron's and Miguel's race. In time she would lose her prejudice. The baby was the opening wedge in creating a division between Maria de Santana y Borjas and her ancestral bigotry. But the process would take time. Years, probably.

Enrique, one of the *mozos de quadra,* a stable boy, came in with wood to build the fire into a roaring blaze. El Cid, Adriana's cat, followed him into the room. The animal was large, nine kilos at least, and looked even larger because of his long, full coat. He sat before the fire looking up at Doña Maria.

"I wish you would get rid of that beast," she said. "He always looks as though he is judging me."

Adriana could not suppress a smile. "Perhaps he is, Mama. The gypsies say cats have magical powers."

Tomasa's dark eyes widened and she made the sign of the Cross on her breast.

Adriana looked at the wet nurse and said, "It's a *cat,* girl, not a devil."

"*Sí, señora.*"

"Just see to it he does not go near the baby," said Doña Maria.

El Cid regarded Doña Maria critically for another full minute before he dismissed her with a flick of his tail and leaped into Adriana's lap.

"I have never liked cats," Doña Maria said. "Sly creatures. I much prefer dogs."

Adriana scratched El Cid behind the ears and was rewarded with a deep, rumbling purr. Don Alvaro had told Adriana long ago that dogs bestowed their loyalty where you chose, cats where *they* chose. "Therefore, affection from a cat should be more highly prized."

El Cid looked at each of the women in turn, then curled up and closed his eyes.

Doña Maria returned to the original subject of conversation. "You are resolved, then, to go back to Santander. When?"

Actually, Adriana had already discussed this with her father, but it would not do to say so, most particularly since her mother had striven to give the impression that El Patron wanted the Marburgs to stay on at Santanilla indefinitely. It was possible—probable—that when Don Alvaro had spoken to his wife about it he had allowed her to think that the decision had not already been made. Years spent with Maria had taught El Patron that direct confrontation was best avoided in the interest of domestic peace.

"Next week, Mama," she said. "Miguel has much to attend to."

"The bank," Doña Maria said. The hacendada of Santanilla had never quite managed to rid herself of her Church-inspired prejudice against the lending of money at interest. It made her uneasy that a German bank held mortgages on Santanilla. Still, if it must be tolerated, she felt secretly satisfied that Miguel Marburg was committed to protecting the family's interests. He was, after all, a kind of Santana himself now.

"Did Miguel ever tell you why we sold no horses to that American?" For two months Doña Maria had tried to sort out the rumors and servants' gossip. Her husband had deliberately neglected to tell her of Aaron's part in preventing the sale to Señor Langhorne Chase.

Adriana, who had heard the entire story from her furious spouse, had been delighted. And like her father, she was proud of what Aaron had done. But she had no intention of telling Doña Maria the details.

"There was some problem," Adriana said, deliberately vague. "Señor Chase could not meet the terms."

Doña Maria's instincts told her information was being withheld, but she was accustomed to this. It was the price one paid, she understood, for being forthright and outspoken.

"Well, then," she said. It pained and angered her that she could find so little to discuss with her daughter. Adriana had never been interested in the things proper for women of her station in life. If she had ever had a taste for feminine conversation, her special relationship with her father had overridden it. She dealt with domestic matters adequately, but only that. She allowed her household servants to bully her because their supervision bored her. She was forever to be found with her nose in a book, ruining her eyes, filling her mind with information useless to a Spanish matron.

All of this must be borne, Maria de Santana y Borjas knew, because Adriana was her father's daughter. She had been stolen from her mother, and this was a great tragedy. Now their conversations were infrequent and difficult, more in the nature of duels than mother-daughter sharings. Doña Maria, who was always slightly angry, grew more so when she regarded her loss. But, she thought glancing fondly at the bassinet, there was another generation of Santanas in the house now.

"Well, then," she said again. "If you have made up your mind."

"I am sorry, Mama. But we must return to town. Please try to understand."

Doña Maria stood, a tiny, ramrod-straight figure in the vast, cold room. "Tomasa," she said sharply. "Keep that baby warm. Do you understand me?"

When her mother had left the sitting room Adriana did not immediately take up her book again. It was Mr. Dickens's new novel, *A Tale of Two Cities*.

These encounters with her mother wearied her. It was so very difficult to talk with her. Doña Maria dropped things haphazardly into the conversation, and it was almost impossible to know whether they were important or simply gambits intended to distract and put one at a disadvantage.

Her mother's question about Aaron, for example. She seldom gave any indication of caring where Aaron might be or what he did. And where *was* Aaron spending his time these days? Adriana wondered. She had seen very little of him since the baby was born, and she found she rather missed his company.

Presently she opened her book again and returned to the heroics of Mr. Sidney Carton. The character was a bit foolish and quite touching, she thought. She could almost imagine Aaron playing the part.

A thoughtful smile touched her lips and she rubbed the top of El Cid's broad head until he stretched and began to purr again. Males were so easily dealt with, she thought, still smiling. Why did her mother find it so very difficult?

In the room of La Casa that served as an office, Micah Marburg sat perusing the estate accounts. The sheets, filled with columns of Aaron's neat copperplate script, covered the surface of the heavy refectory table that was used as a desk.

Micah leaned back in the chair, ran his fingers through his thick, dark hair, and stared pensively through the thick panes of the doors leading to the outside gallery. The rain streaked the glass and from time to time a gust of wind, spinning beneath the eaves of the great house, rattled the doors in their frames. The oil lamps, needed throughout the day at this dark time of the year, flickered in the drafts. The townhouse had new gaslights, but the hacienda was still illuminated much as it had been for all of the two hundred years of its existence. To Micah Marburg, accustomed to the modernity of a German town, Santanilla was medieval.

The accounts were all current. The last item in the ledger was the four wagonloads of oat hay delivered to the horse barns only yesterday.

At this very moment Don Alvaro was overseeing the work crew lifting the bales into the lofts.

When did Aaron do his work? Micah wondered. Since the New Year, he had seen the boy scarcely a dozen times, and then only briefly. Aaron must be doing the accounts late at night, when the rest of the household was asleep. Most of the time he seemed to be away, in the company of Adriana's brothers.

This was a development Micah had not foreseen. On the one hand, he was not displeased to see that some of the hostility Aaron usually showed the Santana brothers had gone (or at least gone into hiding). But on the other hand, Micah could not bring himself to believe that anything good could come to Aaron through so peculiar an association.

Micah wondered if he had not overdone the almost cloistered atmosphere in which he had raised Aaron. The boy had been reared in a kind of closed academy devoted to the theory, practice, and mechanics of banking. He had been force-fed languages, accounting, law, and economics. In Marburg am Lahn there had been a perfectly serviceable *gymnasium*. Given the known laxity of the Marburg family's Jewishness, he could have survived a German education. Micah himself, and Isaac too, had had such schooling. There had been anti-Semitism, of course, but nothing one could not survive. But (and it troubled Micah now, when he could force himself to think about it) no one had ever considered asking Aaron what he wanted. No, Aaron had been trained to become at the earliest possible moment an asset to the Marburg Bank. Seen in that light, Micah's and Isaac's treatment of the boy had been cavalier, to say the very least.

It was hardly surprising that Aaron was very different from other young men his age. Micah had the uncomfortable suspicion that Aaron, at almost eighteen, was still a virgin. It was only a suspicion, because Micah had never spoken of intimate matters with Aaron. The truth was, he admitted bleakly, he and Aaron had never talked in the manner of fathers and sons.

Which brought Micah to the most troubling admission of all. Aaron had never really seemed a son to him. He had always regarded the boy—and treated him—as some sort of a potentially useful younger brother—a sibling too junior to be included in pleasures or confidence, forever on probation, in the manner of an employee.

Micah sat thoughtfully at the large table, drinking the bitter Moorish coffee of Spain and listening to the wind blow through the arches of the gallery and across the sere winter garden. He was reviewing his performance as a father and finding it wanting.

I was too young when Aaron was born, he thought. Only a little older than Aaron is now. And Sarai—what could be said of Sarai? Sickly from the beginning, a sallow and melancholy woman so devoid of passion that her efforts to dissemble disgusted a lusty man. Poor creature, she had been an impossible woman to love. God forgive me, he thought, but that was the simple, terrible truth of it. Now that he had a son by a woman he passionately loved, he understood how empty his first marriage had been—and what that emptiness had done to his relationship with Aaron. *With Aaron.* Why was it so difficult for him to say *with my son?* But it was so, and it was too late for a change. A loveless marriage had made him into a cold father.

He took a cheroot from a case and lighted it with a wooden match. He watched the flame until it died in the damp air.

Don Alvaro liked to say that a man's life was governed by *las Parcas* —the Fates. It was simpler than that, and more complicated. Time was the key. Time and circumstance. As it was written in Ecclesiastes: *To everything there is a season; a time to keep, and a time to cast away.* He had been unready to be a husband when he married Sarai; unready to be a father when Aaron was born. Who could say why?

Now it was different. He thought of his beautiful young wife and her golden infant, and his heart filled. *Now* he was a husband; *now* he was a father.

And what about Aaron? Under the adolescent façade of rebellion, under the sullen mask, was there still a child waiting for a father's love and approbation?

People say we are alike, Micah thought. One would think that would make it easier to touch, to share, to love. But it did not.

With a sigh, Micah Marburg returned to scrutinizing the painfully, exquisitely correct ledgers before him. Next week he would remove his wife and child to the townhouse in Santander. Aaron would remain here at Santanilla.

It should have shamed Don Miguel Marburg that he was relieved to be putting distance between his firstborn and his new family, but it did not. Aaron's hunger—yes, his *jealousy*—was becoming a burden.

S*alud, amor, y pesetas.*" Santiago
Santana lifted his glass of *aguardiente* in a toast to health, love, and
money.

Alfonso laughed and nudged Aaron. "Answer him, *compañero.*
Answer him."

Aaron disliked Alfonso's way of touching, hugging, nudging when
he was drunk. But Santiago said that was just Alfonso's way of being
a good companion. "He is a clown, my brother," Santiago said, "but
he means well, trust me."

"*Y tiempo para gozarlas,*" Aaron said. And time to enjoy them. He
drank his glass of brandy down and Concepción, her enormous dark
eyes owlish in the candlelight, her olive skin gleaming damply in the
overheated room, expressed her approbation with a giggle. Her deeply
cut bodice showed half of her breasts and Aaron found it difficult not
to stare at them. Her nipples showed plainly through the silk. Aaron
had never seen such ripe-looking breasts. In fact, the only breasts of any

kind he had ever seen had belonged to his dreadful cousin Rachel Silber, who had spitefully shown herself to him when she was eleven and he was ten. It was not an occasion he remembered with pleasure. But Concha was not cousin Rachel, and he was no longer ten years old. He was also far from sober. The four of them, Aaron, Santiago, Alfonso, and Concha, had been drinking *aguardiente* since five o'clock. It was now after nine and there was no prospect of eating until eleven or later. No one took meals at a respectable hour in this country, Aaron thought unsteadily.

It was Concha's saint's day, she said. They were in her shabby little house in Liencres. Santiago had hired a trio of *musicos* and they stood out in the gallery, protected from the rain but not from the cold, playing through the *rejas*. It was what Alfonso called *una pequeña parranda*—a little spree.

Aaron had begun the evening thinking about Adriana, and as he had become progressively drunk, he had gone through a period of the most astounding pain and guilt. What could be said of a man who hated his infant half-brother? What sort of person could feel such emotions? But presently he had found himself regarding his troubles at one remove, as though he were someone else watching Aaron Marburg wrestle with his sins. If liquor could distance one from one's problems, there was something to be said for it.

Not only that. When he had walked into the tiny *sala*, Concepción had been a pretty enough but coarse girl with heavy thighs and stubby hands. He had found himself comparing her unfavorably in every particular with Adriana. But after the third bottle of *aguardiente* was opened, her dullness became placid good nature, her peasant's coarseness became sturdiness, her smile became whiter and warmer, her eyes brighter. And then there were those amazing breasts and the deep crease between them.

Among the books in Simon Pauley's library Aaron had encountered a new translation of poems from the Persian called *The Rubaiyat of Omar Khayyam of Naishapur*. The verses had been pleasant enough, but tonight one seemed to stick in his mind most persistently. The last two lines were: *I often wonder what the vintners buy / One half so precious as the goods they sell.*

The poet must have known Concepción, he thought with a foolish giggle. Concepción and *aguardiente*.

Concepción Paredes was a simple girl. A childhood among the dependents of Hacienda Altamira did not stretch the mind or sharpen the intellect. Until she was fourteen years old she had worked as a scullery maid in the kitchens of Altamira, the estate bordering Santanilla, as her mother had done before her.

Children of the *peones* on the haciendas of Old Castile grew up swiftly. They lived among animals: horses, sheep, and cattle. They were surrounded by *vaqueros* and shepherds, lusty men who had few pleasures and who knew that their lives might be hard, dirty, and short. Sexually mature girl children were always at risk in such an environment. Therefore, and with the wholehearted approval of the Church, parents tended to arrange very early marriages for their daughters. Concha Paredes had begun to menstruate at nine. By the time she was twelve, her father had arranged for her to marry one Juan Castro, a thirty-year-old shepherd whose first wife had died of smallpox in the epidemic that had swept northern Spain some few years earlier.

In the normal way of things Concha would have been married, leaving the kitchens of Altamira for the bleak life of the shepherd's wife, living in a cottage at the hacienda in winter and spending the less severe seasons in camp with her husband in the high meadows of the Cantabricas. But a month before he was due to bring his herd down from the mountains, Juan Castro had drowned trying to rescue a ewe in a flash flood.

Concha did not grieve; she scarcely knew the man. But she was now suspect. Her virginity was in question. This was because, in spite of all the priests could do to admonish their congregations, the *peones* had a regrettable tendency to begin exercising connubial rights immediately upon betrothal.

As it happened, Juan Castro, a man of Catalan descent, had been deeply religious and honorable. He had not touched his twelve-year-old bride-to-be. But very few of the eligible men at Hacienda Altamira believed this.

Time passed, but no further offers were made for the hand of Concepción Paredes. Advances, however, were many and grew steadily bolder. It became necessary for the Paredes family to guard Concha's suspect virginity day and night.

Aware of the Paredes' troubles, Doña Alicia, the hacendada of Altamira, took action to end them. She arranged with Señor Pauley, the consul in Santander, to take Concha into his house as a *criada,* a housemaid. She would have been incompetent to serve in that capacity in any proper Spanish household, but for an American she would do.

Concha worked for Pauley a year and some months before encountering Santiago Santana, who dazzled her rather slow mind and unlocked her overdue sexuality. The consul had been furious, Doña Alicia philosophical. One could only do so much to save *peones* from themselves. *Las Parcas nos mandan.*

Concha's pregnancy, now in the fourth month, had troubled her very little. She was a strong and healthy girl. Not without reason did the Santana brothers habitually speak of her as La Yegua—the Mare. She came of a people bred for centuries to survive and procreate in a harsh and unforgiving land. Women of her race and class who had difficult parturitions died, as did their progeny.

She had felt some discomfort from morning sickness in the second month, but only briefly. Her sturdy frame now displayed a small but definite roundness of belly and increased fullness of breasts. Her nipples tended to engorge more easily now, and she found that she was having more erotic dreams than before.

This last development *was* something of a problem. Since telling Alfonso of her condition, she was astonished to have him cease almost completely to engage in sexual intercourse with her. He told her that it was out of consideration for her well-being, but she did not believe him. Having lived most of her life in a one-room stone cottage with a large family, she knew that men (the men *she* knew, at least) did not avoid love with pregnant women. She well remembered the grotesquely humorous sight, spied from under her covers as she lay on her palliasse in a corner of the Paredes hovel, of her brother Francisco humping awkwardly to penetrate his wife a mere month and a half before she gave birth to a son.

But Alfonso refused to do more than fondle her. It was so out of character for him that she wondered if someone had told him that he must behave in this peculiar manner.

He had ceased to strike her, too, and this was equally strange. In fact, he had recently been treating her with such reserve that she had begun to wonder if some mishap had not overtaken his virility. She did not dare to ask. His forbearance would not extend so far as that.

But the unhappy truth was that she missed a man's attention. Santiago had taught her many ways of lovemaking that might be sinful, but were enormously pleasurable. Alfonso had been less inventive, but more *macho.* Her schooling in the bed of the Santana brothers had been extensive, and for the last months she had been celibate. Her body had grown accustomed to sex, and she longed for it.

First Alfonso and then Alfonso and Santiago together had spoken very seriously to her about her future. They had explained that it was,

86

of course, impossible for her to dream of marrying Alfonso Santana. She quite understood this. She was, as they were, the product of a rigid caste system. The daughters of herdsmen simply did not marry men of Alfonso's class. Old Castile was the most conservative of Spanish provinces.

But, the brothers had explained further, it was their duty (one that they willingly accepted) to see to it that provision was made for her and for the child that she would bear in the midyear. This they would most assuredly do.

And then, wonder of wonders, they had suggested that it was possible—very *remotely* possible—that a husband might be procured for her. And if not a husband, at least a substantial endowment that would permit her to live comfortably if not respectably.

She had seen this coppery-haired young relation of the Santanas before, briefly. His status was not quite clear to her. He was of the Santanas, but not a Santana. He was a foreigner and, some said, a Jew. But Jews were dark and slightly built, with long, greasy locks about their faces. The Jews who killed Christ had looked like that. Father Carlos, the priest in the church in Liencres, had described them many times. This Aaron Marburg was handsome. Therefore he could not really be a Jew. The gossips were wrong.

It took time for Concha to accept a new idea of any kind. But this evening it had occurred to her it might be this young man Santiago and Alfonso had in mind for her. She had imagined they meant some impoverished *mozo* or vaquero.

At the point in the evening's carousal when she had noticed how Aaron Marburg was looking at her breasts, she had had one of her very rare flashes of intuition. This was why Alfonso had been avoiding her bed. He had actually been depriving himself so that she might, in good conscience, look elsewhere. Her heart filled and her eyes grew moist as she considered such unselfishness. Alfonso was truly concerned about her welfare.

For only a moment, it troubled her that she could think of enticing young Marburg while she carried Alfonso's baby in her womb. What was being planned here was a thing she knew instinctively she could never tell her confessor. But Concepción Paredes came from a level of society in which one made one's own accommodations with the church. Confession purified the soul, of that she had no doubt whatever. But generations of bitter experience had taught the dark Iberians that confession—like all the rituals of religion—had its limits. One simply did not share with God all the misdeeds one performed in order to survive, only those that could be forgiven by doing a penance that was bearable.

Señor Pauley, during his futile attempts to teach her reading, had shown her books in which it was written that in New Spain the friars had allowed the pagan Indians to incorporate many of their own demon rituals into the liturgy of the Church so that they might make the transference from godlessness to grace more easily. If the priests could allow the worship of gentle Jesus in the blood-spattered temples of heathen gods, then surely what she was contemplating (at the instigation of her betters, let it be said) was not unforgivable in the eyes of God.

And besides, she thought with innocent lechery, to allow herself to be seduced by this handsome, white-skinned young foreigner would be like slaking a thirst. It had been far too long since she had wrapped her legs around a man. There was an itching dampness between her thighs and a tight feeling in her breasts.

Alfonso would not look at her, but Santiago was smiling broadly. She had the uncomfortable feeling that he was looking into her mind.

She is very nearly ready, Santiago Santana thought. He had touched her *aguardiente* with the tincture of cantharides, and to judge from her constant, hungry motion, it was working on her.

He had obtained the cantharides—made from the crushed wing cases of the blister beetle—from the head groom at Santanilla. It was used regularly to ready mares to take the stud. According to Dr. Reyes, the district veterinarian, the so-called Spanish Fly was not an aphrodisiac, as horsemen claimed, but simply a substance that irritated and sensitized the genital membranes. Santiago had found it effective more than once, and he was amused to see that it was acting on Concha.

The woman *was* a mare, and if one wanted results one had to treat her as a mare. Alfonso was squeamish about the cantharides, but Santiago had said, "We want her to give the Jew the ride of his life."

It was true Spanish Fly could be dangerous when given to human beings, but Santiago had used it before. It produced amazing results in women. Alfonso was a timid man at heart and probably jealous of the ride Concha was about to give the Marburg.

Aaron was thoroughly drunk now. It was almost time to bed him down and steal away.

Santiago told his brother to pay the musicians and send them away.

Aaron asked thickly, "What time is it, Santiago?"

"Very late, *compadre.*"

"We should go," Aaron said, rising unsteadily.

"Ah, no. You cannot ride twenty kilometers to Santanilla in your condition."

"I do not feel well." Aaron felt the room spinning. It was a new and unpleasant sensation.

"Lie down in Conchita's bedroom. You will feel better very soon."

"I shouldn't," Aaron said.

"Do as I say, Aaron. Believe me, I know about these things," Santiago Santana said. "*Hola,* Conchita, help me with this bravo."

Aaron felt the girl beside him, very close. She had a musky, animal smell to her. He saw Alfonso scowling at him across the room. He tried to stand alone, but Concha held him, her breast against his side, her arm about his waist.

"I am expected back—" he muttered.

"So are we all," Santiago said, laughing. "We will tell Ana you were detained overnight. It's time she knew you were a man, *compadre.*"

That was the way men spoke to one another in this country, Aaron thought. They were forever telling one another that they were men, or that they should act like men, or that this was the way men behaved. Perhaps Santiago was right. Aaron's mind was too dulled with drink to be certain of anything.

"Alfonso," Santiago said. "Put Estrella in the shed and unsaddle her. This one is riding another mare tonight."

"Santiago," Alfonso protested, "I think we should reconsider—"

"Remember the last knight in all Spain, baby brother," Santiago said. "Then do as I tell you."

When Aaron awoke in the darkness it was deep night and the fire in the *sala* had burned down to a bed of coals. A faint, ruddy illumination marked the door of Concha's bedchamber, but nothing else.

He could hear someone panting, breathing in deep, gulping gasps. Someone was pulling at him too; he could feel a clutching hand on his shoulder, trying to roll him over onto his stomach. It was Concha. She was naked and so was he and she was tugging at him, pulling him, wrapping her legs around him. She was weeping too, but not as one weeps with sorrow. This was an agonized sobbing unlike anything he had ever heard.

"Oh God, oh God," she kept saying. "Wake up, wake up, *please.*"

Aaron had no memory of how he had come to this bed, which seemed to be in slow, whirling motion. The liquor he had consumed seemed to lie puddled in his brain and belly, but the writhing woman rubbing against his skin inflamed his sexuality.

Concha had thrown aside the counterpane. With a series of odd, sideways motions she had managed to place herself under him. Her large thighs were spread wide and he could feel the hot wetness between them.

Aaron's experience of women was near to nonexistent, but he was both young and strongly sexed. Concha's frantic hunger invaded him and he began to respond to her desperate importunities. Her skin was slick with perspiration. It was hot to the touch. With rough, muscular thrusts of her pelvis she rolled against him and moaned. Her hands groped for him, guiding him toward penetration. All the while she gasped and shuddered and pleaded so that Aaron was consumed by a totally unfamiliar mixture of fear and desire.

He was shocked by sensation as he entered her. She seemed on fire. Her back arched and her fingernails tore the skin of his back but he was only dimly aware of the pain. Her cries grew louder and she uttered short, broken screams as she thrust against him so fiercely that he could feel the tendons in her upper thighs against his groin. Her hands sought his buttocks trying to pull him into her as she rolled her hips. He could feel the muscles of her vagina contracting in powerful spasms. He tried to hold back, but it was impossible. He felt himself spurting. She felt it too and shrieked, not with passion but with desperation. "No, no, no, *no!*" For a moment he had been a man, but suddenly he collapsed into childhood. The wracking sensations receded, leaving him with only his confusion and fear. Sexual love could not be like this, brutal, laced with panic, feverish with near-terror.

He backed away from her and she cried out, snatching at him. He scrambled from the bed and stood naked, reeling, looking at her plunging form in the dimness.

She began to scream again, clawing at her crotch. She appeared to be wrestling with some invisible antagonist all the while making terrible sounds. It slowly penetrated Aaron's muddled mind that the girl was ill, or mad. No human being should make such sounds. He had a terrible flash of memory. His mother's screams, very like these, had filled the house in Marburg the day she died.

Shocked into sobriety, Aaron found a match and lighted a lamp. In the flickering yellow illumination Concha was even more frightening. Her eyes were bulging with terror. Her fingers pressed into her crotch and belly. She screamed again and again, her words barely understandable. *"Burns, burns! Oh, God help me!"*

Aaron held her by the shoulders and spoke to her, but she seemed unknowing. He tried to remove her hands from her genitals, but he could not. She was unbelievably strong. Her skin was shiny with sweat and hot to the touch. A fever was consuming her.

He went to the wash basin and poured water over a towel. When he tried to wipe her brow she snatched the wet cloth and jammed it between her thighs. She began to tremble more and more violently. Whatever was afflicting her was not getting better. For the first time it occurred to Aaron that the girl might actually die. The thought terrified him. He tried to wrap her in a blanket, but she bucked and turned as though the touch of the rough cloth against her skin was agony. Her screams had grown hoarse. They came in short, animal bursts. A wracking convulsion shook her and Aaron knew that if he did not bring assistance immediately Concha would soon be beyond help.

He scrambled into his trousers and a shirt and ran from the house into the street. There was no medical doctor in Liencres, but a short distance from Concha's house was an apothecary's shop. Aaron sprinted through the dark, barely conscious of the cold rain or the slick cobblestones under his bare feet. Liencres slept, the houses shut behind their walls and *rejas*. Twice Aaron fell, only dimly aware that he tore the flesh on his knees and hands.

The apothecary's sign, a wooden mortar and pestle, banged and swayed in the wind. Aaron threw himself against the locked door, pounding and shouting. It seemed an eternity before a light appeared in the window above the sign. The *boticario,* wearing a nightcap and holding a lamp, appeared and demanded to know who was disturbing him at four in the morning, and why.

"Help," Aaron shouted, "I need help. A woman is very ill. Please help me!"

The lamp was lifted to throw a dim light on Aaron standing below in the rain. "I am not a physician," the apothecary said testily. "Go away."

Aaron beat on the door with his fists. "Help me! It is Concepción Paredes. She is very ill. I think she may be dying!"

More lights came on in the quarters above the shop. Aaron heard the *boticario's* wife shouting at him. The rain sluiced off Aaron's head and down his back. The wind gusted, swirling the rain down the narrow street.

"Oh, very well. What is the number?"

"Come now!" Aaron screamed.

"Give me the house number, hombre! The address."

Aaron gave it and stood, legs apart, hands on thighs, trying to catch his breath. He tried to calm himself, but he was shivering with cold and fright. He could still see Concha convulsed on the rumpled bed. Was she still alive? Should he have left her alone? But what else could he have done? And through all of his thoughts ran a terrible, corroding streak of shame and guilt.

The *boticario* appeared at the window once again. "Go back, *joven.* Stay with her. My wife and I will come straightaway."

"*Hurry, please!*"

"Yes, yes, yes. Now go back and keep her warm. We will see what can be done. Go."

Aaron turned and ran back down the dark street. He could feel the lacerations of his knees and hands now.

When he reached the house Concha was still convulsing. "I am on fire, *ay Dios,* it hurts me so much—" She rolled her eyes, which were cavernous with terror. She clutched at Aaron and begged him not to leave her alone. Periodically her stomach muscles would contract, forcing her to arch her back. Aaron saw, to his horror, that the wet towel between her thighs was pink with blood.

"Am I going to die? If I am going to die I want a priest." She spoke more calmly now as though she were coming to terms with her pains.

"You are not dying, Conchita," Aaron said. "The *boticario* is coming."

He held her in his arms and steadied her each time a spasm came. God forgive me, he thought, what have I done?

He sat hunched by the fire as a thin dawn light came through the *rejas.* He had dressed and built up the blaze on the hearth and then, because he did not know what else to do, he merely sat, staring at the closed door to Concha's bedroom, and waited.

A half hour ago the door had opened and the apothecary's wife, a blowzy woman still wearing a coat over her nightdress, had appeared, stared coldly at Aaron, refused to speak in answer to his questions, and rushed from the house.

It seemed a very long wait before the door opened again and the *boticario,* in shirtsleeves and wiping his hands, came into the *sala.* He was a porcine man with bushy gray sideburns and eyes like shoe buttons.

"She will recover," he said grimly. Disapproval, even contempt was in his manner. "I have administered a sleeping draught. She will rest now." He began to roll down his sleeves.

"What was the matter with her?" Aaron asked, his voice thin with strain.

The man turned to stare at him again. "Come now. Do you claim you don't know?"

"How could I know? I am not a doctor," Aaron protested raggedly.

"Let me explain then," the apothecary said acidly. "She is suffering cantharides poisoning. It is very dangerous to use the Spanish Fly on a woman. What were you thinking of?"

Aaron stared back dumbly. "I don't understand."

"Of course not. You have never heard of such a thing." The *boticario* spoke bitterly and with emphasis. "You could have killed her. Do you understand that much?"

Aaron shook his head in confusion. He had never in his life heard of the Spanish Fly or cantharides.

"What was it? Wasn't she hot enough for you, *macho?* Did you have to build a fire in her belly?" He began to pull his coat on and close the satchel he had brought into the room. "You had better stay here. Don't run away, or they will find you. My wife has gone for the Guardia."

The mention of the Guardia was like a dash of cold water in Aaron's face.

"The Guardia? Why?"

"You are one of the Santanas, aren't you? Which one?"

Aaron shook his head in confusion. "My name is Aaron Marburg. I—"

"Ah. The son of the Jew. Yes."

Aaron was so stunned that he scarcely reacted to the implied insult. "I don't understand you. Why is your wife bringing the Guardia?"

"I hope so that they may put you in the *cárcel,* where you deserve to be. But things being as they are, I suppose they will only escort you back to Don Alvaro of Santanilla and let him deal with you." He finished buttoning his coat, went into Concha's bedroom, and reappeared with a bloody bundle in a wet towel. "I am taking this with me as evidence. But I want you to see it before I go, young sir. *Look at it.*" He unwrapped the soiled towel and held it out to Aaron. In a bloody nest, a tiny human manikin lay curled like a snail.

Aaron's stomach heaved.

"Yes. It is quite a sight, isn't it?" the apothecary said grimly. "It was a human life, and now it is offal."

Aaron's voice was barely audible. "I didn't know," he whispered.

The apothecary made a sucking sound with his tongue and teeth as he covered the fetus. "What did you expect? Bloody *gentecilla.*" He used the ironic form of the word for gentry with disgust. "Don Alvaro can be proud of you."

When he had gone Aaron went into Concha's bedroom and sat on a chair by her bed. The girl slept fitfully, her hair a tangle, her mouth slackly open. There were deep shadows under her puffy eyes. All her prettiness was gone and she looked worn, used.

In Aaron's mind the images tumbled against each other like frightened animals. He felt numb, battered. He sensed the shattered ruins of his life all around him, but he was too drained, too filled with pity and shame and self-loathing to care.

Luis Torres presented himself to Don Alvaro Santana and his son-in-law dressed in his finest. He wore the full ceremonials of a captain in the Guardia Civil, with all his medals and with the red-lined cape draped over his shoulders and the stiff leather hat set squarely on his head. This was a formal occasion of the utmost gravity, and Torres wished El Patron of Santanilla to know that he, Capitán Luis Torres, so regarded it.

The young Marburg had been escorted back to Santanilla by Torres's second-in-command, Teniente de Este, and two troopers, but Torres himself had hired a carriage to bring him from Liencres so that he might arrive unmuddied by the rain-sodden road. He considered it of great importance that Don Alvaro should see him at his most military, and with clean boots.

The truth was that Capitán Torres was both excited and deeply worried about facing Don Alvaro Santana in the present situation. On

95

the one hand, the comandante was experiencing a certain satisfaction in being in a position to exercise his authority over one of the Santanas. On the other, and almost overriding the satisfaction of the first, was the fact that he both admired Don Alvaro sincerely and belonged to a class of society accustomed to deferring to such formidable men. One didn't behave in a cavalier fashion with such people. Don Alvaro might be in disfavor with the present government in Madrid, but one with his record of gallantry almost certainly had friends at the court of the Regent Christina. Great care and respectful formality were indicated.

Yet the people of Liencres must be shown that justice was being done. The story of Aaron Marburg and the Paredes girl was already the topic of gossip in the plaza of Liencres. By tomorrow it would be known from Asturias to Navarre.

Young Lieutenant de Este, who was from Valencia and unfamiliar with the way things were done here, had been prepared to leave a trooper at Santanilla to guard the Marburg boy. Fortunately Torres had discovered his intention in time to prevent the insult to the hacendado of Santanilla. He despised the Santana brothers, but Don Alvaro was a different matter. One went carefully with him.

Don Alvaro and his daughter's husband (a distressingly handsome man whom Torres had not met before) received the captain in the main *sala.* The comandante had never before been inside La Casa at Hacienda Santanilla, and he was both surprised and daunted to find it so large and so austere. The walls of the room were white plaster over stone, the hearth large enough for the trunk of a small tree to be burning there, the floors Moorish tiles bare of rugs or carpets. The *sala mayor,* the most formal and seldom-used room in the house, was almost completely devoid of furniture. Three large wooden chairs of positively medieval design stood before the hearth, but at the moment there was no suggestion that Capitán Torres should avail himself of one of them. He clicked his spurs together and stood under the scrutiny of Don Alvaro and the foreigner known as Don Miguel and a trio of cold-faced Santana ancestors (two in morion and breastplate and one wearing a magistrate's chain of office) who peered down from dark portraits flanking the stone chimney.

"I have come, Don Alvaro," the policeman said, "to inform you completely concerning the unfortunate events of last night in Liencres."

"I have been expecting you, Capitán," Don Alvaro rumbled. Torres was strongly aware of the hacendado's impressive size and the ominous depth of his voice. He must have been a fearsome hussar in the war, Torres thought.

Don Alvaro said, "May I present Don Miguel Marburg, my son-in-law and the father of the boy Aaron."

Torres brightened a trifle at the courtesy and bowed correctly to Don Miguel. All the district knew Miguel Marburg to be a Jew. A convert, to be sure, but still a Jew. Yet he resembled no Hebrew Luis Torres had ever encountered. He was too tall, too proud, too handsome, and far, far too angry. The expression on the finely modeled face was one of fury.

Don Alvaro indicated the chairs by the fire. *"Sientese,* Comandante."

Torres unshipped his hard leather hat and lowered himself into one of the chairs. It was as uncomfortable as it looked. The seat was uncushioned and the vertical back was so positioned as to make it impossible to use it for support.

A mozo appeared with a small table and a tray with a bottle of Jeréz and three heavy crystal glasses. Don Alvaro made no move to pour the sherry.

Torres had often hoped that he might one day be received socially at Santanilla, but it was austerely obvious that he was here on probation. Don Alvaro was waiting for him to speak.

"I regret that I enter your house on a sad occasion, Patron," Torres said. "But I am a simple officer of the law. Duty commands me."

He balanced his hat against the stiff thigh pieces of his boots and continued. "My officer has given you the essential facts, I assume?"

"No facts have been established, Capitán. You may assume only that we are familiar with the allegations made against Don Miguel's son."

Torres licked his dry lips. "Ah, yes. Well. The *boticario* Ernesto Rojas, of Liencres, was summoned to the bedside of the girl Concepción Paredes at approximately four this morning and found her in distress from a surfeit of liquor and the effects of also having ingested a quantity of cantharides."

He waited to see if either Don Alvaro or Don Miguel cared to comment at this point. He hoped that they would. Simply recounting the charges made against Aaron Marburg by the *boticario* and his wife placed the comandante in the position of adversary to all the Santanas, a thing not to be attempted without trepidation.

Neither Don Alvaro nor his son-in-law spoke.

"It is, of course—and most unfortunately, Patron—a practice

97

among the young bravos to use—ah, special preparations—on unchaste women—"

For the first time, Don Miguel Marburg spoke. His voice was explosive with fury and contempt. "Bravo? Aaron? He is hardly a bravo, Captain!"

Torres spread his hands. "Nevertheless, Don Miguel. The young gentleman and the girl had been drinking heavily. *Aguardiente,* the *boticario* said. The Spanish Fly may have been some kind of lark. Unfortunately—"

Don Alvaro's eyes were like chips of steel. "No lark, Captain. If the girl was given cantharides, it was a reckless and cruel act. Is the *boticario* certain of his diagnosis? He is not, after all, a physician. His testimony would be worthless in a court of law."

"It is true that Rojas lacks medical qualifications, Patron. But we are all country folks hereabouts, even in Liencres. We are all familiar with the use of Spanish Fly on livestock, and unfortunately most of us have seen cantharides poisoning in human beings. I agree that the *boticario's* testimony would not be allowed in a court, but I believe him when he says the Paredes girl was given cantharides."

"And?"

"Patron?"

"You were going to add something. Do so."

"Well. The girl was pregnant, Don Alvaro. The cantharides caused her to miscarry."

Don Alvaro's face turned stony. "Your *teniente* did not mention that," he said. Don Miguel's fists closed on his knees.

"I regret giving you this information, but—"

"Yes," Don Alvaro said. "Duty demands it."

"Just so, Patron. It makes the entire affair more complicated."

"Who is this Paredes girl?" Don Miguel demanded.

"She is the daughter of a herdsman on Altamira," Torres said. "For a time she was a *criada* in the house of the American consul Pauley. Then—" He shrugged expressively. "She was living in a house on Calle San Gregorio." He paused, his discomfort evident. "May I ask you where your sons Santiago and Alfonso may be, Patron?"

"Why do you ask me that?"

"The neighbors say that there was a fiesta at the Paredes girl's house last night. Alfonso Santana was known to have frequented the place often, and both he and Santiago were there last night. There were hired *musicos,* too. They have been questioned by Teniente de Este. They say they were hired and then dismissed before midnight by your son Santiago."

Don Alvaro was on his feet and shouting at the door for a *mozo*. When the frightened servant appeared, Don Alvaro asked, "Where are Santiago and Alfonso? Find them and tell them to come here at once."

The *mozo,* an old man, said, "They are not here, Patron. They rode off to Santander early this morning."

Don Alvaro returned to stand by the fire, his large face like a thunder cloud. "They will be questioned when they return, Don Luis. Rely on it." It was a measure of his discomfiture that he addressed the policeman in the polite form, a thing he would never have done in the ordinary course of conversation.

"Is this Paredes girl a whore?" he asked.

Captain Torres shrugged. "It is a matter of definition, Patron. She is not known to be a professional harlot. But—"

"What is being done for her?"

"The *boticario's* wife sent a message to Altamira, to her family. Of course there is no question of her returning there, and her mother refuses to accept her. But one of her sisters has come to Liencres to care for her until she is able to do for herself."

Don Alvaro's tone was wintry. "Doña Maria will speak to Doña Alicia at Altamira. If she can do nothing with the girl's family, other arrangements will be made for her."

"I expected no less, Don Alvaro," Torres said.

"Let us speak plainly," Don Alvaro said. "Is it your intention to place a charge in law against Aaron Marburg?"

"I would much prefer not to, Patron," Torres said.

"But?"

"The *boticario* talks a great deal. There is already much bad feeling in Liencres. I have had to report the entire affair to my superiors in Burgos. It will take time, but they will almost certainly pass the report on to Madrid. Eventually it may, indeed, come to a criminal charge. I much regret it, but what can I do?"

Don Alvaro fixed the policeman with a look that, Torres thought unhappily, must once have been reserved for the Carlist infantry.

"I see," Don Alvaro said coldly. "We understand the position." His tone indicated that the conversation was now at an end, and Torres came regretfully to his feet. This interview had not gone well. He looked briefly at the untouched bottle of *jerez.* He had hoped that they would have come to terms over a *copa* of sherry, as true gentlemen did. But it was not to be. He banged his spurred heels together and bowed before putting his leather hat back on his head. "I will see to it that you are kept informed, Patron," he said. He was on the verge of asking Don Alvaro for his word as a Spaniard that young Marburg would remain at Santanilla within reach of the Guardia. But though Captain Luis Torres was a courageous man, he was not so courageous as that.

When the policeman had gone, Alvaro Santana poured two full glasses of sherry and handed one to his son-in-law. He stood by the fire in the great hearth, frowning deeply. "I can scarcely believe this has happened," he said in a heavy voice.

"I don't know what to say to you, *suegro,*" Micah Marburg used the formal word for father-in-law. He was pale with anger.

"Had you any idea the boy had a woman in Liencres?" Alvaro asked.

"No. It shames me to admit it, but no."

Don Alvaro's black eyes fixed his son-in-law. "He is almost eighteen, Miguel. I had my first woman when I was twelve."

"You are a different matter entirely, Patron."

"Where is the boy now?" Don Alvaro asked.

"In his rooms. He will see no one."

Alvaro drained his glass and refilled it. "I am not surprised. Has Adriana spoken with him?"

"She tried. He locked his door against her," Micah said.

"Be careful how you deal with the boy, Miguel."

Micah Marburg's face darkened at the caution.

Alvaro placed a large hand on his son-in-law's shoulder. "I know, *yerno,* how angry you are."

"Aren't you, Patron?"

"Yes. If it is all as simple as that *peon* of a policeman says, Aaron has done a revolting thing." He paused, grimly thoughtful. "But do nothing until I have spoken with Santiago and Alfonso."

Micah Marburg was silent. His lips compressed into a bloodless line that made his handsome face strangely cold and ugly. His dark complexion seemed sallow.

"How could he have made the girl pregnant?" Don Alvaro asked. "When? How long has he known her? Was she his mistress? Has he been neglecting his work here?"

"No," Micah said. "That, at least, he has not done. Though I have been wondering *when* he worked. You know yourself, Patron, that he has been sulking for two months. He seems never to be around. Doña Maria has commented on it."

"Doña Maria comments on everything, Miguel," Don Alvaro said dryly. "Aaron is nearly a man. He can't be kept on leading strings forever."

"He should be kept on a chain," Micah said bitterly. "He has humiliated the Santanas before all the district."

"*Me cago* on all the district," Don Alvaro said. "If he has done wrong, we must put it right. That is enough for all the district."

"Will there be criminal charges?" Micah asked.

"We shall see."

Micah, unable to contain himself, began to pace. "What about the girl's family?"

Don Alvaro looked thoughtful. "She has brothers and a father. They might take it upon themselves to avenge her honor."

"Her *honor*?"

"Yes, Miguel. Even a herdsman's daughter has her honor. You should be Spanish enough by now to know that."

"But the girl is a trollop. A whore."

"The girl is sixteen, Miguel," Don Alvaro said. "And she is Spanish."

For the first time Micah Marburg grew concerned for the safety of his son. It made him even angrier.

"However," Don Alvaro said, "this is something we will consider as soon as we know what happened and how it came about. I find it passing strange that Santiago and Alfonso, who never rise before ten in the morning, should suddenly gallop off to Santander at dawn. Aaron has been much in their company lately. Not, I am sorry to say, company I would recommend for such an innocent."

"My son seems a great deal less innocent this morning," Micah Marburg said ominously, "than he did yesterday."

Don Alvaro took his heavy gold watch from his waistcoat pocket and opened it. "I will take Doña Maria to Altamira to see Doña Alicia. Provision must be made for the girl."

"And if they won't have her on Altamira?"

"Then we will make a place for her here," Don Alvaro said. "But Alicia is not a cruel woman. The girl would be better off with her than under Doña Maria's hand. If we offer to settle something on the family, an accommodation can be reached."

"My God, Alvaro," Micah said, red-faced. "It is not for you to spend your money on Aaron's whore. I can do that, at least."

Don Alvaro Santana regarded his son-in-law sternly. "The head of the family makes these decisions, Miguel. It is the way things are done here. Now, if you will excuse me, I want to question Julio and find out what he knows of all this. And I give you one more piece of unsolicited advice. Wait before you speak to Aaron again. You may, of course, ignore my warning. But take it from one who has made every possible mistake with his own sons. A little patience now may spare you both much unhappiness later."

With that, Don Alvaro lumbered bearlike and preoccupied out of the *sala mayor* of Santanilla.

A thin and watery sunlight of the sort that appears between storms leaked in through the clerestory windows of the woolhouse. The vast, empty structure was deserted; it would not be used again until shearing time for the sheep in early summer. In one of the lofts, Julio Santana watched as Chole Segre placed the cards on the dusty floor.

The Three of Cups fell on the Hanged Man and Chole uttered her throaty laugh. *"Hola,* Don Julio! There! Evil fortune for three of your enemies. What fine luck you have!"

Chole was a Catalan gypsy who had appeared at Santanilla last summer with the itinerant shearers and had stayed on to keep house for José Luna, the head groom. Her Christian name was actually Soledad, which meant "solitude" and was the source of much hilarity among the male retainers at the hacienda. Since Julio's falling out with Elvira Ubeda over the *jota desnuda,* he had taken to tumbling Chole in the empty woolhouse. She was heavily pocked by *la viruela* and she was not overly clean. But she had an enormous appetite for sex as well as an inventive personality, and Julio Santana was pleased to have her available. The business with Elvira Ubeda had had the effect of making him a kind of cuckold among the girls of the district, undermining his appeal.

Chole was also skilled, as many gypsies were, in the telling of the Tarot, and though Julio claimed not to believe in such superstitions, he was a gambler enough to know that lives could be affected by something as simple as the fall of a card.

The affair of the nude dance at La Horca last November had savaged Julio's self-esteem out of all proportion to the actual importance of the event. He realized this, but it was his nature to nurse grudges. His brothers had known that the Ubeda slut intended to go on displaying herself to the men of the district even though he, Julio Santana, had chosen to make her his mistress. By failing to warn him, or worse still, by not preventing his public humiliation, they had aligned themselves with those who laughed at his horns. Since that very Sunday, Julio had determined that he would repay Santiago and Alfonso for their treachery.

He had immediately set himself to the task of searching out his brothers' vulnerabilities. Alfonso, a born fool, was easy to injure. But the arrogant Santiago had taken more time and effort.

In matters such as these one struck at the enemy's groin—that is, through his woman. Julio had seriously considered hiring a few vaqueros or shepherds to rape Marta Ordoñez. He had even thought of doing so himself. But on reflection he had decided that Santiago's blood was too cold to make such a revenge effective. Santiago would simply discard the Ordoñez woman.

Instead, Julio had set about accumulating information about Marta Ordoñez. She had arrived in Liencres surrounded in mystery. There had to be something in her past that could be used to embarrass Santiago. Every beast, as the gypsies said, has a tail to be stepped on.

By year's end Julio's persistent enquiries had begun to produce results. He had sent to a friend in Valladolid asking for information about Santiago's woman, and the friend (who owed gambling debts to Julio) had responded handsomely.

No one in Valladolid, he wrote, knew of a Marta Ordoñez. But there had been a great local scandal some years before about a woman of good family, a nun of a teaching order, who had been seduced by a cavalryman from Seville and expelled from her convent. The ex-nun, Sister Gracia by name, had borne a bastard daughter who was now in the care of the sisters of a contemplative order in the city. The description of the debauched nun fit Marta Ordoñez perfectly. Julio was delighted with his find. To discover that her eldest son was fornicating with a former nun would ignite a white rage in Doña Maria.

The lumpish Alfonso had been more of a problem. His lumbering relationship with Simon Pauley's former servant girl Concepción Paredes was totally unremarkable. Young men of Alfonso's class had been keeping servant girls since time out of mind. The fact that Alfonso habitually mistreated Concha was certainly a reflection on his character, but little more than that.

And then, three days ago, Lieutenant de Este of the Guardia had brought the son of the Jew to Santanilla from Liencres under arrest. Before returning to his post, de Este had shared a stirrup cup and the story with Julio Santana.

That very morning Santiago and Alfonso had raced away to Santander, sending word by old Lopez that they planned to remain in town for an indefinite stay. Julio had carefully questioned the *mozo* and had concluded that his brothers were in a state of near panic. For Santiago's supercilious aplomb to have shattered was a remarkable event.

The story about the Spanish Fly raced through the household staff and Soledad Segre, at Julio's instigation, set about asking questions of the grooms and herdsmen.

Julio himself had been closely questioned by his father the morning the Guardia brought Aaron from Liencres. Julio had, of course, maintained a determined ignorance about the Paredes girl. This was a highly perishable fiction, Julio realized. That Concha Paredes was, or at least had been, Alfonso Santana's mistress was too well known.

Julio well remembered the Sunday at La Horca when Alfonso had arrived, ruffled and angry, cursing the Paredes girl. He was certain that Santiago and Alfonso, possibly with the help of Marta Ordoñez, had planned something that very afternoon—something he, Julio, might have known about had he not flown into a rage over the Ubeda whore's dance. Now that the story was spreading that Concepción Paredes had miscarried or, some said, been aborted, the reason for Alfonso's anger that day was obvious.

Recalling the few times since that Sunday when he had accompanied Aaron and his brothers on *parranda,* he remembered how strangely generous Alfonso had been with the son of the Jew. It had seemed to Julio that Alfonso had thrust La Yegua at Aaron repeatedly, though the stupid boy had been too naive and inexperienced to understand what was happening.

Now it all made sense to Julio, and the final confirmation was given him by Chole Segre. José Luna, the head groom, had told her that on the afternoon Don Santiago and Don Alfonso had ridden off to Liencres with Don Aaron, Santiago had taken a bottle of Spanish Fly from the horsebreeding barn with the laughing comment that he intended to build a fire between someone's legs.

Small wonder then, Julio thought excitedly, that the Three of Cups fell so neatly on the Hanged Man. Perhaps the Tarot really did unlock the future. Chole Segre certainly believed it.

It was typical of Julio Santana that he imagined he knew all that Soledad Segre believed. Though the three Santana brothers varied enormously in a number of traits, one they had in common: arrogance. In their defense it might be said (if anyone could be found to say it) that nothing in their heritage or upbringing had been conducive to humility. The training of a Spanish country caballero went back to the fourteenth century and was designed to suit a citizen of the world's greatest imperial power. History had made such attitudes obsolete, but in so conservative a province as Old Castile, only the exceptional individual was aware of it.

Chole Segre was such an individual. She was ignorant because she was uneducated, but she was far from stupid, and she had the gypsy sense of reality. Gypsies were common in Spain, but their ubiquity did not spare them from the prejudice and contempt that had been their lot throughout Europe and for all of their history. Like the Jews, the gypsies of Europe had undergone a savage winnowing. Like the Jews, they were a race of survivors. And like only the very cleverest of the Jews, they had learned the art of manipulating the *gaijo.*

Chole enjoyed all men and Julio Santana served her as well or better than most. She knew that she might have been beautiful had not the smallpox left her face cratered and scarred. But unlike a *gaijo* woman, she knew how to accept what was without wishing for what might have been. Julio was, in a small way, a prize. Most men of his class would have avoided Chole, or at the very least used her seldom. Spanish men tended to be slaves to feminine beauty, a quality that disease in childhood had put out of Chole Segre's reach.

Therefore, Chole knew, it was to her advantage to advance Julio's fortunes. Not precipitously, because too much success would swell the young man's natural arrogance beyond containment. But when, and if, it should become possible to improve Julio's condition in life, it seemed logical to assume that she would be bettering her own. She did not wish to be a groom's whore forever.

106

She did not love Julio Santana. She did not even particularly like him. He was not, after all, a likable young man. But she could regard him quite dispassionately as a possible vehicle for her own advancement. Marriage was out of the question, of course. No caballero would willingly marry a gypsy, even if a virginal one could be found. But few gypsies would wish to be married to a *gaijo.* They were a dreary lot, fit only to be used for the advantage of the People. Since meeting with Julio Santana, Soledad Segre occasionally dreamed of a Santanilla open throughout the year to the gypsy caravans that roamed the north. Now it actually appeared that the dream was not a total fantasy.

Chole knew young Aaron Marburg only from a distance. A lusty woman, she admired his tall good looks (though she found his pale skin and copper-colored hair slightly distasteful), and she appreciated the unfailing courtesy he had always displayed to her, and in fact to all of the dependents and tenants on Hacienda Santanilla.

Under ordinary circumstances, however, Chole would not have lifted a finger to help him. He was a *gaijo,* and stranger than most. He was also a Jew, and Spanish gypsies were devout Catholics. One race of outcasts did not spend itself in helping another.

But Chole was intellectually curious about the Jews, and since coming to Santanilla she had questioned Father Sebastio about them. Unfortunately, it soon became apparent that the old Dominican knew next to nothing about what Jews believed or how they lived and worshipped. As a child Chole had been taught only that the Jews had killed Christ and been punished for it. She had also heard the country tales about strange rites in the synagogues, ceremonies based on the ritual murder of children and animals. Though the stories had given her and the other gypsy children a delicious thrill, few now believed them. Chole's common sense told her that the authorities would long since have rounded up the Jews and exterminated them if they really made a practice of blood sacrifices of gentile children.

Actually, there were very few Jews in Old Castile. They were rarer than Moors. And when Chole became acquainted with handsome Aaron and his even more handsome father, Don Miguel, the wild stories told by the Spanish *peones* served only to increase Chole's contempt for people who could repeat such foolishness. Without realizing it, Soledad Segre was one of the least prejudiced persons living on Santanilla.

To Chole the Tarot was a living thing. The Church frowned on fortune-telling and the other, darker uses to which the cards of the Tarot were often put. But Chole, like all of her people, well knew that there was this world, and then there was another, deeper, more pro- found, more sensitive to the forces of the occult. It was in that other realm, the misty mirror image of the mundane world, that the great events that governed a person's life were determined. The Tarot opened the doorway between the worlds and allowed the adept to search in the shadows for the Powers that led mere humans about the business of living.

When the Tarot said that Julio Santana had it within his grasp to injure three enemies, Chole did not for a single moment doubt that this was revealed truth. The identity of the enemies was clear. The gypsy girl felt sorry that one of them happened to be Aaron Marburg, who had never done Julio harm, but it was Julio's fortune laid out there on the dusty floor of the woolshed, and it was to him that the Powers spoke. She, as the medium, had the ability and indeed the right to influence the *gaijo,* who, like all his people, was blind to the forces alive in the Tarot deck. But the fate was his alone.

Chole drew a deep sigh and continued to deal the cards. The Seven of Swords fell on the Knight. Great sadness for Don Alvaro. The cards were alive today.

"What is it, Chole?" Julio demanded. "What do you see now?"

"Your father at odds with three sons, a daughter, two near sons, and a wife. See, here is the Queen of Swords." Chole turned the card from the stack, knowing what it would be and who it represented. She showed her teeth like a lioness snarling. Of all the women on Santanilla, she disliked the hacendada most of all. At a stroke, the Powers were stripping Doña Maria of most of her family.

It seemed to Chole that this moment of light between two storms was illuminated with truth. She could sense the lifelines of the Santanas all around her, some twisting like gnarled ancient roots into the deep past, others groping like tendrils toward the promise of a distant future. And still others cut short, stunted, cast out of the familiar land—

"Chole, *Soledad!*" Julio was shaking her by the shoulders. "Don't go gypsy on me, you pocked bitch," he said. "Tell me what the cards say."

Chole Segre opened her eyes. In the pallid light from the high windows they were so darkly brown that they seemed black and empty. She began to gather the cards. She wrenched her shoulder out of Julio's grip. "It is done," she said.

"Done? Why?"

The gypsy's smile turned feral. "Now it is for you to do, not for me to say."

Julio sat back on his haunches, his booted ankles aching. He knew perfectly well what Chole meant.

She stacked the cards and tucked them into the rag pouch depending from her waistband. She pulled her skirts high on her thighs and squatted before the Santana like a woman defecating. "Well, Don Julio?"

"Shut up, gypsy. Let me think."

"Yes. But not for too long. I have noticed that a surfeit of thought turns you into a *maricón.*"

Julio restrained an impulse to slap her. Damn the whore, she was right. All that he needed, he had. He not only could pay off Santiago and Alfonso, he could do far more. He could even, with luck and courage, make himself the future master of Santanilla.

He had not aimed so high as that.

"I should speak with Aaron first," he said, knowing what Chole's scornful comment would be.

The girl's laugh was sharp as a dagger. "For three days the boy has been in his room wishing he were dead. What use can he be to you? Are you afraid to go to El Patron?"

Of course he was afraid, he thought savagely. A man would be a fool not to be. The thought of his father's cyclonic rage was terrifying.

She surprised him by not whipping him with her contempt. She caught at his hand and held it between the two of hers.

"Tell Doña Adriana," she said. "Let *her* tell El Patron."

Aaron awoke from a fitful sleep to the sound of many horses clattering on the cobblestones of the outer courtyard.

It was dusk. He had lost track of time and hardly knew which day it was. He had resolutely refused to open his door to either his father or, God forbid, to Adriana. The servants had left him to his own devices, putting his meals on trays outside his door. Some he had eaten, most he had not.

He burned with shame and grief. He thought constantly about Concha Paredes writhing on her sweaty bed and about the tiny, blood-streaked human doll the *boticario* had shown him.

Aaron was too clever not to know, despite his shattered state, what had been done to him and by whom. The poor Paredes girl had been brutally used because a mistake had been made, but the purpose had become agonizingly clear. The cousins held him in such low regard that they had imagined they could bind him to poor Concha. The greatest horror was that they had done this thing laughing, as a joke.

He rolled from his bed and went to the *reja.* In the gray light of evening he could see the horsemen. There were eight of them, six mounted on the pick of Don Alvaro's stables. The riders were Santanilla vaqueros; Aaron recognized them all. The seventh and eighth horses were Santiago's and Alfonso's stallions, lathered and wild-eyed from what must have been a long, hard ride. The brothers stood in a crowd of men, barely visible, facing the arched doorway to the main house. A vast, dark shape, shadowy against the interior lamps, was Don Alvaro. He loomed like a mountain.

The doors were closed and the milling men dispersed, leading the horses back toward the stables. A thin rain began to fall.

There was a knock at Aaron's door.

"Aaron. It is Papa."

Aaron sat on the window ledge. He rubbed his cheek and was vaguely surprised to feel stubble, a soft three-day growth. He became aware of himself. He had not bathed or changed his linen. There was a rusty taste in his mouth and his eyes felt grainy. The pit of his stomach was a cavern. The tiles were icy on his bare feet.

"Aaron. Open the door, son."

He could not remember when he had last heard his father speak to him in that gentle manner. It had been years, surely.

He heard his father murmur something to a companion, and her reply.

Of all the people in his world, Aaron thought, he could not face Adriana.

"Send her away," he said. "Please."

There was a whispered conference outside the massive oak door, and presently Aaron heard the clicking of wooden heels on the tiles of the gallery.

With a great effort he came to his feet and walked across the unlighted room. Against the door he said, "Has Ana gone?"

"Yes," Micah said. "Now open the door, Aaron."

Aaron pulled the bolt and let the door swing open. His father stepped into the room and closed the door behind him. In the darkness he looked even taller than he was. Aaron could smell the sweetness of his pomaded, meticulously combed hair.

"A light," his father said.

"No," Aaron said. "Leave it."

Micah suppressed a swift irritation, and Aaron sensed it. He seemed peculiarly sensitive to his father's feelings at this moment. It was almost as though he shared the older man's nervous system, as though he could read his thoughts. Micah was reining himself carefully, trying to establish a rapport that had never been. The rapport was there for Aaron. He could feel all that his father was feeling, but any hope of sympathy had died long ago.

Micah picked his way through the untidy gloom to a chair and sat down.

Aaron said, "The girl. How is she? Where is she?"

"At Altamira," Micah said. "She is recovering swiftly. She is a strong girl."

"Have you seen her?" Aaron asked.

"I? Good God, no. Doña Maria has. She says she will be on her feet within a week or two."

Aaron thought of Concha's broad back, heavily muscled flanks. Then he remembered her screaming. He sat down on his unmade bed, his belly aching.

"They called her the Mare," he said.

"Who called her that? Santiago and Alfonso?"

"Yes," Aaron said. "They laughed at her."

"Well," Micah said grimly. "They are not laughing now. They are with El Patron. He sent a troop of vaqueros to bring them back from Santander."

Aaron thought of the cousins, and his thoughts were laced with a thin, acid hatred he had never felt before. And yet he was surprised to realize that he didn't care what happened to them, now or ever. What they had done was cruel and despicable, but he, Aaron Marburg, had played a part in it. That was the unforgivable thing he could never forget.

"What will El Patron do?" he asked.

"Santiago and Alfonso will leave Santanilla tomorrow," Micah said. "He is sending them to an old comrade of his, General Diego Viscaya, in Spanish Morocco. There they will stay until El Patron calls them back. He swears he may never do that. He is very angry, Aaron."

Aaron closed his eyes and leaned back against the cold plastered wall. This house, he thought, is like a prison to me. Was it like that to Santiago and Alfonso? He could imagine their terror as they faced El Patron, but would they ever wish to return here once they were free? Of course they would, he told himself. Prison or palace, Santanilla was their home, their birthright. As it could never be his.

"I can't stay here, Papa," he said.

"I know. That Guardia captain—"

"*Not* because of the Guardia," Aaron said violently. "That has nothing to do with it."

His father's irritation was like a familiar wave washing over him. A thousand times or more he had felt it, ever since he was a child. Had he ever before realized so clearly that there was no love for him in Micah Marburg, that there never had been? He must always have known, he thought. Somehow, the clarity of the revelation made what must be far easier.

Micah was saying, "Captain Torres has made it clear that there will be civil—perhaps criminal—charges brought. It would be unthinkable to have you put on public trial in Liencres. The family could not permit it. There is Adriana to think about, and Roberto. This is their home."

Aaron felt a cold hardness suffusing his body, as though his bones were becoming steel, his flesh marble. If a sword were to strike me now, he thought, it would shatter. "I agree, Papa," he said.

"Good. Good, Aaron," Micah said, relief in his voice. There was a subtle shifting of power taking place between father and son, and both sensed it. It was as though childhood and adolescence were dropping away from Aaron, leaving the harsh, bare structure of a man.

"Yes, well, then," Micah said. "I have sent to your uncle Isaac asking him that he write to a Mr. Symington in New York. He is president of the Harlem Bank, who are our correspondents in the United States. Mr. Symington will make a place for you there. You have always wished to see America. It will be for the best."

Aaron, red-eyed in the darkness, stared at his father's shadowy shape. Did nothing *ever* change? Depite all that had happened, despite the rending upheaval that was changing lives all around him, did he still imagine he could order Aaron's life so neatly, so aseptically, as though he were dealing with a clerk or a bookkeeper? It was almost incredible that a man of his father's age and experience could be so insensitive. How could Adriana love such a man?

Micah said, "Simon Pauley is returning to America directly. He sails from Santander in less than a week. You will travel with him. He has already agreed. He is very fond of you, you know." He shifted uncomfortably in his chair. Could he feel the fabric of their relationship dissolving, Aaron wondered? Never strong, it was like silk rotting away. Aaron closed his eyes again. I have always known it, he thought. Always. How foolish of me ever to imagine it could end in any other way.

A silence fell when Micah stopped talking. Aaron felt no requirement to break it. He stood, waiting for his father to leave.

Micah came to his feet and stood too, but awkwardly, as though he did not know what more to do or say. If he touches me, Aaron thought, if he pretends to love me, I may strike him.

But Micah Marburg did nothing more than walk carefully to the door. "You must come out of here tomorrow, Aaron," he said. "There is much to do."

Aaron looked coldly at his father and said, "Yes, Micah. Good night."

Micah, startled, made as if to speak again, thought better of it, and closed the door behind him.

The sea, gray green under a gray mantle of cloud, frothed and rolled with row upon row of whitecaps. The wind, laden with rain and sleet, swept across the canted deck of the brigantine *Dover Light* like a million tiny blades of icy steel.

The ship, on her best point of sail, surged ahead as though eager to leave Europe behind her. Aaron Marburg, alone on the foredeck, gripping the wet railing with gloved hands, watched the water boiling past the fat hull, patterned with spume and spindrift. Somewhere aft a ship's bell rang the changing of the watch and sailors, some of them amazingly barefooted in this weather, raced across the wet decks to exchange their incomprehensible tasks.

Aaron turned to look at the quarterdeck where Simon Pauley and Captain Denver stood, heads together, enjoyably exchanging bits of nautical arcana.

The cold water found its way past Aaron's greatcoat collar and down his neck, but he ignored it. The sea, this vast Atlantic, was a revelation to him. The size and power of it tended to minimize the troubles of mere men and women.

Here on the *Dover Light,* a wooden, rainswept cockleshell on the empty fastness of the sea, accompanied by a handful of crewmen and passengers, the only human life within the compass of his eyes, he remembered his last days at Santanilla.

On the night before departure for Santander and the ship, he had met with Don Alvaro. They had sat alone, as they had once before, in the dark of El Patron's beloved observatory. Even El Cid had come to bid Aaron farewell.

"I should not say it," Don Alvaro murmured sadly, "but I shall miss you far more than I shall miss Santiago and Alfonso."

El Patron had done exactly what Micah had said he would do. He had ordered his first and third sons to leave Santanilla and present themselves to General Viscaya in Spanish Morocco. "I gave them sufficient money to buy commissions in La Legión Extranjera," Don Alvaro said. "They may do as they choose about the army, but they shall not see Santanilla again." Aaron was moved to hear real grief in the old man's voice. Santiago and Alfonso had lived all of their lives as caballeros, taking privilege as their due. But there was a price for such ways, and they had failed to pay it. They had not lived up to a code of honor that was dearer than life to Don Alvaro José Esteban Santana y Avila. And he had cut them from the family as ruthlessly as one might prune a diseased branch from a tree. It had been a fearsome act, medieval in concept, religious in intensity. Santiago and Alfonso could now look forward to years in Africa as soldiers of the Spanish Foreign Legion. Aaron might have felt satisfaction, but he did not. He felt nothing.

Aaron had half expected Doña Maria to defend her sons. She did nothing of the sort. If anything, she was more bitterly set against them than her husband. To mistreat a helpless woman was, to the hacendada of Santanilla, a despicable act. For the tiny, fierce chatelaine, two of her sons had ceased to exist.

Nor did Julio Santana escape. He had been forced to endure his parents' full fury for having lacked the courage to face his father with the truth. He remained at Santanilla, but on sufferance, with only his gypsy paramour for comfort.

Aaron faced the windswept horizon, remembering how sadly Don Alvaro spoke. "You were almost the son I wished for, *nieto.* With you I could have shared my thoughts. My own sons are nothing."

"There is always Roberto," Aaron said thinly.

El Patron shook his head. "I shall do my best for him. I will give him the California land if I can clear the title. It will be something for him. But I shall be old before he is a man. He will be raised by women. No, it is you who should have been the heir to Santanilla."

A dream, Aaron thought with his cold, new clarity. There had never been a place for Aaron Marburg at Hacienda Santanilla.

He remembered Adriana, and there was pain in that.

How could I have been so ignorant, so naive in the ways of the world? *I love her,* he thought, my father's young wife, my stepmother. How, he wondered, could he have hidden that knowledge from himself for so long?

At least now he understood why he could not think of young Roberto without jealousy. Roberto was the son his father had got on the body of the one person Aaron had ever learned to love. The thought was bitter. In another, kinder world Roberto could have been *his* son, and Adriana his beloved. It was twisted, almost incestuous, too dark to fathom.

Above him, canvas cracked and boomed on the straining yards. Ice coated the shrouds and ratlines. The other passengers huddled in their cabins. The pennant at the masthead pointed like a spear in the direction of America. Spray broke over the bows as the *Dover Light* drove westward.

To another life. To a *different* life.

"Pax vobiscum, filius," Father Sebastio had said, strange tears in his rheumy old eyes. "I failed with you. But go with God, young Aaron."

Aaron reached inside his clothes and withdrew the bulky letter of introduction his father had written so carefully to Mr. Symington of New York.

"Micah," he said, and his words were lost on the wind. "All that is finished now."

He drew the heavily embossed paper from the envelope and tore it into strips, releasing them to fly far to leeward where they vanished in the frothing, turbid, frigid sea.

1864

Two hours after dawn on May 4, 1864, Colonel Zachary Isbrandtsen, commander of a regiment of Wisconsin Volunteers, sat on his black charger on the crest of a low hill overlooking Germanna Ford. Isbrandtsen's regiment had been given the task of detaching a single company to cross the Rapidan with the engineers to protect the bridgehead.

The army's baggage train had begun to move out of the Brandy Station bivouac last evening. Now the last of the baggage train, heavily guarded by cavalry, was moving across the Rapidan on the two pontoon bridges.

It had been a strange, brooding encampment at Brandy Station. Though the air was soft and warm, filled with the sweetness of honeysuckle and the tang of camp fires, the Army of the Potomac had seemed oddly somber, subdued. The men, nearly all of them veterans by now, had conversed in murmurs. There had been some singing, among

Isbrandtsen's Germans mostly, and some of the usual visiting of other units. But there had been no real hell-raising, no gambling, no boasting. Only letters home and thoughtful conferences around the camp fires. Isbrandtsen had heard a staff officer say gently, "What would we feel if every man who is to die in the coming battle wore a badge, so that we might know him?" The notion had brought a cold chill down Zachary Isbrandtsen's back. Yet it had been expectation rather than fear in the air. The men were waiting to see what Grant would do. They were weary of inconclusive battles.

The morning air was fresh, bracing, the sky a clear, innocent blue. From down the line of march Isbrandtsen could hear his German immigrants singing. How they loved to sing as they marched! German marching songs, of course. Two-thirds of the regiment spoke no English, or as little as made no difference. They were the sons of German farmers who had come to this country bloodied by the repressions that followed the revolutions of 1848 in Europe. On the isolated farmsteads there was little need to learn English, and so few had. But they were good soldiers—the best—and fiercely devoted to the Union cause.

Isbrandtsen extended his hand for the brass telescope carried by his aide, Lieutenant Eisener. He opened it and studied the long column of blue-coated soldiers. Behind the colors rode Lieutenant Marburg leading Company A. Isbrandtsen had been dubious about accepting Marburg when the officers from General Frémont's headquarters were being reassigned throughout the army. But it had been either Marburg or an impossibly dandified Hungarian ex-dragoon, one of a dozen or so John Charles Frémont had somehow collected into his department headquarters. He had taken young Marburg because he spoke German, and he had not been sorry. Behind Company A, the rest of the regiment swung along smartly, oblivious of the catcalls from the Ohio troops moving across the parallel pontoon bridge. Marburg's once-elegant uniform was worn and shabby now. Isbrandtsen had heard that Jessie Benton Frémont had sent the newly arrived young immigrant to the general's own tailor for it. The tale was probably apocryphal. Lieutenant Marburg's aloof and silent demeanor gave rise to many odd stories. But two years in the real army had worn away any remnants of the ruffles and flourishes of Frémont's little kingdom.

Isbrandtsen lifted the telescope to examine the terrain to the east of Germanna Ford. A dozen miles off, across a jumble of low hills covered with skinny second-growth pines and thornbushes, General Hancock's Corps was on the move, crossing the Rapidan downstream at Ely's Ford, not far from where the lesser river joined the Rappahannock. By midmorning his advance guard should be in Chancellorsville, ready to begin the broad encirclement to the south and west that should put a noose around Bobby Lee and his damned rebels. Ewell's Corps and A. P. Hill's force had been reported advancing to the east along the Orange Turnpike and the Orange Plank Road. Grant's troops knew it, and they were ready to fight if their commander was.

Colonel Isbrandtsen thought of the staff officer's remark about marking the dead before the battle, and shuddered. He could imagine the bloody badge on at least a third of the singing, blue-coated men marching across the bridges. He wondered briefly if Zachary Isbrandtsen wore that invisible stigmata. He was forty-five years old, a lawyer with a good practice, a husband with a loving wife, and a father with two pretty daughters. But none of those grand things would stop a musket ball.

The Rapidan, swift and smooth, flowed under the pontoon bridges and emerged in a complex pattern of ripples. On the banks white dogwood bloomed in luxuriant profusion. The fields through which the soldiers marched were ablaze with wild flowers. Isbrandtsen had written to his wife Elisabeth, "It does seem that the good Lord is trying to tell us not to damage His earth any more than is necessary to bring victory."

Despite the handsome morning and the brave sights and sounds of the army on the move, last night's sense of somber brooding persisted. It was the proximity to the Wilderness, Isbrandtsen thought, that stunted, cut-over forest of scraggy pines and thickets pierced by a maze of narrow roads and walking trails. Some of the Chancellorsville fighting last May had taken place in those woods and unburied bones still lay there, caught in the thornbushes.

"Lieutenant General's staff coming, Colonel." Eisener pointed to a group of well-mounted officers galloping across the nearer bridge.

Isbrandtsen frowned because the staff group had slowed the crossing of Isbrandtsen's own troops. But the aides were swiftly clear of the bridge and cantering briskly up the slope. Grant must be coming, Isbrandtsen thought, lifting Eisener's telescope to search the line of march back along the Germanna Road.

He could just make out a headquarters company trotting forward. A three-starred flag whipped in the breeze. In the morning distance a bugle sang and the sun flashed on polished musket barrels and brass fittings. Regimental colors shone in the clear, pure light. Isbrandtsen handed the glass to Lieutenant Eisener and spurred his horse to a gallop down the hill toward his own regiment. As he went, with the cool air in his lungs and the graceful power of his charger beneath him and the jingle of chains and saber in his ears, he recalled a remark by another, more famous, officer: "It is well that war is so terrible, or we would grow to love it too much." Robert E. Lee was supposed to have said that.

By midmorning Isbrandtsen's Wisconsin Germans found themselves swinging down the Germanna Road into the heart of the Wilderness.

Aaron, whom Adriana Santana might have had difficulty recognizing had she stood by the side of this narrow Virginia lane, rode at walking pace on a rangy army remount whose jolting gait and hard mouth caused him often to remember Estrella with regret.

Two and a half years of war had changed Aaron. He was thinner, harder, deeply tanned by the sun. He wore a drooping, copper-colored moustache and his eyes seemed to have faded to a paler, metallic blue. The callow boy who had agonized over the fate of Concepción Paredes, if he existed at all, was buried deep within the veteran soldier.

In three years Aaron had written two letters to Santanilla. The first, composed as he traveled westward by train with Commodore Simon Pauley's letter of recommendation to General Frémont in his pocket and three hundred gold dollars in his carpetbag, had gone to Adriana. He had posted it at one of the stops on his seemingly endless journey to Frémont's headquarters in St. Louis, a large town called Cincinnati. He had immediately regretted it. Though the letter had actually been formal and as correct as anyone could have wished it to be, he found himself imagining that it had revealed far too much of what he was feeling, alone in this strange and dubious country.

The second letter had been sent later, after his arrival at General Frémont's glittering headquarters and after his interview with a Major Sean Dundalk, the second son of an Irish lord and a former officer in the Irish Guards, who had the task of examining the stream of foreigners pouring into Frémont's almost royal court asking for commissions in the United States Army.

Aaron had written to Don Alvaro to inform him that (much to his surprise) Major Dundalk had unhesitatingly placed his stamp of approval on Aaron's request for employment as a soldier. Undoubtedly the letter Aaron carried from Simon Pauley, a personal friend of the general's, had been a factor, as had Aaron's ability to speak German. Not all the German immigrants in America were in the Wisconsin regiments. Hundreds more, many of them fresh off the boats, were finding their way into the swiftly expanding army, and Frémont enlisted all he could find.

Aaron had left it to Don Alvaro's discretion whether or not to share the letter with Micah. Aaron himself, however, had no intention of writing to his father, and he did not do so. Much later, after President Lincoln's patience with the Pathfinder was exhausted and the command in St. Louis given to someone else, a letter from Simon Pauley had found Aaron.

Aaron had replied to Commodore Pauley, but he had not written to his father. It seemed to him that his own act of rebellion, his refusal even to call upon Mr. Symington of the Harlem Bank of New York, was self-contained and explicit.

For some fourteen months in St. Louis, Aaron had conscientiously tried to become a soldier. He had been given a commission as a second lieutenant of infantry. His first assignment in the headquarters of the Department of the West was to be that of translator on the staff of the general's wife, Jessie Benton Frémont. He had protested to Major Dundalk, only to be told sternly that an officer in *any* army, even the American, followed orders.

The general's wife was the daughter of a United States senator, and no one in the headquarters of the Department of the West was ever allowed to forget this. Jessie Frémont organized a sparkling military court for her husband, who, as Aaron soon discovered, was a legend in America and the particular darling of the radical Republicans.

Aaron had not been in St. Louis a month before General Frémont began to destroy himself. By August 1861 the Pathfinder had come to regard himself as military proconsul of Missouri. He issued a proclamation confiscating the property of disloyal Missourians and emancipating their slaves. An enormous quarrel erupted in Washington as a result of this and other actions taken by the colorful general in St. Louis. Frémont was ordered to rescind his proclamation and he did so, but he and his rash actions caused endless fights between the more moderate Republicans, who supported President Lincoln, and the radicals, who worshipped Frémont.

Life in the headquarters was not what Aaron had expected military life to be. When General Frémont was absent, which was often, his wife was left in command. Military balls and ceremonials took place in an endless social whirl. The headquarters was stiff with foreigners. Aaron Marburg's commission as a second lieutenant was a small favor compared to the far larger ones grandly dispensed by John and Jessie

Frémont. The Pathfinder commissioned majors and colonels by the score, brigadiers by the dozen. The United States Military Academy at West Point had, over the years, produced an officer corps adequate to a small, innocuous army. But when secession came, more than half of the officers of the United States Army chose to honor allegiance to their states rather than to the federal government. The result was that as the army swiftly grew to face the threat of a dissolving Union, it became necessary to take officers where one could get them. They came from shops, offices, schoolrooms, and farms. And they also came from the ranks of the politicians, men who had served as judges, legislators, and administrators—many of whom knew that their future careers depended on a good war record. The leap from politician to brigadier or even major general was made often in these times. Many of these officers were disgracefully incompetent. But as Aaron discovered after the War Department wearied of Frémont and his imperial ways, relieving him of command and dispersing his officers throughout the real army, some temporary officers were surprisingly effective. It was his first hint that one need not be a genius to be successful as a warrior.

As the day aged, the sun fanned through the dust raised by the boots of tens of thousands of Union soldiers. On this spring morning Grant commanded 166,000 men of all branches, and as the Army of the Potomac marched into the Wilderness, it searched for the estimated 70,000 rebel soldiers of the Army of Northern Virginia.

Aaron, riding now with a blue bandanna over his mouth and nose to keep some of the dust out of his lungs, turned to inspect the column of Company A. The men were marching in good order. Yesterday at Brandy Station his Germans had lightened their packs, replacing such useless items as the heavy winter overcoats they had been issued with cartridges for their muskets.

Aaron's men were armed with the U.S. Musket Model 1855, similar to the British Brown Bess that had dominated continental infantry warfare for two generations. As smoothbores, these guns, and others like them, were accurate only at fifty yards or less. This inaccuracy had determined infantry tactics since the Napoleonic Wars. Units preparing to charge enemy forces could form themselves into solid masses of men two to three hundred yards from the enemy, advance in good order, taking only inaccurate fire until within fifty yards of the enemy, and then charge.

But now the rifled barrels with which all infantry muskets were fitted had changed all that. A rifled musket, firing a cone-shaped minié ball, was lethal at two hundred yards. And terrain seldom allowed armies to form up at a greater distance from the enemy. The result was that an infantry charge had become a slaughter. Aaron often wondered what El Patron would have made of the sight of ten thousand men charging through two hundred yards of a killing ground. Don Alvaro had once spoken of war as a matter of sword cuts and maggots. What would he have thought of the sheer madness of this new kind of war, a nightmare of quick-firing rifles and tin cans filled with musket balls fired from cannon at point-blank range into masses of charging soldiers?

Aaron had now seen action at Vicksburg and in a half a hundred nameless firefights. One-half of the men he led out of the trenches at Vicksburg were gone, replaced by new volunteers, who still seemed to come in a never-ending stream from the farms of Wisconsin.

He had seen very little of this country, even now. And he still found himself amazed at the *scale* on which things were done here. The country was vast. Though he had been only as far west as St. Louis, he was somehow aware of the immense distances stretching away farther to the west. That was a land he intended to investigate.

When Aaron had had his first sight of any army—an *American* army —on the march, he had been staggered by numbers. Blue-uniformed men like a moving forest, a thousand battle flags, regimental colors, guidons. Ten thousand horses and thousands of guns. The wealth being squandered here in war was stunning. Because he held a commission, he was technically a citizen of the United States of America. He felt a certain ambivalence about that. Pride, yes; much pride in being a part of something so vast, so powerful. But the power and the glory were flawed. He had been in bivouac near Vicksburg when he heard General Grant's infamous General Order Number Eleven read out to the troops. Grant had been vexed by the rampant speculation in army stores and contracts, and he had singled out, as any European anti-Semite might, the Jews: "The Jews, as a class violating every regulation of trade established by the Treasury Department and also department orders, are hereby expelled from the department within twenty-four hours from receipt of this order."

It had been a pronouncement worthy of Father Sebastio, Aaron thought in a white fury. He had presented himself to Colonel Isbrandt-sen immediately, demanding to know whether General Order Number Eleven applied to himself, or to any of the several German Jews in Company A. "If I am to leave the department, Colonel, I will need to be told where I am to go." He had stood rigidly to attention (he knew how to be a soldier by then), his hand gripping his saber so tightly the knuckles ached.

"Don't be a damned fool, Marburg," Isbrandtsen had said calmly. "Go back to your men."

When Aaron had gone, Zachary Isbrandtsen sat at his field desk looking after him and wondering why it was that simply because one was a great soldier, as Grant was, people expected him to be an equally great man. And were angered and disappointed when he was not. Colonel Isbrandtsen had a suspicion that General Order Number Eleven had deprived the United States of a new and possibly useful young citizen.

The colonel was correct. From that moment Aaron Marburg abandoned any notion of settling in the United States.

By two in the afternoon the Wisconsin Volunteers had reached Wilderness Tavern. Here, in a small clearing surrounded on all sides by the thick forest, they went into bivouac.

Soon camp fires were alight and a haze of smoke drifted through the tangled thickets of the Wilderness.

Sergeant Hauptmann, a young man who had been a schoolteacher in Milwaukee, reported to Aaron that the men were preparing their midday meal, that the company had suffered no casualties on the march from Brandy Station, and that the pickets were on station.

"Thank you, Sergeant," Aaron said, and offered Hauptmann a drink from the bottle of whisky in his rucksack. Emil Hauptmann was a good soldier, conscientious, intelligent enough to be good company, strong enough to command the respect of the men. With Hauptmann Aaron could speak either English or German at need, and though they were not friends—Aaron had made no real friends in the army—they could while away in far-ranging conversations the long hours of waiting that made up most of army life.

A squad of pioneer troops, marching raggedly as did all engineers, passed on the way to repair a bridge over a gulley on Brock Road. With them was a detachment of colored soldiers from General Burnside's IX Corps. There were two brigades of Negroes in IX Corps; neither had ever fought, and wagers were being made throughout the army that they would run "at the first whiff of powder."

The engineers raised their customary halloo when they saw the Wisconsin regimental colors before Colonel Isbrandtsen's tent. Cries of "Hey, Dutchie!" were accompanied by raucous laughter.

Emil Hauptmann paused in his filling of a corncob pipe to sigh,

"Pockenliche Baurn." Proud of his big-city Milwaukee background, the company sergeant always referred to shouters as "poxy peasants." He puffed the pipe alight and said wearily, "Why must it always be 'Dutchie?' " The question was rhetorical. To most Americans Deutsch meant Dutch, and there was an end to it.

Aaron seated himself on an upturned ammunition case and carefully lighted one of his husbanded cheroots. The memory of how Doña Maria used to open windows and flap her shawl indignantly when Don Alvaro fired one of his rank cigars in her sitting room brought a faint smile to his lips.

For a time the two men sat and smoked, each lost in his own thoughts. Aaron was remembering the way Adriana's wheaten hair blew in the wind, and the warmth of her smile. What was she doing at this moment, in the deep Spanish night? The image of his father lying beside her, making love to her, brought a dull ache. But how could one lose what one had never possessed?

The westering sun sent bars of yellow light through the forest. The smoke from the campfires hung over the clearing. The troops were quiet. There was very little larking about. The soldiers spoke to one another in low voices, quietly. The weight of the Wilderness seemed to oppress them.

"How far are the Rebs, I wonder," Sergeant Hauptmann said.

"Not far," Aaron said. He remembered the earthworks before Vicksburg, where one came to know the faces of the men in the trenches a dozen yards away. But for the uniforms and flags, one could tell no difference between Reb and Federal, and after the bodies had lain in the hot summer sun for a few days, even the uniforms made no real difference.

Aaron rose and brushed the dust from his blue trousers. "Let's walk the picket line, Emil," he said.

Together they made the rounds of the company area. The sentries lounged, relaxed but alert, at the edge of the woods and thickets. Other troops, infantry now and not engineers, were moving south along Brock Road in the general direction of Spotsylvania. It was there, clear of most of the Wilderness, that the staff hoped for the army to make its first contact with Lee's divisions.

A group of new and homesick immigrants had gathered around one of the fires and were singing softly.

> *Sie kämmt es mit goldenem Kamme*
> *Und singt ein Lied dabei;*

128

Das hat eine Wundersame,
Gewaltige Melodei—

And Aaron remembered a time, long ago, before Santanilla and all that happened there, when a boy sitting at his work desk could look through a narrow window at the River Lahn and see the girls of the *hochschule* rowing their boat and singing of Die Lorelei in their thin, sweet voices. Was it true, he wondered, that in the presence of death one remembered all of life in such poignant images?

He wished that he could share, for the moment at least, the act of being alive with Emil Hauptmann. It would be comforting. Perhaps the boy who came to Santanilla could have done so; but the bitter young man who left it could not. In any case, Hauptmann did not share Aaron's heritage. He was, after all, and despite his name and blood, an American, born in Milwaukee. To Emil, Marburg am Lahn was a mark on a map in a geography book, the place where Martin Luther had debated religious doctrine with Ulrich Zwingli, nothing more.

When it really comes to it, Aaron thought somberly, we are all of us always alone.

Just before dusk there was a flurry of activity along the Germanna Road. The Wisconsin troopers stood to watch a party of officers canter by on the way to Wilderness Tavern.

Someone shouted, "It's Grant! It's the general!" The soldiers waved their forage caps in the air and cheered.

The general was on his favorite charger, a large bay named Cincinnati. Aaron had seen Grant before. Usually he wore a private soldier's cheap blouse with only his three-starred shoulder straps for decoration. But now he was dressed in a lieutenant general's full regalia: blue frock coat over a blue waistcoat, gold striped trousers tucked into highly polished, spurred boots, yellow string gloves on his broad hands, a red sash around his waist, and a saber on his saddle. Clearly this was a special occasion. As the soldiers cheered him he removed his blue felt campaign hat and waved it at them. "What unit, boys?" he called in his oddly high-pitched voice.

"Wisconsin Volunteers, General!"

Someone in the adjoining regiment laughed and yelled, "Milwaukee Dutchies, General!"

Cincinnati pranced and curvetted. Aaron noted that the general's seat on a horse was none too secure. Grant was no cavalryman. "Good luck to you, boys!" he shouted, and cantered on, followed by his aides, down the dusty road toward V Corps headquarters.

"A grand sight, the general," Sergeant Hauptmann said warmly.

True enough, Aaron thought, though Grant's horsemanship was a pity. But even that would find favor with the troops if all went well. They would say that *their* general was a foot soldier, and the infantry was, as Napoleon had once said, the Queen of Battles. They would say it, that is, if Grant gave them victory. Americans, Aaron thought, were still a simple people. They could love a general who left the battlefields littered with his own dead soldiers—*if* he won battles. Robert E. Lee was such a general. It was said that he wept over the dead at the battle of Fredericksburg, but his grief had not prevented him from spending Confederate lives in order to defeat Franklin's Federals. Lee had even lost two generals, Cobb and Gregg, at Fredericksburg, but he had inflicted almost thirteen thousand casualties on the Union forces.

Aaron wondered what Grant and Lee could do together, and how long the nation, North and South, could continue the slaughter. But even death was on a heroic scale in this vast land.

In the distance Aaron could hear other units cheering the commander. The sun had settled below the scraggy treetops in the west. How far away were the Confederates now, Aaron wondered. Ten miles? Twenty? Somewhere down the long, narrow track of the Orange Turnpike.

Aaron was still speculating about the location of the enemy when the dusk turned to deep night and the camp fires flickered and danced like fireflies seen through the branches of the Wilderness.

icah Marburg had never before realized how damp and gloomy was brother Isaac's house on the river. Spain had spoiled Micah with its dry heat of summer and the sharp cold of the Cantabrican winter. There was a moldy smell in these old rooms that he had occupied as a boy, a chill in the air, a forgotten feeling of fraudulent penury. The old mansion was a countinghouse. How was it, Micah wondered, that he had never before realized that? Shabby outside and heavily opulent inside.

The meetings with Isaac had gone badly and would grow no easier to bear now that decisions were to be made. Micah had imagined that his journey to Marburg am Lahn—his pilgrimage, really—would solve his problems. How could he have so completely forgotten how steely his brother could be when money was the issue?

Isaac had changed in the last years. It had surprised Micah to discover that his brother seemed resentful about his long absence.

More than once he had made it known that he found it strange that Micah had never brought his Spanish wife to Marburg, that he, Isaac, had never seen his new nephew Robert, and that Aaron was gone to America. Isaac, who was childless, appeared to feel that Micah Marburg had handled his life badly.

"You speak German like a Spaniard," Isaac had said on the first day. On the second he had made known his displeasure with the way in which Micah was representing the Marburg Bank in Spain and Portugal. "You have grown careless, Micah. You have too many other things on your mind."

Heaven knew that was true enough. Santanilla was staggering under a weight of debts. The winter of 1863 had been severe. There had been heavy stock losses. A fire had burned the woolshed to the ground, and it had had to be rebuilt. El Patron spent more and more time in his observatory, and with Aaron gone the financial affairs of the hacienda had been left to Julio, who was a fool and a wastrel. Micah himself had had to take charge more and more often, and it was true that the affairs of the bank had suffered.

Micah looked about him and hated what he saw. He despised the cold Hessian spring, the muddy odors of the river, the narrow streets of Marburg, the pale, narrow-minded people. He was aware that it was he himself who had changed, not the town nor its inhabitants. The family dinner given him on arrival, with all the cousins present, had been painful to endure. The food had been strange to his palate, the wine too sweet, the attitude of the family resentful of this Roman Catholic in their midst. It had stunned him to realize that he regarded them as somehow alien, as *Jews,* and that they viewed him now as a *goy.* In other circumstances, he would have found it ludicrous. But there was no humor to be found in his present situation. He had come back to Marburg to ask for favors from his dour elder brother—and matters had not gone as he had hoped.

In the few years since Micah had last seen Isaac Marburg, the elder brother had grown much older. He was bearded now, which Micah had not expected, and bald, with a fringe of white hair that joined the full whiskers hiding the stiff collar and string tie. Isaac had never been a handsome man. It was said in the family that Micah was the young hero, Isaac the patriarch.

In the thin, cold light from the window facing the river, Isaac's skin looked translucent, patterned with blue veins and wrinkles. His eyes seemed more deeply set, sunk in a network of tiny, sharp creases and overhung by bushy brows not yet totally gray. His long, pale, spidery fingers rested on the documents he had carefully aligned on his massive desk of black German oak.

"The affairs of the bank have not prospered," Isaac said. "You should be aware of that."

What Isaac was telling him, Micah thought, was conditionally true. Disregarding his own advice given long ago, Isaac had invested substantial sums in American cotton. He had overreacted to Confederate successes in the first two years of the fighting in America. Now investments in the Confederacy seemed doomed. But Isaac Marburg always hedged his wagers. The Marburg Bank had grown strong, thanks to his innate caution.

"I understand that," Micah said. It was cold in this room, he thought. I never used to feel the cold this way. "But what will it serve to foreclose on Santanilla? What can the bank possibly gain from that?"

Isaac bridged his fingers before his face and regarded his brother impassively. "Micah," he said, "I have been tolerant. Because you are my only brother, I have been patient and understanding. You will admit that?"

"I have never said otherwise, brother," Micah said.

"When you fell in love with your Spanish *shiksa,* I said nothing against it. When you left Marburg to live in Spain among the *goyim,* I offered no objections. Isn't that so?"

"Isaac, there is no need to go over all that again," Micah protested.

"When you married and became a Catholic, did I complain?" Micah shook his head in weary acquiescence. Whatever happened, Isaac Marburg would have his pound of flesh.

"No, I did not complain," Isaac said implacably. "In fact, I made it possible for you to do what you wished to do, Micah. I understand that you never felt any love for poor Sarai Leyden. God knows she was a difficult woman to like, and there was no reason for you to spend the rest of your life mourning, no matter what the family says."

"I have always been grateful for your understanding, Isaac," Micah said.

The long fingers intertwined like pale vines. Micah suppressed a shudder. What had happened here in the few years of his absence? He had never loved his elder brother, but never before had he feared him.

"Your life in Spain absorbs you, Micah. You have changed. Your appearance, your manner, your heart are different. I see it. The family sees it. Do you?"

"Yes," Micah said defiantly. "I do."

The pale lips in the thicket of white beard pursed. Micah remembered a schoolmaster's lips pursing so before the rod fell. For a moment he hated his brother.

"I did not imagine you would cut yourself off so completely from your own people, Micah. That was foolish of me. I should have foreseen it," Isaac said. "I had hoped that you would send Aaron back here to me when you no longer wanted him with you. We invested much time and effort in training the boy. He would have made a fine banker. And now that you have another family, he could have been the son I never had. I would have been pleased if you had done that, Micah."

"There were reasons, Isaac," Micah said tightly. He had never given Isaac Marburg an account of what had happened to cause Aaron's flight to America. He did not intend to do so now.

"He never went to Mr. Symington in New York," Isaac said. "He became a soldier instead. Why, Micah? Our people are not soldiers."

"That was Aaron's decision to make," Micah said.

"Does he write to you? Is he well?"

Micah, agitated, rose and went to the window to stare at the turbid water of the Lahn flowing past the sloping lawn behind the study. The conifers surrounding the house were dark, almost black. A bent old Marburger hoed doggedly in a flowerbed. The day was overcast and bleak, with a silver gray light and no shadows.

"He writes very seldom," Micah said, tasting the lie. "He is young."

"He is twenty-one. A man."

Micah turned to face his brother. "He is my son, not yours, Isaac."

The thin light gleamed on Isaac's waxy scalp as he nodded like a sage. "Yes, That is true."

"About Santanilla, Isaac."

"What about Santanilla, Micah? The mortgage payments are badly in arrears. More than a year. I have been very forbearing, but you are a banker, brother. You know that this cannot continue."

Micah tried to imagine himself telling Adriana and El Patron and Doña Maria that he could do no more to save their ancestral holding, that the mortgages he himself had arranged were to be the instrument of their dispossession, that Roberto's inheritance was lost to the Jews. He felt physically ill at the thought.

"A bargain, Isaac," he said.

"I am listening, brother."

"My shares in the bank are worth considerably more than the money advanced on Santanilla."

"Yes. Perhaps a third more."

"More than that," he said harshly.

Isaac shrugged. "It may be."

Micah stood over his brother, looking down at his naked head. He had a horrible image of himself snatching the heavy paperweight from the desk and bringing it down with all his strength on that fragile skull.

"I offer you my shares in the Marburg Bank in return for the Santanilla mortgages and fifty thousand Hessian marks," he said.

Isaac's lips pursed again. "Unwise, brother," he said.

"That is my concern, not yours," Micah said violently. He felt a thin pain in his chest and arm, but he ignored it. His hurt and anger sustained him.

"I will have to confer with the other shareholders," Isaac said.

"You can make the decision yourself," Micah said. "Make it now."

Isaac Marburg's thin shoulders shook with bitter laughter. "What a man will do for love," he said. "What a fool you are, Micah."

"Decide now," Micah said again. "I want to get away from this place. I'm sick of it and of you, brother." He squeezed his arm to block the angry pain.

"So be it, then," Isaac said. "Remember that I told you it is unwise."

"I will be the judge of that," Micah said, walking stiffly to the tall carved door. "Have the papers drawn."

When his brother had gone, Isaac Marburg stood and went to the window. He had not lived as a religious man, but now as he grew older he felt it proper to return to the ways of his people. He had been mistaken to acquiesce in Micah's defection, but it was too late now to regret what was and would be. The words of Leviticus seemed appropriate: "And I will set my face against that man, and will cut him off from among his people; because he hath given his seed unto Moloch, to defile my sanctuary, and to profane my holy name."

Tomasa Gomez gave a final, delicate tug to the silver-tipped cords that fastened the *chaleco* of Roberto Marburg's riding habit. The tiny boots were of polished black cordovan leather, the spurs silver-mounted to match the buttons of the fitted trousers and jacket. A flat, broad-brimmed hat sat at a rakish angle on the curly blond head and a small riding crop hung on a braided thong from the boy's wrist.

"There," Tomasa said, leaning back to inspect her work. *"Ay, que lindo!"* Her exclamation was one of pure love and admiration.

Roberto smiled at her with affection. She was his *nana*—for him at three and a half, the most important person in his life.

The nursery was bathed with a warm May sunlight. In the corner of the large, airy room was Paco, the elaborately carved and decorated hobbyhorse made for the young master by the *mozos de quadra*. Next to Paco stood a floor-to-ceiling cabinet containing all of El Patroncito's toys and games. On the side of the room opposite the toy cabinet stood the wardrobe, a massive piece of furniture in which the young master's clothes hung in neat rows. Tomasa was a fanatically neat housekeeper and there was never a hint of disorder in the nursery.

This was a special day. Roberto was not quite certain why it was special, but Tomasa and *la abuela,* Doña Maria, said that it was a day he would never forget. Obviously something fine and out of the ordinary was going to happen.

Mama appeared in the doorway. Mama was beautiful, and sometimes she picked him up and held him, though not often and not recently. This was not, Tomasa assured him, because she did not love him. Everyone on Santanilla loved El Patroncito. Mama simply had to be careful because there would soon be a tiny brother or a sister for Don Roberto. But not today. That was not what was going to happen today. It was something else.

Adriana, dressed today in fine lawn, arranged to hang loosely about her swollen belly, regarded her son with a critical eye.

"Yes," she said finally. "My handsome young one." She knelt and allowed him to kiss her. As he did so he could feel her belly, in which she was carrying a brother or sister for him. He hoped it would be a brother. Sisters, from what he had seen about the hacienda, were not great fun.

Doña Maria bustled in from the gallery. She was dressed, as always, in black taffeta. Roberto liked the sound she made when she walked. Her voice was always sharp except when she spoke to Roberto, who was, she said, the handsomest little caballero in all of Old Castile.

"Is he ready? Tomasa, what has been keeping you? Julio is already here. So are all the others. Do hurry *along,* girl."

Flanked by women, young Roberto was led through the gallery and out into the back courtyard. There all the household servants were assembled, and most of the vaqueros and herdsmen. When they saw the boy in his tailored finery the women burst into applause.

Roberto looked about. He had known his father would not be there because his father was far away in Germany, visiting the mysterious and never-seen Uncle Isaac. But El Patron was present, dressed in riding clothes, booted, spurred, and holding a new, silver-mounted bridle. He smiled broadly at his grandson, then shouted through the open gate, *"Bueno pues,* Julio! Come *on,* man."

Uncle Julio came through the gate into the courtyard leading a pure white pony, a tiny Shetland with feathery hocks and a long, fine mane. Don Alvaro expertly slipped the bridle over the small horse's head and one of the grooms appeared with an exquisitely made small saddle decorated with silver conches. Roberto thought his heart would burst. The tiny horse was the most beautiful thing he had ever seen.

Uncle Julio strode over to where Roberto stood with his mother and Tomasa. He picked up his nephew, seated him on his shoulder, and carried him over to the pony.

"This is Blanco, Roberto," El Patron said. "He has come all the way from England to belong to you, *nieto.*"

Roberto, unafraid, reached out to touch the pony's velvety nose. "Oh, he is beautiful, *abuelo!* Isn't he, Tío Julio?"

Julio raised him high and set him down on the saddle. Two of the grooms came forward and made adjustments on the stirrup-leathers. The pony sidestepped nervously, but El Patron had his grandson firmly around the waist and held him on the saddle. He handed a lead rein to Julio, and together they set the pony in motion, walking around in a circle as the household watched.

"Blanco!" Roberto Marburg shouted with delight. "Blanco! Blanco! Blanco!"

Suddenly Roberto realized that his grandfather's hands were no longer balancing him in the saddle. He had a sudden impulse to cry out, to be frightened of falling. But the pony's gait was smooth and steady as though he were gliding through butter. Roberto looked at the faces of the servants and tenants all gathered to watch the young master take possession of his first mount. He knew that he must *not* cry out, must *not* admit to being frightened. He did not know why, but he knew that it was so. He pressed his small lips together and concentrated on staying in the saddle.

The vaqueros uttered shrill cries of appreciation. The women made little shrieking noises. Mama watched with a fixed smile on her face, her hands clenched at her side. Tomasa was fearful and showed it. Ana-Maria Gomez, Roberto's goddaughter, tugged unheeded at Tomasa's skirt. Uncle Julio watched, his face unguarded and not so friendly. But El Patron walked at the pony's side, ready to catch his grandson if he should lose his seat.

"Blanco," Roberto said again.

The pony turned and looked at him out of one dark brown eye.

"Enough now, Papa," Adriana called.

"One more circuit," Julio said. "Let him learn." He flicked the lead rein and the pony broke into a trot. Roberto clutched at the saddle horn. *"Not* like that, *sobrino,"* Tío Julio said sharply. El Patron snatched the boy from the saddle and set him on his feet. He glared at his son and said, "Put the pony up now, Julio. Enough for the first day."

Adriana lifted Roberto into her arms. She too glared angrily at Uncle Julio. Roberto did not know why.

"My adored one," she whispered in the child's ear. "You did wonderfully, bravely. You will be the finest caballero in all Spain."

Roberto Marburg pressed his cheek against his mother's. She smelled of flowers. He did not really understand what she was saying to him, but what did it matter? When he grew up, he resolved, he would be whatever she wished him to be. In that way he would be happy, and safe, and protected, and loved as much as he was today.

In the early hours of the fifth of May, General George Gordon Meade was awakened at his Wilderness Tavern headquarters with the news that Federal pickets had encountered a line of Confederate skirmishers on the Orange Turnpike.

General Meade, in nominal command of the Army of the Potomac, sent a report of this encounter back to General Grant at Germanna Ford and ordered his own skirmishers forward to, as he wrote, "develop the intentions of the enemy." Isbrandtsen's Wisconsin Germans were ordered ahead to support the Federal pickets.

At seven o'clock, Colonel Isbrandtsen marched his regiment onto Brock Road, a narrow path intersecting the turnpike. When they were fully deployed, he faced the regiment to the west and prepared to advance. Officer's call was sounded and he briefed his company and platoon commanders. His information was sparse. The armies had begun to grope for one another in the dense undergrowth of the Wilderness.

The day would be warm, Aaron thought. No breeze penetrated the forest to disperse the dust raised by the maneuvering troops. To the south of the regiment's position was the sound of intermittent firing. To Aaron it sounded like skirmishers conducting what the military liked to call "reconnaissance by musketry." One simply fired into the bushes and tree lines to see if anyone fired back.

Colonel Isbrandtsen's briefing had included the not very reassuring intelligence that the southern anchor of the line was in the hands of a General Crawford's division, which contained two brigades of Pennsylvania Reserves. These were troops that had, to a man, refused to reenlist and now had less than four weeks to serve before their time expired. These summer soldiers were expected to hold the southern flank against the Confederate General A. P. Hill, who was believed to be advancing eastward with a division of veteran infantry.

Aaron returned to his unit and briefed the company noncoms.

"What do we have in front of us, Lieutenant?" Sergeant Beardsley, a man of thirty with a thin, haggard face (the result of a recent bout with dysentery) was acting First Platoon commander. Company A was under strength in both officers and enlisted men. There were fewer than one hundred and ten men in it, and Aaron was the only commissioned officer. Promotions came hard in the Wisconsin Volunteers.

"The colonel thinks there are two divisions on the turnpike," he said. To lessen the impact of that depressing news, he added, "General Hancock's corps is coming from Chancellorsville to support us." He did not say that it would be late afternoon before Hancock's troops could be in position to fight. "Tell the men they can stand easy. Smoking is all right, but don't let them empty their canteens. It's going to be hot today."

"*Zu befehl, Herr Leutnant,*" Beardsley said with a wry grin, his German horribly accented. Not all the soldiers in the Volunteers were German-speakers.

The noncommissioned officers dispersed, leaving Aaron and Emil Hauptmann alone. Aaron listened to the sounds from the company's left. The firing had become more intense, but nothing could be seen. He climbed up onto a fallen stump, trying to see through the smoke and dust to the west.

"Make sure everyone has water, Emil," Aaron said. The certain

141

need for drinking water obsessed him. It would be impossible to resupply the troops in this tangle of cut-over trees and brambles.

"Yes, sir." Sergeant Hauptmann trotted off down the line. Sometimes the soldiers filled their canteens with beer or whisky. Emil Hauptmann would know how to deal with those who had done that.

Aaron took his Walch pistol from its holster and inspected the load. The Walch was a ten-shot revolver that he had purchased from a wounded officer of the Ninth Michigan, the only regiment in the army to have been issued the complicated weapon. Aaron had coveted the pistol because of the number of shots that could be fired before reloading. Captain Lescher, the regimental ordnance officer, had warned him that the weapon was given to double-firing and exploding in one's hand, but so far the Walch had been reliable. Aaron had stopped the dangerous practice of carrying a sword into combat. Swords were the mark of an officer, and certain to draw Confederate fire. The former company commander of Company A had been flourishing a sword when he was cut down.

The fighting at the left of the line was getting heavier. The popping of muskets was punctuated from time to time with the crumping roar of artillery. How the cannoneers could find targets in these woods, Aaron could not imagine. Probably the guns were simply being lined up on the road and fired blindly. The air was growing thick with the stench of burned powder.

Sergeant Hauptmann returned. "Johan Blier had whisky. I poured it out and put him on my list. He has water now, and he can dig latrines when we come out of the line."

Aaron nodded agreement. He seldom interfered with the company sergeant's disciplinary measures. He knew the men far better than did Aaron.

The order came from the rear to fix bayonets. The men took the long, triangular blades from their scabbards and locked them to the musket-barrels. Bayonets made deadly, agonizing wounds that invariably suppurated. Aaron hated them.

Somewhere to the company's front firing began. The Federal pickets had made contact with the Rebels. But time passed and the order to advance did not come. The men waited restlessly, stealing an occasional drink from their canteens. Messengers and dispatch riders galloped along the road. A troop of cavalry jingled by. An hour passed. Two. The Volunteers waited.

The sun climbed over the tree line, but it could not penetrate the dust and smoke. Aaron's lips felt parched, cracked. He could smell his sweat drying in the wool of his blouse. His hair felt damp under the forage cap. He looked back at the regimental command post. Orderlies had put out camp stools and Isbrandtsen and his officers sat talking under the regimental colors.

More cavalry cantered across the regiment's rear. The fight in the south was continuous now. Aaron's map showed a place called Chewning Farm somewhere to the left of the line; the brigades of Pennsylvania Reserves must be fighting there. Presently stragglers began to appear from that direction. Whatever the intention had been, the left was apparently not holding. Casuals milled about behind the line of Wisconsin Germans and officers, still mounted, galloped about waving their swords and cursing the stragglers into some semblance of order. The heavy undergrowth made things difficult, but gradually the streams of blue-clad infantry were contained and organized into a column to be marched back in the direction of the fighting at Chewning Farm.

The appearance of soldiers withdrawing from a firefight made the Wisconsins uneasy, and Aaron walked along the line speaking to his men, looking at equipment, reassuring them.

Somewhere not too far ahead, the skirmishing seemed to be developing into something more serious. The noise of musketry was punctuated with shouts and Rebel yells, but nothing could be seen. The smoke had turned the pallid sky silver.

Several of Aaron's men were relieving themselves, urinating where they stood. Aaron glanced at his watch. The morning had nearly gone in maneuvering into position and waiting. Always, he thought, the waiting. Don Alvaro had never talked about that.

More cavalry galloped south along Brock Road, sending clouds of dust into the already nearly unbreathable air.

Aaron said to Sergeant Hauptmann, "I'm going to see the colonel." It was a useless gesture, but the men expected it of him. He trotted back to the regimental command post and saluted Isbrandtsen, who was not pleased to see him.

"Don't tell me the men are getting restless, Lieutenant Marburg. They are to stay where they are until we receive orders."

"Today, sir?"

"That's enough, Marburg."

"Sir." Aaron said.

Major Anderson, his battalion commander, took Aaron by the arm and walked a short distance with him. Anderson was a ruddy Swede who had served as a drummer boy with Winfield Scott in the Mexican War.

"Don't blame the Old Man, Lieutenant," Anderson said. "He's as anxious to go as you are. The goddamn generals are all back there at Wilderness Tavern arguing. Just keep your company ready."

"Yes, sir," Aaron said.

Anderson turned back, he was grinning broadly, showing long yellow teeth. "Marburg?"

"Major?"

"Is it true Mrs. Frémont sent you to the general's tailor?"

"She did, but I couldn't afford him."

Anderson laughed aloud and struck Aaron sharply on the arm, sending a puff of dust into the air. "Good lad. Go on now. Keep your Dutchies in order."

Aaron returned to the Company A lines. To Emil Hauptmann he said, "We go when we go. That's all."

A mounted officer from General Meade's staff came down Brock Road at a full gallop. He reined in to give one of Isbrandtsen's officers a dispatch, then galloped on as though pursued by Furies.

All of Aaron's men watched the exchange with interest.

A battery of field artillery came down the turnpike and wheeled into position behind the Volunteers. The cannoneers unlimbered the guns and set about digging stops for the trails. They worked swiftly, with quiet efficiency. The noise of battle to the company's front increased in intensity, but it was impossible to see through the smoke and dust. Visibility had dropped to less than fifty yards.

Isbrandtsen's bugler, a sixteen-year-old boy from Kenosha, raised his instrument and blew the advance.

Aaron stepped off the road into the woods, raised his arm, and pumped it forward. *"Vorwärts! Folgen Sie mir!"* He began to walk into the forest, pistol in hand. He had not gone far before he realized that attempting to advance through the tangle of thicket and fallen timber ahead was going to be difficult. The men were already having to detour around tangles of thornbush and climb over cut trees and stumps. But they were managing, moving forward in an increasingly disorganized line abreast. Sergeant Hauptmann was shouting at them in German, trying to keep the line dressed. Ahead, the sounds of battle grew louder. Behind was the rattle of drums and the huzza-ing of infantry. The long blue line of Company A, Wisconsin Volunteers, walked into the Wilderness.

A man learns to live with terror, Aaron thought, but each time he faces it he hates it more. Reason told him that he was in this terrible place by his own choice, that no one had forced him to become a part of this savage war. But reason did not prevent him from blaming Micah Marburg for his presence here. It made very little sense, and Aaron was sharply aware of that, but what his intellect told him did little to assuage the hatred he was feeling at this moment.

Five hundred yards from the road there was no semblance of a path or clear ground. The thornbushes grew in rank profusion around the weedy trunks of second-growth pines. The forest had been logged and abandoned to brush and stump. The acrid smoke of burning gunpowder lay thickly in the air, stinging the eyes and throats of the blindly advancing men.

The artillery behind them had begun to fire over their heads. Aaron could hear the whirring of canister in the air. The tops of the young trees were being shredded by the storm of lead balls. Bits of branches and pine needles fell in a steady rain.

On his right, Aaron heard his men begin firing. But he could no longer see them. The blue line was a line no longer, there were only groups of men marching forward through the thickets, vague blue shapes in the smoke and dust. He heard a Rebel yell ahead of him; the wild, yelping cry raised the hackles on his neck, as it always did. He plodded forward, the heavy Walch in his sweating hand. At times the undergrowth was so thick that as he pushed through he could see nothing to his right or left. Yet he could hear his men moving through the tangle.

A flash of brass and homespun in his path made him bring the pistol into firing position, his breath catching in his throat. But the man was dead, half-seated in the bush, one half of his face leering at Aaron, the other half a ruin of blood and bone. Bits of twig and weed stuck to the already congealing mess. Aaron pushed stoically on. He had no feelings now, only a vast, empty awareness of himself surrounded by invisible danger. He could hear the snap of bullets striking the leaves nearby. The dead man was passed by, forgotten. There was nothing to be remembered about the dead.

A Confederate carrying an old Mississippi rifle materialized out of the smoke and fired at Aaron or someone near him. Aaron raised his Walch and pulled the trigger. The man melted into the bush. Aaron did not know whether or not he had hit him. He fired again, blindly, and saw more Confederates running toward him. All around, the firing became intense and the smoke rolled through the forest, hiding the running enemy. Aaron heard a cry behind him, someone calling out in German for *Mutti!* There was a rattle of musketry, and the Confederates were gone.

On the right there were shouts and more Rebel yells. A fire

starting in the dry brush ignited a small pine. The needles crackled and exploded. Beyond the burning tree Aaron could see some hastily constructed log breastworks and caps of gray and homespun. Someone was waving a Confederate battle flag. It was shredded by bullets even as he watched. There were bluecoats around him now, and he signaled his men to take cover. He called for Hauptmann, who appeared at his elbow, face burned by powder, eyebrows singed, teeth bared in a grimace. Aaron gave him the order to flank the Confederate strongpoint rather than attempt to take it by frontal attack. The sergeant moved off to the right, Aaron to the left.

A heavy explosion warned the Federals that the Rebels too had moved up artillery and were firing fused shells into the forest. A change in the odor of the smoke told Aaron that there were other fires burning in the thickets.

Crouching, he signaled several of his men to follow him around the Confederate position. It was difficult not to lose one's way in the smoke and dust. Aaron, flanked by half a squad, crawled forward. He could hear the Rebels firing, but he could not see them. He lay for a time, his heart pounding against the thick carpet of dry leaves of the forest floor. Overhead, the sun had moved far to the west. Now it was only a brightness in the foul-smelling smoke.

The soldier beside Aaron, a beardless boy who had joined the regiment at Brandy Station with a half dozen other recruits, was sobbing. But when Aaron moved forward, he kept pace, tears and all. He inched ahead, cradling his musket in the crook of his elbows as he had been taught.

Aaron's eyes burned. He said, "Can you see the Rebs, boy?"

"Just ahead, sir. I think they're just ahead. I think so, sir."

"Are you all right? Not hit?"

"Oh no, sir. I'm all right." Tears streaked the grime on his face. "I won't run, sir. I promise I won't run."

Aaron, feeling a thousand years old, managed a brief smile and said, "I know you won't, son. Volunteers don't run, do they?"

"No, sir, they don't, sir." The boy plunged his face into the rubble of dry leaves as a shell burst somewhere overhead.

Aaron raised his head to look for Hauptmann. Barely visible although only fifty yards off, Hauptmann's forage cap was waving from a clump of thornbush. Aaron looked behind him to see how many men had followed him. Besides the Brandy Station recruit, four bluecoats were visible.

In a moment he would have to stand on his feet and lead a charge

146

on the Confederate works. It took him some time to nerve himself to the task. He had a mad vision of Father Sebastio's wizened face. The old Dominican looked very disapproving. "You see?" he seemed to be saying. "You may very well be killed, and what will become of you unbaptized?" Aaron shook his head to rid himself of the phantom.

"Are *you* all right, Lieutenant?" The tear-streaked face beside Aaron was concerned.

"I am all right. Get ready." Aaron checked the percussion caps in the Walch and gathered himself.

"Now!"

Bluecoats rose from the brush and charged at the makeshift breastworks. Aaron pounded forward, feeling the branches and brambles pulling at his clothing. The Rebels were firing in ragged volleys. Now he was at, and over, the piled logs, firing his pistol into the gray-clad bodies. For a nightmare moment gray and blue made a swarming, clawing mass. Muskets exploded in Aaron's ears, the stench of blood and shit was in the air. Someone had fouled himself in the act of dying. And as suddenly as the fight had begun it was over. Six dead Confederates lay behind the piled logs, and three dead Federals. A wounded Volunteer, cut down by Rebel fire in the charge, lay a dozen yards outside the strongpoint, moaning and begging for help. Before Aaron or Hauptmann could prevent him, the Brandy Station recruit was over the logs and scuttling through the brush toward the wounded bluecoat. He had almost reached him when a volley of musket fire came from somewhere unseen but very nearby, and the boy sprawled face down in the brush and lay still. The wounded Volunteer continued to moan and beg for help.

"Everyone, stand fast," Aaron said, and sat down on the ground, leaning against the logs.

The volume of fire was steadily increasing, though outside the strongpoint no soldiers except the dead boy and the wounded man could be seen. Smoke hung thickly in the air; the crackle of the forest burning was very sharp.

Sergeant Hauptmann and one of the men began to roll the dead Confederates over the log breastwork. One of the Rebels, a fair-skinned boy with silky auburn whiskers, was the one who had voided his bowels when his chest was jellied by a minié ball fired at close range.

As Hauptmann and the other lifted the Rebel to the top of the breastwork, the body was struck by several more bullets. They let the body drop and huddled behind the logs.

Aaron removed his forage cap and forced himself to raise his eyes level with the top of the breastwork. He called to his troops in German.

From somewhere came a drawling reply: "Talk English, y'damn Yankee!"

From elsewhere came replies from Aaron's Germans. The entire line of advance had been fragmented and stalled. There were sounds of fighting all around. Aaron could see the dead recruit and little more. The wounded man had begun to shriek and scream for his mother. The men in the captured position drank water from their canteens and tried not to hear him. Presently he was silent.

At dusk there was some activity in the direction of Brock Road. A line of blue infantry could be seen skirmishing forward. To the south was a line of burning brush. Behind it a firefight was going on, lighting the smoke with flashes.

Aaron said, "All right. Get ready to move out." He raised his head expecting to be hit at any moment, but the Rebels had evidently withdrawn to the west. Aaron stood and began to muster his men. He could count only fifty of the one hundred and ten who had started the advance into the forest. He formed them into a skirmish line in the gloom and called to the advancing Federals, "What unit?"

"Eighteenth Vermont," came the reply. In this tangle of woods, the neat order of battle devised by General Meade had broken down to leave isolated units wandering about in confusion. But somehow a line of battle had been stitched together and the attack was continuing.

"What unit are you?"

"Wisconsin Volunteers," Aaron said.

"Where are the Rebs, Dutchie?"

"That way," Aaron said, pointing west.

The Vermonters passed, barely visible in the smoky dusk. To the front the crashing of musketry seemed undiminished, though how one could find targets under these conditions was difficult to know.

"What do we do, Lieutenant?" Sergeant Hauptmann asked, rubbing at his powderburned face.

"What's our strength, Emil?" he asked.

"Fifty-five, all told. Nineteen wounded."

The company had suffered casualties of fifty percent, and the battle was continuing. For a moment Aaron was tempted to take his men out of action. He longed to seek the quiet and safety of the rear area, to save those of his men who were left—and himself.

"We'll move out now, Sergeant," he said.

"Zu befehl, Herr Leutnant." This time Emil Hauptmann of Mil-

waukee, Wisconsin might have been addressing a Prussian *Junker.* Reeling with fatigue, Aaron had a wild impulse to laugh. What would dear Adriana think of all this? That clear mind of hers would know it for what it was, pure madness.

"Speak English, Yankee," Aaron said, a slightly lunatic smile on his blackened face.

"Yes, *sir*," Hauptmann replied.

The company formed into a skirmish line again and pushed into the forest after the Vermonters. Presently there was a great flurry of firing ahead and the Vermont regiment appeared, running toward the rear. Aaron looked for an officer, but found none. He shouted at the New Englanders to stop and take cover, but only a dozen or so did. The remainder vanished in the darkness, running back toward Brock Road.

One of the soldiers who had stopped near Aaron shouted that the Rebels were counterattacking. Aaron called to his men to stand fast and fire low. It was nearly full dark now, and sharpshooting was impossible. Aaron told Hauptmann to tell the men to let the Rebels charge through if they chose, and to take them in the rear.

He could hear the Confederate infantry approaching through the dark, smoky woods. They were coming at a steady pace but Aaron knew that they would no more be able to hold a firm line than had the Federals that afternoon.

Somewhere to the north, no more than a thousand yards away, a vicious firefight began, flared, and died to desultory sniping. The woods were burning up there. Aaron could see the glow of the fire in the smoke and dust.

Aaron's men began to dig themselves in, piling dirt and branches into individual breastworks. He could see them only in silhouette against the glowing smoke.

"Stand fast, Volunteers," Aaron called.

Hauptmann appeared out of the darkness. "How long, Lieutenant?"

"No idea, Sergeant. As long as necessary, I guess."

"It sounds as though the Rebs are having trouble up ahead."

"Yes," Aaron said. It would have been pleasant to believe that the Confederates were being beaten, but he knew better than that. They were being slowed, possibly even stopped, but by the same forest tangle that had stopped the Federal attack.

"How are the men for ammunition?"

"Fair," Hauptmann said.

"Water?"

"All except Private Blier," Hauptmann said grimly.

"Then we wait," Aaron said.

Aaron did not sleep that night, nor did any of the other survivors of Company A. They ate the rancid-tasting canned rations they had been issued and lay waiting for the dawn, a line of men scattered through the tangle of brush and felled trees.

No more Federals appeared from the rear and the fighting to the west flared and died several times before the sky began to lighten. The smoke of battle did not clear. It clung heavily to the ground, shrouding the forest in a silvery, flame-shot pall.

At five in the morning the night dissolved into a ghastly twilight and the noises of battle seemed to have spread to right and left.

Hauptmann scuttled through the undergrowth to Aaron's side. "They are all around us," he said.

The sergeant's voice was hoarse, ragged with fatigue. He and all the remnants of Company A were near the breaking point. Twenty hours in this hellish wilderness under intermittent fire from an enemy seldom seen had taken a terrible toll.

"Can we withdraw, Lieutenant?" Hauptmann asked.

"Listen," Aaron said. There were sounds of battle behind them, as well as ahead and on the flanks. The terrain had triumphed over mere military planning. Aaron guessed that other units, Confederate as well as Federal, were in the same condition as Company A: scattered, decimated, out of touch with the planners of the battle. What was on trial here was no longer strategy and generalship, but simple human endurance. Until the ownership of this worthless tract of woods was decided, the great men, Grant and Lee and the others, were irrelevant. He wondered if they themselves knew it. But of course they must.

From somewhere to the west came a chorus of thin Rebel yells. The Confederates, drawing on God knew what resources, were mounting another attack.

Aaron came to one knee and drew his pistol, looping the lanyard about his neck. "Volunteers, mark your targets!"

A line of homespun uniforms appeared out of the smoke. The Rebels were trying to make a running charge, but the undergrowth slowed them, drove them into clotted masses of men. Aaron estimated that there were a hundred men in the attacking wave. They carried bayoneted rifles and were led by an officer in gray waving a saber. Firing began all along the Volunteers' line and the Confederates began to fall. But the Federals' rate of fire was too slow and the Rebels overran

Company A's positions. Fighting was hand to hand. Aaron fired at the Confederate officer and missed. A soldier in homespun thrust at him with his bayonet, stumbled, crashed against him. Aaron felt the man's hands clutching at his throat. He pressed the Walch to the man's belly and fired.

When he came to his feet again, the ground was littered with Confederate dead and wounded. The survivors of the charge had crashed onward to vanish in the smoke. Aaron could locate only a score of bluecoats standing. The others lay among the Confederates. Someone was screaming wordlessly and thrashing about in the bloodspattered brush.

"*Sergeant Hauptmann!*" Aaron heard the edge of hysteria in his voice and contrived to control it. But Hauptmann had disappeared. Aaron looked about and found him, face up, eyes staring at the smoke-metalled sky, his blue blouse wet with blood. He stooped and picked up the sergeant's rifle. The bayonet was bloody.

More Rebel yells came out of the murk, and Aaron knelt and aimed the musket at the smoke. When he saw the second wave of the Confederate attack appear, he fired into the massed homespun rank and saw a man fall. The last survivors of Company A fired a volley, and more Confederates collapsed into the tangle of thornbush and fallen branches.

Aaron watched the enemy advancing. His mind was wiped clean of any but the most immediate impressions. He saw the faces of the charging Rebels, teeth bared, facial muscles corded with tension. He noted the shabbiness of their uniforms. Some wore cloth wrappings on their feet instead of boots. He watched a black-bearded man pause, raise his musket, and fire.

The ball struck Aaron's arm and spun him around. The pain was blinding and his face felt the sharp spines of fallen leaves against his cheek. The wave of men washed over him. He heard the crackle of the undergrowth, the shrieking noises the wave made as it passed him. *I must get up,* he thought, *I must do something.* He lay face down in the tangled vines and bushes like a puppet whose strings had been cut. The pain in his arm rose to his shoulder and spread through his body.

He forced himself to roll over onto his back. It was the most agonizing thing he had ever done. What followed was worse. Somehow he unfastened his sash and began to bind his arm, or what he thought might be his arm. He could not be certain, because all he could feel was a stump ending in fire.

He had almost finished when his reserves of consciousness failed him. He drew a shallow breath and noted with a vague and diminishing interest that night seemed to be falling again. But it was a very strange night, he thought, that began at the edges of his field of vision and slowly closed in to shut off the light.

Wounded men burned to death in the Wilderness that day. The shrilling of one of them, coupled with the stubborn resistance of his own young body, pulled Aaron briefly out of his night-dream of dying.

Far beyond and above the smoke of battle, the sun could be seen as a vague, silvery disc. The battle had lighted many fires and the soldier being consumed within earshot of Aaron was not the only one who died the heretic's death.

For a time Aaron listened, hearing first cries for help, then yells of protest, then shrieks of terror, and finally the screams of burning agony.

He lay staring at the sky, his own pain growing old and distant, so that his mind seemed to float in space, only loosely tethered to the bloodstained casualty sprawled in the brush.

Don Alvaro had spoken of war as something men did because it was their nature to do it. "Sword cuts and maggots," Aaron remembered. But there was war of riding blood horses through the Pyrenees and seeing an occasional friend die or be wounded; and there was slaughter.

The soldier in Aaron's war had discovered that his options were those of a steer in an abattoir. He pondered this as the burning soldier screamed.

The beast about to be butchered might feel terror, surely he must. But he did *not* feel compassion, or sympathy, or love. Not at the moment when death was nearest.

I saw the tearful young recruit from Brandy Station die, he thought. And felt nothing. I saw my company wiped out to a man. And felt nothing. I saw Emil Hauptmann—and how many others?—dead before they were fully men. And I felt nothing. I may be dying. And I feel only fear of the fire—

Did those *Marranos,* bound to the stake with the iron pear jammed between their jaws, feel God's grace because they were dying for their faith? They did not. Aaron was certain of it now. They felt only fear of the fire.

He heard the sound of burning brush coming closer.

This I promise myself, he thought. If I live—*and God, I want to live*—I will fight no man's battles but my own. If I live to have a son—*please,*

God, let me live to have a son—I will protect him from this. No son of mine will ever take up arms or fight in another man's cause—

He could smell the fire now as it spread through the dry forest. The sounds of battle were gone and there was only the crackle of flames.

With all the power of his will he reached out to dig his right hand into the earth and pull himself along. The broken twigs and branches caught at him, probed his wounded side with the touch of knife blades.

Again he reached, pulled, moved. Away from the fire. And again.

The darkness plucked at the edges of his vision, but his desire to live kept it at bay. Reach. Dig. Pull. Not the *fire,* not the *fire.*

His digging hand struck a round stone. He clawed at it and found himself staring into the empty eyes of a human skull. Broken teeth smiled at him and he uttered a moan of terror. This was not the first battle fought in the Wilderness. The skull was the unburied head of a soldier who had died here the year before. There were many caches of human bones in this terrible place.

Aaron rolled over on his back, despairing. He called out, unaware that he spoke in his native German.

A dozen yards away, a pair of Quakers in blue coats, men of conscience relegated to caring for the dead and the near-dead, heard. "Over there," one said.

Aaron listened to the cracking of dry twigs. In sudden fear he fumbled for his pistol but could not find it. Someone cradled his head gently and put a canteen to his lips.

" 'Tis all right," a voice said. "Thee be safe now, Dutchie."

1866

18

The cards foretold it," Chole Segre
said, half smiling. "I said to you that it would be."

Julio Santana resolved not to argue with the woman. If she wished
to claim clairvoyance, who was he to deny her? She had been right
enough often enough to make her advice invaluable.

The hacienda was in mourning. Capitán Santiago Santana y Borjas
had come home from Africa in a sealed coffin, killed (and mutilated,
Don Alvaro had bleakly confided) by the Riffs in Spanish Morocco. He
lay now in the family crypt with his siblings and grandparents. It was
a dreadful price to have paid for the mischief he had done to the young
Jew and the Paredes girl, but Julio Santana felt no particular sympathy
for the dead man. Chole Segre said that Santiago had been born to this
end, and she was right.

Julio drew in a deep puff of smoke and stubbed his cigar in the dry
grasses. He sat with Chole on the hillside overlooking the new woolhouse, rebuilt at such great expense after the fire.

The day was cool, the breeze steady from the Mar Cantabrica. The white clouds of early summer floated motionless in a pale sky where hawks flew, searching for young lambs.

Beyond the woolhouse, in the riding ring near La Casa, Julio could see his young nephew, Roberto Marburg, cantering his white pony under the critical eyes of a vaquero. He wore a mourning band on his riding jacket.

"Will El Patron allow Alfonso to return now?" Chole asked.

"I see no sign of it," Julio said.

"Doña Maria? She might want him back."

Julio gave a short, harsh laugh. "After this long, you should know my mother," he said. "To her, Alfonso is as dead as Santiago."

Chole Segre smiled, teeth white in her scarred face. "She could have been *rom*—one of us—that one."

"Never let her hear you say that. She will have you whipped off the hacienda."

"The cards tell me that I shall die here. As a very old woman."

Julio snatched at Chole's hair in a gesture of cruel affection, *"Caray, vieja*—you and your cards."

Soledad pulled away from him and stood on her bare feet, looking out across the land to the distant sea. "The cards tell me more than that. They say you are the heir to Santanilla."

Julio rose to stand beside her. He wore the rough clothes of a working vaquero. For almost five years he had labored like a *peon*. El Patron had seen to that. Sometimes it was difficult to believe the things that the gypsy witch told him would be. But still—

Adriana's Jew was ailing. Aaron Marburg was swallowed up across the sea. There was only that bright-haired little demigod down there in the riding ring to think about now. All things were possible, weren't they?

Yet he said, *"There's* El Patron's favorite, gypsy. There's the heir to Santanilla."

At times he was filled with angry despair and asked himself what did it matter? The fortunes of the hacienda had declined. The horse herd was small, the sheep were few, the price of wool paltry. Miguel had somehow managed to clear the mortgages held by the Marburg bank, but in the process he seemed to have impoverished himself. He had actually sold land. Now they must sell the townhouse in Santander. Julio was not included in the family conferences about money, and it was just as well. He was no longer allowed to live as a caballero, as he had been trained to live. His visits to La Horca were few and infrequent, and when he went there he was not treated with respect. El

Gallo was dead of typhoid and his son was neither generous nor gracious. Life was changing, always changing.

Far below, a tiny black figure appeared near the riding ring. Doña Maria, come to oversee little Roberto's horsemanship. Beside her stood Tomasa Gomez, a woman with the face of a devil and the body of an angel, whom Julio, to his regret, would never know carnally. As the boy's *nana,* she was sacrosanct.

Where, Julio wondered, was one's beloved sister? Nursing her Jew, no doubt. Or possibly conspiring with El Patron. The old man grew stranger and more suspicious year by year. What was it Santiago used to call him? Yes, "the last knight in all Spain." Well, the armor was growing rusty and times were changing. But in what direction, who but the Holy Virgin knew?

"Don't be so sad, *gaijo mio,* " Chole said, slipping an arm under his shirt and around his waist. "The cards promise much."

Perhaps, Julio thought, but what was "much?" How could a gypsy know?

"Don Miguel wrote to America," Chole said. "Months ago. There has been no reply. But there will be."

Julio looked into the pockmarked face. "How could you know that?"

Chole laughed musically. "Doña Adriana's maid is a slave to the Tarot. Tit for tat."

"Felicia spies for you? On Adriana?"

"She tells me things. I tell her things. Why not?"

Why not, indeed? Gossip was common coin in any hacienda. The *criadas* formed an information network that could be invaluable if one knew how to tap into it.

Chole said, "Don Miguel sent to the tall American, the one who used to live in Santander. He asked him to find his son."

"To come back here?" Julio was dismayed at the thought.

"Oh no. Don Miguel is still angry because he chose to become a soldier. Not to come back here."

"Then for what?"

"Feli could not say."

Of course, Julio thought. He had forgotten that Felicia, despite all his sister's attempts at education, was illiterate.

"Something about the California land, I think," Chole Segre said.

"How do you know that?"

"I listen too, *macho.* "

"You are guessing," Julio said.

"Perhaps. We shall see."

Julio kicked at the barren earth with his boot. "What difference can it make, anyway?"

"Maybe none at all. There has been no letter from Don Aaron. Maybe there will be none. Maybe he is as dead as that one." She indicated the mausoleum in the hollow of ground near the stone chapel. "But one can wait and see."

"God, you would try the patience of a saint," Julio said irritably.

"Which you are not," Chole said calmly.

"Sebastio assures me of *that* often enough," Julio said.

"Do not be disrespectful to a priest of God, Julio," Chole said primly. Religion was not a matter for levity to Soledad Segre. "You must learn to wait."

"I have been waiting all my life, gypsy."

"If something can be done about the California land, there will be more for all of us."

Julio erupted into unkind laughter. "For all of *us?* For you too, gypsy?"

The woman's black eyes were stark and cold. Her basilisk gaze swiftly cooled Julio's contempt.

He said quickly, "I am joking with you, *vieja.* Joking."

"Don't joke with me," she said evenly.

Julio searched for a partial change of subject. It made him uneasy when Soledad Segre turned steely. It had been more than four years since he had taken another woman. He had become almost totally dependent on the gypsy; at times like this he was even afraid of her. "What about the California land, *vieja?"*

The woman shrugged her shoulders. "You are too stupid to understand," she said, and walked away down the path toward the hacienda.

Julio Santana watched her go, watched the way her slender, sinuous body swayed as her bare feet trod the descending hillside path. Simply watching her movements brought a tightness in his loins. She is my own personal succubus, he thought bleakly.

It was a measure of what was happening to the Santanas. The eldest son lay rotting in the grave, the tame Jew was no longer able to keep the debtors at bay, and gypsy devils roamed the ancestral lands at will.

Adriana Marburg put aside the copy of *La Gaceta* she had been reading to her husband. His hand on the counterpane looked translucent, the veins visible beneath the fine, delicate skin. Micah's bed had been arranged so that, propped on the bolsters, he could see through the window to the riding ring where Roberto was working his pony.

Micah was mending; Adriana demanded that assurance from both the new French doctor from Liencres and from herself as well. He *was* mending. It had to be.

The seizure that had felled Micah had happened nearly a year ago, but Dr. Danton had warned them all that recovery would be slow. "It is *angina pectoris,* madame, and I must make it clear to you that he will never be as strong as before. But with care and rest he may live for many more years." Now, at Adriana's insistence, Micah was confined to his bed for at least half of every day, and when he was allowed to go about it was with his wife or Doña Maria at his side to make certain that no excitement disturbed his convalescence.

He rested now, having listened to the excruciatingly boring items that comprised the *Gaceta,* his head resting on Doña Maria's favorite linen. It amazed Micah that he appeared to have won the hacendada's affection at last by the dreadful expedient of having a heart attack. Whenever Adriana was not with him, Doña Maria was, chatting companionably with him about everything from local gossip to the ancient controversy concerning the Borjas family's problematical relationship to some obscure and short-lived Renaissance pope.

Adriana, dressed all in black for Santiago, looked golden in the luminous morning sunlight. There was a mature purity in the thin, regular features, the straight blond hair skinned back over her narrow brows and caught in a knot at the nape of her long, slender neck. So short a time ago she had been a girl. Now, twice a mother and slender as a willow, she was more beautiful than ever.

Through an open doorway to the gallery came the sound of Cecilia shouting with laughter. His daughter was a tiny creature, elfin, black-eyed, black-haired, a miniature replica of Doña Maria. They had christened her Cecilia Morena Borjas Marburg y Santana. A weighty name for so small and happy a child, Dr. Danton said. And one would have imagined that Cecilia would swiftly become the hacendada's favorite. She resembled Doña Maria, after all, and carried her precious family name. Don Alvaro had even (at great expense, and risking Father Sebastio's pride) had the sacrament administered by the Bishop of Liencres, Doña Maria's kinsman.

But though Doña Maria liked her new granddaughter well enough, Roberto remained her unquestioned favorite. *"Mi caballero dorado,"* she called him.

Doña Maria had even insisted that Tomasa Gomez undertake to

be Cecilia's *nana* as well as Roberto's—a thing heretofore unheard of at Santanilla. Adriana was aware that this was done in order to weaken the ties between Roberto and his doting nurse, and transfer some of the affection given her to Doña Maria herself.

Young Roberto, however, seemed to have enough affection for all. Adriana had never known a more loving, forthcoming child. If Don Alvaro Santana was the last knight in Spain—and Adriana knew that those who so named him did not always mean it kindly—then Roberto was like Galahad, gilded, affectionate, and promising to be more handsome even than the illness-faded but still beautiful man in the high feather bed.

"I will tell Tomasa to keep Cecilia more quiet," she said.

"No, no. Let be, Ana. I like to hear her playing," Micah murmured.

Cecilia, like Roberto, should, he thought, be only a source of joy to him. But though it was years premature, he now found himself fretting about the girl's future. Girls of good family did not marry in Spain without dowries, just as young men did not go off to university without large purses. And whence, Micah asked himself, were these things to come? Since he had parted company with the bank and taken over the direct management of Santanilla, money had leaked away in a dozen small but steady streams. With the end of the war in America, wool prices had crashed. No one seemed to want to buy horses for any purpose. The railroad had been extended to the east, into the Pyrenees, but Santanilla had been bypassed. The estate was falling slowly but steadily into decay, and since his illness he was helpless to stop it.

The change in Adriana was profound. Micah did not know whether it was his heart attack or the deteriorating state of the Santana finances or both that had brought about the metamorphosis, but Adriana Marburg was no longer the feckless girl who had once supposed that Isaac Marburg would send money on demand.

Exercising great care not to fatigue him, she had set about having him teach her what she needed to know about accounting and business. He had resisted at first, unwilling to lose the charming innocent he had married. But a woman of Adriana's intelligence was not to be denied. With gentle insistence she extracted useful information from him until now, only a year since he had been leveled by the angina, it was largely Adriana who conducted the financial affairs of the hacienda.

Micah could not be certain whether or not he was sorry that she did not do this under the supervision of El Patron. Since the business of the Paredes girl and its explosive consequences, Don Alvaro had begun to fail. He was still the same ursine aristocrat he had been when Micah first knew him, but with a difference. Since the departure of Aaron (for whom he had felt a real affection) and his two sons (whom he had actively disliked, but to whom he felt he owed some protection), Don Alvaro had begun to separate himself from the practical business of everyday life. He had announced that Roberto was to be regarded as the heir to Santanilla in all its aspects, and then he had withdrawn into his library and his observatory. Certainly he had been of no help whatever to his son-in-law when Micah had quite literally ruined his health trying to put Santanilla on a sound financial basis.

Now that Adriana conducted most of the affairs of the hacienda, Micah supposed that she consulted from time to time with her father —but he was not certain of it.

The wonder of it was that Adriana could daily face the multiplying problems and their diminishing solutions and still be the loving wife and constant nurse to an ailing, near-to-useless husband.

When he permitted himself the anger, Micah discovered that he blamed Aaron for much that had happened. If the boy had been more clever, if he had been more mature, many of the ills that had befallen Santanilla would never have happened. It often infuriated him when Adriana spoke of Aaron, wondered about him and where he might be, if he was well, or alive at all. She seemed genuinely to miss the boy, and at such times Micah could not suppress a corroding jealousy. He could not forget that Aaron and Adriana were but three years apart. These thoughts became more corrosive still when he looked at his own face in the mirror and saw what his illness had done: the graying, receding hair, the hollow cheeks, the pouched eyes and thinning, bladelike nose.

He had, in a moment almost of desperation, written to Simon Pauley in Washington, D.C., first seeking to know—as surely he had a *right* to know—whether his firstborn son were alive or dead.

To have cast away the opportunity he, Micah, had arranged for Aaron in New York had been the act of a petulant, spoiled child. To have become a soldier in the Americans' war had been the act of a fool. Marburgs were not supposed to act so willfully.

But Aaron had done so, and there was an end to it. One might have expected him at least to write, to tell those who cared if he were alive or dead. But no, there had been only leaden, churlish silence.

And so Micah had written—not to offer forgiveness; oh no, matters were too far gone for that—but to offer *employment,* which was the proper thing. He had asked Pauley to locate Aaron, if that were possible, and to offer him the task of traveling to California to investigate the standing of the Santana claims to their old and clouded royal grant. He had asked Pauley to advance Aaron one thousand American dollars for the journey and as compensation. But Pauley had written back that so far he had not yet found Aaron, and that he would continue his inquiries through friends in the War Department.

But months had now gone by and there was still no word. And in the dark night, when Adriana was quietly asleep beside him, Micah Marburg sometimes imagined his son dead, and shamed tears would fall on the pallid, porcelain cheeks.

It was not easy, Micah thought, to be old and dying before your time.

Roberto Marburg walked in the direction of the stables, leading his pony. The boy's blond head had become almost silvery from exposure to the Spanish sun.

Behind Roberto, glancing from time to time at the white pony, walked Ana-Maria Gomez, a small, dark girl with flat features, sturdy legs and bare feet.

"You see, Anita," the boy was saying earnestly, "I must have my riding lessons every single day so that I can become a knight."

The little girl clapped her hands delightedly. "And fight the Moors, Roberto. You must fight the Moors." Tomasa's daughter was often allowed to stay in the nursery when Doña Maria or Doña Ana read to Roberto from the big book with the stories in it about El Cid and Rollando.

"Not the *Moors*, Ana," Roberto said with tolerant exasperation. Girls really knew so little about fighting. But he must never hurt Ana-Maria's feelings. She was his goddaughter. He was not sure he understood all that this entailed, but Mama and Tomasa always said he must treat Ana-Maria with consideration.

"Then who, Roberto?"

He led the way across the compound. A *criada* carrying water to the washtubs behind the kitchen stopped to bob at him with a doting, *"Buenos dias,* Don Roberto." He inclined his head to her gravely, as he had been taught to do with servants.

Ana-Maria tugged at the sleeve of his riding coat. "Tell me, Roberto. Who?"

That was a problem. The Moors were long gone from Old Castile, he knew, though the vaqueros said that some still ghosted through the

163

high mountains and sometimes killed the sheep. But Mama said that was not true, that there were no ghosts of any kind.

There were the Riffs, of course, who had killed Uncle Santiago. They were Moors of a sort. But they were far away in Morocco. El Patron had shown him where Morocco was on a map. It was colored red. And knights no longer fought Riffs. Soldiers did.

El Patron had fought the Carlists. Roberto was not at all certain who the Carlists were, only that they were hiding in France and might come back one day. Abuelo Alvaro had fought them on horseback. On a much larger horse than dear Blanco. Larger, but no better or braver, he told himself stoutly.

They reached the stable and Roberto led Blanco into his loosebox. The pony tried to eat from the manger, but Roberto restrained him gently, cross-tieing him with the ropes spliced into the rings on the stall walls. He set about unsaddling the pony.

"Rober-*to*," Ana-Maria said petulantly.

"What, Anita?"

"*Tell* me. Who must a knight fight? And why?"

Roberto disliked not having a specific answer to a specific question. His was a literal and precise mind. Even his fantasies were exact.

He put the small, silver-decorated saddle outside the loosebox and began to wipe Blanco down with a damp cloth, as the vaqueros had taught him to do.

"I will go to New Spain one day," he said, "and fight the slavers with my brother, Aaron." Somehow he saw Aaron, who Mama said looked very like Papa, on a great warhorse, wearing a breastplate and morion like the ancestors in the paintings in the *sala mayor*.

"I don't remember Don Aaron," Ana-Maria complained.

"I do," Roberto said. Not very well, of course, he thought. I was only a baby when he went away.

Ana-Maria, with the beginnings of Iberian practicality, asked, "Was my mother Don Aaron's *nana?*"

"Certainly not. Aaron was my brother before I was born. Before Papa came to Santanilla."

This was a concept totally beyond Ana-Maria's grasp. She did not understand how such a thing could be because to her the world beyond Santanilla was vague and somehow menacing. Don Miguel had always been at Santanilla. She fell silent.

Roberto finished grooming Blanco and then freed him to eat and drink. He kissed the velvety nose before closing the bar across the loosebox.

He started back toward La Casa. It was time for him to wash, change his clothes (Tomasa would be waiting to help him), and then present himself to his grandfather in the observatory for his mathematics lesson. Roberto was almost never tardy. It would be disrespectful to the *abuelo.*

Ana-Maria Gomez dogged his footsteps. "Tell me about Don Aaron," she demanded. "Is Don Aaron a knight?"

"Maybe not a knight. There are very few *real* knights anymore. But Mama says that he is brave and noble and that one day he will come home to Santanilla."

"Will he, *padrino?*" His goddaughter regarded him with eyes as black and bright as shoe buttons.

"Of course," Roberto said firmly.

"What if he decides to stay in New Spain? The *mozos* say he will never come back."

"Then I will go to see him," Roberto said. "He is my *brother.*"

The children reached the gallery leading into the family wing of La Casa. Geraniums flamed in hanging baskets between the arches. The hill breeze carried the smell of new grasses. Roberto longed to go back to the stable, fetch out Blanco again, put his playmate astride behind him (Tomasa frowned on that), and gallop to the ridge whence one could see the broad, flat blue of the sound. He loved it up there.

But it was time for a mathematics lesson, and no allowance was made in Don Roberto's schedule for missed lessons. He sighed and said, "Go and play now, Anita."

The little girl watched him vanish into the deep, cool shadows of the big house. How very difficult it must be, she thought sympathetically, to be one of *la gente fina.* But how else could the world be ordered? Someone, her mother often told her, must see to the running of things. She picked a red flower from one of the baskets, threaded it through her stringy hair, and ran off to look at the new lambs.

Flag Officer Simon Pauley, only days from his return to civil life but still resplendent in naval uniform rich with gold lace, regarded the austere young man seated across the table from him. Frankly, Pauley told himself, I would not have known him, he has changed so.

In the softly reflected summer sunlight that filled the dining room of the Senator Hotel on Washington's Michigan Avenue, Aaron Marburg ignored the meal set before him and toyed tensely with his wineglass.

Pauley found it difficult to believe that the man who sat across from him was not yet twenty-five. Thin almost to emaciation, with the drawn cheeks and deep-set eyes of a long convalescence, there was gray in his coppery hair and full beard. He used his left arm sparingly—scarcely at all—and the clenching movements of his fist were continuous. "The surgeon recommended I exercise it," he had explained curtly, "and by now it has become a nervous habit."

Aaron Marburg was dressed in civilian clothes, dark and so trimly cut that they resembled a uniform. He sat erect in his chair, a somehow angry figure. Pauley, who had access to Aaron's military records through his connections in the War Department, knew what he had endured. A year's convalescence in a military hospital was not a pleasant thing to contemplate.

"It does not trouble you to speak of it?" Pauley asked. Since sitting down at table he had said the same thing at least three times, in different ways.

Aaron's light eyes drifted from table to table where prosperous Washingtonians and officers still in uniform sat eating and conversing. "No," he said. "The doing troubled me, but that is over now."

"You are clear of the sawbones, then? Discharged?"

Aaron looked across the table with an expression of solemn pity. Pauley sensed that there was no way he, who had spent the war in the Navy Department here in Washington City, could ever know what a foot-soldier's war had been like. My God, he thought, with that expression on his face he looks like Old Abe. A tightness moved into his throat as he remembered the dead president.

"There is nothing more to be done," Aaron said. "This—" He moved his left arm slightly. "—will never be whole. But it will serve." He essayed a slight, humorless smile. "I have been working at the Freedmen's Bureau when I can. You have no idea how badly they handle money there. They will accept anyone who can read and add."

In March of the previous year, a day before President Lincoln's second inauguration and thirty days before his murder, Congress had formed the Bureau of Refugees, Freedmen, and Abandoned Lands and gave it supervision of all displaced Southerners, black and white, and all Southern property confiscated or taken by the Federal military. Radical Republicans—men with whom Simon Pauley closely identified —had packed the bureau with freed slaves and Northern Negroes. Unfortunately, not all of these appointees were literate, and therefore the need for persons with Aaron's skills was desperate.

"Have they paid you well?" Pauley asked.

"Well enough," Aaron said in his curt, impatient way. "My requirements aren't great."

"My sources in the War Department mentioned a chest wound as well, Aaron."

"The ball that hit my arm slivered. A piece of it collapsed a lung. That accounts for most of my year in the loving hands of the army medical department, Commodore."

"You were lucky," Pauley said before he could restrain himself.

It was a stupid thing to say, yet when any sort of wound in a limb meant almost certain amputation and a wound in the chest meant unpleasant death, Aaron Marburg *had* been lucky. Relative to hundreds of thousands of his comrades, at least. "Forgive me. That was foolish."

"No. You are quite right. I lost my entire company in the Wilderness. I must have had some luck to survive. Luck and a pair of Quaker conscientious objectors."

"But you are truly mending now," Simon Pauley said. "I want to know on my own, of course, but I have another reason for asking."

"Another year, they tell me, and I'll be as well as I will ever be," Aaron said.

Simon Pauley toyed with his food, sipped wine. Presently he said, "Have you had word from Spain?"

Aaron shook his head briefly. There was no expression in the harrowed young-old face.

"I didn't think so," Pauley said. "You have not written to them, have you?"

"I wrote to my stepmother while I was on the way to Frémont. That is all."

Pauley studied the color of his wine. Damn the boy—who was certainly a boy no longer—he didn't make it easy to talk to him. He smiled, seeking the youngster with whom he had spoken Spanish and English a very long time ago in Santander. "You have lost your accent, Aaron," he said.

"My troops were mostly Germans—dead Germans now," Aaron said somberly.

"I am sorry, lad," Pauley said. "But you could have joined Frémont as a quartermaster, you know. I suggested that once."

"I remember."

Pauley sighed. This conversation was progressing like a barefoot walk through a field strewn with broken glass.

"You once spoke of going out to California," the older man said.

"Did I? I may have done."

"Is it still in your mind to do that?"

"I have thought about it. California or Mexico. Though I wouldn't be much use to Juárez now."

"You weren't thinking of going as a soldier again?" That was a possibility Simon Pauley had not even considered.

"No." The denial was flat, definitive, weighted with intense feeling. "I've had enough war, Commodore."

"In any case the French and their fancy Maximilian will be out of

Mexico in a year more or less. Napoleon won't send more troops now that the war is over here."

Aaron leaned forward slightly, his crippled arm resting on the edge of the table. "I shall not remain in this country, Commodore. If not Mexico, it will be South America or some such place. I will not stay here."

Pauley was taken aback by the harshness of his manner.

"But you are an American citizen now, Aaron. You earned it in battle. You have every right—"

"I am a Jew," Aaron said in a stony voice.

"God blast and damn that Grant," Pauley said, rattling the silverware with a gaunt fist. The other diners heard and looked uncomfortable. One did not curse war heroes in Washington City these days.

"It's that damnable General Order Number Eleven, isn't it," he said.

Aaron did not reply.

"I suppose it would be of no use to say that not many Americans feel that way, Aaron?"

"How many is not many?" Aaron asked coldly.

"I am truly sorry. Grant paid for it, you know."

"I saw how he paid for it, Commodore. They made him commander of all the Federal armies. It was a cruel price."

Pauley sighed. "The man is a fool, lad. A great general, but a fool all the same."

Aaron gave that short, hard laugh again. "He will be President. Just as soon as Congress is rid of Johnson. You know that. No, I served in Grant's army but I won't live in his country."

Pauley smiled thoughtfully. Few soldiers fresh from the mind-numbing womb of the army thought about politics with such clarity. But this boy was not the ordinary veteran. "Why do you say Congress wants to be rid of President Johnson, Aaron?" He drained his wineglass and refilled it from the carafe on the table. "It is quite true, but is it so obvious to everyone?"

"Johnson is too soft on the Rebels," Aaron said. "I think that is the way you yourself would put it, Commodore. You are friends with the Radical Republicans, you share their views. Or you once did."

"I still do," Simon Pauley said. "But tell me why you think I am wrong, lad."

For the first time Aaron sipped at the wine. He put the glass down carefully. "The war was fought to end slavery because slavery had to be ended. No one who fought on the Union side will argue with that.

It was always what you and your friends wanted. True, Commodore?"

"A simplified statement of what we Abolitionists believed in, but yes, true."

"I will tell you a little war story," Aaron said. "I think it illustrates the fact that nothing is so simple as one believes it to be."

"Go on."

Aaron looked out across the room. It appeared to Pauley that he was not seeing the well-appointed chamber, the wood-paneled walls, the tables and diners. "After I was wounded," Aaron said, "I was put on a wagon heading north from Chancellorsville. A field surgeon had cleaned up my arm and my chest had not yet begun to rot— Forgive me, Commodore, this isn't luncheon conversation."

"Please, lad. Go on. I am listening."

"Very well, then. The wagon train was moving north toward Washington with more than a thousand casualties. The ones the surgeons thought could be saved. Of course, at every stop bodies had to be taken off and left for the Quakers to bury. But we had the best care the army could offer. There were medical supplies and orderlies, even some doctors. The Army of the Potomac did the best it could for its wounded. I will give Grant that. He butchered his soldiers by the thousands, but those who came through got the best care he could arrange for them."

Aaron held out his glass so that Simon Pauley could refill it before going on.

"Near Nokesville or Manassas—somewhere in Virginia, I was too filled with laudanum to be sure—we overtook a column of Confederate prisoners on the road. I don't know which prison camp they were being taken to, I never did find out. But they were in a bad case, Commodore. Wounds, fever, dressed in rags. Most of them had long since worn through their boots. They were being fed by the infantry guarding them, but that was about all. They were dying along the road, Commodore, just as we were. But much more swiftly, and sometimes for far less reason. Defeat is like that." He paused to look thoughtfully, distantly into space, and Simon Pauley shivered inside his fine blue coat.

"Manassas, did I say? Well, wherever. Our wagon train and the column of Rebs stopped near a road junction. There must have been three thousand Confederates, Commodore, maybe more." He picked up a knife and began idly to draw lines on the tablecloth with it. "Grant turned south after the Wilderness and Spotsylvania, you know." He smiled briefly. "Before the battle I remember the troops were waiting to see what he would do. Whether or not he would stick to Lee and make him keep fighting. 'A turn to the north,' they said, 'and it's Joe Hooker all over again. A turn to the right, and it's hooray for Grant.' Well, the army turned south all the way to Cold Harbor, Commodore, and that's where some of these Confederates had come from. On their feet. Wrapped in rags. Wounded men, sick men. Until we came up with them at Manassas junction."

He dropped the knife and used his free hand to massage the injured arm. "I couldn't stand the stink of the wagon, you see. So I got out to walk about and breathe some clean air. Of course there was none, because there were four thousand rancid, wounded soldiers in that one place. But I did the best I could, nursing my laudanum and canteen of water. And then amidst all those Confederates sitting by the side of the road, I saw a black man. He wasn't the only one with them, Commodore. There were hundreds. The Federal troopers tried to drive them off, but they wouldn't go. I imagine that the Negroes who could be driven off, had been, farther south. But the bluecoats kept trying. They yelled at them that they were *free,* and that they had no cause to stay with a mob of captured Rebels. From time to time they even used their rifle butts on them, but the Negroes who were there were determined to stay." Aaron looked strangely at Simon Pauley and said, "This particular black man I saw, Commodore, was very tall. Thin, long-headed, with fine features. He was dressed like all the others in that column of prisoners, in gray rags and homespun. But in a strange way he was as elegant as the day I first saw him at Santanilla."

"Good God, Aaron. Not that fellow Chase's slave? What was his name? Randolph, that was it!"

"None other, Commodore. The redoubtable, elegant, dignified Randolph. There he stood, guarding a wreck of a Confederate major sitting in the dirt by the roadside. It was Langhorne Chase, though if it had not been for Randolph I would never have known him. I'm no physician, Commodore, but even I could see that he was dying. He stank of dysentery and corruption. He had a belly wound. Not deep, but deep enough under those conditions.

"I wouldn't have believed it possible, but I spoke to Randolph and he remembered me. Maybe it was because I was the one who insulted Chase that day at Santanilla. You know I told him that if he didn't leave at once, Don Alvaro might shoot him. Maybe that was what Randolph remembered. But whatever it was, he spoke to me just as though nothing had changed. He was sorry, he told me, that the major was indisposed—that's what he said, indisposed—but that whenever it became possible, he would tell him that he had seen me. Then he unbent just the tiniest bit, Commodore. Just enough to say that he knew Massa Chase was in pain, and did I have anything I could give him to offer the major, who still had many miles to walk."

Aaron drank another glass of wine, slowly, to the dregs. "I gave him my laudanum and my canteen. I guessed I could do that much for the man I insulted at Santanilla. But I didn't do it for him. I did it because Randolph asked me with such dignity. Does that seem sensible to you?"

"Yes, lad. It does indeed."

"Then I asked him what he would do if Major Chase died. I *think* I said if, and not *when.* I hope so. He told me that he would do what was proper. I assume by that he meant he would bury Chase. And that then he would slip away and make a life for himself. 'I am now a free man, sir, after all,' is what he said. And then I got back into my wagon and we went off north, and the last I saw of him he was holding Chase's head in his arms, giving him water from my canteen."

Aaron regarded Simon Pauley speculatively. "How do you account for that, Commodore? What price your simple pickaninnies? Do you have any idea what has happened to this country? Are you absolutely certain you know where you are going? Are you really going to give those people everything you promised them? Because if you do not, sir, something terrible may happen here one day." He straightened in his chair abruptly. "But I don't intend to be here when it does. One war is all I have in me."

Simon Pauley selected a cigar and, as Don Alvaro used to do, made a ceremony of cutting and lighting it. Aaron watched him, wondering if his long tale had meant anything at all to him. Perhaps it had. Aaron himself was not certain he knew the meaning of it, if there *was* any meaning.

"I think your father would be proud of you, Aaron," Pauley said presently.

"Don Alvaro Santana, perhaps. Not my father," Aaron said. "Not that it matters."

"You should not hate your father, lad. Remember the Commandment."

"I don't hate him, Commodore. I am indifferent to him."

"Is that true?"

"On my honor as an officer and gentleman," Aaron said ironically.

"Then would you do a thing?"

"A thing, Commodore? What sort of thing? And for whom?"

"For your family."

Pauley noted that the color drained from the thin, bearded face. "For your stepmother. For your friend, Don Alvaro," he said.

"How can I serve the Santanas?" Aaron asked coldly.

"Don Alvaro wrote to me some time ago to ask if I could find you."

"Which you have done," Aaron said.

"Quite so. Which I have done. He asked if I could find you and ask you to undertake a journey to California for him. To the old state capital at Monterey. To search the documents and establish the status of the Santana land grant."

Aaron remained still and silent, his pale eyes icy.

Simon Pauley said uncomfortably, "Look, lad. I have become something of a businessman. It could not be helped. Long ago, when I was at sea, I backed a merchant in San Francisco. I don't know what possessed me. It must have been a lucrative voyage, I forget now. The man is getting on in years and wants to retire. It is a matter of importing copra—you know what copra is?"

Aaron nodded.

"One crushes it to make coconut oil. It has many uses. More and more these days, it seems. Now the firm has bought a factory to do the crushing and make the oil. There is money in that. Quite a lot of money. The plant is in a town on the Mexican coast, a town called Tihuacan. I need someone to go there and organize things. I don't like to leave it all to strangers. Might you be willing to do that for an old friend?"

"You are offering me a post, Commodore? If I do what my father wants done in Monterey."

"Don Alvaro, Aaron."

"My father, sir. Did he offer to pay money?"

"Well, Aaron—"

" I am not insulted, Commodore. My relationship with my father has always been that of an employee to an employer. He *did* offer money?"

Damnation, Pauley thought. How was it that a boy less than half his age could make him feel so uncomfortable?

"Yes, Aaron. There is a thousand dollars for expenses."

"Not very generous, wouldn't you say, Commodore? A voyage to San Francisco will take nearly half that sum."

"I believe things have not gone well at Santanilla, Aaron."

Aaron had a single bright flash of memory. Adriana was before him, bright and golden in the Spanish sun.

"Very well, Commodore," Aaron said. "Yes."

"Yes?" Pauley said. "Like that?"

"Yes to both offers. And my thanks to you." The stress on the final word could not be missed.

They finished their meal in silence. Pauley was conscious of the rolling of the black bunting on the arches of the windows. Much of Washington remained stubbornly in mourning for the dead president, though a year had passed.

When they rose to leave, Pauley said, "I should tell you, Aaron. Your father has not been well."

"I see." It was said without any emotion whatever.

"And Santiago is dead. Killed by the Riffs in Morocco, I understand."

Simon Pauley was shocked by the cold contempt in the thin, copper-bearded face. "That is good news, at least," Aaron said.

" 'Vengeance is mine, saith the Lord,' " Pauley said reprovingly.

"Quite so, Commodore. Perhaps there is a God, after all."

Pauley looked away and sighed. How strange it was that his sojourn in a foreign land had made young Aaron more Spanish rather than less. I am too old to deal with such intensity, he thought. Though God knew the boy had a right to be bitter.

He said, "When could you undertake the journey, lad?"

"When you please, Commodore."

"Very well, then. Come to my house tomorrow and we will complete the arrangements."

1867

Good Friday was a day of cold winds and low clouds. The sun cast the shadows of the racing clouds on the land in rays of swiftly moving darkness. The scattered stands of scrub oak on Santanilla had not yet begun to leaf out; the thin, twisted branches stood stark against the sky, moving in the icy gusts that swept down from the ridges of the Sierra Cantabrica.

Adriana Marburg, wrapped against the cold in a dark blue riding habit, her pale hair caught under a flat, wide-brimmed hat, hands covered by string gloves, shivered as she sat firmly on the sidesaddle. Estrella, given her head, had turned her rump to the wind from the mountains and stood like a statue on the crest of the ridge overlooking Santanilla.

Early this morning there had been an argument between Adriana and her mother. Doña Maria, with Tomasa Gomez and the children, had departed from the hacienda for Santander and the Viernes Santo celebrations—Mass and the procession of hooded penitents. The hacendada had expected that her daughter would go with her. She customarily took Father Sebastio on this yearly occasion, which meant that there would be no Mass at the family chapel. And though the men of the family seldom made the Good Friday pilgrimage to the cathedral in Santander, it was a tradition of long standing that the women and children never missed it. The robed penitents in their steeply peaked hoods, the chanting and the swinging of the brass censers were among Adriana's earliest memories. Even the female servants were given the entire day to attend, either walking the twenty kilometers as their own penitence, or, if they thought prudent, riding in one of the hay wagons driven by a *mozo de quadra.*

But today Adriana had declined to go, and after an unpleasantly acrimonious exchange between mother and daughter, Doña Maria had driven off in the landau with Roberto, Cecilia, Ana-Maria, and Tomasa, and Father Sebastio perched on the seat with the driver.

Adriana could not explain to herself why she had suddenly abandoned a ritual in which she had participated all of her life. She had simply revolted and refused to go. Now, seated on the back of old Estrella, she knew only that something remarkable had taken place.

The cold wind on her face felt fresh and clean after months of spending most of her days in a sickroom. She could not clearly recall how long it had been since she had ridden alone. She knew only that to have spent the day in church would have been unbearable.

Adriana had left Felicia to watch over her sleeping husband. She had not tarried to look in on her father, who was, as usual these days, mewed up in the observatory.

She had dressed for riding, driven by an almost panicky urge to be out and away before some necessity should rob her of this one swift moment of freedom. She had chosen to ride Estrella because the old mare was seldom ridden these days, and deserved better. *These days.* It was odd how often that phrase rose in her mind, Adriana thought, gripping her riding crop tensely.

There was reason enough, God knew. To think that Santanilla land had actually been sold. Not much, it was true, but still it was a thing that had not happened in the memory of any man or woman now living on the estate. And the townhouse was gone now. Not that she missed living in the town. She had never been totally comfortable there, with other people pressing in around one. But the house had been sold not by choice, but because money was needed to keep the hacienda functioning.

Gently Adriana urged Estrella into motion along the ridgeline. She knew this ground so very well, and barren though it might be, she loved it with a passion. Santanas had held this land for two hundred years, had lived from it, guarded it, treasured it. It was the land that gave the family meaning—the land and the things that grew on it and from it. But all of that was changing. It brought an ache to her heart, and a sense of loneliness. Because it seemed to Adriana Marburg that she, and she alone, realized what was happening. All would have been well, she thought with sudden bitterness, if only Miguel had not become ill.

But he had, and his strength had drained away. The tragedy of sickness was not only that it opened the door to death, but that it became one's single preoccupation, the object of all thought, the subject of all conversation, the only reality.

Miguel was not getting better. Though Adriana maintained the fiction that he was as best she could, it *was* a fiction. Miguel Marburg was slowly dying, and his mortality was central to his every thought. After his first seizure he had still had enough hope to spend some of himself in teaching Adriana what she needed to know to keep the hacienda going. After the second and third attacks, Miguel had nothing to spare. The illness became his obsession.

Adriana urged Estrella to a faster pace, as though she could somehow escape the darkness of the thoughts that pursued her.

In the last year the change in Miguel had been profound. All that remained of the virile, handsome man she had married was an emaciated ruin of parchment skin, deeply etched features, high, broad forehead over sunken haunted eyes that looked far beyond the confines of the sickroom into some approaching eternity no other could see. Miguel, her passionate, exotic cavalier, had slipped away, leaving behind an increasingly cranky, aging man. She loved him still, but her heart longed for the man he had been and would never be again. In the stillness of the long winter nights she dreamed, foreseeing, of the day that would come: Miguel Marburg's requiem Mass and the terrible, final closing of the bronze door of the mausoleum near the family chapel. What then, Adriana? she wondered.

Because she must, she had made an unspoken pact with her brother Julio. She continued to conduct the financial affairs of the estate, but to Julio was left the actual running of the hacienda. It was a formula for slow surrender, she knew, and she hated the need for it. Julio had always been a fool, and nothing would ever change that. Adriana despised the woman he kept, the gypsy Segre. But Segre could not be faulted for lack of cleverness. Though it pained her, Adriana was willing to acknowledge that. What brains Julio possessed resided under Chole Segre's greasy gypsy curls.

A large part of the woman's cleverness was devoted to maintaining a kind of uneasy peace between Adriana and her brother. Chole Segre was unfailingly diffident in dealing with Adriana and Doña Maria. Diffident and somehow, behind those veiled *gitana's* eyes, watchful and knowing.

It is wrong for me to feel as I do about the gypsy, Adriana often thought. It is not the way I was raised to think. I was not given my education so that I could wallow in prejudice as Spanish gentlewomen have done for four hundred years. But saying it to oneself and feeling it in the Spanish marrow were different things.

Adriana tapped Estrella with her crop and gave the mare her head. The animal broke into an eager run across the length of the ridge. Adriana did not hold her to a canter or restrain her in any way. Instead she lifted her face to the wind and let the mare's speed flow through her like a tonic. Her hat blew off and hung behind her back. She reached up and pulled the combs from her hair.

The mare, as smoothly as though running through air, galloped up the ridge, her head extended freely under Adriana's sure hand on the reins. Without breaking stride she leaped a shallow gully cut by the winter rains, and raced on. Adriana, liberated, uttered a wordless cry of pleasure that was snatched away by the wind and lost in the soft thudding of Estrella's delicate hooves.

Estrella stumbled and would have fallen had not Adriana Marburg been a skilled horsewoman. She slowed the mare's flight to a canter, to a trot, and finally to a walk. The beast's breathing was deep and labored, her flanks lathered. Adriana ran her hand along the delicate, muscular neck.

"*Yeguita,*" she said. "Little mare. Go gently, go gently now. You are a venerable lady, so go gently now."

The momentary burst of joy was gone. I am a fool, Adriana told herself. If I had fallen, what then? To die out here in the hills of Santanilla would be a foolish thing. What would happen to the land? To Miguel? To my son and daughter? Who would care for them if I should die?

How odd it was, she thought, that she had never actually thought of herself dying, never considered what would happen if she did. We Spaniards are said to be in love with death, she told herself. And yet it is a self-centered preoccupation, with almost never a thought to the problem of who will meet our obligations when we are in the earth. She allowed herself a mirthless smile. Tomasa and Felicia constantly talked of dying, and they were barely out of their teens. But nevertheless the subject fascinated them; they had grand dreams of funereal pomp, of mahogany coffins and black taffeta and sable plumes on shiny jet horses drawing magnificent hearses. It was as though they planned to attend their own funerals, whenever they might take place, walking behind the hearses in dark finery (for which they would have saved and scrimped all of their lives) among the grieving mourners. What a strange people we are, Adriana thought, so to love the ceremonies of the grave.

El Patron had once said that only a Spaniard could truly appreciate the pleasures of death. It was one of her father's ways of saying that he —and she; all of them—were still far from enlightenment.

She turned Estrella down the mountain. It had been a very long time since Don Alvaro had spoken to her in that companionable, ironic way. She found that she missed their conversations very much. With Miguel ill and Aaron long gone, who was there at Santanilla with whom she could talk?

El Patron had not loved Santiago. Who could love such a man? Yet some of her father had died when they brought her brother home from Morocco. Perhaps because it was El Patron who had sent him there.

The granite strength that had made her father the man he had been, rebel and knight, was slowly crumbling. She could sense this and it filled her with sadness, sometimes even with despair. Time and circumstances were wearing away the old man's vitality and assurance. But never his convictions, she thought firmly, never those.

Roberto was too young to carry on; perhaps in a sense he would always be too young and too sweet to become El Patron of Santanilla. She dearly loved her son, but she had begun to suspect that he would always need someone else's strength nearby to sustain him.

Julio—well, what could be said of Julio and his gypsy paramour? His hands were grasping at Santanilla, but would they really be able to hold it?

Aaron might have been the son El Patron should have had, but he was far away.

What, then, was left? she asked herself.

The answer was plain, self-evident.

I am left, she thought. Whatever becomes of the Santanas, I will decide.

Why else had she been raised as she had been? Why else had she been spared the narrow, religious upbringing of other women of her class?

One day soon, she thought, the family will be in my hands. It will come.

The thought did not fill her with exultation. Quite the reverse. She found that she faced the future with a certain anger and much sadness. How quickly, she thought, one begins to grow old.

She came down from the foothills onto the crest of a knoll above the track from the main gate to the estate. A lone horseman was cantering in the direction of La Casa. It was a post rider from Liencres, almost certainly. Adriana sat on Estrella and watched until the rider vanished over the crest of the hill. What could bring a rider out to Santanilla on Viernes Santo? With a tap of her crop she set Estrella in motion again in the direction of the road.

The cypress trees planted by the ancestors along the track swayed in the wind. They made a softly soughing sound, as though their tips were brushing the low, scudding clouds.

The road curved as it topped the hill, and when Estrella jogged to the crest, tossing and bobbing her head with the residual excitement of her run, Adriana looked down into one of the north pastures and felt her temper flare.

A small gypsy caravan was camped in the field among the rangy cattle. The brightly painted wagons had been arranged in a circle and the gypsy's animals, six donkeys and a swaybacked horse, had been hobbled and were sharing the sparse feed in the pasture. A half dozen people were gathered around a small fire and swarthy children tended a small herd of goats. Adriana, her face like a thunder cloud, cantered forward.

As she approached the camp, she was not surprised to see that Julio and Chole Segre appeared out of one of the wagons. All the gypsys stood respectfully as Adriana approached.

The patriarch, a burly man with a great mop of oiled ringlets under his cap and gold earrings in his ears, stepped forward. He removed his headgear with a flourish and said, *"Buenos dias,* Patrona."

Adriana was unable to restrain her feeling of disgust. The man's body had a pungent odor. Bathing was not easy for gypsies on the road, nor did they trouble themselves much about it. She saw that they were cooking a lamb and wondered darkly where they had obtained it. Not from the Santanilla flock, which had already begun to move into the mountains.

Julio approached and stood at Estrella's shoulder, looking up at his sister with an expression of mingled apprehension and defiance. "Not off at church, then, little sister?" he said.

"Who gave these people permission to camp on Santana land?" Adriana demanded. "Was it you, Julio?"

Chole Segre stood with the others, not speaking, but looking up at Adriana on Estrella.

The children gathered to join the adults, their dark eyes wide at the sight of the golden-haired lady on the half-Arab mare. Plainly, they had an eye for horseflesh. And for anything else that could be stolen, Adriana thought angrily.

Just below the level of her consciousness Adriana felt the beginnings of shame. What harm could these people do? The children were darkly alien, but really quite beautiful. But they stole things, killed livestock, littered the pastures.

Chole Segre moved closer to Julio and murmured in his ear. Julio showed his teeth in an uneasy smile. He said to Adriana, "Yes. It was I, sister. I told them they could camp here."

The gypsies spoke among themselves in their own Romany chatter. Estrella danced and curvetted nervously at the strange smells and animals. Adriana controlled her with unconscious skill and the patriarch flashed a smile in appreciation of her horsemanship. Suddenly Adriana felt petty. In Old Castile one did not offer hospitality to gypsies, but neither did one behave unfairly toward them. They had asked, and they had been granted permission by a Santana. Whatever Adriana might think of the wisdom of Julio's decision, it had been made.

"If you wish to wash," Adriana said abruptly, "you may use the well in the stable courtyard." She reined Estrella back, ready to turn for the road.

"A thousand thanks, Doña Ana," Chole Segre said, smiling.

Adriana felt her temper flare. What right had that women to use her family name? Julio caught her anger and touched Estrella's bridle. "Let me speak with you a moment, Ana," he said.

He walked beside Estrella to the road. When they were out of earshot, he said, "This is not what our beloved father taught you, is it, sister?"

Adriana snatched the reins from his hand. "It is not for you to talk to me about prejudice, Julio!" It had been a long time since she had heard of Julio referring to Miguel as "that Jew," but she had no doubt that he still did so among his low friends at La Horca Francesa.

"Peace, Ana. Let's not argue." He took a bundle of filthy peseta notes from pocket of his work clothes. "They pay, sister," he said.

Adriana was horrified. "You take money from them?"

"Where else am I to get it, sister of mine? Every penny this place earns now gets eaten up either by your pretty son or your sick husband. A man has a right to live."

Adriana drew back her crop and would have struck him, but he danced backward out of reach and laughed at her. "Go home, little sister. Go home and see what the last knight in Castile has to say." He slapped Estrella sharply across the rump and set the little mare galloping for the road. Adriana rode in furious silence for Santanilla.

She galloped Estrella into the stable courtyard and threw her crop and reins to the groom who hurried from the horsebarn to meet her.

Without pause, she strode straight for the path leading up the slope to the observatory. Felicia, who had heard her arrive, ran from the family wing waving and calling.

"Doña Ana! Don Miguel is awake and asking for you. *Señora,* do you hear me?"

Adriana did not pause. Her boot heels clacked on the flagstones, her blond hair, waist length when unbound, was like a battle flag.

At the door to the observatory, Adriana rapped once out of life-long habit, then pushed the studded oak portal ajar and marched in.

The room was untidy, littered with piles of books and unread scientific periodicals. The telescope, made especially for Don Alvaro by Professor Fraunhofer, had been partially dismantled for cleaning, but the task had not been completed. Oculars and the objective lens lay on a work table exactly in the same position they had occupied when Adriana had last visited the observatory.

Her father sat at his table, a stack of foreign newspapers, months out of date, lying on the floor beside his chair. On the table was a pile of legal-looking documents that he had apparently been inspecting.

Quite suddenly Adriana was struck by the big man's appearance. He wore trousers, felt slippers, and a soiled quilted robe. His hair was untidy and he had not shaved. El Patron, Adriana thought with a shock, looked *old.* And there was a neglected mustiness in the air of the cold room. For months, she realized, she had had this portrait of deterioration before her, yet because she had been preoccupied with other things she had not really *seen* it.

It did not dampen her anger, but it chilled it, adding an element of fear.

"Ana," El Patron said, removing his spectacles. "There you are. I was going to send for you, but I couldn't find Felicia."

There was a vagueness in his manner that could not be new, but Adriana had not noticed it before this moment.

She drew a deep breath and said, "Papa, I want to speak with you about Julio."

Don Alvaro waved a hand as though brushing away a cobweb. "Ah, Julio. What has he done now? Or not done, is that it?"

Adriana stood straight and still as she had been taught to do when discussing family matters of importance. "He is taking money from the gypsies," she said.

"Yes, well." To her amazement, her father shrugged without a sign of anger or disapproval.

"Papa," Adriana said, "do you understand me? He is accepting money from gypsies in return for allowing them to camp on Santana land."

"Well," her father said again. "Of course he should not do that. He has grown very fond of the gypsies, though, since that woman—what is her name?—came."

Adriana felt the blood draining from her cheeks. "Papa," she said more gently. "Don't you hear what I am saying? Julio is accepting payment for use of Santana land from gypsies."

Her father's hands trembled on the desk. "Yes, yes, Ana. I know. I have heard about it from the servants. He should not take money, of course."

The last of her anger leaked away, leaving Adriana empty. "If he accepts payment from squatters, Papa, it gives them rights. You told all of us that many times."

Don Alvaro rubbed at his eyes with his fingertips. Adriana noted how stained they were from his constant smoking. His wrists looked thin and fragile.

"I will speak with Julio," Don Alvaro said. "Yes, I will do that. Can you reach me a match, daughter? Just there, on the work table."

Despair crashed over Adriana in a wave. What was happening to the Santanas? While she devoted all of her attention to Miguel, the hard core of the family seemed to have begun to dissolve. She walked to the work table and found a *cerillo*. She struck it and held the flame to the cheroot trembling in her father's lips. Then she stooped and held his head in her hands and kissed his graying hair. Her eyes felt hot and wet.

"Ana," the old man said. "Look. See what came with the post. A packet from Aaron. From *Aaron, hijita.*"

Adriana brushed her eyes and found a chair. On the desk lay a stack of legal documents, some in Spanish, others in English. And a letter.

"Read it, Ana. Go on, read it. See what Aaron has done," El Patron said, his voice tremulous. "About the land in Alta California, daughter."

Adriana took the strange, slick paper in her hands and lifted it to the light. It was covered with lines in Aaron's Teutonic copperplate handwriting.

"Estimado Patron," he wrote.

Last summer, in the city of Washington, Señor Comodoro Simon Pauley entrusted me with a task upon behalf of you and the Santana family. Since the request originated either with you or with my father, Don Miguel Marburg, you will be aware of what the task entailed. However, so that there will be no misunderstanding, I will repeat for you the instructions I received through Señor Pauley.

He requested that I go to California and determine the present status of the property granted to your ancestor, Don Esteban Santana, by the Spanish Crown in 1722. He asked, on your behalf, that I investigate the title to any land in California still subject to claim by descendants of the original recipient of the royal grant.

In the event, Patron, the task was more complicated than el comodoro expected. But the travel required fit in with certain plans of my own, and so I have been able to complete the search with what I hope you will regard as satisfactory results.

In the old capital of Alta California, Monterey, I found mission records for several years, including the year 1722. One of the friars, engaged for the task by the alcalde, listed the royal grants registered in that part of New Spain. There was an entry setting forth, in very general terms, the extent and location of the Santana grant. It consisted, in modern measure, of approximately 15,000 hectares of land situated on the coastal slope of the mountains known as the Santa Lucia Range. The benchmark was listed as being 36°31' north latitude, and 122°17' west longitude. The county surveyor warned me that benchmarks located before 1850 were notoriously inaccurate. There was no record in Monterey Presidio that the land was ever occupied or ranched by Don Esteban, who was a member of the military garrison between 1718 and 1725. A local historian believes Don Esteban used his grant as a hunting preserve, as wild boar abound on that coast.

I engaged horses and visited the most accessible parts of the property, and it is my opinion that ranching or farming would be difficult there, but not impossible. There are a number of vistas on the first range of foothills that are impressive, with a view of the Pacific Ocean and many sheer drops to a rocky and turbulent coastline. The terrain itself is not dissimilar from that around Santanilla, though the climate is very different, with fogs and Pacific storms prevalent in winter and spring.

I also discovered that much of the original grant has been claimed by settlers and ranchers, so that of the 15,000 hectares, perhaps no more than 2,000 remain, much of it steep and mountainous. I established the fact that most of the settlers are protected by homestead laws of the United States, and some have held what they claim to be clear title since 1850, when California was admitted to the United States.

These titles I examined at the state capital of Sacramento, where I was shown much courtesy by the governor, Mr. Henry Haight, a personal friend of Comodoro Pauley.

In Sacramento I took it upon myself to register your claim to title of the land that remains unhomesteaded. Though titles to royal grants are difficult to confirm, the state government of California prefers to recognize them if any evidence of their bona fides can be established.

In order to assure that your title be recognized—and since, thanks to Simon Pauley, I was about to take up a post in the town of Tihuacan, in the Mexican state of Sinaloa—I took it upon myself to travel to Mexico City, there to examine the records of land tenure in Alta California that were removed from Monterey after the signing of the peace of Guadalupe-Hidalgo in 1848.

As you may know, the political situation in Mexico has been chaotic for some years since the French persist in forcing upon the Mexicans an emperor sustained by bayonets. But matters are resolving themselves swiftly now, and the forces of Benito Juárez have all but driven Maximilian and the French from the country.

In Mexico City I was able to engage the services of a lawyer whose brother is a general with Juárez. In this country it is always wise to retain those whose political connections are current. With the lawyer's assistance, I was able to find, in the National Archives, a certified copy of the royal grant to Don Esteban, a document signed by King Philip V, and dated July 17, 1722, at the Escorial. This, the lawyer assures me, will be considered confirmation by the Americans in California.

I now have, I believe, completed my commission, Patron. I enclose with this letter notarized copies of all the pertinent documents and I have dispatched other copies to Governor Haight in Sacramento, asking that they be registered as evidence of your ownership of the remaining property. From

*this day forward, you will be expected to pay taxes on this land to the State
of California, but I am assured that the amount is nominal.*

*Therefore you may now assume that the land described in the enclosed
title deed is yours without encumbrances.*

*I hope, Patron, that this finds you well and that Santanilla prospers.
I have taken the liberty of enclosing a short note for Doña Adriana.*

*Su seguro servidor,
Aaron Marburg*

Adriana looked up from the handsomely scripted pages. A strange
excitement tightened the breath in her chest and made her fingers
tremble imperceptibly. "A letter, Papa? For me?"

Don Alvaro searched among the papers on the desk and produced
a single page that had been sealed, but was now open. Adriana felt a
thrill of mingled anger and, strangely, apprehension that her father had
so casually opened and read a letter clearly intended for her eyes alone.

The angers, annoyances, and uneasy fears of the day seemed to
overwhelm her. She felt like a girl at puberty, seething with fantasies
of parental oppression and intrusiveness. "Papa," she said, "you
opened a letter addressed to me?"

The moment the words were spoken she realized she must sound
a fool. A letter from a *boy,* after all, and her stepson at that.

Yet there had been another letter, written long ago. She remembered it now, as she had not for many months, and her cheeks burned.
If this letter were in the same vein, what would she say to her father?

Don Alvaro said, "It is a letter from *Aaron.* From Aaron, *hija.*"

Adriana held the single page without yet looking at it. Her father
was regarding her with a perplexed expression.

Yet a year ago he would have understood her. A year ago he
would not have opened the letter. He himself had raised her to be an
independent woman, with her privacy intact. The manner of his dealing
with her, even as a girl, had been the scandal of the district—and his
delight. I would have expected this from Doña Maria, she thought, but
not from him. Apparently time and circumstances were eroding convictions Adriana had thought immutable.

She was struck by a sudden and seemingly errant thought—one
that, regarded seriously, was not errant at all but painfully pertinent to
the present situation of all of them at Santanilla. It was as simple and
straightforward as an axiom.

When one was rich—when one was *safe*—it was not too difficult

187

to be high-minded. One could be kind to inferiors, generous with the less fortunate; one could easily bestow upon one's children the rights of individuals. One could graciously abjure prerogatives of birth and class.

But when money grew scarce and life was no longer so safe and certain, one unconsciously became meaner, more protective of privilege, less free to embrace the new. She had expressed that axiom this very morning with her arrogant treatment of Julio's gypsy friends. Don Alvaro's liberal daughter, who had been the talk of the province, would never have behaved that way. Why, then, should it surprise her that Don Alvaro, who once had opened his daughter's mind to the new ways of thinking, now unhesitatingly opened her mail?

Adriana succumbed to a strong sense of having lost something of great value, something she had not before realized was so fragile.

The great liberal thinkers of the Enlightenment, her father's idols and her own, had all, almost without exception, been rich, privileged, aristocratic. This little incident of the letter from Aaron now made her wonder if their courage had been so great as she had always been taught to believe.

It was creeping poverty that shattered ideals, she thought. That was a truth so self-evident that she wondered why it had not occurred to her before.

Adriana would never bring herself to share this epiphany with her mother. Doña Maria would regard it with such satisfaction. She had, after all, never wavered from her reactionary convictions. This was evident in her iron determination that Roberto and Cecilia receive a full measure of traditional education, complete with an awareness of religion and the ancient privileges of their class.

For a moment Adriana felt lost. To whom could she turn now? On whom could she rely to give her the free and independent life she had been promised? Not Miguel, God help him, who now thought only of sickness and death. Not her father, whose eager liberalism and joy of life had dulled as his estate deteriorated.

I am Adriana Marburg, she thought. I am a Santana. Women of my blood held castles as chatelaines against the Moors. They must have known, as I do now, that when all is said and done, there is only oneself to do what must be done.

"Adriana? *Hija?* You don't look at Aaron's letter." El Patron sounded querulous. She regarded him with love and pity.

"Yes, Papa," she said. For the moment she had forgotten Aaron, but she thought of him now differently from ever before. We cast him away, she thought, as though he were of no use to us. That was a bad thing to do. A young man, so bright and full of promise, should never be discarded so cavalierly.

The letter was not what she had expected, but it was what she deserved, she thought. Cool, formal, distant. Not at all like the other.

"Estimada Suegra," he wrote.

> *I hope that this finds you well and happy. Comodoro Pauley tells me that my father has not been in good health. I am sorry to hear of this and trust that he is recovering.*
>
> *I am remiss for not having written to you, or to Don Miguel, before this time, but I am a poor correspondent and I fear I will remain so. It is not for lack of thinking of you.*
>
> *I have settled here in Tihuacan and have begun, in a small way, to prosper. Here I shall remain for the foreseeable future and make my life.*
>
> *Please convey my good wishes to my small brother Roberto and to my little sister Cecilia, whom I have never seen.*
>
> > *I sign myself*
> > *su hijastro y seguro servidor,*
> > *Aaron Marburg*

Adriana folded the letter carefully and tucked it into the bosom of her riding habit. She felt a deep sadness.

"He says that he prospers," El Patron said. "That is good to hear."

"Yes," Adriana said softly. "Good to hear, Papa."

Don Alvaro, suddenly conspiratorial, spread his hands over the documents Aaron had sent. "He has done well for us, marvelously well. This will be Roberto's. I always intended that it should belong to him. We will say nothing about it to Julio, Ana. Nothing."

Adriana straightened her back and stood erect. "Yes, Papa," she said.

Don Alvaro caught his daughter's hand and held it. "Things are bad here, *hija*. They are bad and will get worse. Spain—*mi hermosa España*—is failing. There is no honor here any longer." He released her hand and fumbled through a pile of periodicals on the floor until he found what he was seeking, a Paris newspaper six weeks old. "See this. Look at it, Ana." He thrust the folded sheet into her hands. It was a scurrilous piece about Isabella, the Spanish queen, and her latest lover, Carlos Marfori, a cook's son whom she had made a minister of state.

"See what is becoming of us here, Ana," El Patron said, his voice suddenly trembling with anger. "There is fighting in Extremadura. O'Donnell is sick and will surely die. Then the Carlists will come back. No, my beautiful Spain is done for, done for." He touched the documents on his desk. "Here. Here is where we will go. It will belong to Roberto and we will live there on a new Santanilla. Yes, a new place in a new world. We will not tell Julio and his gypsies. This will be our secret, daughter."

Adriana closed her eyes for a moment. They were moist with tears. "Yes, Papa," she said.

"It will take money, *hija*. It will take time and money, but we will take the time and find the money. Perhaps Miguel's brother will help us. Do you think? Well, no matter. I will provide everything we need. The Santanas will go to the New Spain. Aaron says there are vistas overlooking the Pacific. Imagine that, *hija*, Balboa's great ocean-sea! You will see, daughter. You will see—"

He stopped, breathless. Adriana knelt at his feet and hugged his knees, the tears flowing down her cheeks. "Yes, Patron," she said. "It shall be as you say."

The old man bent and kissed the crown of her head, running his hand gently over her golden hair. "Now, you must go, *hija*," he said. "I have mountains of work to do. Plans to make. So many plans."

She left Don Alvaro at his desk and walked out of the observatory into the cold and blustery April daylight. The tears were icy in the wind. She walked with her face lifted to the silvery sky and her long hair blowing about her cheeks.

There is no one but me, she thought. No one.

Sorrow gave place to a steely resolve. If that is so—and it is—then so be it. Her father might be a foolish old man, tired and disappointed, his sons dead or wasted, his blood thinning. But El Patron's dream, impossible as it might seem to be, was *not* so foolish.

Her eyes narrowed against the metal sky, she thought: I am Adriana. What must be done, I will do. And God help anyone who stands in my way.

Felicia, visibly agitated, said, "Patrona, Don Miguel has been *asking* for you."

Adriana, standing in her room before the pier glass trying her hair back with a ribbon, said coldly, "Is he worse?"

"No, Doña Ana, I don't believe so. But he wants—"

Adriana cut her off abruptly. "Then I will have my bath first. Go tell him so, and then draw a tub for me."

"*Sí,* Patrona," Felicia said, subdued.

For a time Adriana stood before the glass looking at her reflection. Then she began to undress, pulling the heavy habit off and throwing it to the floor. It was icy in the room, the wind stirring the heavy drapes at the windows. Adriana's bare feet took the chill of the tiled floor. The scudding cloud shadows alternately darkened the room as they passed over the hacienda.

She stood naked before the mirror, examining herself dispassionately. She was thin, too thin. But her breasts were still high and firm. There were tiny stretch marks on her belly—Roberto's gift, and Cecilia's. But her thighs were still round and firm, her legs straight.

Yet the girl she remembered was gone. This was a woman fast approaching middle age. In this land, a married woman of twenty-eight was old.

No, she thought. Not yet. There is too much to be done. She cupped her breasts in angry sensuousness, thumbed the dark nipples erect. Miguel had not been able to touch her for nearly two years and she longed to be made love to.

She stepped to her dressing table and opened a drawer. From it she took a small silver casket inlaid with cloisonné. Inside was Aaron's letter written on his journey to St. Louis. She drew out the letter. It was a love letter, written by a young boy deeply in love with a woman he could never possess. The phrases were clumsy, touching, endearing.

It ended with a tender, hopeless farewell. "It is not likely that we will ever meet again, dear Ana, but I will never forget you."

Adriana refolded the letter carefully and together with the new, replaced it in the casket. She returned to the pier glass and stood for a moment, strange and dangerous fantasies flowing like a dark river through her mind.

I am the only capable Santana, she thought at last, and I will do whatever I must do to protect my family. At this moment she could only guess what that might involve, but she knew with an absolute certainty that whatever the cost, she would pay it.

The road was little more than a track in the hard sand. It ran out of Tihuacan, straight to the northwest between the sea and the linked lagoons that glistened like sheets of polished glass in the high sunlight. June on the Tropic of Cancer was the heart of *el tiempo de calor,* the hot season, when the sun burned directly overhead at noon and the sea lay flat and oily-calm except when the *chubasco* blew. Then the typhoon waves would wash over the flat land between the lagoons and the ocean, smashing with exploding spray against the breakwater of the Malecón, and drenching the curving Paseo de las Olas Altas and the red-tiled roofs of the houses built facing the sea.

On this day, the air was calm. The buggy and the handsome bay gelding in the traces stood on the road that ran from Tihuacan northwest to La Cruz, their shadow the only shade in view. Aaron had bought the horse and rig from an *imperialista* family that had fled with the last troops of the French garrison. It was the finest outfit in Tihuacan.

The woman sitting beside him wore a broad-brimmed bonnet and a dress of white lawn decorated with Italian lace. Her skin was olive, what the Mexicans called *morena,* her hair shiny black and caught at the back of her slender neck in a tight knot, held there by a comb made of amber and decorated with silver filigree.

Among the eligible bachelors of Tihuacan Julia Marini was not accounted one of the most beautiful women, but she had a devoted following. Her face was oval, with narrow brows, a full-lipped mouth, and large, expressive eyes of a startling green.

Aaron Marburg acknowledged that there were prettier girls among the unmarried, but it was Julia's quick mind and shrewd good sense that attracted him to her.

Her father was an Italian, a naturalized citizen of Mexico and the prosperous proprietor of Tihuacan's largest and most profitable general store. In a country where a merchant class was still a novelty, Marcello Marini was regarded as a valuable citizen of the town.

It was the Marini establishment that supplied the new farmers, formerly landless *peones,* who worked the small holdings surrounding Tihuacan. The land reforms of Presidente Benito Juárez had broken up the large estates, and most of the hacendados had run away as the *Juárista* armies drove off the French imperials. But the newly propertied *peones* lacked money to buy the seed and farm implements they needed, and Marcello Marini had imported what was required, selling it to the *peones* on credit, with the land as collateral.

Many waves of land reform had rolled over this country, Aaron knew. The pattern was always the same. The large holdings were expropriated by reforming governments and the land parceled out to the poor tenants. Since the land was not suited for growing crops other than corn, and since the governments invariably gave out the land in parcels too small for efficient farming, the *peones* were forced to encumber it to merchants and bankers in order to obtain what they needed to work their holdings. Then, as each *peon* family succumbed to economic reality, the land accumulated in the hands of a new landed class and the *peones* became tenants once again.

Aaron had no particular feeling about this seemingly endless circle of idealism gone wrong. It was simply the way things were done in Mexico—indeed, in all of Spanish America. The system had made Marcello Marini a rich man in the first wave of *Juárista* reform in the late 1850s, rich enough to allow him to survive the uncertain fortunes of the war between Benito Juárez and Napoleon III's puppet Maximilian, and to begin the process all over again, now that the French had been driven out of the country, allowing the idealists to return.

One of the things that most attracted Aaron to Julia Marini was her clear and lucid understanding of the realities of life in this country. Unlike any of the other husband-hunting girls of Tihuacan, Julia thought about—and understood—Mexican politics as well as the business that had made her father into a rich man and herself into an heiress of some proportions.

In many ways, Aaron often thought, Julia was as Adriana had been, *different* from the ordinary run of her peers. And since rural Mexico was even more provincial than Old Castile, she, again like Adriana Marburg, was the object of endless gossip and envy.

It was true, as Aaron admitted to himself quite freely, that Julia lacked Adriana's elegance and style. That was to be expected. Don Marcello had come to Mexico in even more straitened circumstances than had Aaron himself. He was the son of a family of Genoese fishermen so impoverished that he had arrived in Vera Cruz with forty pesos in his pockets and a rubber stamp with which to sign his name. That had been in 1822, about the same time that Augustin de Iturbide had managed to drive out most of the Spanish colonial troops, declaring himself Emperor of Mexico. One of Julia's prized possessions (she wore it now, on a golden chain around her neck) was the first gold coin her then-fifteen-year-old father had earned in the new land. It bore a Mexican eagle and the legend *Augustinus Dei Providentia* on one face and *Mexici Primus Imperator Constitutionalis* on the other. The regime of Augustinus, by God's providence Emperor of the Mexicans, was all but forgotten now. But Don Marcello, who had worked and grown rich, and even learned, in time, to read and write, could look at that coin at his only child's throat and remember how far he had come.

Don Marcello had married a Mexican girl of good family, the Arsellos of La Cruz, late in life. Doña Lucilla had died giving birth to Julia, and Don Marcello had never remarried. This had left Julia Marini the undoubted heiress to all that the old Genoese owned and made her extremely popular among the *bravos* of Tihuacan.

But Julia had met Aaron a month after his arrival in Tihuacan and she had made a decision. Now she waited calmly for him to make the same decision. In her mind, there was no doubt whatever.

The shadow of a hawk flying far overhead disturbed a fleet of mudhens on the lagoon and they whirred into flight, leaving long wakes interlocking on the glassy surface of the water.

Julia, her elbow resting on the wicker hamper on the seat beside her, removed her bonnet and fanned her face. The vertical rays of the sun on the black top of the buggy radiated a dry, salty heat. The road to La Cruz stretched out before them, two shallow ruts in the packed sand between the ocean beach and the lagoons. The sea looked unreal, a deep purple blue. The tide was slack and the waves washing the long shingle of beach were small and regular. Julia loved this isthmus between the marshes and the sea. It had a stark, austere beauty.

"Which shall it be, Julia? The sea or the lagoon?" Aaron asked.

"The sea," Julia said. These excursions were precious to her, though she knew that they were the subject of endless gossip among the ladies of Tihuacan. She was the only young woman of the town defiant enough of custom to ride out with Aaron Marburg (or, for that matter, any young man) without a *dueña*. The Marini servants thought it a scandal, but Don Marcello knew his daughter well and trusted her. He was developing a fondness too for Aaron Marburg, which pleased Julia very much.

Aaron flicked the reins across the gelding's rump and turned him off the road onto the broad, flat expanse of ocean beach. A single broad-winged *alcatraz* soared silently high above the sand, banked and glided out to sea.

At the edge of the almost featureless dunes Aaron stopped the buggy and set the brake. He dismounted and loosened the gear on the gelding. Julia noted that Aaron habitually took better care of his animals, his buggy horse and his thoroughbred saddle mare, than any of the other young men of her acquaintance. She approved of that. Horses were valuable and should be handled accordingly. She was not a merchant's daughter for nothing.

Aaron assisted her to the sand and she walked swiftly to the water's edge while he unloaded the hamper and a blanket. She stood looking out to sea, across the wine-colored expanse toward the single small cloud in the western sky. Though she could not see the land under it, she knew that it had formed over the very tip of the Cape of San Lucas at the southernmost point of Baja California. Only weeks before, a Honduran steamer had gone aground on that rugged coast, with a loss of ten sailors. The wreck still lay grinding on the rocks with its valuable cargo of hardwoods. Her father had hired fishermen from La Cruz to salvage the wreck. Marcello Marini missed few opportunities like that.

She turned and walked back to the buggy. Aaron had removed his seersucker coat and rolled up his shirtsleeves, but he quite properly still wore his high, starched collar and silk tie.

He bowed to her in that curiously formal European way of his to indicate that he was ready for her to serve the picnic lunch he had had his *cocinera* prepare for them. His cook, like all his servants, left a great deal to be desired, but that was to be expected in a bachelor's household. Julia spread her long skirt and sank down onto the blanket.

She watched Aaron as she served out the cold *pollo* onto the fine china dishes. She wondered who had helped him select them and the heavy silver tableware. Perhaps he had done it unassisted. Aaron Marburg was obviously a young man who had lived surrounded by objects of good quality.

She often wondered what he would look like without his beard. The coppery color of it was interesting, but it did make him look older than he was. His forehead was high and broad. She liked that. Her father's was the same. But it suggested that, like her father, Aaron might one day be bald. A pity to lose that fine head of hair he now possessed, but he would be an impressive older man.

His arms were brown and thin. She knew that unlike many others who managed the various enterprises in Tihuacan, he was quite willing to work side by side with his men at Trituradora de Aceites, S.A., his copra-crushing plant on the south edge of Tihuacan. He was already a partner in the factory and hoped, eventually, to buy out the American owner, Señor Pauley.

The Trituradora was a noisy, dirt-floored sheet-metal shed containing four huge machines called expellers, powered by a converted ship's steam engine and a whirring cat's cradle of shafts and leather belts. The copra, broken pieces of sun-dried coconut, was fed into the vats atop the expellers to be ground, heated, and pressed. It came forth as clear, glistening oil and dried copra cake. The cake was valuable as feed for livestock and the oil was shipped in drums by steamer to the United States. Aaron explained to Julia that it was used in the manufacture of soap and other products. Given a complete tour of the Trituradora and the vast warehouse where the copra and the cake and oil were stored, Julia found it fascinating. The workmen had been delighted to show *"la señorita del patron"* everything.

She placed the plates of cold chicken and potato salad on the blanket and waited, hands demurely folded, as Aaron poured crystal glasses full of dark Chilean wine.

Julia Marini watched attentively. She noted that he appeared now to have better use of his left arm than when he had arrived in Tihuacan. But he could still not straighten it completely, and it seemed certain he would never be able to do so. The inside of the elbow was deeply scarred, as though a two-inch trench had been dug in the flesh. He had been wounded in the American war, though he seldom spoke of it.

There had been a chest injury as well, and when he first appeared in Tihuacan the local *curandera* had attended him. Her treatment had evidently been efficacious, because he was now less gaunt and seldom coughed. He did not, however, believe in the *curandera*'s powers, which was not surprising, since he had lived all of his life in Europe and the United States, where medical doctors were always available.

Six months ago a doctor of that sort had arrived to set up practice in Tihuacan and Aaron no longer patronized the *curandera,* but he never failed to give her a coin whenever he encountered her on the street, and so avoided being cursed. It was a wise precaution, Julia thought. One could never really be certain what mischief the *indios* might contrive with their pagan powers. And *el doctor* Juan Amaya-Ruiz was a charming man (though suspected of having served in the imperialist army); both Aaron and her father, Don Marcello, liked to play chess with him and seemed to enjoy his company.

"Your wine," Aaron said, handing her a glass and lifting his own. *"Salud y pesetas, estimada señorita,"* he said with a smile.

She smiled back, amused by his lisping Castilian accent. No one else in Tihuacan spoke Spanish with the accent of Old Castile. It was both elegant and slightly humorous. The language of Sinaloa was the Mexican *idioma,* harsher, less sibilant, and far less formal. Often Aaron appeared to have difficulty understanding the slangy speech of the common folk, laced as it was with words taken from the language of the conquered race, Náhuatl, and others simply made up by the people of the barrios.

Julia had struck a bargain with Aaron. He would speak to her in English and she to him in Italian. But it was a bargain more often broken than kept. Their conversations always became too intense to be carried on in the manner of language lessons.

"The toast is *'Salud, amor, y pesetas,'* Don Aaron," she said lifting her wineglass.

"Perhaps it has been too long since I have had any of those things to remember," he said.

She shrugged prettily and said, "How sad to hear so young a man say a thing like that."

Aaron sipped some wine and replied, "A great man I once knew used to say, *'Las Parcas nos mandan.'* Is that a saying here as well as in Spain?"

"Yes. We say it here. 'Fate rules us.' But we do not believe it. This is the New World, after all. We don't really believe in fate. We make our own destiny."

"Admirable," Aaron said. "I must remember to tell that to the captain of the next steamer that carries oil to the north in the time of the *chubasco.*"

"Of course we do not do foolish things," Julia said.

Aaron shook his head and said ruefully, "I cannot imagine you ever doing a foolish thing, Julia."

Julia stretched her arms skyward and lifted her face to the sun. It felt like a caress to her, familiar since childhood. Aaron mopped at his face with a handkerchief.

"Are you too warm?" she asked.

"Yes. But I am growing more accustomed to it," he said. "Juan Amaya tells me it is good for me."

"It must be. You are looking much stronger."

"Was I so feeble when I arrived in Tihuacan?"

She nodded wisely. "You were ill. That was plain to see." She nibbled at some chicken, daintily, as the convent sisters had taught her she should do in the company of a young man. It seemed so foolish to pretend that one did not enjoy one's food, but if that was the way of things, she could endure it. When she got home she could have a proper meal.

"Papa received word this morning," she said, "that Maximilian has been shot in Querétaro. Presidente Juárez refused him clemency. It is very sad."

"Maximilian was a stupid man," Aaron said shortly. "He should never have come to Mexico. Juárez could not pardon him. Too many Mexicans died driving the French out of the country."

"People will make a legend, though," Julia said thoughtfully. "Of Maximilian and poor, mad Empress Carlotta."

"You find that romantic?" Aaron asked.

"Yes, I think I do. A little."

"Death by gunfire is never romantic, Julia. Never."

The gelding stamped and Aaron rose and carried some water to him. Julia listened to the soft, snuffling sounds the beast made drinking. The sun glared on the white sand. The pelican returned to soar just above the surface of the sea, where the waves broke in neat, glistening rows of diamonds.

Aaron returned and sat beside her. "You haven't touched your *pollo.* What will I tell my *cocinera?* That you don't fancy her way of preparing chicken?"

Julia flashed a quick and spontaneous smile. "I was taught in the convent that young ladies eat like birds."

"There are birds and there are birds. I know you are hungry," Aaron said. "I am. Eat."

They laughed companionably and fell on their meal with gusto. Aaron watched sidelong as Julia neatly demolished a breast of cold *pollo.* What a *likable* girl she was, he thought. He had never before thought of a woman in terms of friendship. Not that it lessened her sexual attractiveness, far from it. The swell of her breasts under the thin lawn, the turn of her calf exposed by the slightly lifted skirt affected him powerfully. Quite suddenly he was reminded of Concha Paredes, and he was inwardly stirred by the memory and at the same time ashamed that he had thought of the Spanish girl so seldom since leaving Santanilla. He did not exactly blame himself for having avoided memories that were painful, but he thought that a kinder and more generous man would have at least wondered what had become of Concha.

He made no apologies for his feelings about "the cousins." When Simon Pauley had told him that Santiago had been killed by the Riffs in Morocco, he had felt no pity. Santiago had done nothing in his short life to deserve pity. Neither had Alfonso or Julio. Quite the reverse, in fact. They had disappointed Don Alvaro and Doña Maria and, yes, Adriana, as well.

He looked out at the empty expanse of the Pacific, remembering the view from the ridge overlooking Santanilla: the gray sound of the Mar Cantabrico, the rough, barren land, the dull red-tiled roofs of La Casa, and, once again, Adriana.

She had written to him, a kind, rather sad letter to which he had made no reply. He felt no emotion at the thought of Micah Marburg's illness. He had separated himself from his father that cold morning on the deck of the *Dover Light.* He thought that he had separated himself from the Santanas as well, but that had been more difficult as the letter he had so foolishly written to Adriana from Cincinnati had proved. And even now, after so long and so eventful a time, he still missed Don Alvaro, who in a few short months had been more of a father to him than Micah had ever been.

He thought, too, of his half-brother Roberto and wondered at the envy he still felt. There was a sister now, a girl of four. Adriana had sent a small daguerreotype of the two children. A tiny, smiling, elfin girl with dark hair and the bright eyes of a mouse, and the solemn, beautiful, golden boy in the riding kit of a hacendado. She would have done better, Aaron thought, to have sent one of herself.

"A centavo for those thoughts," Julia Marini said.

Aaron shook his head evasively. He had no wish to speak to Julia of his life at Santanilla. When that nightmare of the Paredes affair was ended, it was as though a barrier had fallen across the years of his life. He knew with absolute certainty that no matter how long he lived, he would forever divide his life into two realities. What took place before that horrible night in Liencres would not be forgotten, but he would speak of it only under pressure of the greatest necessity.

Julia sensed that she was in danger of intruding into a part of Aaron's past he did not wish to share. This saddened her, but did not surprise her. Many people came to Tihuacan and other places as isolated with a wish to forget what went before. Gossiping about immigrants from abroad or from the United States was the daily amusement of half the men and two-thirds of the women in Tihuacan. She knew that there was endless curiosity about Aaron Marburg, with his Castilian speech and romantic wounds. But she also knew, instinctively, that the woman lucky enough to get him for her own would not do so by prying into his past. When and if he ever chose to speak, she resolved that she would listen and understand. Until such time, she would be his friend, accepting what he offered of himself, demanding no more.

Far out on the sea, from beyond the sharply limned horizon, a thin plume of black smoke rose into the white sky like a thread.

"A ship," Julia said.

"From our harbor, I think. The *Orizaba* sailed this morning."

"With oil from La Trituradora?" The momentary tension between them vanished as they spoke of everyday, practical things. Far better this way, Julia thought.

"Two hundred metric tons, bound for San Francisco and Seattle," Aaron said. He grinned at her suddenly. "At a very good price, too."

She laughed easily. "You know how to charm a merchant's daughter, Don Aaron," she said. "I hope you dealt firmly with *los gringos.*"

"Profitably," Aaron said.

"We need to keep them in their place, or they may take it into their heads to come back," Julia said. "What was it Presidente Juárez said? 'Poor Mexico—so far from God—' "

" 'And so close to the United States.' It was well said, I think. They are a strange people, the *norteamericanos.*"

"I read in *La Prensa* that they have just paid the Russians seven million dollars for Alaska. Seven million—that is fifteen million gold *pesos.*" She spoke wonderingly and touched the golden *augustín* at her throat.

"A waste," Aaron said. "A fantasy."

Julia said thoughtfully, "I wonder. Who knows what it may really be worth someday? They are good at picking up bargains, the *yanquis.* Look what they did when they bought Louisiana. They are to be reckoned with."

She wondered if he would make some comment on his service in the American war against the Confederacy, but he did not. He only shrugged his slender shoulders and got to his feet, extending a hand. "A walk along the shore, Julia?"

"Wait," she said, and kicked off her shoes. "Look away," she commanded. He did so, and she peeled off her white lisle stockings. The sand felt hot and grainy beneath her naked feet. "Now," she said, and stood to run for the water's edge.

Aaron followed her slowly, watching the way she lifted her skirt above her ankles and waded in the tepid waves.

There was a quality of earth and sea in Julia Marini, a straightforwardness that was immensely appealing. A man could make a life with such a woman. He still had a very long way to go before he could ever think of marriage, but when the time came, he told himself, one could do far, far worse than Julia Marini.

Winter descended with uncharacteristic mildness on Santanilla that year. There were few storms on the Bay of Biscay, and those that did develop did so with a lethargic gentleness unknown in that sound for fifty years. There was rain where there had been sleet, and snow and winter freshets where there had been frozen streams in the folds of the Cantabricas.

Doctor Marcel Danton, a stately and elegant man of affluent middle age, sat in the *sala mayor* of La Casa of Santanilla sipping sherry with Doña Maria Santana and Doña Adriana.

A fire burned in the great hearth, and for the first time that the doctor could remember the *sala* was comfortable on a December afternoon.

Danton removed the monocle he affected and studied the women he had been lecturing with regret. He genuinely wished that he could speak more cheerfully about Don Miguel. He wished even more that his craft were sufficiently advanced so that he could offer hope of a cure.

But this he could not do. Twenty years before he had learned at the Sorbonne that angina was the symptom of a progressive—and irreversible—congestion of the heart, and that it was fatal. Soon or late, and more likely soon, Miguel Marburg was going to die.

From what he had seen of his patient's condition this afternoon, soon would be a mercy.

He was filled with admiration for Doña Adriana. For so young and beautiful a woman as she, the task of nursing the patient now sleeping beyond the arched gallery must be one of incredible difficulty and tedium. Yet she performed admirably, with a skill and dedication Dr. Danton found astonishing. Love, he supposed, was the great motivation. As a Frenchman he had an enormous faith in the idea of love, but precisely because he was a Frenchman he found himself wondering how such a woman could continue to love the wasted skeleton of a man in the sickroom. Celibacy, Danton thought, was all very well for holy nuns and saints. But for a woman with the appeal of Doña Adriana, it must make life joyless.

"You may certainly seek a second opinion, Madame Adriana," he said. "In fact, I urge you to do so. My colleague Dr. Martinez, who presided so skillfully at the delivery of your own two children, would be quite willing to examine Don Miguel."

"There is no question of that, Doctor," Adriana Marburg said calmly. "We have confidence in you." Doña Maria, a tiny husk of a woman but still straight as a sword blade, nodded her agreement. "I only ask if you can do anything to ease Don Miguel's pain."

Danton made a Gallic shrug and replaced his monocle. "I have heard that the profession in Germany is using a new drug, the nitric acid triester of glycerol, in the treatment of *angina pectoris,* but I am doubtful of its value. It was discovered ten years ago by an Italian and it is being used, *mon Dieu,* in the manufacture of explosives by a Swede named Nobel. Hardly a recommendation for inclusion into the pharmacopoeia, dear Doña Adriana. I would not ordinarily assault the ears of a lady with such technical talk, but the range of your intellect is famous in the district." He again removed the monocle and let it hang from a ribbon around his neck. "The Germans are said to be very advanced, but I find it impossible to believe that ingestion of so violent a compound as nitroglycerine can be of value to a patient with Don Miguel's complaint. No, dear madame, bed rest and laudanum. That is all I can, in conscience, prescribe."

"My husband dislikes taking laudanum," Adriana said. "He does not wish his mind clouded."

"Don Miguel is a brave man, Doña Adriana. But laudanum is, I regret to say, science's only specific for pain."

"You forget prayer, Doctor," Doña Maria said severely.

"Ah, yes. Well, of course. Every medical practitioner knows the value of prayer."

"Father Sebastio spends many hours with Miguel," Doña Maria said.

"And is a great comfort to him, I am sure, Patrona," Dr. Danton said.

Adriana said, "It is difficult to keep Miguel in bed, Dr. Danton. He insists on trying to be active, and he simply hasn't the strength for it."

"You see," Danton said, spreading his white, tapering hands. "Bed rest and laudanum."

"So be it, then, doctor," Adriana said.

Doña Maria poured more Jerez into the doctor's glass and declared forcefully, "A journey to Lourdes would do more than all your laudanum, Dr. Danton."

Marcel Danton controlled his impulse to roll his eyes. For nine years, ever since some demented peasant girl claimed to have seen the Holy Virgin in a grotto in the Hautes-Pyrénées town of Lourdes, the medical profession had been plagued by the competition of religious fanatics. While he did not consider Doña Maria de Santana y Borjas a fanatic, she was too religious by half in her notion of how best to treat a sick man.

"Of course, Doña Maria," he said silkily. "A visit to the holy shrine would undoubtedly do much to improve Don Miguel's condition. But unfortunately, I could not possibly recommend that he travel. At least not for the foreseeable future."

Doña Maria accepted this opinion with unexpected grace. "Sebastio agrees," she said.

Adriana said, "Thank you, Dr. Danton. We will expect to see you next week, then."

Danton, knowing himself dismissed, stood and bowed to the older woman. With Adriana at his side he walked through the gallery to the courtyard, where his buggy waited.

There was something infinitely sad about Santanilla this last year, he thought. There was an almost imperceptible, but very real, deterioration about the estate. Work that needed to be done, painting and minor repairs, was not being done. Clearly the land and buildings were now in the care of the middle son, Julio, whom everyone knew to be an oaf and a wastrel. Don Alvaro was seldom to be seen, and though one could not be absolutely certain, there seemed to be fewer servants and tenants about.

It seemed to Danton that just in the short time he had been in practice in this part of Old Castile, many of the old families were having difficulties. Miraflores, the hacienda bordering Santanilla on the west, had actually been sold, lock, stock, and barrel, to a rich merchant from Huelva, a man suspected of being more Portuguese than Spanish (to the horror of the conservative Old Castilians), as well as entertaining illusions of social advancement. The family name, Alvarez, could be anything, Dr. Danton thought. In a very short time Marcel Danton had assumed many of the prejudices of the district.

He asked Doña Adriana's opinion of the change in ownership of Miraflores, one of the oldest haciendas in the north.

"I don't know the people," Adriana said. "But I shall make them welcome."

Well, of course, Don Alvaro Santana's daughter would say that, Danton thought with grudging admiration.

"Are they a large family?" he asked.

"Several sons, I believe," Adriana said. "And a daughter near to Roberto's age."

Danton pondered that as they walked along the arched gallery. Could the beautiful but, one suspected, impoverished daughter of El Patron of Santanilla be thinking in terms of dowry? Marriages were often arranged and children betrothed in this medieval country. No, it was too feudal a concept to be entertained by so liberated a woman, one who might even be mistaken for French. Quite out of the question, the doctor thought.

As they reached the courtyard at the end of the gallery, a horseman came cantering through the gate. It was Danton's cousin, Jean-Claude Raymond, a young man who had descended upon Danton's establishment in Liencres after being banished from Paris and his regiment of Chasseurs over some petty embroilment concerning a ballet dancer, a duel (bloodless, fortunately), and a fellow officer. A handsome, feckless young man far richer, unfortunately, than Danton himself. But personable, for all that.

Jean-Claude stopped his Arab chestnut with a flourish and removed his Spanish riding hat with a broad gesture. "A thousand pardons, madame. I do not mean to intrude, but my cousin is wanted in Liencres at once. Something about a fisherman and a dockline and a leg that will probably have to be removed. The details escape me, but the *boticario* seemed most agitated. He cannot do the job himself, it seems."

"Madame Adriana Marburg," Dr. Danton said formally. "May I present my cousin, Jean-Claude Raymond." He could not resist adding, "One-time lieutenant of the Chamborant Chasseurs. Three hundred years of military *gloire* have not taught him enough manners to dismount when being presented to a lady."

Jean-Claude Raymond, apparently a young man given to larger-than-life gestures, flung himself from the saddle to bow and kiss Adriana's hand extravagantly. He was handsome and knew it, she thought. And somewhat empty-headed, she had no doubt. He was staring at her with admiration.

Danton said acidly, "Doña Adriana's husband is my patient, cousin."

The young Frenchman actually blushed. Adriana found that touching in one who obviously thought of himself as something of a gallant.

Danton lifted Adriana's hand to his lips and said, "I regret I could not be more encouraging, Patrona. But Don Miguel is a man with much will. Let us hope always for the best."

"Until next week, Dr. Danton," she said and watched him mount to the seat of his new American buggy. He clucked at his horse and rolled through the gate.

Jean-Claude Raymond had mounted and was making his mettlesome Arab dance and curvette.

"Arabs have tender mouths, Monsieur Raymond," Adriana said looking at him coolly. "They respond best to gentle hands."

"Ah, madame," he said, "you see through me. I was showing off, I confess." His Spanish was so heavily accented with French as to be nearly unintelligible.

She replied in his language, "Not always safe, monsieur, in this country."

He smiled at her dazzlingly. He had a square, fair-skinned face and dark brown eyes. Could he be twenty-three? Not more. She smiled back at him, amused by his theatrical gallantry. He raised his hat once again, made the little Arab rear and paw the air, and was gone. She listened to the hoof beats dying away as he galloped off after his cousin. Then she turned back into the house and forgot him.

Father Sebastio, his shabby cassock
rustling about his ankles, hurried along the gallery from the kitchen to
the family wing of La Casa. A steady, gentle rain was falling. He could
hear it striking the broad leaves of the plants growing in the courtyard.
From time to time, as he passed a dimly lighted window, he could see
it glistening and puddling on the flagstones beyond the broad Roman-
esque arches.

It was near to nine o'clock, and it was his turn to sit the night with
Don Miguel. Nowadays the *señor* was never left alone. When Doña
Ana's duties took her elsewhere, Doña Maria kept watch, and when she
was unavailable the *criadas* sat with the sick man in a rota. Sebastio was
the only male member of the household to be included. It was at Doña
Maria's command, but Father Sebastio was secretly pleased that Don
Miguel seemed to take comfort from his presence. A convert he might
be, the old priest thought, but time had proved him to be a good and
dutiful Catholic.

The coming year's April would be the sixtieth anniversary of Sebastio's service to the Santana family. Lately he found that he spent more and more time remembering the past, which seemed now to return to him with so much more clarity than events of a month or a year ago. A mark of old age, he knew, this two-tiered memory: yesterday confused, the distant past bright and shining.

He had been eighteen years old when he had walked, for the first time, up the dirt road and through the gate of Santanilla. He could see himself as he was then, a seedy and impoverished Dominican in brown homespun with sandals on his bare feet, the implements of his holy office (all that he possessed) in a cloth sack slung over his shoulders.

Father Baldomero, the Santana's chaplain for the previous twenty years, lay sealed in his casket in the family chapel awaiting the good offices of his successor. The old chaplain had died suddenly of a stroke while on horseback in the company of the then-Patron, Don Alvaro's father, and so he waited unshriven in his pinewood coffin.

The young Dominican's first task at Santanilla had been to dispatch the soul of his predecessor to Paradise. Or at least to Purgatory, where the Judge who knew him better than the eighteen-year-old Sebastio would decide his fate in the world to come.

Sebastio, born Ramon Diego in a shepherd's hut in the high Cantabricas, had been given to the Church by his poverty-ridden parents at the age of ten. Learning had come hard to him, but he had persevered. The Dominicans had trained him, chastised him, and finally ordained him. But he knew himself to be an ignorant man that Lenten day in 1808 when first he saw Santanilla, and his opinion of himself had not changed in nearly sixty years. If my people had given me to the Jesuits, he often told himself, I would never have been made a priest of God. He considered himself one of the most fortunate of men.

His sandals slapped on the damp flags of the gallery and his breath came hard. He was remembering Don Alejandro, Don Alvaro's father. Large, like his son, with a chest like a barrel and a voice like thunder. A swordsman, a lecher, and sinner—and yet, and yet—Father Sebastio smiled as he hurried along—always kind to his chaplain. "Sebastio," he would say, "you may be only a priest, but remember, when you get to heaven, that I always treated you like a man. You must speak for me." El Patron-that-was had been so certain that his scrawny, underfed chaplain would stand at the Throne of God before him. Yet a fighting bull had broken his lance and gored his fine horse and killed him these fifty years past.

Many times in the last half-dozen years Sebastio had wondered what the old *señor* would have thought of his granddaughter's husband. It was difficult to know. Racial antagonisms had been stronger in his day, but he had been a man to whom no one dictated likes and dislikes. He might well have approved of Don Miguel. Certainly he would have approved of Don Miguel's efforts to maintain Santanilla as it should be. Steeped in his own concept of chivalry, the old Patron would have appreciated a man who had fought so hard, even at the cost of his health, to sustain the Santanas.

From time to time Father Sebastio could hear faint snatches of music in the air. Don Julio and his friends had turned the woolhouse into a cantina in all but name, and strange gypsy melodies could often be heard on the night wind. It seemed that Don Julio and Doña Adriana had reached some kind of understanding. Two kinds of life, separate and vastly different, were going on at Santanilla. Julio performed the work of the hacienda—not well, but adequately—while Doña Adriana and her mother conducted the affairs of the family as though nothing whatever had changed. The strain of this division was palpable in the air, but Sebastio thoroughly approved of the way in which the hacendada and her daughter maintained the old standards. The Santanas, despite Julio's taste for the commonality, were still a great family.

At the door to Don Miguel's room Father Sebastio encountered Doña Maria and Tomasa Gomez herding the children from their nightly visit to their father toward the nursery wing. Doña Cecilia ran to kiss Sebastio and he lifted her in his arms with an effort. The child touched his heart, and had from the moment he had first seen her in the bassinet. A smiling, happy girl with a strange, but to him moving, propensity for playing with religious objects. He often found himself wondering if she were a destined bride of Christ.

He set her gently on her feet and acknowledged Don Roberto's solemn, formal greeting. As always, Tomasa had dressed the boy impeccably, as though he were the miniature *patron* of the children's kingdom. Which perforce he was, Sebastio thought. From birth, Roberto Marburg y Santana had been given—and burdened with—all the privileges and responsibilities of his class. Perhaps, Sebastio thought with an old man's acerbity, there would come a day when the ladies of Santanilla would come to question the wisdom of what they were doing to this gentle and handsome boy.

"Don Miguel is asleep," Doña Maria said in a low voice. "There is coffee for you in the hearth. Doña Ana is in the office. She will look in on you later."

"*Sí,* Patrona."

"And wrap yourself in a blanket, old man. It may turn cold before morning."

"Patrona."

"And don't let those beasts get on Don Miguel's bed." She indicated two half-grown kittens, offspring of El Cid and one of the stable cats, sleeping on the hearth. "They will disturb him."

"Yes, Doña Maria," Sebastio said dutifully. He knew, as did the hacendada, that since his illness Don Miguel liked having the household cats about. "They bring life into the room," he often said.

"Remember, Sebastio. A blanket."

"Good night, Patrona," he said.

He entered the room quietly. The fire on the hearth burned well, with glowing coals casting a ruddy light across the tiles. On the bed, Don Miguel slept, propped up on bolsters. Father Sebastio went to him, knelt at the bedside for an *Ave Maria,* then stood and made the sign of the cross in the air over the sick man's forehead.

It pained the old priest to see how ill Don Miguel looked. He was gaunt, his facial bones seeming to thrust from his skull. The bearded cheeks were hollow, etched with lines of grief. Once, many years ago, Sebastio had traveled with Don Alvaro to the Alhambra, and there he had seen a painting by El Greco depicting the Christ. Don Miguel's resemblance to that painting was startling. Sebastio wondered if it were blasphemy to make such a comparison. But the resemblance was real, and *El Señor Jesu Cristo* had been born a Jew, had he not?

It troubled the old priest that Don Miguel had not yet received the sacrament of extreme unction. But Doña Ana had adamantly refused to let it be done. She would not accept the evidence of her eyes that her husband was slowly dying. There was a ferocity in the love of a woman for a man that frightened Sebastio, had always done. The old Patrona, wife of Don Alejandro, had been like that. When he died in the bullring she had indulged a howling, furious grief that had marked the family to this very day. The way of Don Alejandro's dying was largely unknown among the younger folk of Santanilla because there had once been a time that the mention of it would bring down a raging, blasphemous sorrow from Doña Elvira, and she would curse God in her agony. Still, Sebastio remembered, when she lay dying she had at last accepted the sacrament and reconciled with Mother Church. To Sebastio that reconciliation had been his first proud, if fearful, moment of accomplishment among the Santanas.

He made the sign of the cross over Don Miguel once again and settled himself down in an armchair before the fire. One of the kittens climbed into his lap, turned several times about to make a nest, and settled down with a sleepy sigh.

Sebastio watched the glowing coals dreamily and surrendered to old men's thoughts.

Father Sebastio awoke from his doze to hear the distant sound of the striking clock in the *sala mayor.* The fire had burned low and the cats were gone. There was a soft wind chuckling under the eaves of the old house and the wet dripping of rain outside the window. With a start, Sebastio realized that there was someone else beside himself and Don Miguel in the room. He caught the fragrance of violets in the air and the rustle of taffeta underskirts.

He felt Adriana drape a blanket over his shoulders.

"Forgive me, Doña Ana," he whispered. "I must have dropped off for a moment."

"No matter," Adriana said. "He is sleeping quietly."

Sebastio watched her slender figure, a shadow in the dimness, as she stooped to kiss her husband's cheek. Holding the blanket in place (not because he was cold, but because Doña Adriana had placed it there), the priest stirred the coals on the hearth and added another log. Blue flames, tiny as witchfire, fed on the oily blood of the greasewood. The rising firelight illuminated Adriana's pale face and yellow hair.

"What time is it, Patrona?" Sebastio asked.

"Just after two," she said. "Why don't you go to your bed? I will watch with him."

"No, Doña Ana. Old men don't need much sleep. Only a wink now and again. I will stay."

She moved and he could hear the jingle of keys at her waist. Strange how such small things heralded profound changes, he thought. For more years than he could remember, those keys were worn only by Doña Maria, her symbol of household authority—even despotism. Now Adriana wore them. The golden-haired girl upon whose head he had sprinkled the holy water was a child no longer, but the true mistress of Santanilla.

"The coffee is still warm," she said. "Shall I pour some for you, Father?"

"I thank you, Doña Ana. But no. Have you only now stopped working?"

"The accounts need to be done. Julio sold the last of the horse herd today."

"And kept more of the money than he should, I'll wager," Sebastio murmured crossly.

"You are not to worry about such things, Father," Adriana said. She looked across the firelit room to the bed. "If he wakes, see if you can persuade him to take his laudanum. Dr. Danton says he must sleep as much as possible."

"I will try, Patrona," the priest said.

She stood over her husband for a time, as though unwilling to leave him. She is remembering the man she married, Sebastio thought. And he too remembered the tall, handsome foreigner he had wedded to the daughter of Santanilla in the sunlit chapel. Was it only nine years ago? As little as that?

Adriana moved with a rustle of petticoats. "Call me if he awakens, Father. He may not take his medicine for you." She bent and kissed her husband once again and was gone.

Sebastio sighed and settled again into his chair before the fire.

"Sebastio." The voice was as thin as the winter wind.

The priest came to his feet and went to the bed. "You were not asleep, Patron," he said accusingly. "Shall I recall Doña Ana?"

"She needs her rest, padre. Let her be." Miguel spoke without moving. It seemed that his voice came from the air and the darkness.

"Will you take your laudanum?" the priest asked.

"Enough, padre. No potions tonight." There was a pause, then Sebastio heard the long, soft whistle of his breathing. He must be in pain. "Come sit here," Miguel said. "Talk to me."

Sebastio moved his chair to the bedside. He took a limp, cold hand in his own brown and wrinkled one. "Dr. Danton says you must sleep, Patron."

"The devil take Danton and his damned poppy. I'll sleep soon enough and long enough."

"Gently, Patron. Don't excite yourself."

Miguel made a sound that could only be laughter, though it was very near to silence. "It has taken you a long time to call me Patron, Sebastio," he said in that thready voice.

"Mea culpa," the old Dominican intoned. *"Mea maxima culpa."*

"For months I have lain here thinking, padre," Miguel said. He

212

sighed and presently went on, "It has been a long time since I have made a confession."

"Is that what you wish, Patron? I am not properly vested."

The soft laughter came again. "What a conventional priest you are, Father Sebastio. Should I send you out in the rain for the vestments? That would be ill-done, I think. Just talk to me, Father. And listen."

Sebastio's eyes felt damp. Old men's tears come easily, he thought. "I am here, my son."

"Good," Miguel whispered and held onto Sebastio's rough hand.

Presently Miguel said, "Ana will not let me speak with her about dying, Father. She won't hear of it. And I need to talk, you see. I need someone to share the fear with me."

"There is no need for fear, Patron."

"That is well for a holy man, padre, or a saint. I am neither."

"You are a good man, Don Miguel."

"Ask my son if I am a good man," Miguel said so softly that Sebastio had to strain to hear him. "Ask Aaron."

The old priest lowered his eyes and said a silent prayer.

"Well, what's done is done. I never loved him, Sebastio. God forgive me, I never did, and he knew it."

"Oh, Don Miguel—" Sebastio felt a terrible, unpriestly urge to close his ears. It was not seemly that one should hear such naked sorrow in another man's voice. Yet he had heard similar things all of his priestly life. It was his task, assigned by God and Mother Church, to help penitents to bear their sins.

"Is there a heaven, padre?" Miguel whispered. "If there is, then there must be a hell. I wonder where I shall spend eternity."

Sebastio wondered if Don Miguel were weeping, and then he heard that thin, thready laughter once again.

"There is a thing that troubles me, Father," he said.

"What thing, my son?"

"I was never a religious Jew, padre. I could never convince myself that Jehovah concerned himself over whether I ate milk and meat from a single dish."

"Those are rules made by men, my son, not by God," Sebastio said. "But you embraced the True Church, to the everlasting salvation of your soul."

"I embraced the Church, padre. But not for my soul's sake. I did it for Adriana." Again there was a long silence, and then Miguel said. "For my beautiful wife, padre. If I had to make the choice again at this

213

very moment, I would do the same. If I had to do the reverse—if I had to renounce God to have her, I wouldn't hesitate."

"My son, my son. Don't say such things, I beg you."

"Do not worry, old man. I won't need to prove myself now. Not in the time I have left. I am of the Church, Father. As much as I can be of anything."

"Then you have no cause to be troubled."

"A good and simple man can believe that," Miguel said gently. "But I still ask myself: Am I any better Catholic than I was a Jew?" He drew a series of deep, labored breaths before going on. "The truth is that I hated being a Jew. I despised my people and their ways. I disliked the cold, dark rooms I lived in when I was a boy. We were rich, padre, but we lived poor so as not to arouse the envy of the gentiles. It never worked. We were always apart, mistrusted, suspected. At school I used to pretend I was not a Jew. I could pass for a *goy,* you see. No, becoming a Catholic was no struggle for me, Sebastio. I would have done far more than that for Adriana. So now I ask myself, am I a fraud? How Catholic am I, really? This is a time when I should know the answer. I don't want to die uncertain."

"My son," Father Sebastio said in an agitated voice, "Do not torture yourself with such useless speculations. You are a son of the True Church. You have accepted the sacrament of baptism and the authority of the Holy Father. You have taken Communion and are in a state of grace. That is all a Catholic needs to know, the rest is in the hands of the ghostly powers—of God."

Miguel sighed again. "So it is as simple as that, Sebastio."

The old Dominican said unhappily, "I am not a learned man, Don Miguel. My theology is that which an unlettered country priest can understand. All I know is that God is merciful and that you are an accepted son of God's Holy Church. Be at peace, Patron." He squeezed the cold hand gently and placed it beneath the counterpane. "Now sleep, my son. Rest. We will speak some more tomorrow."

Miguel Marburg closed his eyes. In a voice that was barely audible, he said, "How very strange."

For a time Sebastio sat by the bed in silence, listening to the rain and the thin, reedy sound of the sick man's breathing. Presently he moved his chair back to the fire and there, wrapped in a blanket, kept watch.

At five in the morning, as the clock in the *sala mayor* struck the hour, Father Sebastio became aware that there was only the sound of the soft rain falling in the darkness. The faint, labored breathing had stopped.

The old priest rose heavily to his feet and went to the bed. He said a silent prayer, brushed his fingers over the half-open eyes, and made the sign of the cross. Then he turned to shuffle from the room to tell the household that Don Miguel Marburg had died quietly in his sleep.

Adriana's letter telling Aaron of Micah's death arrived at Tihuacan on the day after Christmas. Work at the Trituradora had been suspended since mid-December while the workmen, and Aaron himself, had participated in the celebration of Las Posadas. For nine nights, beginning on the fifteenth day of the month, until Christmas Eve, bands of townspeople had roamed through the streets of Tihuacan singing outside homes designated as "inns." Their songs were traditional pleas for shelter for Mary and the Christ child, and it was the custom for them to be turned away until the night of December 24, when they were then welcomed and a massive fiesta took place.

Aaron had never before participated in celebrations so good-natured and touching, and with Julia Marini at his side he had paraded with his group from the Trituradora and their wives and children singing the Christmas songs with gusto.

He had taken Christmas dinner at a huge gathering of local notables at the Olas Altas home of Don Marcello, a feast that had ended
with the guests departing from the house (some revelers sober, most
not) in the light of a clear December dawn.

The letter was waiting for him in the *corredor* of his rented house
near the Trituradora.

The *ama de llaves*, Señora Maria Macías, a *mestiza* woman he had
engaged as housekeeper, shuffled barefooted and sleepy into view with
a pot of coffee on a tray and followed him into the small *sala* off the
central patio.

Señora Maria (the title was honorary; she had never been married,
though she had borne two children) had been a *soldadera* in the ranks
of the *brigada* commanded by the young hero of the war against the
French, Porfirio Díaz. Her children had been lost in the course of the
war, one dying in the battle for Puebla, the other of the amoebic
dysentery that had decimated the ranks of *Juáristas* and imperialists
alike. At the age of forty she could easily pass for a woman of sixty, but
her instinct for motherhood remained powerful. Juan Ortega, Aaron's
capataz at the Trituradora, had recommended her for employment.
Ortega was a good foreman and a shrewd judge of his *mestizo* country-
men. Señora Maria ran Aaron's household with a military discipline
that freed him totally from domestic concerns. She also tended to
mother him.

Now, as he recognized the handwriting on the envelope, Señora
Maria saw that he paled. She immediately herded the young Patron into
the *sala* and poured the cold, syrupy coffee into a cup and covered it
with scalding milk.

She stood waiting for further instructions, an expression of concern on her broad Mexican features, her thick body wrapped in a
shabby robe, her brown, splayed feet firm and unmoving on the tiled
floor. Maria was fond of the Patron, who was decent, for a foreigner.
She had never been able to clarify in her mind exactly what sort of
foreigner he was. He had been a *gringo*—or at least he had served in
the *gringo* army, a thing of which she thoroughly approved. She had
spent her youth among soldiers, and a part of her middle age as well.
The life of a *soldadera* was no bed of blossoms, but Maria Macías would
have spent hers no other way. Though she did not know it, the five-
sixths of her blood that was not Spanish came to her from a warrior
race, a people who fought with clubs and obsidian saws, not to kill, but
to capture prisoners whose human hearts were relished by the gods.

Maria was a firm and believing Catholic, but under the cheap mezzotint of the Virgen de Guadalupe and its altar lamp kept burning in her room, there was always a dish of clear water in memory of Quetzalcoatl, the Feathered Serpent. The Church in Mexico had overturned the idols, but not the old ways.

Maria watched the Patron as he read the letter. It was something vastly disturbing to him, she could see that at a glance. She could not read, but the post courier who had brought the letter had told her that it had come from Europe. Maria was not sure, nor did she care, where exactly Europe was. Somewhere across the eastern sea. Not the Pacific that washed the rocks off the Malecón of Tihuacan. Nothing good came to Mexico from Europe. From Europe had come the French soldiers who had killed one of her children and a dozen of her lovers. From Europe had come the Austrian *maricón* Maximiliano.

It suited her to think that the young Patron had come to Tihuacan from the land of the *yanquis*. While it was true that a long time ago the *norteamericanos* had sought to steal Mexico from the Mexicans, in more recent times they had learned better manners. They had sent guns and artillery to the *Juáristas* during the war. She herself had served a field-piece from the north at the siege of Puebla. And there had been many volunteer *yanquis* in the *Juárista* army. That was to their credit. El Presidente Juárez (whom God protect) said that the *gringo generalisimo*, Abraham Lincoln, had been a man of the people and a great war leader. Of course he had been *fusilado*. The work of some European, no doubt. And now here was a letter from Europe to upset the young Patron. If she had not been tipsy on *mescal* (the Patron being away) last afternoon, she would have destroyed the letter.

Aaron said, "You can go back to bed, Maria. I won't need anything more this morning." His voice was thin and strained.

"The letter has distressed El Patron," Señora Maria said. The concept of privacy was alien to her. In the army one shared with comrades the bad and the good.

Aaron closed his eyes and rested his head on the carved wood back of his chair. *"Mi papa murió,"* he said.

"Ay, pobrecito! Pobrecito patron!" She buried her face in her hands and wept freely. To such a woman grief was a common commodity, a thing to be expressed openly and without restraint. It did not matter that she had never known the dead man, or that he had died far away across an alien sea. He was her Patron's father, and as such was worthy of sincere and instant mourning. If he had lived and died in Tihuacan, even though Don Aaron was a newcomer, his funeral would be a civic occasion with hundreds of mourners winding through the narrow

streets behind a band playing dirges and a hearse drawn by black horses with sable plumes on their harness. That was the proper way of displaying sorrow. But since the young Patron's father had died far away, all she could offer were her tears.

Aaron stood and put an arm across her shoulders. "I thank you for your concern, Maria. But go to bed now. I wish to be alone."

The *ama de llaves* clutched his hand and kissed it. Then she patted his cheek familiarly and shuffled from the room, sobbing generously.

For a long while Aaron sat in the *sala* watching the light of the winter sun slant more and more steeply into the stand of philodendrons and palms in the patio beyond the narrow glass doors.

There was an empty ache in his chest and his eyes felt hot and wet. The intensity of his own reaction to the news surprised him. Adriana's letter had not been totally unexpected. He knew Micah had been in ill health. As long ago as his last meeting with Simon Pauley, he had possessed that information. But he had never once given thought to death. It was as though he had somehow imagined that his father was immortal, as well as unreachable.

He shut his eyes and tried to recall the last hours he had spent alone with Micah. There arose images of his own darkened room at Santanilla and the pain and anger he had felt when it became clear that he was to be shunted off to America to protect the good name of the almighty Santanas. He had lived with those emotions bottled up inside him for nearly seven years. The shame of the way the Paredes girl had been used—and how little thought he had given her—that was still there too, and would probably always be.

He had so wanted Micah to love him, but it had never happened. It was Roberto whom Micah had loved at the end. Roberto, and perhaps the pretty dark-eyed child in the daguerreotype with the musical name of Cecilia Morena. For her sake, he hoped that Micah had had enough love left over after lavishing it upon Adriana and her golden son.

There was enough hurt and resentment in Aaron for a lifetime. And yet what he felt now at this moment was, to his surprise, genuine grief. Not the uncomplicated, cleansing hunger to mourn one encountered in a Maria Macías, but something infinitely more subtle and, he feared, long-lasting.

He looked again at the open letter in his lap. Adriana had written: "Father Sebastio was with him often in his last months. They had become close friends, and I think this gave Miguel much comfort.

Sebastio was at his bedside when he died, and he swears to me that death came peacefully, as to one in a state of grace."

How like the Adriana Aaron remembered, to concern herself with whether or not her husband was "in a state of grace." Yet how strangely and uncharacteristically detached her statement seemed. Had she watched, knowing, all these months, knowing that she must prepare herself to live on without Micah? Yes, the words had that ring of sorrow armored against the dark angel's inevitable triumph. The Adriana who wrote this letter, Aaron thought, was a girl no longer.

Tears ran down Aaron's cheeks. He knew that he was not weeping for what had been. There were no tears to be shed for that. But there were tears aplenty for what might have been, for a father and son who should have loved one another better.

Who would have imagined, Aaron thought, that old Father Sebastio would have been Micah's staff on those last, rocky miles? The old Dominican was surely near to ninety now. A raw, unlearned, bigoted ancient. Yet a man with a mission, for all that. It had been his task, assigned by God, he surely thought, to save all Santana souls. A thin, sad smile touched Aaron's lips. He thought of the long, wrangling hours he had spent receiving instruction in the ways of Mother Church from the half-educated, struggling old priest. How hard he tried with me, Aaron thought, and how I frustrated him.

Even after all this time, those memories saddened Aaron. It had seemed to him then, and it still seemed to him now, that religion should be a blaze fueled from within. If one were a truly secular man, the inner fires were simply absent, and no amount of instruction or importuning could substitute for them.

Micah Marburg had become a Catholic for one reason only, to be allowed to marry Adriana Santana. That had seemed good and sufficient reason to him. How, Aaron wondered, had such a religious conversion served him in the hour of his death? There was something pitiful about the image of a man pretending faith in his final hours. He hoped that Micah had not been reduced to that.

Though he did not wish it, Adriana's letter set him to thinking about his own future in this Catholic land. By now he was old enough to admit that a part of his own recalcitrance in the matter of conversion had been rooted in adolescent pride. The whole of his frigid relationship with his father had been focused, like a wintry sun through a glass, on the contest of wills that his conversion had become. For both men, faith and religion had had almost nothing whatever to do with it.

If anyone had "won," it had been Aaron, and not Micah. The son had set himself against the father's will and carried the day—to an empty victory, to be sure, yet a victory none the less.

But victory was not permanent. The longer Aaron lived in Mexico, the more certain he became that eventually he would have to face the problem again, and this time in the same practical terms as his father had done. The irony of the situation was not lost on him.

One day, perhaps soon, he thought, I will wish to marry. Julia Marini seemed the obvious choice. But this was Catholic Mexico, and Julia and her father were unquestioning Catholics.

He had spoken on several occasions to Don Marcello and to Julia about his Jewish ancestry and his convinced secularity. Don Marcello had refused to see it as a problem, clearly regarding Aaron's eventual conversion as inevitable. Julia, perhaps because she had been born in the New World, had an even more indifferent attitude about Jews in general and Aaron's antecedents in particular. To Julia Marini "the Jews" were scarcely a part of the modern world at all. She thought of them, as a people, as contemporary with the Babylonians and other lost nations. And when, nettled by this educational lacuna, Aaron would point out to her that Jews and Jewishness were still very much a part of the modern world and that they partook of its problems every day, she would shrug and say, "Oh well, in *Europe,*" as though Europe was not to be found on the same planet as Mexico.

Nor did it change her outlook when Aaron would tell her, with some heat, that pogroms still swept Russia and Poland yearly, and that Jews died in these racial spasms of hate. It was during these discussions that Aaron came to realize that Julia's education had been unworthy of her intelligence, and that her mind had been molded by well-meaning, but unlearned and narrow, religious teachers in her convent. Things that pertained to Mexico, her country, and to the life around her here in Tihuacan, Julia grasped with a sure and sharp intellect. Things outside her immediate environment simply had no importance and no meaning to her.

Aaron had been a Jew? What did it matter? Eventually he would conform.

And so the struggle to remain true to himself that he thought he had won when he fled Spain was still with him. Aaron wondered if Father Sebastio would think this righteous punishment for his sin of stubborn pride.

Aaron remained in his house all that day, reviewing the memories—some few sweet, but many bitter—of his life with his father. It was strange and sad to think that even if he should one day return to Europe —to Santanilla—there would be no Don Miguel Marburg, no handsome cavalier, at Adriana's side.

As evening fell he called Maria to bring him writing materials. For a very long time he sat staring at the blank paper, searching for something to be said. In the end he penned a simple note to Father Sebastio.

He wrote: "I thank you for your kindness to my father. I enclose my contribution to the funds the family will allocate to pay for Masses in the cathedral of Santander. God be with you." He enclosed all the money he had in the house, some eight hundred Mexican pesos.

It seemed a cold missive, but it was a cold grief that he felt.

1870

It seemed to Soledad Segre that each year the Spanish *gaijo* required some new scandal with which to divert their minds from the really important matters in life, which were the acquisition of land, legitimacy, and money.

The most recent affair to set the district tongues clacking was the killing of the woman Marta Ordoñez, the mistress of Capitán Torres, commander of the Guardia Civil garrison in Liencres.

The story was that Ordoñez, who was rumored to be a debauched nun, had spent a number of unhappy years as Luis Torres's woman, but that she had been blameless despite his ferocious jealousy. Nevertheless, it was known that he regularly beat her and accused her of infidelities that would have taxed the strength of a Messalina.

One evening (during Lent, the scandalized gossips said), after a day-long debauch with his friends at the *cantina* of La Horca Francesa, the captain indulged his fists with excessive vigor and Marta Ordoñez fell into unconsciousness for three days (during which time she was attended by Dr. Marcel Danton of Liencres), after which she meekly died.

Captain Torres was immediately brought up on charges by the Guardia. The specification was manslaughter, because in the opinion of the senior officers of the court-martial, the captain had been acting in defense of his honor and without malice.

The trial was held in Santander and was heavily attended by the people of the district. Old gossip was revived, and for two weeks the folk of Santander and Liencres spoke of little else. The defense counsel, a dapper Madrileño of good family, spared no effort or expense to investigate the Ordoñez woman's past and blacken her character. He was able to prove that she had indeed been expelled from a convent in Valladolid (where an illegitimate daughter was still cloistered), and that she had been formerly the mistress of Santiago Santana y Borjas of Santanilla. The Madrileño, eloquent in his condemnation of the dead woman, suggested that Ordoñez had in some way been responsible for Santiago Santana's estrangement from his family and for his subsequent flight to Spanish Morocco, where as a gallant member of La Legión Extranjera Española he had met his soldierly death in battle against the Riffs. The defense counsel regretted that he was unable to obtain the direct testimony of Captain Santana's brother, Major Alfonso Santana y Borjas (who had loyally accompanied his brother into exile in the legion), but he was able to produce an affadavit stating that Marta Ordoñez had in fact been his brother's mistress. Julio Santana, who was available (and often present in the courtroom) was not asked to testify. Chole Segre had heard that Don Julio's recent association with gypsies would have made his testimony unsuitable to the defense of an officer of the Guardia. Julio himself told Chole that wild horses could not have made him give evidence in defense of Torres, who had had the effrontery to buy the Santana townhouse in Santander and live there with his whore.

In the event, it had apparently been a mistake to involve the Santanas in the testimony. Santanilla had fallen on bad times, but old Don Alvaro was still admired in Old Castile and the ladies of his household, even including his excessively forceful daughter, the Widow Marburg, were widely respected.

Furthermore, the defense counsel's big city ways annoyed both court and spectators. Unfortunately for Luis Torres, Marta Ordoñez was remembered as a quiet, long-suffering woman, devout and kind to the poor, while Torres was remembered mainly for his ludicrous claims to family distinction.

At the end of the four-day trial, Torres was brought into the courtroom to face the five senior Guardia officers, and there found the naked sword on the table pointed in his direction, indicating that he had been found guilty. This method of informing the accused had been borrowed from the British during the Peninsular War, and it appealed mightily to the Spanish sense of theatre.

Chole Segre, who was in the crowded courtroom that day, appreciated the drama, but she enjoyed the irony of Torres's sentence far more. Like most gypsies, she had little love for the Guardia.

The president of the court announced that forthwith Captain Luis Torres would stand in the town plaza of Liencres, there to be stripped of his rank and service and declared cashiered from the Guardia Civil. He would then be given a choice of thirty years in prison or immediate transportation to Spanish Morocco, to be enlisted for life as a private soldier in the Spanish Foreign Legion.

Within forty-eight hours, and under an unseasonably gray and lowering sky, Preso Militar Luis Torres was thrust into a black prison wagon for the journey across Spain to Cartagena, where he would be put on board the first ship departing that port for Ceuta on the African coast.

For some weeks the trial provided the local gossips with speculations and revived old scandals. Chole Segre watched Doña Maria and Doña Adriana going about their business on the estate and felt a grudging admiration for them. They were *gaijo,* but their family motto was apt. They knew how to endure.

For a time the Alvarez children from Hacienda Miraflores were not seen at Santanilla. Doña Maria, with a patience her own children would have found uncharacteristic, had established a good (if not close) relationship with Don Silvio and Doña Consuelo Alvarez. But the scandalous chatter created by the trial of Luis Torres had caused Doña Consuelo some concern. While it pleased her enormously to be noticed by Doña Maria, a Borjas and the hacendada of one of the most venerable estates in Old Castile, as a parvenu (and Doña Consuelo had no illusions about her status in the district) one had to exercise care in the selection of one's associates.

The two women had, in fact, reached a tacit understanding that for a time—at least until tongues stopped wagging again (as they surely would eventually)—the families should maintain a discreet distance from one another.

To Roberto Marburg, this decision brought a certain unhappiness.

He had rather begun to like Maria-Elena Alvarez and her brothers. He missed their company.

Loneliness was never far from Roberto. Even his goddaughter and shadow Ana-Maria Gomez was gradually being taken from him. Differences of caste were disrupting the easy companionship of infancy. The tutors who regularly journeyed to Santanilla were becoming the instruments of separation between the yellow-haired hacendado's grandson and the Iberian daughter of shepherds.

Roberto, already showing an intellectual bent despite his grandmother's suspicion of learning, tried hard to interest Ana-Maria in the wonderful things his tutors offered.

But Tomasa Gomez's daughter was simply not interested in the history of the Caesars or the decisions reached at the Congress of Vienna. Tomasa herself saw to it that her daughter learned what was needful and ignored what was not. Tomasa was devoted to her youthful Patron, but her entire life's edifice rested on foundations of firm belief in the fitness of things. It was expected of Anita, even demanded of her, that she love her *padrino* and defer to him in all things. But it was right and proper that as the two children grew older, their interests in life would diverge. Roberto would in time take his place among *la gente fina,* make a proper marriage, and raise sons to inherit the estate. Ana-Maria, at a far earlier age, would be given in wedlock to a suitable good man of her own class. She would be blessed and endowed by Roberto as her godfather and if God granted, she and her husband would spend their lives as Roberto's servants. For this kind of sensible future, too much of the sort of education Roberto must undergo could only be bad for Ana-Maria.

So though Roberto Marburg and his goddaughter still roamed the hills and rode his white pony together, these pleasures came less frequently. Ana-Maria now spent much time among the *criadas* of the household, learning to do the domestic work that was destined to be her task in life.

Roberto turned to his sister Cecilia for company from time to time, but she was so gentle and so delicately made that he regretfully had to conclude that though he loved her as a brother should, she simply was not much fun to be with. She spent much of her time with old Father Sebastio at the chapel. So much of it, in fact, that there was already talk of preparing her to enter the Convent of Santa Teresa at Avila, where her grandmother had been educated.

Occasionally Roberto would seek to play with the gypsy children who always seemed to be about the estate these days, but Doña Maria disapproved, and even Chole Segre, Uncle Julio's friend, discouraged him. "They will steal the gold from your hair, little one," she told him, laughing. "You are far too tender a morsel for a caravan child."

So Roberto spent such of his time as was not needed for studies with his tutors or with Don Alvaro riding in the foothills of the Cantabricas, following the sheep and the cattle and wishing with all his young heart that Maria-Elena and her brothers might soon return to Santanilla to visit as they used to do.

It was Uncle Julio, of all persons, who provided Roberto with an occupation for his spare time.

Much against his father's advice, Julio Santana had invested money in a small herd of fighting bulls. This had been tried at Santanilla before, and it had failed. The pasturage offered by the Santanilla land was too sparse to meet the requirements of brave bulls. In order for them to grow large and strong enough for the ring, they had to be fed constantly on grain, which was expensive. And because he could not afford the Miura bloodlines his father had once tried, Julio was forced to accept an inferior Asturian stock, which bred up rangy and treacherous. But he persisted, and a ring was built in one of the northern pastures, where the gypsy boys, and even occasionally Roberto, were allowed to cape the calves, testing them for bravery.

Adriana fiercely objected to this, as did Doña Maria. But Roberto, expressing the nearest thing to rebellion he had ever shown his mother, appealed to Don Alvaro, who distractedly accused the women of keeping his grandson in leading strings too long. "Let the boy be, Adriana," El Patron said, petulant at being disturbed amid his now-permanent litter of books and papers in the observatory. "Give him a chance to be a man."

But Doña Maria, remembering how her father-in-law had died, did not cease to brood and complain.

On a sparkling morning, two days before the new national holiday of El Cinco de Mayo, Aaron Marburg and his foreman, Juan Ortega, stood in the dirt of the road watching a painter put the finishing touches to a new sign on the arched facade of the Trituradora. Others of the work crew—all, in fact, not currently engaged in keeping the conveyor belts to the expellers clear—had joined them in the street to watch the legend *Aaron Marburg, Propietario* take shape under the name, *Trituradora de Aceites, S.A.*

The evening before, Aaron had received acknowledgment from Simon Pauley, now retired in Boston, that his indebtedness was at an end and his title to the enterprise in Tihuacan was now unencumbered.

As the painter finished with a flourish and turned around on the scaffolding to accept the plaudits of the spectators, the workmen raised a cheer and Juan Ortega, flushing with pleasure, poured a glass of tequila for El Patron and then emptied the bottle into the tin cups and thick china mugs in the hands of the off-duty workers. Though he had to shout to make himself understood over the roar of the machinery, he managed to deliver a rather flowery speech of congratulation that his wife, who had heard it three times, said was an oration worthy of any senator in *la capital.*

"And so good fortune, *Jefe,*" Ortega finished grandly, "especially to you and to your many sons to come who will command this great enterprise when we are all dead." There had been considerable discussion among the men when Ortega was laboriously writing down his speech. Should one mention El Patron's sons? He was not, after all, married yet. Yes, it was known in the town that Don Aaron had a great interest in Señorita Marini, but no one had mentioned a betrothal. Still, there could be nothing amiss in giving the boss a strong hint that the men of the Trituradora would like to see him married. They approved of Señorita Marini, a young lady who took an interest in them and their families. She was intelligent, of course, and that could cause trouble. On the other hand, she was also rich, and no one could find fault with that. Once Don Aaron settled down and started producing sons who could inherit the Trituradora, the men who worked there—and their posterity—would be assured work and fair wages in the future. So the hint about sons in the speech met with approval.

Aaron, who by now knew how to respond, raised his glass in a toast. *"Viva el trabajo. Viva la Trituradora. Y viva Mexico!"* Without exception, these men were patriots. Aaron knocked back the tequila, wincing. Five years in Mexico, and he still seemed to be drinking the spines rather than the juice of the *maguey!*

The *capataz* drank, raised a cheer among the men, and then shouted for the expeller crews to return to work. "You can get drunk tonight at La Gallineta, courtesy of El Jefe! But today we work and make oil like any day!"

The men returned to the reverberating tin-roofed building laughing and shouting their thanks. Aaron had, as custom dictated, arranged for the *cantina* on the La Cruz road, an adobe hut surrounded by thatched lean-tos with dirt floors pounded smooth by dancing feet—an establishment with the unromantic name of The Mudhen—to be taken over for the night by the men of the Trituradora. They would dance and whore and get drunk (their women would *not* attend the festivities), and in the morning Aaron would have to go down to the *cárcel* and retrieve a substantial proportion of his work force. The Trituradora would work a short shift tomorrow morning, and Aaron would have to soothe the wives and quasi-wives of his people with bonuses (delivered directly into the women's hands). But to have done otherwise would be thought mean-spirited and unworthy of the loyalty of so many brave men.

Aaron took one last pleased look at the sign on the plaster façade of the galvanized iron building and walked back into the small room that served as an office.

The golden oak rolltop desk, scratched and gouged by years of hard use, was stacked with work. With a sigh, Aaron slipped the paper cuffs over his white shirtsleeves and addressed himself to the basket containing bills of lading and the schedule of arrivals and sailings from the port. He had never lost the habit of neatness learned first from Uncle Isaac and later, at Santanilla, from his father.

The *Orizaba* was once again anchored in the harbor, ready to take aboard three hundred metric tons of oil and, for the first time, a small shipment of copra cake. A consortium of ranchers and farmers in California had decided to experiment with the mealy cake as an agent for fattening cattle. Though Mexican farmers in Sinaloa had been feeding the cake to their animals for several years now, this was the first indication of interest by the Americans. Aaron believed that it could be a major innovation, and very lucrative if successful.

The sun burned through the grimy windows facing the street with an intensity that brought a sheen of perspiration to Aaron's forehead. The tiny flies that bred in the steaming piles of copra in the warehouse buzzed confusedly in the warm air of the office.

The boy who brought the newspapers came weaving up the dirt street on his rusty bicycle. A dark *mestizo*, no older than seven or eight, with enormous black eyes and a flashing smile, he scurried past the workmen and into the office laden with a canvas bag filled with papers. His burden came near to dragging on the floor. He wore the ubiquitous white pajamas with trousers that ended well above his thin ankles and already leathery bare feet.

"*Periódicos, mi Jefe,*" he sang cheerfully. Don Aaron was one of his premium customers, a man who bought one copy of each of the three Tihuacan journals daily.

It never ceased to amaze Aaron that the children of people who lived in such poverty could be so unfailingly cheerful. Yet this handsome boy would be, in a short thirty years, a wizened and exhausted man—if he did not succumb first to malaria or typhoid fever. The harsh realities of Mexican life were the engine that drove the never-ending cycle of political upheaval in this vast land.

El Diario Tihuacanteco, the journal of the conservatives in this part of Sinaloa, sold for a *tostón,* fifty centavos. The price placed it beyond the reach of the few literate workers in the town—as it was intended to do. It was read by landowners, merchants, and factory owners. Industrialization was slow coming to Mexico, but there were several manufacturing enterprises in Tihuacan: a shoe factory, a textile mill, and, of course, the Trituradora.

La Prensa Libre, scarcely more than an angry broadsheet, was the voice of the radical-anarchist movement, always strong in Mexico. It could be had for one centavo—or gratis, if the potential convert had no money. Rumor had it that *La Libre,* as it was familiarly called, was financed from abroad, possibly even from the United States, as a provocation to bring on another American intervention. Aaron thought this unlikely. If the United States should consider it the nation's "manifest destiny" (a phrase one heard often these days) to intervene in Mexico, the United States would do so without excuses. But Americans were looking elsewhere in the world. They generally did. Mexico was curiously terra incognita, and likely to remain so.

The paper with the largest circulation was *El Observador de Tihuacan.* It expressed the slightly socialist opinions of the liberals—the largest and most undisciplined party of all. It was sold for a modest five centavos and tended to be stodgy, noncommittal, and dull. It ignored, whenever possible, the fact that the Liberal Party was continually torn by dissension.

In Europe a town of twenty thousand people with three newspapers would have been remarkable. But here in Mexico each political faction felt it imperative to have its own voice, and since the end of the War of the Intervention, newspapers had proliferated wildly.

Aaron greeted the newsboy with a broad smile. *"Hola, Pepe. Como te va, pequeño?"*

"Bien, Jefe. The sun is shining and there is plenty of news," the boy sang. It was his cheerful daily litany.

Aaron flipped a silver peso and the boy caught it expertly. *"Mil gracias, Patron!"* Like fully two-thirds of the street children in Tihuacan, Pepe was a private entrepreneur. He bought his newspapers at full price and relied on the well-established custom of *propinada,* tipping, for his profit. Aaron was aware that Pepe was one of fourteen children in his family, all under the age of sixteen, whose father had died in the war against the *imperialistas.* Somehow they and their widowed mother (who worked as a *criada* at the town's one hotel, the Belmar) had survived and were seldom hungry. Aaron's battalion commander in the Wisconsin Volunteers, the man who had served with Scott in the Mexican War, always used to say that Mexicans were lazy, with no understanding of the work ethic. But Aaron had discovered that this was far from the truth. Mexicans were capable of enormous effort once they had decided it was necessary. The difficulty lay in convincing them.

Pepe placed the papers on the corner of Aaron's desk and hurried out into the factory, detouring through the warehouse to fill his pockets with pieces of sun-dried coconut, as was his custom. Presently he reappeared and mounted his bicycle, his mouth filled with copra. He waved to Aaron, and was gone. Aaron opened the papers. It was an absolute requirement for a businessman in Tihuacan to stay current on what the various political factions were saying about the world and one another.

Since the beginning of Benito Juárez's second term in the presidential palace, the coalition of divergent political factions that had combined against the imperialists had begun to show signs of strain. To the right of center, and claiming the support of the Church and some of the leaders of the nascent merchant class, together with many ex-military men and some bureaucrats, a kind of proto-party was forming around the colorful figure of Porfirio Díaz, the young general who had commanded the *brigada* that had carried the day at the defense of Puebla—and, incidentally, won the victory that would be celebrated as a national holiday in two days' time: *El glorioso Cinco de Mayo,* an anniversary comparable to the North Americans' Fourth of July.

Aaron heard the praises of General Díaz regularly from Maria Macías, who would not ordinarily have been expected to support the conservative cause, but who remembered her days as a *soldadera* in Díaz's brigade as a golden (if somewhat risky) time in her life.

Aligned with Díaz in an uneasy partnership was another faction of the right headed by Sebastian Lerdo de Tejada, who claimed that *he* spoke for the landowners, the professional men, and the Church, while Díaz's true supporters were only disgruntled military men who wanted a *caudillo* for Mexico, and disappointed office-seekers who wished to milk the public treasury.

In the center stood the stocky, beloved figure of Benito Juárez, a president who had won a great victory and was now watching it erode in still another round of the endless factionalism that had plagued Mexico since the days of Augustín Iturbide, the faintly comic figure of an emperor whose golden daric Julia wore around her neck.

The anarchists, who seemed to plague Mexico no matter who sat in the presidential chair, had recently decided to reject the results of the election that had given Juárez his second term. To express their displeasure they had formed an army of sorts and shot up the town of

Esperanza, in the neighboring state of Jalisco. Sixty-five people, twenty of them women and children, had been gunned down in the town plaza and inside the church. *El Diario* was calling it an outrage and a massacre of the innocents; the liberal *Observador* cautioned against overreaction; *La Libre* declared it a bitter but necessary blow against the forces of reaction that were stealing the revolution from the people.

Aaron pushed the papers aside with a feeling of revulsion. The pleasure of the morning was gone. This land was so rich, so much needed to be done. Yet the Esperanza raid was not an isolated event. There had been a dozen or more such attacks on conservative towns and villages by anarchist *guerrilleros* since Juárez's second inauguration.

Not only did the killing sicken Aaron, it offended his Teutonic sense of order. If this sort of thing could not be stopped, Mexico would never be a real nation.

He slammed the rolltop desk closed and walked out of the office into the street, letting the soft breeze from the harbor cool him.

Hands in pockets, he walked down the dirt street looking at the plaster walls crowding the roadway, the wrought-iron gates and *rejas* over the windows through which could be caught glimpses of tropical patio gardens and fountains where the rich lived, the adobe hovels with rusty galvanized iron roofs that were the homes of the poor. This country was both Spanish and not Spanish. It was as though Aaron were looking at Spain through a glass that altered and magnified so that the total effect was unique. In the narrow streets of the town one heard the language of Castile and Aragon spoken in accents and cadences that would sound strange even to those men who had brought it, together with horses and armor and gunpowder, to this new land. And in plazas and *mercados,* one swiftly became accustomed to the sound of Náhuatl, as musical to the ear as the frequent sonorities of church bells and the cries of vendors.

What would Adriana make of this country, Aaron wondered? What would the descendant of Vandal and Visigothic conquerors think of these strange folk Hernando Cortes and his freebooters had marked forever with the Spanish brand? The Mexicans were independent now and would very probably remain so, but they were set in the Hispanic mold forever. There were foreigners to spare in Tihuacan, as there were all over the country. And they were accepted as Mexicans readily enough. He was himself a case in point, as was Don Marcello and his family, and many others. But the country was governed—sometimes misgoverned—by a race that had not existed before the Spaniards came looking for gold. It was the *mestizo* who ruled here, the descendant of millions of the conquered race and a few hundred thousand Spaniards who had spread their blood thinly, but widely, among the Mexici, the Toltec, Olmecs, Mayans, Chichimecs, and a score of other nations.

Europeans and Americans might live here, might exploit the land and its people, might bring their grand gifts of plough and lathe and steam engine. But Mexico would always belong to the Mexicans. Foreigners would never rule here. Ferdinand Maximilian Joseph of Hapsburg had learned that in front of a Mexican firing squad. It was a truth worth remembering.

But despite the harshness of the lessons Mexico taught the stranger, Aaron suspected that Adriana would love this country for its vitality, its bottomless reservoir of hope, its exuberant people, and its grandeur. Why, all of Spain could be lost in a third of Mexico. Yaqui Indians roamed freely over a territory greater than a Spanish king had ever truly ruled. Benito Juárez, his narrow *mestizo* eyes coldly glittering under the Lincolnesque stovepipe hat he loved to affect, had expropriated more land from the church than a dozen popes had ever dreamed existed.

Aaron bought a *burrito* of beans wrapped in a *tortilla* from a street vendor and started back toward the Trituradora. He ate it hungrily and tossed the last of it to a ribby street dog. How very strange it was that even after all this time so many of his thoughts turned on Adriana— what she might think, what she might enjoy. How was it at Santanilla now, he wondered. She had written to him in Sebastio's name after the old priest had received his letter with the eight hundred pesos. Sebastio's hands were too gnarled to hold a pen, she said. Possibly, Aaron thought. But *she* had written, not Don Alvaro, not Doña Maria. A half-dozen letters now, in almost ten years. He wondered if she saved his letters as he saved hers.

Adriana had a plan, it seemed. Julio was allowing Santanilla to crumble away, but she had resolved to make a new Santanilla in California. It would take time and money, she said firmly, but Aaron had no doubt that if anyone could manage it, Adriana would.

He had asked himself many times what he felt about that, and found that he had no wish to answer. The past was filled with events best forgotten and thirsts better left unslaked.

The sun was past the zenith when Aaron returned to Trituradora. It had grown very hot and the smell of copra was thick in the air, a tangy, tropical odor that he had learned to enjoy.

From up ahead came a great clatter and shouting, and street urchins ran past him laughing and calling out to one another. The clear, unmistakable sound of a bugle pierced the afternoon.

The district where the Trituradora was situated had not yet been totally built up. The road ran through scattered blocks of poor houses, small businesses, and market stands. Across from the Trituradora's warehouse lay a broad field gone to scrub thorn and wild grasses.

As Aaron approached he saw that soldiers, fully a brigade of them, were busy setting up a bivouac in the grassy field. Tents had sprouted and picket lines tethered the mounts of the officers. A headquarters tent faced the road and the warehouse. Several officers stood about in the shadow of a stand of flags. Aaron estimated that there must be at least eight hundred soldiers in the process of setting up their camp.

Evidently they had come from the south, perhaps from some fruitless chase after the anarchist guerrillas who had attacked Esperanza. The uniforms and equipment were dusty, but they were new and in good condition.

Aaron's military memory stirred and he found himself wondering why, if this unit had been seeking guerrilla raiders, so much of it was infantry. Foot soldiers were worse than useless for a pursuit in the rugged mountainous terrain of Jalisco.

He nodded cordially to the soldiers as he passed on toward the front of the Trituradora. The men were young, but oddly distant in their demeanor. Most Mexican troops were not nearly as disciplined as these, Aaron thought. Whoever commanded them ran a strict unit.

As he turned into his office, Juan Ortega, the *capataz,* appeared, looking round-eyed, even awed.

"*Jefe,*" he said. "While you were out a messenger came from Don Marcello." Ortega was highly conscious of the Federales in the field. He kept glancing at them through the window.

Aaron said, "They will still be there when you have given me Don Marcello's message, Juan."

"*Perdóneme,* Patron," the foreman said. "It is only that we haven't seen the military in Tihuacan since the Frenchmen left."

"The message, *hombre.*"

"*Sí,* Patron. Don Marcello requests that you dine with him tonight at nine at las Olas Altas. He says it is of great importance. He sent his *mayordomo, Jefe.*"

"Thank you, Juan," Aaron said, and prepared to open his desk again. But Ortega remained in the office expectantly. "Was there something else, Juan?"

"*Sí, mi jefe.* The *mayordomo* told me why you are invited, Don Aaron."

"And now you are going to tell me, aren't you, Juan." If the *capataz* had a fault, it was a tendency to make a great tale out of small events.

"You are to meet General Díaz, Patron!"

"Thank you, Juan."

When the foreman, visibly disappointed at Aaron's reaction, left the office, Aaron stood at the window looking thoughtfully at the troops bivouacked in the field across the road.

So Porfirio Díaz had finally come calling on Tihuacan. And he had not come alone.

$$27$$

on Marcello Marini's house was built on a large plot of walled land in the approximate center of the broad crescent of the Paseo de las Olas Altas. This was a broad street along the breakwater and the ocean beach, a long, gently curving avenue along which the gentry of Tihuacan took their Sunday promenade.

Don Marcello had created for himself a Mexican version of the Mediterranean palazzos outside of which he had sold fish from a cart in his youth. From the open *corredor* facing the Pacific could be seen the long, graceful line of the Malecón that ended among the stunted pines and cypress trees of Cabo Sur, the small, steep cape dividing the shallow northern bay from the deep-water harbor and roadstead facing the southern commercial districts of Tihuacan.

All of Tihuacan's most important citizens lived on las Olas Altas, or as near to it as they could manage. Here, side by side, were the townhouses of the few large landowners who had been able to maintain their state through the War of the Reform and the war against the imperialists. Here too lived the members of the town administration, including the mayor (a pleasant, ineffectual man given to long absences in Ciudad Mexico), as well as the newly rich members of the growing merchant class. It was the handsomest location in Tihuacan, and the place best situated to catch the ocean breezes in the *tiempo de calor.*

Rather than compel his old *mozo* to spend the night hours waiting with the horse and buggy, Aaron Marburg chose to walk from his own house in the less fashionable part of town to Don Marcello's. It was not far, less than two miles. Tihuacan was built in the manner of most seaports, in a narrow band of development hugging the water. Distances north and south were considerable, but in an east-west direction no street was far from the sea.

The transition from daylight to dark in these latitudes below the Tropic of Cancer was swift. A thin crescent moon hung in the west above the sea and the last red band of the sunset limned the western horizon. As he walked through the unlighted, narrow dirt streets (in Tihuacan only the Malecón and the streets immediately bounding the cathedral square were paved), Aaron could hear the sounds of music and dancing in the cantinas. Tihuacan was filled with cantinas. They ranged in elegance from barrooms with tiled floors and walls (as in the Belmar Hotel) to *ramadas* such as La Gallineta, where the men of the Trituradora were celebrating his ownership tonight. Under ordinary circumstances Aaron would have been expected to appear at La Gallineta to share *una copita,* a "little drink," or two, with his men. But by now Juan Ortega would have rather importantly told them that *el Jefe* had been summoned to meet a hero of the nation, General José de la Cruz Porfirio Díaz, the victor of Puebla.

As he walked, Aaron pondered Don Marcello's summons. Julia's father was deeply involved in politics, as were most men of substance in Mexico. Rich men supported the factions they favored with large contributions of money and goods. It was expected and required of them. What made Mexican politics rather different from the politics of the North or of Europe was that these same men also contributed substantial sums to factions opposing theirs, on the not illogical theory that it was always best to consider all the possibilities. His years in Mexico had already taught Aaron that no matter in which direction the *politicos* took the republic, they would always be indebted to the men who had paved their way with money. Men with the hard, clear principles of a Don Alvaro Santana—men who supported a cause even at the risk of family fortunes—were rare.

Aaron concluded, as he approached the high iron gate of Don

Marcello's house, that his summons had two possible interpretations. Don Marcello was fond of him and approved of the tacit arrangement that existed between himself and Julia. Therefore it was to be expected that the merchant would invite him to any social function honoring a national hero. If the gathering were large and included many Tihuanteco notables, that simple explanation would suffice. But if the dinner were small and intimate, even secret, then something would be required of him. Not money, certainly, because Don Marcello had plenty of that. But something.

Don Marcello, a short and muscular man with muttonchop whiskers and the hard brown eyes of a seagoing Genoese, greeted Aaron in the *sala.* He was dressed conservatively in black, with a heavy gold chain glittering on his small but prominent belly. There were diamonds in his stickpin, and his still-dark hair smelled of English pomade.

Aaron looked for Julia, but she did not appear. Nor were there as yet any other guests. The dinner, he surmised, would be even more private than he had supposed.

Don Marcello embraced Aaron with a hearty *abrazo* and guided him from the *sala* out to the open-arched *corredor,* where a table had been laid for three people. At the north end of the gallery were wickerwork chairs and a cabinet containing an assortment of Mexican and European liquors. A white-coated mozo stood waiting to serve.

"Don't look for my daughter tonight, *hijo,*" Don Marcello said familiarly. "This is not a ladies' night."

Aaron resigned himself to the situation. It was customary in this country to sequester the women of a household when the men gathered to drink and talk politics and business. It always surprised Aaron when Don Marcello acquiesced in this practice because Julia Marini was not one of the ordinary run of empty-headed belles of the town, and she was often allowed to participate in the animated discussions that took place between Aaron and her father. But tonight the merchant was obviously deferring to the Mexican prejudices of his third guest, who had not yet arrived.

"Sit, *hijo,*" Don Marcello said, waving at a chair. *"Una copa?* I have some grappa just off the boat. The nectar of my youth. Or perhaps you would prefer American whiskey." He smiled. "Our guest has a fondness for things North American. It is said he once raided a train because it was carrying a shipment of *yanqui* bourbon."

Aaron accepted a tall crystal glass with a generous portion of whisky.

Marcello raised his glass of grappa in a toast and sipped at it. He made a satisfied sound and said, "A peasant drink, *joven.*" He always called Aaron "son" or "youngster." It was to be taken as a measure of his regard. "Yes, a drink for peasants and fishermen. I never lost my taste for it. Sometimes I think it rather scandalizes our local *gentecilla.*" He often used the derisive Spanish word for "gentlefolk." Don Marcello was a man who would never lose sight of his own heritage. His love for his adopted country was rooted in the freedom it had given him to rise in the world.

"*El general* will be along presently. He is at the moment doing something or other military. You would know more about that than I."

"There are eight hundred Federales bivouacked near the Trituradora," Aaron said. "Are we expecting a *guerrillero* attack in Tihuacan?"

Don Marcello laughed softly. "I do not think so, *joven.* Our guest never goes anywhere these days without a herd of soldiers. There is trouble in paradise." It was Don Marcello's habit to refer to the capital at Mexico City in that scornful way. Many of the newly rich of Tihuacan were building themselves summer homes in the Valley of Mexico, where the heat was less intense and where the senators who made the laws of the land could be more easily entertained. And bribed, Aaron knew. Don Marcello was not above bribing politicians, but he felt no need to live among them in order to do it.

Don Marcello turned and dismissed the *mozo.* When the servant had gone, he leaned forward and said, "Juárez is in bad health, *joven.* The cats that he keeps together in his bag are beginning to fight. The largest cats, and the two with the sharpest claws, are Lerdo and our distinguished guest. I offer this as background for what will be an interesting discussion this night."

Sebastian Lerdo de Tejada was now chief justice of the Supreme Court in the capital, a position of enormous legal power, but without military force. Like everyone else, Aaron was aware that Lerdo and Díaz had been rivals for years, but that their respect and affection for Benito Juárez kept them (sometimes precariously) in double harness within the Liberal Party.

In Tihuacan it was said that the anarchists to the far left of the *Partido Liberal* had no following. Aaron knew this was not so. Many of the men who worked on the waterfront, loading and unloading the fleets of lighters that carried ashore the cargoes from the freighters in the roadstead, were fiery believers in the promises made by the leaders of the left, as were the small farmers of the neighboring *campo.*

These men, most of them, had fought in the war against the imperialists. Their commanders, many of them as unlettered as their troops, had made populist promises (the abolition of money and property, total distribution of all church lands, the sharing out of the wealth in the national treasury) that President Juárez had repudiated. The radical left was not well organized. The very nature of its aims made it impossible to regiment. But it was angry, disappointed, and resentful. The activities of the *guerrilleros* were evidence of that.

To Aaron Marburg, conditioned as he was by his background to the orderly and businesslike conduct of affairs, the angry rebelliousness of the anarchists was Mexico's tragedy. Over and over again in the nation's past, the poorest of the common people had been promised a golden age. When it failed to materialize, they exploded into violence and murder. Then the forces of the right, never sanguine about the wisdom of the revolution, would strike. Since Augustín de Iturbide's day the pattern had been repeated many times. Aaron hoped that the current troubles in Jalisco were not simply the precursors of still another cycle of violence. Chief Justice Lerdo de Tejada had recently made some very harsh judgments against the left wing of the Juárista coalition, and he now claimed to speak for all of the conservatives of the nation. Fortunately, Díaz largely controlled the army, and though he was known to disagree with the president about how best to deal with the guerrillas, he had not made common cause with the Lerdistas. He was, in fact, at odds with them and seemed likely, Don Marcello said, to remain so.

Aaron and Don Marcello sat in the semi-darkness of the open gallery talking and listening to the rush of the surf on the breakwater across the Malecón. It was a spring night of singular beauty, the stars brilliant in a sky of an almost royal purple-blue. The thin sliver of moon, half-enclosing a lighter darkness, sank slowly toward the western horizon. The music of a distant cantina, faint and poignant, could be heard across the silent rooftops of Tihuacan. Aaron could hear a *campesino* singing, in a sweet tenor voice, a song of the soldiers in the French war.

"Borrachita, me voy/ Hasta la capital/ a servir el patron/ que me mandó llamar/ ante ayer—"

The song was a lament by a soldier going off to fight for the capital because his Patron commanded him. Mexican songs were often laments, thought Aaron. It spoke volumes about the history of this lovely, troubled land.

"How sweetly they sing," Don Marcello murmured.

And how sadly, Aaron thought.

Outside, on the Malecón, there was a clatter of cavalry and the sound of carriage wheels.

The *mozo* minding the gate called out to the house and an honor guard of servants lined the graveled way from street to house. Aaron stood, and from under the broad eaves saw a dozen brilliantly uniformed soldiers taking up positions around the grounds. The gate was opened and a carriage drawn by a pair of black horses drew up to the portico. Two officers alighted, one heavily built and wearing a cascade of aguillettes over his shoulder, and a second man in a plainer uniform.

Porfirio Díaz had arrived.

A parade of *mozos* bearing the hurricane lanterns used to illuminate the open gallery appeared, turning the long verandah bright as day. A horde of insects gathered to flutter against the glass hoods, making the light flicker eerily.

"The general dislikes dark corners," Don Marcello said quietly to Aaron.

The *mayordomo,* splendid in white duck coat and black trousers, led the two soldiers into the *corredor* and said, *"Patron, General Díaz y Coronel Dundalk."*

Aaron started at the remembered name. The man with Díaz was, indeed, the Sean Dundalk he had known briefly at General Frémont's St. Louis headquarters in '61, nine years older but still large and ruddy. He wore a magnificently decorated uniform brilliant with bullion and gold lace, the aguillettes of an aide-de-camp on his shoulder and an enormous revolver in a polished holster at his waist.

Don Marcello was saying, *"Mi General,* I present Don Aaron Marburg, of whom I have written to you."

Díaz, a well-proportioned man of middle height, examined Aaron carefully. His face was smoothly shaven except for a drooping moustache. His hair was cut short and neatly combed. His dark eyes, under level brows, were intense and searching. He was forty years old and had been a soldier since he was sixteen. For eight years, since the battle of Puebla, he had been a national hero.

Díaz did not immediately acknowledge Don Marcello's introduction. Instead he turned to his companion, Dundalk, who looked long and hard at Aaron and then nodded. Díaz said, "I present my aide, Colonel Dundalk, gentlemen." His Spanish was precise, but in the idiom of the people. His pronunciation of Dundalk was like the *mozo's.*

Aaron spoke up immediately. "Sean Dundalk, don't you remember me? St. Louis? Frémont's headquarters?"

Dundalk stepped forward and took both of Aaron's hands in greeting. In loud, Irish-accented English he said, "Of course I do, laddie. I don't remember the beard, though. How grand you look."

Aaron said to Don Marcello, "This is the man who gave me to General Grant, Patron. The one who saved me from the Quartermaster Corps."

Don Marcello led the way to the end of the gallery, where the *mozo* stood ready to pour drinks. Díaz signalled to Colonel Dundalk and spoke with him privately for a moment. Aaron saw Dundalk reply to something affirmatively and then fasten the flap of the polished holster over his pistol. It struck Aaron like a bolt of lightning that Dundalk had come with Díaz to make certain that the man "of whom Don Marcello had written" was actually who he claimed to be. Sean Dundalk, the far-roaming Irish soldier of fortune was not only Porfirio Díaz's aide, he was his bodyguard.

Dundalk stepped back and saluted formally. *"A sus ordenes, mi General."* His accent was execrable, unabashedly so.

Díaz said, *"Lo siento,* Don Marcello, but my aide has military duties to attend to." To Aaron he said, "You will be able to renew your acquaintance tomorrow or the next day, Señor Marburg. We will be in Tihuacan until after the Cinco de Mayo."

Dundalk gripped Aaron's left arm hard enough to make him wince from his old injury. "I am sorry, Aaron. I heard you were wounded. Forgive me, laddie. We'll talk tomorrow." He offered Don Marcello a soft salute and marched from the house.

It was well after midnight when the last of Don Marcello's excellent dinner had been cleared away and balloon glasses of *aguardiente* served. Throughout the meal Porfirio Díaz had displayed a polished charm. The conversation had ranged across an impressive number of subjects, from politics to economics to the explosive energy of the new revolutionary art of Mexico. But it was plain to Aaron that Díaz had not yet broached the reason for his presence in intimate discourse with two businessmen of Tihuacan.

Presently the general pushed back his chair and stretched his booted legs. All three men accepted Cuban cigars from the silver humidor offered by a *mozo.* Díaz drew in a mouthful of the aromatic tobacco smoke and seemed to nod imperceptibly at Don Marcello. The host signalled the *mozo* to remove most of the lanterns; the whirring of the night-flying insects died. Through the broad arches of the *corredor,* beyond the pale band of the Malecón and the breakwater, Aaron could detect the soft phosphorescence of the breaking waves. The night air had the feel of velvet and the mingled odor of the sea and the flowering plants on Don Marcello's gardens.

"One can live very well in Mexico, Don Aaron," Díaz said quietly.

"It is a beautiful land, General," Aaron said. "Full of promise."

"This is a long way from the Boccadasse of Genoa," Don Marcello said in a satisfied tone. "Mexico has been very good to me."

"Yet," Díaz said, tapping ashes in to a glazed pottery bowl, "one must always think of the future. The revolution is never totally secure. Don't you agree, Don Aaron?"

"I seldom involve myself in politics, *mi General,*" Aaron said cautiously.

Díaz smiled whitely in the dimness. "But you think of it, surely. No one can live in this country and not have political opinions. You admire Benito Juárez, surely?"

"Very much," Aaron said. "He has performed miracles."

"My dear friend," Díaz said. "Miracles are in the eyes of the beholder. They said we performed a miracle at Puebla, but believe me, our victory was not the product of divine intervention. A thousand women crawling on their knees to beseech the Virgin of Guadalupe could never achieve what six batteries of field artillery can do. I sometimes think our *presidente* is inclined to forget this."

"I never heard that Juárez was a man to ask God's help," Don Marcello said. The president's anticlericalism made Juárez suspect in Don Marcello Marini's eyes. The merchant was devout.

"God's help, yes, Don Marcello," said the general. "Not often the Church's, however. Well, that is as may be. The Church has not always been a friend of the people in this country. It must take what comes." He reached over and squeezed Don Marcello's arm familiarly. "It will not be too bad, *amigo.* I promise you that."

"The Lerdistas promise total restitution of Church property, *mi General,*" Don Marcello said. "They have a following."

"You do not number yourself among them, I hope." Aaron clearly heard the steely cutting edge in Porfirio Díaz's voice. The man projected a vibrant charm, but plainly one crossed him at one's peril.

It was common gossip that both Díaz and Sebastian Lerda de Tejada would stand for the Presidency in 1871, though neither was given much chance of election if Benito Juárez were to seek a third term, as he was almost certain to do.

"I am a son of Mother Church," Don Marcello said firmly. "But I believe that church and state should be separated here, just as they are in the United States."

Díaz laughed easily. His admiration for the Colossus of the North was well known. He had made many public statements of Mexico's need to be open to American investment and exploitation. But Aaron thought it best to remember that José de la Cruz Porfirio Díaz was a Mexican, and a soldier. His admiration might not stretch so far as to include the *yanqui* devotion to individual liberties and rights.

Díaz seemed to divine his thoughts. "As a European, Don Aaron, you can stand aloof from us and see clearly."

"I plan to live out my life in Mexico, *mi General,*" Aaron said. "Surely that makes me a Mexican?"

"I do not mean to offend you, *amigo,*" Díaz said. "I only mean that you are not filled with the political fevers that rage so freely in the children of this land. I am such a child, and I know how hot they make the blood." He took the time to relight his Havana before going on. "Mexico is like a boiling river, my friend. You stand on the bank, but I stand neck deep in the water. If *I* can see certain things from my precarious vantage point, surely you can see much more from where you are. Regard us dispassionately, if you can, Don Aaron." He got to his feet and walked to the balustrade overlooking the gardens. He was a compact, erect shadow against the night.

He dropped the cigar into the garden and turned, resting his weight against the iron railing spanning the arch. "You have lived in Spain, Don Aaron. And you have lived among us now for how long? Five years or more. You were a soldier among the *yanquis.* When I commanded my *brigada* at Puebla, you were in the trenches before Vicksburg. Colonel Dundalk has told me of your military service, so I am assured that you can see matters with the eye of a soldier." He returned to the table and seated himself once again in one of the creaking wicker chairs. "Mexico—in fact, all Latin America—is unique in the world, my friend. Our political institutions are modeled on those of the United States of the North. We have a president, a legislature, a Supreme Court, our country is made up of states. We are, in fact, legally Los Estados Unidos de Mexico. The rest of Latin America is very similarly organized, but let the southerners stand for the moment. What I say of Mexico is largely true of all the countries to the south of us.

"*Bueno pues,* here we find ourselves in a nation that might have been organized by the English aristocrats who made the United States. *But—*" He leaned forward and thrust a finger at his listeners. "We are *not* English aristocrats. We are *not* Anglos of any sort. We are *Mexicans.* By this I mean that our culture came to us with the *conquistadores,* from *Spain.*

"Now you, Don Aaron, should know best exactly what that means. We take in our Iberian heritage with our mother's milk. Oh, we are a nation of *mestizos,* right enough. But for three hundred years we have been taught that all true culture, all honor, all glory is Hispanic. Even as we drove the Spanish colonialists from our soil, we kept their language, their literature, their music—yes, their love of death, too—for our own. Please note, my friend, I have not spoken of a Spanish love of individual liberties, of the rights of man, of political freedom or fairness. And why? Because they do not exist. It is as simple as that. We have the character of Spaniards in a nation pretending to derive its legitimacy from a constitution aping the Constitution of the United States—a noble document, *señores,* but not one a Spaniard—or a Mexican—is ever likely to regard as Holy Writ.

"We make revolutions easily in this country, but we do not take seriously the notion that revolutions are made to ensure the Rights of Man. We are too Spanish for that, my friends. And too Spanish we will always be. Even now, with the last invaders of our country gone only a few years, Mexico longs for a *caudillo."*

A silence descended on the gallery. Porfirio Díaz raised his goblet of *aguardiente* in a silent toast and drank it slowly.

Presently Aaron said, "And you are that *caudillo,* General?"

Díaz gave a low laugh. "I may be, my friend. Or it may be another. But always remember this. Mexico will forever be Mexico. It will never be the United States. Nor will any of the countries of the Isthmus, or of South America. We took our political institutions from the Northern Anglos, Don Aaron. But we had our souls from the dark heart of Spain."

He looked questioningly at Don Marcello, who seemed to shrug in reply. Díaz said quietly to Aaron, "I ask a favor of you, Don Aaron. It is a small thing, but it is a matter of some importance to me."

"Be free to ask, *mi General,"* Aaron said, and knew in that moment that here was the reason for this private meeting.

"The *Orizaba* is in the harbor. It arrived from San Francisco this morning. There is a cargo aboard that my men will be unloading tomorrow. I ask permission to store it, under guard, in your Trituradora warehouse."

Aaron felt the prickle of danger along his spine. But all that he had heard tonight from this charming and dangerous man made it clear that to refuse was to make an enemy. With sinking heart he said, *"Mi casa es su casa, General."*

Don Marcello rose from his chair and gave Aaron a strong *abrazo.* "You will not be sorry for this, *hijo.* I give you my promise."

247

28

Through the open window the sea wind carried the sound of church bells. In the distance could be seen the roofs of the village of Quejo, and beyond them the flat, hard blue of the Mar Cantabrico. The tiny villa on the hill was charming, with a fine view and a lovely garden. The single *criada,* an old woman named Pilar, was quiet, efficient, and discreet. Her husband, who cared for the gardens, was a leathery graybeard who bowed his head when he saw Adriana and never spoke a word. Jean-Claude contended that the old fellow was mute, and he may well have been, though he understood orders well enough.

I shall miss this place, Adriana thought. But all pleasant things come to an end.

She lay at her ease in the deep feather bed, comfortably sated with lovemaking. A boy he might be, she thought amusedly, but there was a man there, under the smooth, fair skin and hairless chest.

He stood now at the window, an opulent brocade dressing gown draped over his slender shoulders, frowning at the distant sea. He was perilously close to sulking, or perhaps that was too unkind a judgment. He was very young, after all. Still, she had warned him that it would come to this. She succumbed to a delicious sadness that was, she knew, as indulgent as the excitement at the beginning had been. Jean-Claude had given her respite from the realities of life at Santanilla. With the young Frenchman she had been able to be a girl again, to laugh again. And if it had not been love as she remembered it, at least there had been passion enough to sate her Spanish hunger. Twenty afternoons in this secret place, twenty, one each week. They seemed so many, and so few.

The outside world came seldom into Old Castile. In Madrid there were quarrels among the royalists and politicians. The queen had fled to France—presumably with her cook's-son lover—and had been declared deposed. The *caudillos* fought among themselves, and in the radical South the Republicans troubled the countryside. A half-dozen royal incompetents, sought all over Europe, were not so incompetent as to take on the wearing of a Spanish crown.

Had her father been what he once was, these events would have been of vital interest at Santanilla. But he spent his days planning and replanning a new Santanilla across the sea, and from one week to the next he was not seen outside the littered observatory.

It was the loss of Don Alvaro's companionship as much as anything that had brought Adriana Marburg to these secret afternoons in the little villa above Quejo village.

Among the many who had been offered the Spanish crown was the Hohenzollern Prince Leopold, an appointment that had aroused the French emperor, Napoleon III, to protest to Kaiser Wilhelm of Prussia. The exchange of secret messages had become acrimonious and Napoleon III, never noted for his good sense, had dispatched a telegram to the Kaiser (who was taking the waters at Ems) demanding a letter of apology for having put forward a Hohenzollern as a potential Spanish king. Suddenly and deliberately the insolent message, now known all over Europe as the Infamous Ems Telegram, was made public by Count von Bismarck, together with the Kaiser's rejection.

Within a week of the publication of the telegram, Jean-Claude Raymond had received a telegram of his own, from the colonel of the Chamborant Chasseurs, directing him to return to his unit at once because war between France and Prussia was imminent.

And so, in the end, the tangle of Europe's childish quarrels had found its way into Old Castile after all, Adriana thought with wry amusement. A German warlord received a telegram about the Spanish succession, and these warm afternoons at Quejo were over. Adriana sighed and stretched in the soft bed. Well, it was past time for farewells. Jean-Claude should get on with his life, as should she. There was still so much to be done, years to live, money to be put by, alliances to be made, before the new Santanilla could become a reality, a place for Roberto in the new world.

Jean-Claude turned from the window and stood looking at her intently. "I cannot accept this, Adriana," he said.

"Las Parcas nos mandan," she said gently.

"Come with me. We will marry. I beg you."

"You know that is impossible, Jean. You have always known it."

"Shall I get on my knees? Adriana, I cannot leave you." He flung himself dramatically onto the bed and kissed her hair, her shoulders, her breasts. "You *belong* to me," he cried out.

"I belong to others, Jean-Claude," Adriana said, less patiently.

Seeing her unmoved, he sat on the edge of the bed and buried his face in his hands.

Adriana did not want to be unkind. These afternoons with Jean-Claude had given her the strength to carry on as she knew she must do. But she did not love him, and she had told him so from the beginning. She ran a hand through his rumpled hair and half-chided him. "There now, my beautiful young man," she said in his language.

He raised his head to look at her with brimming eyes. " 'Am I beautiful? It is for you alone. Say that you love me, for without you I cannot live.' A Persian poet wrote that two thousand years ago, Adriana. He must have known you in another life."

"Such a pretty speech, Jean. You are a lovely man and I will never forget you," she said. "And now make love to me one last time, because it is growing late and I have a long way to ride."

He helped her to mount the old half-Arab she often rode and then stood looking up at her, his chest aching with loss. She sat her horse like a queen, he thought, like a goddess.

I will stay, he thought. I will not answer my call. I cannot give her up.

She leaned forward and kissed his forehead. "Good-bye, Jean-Claude. Go with God."

He watched her ride down the path to the road leading to Santanilla, out of his life and into that dark Spanish world of her own that he would never know.

The following morning, the fourth day of May, little Cecilia discovered Father Sebastio prostrated like a young priest at his ordination before the altar of the family chapel. In his eightieth year, and while performing his own private penance (for what imagined sins, no one could know), Sebastio had died in his beloved church.

Doña Maria, dry-eyed but grieving, dispatched a message to her cousin, the Bishop of Liencres, demanding that he, and he alone, perform the obsequies for Sebastio, who would be buried in the family crypt among the Santanas, as was his due.

El glorioso Cinco de Mayo in
Tihuacan was a day of extravagant celebration, the more so because it
happened that the hero of Puebla, Porfirio Díaz was in the town together with a full brigade of Federales.

The day dawned bright and still, with public buildings and private
homes decorated with red, white, and green bunting and displaying
hundreds upon hundreds of flags of the state of Sinaloa and more
hundreds bearing the eagle-and-serpent device of the national ensign.
In the Plaza Mayor, the broad, tree-shaded square before the cathedral
where, on ordinary summer nights, mariachis played in the wooden
bandstand, a military band composed of Rurales began to play patriotic
airs at eight o'clock.

The Rurales were a national police force created by Benito Juárez.
Patterned after the Guardia Civil of Spain, the Rurales were nominally
responsible for the enforcement of the law in the vast hinterland of the

coastal plain and the mountains of the Sierra Morena Occidental. They were a reasonably effective force, but one with minimal discipline and training, so that in times of real trouble it always became necessary to call in troops of the federal army. In Jalisco, the Rurales had been repeatedly routed by the anarchist insurgents, but in Sinaloa they had yet to be tested, and so spent most of their time in parading and playing band concerts. The occasion of a great national fiesta displayed them to advantage, resplendent in their gray *charro* outfits with silver braid on their trousers and broad *sombreros* on their heads. There had already been a number of bar fights between the Rurales and off-duty soldiers from General Díaz's elite brigade.

On the Malecón, across from the hotel, a stand had been built and decorated. From this vantage point the vice-*alcalde,* Don Mauricio Perez de Lebron (one of the few Mexican bureaucrats of pure *criollo* descent), General Díaz, and a selection of Tihuacan's more affluent citizens would review the parade that would muster at the Plaza Mayor, wind through the town, and end in the parkland of Cabo Sur. The night would bring a great display of fireworks, dancing in the streets and squares, and plenty of free tequila, mescal, and cerveza, courtesy of the town merchants.

Aaron had been invited to sit beside General Díaz on the stand— a singular honor. But he would have much preferred to spend the day with the minimum crew of workmen who had volunteered to keep the boiler stoked at the Trituradora in return for double their ordinary wages of three pesos a day.

On the previous morning, Aaron had gone to the harbor front, there to watch several companies of soldiers, under the direct command of Colonel Sean Dundalk, unloading wooden crates from the lighters plying between the anchored *Orizaba* and the shallow water dock.

Captain Jonas Willard, the American master of the *Orizaba,* had come ashore with the first lighter-load to confer with Dundalk. Aaron, who knew Willard well, had joined the conference unasked. He had seen crates like those being brought ashore many times. Though they had been labeled "Farm Implements," their contents would be familiar to anyone who had ever served in the Union army. They were rifles and ammunition, American surplus, enough to arm a full division of infantry.

Willard touched the peak of his battered cap to Aaron and said, "So it's to your place they'll be taking these rakes and hoes, Mr. Marburg?" He looked sidelong at Dundalk, sweating in a woolen fatigue uniform. "Better there than on my ship, but I hope you have plenty of *soldados* to keep watch on them."

Aaron said to Dundalk, "You could have warned me."

"And when and how could I have done that, laddie?" the Irishman said. "I am only a simple hired soldier. *He* tells people what he thinks they need to know."

Willard narrowed his eyes against the sun's glare on the water. Besides the *Orizaba,* there were three other ships in the Tihuacan roads, two side-wheel steamers, with hulls more rust than steel, and a Chilean trader that had put in last week for repair. A storm had carried away her foremast in the southern ocean, and leaks had damaged her cargo of nitrates. It was unlikely that she would ever leave Tihuacan. There had been some talk of running her aground near the shore and using her as a pier. But the dangerously explosive nature of her cargo made this plan impracticable. It was more probable that she would eventually be taken to sea and scuttled. This had not yet been done because several businessmen of Tihuacan, including Don Marcello (who knew about ships and cargos), felt that the nitrates were too dangerous in their present condition.

"Another two hours should see the job done," Willard said to Dundalk. To Aaron he said, "We can start loading your oil then. I'd like to be out of here on the evening tide."

"No chance of that," Aaron said. "Unless you can borrow the colonel's soldiers. The stevedores are getting an early start on Cinco de Mayo."

"Well," the shipmaster said sourly. "I could do without still another fucking fiesta, but that's the way of it in greaserland." Scowling, he lumbered back to an empty lighter setting out for the *Orizaba.*

"Charming man," Sean Dundalk said, wiping his wet face with a bandanna. "Is he always such a delight?"

"He loses a fifth of his crew each time he makes port on a holiday," Aaron said. "Maybe his disposition will improve when you get all the explosives off his ship."

Dundalk put an arm across Aaron's shoulders. "Ploughs, you sweet man. Ploughs and mattocks and posthole augers. And don't be concerned. They will be very carefully guarded. Díaz wouldn't be pleased to have them stolen."

"How long have you been with the general, Sean?"

"Two years, or as near as makes no difference. I tried the regular army, but they wouldn't have me. Then a bit of ranching in the Wyoming Territory. But that is incredibly hard work, laddie, and not for a Dundalk. So I came south and signed on with the general. He is a remarkable soldier, Aaron. And an even better politician, which is far more important in this country."

"Would you have any idea what he plans to do with so many guns?" Aaron asked. "Could you venture a guess?"

"A guess, is it? Well, if you repeat it I will say you're a liar, but a betting man might wager that more Lerdistas than anarchists will see the sharp end of these toys," Dundalk said.

"There are very few Lerdistas in Tihuacan," Aaron said.

"I am delighted to hear that, laddie. It makes my job so much easier."

"There are insurgents in the hills twenty kilometers from here," Aaron said.

"Have they been active?"

Aaron shook his head. The *campesinos* who formed the radical movement's guerrilla bands were unpredictable. If the corn grew well, the bands dwindled. If there was drought, or too much rain, or if the corn simply died, as it often did, the men were apt to take their rifles out of hiding and go on a rampage. The massacre in Jalisco was said to have been precipitated by a bad crop. Then there was the unknown factor of the Church. Though the bishop in the golden cathedral of Guadalupe preached peace, the peasant priests sometimes preached rebellion.

"Well, then," Dundalk said. "There's naught to worry us. First let me get these goods put away in your warehouse, and then I will be graciously pleased to accept your offer of a bath, a bottle, and a bed, laddie. In return for which I will bruise your ears with my war stories. You *did* offer, didn't you?"

Aaron grinned in spite of himself. Dundalk had always been the raconteur and professional Irish charmer of General Frémont's headquarters. "I seem to have done," he said.

After the unloading had been accomplished and the crates transported across the town to the Trituradora, Aaron and Dundalk had spent a long evening in Aaron's *sala,* served drinks and a late supper and then more drinks by Maria Macías, who, with little encouragement, had war stories of her own to tell. "The *soldaderas* of today," she concluded scornfully, "are only *putas.* My *compañeras* could love a man, bear a child and fight, all in one day."

Aaron and Dundalk spoke of General Frémont. "The poor foolish man has lost all his money on that railroad he tried to build to California," Dundalk said, "and while he poured good money after bad,

Senator Stanford and his nabobs beat him to it by using coolies. Ah, the sad darlin' never quite gets it right, somehow. He was always too grand for a simple soldier. He should have come to Mexico, laddie. He would have made a brave *caudillo.*"

The night was long and filled with reminiscences. Being with Dundalk put Aaron in mind of the raw boy he had been when first he had arrived in the United States. He remembered the letter he had written to Adriana at the nadir of his loneliness. He remembered her now, as he had then, riding across the fields of Santanilla in the hot Spanish sunlight, her bright hair like a banner in the wind.

"You look so sad, Aaron laddie," Dundalk said. "You are not a crying drunk, I trust. That's an Irish trick, weeping and dreaming of emerald Erin. Or is it our hoes and rakes that have you gloomy?"

That brought Aaron up sharply, aware of who he was now and where. For the rest of the night he remained uneasy in his mind, thinking of the dozens of cases of guns and ammunition stacked under the tin roof of the Trituradora, which was everything in the world that he could call his own.

His frame of mind did not improve in the morning as he watched Tihuacan girding itself for a patriotic celebration.

At ten he made his way in Colonel Dundalk's company to the Trituradora. The expellers were running. They were seldom allowed to stop because it took such effort to get the old ship's steam engine up to full power. The men who had agreed to work through the holiday were in a festive mood, and Aaron wondered if they had secreted bottles in the copra to help them celebrate the day. He hoped not, but it would have been a serious breach of trust for him to search the factory. Instead, he took Juan Ortega aside and cautioned him.

Ortega complained about the two dozen armed soldiers who paced about the grounds. "They get in the way, *mi Jefe,*" he said, "and they are insolent to the men."

"They are necessary, Juan. Until those crates in the warehouse are moved," Aaron said.

"*A sus órdenes,* Patron."

"Remember, Juan. The men are to stay sober. It is dangerous to be drunk around the machines."

"*Sí,* Patron."

The problem was that the *mestizos* who ran the machines considered it a reflection on their *machismo* when they were reminded of the incompatibility of tequila and whirling machinery. Nothing that Aaron had learned in Hessen, or even in Old Castile, had given him a formula for dealing with the pride of the Mexican laboring man. In the tiny fishing village of Acapulco, a thousand kilometers down the coast, young boys made a sport of diving from a two-hundred-meter rock cliff into the sea. It was considered *macho* to finish a liter of tequila before launching oneself into space.

The bivouac across the road from the Trituradora was lightly populated. General Díaz had ordered his officers to allow all soldiers not actually on duty guarding the horses and supplies to join the celebrations. The Cinco de Mayo was, after all, a soldier's holiday.

Colonel Dundalk inspected the guards and settled himself down in Aaron's office. "Here I stay, laddie," he said. "Alert and regimental. You can enjoy the fiesta with an easy mind."

As he left the factory to join Julia Marini and her father on the Malecón, Aaron told himself that all would be well. He would have been less worried had he not remembered that in his time at Frémont's headquarters, Sean Dundalk had been convinced that the sovereign remedy for the aftereffects of a night of drinking was, as he quaintly put it, "the hair of the dog that bit you."

The excitement and gaiety of the day was contagious, however, and by midday Aaron had begun to think that he had allowed himself to become overly concerned. The men of the Trituradora had managed to survive other fiestas without falling into the machinery, and the general's guns would surely be carefully watched by Dundalk and his men, who were, after all, professional soldiers.

The early part of the afternoon was spent with Julia and her father, promenading (along with all the other prominent citizens of Tihuacan) in open carriages to and fro on the Malecón. Young men and women, some accompanied by *mariachis,* formed two lines of traffic on the broad avenue, throwing confetti and serpentine at one another. Young bravos dressed in ornate, silver-laden *charro* outfits and mounted on the mettlesome horses that were a Mexican pride, galloped through the traffic with vaquero yells and an occasional fusillade from the silver-engraved, bone-handled revolvers they all carried. Aaron noted that a double file of federal soldiers had already formed around the reviewing stand, where later in the day General Díaz would be seated among the notables.

In the town squares, real *charros* in somewhat less fancy leather outfits danced *jarabes* with buxom girls wearing the brilliantly colored, flounce-skirted dresses known as *"vestido china poblana." Chinita* was the slang expression for a young girl. No one could explain to Aaron why this was so. Mexico was ripe with such mysteries to confound the European.

There was little of Spain in all this musical display, though from time to time the dancers would slip into movements and rhythms that touched a chord in Aaron's memory. For the most part the songs and dances were exclusively Mexican, with staccato sounds and stampings, intricate steps around the brim of a thrown sombrero, and the whole punctuated with enthusiastic yelps that reminded Aaron of nothing so much as the rebel yells of Confederate soldiers.

To Julia, who had lived in Tihuacan all her life, these scenes were familiar. Each year there were dozens of fiestas in the Mexican calendar, with the greatest of all Carnaval, the country-wide party to prepare for the austerity of Lent. But the Cinco de Mayo was a new celebration, intended to appeal to the strong Mexican sense of patriotism. She rode in the Marini carriage between Aaron and her father, her face flushed with excitement. Aaron lost himself in her laughter.

At three in the afternoon the Rurales began good-naturedly to attempt to clear the streets for the planned parade. By four-thirty they had just managed it. The carriages paused, each in turn, at the gaily decorated stand and the men descended, while the ladies dispersed to watch from the windows of the Hotel Belmar or the *corredores* of the houses along the Olas Altas. Most of them would even now begin preparing for the series of balls and dances to be given in the great houses, a process that could take a really dedicated *señorita* until nine, at which time the evening festivities would begin.

At five, leading the parade, General Porfirio Díaz appeared at the head of a detachment of cavalry and two polished companies of infantry. As he reached the stand where the businessmen of Tihuacan awaited him, he dismounted and accepted the plaudits of the throngs lining the streets. Then the soldiers were allowed to continue on to Cabo Sur, led by one of Díaz's colonels.

Behind the soldiers came marchers from the town, Rurales and costumed civilians, and at the tag end of the line of march, hordes of ragged, barefoot, excited street children waving homemade Mexican battle flags. The Rurales band had taken up a position across from the reviewing stand, and the noise was deafening.

As is customary with such things, Tihuacan's parade ran late, and so, therefore, did the speeches made by the vice-*alcalde* Don Mauricio Perez de Lebron, by Don Quintano Rivas, the local banker, by Don Marcello, and finally by General Díaz himself.

Sitting in the dusk illuminated by torches and lanterns, Aaron was not surprised to find that Porfirio Díaz was an orator of some dimensions. One did not succeed in Mexican politics without the ability to stir the emotions of crowds.

By seven in the evening, with only a rim of light remaining on the ocean horizon, the order was given to begin the pyrotechnic displays. One after another, rockets climbed into the air, to burst with a dazzling shower of multicolored fires. The townspeople shouted and applauded. Occasionally a particularly fine aerial explosion would draw a *diana* from the Rurales brass band: a short, brisk musical theme used by Mexicans to denote approval in the bullring.

For fully an hour and a half the fireworks continued to delight the Tihuacantecos. The bright flashes were reflected in the sea, dimming the waxing moon high in the sky. The pungent smell of burnt powder drifted over the town, reminding Aaron suddenly of the stench of the Wilderness.

Presently the men on the stand became aware of a disturbance among the people on the high backbone of Cabo Sur.

"Incendio! Incendio!"

The crowds began to run across the peninsula toward the harbor, where the cry of "Fire!" grew in volume. Concerned for the drums of oil ready to be loaded on the *Orizaba,* Aaron leapt from the stand and ran for the docks. When he reached the waterfront he could see that the entire roadstead was bright as dawn. The Chilean sailing ship filled with nitrates was alight and burning like a torch. Sheets of flame climbed the masts and rigging and towered five hundred feet into the sky, spewing sparks and burning debris.

In the red firelight Aaron was surprised to see that the Trituradora's shipment of oil drums on the concrete pier had been much reduced. A train of lighters moved across the water toward the *Orizaba,* which was brightly illuminated by its working lights. Somehow Captain Willard had managed to scrape together enough of a working crew of longshoremen to get the lading under way.

The Chilean ship was afire from stem to stern now in a holocaust of burning wood and chemicals. There was no knowing how the abandoned vessel had been set alight, but it roared with flames, a pillar of fire so intense it hurt the eyes. It seemed that everyone in Tihuacan was at the waterfront to watch the spectacular display, which made the fireworks of the celebration pale into insignificance.

"Los bomberos! Los bomberos vienen!" People took up the cry that the fire fighters of the town, with their hand-pumped engines, were trying to get through the crowd to the water's edge. It was a useless attempt.

The fire wagons were hopelessly hemmed in by the excited crowd. Even if they had been able to approach the waterfront, their equipment was totally inadequate to attack a blaze so far from the shore and so intense.

Nevertheless, Rurales and soldiers could be seen trying to clear a path for the firemen with shouts and an occasional blow.

Aaron retreated from the water's edge and walked up the slope of the small peninsula of Cabo Sur for a higher view. Women were chattering excitedly and barefoot children ran wild amid the stunted trees and straining spectators, their voices cracking with wonder at the grand sight in the harbor.

Aaron was happy to see that the burning derelict posed no threat to the *Orizaba* or the other ships in the anchorage. The still, windless evening made the sparks rise high in the air and fall in a wide but contained area around the burning ship.

Almost inadvertently, Aaron turned to look behind him, across the roofs of the town. He felt an iron hand close around his heart. To the southwest, between the outskirts of Tihuacan and the road south, another column of fire was rising into the night sky. Even as he watched, a deep explosion shocked the night, sending tiny spirals of white fire spinning.

The people around him turned now and began to shout and point. A fire in the harbor was an amusement. A fire in the town was a peril to them all. Aaron shoved his way through the milling people and began to run toward the Trituradora.

A crowd had gathered, blocking the streets, and when Aaron, sweat-drenched and dirty, pushed his way to the front it was only in time to see the steel framework of the warehouse, melted and collapsing, fall on the roaring inferno of burning oil and copra. The stench of this fire was pungent, like burning flesh. Someone shouted: "They are all out but one."

A series of sharp explosions drove the people back. There were screams from onlookers burned by fragments of hot metal. Through the blazing façade of the factory, Aaron could see the Number One expeller, its railroad-tie foundation burned away, crash over on its side. Through the office window, boxes and office machines were being thrown out onto the street. Aaron was horrified to see that there was a man still inside, rushing about to save the now-useless furnishings. It was Juan Ortega.

Aaron broke free of the crowd and yelled at the foreman to leave

260

it and come out. The roar of the fire drowned out the sound of his voice. Soldiers from the bivouac across the road were trying to push the people back, away from the heat. One shouted at Aaron, but he dodged around him and ran for the entrance to the factory building. It was like assaulting the open mouth of a blast furnace. Aaron was forced back by the searing heat of the flames. A soldier, guessing at what he was attempting to do, removed his blouse and tossed it to Aaron, who threw it over his head and ran under the open arch and into the office. The walls were blistering and papers scattered about the floor had begun to smolder. The roaring of the flames was deafening. The buttons on the soldier's blouse had grown too hot to touch.

Ortega, ruddy-faced from the heat and wild-eyed, mouthed, "Patron! Patron!" Aaron could not hear anything but the fire. Suddenly Ortega fell. He writhed in pain from the heat of the nearly ignited floor.

Aaron lifted him, feeling a stab of agony in his half-crippled left arm. He hoisted Ortega to his shoulder and stumbled out of the office. A wall of flame blotted out the rest of the building. There were more popping explosions from the pyre of the warehouse. A hot fragment struck Aaron on the forehead like the touch of a branding iron.

He stumbled out into the street, staggering under Juan Ortega's weight. Soldiers rushed forward to help him and guide him away from the fire.

Someone put a canteen of water to his lips, someone else wiped his face with a damp, hot cloth. In the brilliantly lighted night he saw a squad of Díaz's troopers standing with their rifles at the ready. A small man in white pajamas was digging a shallow trench in the earth. An officer was loading a revolver.

The reality of the situation hit Aaron like a fist. He struggled to his feet and approached the officer, a young, very angry *subteniente*. "What are you doing, for God's sake?"

The lieutenant said, "The others got away. This one we caught." He snapped the action of his revolver closed and said to the man in the trench. *"Basta, chingado!"*

The *peon*, eyes white in the firelight, dropped the entrenching tool he had been using.

The lieutenant shouted to his men, *"Buenos, muchachos! Apunten!"*

The men of the firing party formed a rank and raised their rifles.

"No, por Dios!" Aaron shouted. "Where is *el coronel* Dundalk?"

The lieutenant's expression was as hard and alien as the Sphinx. *"Quien sabe?"* he said, and turned his back on Aaron.

"Fuego!"

The bullets tattered the white pajamas, spattered black blood on the edges of the grave in the firelight.

Soldiers began to shovel earth on the executed man.

Aaron stumbled back to where helpful bystanders were bathing Juan Ortega's burns with cool water. The *capataz* looked up at Aaron with tears streaking the blistered grime on his face. "I am sorry, Patron," he sobbed. "I am sorry. I swear it, Patron, it was not the men. I swear it was not they."

Aaron knelt and put a hand on Ortega's shoulder. "It is all right, Juan. It is all right. We will begin again." Though God knew how, he thought, or when. Or with what.

He stood and looked across the field to where the soldiers had finished covering over the insurgent raider, and then back to the weeping Juan Ortega. One life lost, one life saved. He turned to look once more at the still fierce blaze of the Trituradora. Thank God the men had all got out in time. Or had they? Where was Dundalk?

He was suddenly too weary and despondent to think or do more. Rubbing aimlessly at his burned and aching arm, he pushed his way back through the crowd and down the narrow street, still ruddy with firelight, toward his own house.

Maria Macías met him at the street door with tears in her eyes and anger in her voice. "I heard, Patron. I heard that the Lerdistas fired the Trituradora. May God curse them and all their children." She ushered him solicitously into her kitchen, where he was seldom welcome, and sat him down to wash the grime from his face.

"It wasn't Lerdistas, Maria," he said wearily. "It was a little *peon,* not so tall as you."

"Whoever they were," Maria said, wiping gently at his scorched forehead and cheeks with a cloth wet with olive oil, "may they swim in *mierda* for all eternity. *Ay,* Patron, your beautiful, white skin. And you have a cut just here, above your eye." She finished her rough *soldadera*'s first aid and produced a bottle of *aguardiente.* "You need a *copita,* Patron. A little drink makes all the world look better."

At the moment, Aaron thought grimly, it could hardly look worse. God damn Díaz and his guns. The thought of the Trituradora, to which he had devoted so much time and such effort, a smoldering ruin made him sick at heart.

He was suddenly struck by something Maria Macías had said.

"Maria," he said. "How did you know about the Trituradora?

There hasn't been time for the news to spread. How did you know it had been set afire?''

The big woman stood, hands clasped beneath her apron, eyes downcast. "Patron," she said apologetically. "I swear I did not seek to deceive you. I would have told you as soon as you were rested."

"Told me *what*, Maria?" He stood, still unsteady but very angry. "Where is he? *Where*, Maria?"

"Ah, laddie. Here. Here am I, and totally at your mercy." Dundalk stood in the doorway to the *corredor*, his face as scorched as Aaron's, his uniform coat ripped and tattered, his right hand bound—by Maria, Aaron had no doubt—and resting in a sling.

"What happened?" Aaron shouted furiously. "Where were your Goddamned soldiers? Where were *you*? Were you drunk?"

"Aaron, lad, for the Lord's sweet sake. Don't lose your temper." The brogue in Dundalk's speech rasped across Aaron's nerve endings like a knife's edge.

"You *were* drunk, you stupid man. You got drunk and let your soldiers do the same."

"Please, laddie. I am sorrier than I can say."

"Sorry? You're *sorry*? You've beggared me, you worthless piece of shit, and damned near killed Juan Ortega. What *happened?*"

Dundalk lowered himself into a chair like a man in pain. "It was the Lerdistas—"

"Don't lie to me, you bastard."

"Well, yes. It was the mother-raping insurgents, laddie. Who would have thought it of them? You told me they were not active hereabouts. You did, you remember. Well, there were a dozen of them, maybe more. They sent someone to make a diversion in the harbor. We could see it from the street, and everyone was rather careless because there had been some drinking. Some, I said, laddie. Your people as well as the soldiers. That Ortega fellow tried to keep your workmen sober, but he didn't have much luck with them—"

"Or with you, *Colonel*," Aaron said bitterly.

"Aye, I must admit to that. Well anyway, laddie, when the fire started in the harbor and we heard the *bomberos* heading in that direction, all of your people ran to see what was happening. And so did some of my soldiers. I tried to stop them. I swear I tried. But you know what discipline is among these people." He glanced guiltily at Maria, but she gave no sign of understanding English.

"And who obeys a drunken colonel in any army?" Aaron asked.

"Believe me, laddie. You can't say anything one-half so harsh as

263

I have already said to myself. But there it is. No sooner had most of my soldiers run off than I really began to worry—"

"Did you, now? Did you really? How professional of you."

"I set out for the bivouac to get some people to take my company's place, and that's when they hit us. Ten or so black bastards in white pajamas. I didn't think even then they were anybody but some *peones* come down from the hills to get a skinful at the fiesta." He looked longingly at Maria Macías and she poured him a glass of aguardiente. Aaron back-handed it furiously against the wall.

"You're quite right, Aaron. You were right to do that."

"Get on with it," Aaron said in a steely voice.

"Well, there's little more, and that's a fact. They weren't even armed, so how could I know? Think on it, laddie. How could I guess? They came running out of the dark with cigars in their hands, and before I knew what they were about they had sticks of dynamite out of their pockets, lit, and away into the oil storage and the mother-raping copra. The place was a torch in less than a minute."

"And so you ran away."

"What could I accomplish by staying? Some of the officers from the bivouac were charging in, but it was too late by then. The general's precious rakes and hoes were going up like a houseful of Roman candles. Those young tigers of the general's were very angry, laddie. So, yes. I ran."

"And you came here. You should have thought it over. Have you considered the possibility that I might just shoot you?"

"Well, I did think on that, laddie. Actually, I didn't believe you would. But the general will certainly shoot me if I can't get away. There won't be a court-martial, nothing so grand. Just a hole in the ground and a bullet or two in the head. They do that, you know."

"Yes, I know. I saw them do it to the one man they caught."

"You have to help me, laddie." He looked up at Maria, who stood like a carving, still holding the bottle of *aguardiente* and another glass. "*She* knows," Sean Dundalk said. "Look at her. She's been a soldier in this country. She knows, laddie."

"My God," Aaron said. "You bloody man."

"I'm asking you, Aaron. As a former comrade in arms, I am begging you to help me get away. You can't let Díaz find me. He's a fair man, laddie, as fair men go down here. But he'll have me shot as an example to his officers, I promise you. No one will lift a finger to help me, either. *Gringos* are expendable here."

"You're no *gringo*," Aaron said automatically.

"*Gringo,* Irish, the same damned thing or as near as makes no difference. In God's name, help me."

"Be still for a minute," Aaron said. With only the slightest encouragement he could gladly turn this drunken fool over to General Díaz and let matters take their natural course. But he realized that he could not do that.

"The *Orizaba* is still in the harbor," he said.

"She won't sail for a full day, laddie. That's the first place they'll look for me."

"No. Willard found workmen somewhere. He was almost loaded when the fire started on the sailing ship. Willard's a cautious man. He knew something was in the wind. He could smell it," Aaron said. "If he hasn't gone yet, he'll sail on the next tide."

Dundalk caught Aaron's arm with his unburned hand, making Aaron wince with pain. Dundalk was too frightened to be aware. "Ah, laddie. Get me on that ship. Get me on that beautiful ship. I don't care where she's going. To Japan or to the moon. Just get me on board her, I beg you."

"Nothing so exotic," Aaron said. "She sails for San Francisco."

"Heaven," Dundalk said.

"I have no money to give you," Aaron said.

"I'll sell my broad back to Willard for passage. God help me, I'll sell him my backside, if that's his taste. Just get me out to his ship."

"I'll try," Aaron said. "I should kill you myself, but I'll try. Come."

"What, now?"

"This minute, you awful man. The Federales must be searching the town for you. It won't take them long to think of coming here." Aaron turned to Maria and explained what he planned to do.

"That is brave and honorable," she said stoically. "And to be expected. *El coronel* says that you were a true soldier." She poured *aguardiente* and offered a glass to each man. This time Aaron allowed Sean Dundalk to drink it.

They walked through the dark streets, still astir from the night's excitement even though it was approaching the hour of dawn. Aaron carried the *aguardiente* bottle by the neck and managed to walk a path that was not quite straight. Once they encountered a pair of Rurales, but they were as drunk as Aaron and Dundalk pretended to be. And near the waterfront they hid in a narrow alley to avoid a squad of soldiers searching the side streets.

265

They reached the water's edge and Dundalk looked out over the dark harbor searching for the *Orizaba*. "Be there," he breathed. "Oh, be there, Holy Mother of God."

The anchor lamp on the *Orizaba*'s foremast made a shimmering train of beads on the harbor's surface. The moon was down and the early morning constellations were brilliant in the clear sky. Listening, the two men could hear the unmistakable sound of a donkey engine on board the ship, and the slow clank of iron links. The *Orizaba* was raising her anchor and getting ready for sea.

Aaron ran down the stone steps to the fishing dock, where a boatman always slept to discourage theft of his boats. He shook the man awake. It was a fellow with whom he had gone fishing for marlin and *sierra*. They had caught nothing. Aaron hoped that his luck would be better this morning.

"Don Aaron," the man said sleepily. "*Que pasa,* Patron?"

"I need to go out to the *Orizaba, viejo.* Right now, before she makes for sea."

The old boatman moved with amazing speed for one so fresh from sleep on the stone pier. Aaron signaled Sean Dundalk to join him. They clambered into the skiff and the old man shoved off and steadily began to row.

"Shall we not help him row, laddie?" Dundalk said, shivering— though the night was warm.

"Shut up, Sean. Don't talk," Aaron said.

Ahead of them they could hear the splashing as the *Orizaba*'s hook came clear of the sea. A faint opalescence had begun to form in the east over the Sierra Morenas.

Aaron hailed the ship. "Ahoy, *Orizaba!* It is Aaron Marburg. Call Captain Willard."

Willard's voice came down from the bridge. "Is that you, Mr. Marburg?"

"I have a passenger for you, Captain."

Willard gave a short, hard bark of a laugh. "Is he legal or not?"

"You can talk about that at sea. It's Colonel Dundalk."

"Put him aboard, sir, if he can pay." The men in the skiff heard the rattle of a wood and rope ladder on the side of the ship. The great single screw turned lazily, not yet committed to driving the ship.

"He'll take it out of your hide," Aaron said.

"Ah, laddie. A soldier always keeps a few gold *pesos* about his person in case of need. Willard won't be out of pocket."

The skiff bumped against the rough steel of the *Orizaba*'s hull. Her pumps were running; a rank bilgewater cascaded from an outlet above the waterline. A fine mist of coal dust from the stack settled on the water around the ship in the windless morning.

Dundalk seized the rope ladder and swung himself onto the lowest rung. "Aaron," he said emotionally, "I thank you, laddie, from the bottom of my useless Irish heart. I owe you my skin, and I won't ever forget it."

"*Adios,* you terrible man," Aaron said. "Go with God." He pushed the skiff off and the old boatman began to row. He asked quietly, *"Es fugo el coronel?"* Is the colonel a fugitive? The realities of life in this land were not the exclusive domain of the propertied classes, Aaron thought. The poor said little, but they watched and understood. And then, as the boatman rowed steadily for the shore and the *Orizaba,* white froth under her stern, moved out of the harbor of Tihuacan, Aaron thought: The poor? Who could be poorer than he? What property did he own now, save a pile of rank ashes and twisted metal? He had come a very long way to be a pauper in a foreign land.

What now, Aaron Marburg? he asked himself. Whatever now?

His answer took the form of a squad of Federales and a dark-faced officer standing on the dock as he stepped ashore. The lieutenant studied him carefully in the twilight of dawn.

"Señor Marburg?"

"Yes."

"You are to come with us."

He was escorted, not to the *cárcel,* as he had expected, but through the litter of yesterday's celebrations to the Hotel Belmar.

The lobby, built around an open patio where broad-leafed plants grew, was thronged with soldiers. Aaron was passed along to a stocky major who led the way up the pink marble stairs to the second story. There were more soldiers here, and they regarded Aaron curiously as the major rapped once on a door and then opened it. "Go in, *señor,*" he said, and closed the door behind Aaron.

He found himself in the *sala* of the Belmar's only suite. Seated on the antique davenport were Don Marcello Marini and Porfirio Díaz.

Don Marcello showed the effects of a sleepless night, but Díaz looked fresh, clean-shaven, his drooping moustache neatly trimmed, his dark, short hair gleaming with oil.

Aaron tried to read Don Marcello's expression but he could not. The Genoese's face was composed, noncommittal.

Díaz said, "You have had a loss, Don Aaron."

"Yes, *mi general,*" Aaron said carefully.

"I am sorry for that. But we live in dangerous times."

"Yes," Aaron said, feeling suddenly very weary.

"Please. Sit," the general said.

Aaron collapsed into a chair. Don Marcello still did not speak.

Díaz said, almost gently, "My aide, *el coronel* Dundalk. Where might he be, Don Aaron? On the *Orizaba?*"

"Yes, *mi general.*"

The black *mestizo* eyes glittered dangerously.

"You assisted him to desert."

"Yes," Aaron said. It would be pointless to dissemble.

Díaz said, "I would have had him shot, Don Aaron. He deserved no less."

"I know, General."

For the first time General Díaz addressed himself to Don Marcello. "The loyalty of a former comrade in arms, *amigo.* What is one to do?" Before Marcello Marini could reply, Díaz turned back to Aaron. "Well. Dundalk owes you his life. I hope he knows it and remembers."

Aaron felt a loosening of inner tension. Then Díaz did not intend to send a boat after the *Orizaba.*

"I too am in your debt, Don Aaron," Díaz said. "It was a mistake to store my weapons in your factory. It may even have been a mistake to bring them into the country. It appears that my time is not yet."

"It will come, Don Porfirio," Don Marcello said.

"Oh, be certain of that, my friend," Díaz said. "But I have been responsible for the destruction of Don Aaron's property. What shall we say to him about that, Don Marcello?"

"Money is to be used, *mi general.* We both believe in that simple truth," Don Marcello said. "Agreed?"

"Agreed," Díaz said. He fixed Aaron with his intense and level gaze. "The loss of the Trituradora is not only your loss, Don Aaron. It is Tihuacan's and Mexico's loss as well. This country needs industry and progress as much as it needs order."

Aaron kept a puzzled silence. Was it possible that the general meant what he seemed to mean?

To Don Marcello, Díaz said, "I will leave you to conclude our business with Don Aaron." He stood and walked to the door. He turned and looked back. "I hope, *señor,* that if the need ever arises, you will be as loyal to me as you have been to Colonel Dundalk."

When he had gone, Don Marcello said, "You are either a very brave man, *hijo,* or a very foolish one. But whichever it is, you are certainly a *lucky* man." He stood and went to the window which over-looked the Olas Altas and the beach.

"The factory," he said. "It is a total loss?"

"Total," Aaron said.

"Well, no matter. You must rebuild. There must be a new Trituradora, with the best of everything."

"I am beggared, Don Marcello," Aaron said.

"You are no such thing. Will you make a partnership with me, Aaron? And with him?"

"With Díaz?"

"He will be president one day. He is already a rich man. He will be much, much richer."

Aaron felt his pulse quicken. To have Porfirio Díaz as a silent partner in any enterprise in Mexico might be risky. Politicians could rise and fall in this country with stunning quickness. But somehow it was hard to believe that General Díaz would fall. He was too swift to correct his mistakes, too willing to take whatever action must be taken to succeed.

"We will make a partnership, Aaron," Don Marcello said. "I—and he—will supply what money is needed. He means it when he says that Mexico needs the Trituradora. The country needs many new things. Factories and railroads and businesses of all kinds. Will you make a pact with us?"

Aaron was at a loss. He had not expected this.

"For my daughter, Aaron?" Don Marcello said with a smile. "I can't have Julia wed to a poor man. Do you agree?"

"It will take a year, perhaps two, to rebuild the Trituradora," Aaron said.

"With capital all things are possible, *hijo*. First the site will be cleaned. Then more land will be purchased. Then you must go to Germany to buy the latest machines, new engines—those diesels that are all the rage. The Trituradora can be bigger and more efficient than ever before. And when all that is done, we will sit down and have a serious talk about Julia's future. I promise you, my son. One day you will be a very rich man, and a happy one."

Images of the future crowded Aaron's mind. A new beginning with powerful friends. Julia. A real life.

And Europe. He would travel to Hessen to see Uncle Isaac. To Hamburg and Cologne to buy the new machines.

And he would see Santanilla again. Surely he owed Don Alvaro Santana that. He saw in his mind a golden woman in the bright Castilian sun. What harm now, he thought, what harm can there be in seeing Adriana just one more time?

"Done," he said. "Done, Don Alvaro," and he extended his hand to confirm his bargain.

30

One effect of the fire at the
Trituradora that Aaron could not have foreseen was the nightmares.
They began on the night of the first day he spent among the workmen
clearing the burned-over site, and for a month became steadily worse.

Returning home after dark, grimy and with the stench of the
burning still in his nostrils, he would fall exhausted into bed. But sleep
brought no rest. He would find himself once again in the smoky hell
of the Wilderness, with the cries of the dying all around him and the
bitter odor of spent gunpowder gagging him. He would awaken in a
cold sweat, shaking and on the verge of tears. Sometimes his cries
would awaken Maria Macías, and with a veteran's sympathy she would
appear at his bedside with her own patent nostrum for the soldier's
horrors, hot coffee laced with *aguardiente.*

The actual work progressed with an efficiency that was unusual in
Tihuacan. The entire labor force of the Trituradora was put to work

with picks and shovels, and drays were engaged to haul the blackened hulks of the expellers and the remnants of the old steam engine to a scrap-metal dump newly established on the edge of one of the lagoons south of the town. The twisted, half-melted metal parts of the general's rifles and the empty shell casings were all retrieved and hauled to the harbor, where they were loaded onto lighters and sunk in deep water. This part of the work was done under the close supervision of a picked company of Porfirista soldiers Díaz had left behind when he moved his brigade inland.

According to the *Prensa Libre,* Díaz was preparing for the coming national elections of 1871 by gathering under his command all the elements of the army left unsatisfied by the centrist policies of President Juárez. The right-wing *El Diario* reported a speech made by Díaz in Durango, in which the general denounced President Juárez's intention to seek reelection as a direct violation of the Constitution of 1857. "A man who was once the pillar of constitutional liberalism," the general was quoted as saying, "has become prey to the myth of indispensability and the sinful desire for power." Even Sebastian Lerdo was reported to be forming a *partido* to promote his own candidacy for president, using as an excuse the same accusations as Díaz. The country began to prepare for a violently contested election in 1871.

At Julia's insistence, and because he seemed unable to throw off the aftereffects of the fire, Aaron put Juan Ortega in charge of the work on the Trituradora site. He limited himself to a single daily visit to see to it that the work was being conducted in accordance with the plans drawn by John Steinhart, a dour American mechanical engineer imported from the north to create a copra processing plant of the latest and most efficient design.

Steinhart disliked Mexico, loathed the climate and the food (which kept him in a constant state of gastric upset), and he was soon gone back to California, leaving behind him an elegant set of blueprints to guide the workmen when the new construction began.

With the coming of the *tiempo de calor* and the *chubasco* of late summer, the work slackened, though it never completely ceased except on those occasions when the edges of a Pacific typhoon lashed Tihuacan with heavy rains and seventy-mile-an-hour winds.

A new *sociedad anónima,* a corporation, had been formed with Don Marcello and Aaron as the principal shareholders and Porfirio Díaz a silent partner. The articles of incorporation were written loosely enough to allow Trituradora-Fénix, S.A. (the addition of the word phoenix had been Julia's suggestion) to expand into other enterprises as opportunity presented itself. The merchants of Tihuacan and the local politicians were delighted, convinced that this was the beginning of a trend to make Tihuacan the industrial center of the west coast.

As the year waned Aaron found that the nightmares grew less frequent, though from time to time he still dreamed of the executed *campesino*'s spattered blood, black in the firelight.

But as the aftereffects of the fire faded, other strains and pressures began to tell on Aaron. His new arrangement with Don Marcello was amicable but increasingly demanding. The Genoese was a successful man of business and enormously ambitious for himself and for his daughter. Moreover, as the person who was contributing most of the capital for the new venture, he was proud and possessive not only of the Trituradora-Fénix, but of Aaron Marburg, whom he now regarded as a son-in-law in all but name.

Don Marcello had begun to make plans regarding Aaron and Julia's marriage. On several occasions he had pressed Aaron to commit himself to an enormous wedding in the cathedral of Tihuacan immediately upon Aaron's return from his projected trip to Europe. Julia, who was totally at home with her father's ways, remained silent on the subject, but Aaron grew acutely aware that she was patiently waiting for him to speak to her directly. Had he not allowed himself to become so completely beholden to the Marinis, Aaron might simply have done what was obviously expected of him. But having escaped, nine years before, absorption into the Santana clan, he found it hard to accept now the requirement that he become a Marini—and on essentially the same terms as before.

His planned visits to Hessen, to see his Uncle Isaac and the Marburg cousins, and to Santanilla, to see the Santanas, began to take on deep and emotional meaning.

Julia's quiet assumption that he would be baptized and marry her awaited his confirmation. He could delay it until his return from abroad, but not one day longer.

In September came the news of the French defeat at Sedan and the end of the Franco-Prussian War, and with that the last reason for delay of his journey vanished.

With Julia an interested onlooker, he began to plan the voyage. It was a complicated business; Tihuacan was isolated from the rest of Mexico by the Sierra Morena mountains and from the west coast of the United States by fifteen hundred kilometers of nearly impassable roads. Aaron arranged, therefore, to embark on the *Orizaba* or one of the

273

other freighters that called at Tihuacan, and journey by sea to San Francisco—a week's voyage if sea conditions were good, half again that long if they were not. Then from Oakland, on the eastern shore of San Francisco Bay, he would board a Central Pacific train for New York. There he would embark once again on a steamer, a passenger vessel this time, for the Atlantic crossing to Hamburg.

To accomplish the business needed to reequip the Trituradora-Fénix with the machinery called for in Steinhart's impressive plans would require a stay in Germany of thirty to sixty days. It was impossible to judge the time required more accurately than that.

In all, he would be absent from Tihuacan for six months or more, and he knew that he could not in conscience remain away from Julia so long without doing her the courtesy of assuring her that upon his return, all would be as both she and her father assumed it would be.

Yet as September became October and then November, he had not done so. The commitment, he told himself, was *made*. But he could not bring himself to acknowledge it, and the sense of finding himself trapped by circumstances of his own making grew.

It annoyed and discomfited him that he was both eager and reluctant to return to Europe. His innate sense of order was outraged by ambivalence of any sort. To discover it in himself was almost more than he could endure.

Here in Tihuacan was a life, one he intended to live for the remainder of his days. Yet the time was swiftly approaching when he must face—wanted most desperately to face—what remained of that other life he had left behind him. And at the center of that other life stood Adriana.

Julia and his friends sensed his tension and did their best to ignore it. But they could not, or would not, avoid an occasional gentle reminder that Aaron appeared, at least, to have made a choice about his future, and that he must acknowledge that he had done so. Occasionally these reminders were couched in ironic, even humorous, terms.

Dr. Juan Amaya-Ruiz and Aaron came often to Don Marcello's house during the hours of siesta, when all business in Tihuacan came to a halt. Don Marcello did not play chess, but, always the collector, he had acquired a magnificent ivory and silver set of Italian chessmen, and he liked to have Aaron and the doctor use them while he retired from one until three in the afternoon.

At these times Julia contrived always to be present, pretending she wished to learn the game from the doctor, who was an expert. She was, in fact, too active and impatient for chess, and simply used the time to be near Aaron. On this afternoon, handsome in yellow batiste, she moved among the hydrangea bushes planted in stone urns under the arches of the *corredor,* cutting blooms to float in water-filled dishes in other parts of the house.

In seemingly idle talk, the subject arose of the first true Mexican *caudillo,* General Antonio López de Santa Anna.

Aaron moved a chessman and said, "All that I know of Santa Anna is that he fought the Americans at the Alamo and managed to lose Texas."

Julia came and sat on the arm of Aaron's chair. "There is a great deal more to him than that," she said.

Juan Amaya studied Aaron's move and said with a laugh, "Indeed there is, Aaron my friend. A great deal more. Shall we tell him, *señorita?"*

Julia looked reprovingly at Amaya. "He was a very great patriot, Doctor."

"He most certainly was that. But odd. A foreigner would find him odd. You agree?"

Julia suppressed a rueful smile. "Well, yes. A foreigner might think him odd."

"Bueno pues. The odd patriot," Amaya said, making his move. He addressed himself to Aaron. "Santa Anna began his career at the age of sixteen as a subaltern in the royal army in the early years of this century. He was *criollo,* very aristocratic. But very *Mexican.* And not an intellectual or a scholar. We can safely say that, *señorita?"*

"If you think it pertinent, Doctor," Julia said primly.

"At the age of twenty-seven he was aide-de-camp to the Viceroy Apodaca in Mexico City. A great honor, even for one so well born as Santa Anna," Amaya said. His finger rested on the silver crest of a knight mounted on an ivory charger. "But when our first great liberator, Miguel Hidalgo y Costilla—we have had many great liberators in Mexico, my friend—when Hidalgo rebelled against the Spanish crown, he had as allies Augustín Iturbide—he of Señorita Julia's golden coin —*and* Antonio López de Santa Anna, who had turned his coat against the crown."

Julia touched the coin and said, "Then Augustín declared a Mexican empire and himself an emperor. And Santa Anna rebelled against *him* and declared for a republic."

"I am growing dazzled," Aaron said.

"So you should be," said Julia. "In those days General Santa Anna was very progressive."

The doctor abandoned the silver-helmeted knight and took a *ciga-*

rillo from a handsome silver case. He looked inquisitively at Julia. *"Permiso?"*

Julia gave him permission to smoke and he struck a match. "Under a compact known as the Plan de Casa Mata—named for the place where it was conceived—Santa Anna led the forces of the new republic against Iturbide and defeated him. There were a number of minor troubles after that, but in 1833 there was an election by the legislatures of the states and Santa Anna was made president. It was then he began to become—" He looked at Julia over the flame. "Odd?"

"Odd," Julia said with a sigh.

"For the first time in his career, the great cavalier could not gallop about the country fighting battles and deposing emperors. He was asked to stay in the capital and work. He did not like the sort of work he was given. Indeed he did not. But being Mexican as well as president, he solved his problem by allowing the vice-president, Gómez Fárias, to run the nation while he himself returned to his family hacienda in Vera Cruz to do whatever it is that great cavaliers do when they are not fighting battles and accepting twenty-one-gun salutes."

"Gómez Fárias was an evil politician—" Julia began.

"Another liberator," Amaya said dryly.

Julia's green eyes flashed her disapproval of the comment. "Hardly that, Doctor. Fárias took advantage of his position to attack the Church. He closed the University of Mexico because the faculty consisted mostly of learned priests. True, Doctor?"

"Absolutely true, *señorita*," Amaya said.

Julia went on. "He passed laws declaring that the clergy could make no political comments from the pulpits. He expropriated Church treasuries. What was Santa Anna to do?"

"Become president again?" asked Aaron.

"Of course."

"And then he lost Texas?"

"Oh, the *yanquis* had already stolen Texas," Julia said. "There came a war with the French."

"The *first* war with the French," Amaya said. "There have been several. This one took place because Louis Philippe demanded special trading concessions and sent a naval squadron to make his point. We Mexicans do not respond well to threats, Aaron. The Congress in Mexico City promptly declared war on the French, who were ill-mannered enough to show their resentment by bombarding the fortress of Vera Cruz and occupying the town. Santa Anna led a Mexican army to

Vera Cruz and drove the French away. That was the *first* time we learned that the French do not wear well."

Dr. Amaya-Ruiz, rumored to have served with the French-backed imperialist forces in the last war, might have good reason to know whereof he spoke when he accused the French of a lack of stamina.

"It was in that engagement that General Santa Anna lost The Leg." The word was so clearly capitalized that Aaron repeated it.

"The Leg?"

Julia was smiling and so was Amaya.

"Indeed, *amigo*. There you have it. The oddest oddment of all. A French cannonball killed the general's horse and took off his leg above the knee. He recovered with astonishing swiftness, but The Leg, alas, had to be sent to his estate, Manga de Clavo, to be interred. Temporarily."

"Temporarily?"

Juan Amaya-Ruiz blew a series of perfect smoke rings. "The general-president then returned to Mexico City, where he established a *caudillato* of such magnificence—and such corruption—that it remains to this day a model for any government wishing to enrich its adherents at the expense of the nation."

"But The Leg, Juan."

"Ah," Amaya said. "The Leg."

Julia's laughter was infectious. Aaron, smiling perplexedly, said, "Go on."

"Perhaps, Señorita Julia," Amaya said, "because we are truly Mexican and still mourn the loss of Texas, we are being unfair to the general-president. It may be that the affair of The Leg was not, after all, odd, but rather a seeking after lost grandeur."

"That may be so, Doctor," Julia said seriously. "I am certainly prepared to believe that."

"The *Leg*, if you please?" Aaron said.

"Well," Amaya said, studying the tip of his *cigarillo*, "in 1842, after the general-president's unfortunate member had been in the earth at Mango de Clavo for five years—dry years, I hope—it was dug up and transported to Mexico City in great state, where, after a parade and a *Te Deum* in the cathedral, it was reentombed with full military honors in the cemetery of Santa Fe. The procession and the ceremony were attended by the presidential guard, units of the army, the entire cabinet, the diplomatic corps, the cadets of the Chapultepec Military Academy, and the Congress."

"There were speeches, many speeches, songs written for the occasion, and, I understand, poems," Julia said.

"The man was mad," Aaron said.

"Ah, no," Amaya-Ruiz said. "The man was *Mexican,* my foreign friend. The history of Mexico can be truly understood only by Mexicans." He lifted a silver-mitred bishop. "When you are truly one of us, you will know." He placed the bishop next to Aaron's king and said, "Mate."

At two o'clock of a blustery, cold December day, Adriana and her father followed the path down from the Cantabricas toward Santanilla. Don Alvaro rode his aged stallion, a rangy English thoroughbred for which he had given, eighteen years before, the price of a thousand lambs. The stud was gray around the muzzle and carried less weight than he once did, but the proximity of Adriana's mare, Estrella, still made him snort and prance as he negotiated the muddy ground between the down-sloping range and the freshet of icy water dividing two pastures.

It had taken enormous effort for Adriana to entice her father into riding with her this cold and windy day, but she had resolved that El Patron simply must be lured from his endless—and useless—labors amid old documents in the observatory.

Don Alvaro would be seventy in three months, and though he was still a large man, his riding clothes hung on him loosely and there was about him the same slackness of flesh displayed by his mount. Man and horse, Adriana thought sadly, showed the ravages of time.

Yet today, riding through the near mountains with his daughter, Don Alvaro had shown more animation than he had for months. Several times he had urged Espada, his stud, to break into long, loping gallops, scattering the herds of sheep through which they rode and eliciting cries of greeting and cheers from the Santanilla shepherds.

Most of the livestock on the estate no longer belonged to the Santanas. Adriana, with Julio's acquiescence, had managed to lease sufficient pasturage to buy feed for the few Santana animals when deep winter arrived, as it seemed about to do. Adriana had discussed the transactions with her father, but today as they rode through the white-fleeced flocks parting like a turbulent sea before them, the real mistress of Santanilla was unsure whether El Patron understood that the bleating herds belonged to others.

It hardly mattered. What was of concern to Adriana was that her father was up and out of the musty observatory, taking in the snow-promising air and showing more animation that he had since Santiago died. El Patron must stay strong and alert enough to make the journey to California when the time came, Adriana thought. It could not take place soon, because it required a large sum of money—money Adriana was accumulating with a single-mindedness that would have done credit to a Chole Segre. But soon or late, Adriana was resolved that it would be done, and Don Alvaro must be physically as well as mentally prepared to leave these ancestral lands for a new life in a new place. Sebastio had lived actively until his eightieth year, she thought. Surely a Santana could do as well.

El Patron reined in and turned to look behind him at the looming Cantabricas. The wind that blew down the slopes carried an ancient, glacial cold. There were caves in those mountains, caverns upon whose walls Celtiberians in wolfskins had painted woolly mammoths in colors that still glowed in the light of a seeker's lantern. As a boy Don Alvaro remembered sifting through the dirt of cavern floors, searching for flaked flints and reindeer-bone needles. It had always fascinated him to know that this land had been the home of men for ten thousand years before his own ancestors had come down from the north on shaggy ponies and carrying black iron swords.

Today he felt better and stronger than he had for a very long time. The icy air was bracing. The lively movements of the old stallion between his thighs made his blood quicken. He watched his daughter, seated near him on her mare—the same mare he had given to young

Aaron ten years ago, when she was a three-year-old filly and all the world was very much younger. The thought of Aaron Marburg brought a momentary frown and a sadness and quick, septuagenarian tears. He brushed his eyes with a gloved hand. It was a bad thing, he thought, to have sent the boy away because of that wretched Paredes girl. He had heard somewhere that she was now dead, killed by a lover, that parvenu Guardia person who had come once to La Casa. Or was it someone else the foolish man had killed? The memory fell into that middle ground between yesterday and very long ago that was so irritatingly difficult for an old man to recall. Well, what did it matter? *Las Parcas nos mandan.* And a stupid, bad job they did of it, too.

He touched Espada's ribs with his boot heels. Once he had whipped a groom for using spurs on Espada. He remembered that well enough, and enjoyed the memory.

The old stallion fell in beside Adriana's star-faced Estrella, nipping at her neck as though he were still master of a harem of lusty mares.

"Here, control your old *macho,* Papa," Adriana said. "He has the manners of the breeding barn."

Alvaro Santana laughed aloud and leaned in the saddle to touch his daughter's cheek. What a beautiful woman she was, he thought. How did tiny, dark Maria and I produce such a *dorada,* a golden one? He regarded Adriana with admiration and love.

On slack reins Espada and Estrella picked their way along the track toward the hacienda. Adriana, watching her father, felt once again the old warmth and companionship. Today had been good for him. He had always been an active man, with a real need for the sun, even the cold sun of winter, and the wind and the smell of his proud Spanish earth. She resolved that from this day forward she would insist that he ride with her at least once each week.

Even his old obsession with politics had reappeared today. The anti-Carlist in him had been stirred by the news—late, at Santanilla, as all news was—that his old enemies had sought to take advantage of the abdication of the queen, Isabella, in favor of her twelve-year-old son Alfonso. They had scraped together a force (it would have been presumptuous to call it an army) and lost a battle at Oroquista.

The new king's youth had, as usual, attracted the customary stew of European royal pretenders. One had arrived in Madrid, a son of Victor Emmanuel II of Savoy, calling himself—rather grandly, Adriana thought—Amadeo I. Don Alvaro's comments that morning had been worthy of a far younger and lustier man. "Republicanism is on the rise," he had said with a vigor reminiscent of earlier days. "I give this

Savoyard intruder a year, maybe two, before the Cortes comes to its senses and declares a Spanish Republic."

Recently Adriana had had no time for thinking about the complex patterns of Spanish politics, but it pleased her to realize that her father had been reading the torrent of European newspapers that were still delivered to the observatory each time a post rider came to Santanilla. It gave her reason to hope that once she could begin to implement her new plan for the family, the old man would be ready to take part in it.

She had come to an agreement with Julio over the distribution of Santana property. She had even begun to feel a certain grudging regard for his gypsy paramour. Chole Segre was, at this moment, hugely and unashamedly pregnant. Within the month there would be a new Santana bastard. Adriana still bridled at the thought of her brother contemplating marriage to a gypsy, but in all honesty she had to admit that Soledad seemed to have no particular desire to marry him. At least, Adriana thought likely, not until he was well and truly confirmed by the family as hacendado of Santanilla. That she was about to bear an illegitimate child appeared to trouble Chole Segre not at all. She bore her burden—and carried her belly—with a total disregard for the disapproving looks of Doña Maria and the servants.

Tomasa and Felicia were convinced that Chole's child was the work of the devil and would be born with horns and a tail. Doña Maria told them tartly that if it were a male, it would be born with only one horn, the one between its legs, with which it would plant as much trouble as its father had with his own.

Doña Maria, in her sixtieth year, prowled the deteriorating grandeur of Santanilla clucking her disapproval. Moving her to California, Adriana thought, would not be as difficult as she had once believed it might be. The hacendada maintained her starchy standards within the household, tyrannizing the servants as she had always done, overseeing the care of the children with particular emphasis on the education of her grandson Roberto as a true caballero and her granddaughter as a potential religious. But she had ceased to bridle over the constant presence of Chole Segre's gypsy friends and relations, from time to time even unbending enough to doctor their sick children. "To make certain they do not bring some child's plague to Santanilla," she said.

Doña Maria had once again begun to cultivate the friendship of the Alvarez family of Miraflores, loftily ignoring Don Silvio's background as a tradesman. This very day the Alvarez children had arrived for a three-day visit, and Roberto was beside himself with the excitement of their company. As Adriana and her father had ridden out in the dawn, Roberto had already mustered the children, including Ana-Maria, his sister Cecilia, and Maria-Elena Alvarez (a dark doll of a child of nine), into a children's quadrilla for the *tienta* at Julio's Folly (the family's private name for the bullring and paddocks in the north pasture).

The white, wintry sun was high as Adriana and her father approached the hacienda. By now, Adriana guessed, Julio would have his customary ragged troop of gypsy boys out caping his rangy yearling bulls, testing them for courage. They were a scruffy lot, Adriana thought, more like beef cattle than fighting bulls, displeasing to the eye, and treacherous to boot. On a number of occasions one or another of the nasty beasts had injured a boy, once delivering a quite respectable *cornada* that had put the would-be *torero* flat on his back for seven long weeks. Dr. Danton had had to be called to douse the wound with carbolic and sew it shut, with straw drains in place. Each time she saw Roberto caping yearlings, a cold hand seemed to close on her heart. But she had Julio's assurance that neither Roberto nor any of the Alvarez boys would be allowed to work the bulls today. "We do not need to send an Alvarez back to Miraflores on a litter," she had said, but everyone knew whose safety most concerned her. She would never have allowed Roberto to participate in a *tienta* if her father had not taken the boy's part in the argument.

As he rode, Don Alvaro turned often to look back at the rocky slope of the mountains behind him. He was thinking again of the caves and the artifacts he had gleaned there as a boy. He tried to remember something he had been reading in a two-month-old issue of *Los Tiempos,* a Spanish language journal published in Toledo for the minute brotherhood of Iberian archeologists.

"Schliemann," he said suddenly. "Heinrich Schliemann."

"What did you say, Papa?" Adriana asked.

"I said Schliemann, Ana. He is a naturalized American, you know. He became rich in California. People say he made his money as a usurer and a profiteer in the Crimean War. They only say that because he has them by the ears." Don Alvaro laughed with satisfaction and said. "Schliemann. I knew I could remember his name."

"Who is Schliemann, Papa?"

"Hija," Don Alvaro said reproachfully. "Have you stopped reading entirely? Schliemann is the man who is looking for Troy. For the city of Priam and Hector, Ana. And finding it too, *Los Tiempos* says. Think of it, Ana. To turn a spade of earth and find a stone from the walls of Homer's Troy! No wonder the professional archeologists say

such things about him. It is as I have always taught you, daughter. The true amateur can master any science."

"Yes, Papa," Adriana said, suppressing a smile.

Don Alvaro turned to regard his daughter down his imperious crag of a nose. "You are humoring me, Ana."

"No, Papa."

"When one grows old, Ana," he said with great dignity, "the mind jumps about like a cricket. I have been trying to remember that wretched German name all morning. Schliemann. What a pity it could not have been a Spaniard who found Troy. But it is still a great achievement."

"Yes, Papa."

"Yes, Papa," Alvaro mimicked her irritably. "I know you have much to do these days, but you should not stop reading the scientific journals, daughter."

"I will try to keep up, Papa," Adriana said meekly.

"You are not an ordinary woman, Ana," Don Alvaro said. "I gave you a man's education. Do not waste it. Remember."

"I will remember, Papa."

Espada, sensing his rider's mood, began to pace sideways and snort steamily into the frigid air. "What a bore it is to grow old," Alvaro said, and urged his mount into a canter down the hillside toward the hacienda. Adriana followed, looking at her father with affection.

There was a small crowd gathered around Julio's Folly in the north pasture. A half-dozen yearling bulls milled about in the paddock, and in the carelessly sanded ring a tall roan-and-white was trotting about, blowing importantly, and occasionally stopping to paw at the ground with a narrow hoof. It was an unattractive animal with an impressive spread of horns.

A trio of vaqueros leaned across the *barrera* dangling improvised capes to distract the bull. Some gypsy boys lined the paddock fence, looking at the ugly roan-and-white, and making laughing comments. Little wonder, Adriana thought. Julio's stock would never make it into a respectable ring. Not even the *plaza de toros* of Santander would accept such beasts.

Adriana looked for the Alvarez children and found them standing on a hayrick with Julio and Chole Segre. They were shouting with excitement. Ana-Maria Gomez and Cecilia were with them, holding on to Chole's skirt.

Everyone's attention was on the slender blond boy approaching the yearling bull, a silk cape in his extended hands. Roberto.

Adriana felt a deep chill. She kicked Estrella into a gallop and raced to the hayrick to face her brother.

"You promised me you wouldn't let him in the ring today!" Her voice was shrill with anger.

Julio smiled at her with the expression of a lolling dog, "Ana, *por Dios,* let the boy alone. He can cape a calf with the best of them." He looked apprehensively at his father, who had ridden up on Espada.

"I don't want him playing your gypsy games," Adriana said furiously.

The children broke into cries of protest. They wanted very much to see Roberto, who was the designated leader of their quadrilla, cape a bull calf.

"One calf, sister," Julio said, fortified by the children's excitement.

Adriana turned to her father. Don Alvaro was watching his grandson. Adriana was dismayed to see the pride in his expression.

"The boy is very good, Doña Ana," Chole Segre said. "There is very little danger."

Adriana bit back a slashing retort. She wanted to say, "What does danger mean to gypsies?" But she bit her lip and forced herself to remain silent. She turned in the saddle to look at her son in the ring.

He was slightly built, as his father had been, but tall for his age. His pale hair blew in the wind. He carried himself proudly as he walked up to the ugly yearling and enticed him with the cape.

The calf pawed the earth and backed away. Roberto challenged it again. Again it backed away, and the vaqueros shouted with derision. The animal was cowardly.

Don Alvaro allowed Espada to walk to the *barrera* and he sat watching his grandson work the animal.

The purpose of a *tienta* was not to kill, or even to injure the bulls. Their time would come later, as three- and four-year-olds, when they would meet their matador in the true ring. This was simply an exercise to cape the animals one or two times to test their courage.

The roan-and-white seemed to have none. Roberto jogged the extended cape and said in his childish voice, *"Hu, toro!"*

Trapped against the *barrera,* the bull finally made a charge. Roberto passed him with a very respectable *verónica.* The vaqueros and the gypsy boys shouted *"Olé!"* Adriana saw her son's back arch with pride.

He stamped his foot and the bull charged again. He made another *verónica* and the bright cape sculpted itself gracefully around his slender body. The vaqueros again shouted their approval of the young Patron.

The wind blew across the pasture and the ring, fluttering the edges of the cape in Roberto's hands. One of the gypsy boys called for him to come to the *barrera* and wet the cloth to make it heavier, but Roberto ignored him and advanced on the uncertain animal. Adriana felt the beating of her heart against her ribs. It seemed suddenly very cold, and she shivered.

The young bull was once more trapped against the *barrera* and it pawed at the ground nervously. There was an eerie intelligence in its white-rimmed eyes. Adriana said to her brother, "Enough now, Julio. Send the brute out."

Before Julio could order the roan-and-white returned to the paddock, the animal charged, hooking viciously. Roberto, caught unawares, stumbled. The bull hit him squarely with his broad forehead. The boy's head snapped back and he sprawled in the sand.

The vaqueros and the gypsy boys, surprised, did nothing. The bull lowered his head and began thrusting at the stunned boy with his horns. A horn tip caught fast in Roberto's jacket. Roberto tried to get to his feet and the bull tossed him, lost track of him, began hunting still again with the horns. Roberto's nose was bleeding. The gypsy boys shouted at him to stay down and still as they began to clamber over the *barrera* to the rescue. To Adriana they appeared to move in a dreadful, slow motion.

She heard Espada utter an angry stallion's cry as he shied and galloped away, riderless. Don Alvaro had thrown himself off the horse's back and into the ring. He ran at the bull, bellowing furiously and waving his hat to distract him from the boy. The bull, panicked into courage, caught sight of this new enemy and charged.

A horn caught Don Alvaro in the body. It seemed to vanish into the white ruffled shirt, which turned instantly red. Adriana watched her father fall off the horn as the boys formed a circle around the bull, shouting and waving capes.

Don Alvaro lay on his back in the sand, bright blood from chin to waist. Roberto stumbled to his side and knelt there sobbing, *"Abuelo! Abuelo!"*

Then Julio was among the gypsy *mozos,* shouting orders. The vaqueros rushed across the sand to Don Alvaro and carried him out of the ring. They put him down on the ground, and when Adriana reached him, they stepped away in frightened silence.

Adriana felt the wail of grief begin in her chest and burst from her lips. Chole Segre tried to pull her from Don Alvaro, but she struck at the gypsy woman with her fists until she released her. Adriana fell on her father's body, his blood staining her clothes.

She heard Chole say to someone, "Send to La Casa for Doña Maria."

One of the vaqueros herded the children away. Adriana could hear Roberto still sobbing and calling for his grandfather.

Presently she straightened into a kneeling position and looked dazedly at the blood on her hands, on her riding habit.

Chole Segre said, "Please, Doña Ana."

Adriana ignored her. She thought: Mama will be very angry with the Bishop of Liencres for not having sent us another chaplain to replace Sebastio. Who will give El Patron the last rites?

She began to tremble. "Papa," she said.

The old man's face was set, stern. His open eyes glared at the winter sky.

"Papa," she said again.

"Doña Ana, please," Chole Segre said in a whisper. "It is too late. *Está muerto, Patrona.*"

Adriana's trembling stopped, though the cold had invaded her very marrow. She made the sign of the cross on Alvaro's forehead. Then she removed her heavy woolen riding jacket and spread it over his face.

She looked up to see Julio, stricken, staring down at the dead man. In a voice that seemed to come from some glacial depth within her, she said to him, "You tried to kill my son and instead you have murdered our father. May God curse and damn you forever."

1871

The sparkle of sun on the water, the soaring flight of gulls against the clear blue sky, and the happy music of the *mariachis* strolling the deck of the ship among the guests contrasted with the melancholy Julia Marini felt as she considered six months without Aaron.

She stood, apart for the moment, at the rail. She looked across the harbor at the waterfront of Tihuacan: white houses, tiled roofs, the green treetops of the Plaza Constitución, the pink Spanish bell towers of the cathedral, the distant mountains beyond. So familiar was this scene to Julia that she seldom, as now, paused to consider its beauty.

The ship, a newly built fruit carrier belonging to a North American company, had accommodations for six passengers, but only Aaron Marburg had booked passage for the voyage from Tihuacan to San Francisco. At the moment there were a hundred people, most of them young, strolling about the cabin deck of the *Tolteca,* drinking *sangría,* inspecting Aaron's cabin, listening to the *mariachis*. The nature of the fiesta, which Julia had planned with great care, was such that it was nearly impossible for it to take the customary path of social gatherings in Tihuacan, with the men huddling together to drink and talk business and politics while the women gossiped. There had been a series of parties of that sort over the last ten days as Aaron's friends and associates gave him the usual round of *fiestas de viaje*.

But the last, on the *Tolteca*, had been left by common consent for Julia to organize, and she had done so with her customary efficiency. There were a dozen *mariachis* aboard, the food had been prepared by the Hotel Belmar, the sangría made and served by her father's servants. Two of the newer boats of the fishing fleet (in which Don Marcello had a one-third interest) had been painted and decorated with colored bunting to act as launches, transporting the guests to and from the *Tolteca*.

The fiesta was three hours old and the *Tolteca* one hour from sailing. The party was noisy and animated, and no one was too drunk. A successful fiesta, everyone would say.

Except, thought Julia ruefully, that I have made it all but impossible for Aaron and me to be alone.

Many times in the preceding weeks she had been certain that he would say to her the one thing she wanted most to hear. It was not that the future was so uncertain. Plainly, her father and Aaron had spoken privately of what would happen when Aaron returned in the fall. But somehow the moment *she* wished for had never quite materialized. She had known Aaron for several years now, and loved him for very nearly that long. He had come to Tihuacan from the north, a handsome, rather romantically mysterious figure in a town as isolated and provincial as this. He had spoken—to Julia, at least—very little about his life before coming to Tihuacan. She knew, of course, that he had lived among great ones in Spain.

When she thought about this, she felt a bead of apprehension forming. He had left something behind in that previous life, something that had a strong hold on him still. A woman? Julia, unlike most of her Tihuacanteca peers, kept her romantic fancies on a short leash. She was intelligent and observant enough of the life around her to know that the convent fantasy that every handsome stranger burned with unrequited love was exactly that, a fantasy. But in Aaron Marburg's case, the fantasy might well be real.

Something kept him from speaking out to her. It was not that she expected songs of love—not that, she told herself. There were infinite gradations in the affection between a man and a woman, and to be regarded as a friend and companion was at least as desirable—perhaps even more so—as being the object of a passionate obsession. Still, she could wish that Aaron would speak to her of love.

Across the deck from Julia, Aaron stood in conversation with the captain and the mate of the *Tolteca,* a pair of *norteamericanos.* She wondered what they were discussing with such animation.

Aaron looked at her and smiled. Since the fire he had abandoned his beard and now, clean shaven, he looked younger and, she thought, even more handsome. She loved the coppery color of his hair, like burnished bronze in the bright sunlight.

Caray, she thought, how she would miss him. Though everyone in Tihuacan thought of Julia and Aaron as betrothed, they were, in fact, not. At least, not yet. That meant that Julia's old suitors would now take advantage of Aaron's absence to place themselves forever underfoot. There was Juan Carlos Rivas, the son of the local banker, a young man with dandified manners and a swiftly developing tendency to drink too much; Jorge de Lebrun, the vice-*alcalde*'s son, plain as a stick and overproud of his *criollo* ancestry; Ramon O'Higgins, thirty years old, totally bald, very rich, and tedious beyond belief, with his endless claims to a relationship with the family of the liberator of Chile; and a half-dozen others, not one of whom were to be considered even slightly suitable as rivals to Aaron Marburg. Jorge de Lebrun's sisters, Laura and Dolores, were quite possibly the worst gossips in Tihuacan. It was they who set the town whispering about the impropriety of Julia riding out with Aaron *sin dueña.* Dolores de Lebrun had even had the cheek to take Julia aside and warn her that such behavior seriously imperiled one's chances of making a suitable marriage. Their concern for an unsullied reputation had never prevented them from making long eyes at Aaron from behind their fans as they promenaded each Sunday on the Malecón.

Of course they were here today. Everyone was here. That, thought Julia, was the trouble. She would much have preferred to spend the last hours alone with Aaron on their favorite stretch of beach between the lagoons and the sea.

"What an elegant fiesta, Señorita Julia." Juan Amaya-Ruiz, impeccably turned out in a white linen suit and holding a cup of *sangría* untouched in his hand, stood beside her. He glanced through the crowd at Aaron, still speaking to the captain. "I will miss him," he said. "So will you, I imagine."

"Very much," Julia said.

Amaya leaned against the rail. "He is something of a treasure, our mysterious Aaron. Tihuacan gets few like him."

"Do you find him mysterious, Doctor?" Julia asked.

"Perhaps mysterious is too strong a word. But there is an aura of the unknown about him, you'll agree?"

"He is not a talker," Julia said with a smile.

Amaya grinned at her. "Not like all the rest of us, you mean. Well, it is our national character, is it not? To spin grand tales and make much of ourselves."

"Surely not you, Dr. Amaya," Julia said, her green eyes amused.

"Even I, *señorita*. As modest as I am."

"Did you really fight for the *imperialistas,* Doctor?"

"I am a healer, dear Julia. I fight for no one."

"Well said, Doctor. You are as mysterious as Aaron."

"A thrust and a touch, *señorita.* You have the instincts of a swordsman," Amaya said with a half-bow. "I hope you will not be too lonely with our friend gone for half a year."

"Lonely enough. I can say that to you, I think. Tihuacan won't be the same without him."

"Very true, *señorita.* Though if you played cards with him as I do, you might find his absence profitable," the doctor said. "He is a formidable card player. But fortunately for my self-esteem, abominable at chess."

Julia's laughter was free and unaffected. Aaron looked at her again and disengaged himself from the ship's officers.

"Is this a conspiracy of *paisanos?*" he asked.

"It is a lament," the doctor said, "for us poor stay-at-homes who will miss the world traveler. No more than that."

Aaron looked at Julia and said, "The time will pass quickly."

"For you, perhaps," she said, with more feeling than she intended.

Aaron touched her cheek lightly with his fingertips. There had been times, during the last three years, she thought, when he had felt real desire for her and had come close to expressing it. But they were circumscribed by the rigid mores of the small provincial town in which they lived. The gossip of the Lebrun girls and the older, black-clad matrons of Tihuacan did affect what one did and how one lived. It was inevitable. Julia wondered what she would have done if on one of their isolated afternoons he had simply said to her, "I want you." The nuns who had had the care of her through childhood and adolescence might have been shocked and horrified by what her response might have been.

But he had never put upon her the burden of making such a choice between chastity and pleasure, and she supposed she should be grateful for that. Still, he could have done otherwise, and she suspected that if he had, she would have given herself to him without conditions.

Often at night she would wake to the sound of the surf across the Malecón from her bedroom window having dreamed of herself lying naked in Aaron's arms. At such times she would think of him with other women—and surely he went with others, because there was no shortage of *campesino* girls come to Tihuacan to earn their living with their bodies. When she thought of him with such women, it filled her with a jealousy she promised herself she would never betray. After all, it was known to all women that men's physical needs did not necessarily have to do with love.

But the fear that he might love another, that he might give to someone else what she herself most desired, could reduce her to secret tears. To soothe her longings and calm her never-spoken fear she said to herself a dozen times each day and night, *He will be my husband. He will marry me.*

"Julia?" His blue eyes were concerned. "Don't be sad, *niña.* The time will really pass quickly. You'll see."

But can I be sure you will return? The thought was as swift and as painful as a thrust from a stiletto. She said, smiling, "Papa says I must not worry you with complaints about how long your business will take. But I shall write to you every week and tell you to come home."

She heard the archness in her voice, and hated it. Perhaps he had never been as forthcoming as she wished him to be, but they had never played these silly games with one another either. She wanted him to know that she loved him, that she would be lonely without him, and that she would be waiting for him to return to her.

"The time is getting short," she said. "I wish we were alone. Completely alone."

Amaya said, "I will make you the grandest gift. I will remove myself and see to it that there is a circle of silence around you." He lifted Julia's hand to his lips. "I will keep everyone away from you—" He took his watch from his waistcoat pocket. "For ten minutes, at least." He replaced the watch, gave Aaron a strong *abrazo,* and began herding the fiesta-goers away from Julia and Aaron like some tall sheepdog in linen.

But even standing alone, apart from the others, Aaron could not find the words that were needed. He knew exactly what it was Julia wished to hear. He knew too that upon his return he would perform what he had promised—if not in so many words, at least by his actions these last few years.

He looked at Julia in the brilliance of the day, pleased by the way the reflections off the green water and the green of her dress heightened the clear color of her eyes. He liked the smooth line of her cheek, the slightly quizzical arch of her dark brows, the way her cap of straight, black hair made a glossy helmet on her small, well-shaped head. He liked the way she looked, just as he liked the quickness of her wit, the clarity of her mind, and her eagerness for the new. She made the other young women of Tihuacan seem silly and empty-headed.

A man could build a life with Julia. One could share the good and the bad with her. One need never be alone. Marriage to Julia could be what marriage was supposed to be—a partnership of shared affection, respect, and achievement.

But in the end, all that he could bring himself to say to her was, "Things will go quickly for us when I return." And when the captain and the mate of the *Tolteca* circulated among the guests, warning them ashore prior to the ship weighing anchor, and Aaron at last took Julia in his arms and kissed her good-bye, there was another, brighter, image in his mind.

Exhausted by the day, and sad beyond her worst imaginings, Julia sat in her negligée before her dressing table, her hair unbound to be combed by Eufemia, her aged maid and *nana*.

The old *mestiza* kissed the top of Julia's head and crooned, *"Ay, pobrecita mi muñequita.* Her *novio* has sailed away on the *yanqui* ship." She looked mournfully at Julia's reddened eyes in the mirror and began to brush.

Julia snatched the brush from Eufemia's hand and snapped tearfully, "I am *not* your 'poor little doll,' Femia. I am a grown woman. Oh, leave it and go to bed!"

Eufemia regarded her reproachfully and then shuffled from the room, her *huaraches* slapping on the tiles. Julia suppressed an urge to call her back and apologize for her bad temper.

Instead she began to pull the brush through her long hair with all the strength she could manage. With each stroke she said in a low, intense voice, "He *will* marry me. We *will* be married. He *will* marry me."

She kept at it until she had cried herself out and then went to bed. Tomorrow she would face the first day. There would be almost two hundred more before she could see Aaron again, and she would have to take them one by one.

The linden trees standing against
the façade of the *bahnhof* of Marburg am Lahn were not so tall as he
remembered them. The stone buildings around the narrow square
were grimy with coal soot, and the cobbles underfoot were littered with
red and golden leaves scuttering in the wind. He smelled the familiar
tang of the river.

Aaron, in dark broadcloth, stick in hand, a new homburg on his
head, stood breathing the memory-laden air as the porter from the
Neues Lahnerhof stacked his cases into the waiting hack. When he had
finished, he clicked his heels together, military as a Prussian sergeant,
saluted, and waved Aaron into the carriage.

There was more traffic on the streets of Marburg than Aaron
remembered. The town had a strangely frenetic, proud atmosphere.
Military uniforms were numerous, not only the *opéra comique* red and
yellow of the local Hessians, but others that the porter pointed out as

belonging to important Prussian regiments. The old man had snapping blue eyes and enormous muttonchop whiskers. There were medals on his long, dark green infantry-style frock coat, and he wore a stiff, patent-leather peaked cap on which the name of the hotel had been embroidered in gilt bullion.

In January, while Aaron was still in Tihuacan preparing for his journey, the Second Reich had been proclaimed at the Hall of Mirrors at Versailles, a new German Empire created by Count Otto von Bismarck from eighteen duchies and principalities, three free cities, and the kingdoms of Württemberg, Bavaria, Saxony, and Prussia. All were now ruled by Kaiser Wilhelm I.

By the time Aaron had reached Hamburg, Paris had surrendered to the victorious Prussians (a belated acknowledgment of the defeat inflicted on the French months earlier at Sedan, where Napoleon III had been captured).

While Aaron was in Cologne, dealing with the agents and engineers of the Blohm and Voss manufacturing cartel, France had ceded Alsace and Lorraine, agreed to pay a five-billion-franc indemnity, and erupted into a spasm of political recrimination.

Surrounded by jubilant new Pan-Germans, Aaron had read the news dispatches that told of Paris in turmoil. The infant Third Republic, struggling to contain the humiliation of the defeat of French arms, found itself challenged by the establishment of a Paris Commune. From March until May, 25,000 Frenchmen died on the barricades before the authority of the French Assembly could be reestablished in the city.

Now in early autumn, his business complete, Aaron had telegraphed Isaac Marburg telling him that he wished to visit him. He had received for reply a wire that read simply: "You will be welcome." It was signed "Uncle."

The hack's iron tires and the horse's steel-shoed hooves clattered on the cobblestones. The hood had been laid back and Aaron rode in the open, muffled against a slight damp chill in the air, looking up at the tall, narrow buildings with their arrow-slit windows and ornamental wrought-iron balconies. It had been many years since he had traveled these streets, and he had forgotten the shut-in closeness of a German town. Some of the streets were tree-lined, but the leaves were falling and the branches stood stark and naked against the silver overcast. Somewhere a military band was playing. Aaron could feel, rather than truly hear, the reverberating beat of the bass drum.

The porter, seated on his perch by the driver, but facing Aaron, said in his liquid Hessian accent, "It is the band of the *Potsdamer Grossin-*

fanterie. They are stationed here and play concerts every day between one and four in the afternoon. Would the *gnädiger Herr* condescend to hear them before driving to the hotel?"

"I think not," Aaron said. "But I wish to drive down the Lahnen-strasse, if you please."

The porter relayed his orders to the driver, and the hack turned onto the street facing the long bend of the Lahn where it divided the town.

Barges were moving on the river, drawn against the languid current by teams of draft horses on the towpath. The street was broader than most, and between the Lahnerbrücke and the Flussplatz stood the buildings that housed the offices of Marburg am Lahn's more prosperous business establishments.

Aaron rapped with his stick and said, "Stop here."

The hack stood before an ancient, sooty structure tightly wedged between two larger buildings. The façade consisted almost entirely of a stone-arched door of aged black wood polished to a high gloss by a hundred years of daily waxing. Aaron remembered it well. He had taken his turn at the waxing and the burnishing of the gleaming brass fittings.

Above the door, the second-story windows of the counting-room faced the river. They were as grimy as ever. Uncle Isaac had ordered them cleaned only twice each year, in the spring and fall. A clear view of the river and the barges could only distract apprentices from their work. Aaron smiled slightly, remembering.

But the brass plate fixed to the door now bore a shield rather than the spray of linden leaves that Uncle Isaac had taken years ago as an escutcheon for the Marburg Bank. The shield was the mark of the Rothschilds.

The Cologne bankers to whom he had presented his letter of credit from Don Marcello had told him that the Marburg had been sold to the House of Rothschild in 1866, and that Isaac Marburg was in retirement. Aaron wondered if anyone had ever told Micah. There had been an estrangement between his father and uncle; Adriana had not said so, but it had been implied in her few letters.

Isaac Marburg was now seventy-two years old. He had been born in the last month of the eighteenth century. To Aaron, 1799 seemed infinitely distant in time. He tried to imagine a world without railroads, without the telegraph, without steamships. A world of water power and wind power alone, of goods moved over land by the muscles of men and beasts. In that last year of the century George Washington had died at Mount Vernon and Napoleon Bonaparte abandoned his forces in Egypt and returned to Paris to be named First Consul on the eighteenth day of Brumaire. A different world.

He signaled for the driver to proceed to the Neues Lahnerhof. He leaned back and looked dreamily and unseeing at the gray clouds overhead. Uncle Isaac was the last of the Marburgs in this town from which they had taken their name. He had never married, and Micah had been his only sibling. Aaron's cousins were all children of collateral branches of the family, and not one of them carried the Marburg name. Only young Roberto's children and his own would do that.

It was a brooding thought, and it stayed with him as he drove, a half-stranger, through the streets of the town where he had been born.

In the late afternoon he crossed the Lahnerbrücke and presented himself at the door of the old house on the riverbank. Here, amid a jumble of narrow streets and alleys, had once been the Judengasse of Marburg. The new Germany considered itself too enlightened for ghettos, but old habits died hard. Isaac Marburg had lived in this dark and gloomy house for forty years. It faced the street, dissembling; it was far larger than it seemed, with a dank park of lawn and flowerbeds and old pines behind it stretching down to the stone embankment of the Lahn.

Aaron recalled how much his father had always disliked Isaac's house. The shabby face it presented to the street and the heavy Teutonic opulence of the many rooms had filled him with distaste, and he had communicated this feeling to Aaron. Micah preferred to live more grandly, at a distance from the Judengasse. Once he had said, "We lived in places like this when I was a boy, hiding our affluence from the gentiles for no reason." It was the only time Aaron could remember his father speaking of his youth as Jewish.

Aaron dismissed the hack that had brought him across the river and climbed the worn stone stairs to the shabby door. The brass plate with his uncle's name on it was exactly as he remembered it, still decorated with the linden leaves of the Marburg Bank. But now there was a *mezuzah* set into the fretted stonework of the entry. That had not been there when last he pulled at the bell handle.

The door was opened by a pale-haired, stooped old man. Aaron did not know him. Behind was the familiar dark foyer.

"I am Aaron Marburg," he said.

"Herr Isaac is expecting you, sir," the manservant said, taking Aaron's hat, coat, and stick.

Aaron asked if Wilhelm, Isaac's butler for many years, was still with the household.

"Oh, no, sir. Wilhelm passed away five years ago. I am Gerhardt, *mein Herr.*"

"I am very sorry to hear that," Aaron said. "Wilhelm was good to me when I was a boy." He remembered the old butler, sallow and lean as a whippet, presiding over a household staff of eight servants, all of them gentiles. None of the Jews of Marburg am Lahn ever hired other Jews as domestics. Aaron had thought it curious, but it was the custom. "Jews are too stiff-necked to make good servants," Micah had said. "Every one of them thinks he is a rabbi, a talmudist, or a lawyer. One can't order breakfast without a disputation." The memory made Aaron smile thinly. "And Klara?" he asked. Klara Meitner had been his uncle's housekeeper—and, some said, a bit more than that.

"Klara retired some years ago, *mein Herr.* There are only three in service here now. Except for the kitchen staff. They live out."

"I see." So Uncle Isaac now kept a kosher kitchen. That was plainly Gerhardt's meaning.

"Herr Isaac is expecting you in the library, sir. If you will follow me."

The long hallway was as gloomy as ever, lined with dim landscapes in ornate, gilded frames. No one had ever seen the old paintings clearly. The light was too poor, and the varnish was dark and yellowed.

Aaron followed Gerhardt through the badly proportioned rotunda. Here a chilly light filtered in through a skylight three stories overhead. A narrow stairway circled the rotunda, giving access to the bedrooms and parlors on the upper levels. The air smelled slightly of cooking. The kitchen staff was at work.

The butler opened the double doors to the library and said, "The young sir is here, *mein Herr.*"

Isaac Marburg sat in his winged chair near the French doors leading to the garden. Aaron remembered that this was the pleasantest room in the house, with adequate light and floor-to-ceiling rows of old books in tooled leather bindings.

"Come in, come in, boy."

An old man's voice, Aaron thought. He was shocked at the changes in his uncle.

Once Isaac Marburg had been a robust, strongly made man. Now he seemed to have diminished in size. His head alone was still large and shiny-bald. He wore a *yarmulke,* which Aaron had never before seen him do, and a black suit with a long coat similar to that worn by *hassidim.* A white beard, bushy and untrimmed, gave him the look of a patriarch.

He gestured with hands deformed by arthritis. "I can't see you there, Aaron. Come greet your uncle."

Aaron walked across the room and kissed the old man's cheek. The skin felt like parchment under his lips. The heavy clothing smelled musty.

"So you've come back," Isaac said. "Back to Marburg." Aaron was surprised and touched to see that Isaac's eyes were swimming with tears.

"To see you, uncle," Aaron said.

"There have been changes."

"Many," Aaron said. "But the house looks the same."

"The bank is gone. But you knew that, I suppose," Isaac said.

"Yes. They told me in Cologne."

Isaac Marburg folded his hands under his long beard. The tears were gone and he regarded his nephew narrowly. "There is no money for you, Aaron. I paid your father his full share."

"I didn't come to ask for money, uncle," Aaron said.

"I paid your father fifty thousand marks," Isaac said. "What he did with it is not my problem."

"I know, uncle."

Isaac said querulously, "The bank would have been yours. But *he* wouldn't have it. What could I do? I sold to the Rothschilds."

Aaron took a chair facing the old man. "It's done," he said. "You did what you thought best."

"I am not leaving my money to you, Aaron."

"I didn't come here for that, Uncle Isaac," Aaron said. Why did I come? he asked himself. To listen to an old man complain of what was past?

"Are you doing well in Mexico, boy?"

"Reasonably well, uncle."

"But not married yet."

"Not yet." He thought of Julia. What would she make of this cranky, aged Jew?

Isaac shook his head and rocked to and fro. "Lost," he said. "A Marburg lost. Thanks to Micah. Thanks to *him.*"

"That's not fair, uncle. And I don't think of myself as lost. I am sorry if you do," Aaron said. He was tempted to add that Isaac himself had not been so religious in the past, but he did not.

"That woman Micah married," Isaac said. "Was she very beautiful?"

Aaron nodded slowly. "Very," he said.

Isaac Marburg said, "You are the last Marburg, Aaron."

"I have a brother and sister, uncle. Your niece and nephew."

Isaac shook his head emphatically. "Spanish *goyim*. They are nothing to me."

Aaron stood and walked to the window to look out at the sere, colorless garden in the cold afternoon light.

"Pull the bell cord," Isaac said. "I want tea."

Aaron did as he was ordered and studied the shadowed room. Each object in view was placed precisely where he remembered seeing it years ago. The Marburg sense of order, he thought.

"How do I look to you, Aaron?" the old man asked.

"You look well, uncle."

"I shall be seventy-eight this year." It was said proudly, but Aaron knew it was not so. He had heard that senescence sometimes took the form of claiming more years than one actually had. When one grew old enough, Aaron supposed, longevity itself became a cause for self-congratulation.

"Look around you," Isaac said. "The house is just the same. You remember it?"

"Very well," Aaron said. Like his father, he had always disliked this dark and opulent warren.

Gerhardt opened the library door and Isaac said sharply, "Tea."

The butler bowed and retreated, closing the door behind him.

"Wilhelm died," Isaac Marburg said. "He was a troublesome old fool but he knew my ways. Now I have to make do with that one." He glared at the closed door. "They all hate us, you know. Every one of them. They always have."

Aaron made no comment. He had expected his uncle to be as he always had been in his memory: harsh, perhaps, and demanding, but the same hard-bitten secular man he remembered. He had not been prepared for this Orthodox patriarch who now lived in a world Aaron had never known and had no wish to know. He felt an intruder here.

The tea was wheeled in on a cart and served in glasses in silver holders.

When Gerhardt had gone again, Isaac said, "You have a right to know what I shall do with my money."

"What you do is not my business, uncle," Aaron said. "I told you I did not come here for money."

"No, I want you to know."

Aaron sipped the sweet tea and waited. If Isaac wanted to tell him what disposition he was making of his fortune, he could do the old man the courtesy of listening.

"I have willed everything to the Colonization Society in Frankfort," Isaac Marburg said.

"I don't know what that is," Aaron said.

"No, I do not expect you do, living among the *goyim*," Isaac said testily. "A rabbi named Hirsch Kalisher—a Russian—has begun to buy land in Palestine. In *Eretz Yisroel*, Aaron. Think of it!"

A homeland for the Jews. The ancient dream of the Return. It rang in the greetings Jews exchanged on holy days: "Next year in Jerusalem."

"A worthy cause, uncle," Aaron said.

"That's all it means to you, boy?"

"I'm sorry. What else should it mean to me?"

Isaac began again to rock to and fro as though mourning. Aaron was struck by how much he resembled Father Sebastio.

"That a Marburg should be so lost," Isaac said. "Poor Sarai would weep and eat bitter herbs."

Aaron's sense of having fallen into an alien world oppressed him. "Forgive me, uncle. I don't mean to distress you."

"Well, what can be expected?" Isaac said gloomily. "We never taught you, Micah and I. He never even permitted you to be bar-mitzvahed. You know nothing, but it is not your fault."

The old man sipped noisily at his tea, his mind skipping and dancing. Presently he said, "Did Gerhardt take your things to your room? I ordered him to make a place for you."

"I am staying at the Lahnerhof, uncle. I thought it best not to trouble your servants."

"So. You prefer to stay in a hotel and eat filth. Yes, you are Micah's son. When he last came here he was uncomfortable with my ways."

"I don't mean to offend you, uncle," Aaron said again.

"Yes, well," Isaac Marburg said irritably. "Do as you wish. How long do you plan to stay in Marburg?"

"I must leave on Monday. I have a very long way to go."

"I have asked some of your cousins to come for dinner tomorrow. Not all of them, only the ones you remember. I don't like them, but they are all the family we have. You won't disappoint them, I hope. It is *Rosh Hodesh*, you know. They all expect to see you, to have a look at their *goyische* cousin from the New World. Well?"

Aaron suppressed a sigh of despair. He had thought he might see one or two of his second cousins, but one at a time, and in a more congenial atmosphere than this grim house. And he had forgotten that tomorrow was *Shabbat*. Not only *Shabbat,* but the special sabbath that marked the beginning of a new month. Not a high holy day, but if Uncle Isaac had truly become observant, an occasion of some importance to him.

It rather shocked him to realize how like an outsider he felt here. Was it for this that he had given Micah and Sebastio and the Santanas such unhappiness?

"I will be pleased to come to dinner with my cousins, uncle," he said, tasting the polite falsehood. After all, he asked himself, one evening—how bad could it be?

It was worse than he could have imagined. Uncle Isaac had invited seven of his cousins, four of whom were married and arrived, of course, with their spouses. All were within ten years of his own age, which, he supposed, made them his contemporaries in Uncle Isaac's mind.

They arrived in carriages and landaus, dressed in furs and dinner clothes, the women in velvet and taffeta and diamonds. It was plain at the outset that each cousin was resolved to impress the visitor.

The first to arrive, and in Aaron's opinion, the least welcome, was his cousin Manfred Stein. He remembered Manfred as a truculent and overweight boy ten years older than himself who had bullied him at every opportunity. Manfred had attended the *gymnasium* in Marburg, while Aaron had been educated by private tutors. This had presented Manfred with an unlimited source of stinging comments and an occasional chance for pummeling Aaron on family outings.

Now Manfred was balding, gone to fat, and three inches shorter than Aaron. A civil servant, he was the least successful of the cousins and, at nearly forty, still unmarried. He greeted Aaron with Teutonic officiousness and regaled him with tales of his blooming career in the Ministry of Transport and his service to the state in the recent war with the French.

Jacob Farber, the next arrival, was a pale and nervous young man of Aaron's age, a banker, the senior clerk at the one-time Marburg Bank. Aaron remembered him as a sickly and nervous child too, given to sudden attacks of asthma that required injections of adrenaline. His wife Malkah was an heiress of some substance, a small woman resplendent in burgundy velvet and a diamond necklace (which she assured Aaron was an heirloom taken from the Rothschild Bank's vault only on special occasions such as this). She appeared to be fascinated by travel, which was denied her by her husband's health and importance to the bank. "How I envy you, cousin," she said to Aaron. "Think of it, roaming about at will across the oceans. How marvelously liberating."

Aaron assured her that he did not actually roam at will, and that he had come to Germany on business.

Her brother-in-law, Aaron's cousin Theo Farber, was also an officer of the Rothschild Bank. He was two years older than his brother Jacob and the head of the foreign credit department (which Micah had established years before). This allowed him and his wife Marianne, an overweight matron also displaying a startling collection of gems, to travel between Marburg and Paris. "Though I had to arrange to meet Baron Phillippe in Berlin last month," he informed Aaron, "because the French have not really managed to establish order in Paris yet, no matter what one reads in the papers."

At the mention of Baron Philippe de Rothschild, Malkah Farber's face darkened, and she turned her back to make much of Uncle Isaac, who sat like a biblical ancient surrounded by his tribe.

The last arrivals were the Silbers, Cousin Rudolph (five years Aaron's senior and the owner of a large store in Marburg), his rather pretty, silent, wife, Arielle, Cousin Hildegard Silber and her husband, Hillel Montara, a teacher at the University of Hessen, and Cousin Rachel.

It was astonishing, Aaron thought, how much Rachel still resembled the creature who had tormented his childhood. She was over thirty and not married—a circumstance that, in this environment, should have taught her humility. It did not surprise Aaron to learn that it had not. Rachel was still the same intrusive busybody and arbiter of family values that she had always been. She had grown slightly plumper and her breasts (those quivering globes that had troubled Aaron's adolescent sleep) were even larger and more prominent than he remembered them. Her downy black moustache had grown darker, and her tongue sharper.

"Why aren't you married?" she demanded almost at once.

"I plan to be soon," Aaron said. He found it ironic that he had not spoken so plainly in any one of his dozen letters to Julia, but would parry Rachel's initial thrust with the very words Julia would have given much to hear.

"To a *shiksa*, I'll warrant," she said testily.

"To a Roman Catholic, as a matter of fact," Aaron said.

"Thank God in His Heaven that Aunt Sarai is not alive to hear you say such a thing," Rachel declared. She glanced across the room to where Uncle Isaac sat with the Farbers around him. "Does *Der Alter* know?" Aaron had already heard several of the cousins speak of Isaac as "The Old One." It seemed the general practice when out of Uncle Isaac's hearing.

"He thinks it likely," Aaron said. He could not completely suppress a teasing smile. Rachel had always asked to be outraged.

"He'll cut you off," she said. "I suppose you know that."

"I didn't come here to earn a mention in his will, Rachel."

"Didn't you? Then why did you come?"

Aaron was tempted to say that he had come to Marburg to see if Rachel were still as charming as she had been when they were children. Instead he said, "Nostalgia."

"Are you rich?" Rachel asked.

"No."

"What do you do in Mexico?"

"I work. And make plans."

"Well, I wish you joy of them," Rachel said. "Look at Marianne. Whenever we come here she fawns over *Der Alter.* It is enough to make one sick." She fixed Aaron with her dark, glittering eyes. "He has become very religious, you know. He saves his hair and fingernail cuttings."

"It's his privilege," Aaron said. "Old people often become devout."

"Devout. That's a *goyische* word."

"So it is, cousin," he said. "Observant, then."

"Your father wasn't."

"Not at all. Even less so than you could imagine."

"Well, none of the rest of them are either. They are all very liberated, very assimilated, very German. Now that the Prussians own the world."

"Times change, Rachel. People change."

"You won't guess it to see them tonight. The women will be meek, the men will cover their heads at dinner. They will all pretend to be what Uncle Isaac wants them to be."

"And will you, Rachel?"

"I do what is right," Rachel snapped.

"I remember," Aaron said dryly.

"You haven't changed, Herr Aaron Mighty Marburg," Rachel said waspishly. She fixed him with an intent, burning look laden with years of anger. "I would have made you a good wife," she said, "but no, you wouldn't have it, you and your so-elegant father. Go away,

Aaron. There is no place here for you." She turned and walked away as old Gerhardt came into the library to announce that dinner was ready to be served.

Aaron sat alone on the plush bench of the first-class compartment, listening to the clicking of the rails and staring unseeing at the steep, terraced hillsides containing the mighty Rhine.

It had been as Rachel predicted: all the hopeful cousins who imagined Isaac Marburg's fortune was their heritage behaved like *hassidim*. Despite his cousin's angry admonition, Aaron had been unprepared for the sense of exclusion and alienation he had felt at that richly appointed Jewish table. The sweet wine had cloyed, the kosher food had been unfamiliar. Only Rachel, in her bitterness, had spoken to him truthfully. She had said what none of his other cousins had had the courage to say. And as he sat with Uncle Isaac on his right and Arielle Silber to his left, his homburg absurdly on his unbelieving head (all the other men had brought *yarmulkes*), he had realized that Rachel Silber, for all her bad temper, saw him clearly.

And so on the day after *Shabbat,* the Christian Sunday, he had taken himself to the Jewish cemetery to place flowers on Sarai Leyden Marburg's grave and ask her pardon. The flowers would wither and they would not be replaced, and he asked her forgiveness for that too. But a man could not feel what he had never been taught to feel, and even the prophets knew that blood has no memory.

From the swiftly moving train he looked down from the heights to the great gray river below and knew that he was seeing it for the last time.

Isaac Marburg shed more old man's tears when he kissed Aaron good-bye, and it had touched Aaron sincerely. But it was as Rachel had said, there was nothing left to tie him to Marburg. He had no place there. Micah had seen to that years ago.

L ate summer lingered in the dry
hills of Santanilla. The gusting of the southern wind, the smell of the
dusty land, and the tall black shapes of the cypress trees lining the road
stripped away the years and made Aaron remember his first journey
from Santander to the hacienda.

He rode a rangy horse from the *caballeriza* in Santander; he somehow could not picture himself arriving at Santanilla driving a rented
buggy. Adriana would think him grown staid.

He rode at a walking pace, saddened by what he had learned from
the townsman who operated the stable. The man had told him, with all
the usual Spanish embellishments, that Don Alvaro Santana y Avila was
dead, killed by a fighting bull last December. Aaron tried to imagine
what Santanilla would be like without Don Alvaro's robust, domineer-
ing presence. He wondered if Adriana had written to him with the
news. If she had done so, her letter had crossed his path while he was
in the United States or on the way to Europe.

In Santander there had been no one whom he could ask about Santanilla. Simon Pauley's post as consul was now held by a wizened Midwesterner who was reputed never to leave the limits of the town for fear of the republican insurgents, bands of dispossessed *peones* and small landowners intent on disrupting the customary apathy of the district with their attacks on isolated members of the Guardia. The government of King Amadeo I was not respected in stolid Old Castile, and for the first time republicanism (indigenous to the south only) was finding converts among the peasants of the Cantabrican coast.

Aaron had not given Santanilla advance notice of his visit. He had been undecided even as his train rolled through Bilbao. Uncertain of his welcome after his experience in Marburg, he had considered simply returning to Le Havre to take ship for New York or Tampico.

But having learned of Don Alvaro's death, he wanted very much to see Adriana, to offer her comfort. So he had come on, and now he rode through the familiar dry heat of midday, with memories growing stronger at each milestone.

He wondered how it could have been possible that El Patron was killed by a fighting bull. Aaron recalled that long ago Don Alvaro had taken a fling at raising such beasts, but the experiment had not been a success and it had been abandoned long before Micah and Aaron arrived at Santanilla.

In his youth, Don Alvaro had practiced the skills of the *rejoneador,* fighting bulls on horseback—the sport of the Spanish gentry. But the tale told in Santander was that El Patron of Santanilla, at the age of seventy, had flung himself into the ring and had taken a fatal *cornada* from a scrub yearling, ill-bred and treacherous.

There was a Santana family story, seldom retold, that Don Alvaro's father, Don Alejandro Santana, had also been killed by a fighting bull. Aaron had always assumed it a romantic fantasy.

As he rode, Aaron remembered El Patron's favorite saying: *Las Parcas nos mandan.* Perhaps fate operated with a darker certainty in this sere Spanish land.

In the midafternoon he rode through the stone arch of the gateway, under the wrought-iron S, stained red with years of rusting in the winter rains. Almost at once he was struck by the atmosphere of neglect and disrepair. The dry-rock fences that separated the northern pastures had crumbled in places. The rains and flash floods of spring had etched and eroded the ranges, and no workmen had been put to the task of filling and recontouring the damaged land.

There were sheep in the pastures, and some cattle in the adjacent fields. The sheep were being tended by gypsies, whose painted caravan stood in a stand of scrub oaks. The shepherds watched Aaron as he rode by, but did not raise their crooks in greeting.

As Aaron topped the low ridge some miles from the gate, he stopped and sat in the saddle, looking at the distant compound of Santanilla. The house looked unoccupied. There were no servants at their work in the courtyards between La Casa and the cattle barns. In the hollow below the house stood the chapel, its black door shut, the flower gardens that had once surrounded it and been cared for with such pride by Father Sebastio were gone to thorn and wild grasses. The stumpy bell tower was empty; the bronze bell, cast for the Santanas in Italy in 1750, was missing.

The wind was warm and filled with the smell of the Spanish mountains, but it blew cold on Aaron's face, like the palpable breath of the earth's own melancholy.

He touched his heels to his mount and moved down the road to the stone mausoleum that stood near the silent church. Here he dismounted and stood, hat in hand, before the metal doors, looking up at the almost vanished family arms on the lintel. On two stelae beside the Roman archway were carved the names of the occupants of the crypt, each with his death date.

Santiago was here, brought home from the deserts of Morocco. He lay with his infant brothers, Alfredo and Guillermo, and his grandparents, Don Alejandro and Doña Elvira, whom the servants used to say had cursed God. All around the mausoleum were the graves of Santana servants, marked by small stones and crosses, but Father Sebastio lay within the crypt, still watching over his private flock. Aaron was touched by someone's gesture—it must almost certainly have been Doña Maria's—of placing the old Dominican with the family dead.

He reached out to touch the letters, already weathered, that spelled his own father's name. Miguel Marburg, Anno Domini 1867. Below it had been carved Don Alvaro's. Micah lay surrounded by Santanas, Aaron thought. His conversion was indeed complete.

"*Hola! Hombre!* What are you doing there?"

Aaron turned to see a man sitting on a shaggy roan horse, a shepherd by his dress: stiff leather trousers, homespun shirt, straw *sombrero* hanging from a cord over his shoulder.

"*Hola,* Julio," Aaron said.

"*Me cago!* You!" Julio Santana's face, darkened by exposure to the Iberian sun and lined as though someone had carved at it with a knife, showed his amazement. He dismounted and strode forward to seize Aaron by the shoulders. "Let me embrace you, *hombre*. God, you look prosperous." In Julio's *abrazo*, Aaron could smell his sweat.

Aaron looked about and asked, "What has happened here?"

"My God, what has not! You know about Papa." Julio gestured at the name on the stele.

"They told me of it in Santander," Aaron said. "How did it happen?"

"Madness, Aaron, madness. Roberto was caping a yearling and the beast knocked him down. Papa went crazy and ran into the ring."

"Bulls here at Santanilla?"

Julio shook his head in despair. "They were mine. I brought some Asturians in to try to raise money. Filthy creatures, but they were all I could afford. Nothing has been the same since then."

"Where is Adriana?"

"At La Casa. Where else would she be?"

Aaron started toward his horse, but Julio held him back. "Wait. Before you go up there, come to my *finca*. There are things you should know."

Aaron found it strange that the eldest son of the house on the hacienda should speak of his "farm" as though he were a tenant on the land.

"Is Ana all right? She's not ill?"

"No, she's well enough. If a madwoman can be well," Julio said, almost plaintively.

"She's not still grieving for Don Alvaro? It has been almost a year," Aaron said.

"I don't see her often, Aaron, and that's the truth."

"I don't understand you, Julio. What do you mean you don't see her? You both live here, don't you?"

"*Hombre,* I have not set foot inside La Casa since Papa was killed. Not once. She holds me to blame for it. What can I tell you? Maybe I am responsible. The bulls were mine. But she as much as accused me of murder. You know her. You know how she can be."

"You had better tell me exactly how El Patron died," Aaron said.

"It happened the way I said, Aaron. We were having a *tienta.* Roberto wanted to cape a yearling. He'd done it before, and I let him do it. The animal knocked him down. Papa had been out riding with Ana. He was sitting on Espada beside the ring. When he saw the boy go down, he ran into the ring and the bull hit him in the chest. There was no need for him to do what he did, *hombre.* There were a dozen *mozos* there to take the animal away from Roberto. But Papa did it anyway. A man nearly seventy should have had better sense, *por Dios.* I suppose he thought the boy was in danger."

"Ana saw this?"

"Yes. She was there. She went mad. She said that I tried to kill her son and instead had murdered our father. She had not addressed one word to me since that day, Aaron. My own sister. Not one single word." Julio's dark eyes glistened with tears. "I was never a good son to him, Aaron. None of us were. But I loved him, in my way. I swear on my hope of salvation that I did love him."

Aaron found it strange that Julio, whom he had never liked, should move him this way.

"Come with me, please. Before you go up to La Casa. I want you to see my son."

"You are married?" Aaron asked.

"Who marries gypsies? But the boy is a tiger. Come see."

The two men mounted and cantered across the first ridge of hills into a hollow of land where an abandoned bullring stood in a fallow pasture. A cottage, only slightly larger than those given the shepherds, had been built there of the native stone. The roof was raw hides held down with rocks. Chickens scratched for seeds in the rammed earth clearing behind the three-room structure. The remnants of a small corn crop were heaped in one corner of the pasture. A brightly painted gypsy wagon stood near the house and hobbled donkeys mingled with the three riding horses in a post and rail paddock.

"This is where you live?" Aaron asked.

"It is not much, is it? Yes, I live here," Julio said. "One gets accustomed to it."

Aaron remained silent as they approached the house where a woman with smallpox scars and an enormous belly stood in the doorway to greet them. A small, dark-skinned boy, just old enough to stand, clung to the woman's skirt.

A gypsy boy from the caravan appeared to take their horses and Julio said, "This is Chole Segre, my *vieja.*" He snatched up the swarthy child and lifted him over his head. "And this is Paco. Who will soon have a brother, as you can see."

The child gurgled delightedly and looked at Aaron with Santana eyes.

Aaron greeted the gypsy woman formally as Doña Soledad and she inclined her head with gypsy dignity. "My house is your house, Don

Aaron." She said it as though the hovel were a palace. This was a woman who knew how to wait, Aaron thought.

"It's too hot inside, *vieja,*" Julio said. "Bring us *aguardiente.* We'll sit out here." Tattered wicker chairs that Aaron remembered as part of the furnishings of the *sala mayor* in the great house stood at a rough wooden table under the overhanging eaves.

Julio threw himself into one of the chairs and sighed heavily. "Nothing has gone right here since you left, Aaron. You took our luck with you."

Aaron regarded his "cousin" with raised eyebrow. Julio had the grace to be slightly embarrassed. "I swear to you," he said. "I had nothing to do with planning that foolish business with Alfonso's slut. I swear it on my son's head."

"If you say so," Aaron said. "It doesn't matter now. I have grown up since then."

Chole Segre appeared with a bottle and glasses on a tray. Aaron got to his feet and held a chair for her. Julio poured three drinks. No one made a toast.

Chole Segre said, "You come from Mexico, Don Aaron."

"Yes," Aaron said.

"Is it strange there?"

"Only at first. Then it is much like here, Doña Chole."

Chole Segre looked about her at the fallow, weary land and said with feeling, "I cannot imagine ever leaving Spain, this land." She regarded her surroundings with such a hungry possessiveness that Aaron was moved to remember that to a gypsy the ownership of land was the most important thing life could offer. To Soledad Segre, this piece of Santanilla could not be more valuable if it had been sown with gold.

"Spain, *Doña,* or Santanilla?" he asked.

Her smile flashed in her dark face. "Is there a difference, Don Aaron?"

To Julio Aaron said, "How has Doña Maria taken all this?"

"Better than Ana has," Julio said. "I would not have expected it. She blames me, too, of course. But she speaks to me from time to time, my *hidalga* mother."

Julio refilled the glasses with the harsh *aguardiente.* "Mama is at Miraflores. She took the children and Tomasa Gomez for a fortnight's stay with the Alvarez clan."

"Alvarez? I don't remember them," Aaron said.

"The family bought Miraflores while you were in the United

States. They have a daughter Mama wants for Roberto. The family has no breeding to speak of, but a great deal of money. Do you want me to send someone to Miraflores and bring them back? How long will you stay?"

"Don't disturb them. I can see them when they return."

"Don't tell Ana you came down here to the *finca*," Julio said. "She will fly into a rage if you do." Chole Segre caught Aaron's eye and shook her head.

Little Paco, crawling on the packed earth, pulled at his father's leather trouser leg. Julio picked him up and placed him on his lap. How very different from her own golden son this dirty, happy boy must seem to Adriana, Aaron thought.

"Before you go up to La Casa," Julio said, "I had better tell you that you'll find the place very changed."

"I already find Santanilla changed," Aaron said.

"I mean the house. It is like a monastery, the *criadas* tell us. Ana has sold off everything of value. She has even sold as much of the land as she can. The rest is entailed, or we would all be on the roads, begging."

"That is not true, Julio," Chole Segre said. To Aaron she said, "There is an agreement, Don Aaron. When Don Roberto is old enough to marry, the California land is his. Santanilla comes to—" Aaron realized she had come near to saying "to us," but instead she finished, "—to Julio. It was in Don Alvaro's will."

"Ana and Mama are going to marry Roberto off to the Miraflores girl just as soon as they can manage it," Julio said. "If he were eighteen, they would do it today."

"And Cecilia?" Aaron asked.

"Ah, well," Julio said. "Sebastio started Cecilia in the direction of the convent years ago."

Aaron got to his feet, and Julio did so as well. Chole shouted for the gypsy boy to bring the visitor's horse.

Aaron thanked "Doña Soledad" for her hospitality, and she gave him a wry gypsy smile. "I will treasure your visit, Don Aaron," she said. "It isn't often I am treated as though I were a lady. I find it pleasant."

As Aaron was mounting his rented hack, Julio said in a low voice, "The *vieja* thinks she may be hacendada here one day."

"You could do worse," Aaron said shortly.

"If you want someone sent to Miraflores," Julio said, "come see me. There are only two *mozos* left at the big house. Adriana won't pay more of them. She saves every peseta for her grand hegira to America. She is *loca,* my sister."

Aaron put his mount to a canter and rode over the hillcrest to the road to La Casa. The sun lay low in the west, deep red from the blowing dust in the warm wind. There was a tightness in his chest and more excitement than he remembered feeling for years.

Long shadows were stretching out across the land when he reached La Casa, his horse's hooves clattering on the rock-hard earth.

A *mozo* appeared from the direction of the cattle barns to take the animal. Aaron dismounted and removed his saddlebags. For a moment or two he simply stood looking at the great white house in the red sunset light. It was silent, with a brooding look of emptiness. The long *corredores* and arched galleries were deep in russet shadows.

A slender figure all in black appeared in the flagstoned gallery. Her face was pale, with skin so fine it seemed translucent. Straight golden hair was skinned back on the narrow, well-shaped head and caught there with a single silver-fretted comb. Aaron, his heart thudding in his chest, breathed her name. *"Ana."*

She raised her arms to him, with pale, slender hands extended. "You have come back," she said. "Welcome, Aaron. Welcome home."

With the fall of night the wind had died; there was a heavy stillness in the old house. Aaron and Adriana sat at table in the *sala mayor,* a pool of light between them from the tapers in the silver candelabrum, the ends of the huge room lost in shadow. From time to time the windows would come alight as heat lightning played across the ridges of the Cantabricas to the south of the hacienda. Felicia came and went in shuffling silence.

From the moment they had met in the gallery, their conversation had progressed in rushes and silences. With years to fill in, Aaron thought that talk would consume the first hours of their meeting. Instead he found this almost electric tension between them that turned them from the casual into dark avenues filled with danger and wonder.

Across the candle flames, Adriana's pale face floated like the image of a madonna, her eyes fixed on his own.

"What are you thinking, Aaron?" she asked, so gently and tenderly that his heart seemed to turn over. Was this the query of a grown woman to a boy? He did not think so. Adriana was seeing him as he was now, not as he had been. He could feel it like a caress.

"You know, Ana," he said. "You have always known."

She closed her eyes for a moment and then opened them again, as a mingled wave of hunger and sadness passed through her. There, across the flames, sat Miguel reborn, and something more: the man she had seen forming all those years ago. When he said, "You have always known," it was no more than the truth. She had always known he loved her, but she had never quite believed that he would reappear to look at her with desire so naked in his eyes. Long ago it had been a game she played, but it was a game no longer. Her awareness of him was a palpable presence.

And Aaron thought, What have I done by coming here? He had told himself time and time again that he wished only to see her once again, nothing more. He hadn't come back to Santanilla to become her lover. Only to be with her, to talk to her, to share her friendship, to serve her if she needed his help and support. And all the time he had lied to himself. There was a skein of fascination that bound him to her, that had become a part of him, and of which he would never be free. He felt a kind of wild joy in accepting this truth at last, a joy in her company, in her touch, and in the passion he saw in her eyes and heard in her voice.

There was so much to be said, he thought. He should tell her of his life, the new life he had made for himself without her. But since the russet sunset light had gone from Santanilla, all of that had faded away with the colors of the day, leaving only Adriana, whom he had loved for as long as he could remember, and whom he loved now. Everything else was unreal.

She rose from the table and said, "Come with me."

With the candelabrum in her hand she walked through the dark corridors and galleries and nearly empty rooms until they stood in the grand *alcoba,* the room Don Alvaro and Doña Maria had once occupied.

"Only this room is unchanged,' she said. "Everything here is as it was." Her hand trembled slightly, making the candle flames sway, and she placed the candelabrum on a massive table beside the great bed.

He looked at her, slender and austere in her black dress. In the uncertain light her hair gleamed more silver than gold. He looked at the soft curve of her cheek, the feathery arch of her brows, her parted lips.

"You should not look at me that way," she said.

Go, Ana, he thought, *run.*

She said, with a ghost of a smile, "Oh, Aaron. There is no Adriana in the calendar of the saints."

"Nor any Saint Aaron, Ana," he said, and took her in his arms so violently they staggered, kissed her, open-mouthed and searching.

Adriana was drowned in sensation. She thought for just an instant of poor, sweet Jean-Claude, who had always said that love could be *un coup de foudre,* a crash of thunder. How could I have doubted it, she wondered, how could I have not known?

She felt Aaron's fingers working at the buttons down the back of her dress, felt the touch of his hand against her naked skin. She dropped her arms and let the dress and all slide to her hips and for a moment they stood apart, looking at one another.

She would never afterwards quite remember whether they walked to the bed or if he carried her. She lay naked, watching him strip. She saw the scars on his arm and chest and shivered at the thought that his slender body had been pierced by steel. And then he knelt on the bed over her, searching her face with eyes in which she saw the man's love and the boy's adoration.

Aaron touched her breasts, cupped them, ran his hands down her flanks, over her hips, her mons. He bent and kissed her knees, the inner softness of her thighs. His hands explored her back and buttocks until she arched herself against him, pulling him down to cover her.

As he entered her he looked at her opened eyes, her parted lips that formed his name. Then her arms and legs were around him and he thrust against her and she against him with a strength that astonished him.

He had never before had a woman he loved. After this, how could he ever be satisfied with less?

Adriana thought: I have known love, but not like this. It was like a fire in her blood. Because she was a woman, her mind was clear while her body responded with passion. She knew that conscience and all that made her Adriana Marburg would return when the blood cooled. But for this moment, with her lover deep within her, she could hear the distant thunder rolling down from the mountains and smile without guilt. For tonight, she thought, and tomorrow, we are lovers. The day after must fend for itself.

In the dawn Adriana awoke and lay still, relishing the feel of the rough linen sheets against her naked skin, the warmth of Aaron's arm across her breasts, the deep and regular sound of his breathing.

Oh, Father Sebastio, what would you give me for penance now?

319

How shocked and dismayed the poor old man would be, troubled by images of unchastity, adultery, and even incest. She drew in a deep breath of the cool morning air and wondered why she felt so marvelous, so renewed. What a lovely thing it was to love and be loved. She had forgotten, through all the bitter years.

She turned to look closely at Aaron's face. Memory and desire could so easily mingle, she thought. Long ago, as a girl, she had seen this same face on the bolster beside her. In her sated state she could not bring herself to think of last night as a betrayal. She had truly loved Miguel, but she had never known him as a young man, filled with fire. There had always been some small part of her left untouched. Until now.

She traced Aaron's straight brows with a fingertip. He murmured and buried his face in her breast. She sucked in her breath at the touch of his lips. Half-waking, he spoke her name. "Dear Ana—"

She cradled his head with her hand and pressed him against her bosom, feeling her nipples rise and a wetness in her loins. Don't judge me, Sebastio, she thought. You never knew the love of man and woman. The shades of Miguel and Don Alvaro were distant, but she could almost hear her father saying, *"Las Parcas nos mandan,* daughter. Take what life offers you and look straight at those foolish Fates. Hold, but do not cling. You are a Santana."

She was supremely happy, happier than she could remember. Each moment was precious. Aaron said, "Adriana, Ana, Ana." She looked at him with love-drowned eyes and spread herself to possess him.

The sun was high when Felicia scratched at the door. Adriana looked at Aaron to see what he would say. He smiled at her and shrugged.

"Come in, Feli," Adriana called from the depths of the great bed.

The *criada,* bearing a tray with coffee and biscuits, came scuttling into the room, a sidelong smile on her broad face.

"It is a beautiful day, Doña Ana," she said, not meeting Aaron's eyes.

Adriana, propped on the bolster, her blond hair tumbled about her face, looked at Aaron. "Shall we ride today?"

"I would like that," he said.

"Feli, tell the *mozo de quadra* to saddle Estrella and Espada. We will ride before breakfast."

"*Sí,* Doña Ana," Felicia said. At the door she turned quickly to bob her head at Aaron. "Good morning, Patron," she said, and vanished in a flurry of giggles.

320

Adriana, sitting proudly, naked to the waist, poured the tiny cups of Moorish coffee. Aaron could not remember ever having seen anything quite so beautiful.

"I love you, Ana," he said.

"Yes," she said caressingly.

"You've always known, haven't you."

"Of course, *corazón,*" she said. "Always."

He went to the window and let the warm morning breeze blow against his skin. Above the red tiles of the kitchen wing of La Casa he could see the distant ridges of the Sierra Cantabrica. Hawks were soaring there, black dots against a sky that seemed limitless. "What now, *querida?*" he said softly. "Whatever now?"

"No plans, Aaron," she said. "No tomorrows. Not yet."

He turned and smiled at her. "You are right, as always. The tomorrows come whether we want them or not. Let's not rush them."

Her clear blue eyes were steady. "Shall I send a *mozo* to Mama and the children at Miraflores?"

Aaron slowly shook his head. "When *las Parcas* offer a gift of time, we'd be fools to refuse it," he said.

Day followed day and night followed night. Even the weather was kind, with only a warm breeze blowing the scent of the dry grasses in the air and drifting the towering cumulus clouds across the deep sky.

They rode—Aaron on old Espada, Adriana on the venerable Estrella—along the foothill ridge trails and through the high pastures where the sheep stood drowsing in the late summer air.

Sometimes, at a distance, they saw Julio working with the stock on the leased grasslands. Adriana ignored him and Aaron felt no need to seek his company. Except for the few servants at La Casa, Felicia and the two *mozos,* they were alone together, and wanted it no other way.

Lying drowsing under a stand of scrubby oaks, Aaron leaning against a tree, Adriana with her head on his shoulder, they spoke of the recent past, of Mexico and what Aaron was trying to do there. Of the distant past, of Micah, they never spoke.

Eyes closed, Adriana asked, "Will you be a great man in Mexico, Aaron?"

His laughter was wry. "I thought so when I left, Ana. Great plans. But there has been an election in Mexico, and the man to whom I pawned my soul seems to have lost it." In Germany he had learned that Porfirio Díaz and Sebastian Lerdo de Tejada had both challenged Benito Juárez, and both had been defeated. Díaz had attempted an armed insurrection and was presently in revolt against the government of Mexico. What this would mean to Aaron's association with Díaz and Don Marcello Marini, he could only guess. And somehow all of that, even Julia, seemed enormously distant and unreal.

"There is a woman, of course," Adriana said gently. "There is always a woman, no?"

"Yes," Aaron said.

Adriana touched his lips with her fingertips. "Don't feel guilty, *corazón*. This has nothing whatever to do with her."

He said, "I have never been so happy, Ana. Or so unhappy."

"I know, my love."

"What are we to do?" He pressed his lips against the silky hair of her temple, breathing in the scent of her.

"We will do what we must do," she said with a faint smile. "We always have."

That afternoon, when they returned to La Casa, Felicia met them with an envelope bearing the stamps of the *Servicio Postal*. She was trembling with excitement. Never before had she met a postal courier and accepted an official document of any sort.

"It is for you, Patron," she said. "It was sent from Santander."

Aaron accepted the envelope and carried it into the *sala mayor*. Adriana asked, "Who knows you are here?"

Aaron, holding the heavy envelope, reluctant to open it, said, "Only my uncle."

Adriana said quietly, "You had better open it."

"Yes," Aaron said, and broke the seals.

There was a short note from Isaac Marburg and a much-traveled cable. Aaron looked quickly at the signature. It was Juan Amaya-Ruiz. He returned to the note from his uncle. It read: "This cablegram arrived for you the day after you left. God be with you."

Aaron handed the note to Adriana and read Juan's cable. It was six weeks old, having followed him from Cologne to Marburg and now to Santanilla by special post. "Aaron Marburg, Hotel Grosser Köln, Köln, Grossdeutschland. Don Marcello has had a stroke, political reverses. Imperative you return at once. Amaya-Ruiz."

Aaron stood, holding the cable, until Adriana took it from him and read it. She looked up with brimming eyes. "You must return," she said.

"Ana—"

She touched his lips with her fingertips. "Hush, my love. We knew it had to end."

He crumpled the telegram and threw it despairingly into the dark fireplace. He stared at the motto of the Santanas carved into the stone of the mantelpiece. *Yo perduro.* I endure. Yes, Adriana was a Santana. But what of me? he thought. How will I live? How will I endure?

He took her in his arms and held her. He put his lips against her pale hair and closed his eyes.

"Soon or late, *corazón,*" she said. "It had to be." There was grief in her voice, and tenderness. Her fingers dug into his back and she clung to him with all her strength, as though to keep at bay the coming loneliness. "When shall you go?"

"Tomorrow," he said.

"Then we still have tonight."

He kissed the tears on her cheeks. We spent the time like prodigals, he thought, uncaring and happy. Now there is only tonight. To last us all our lives. To last us until we die.

36

The stables at Miraflores were new
and very grand, with looseboxes for the ten saddle and carriage horses
and a vast stone room for tack.

It was in the tackroom that Roberto Marburg had called his secret
meeting of the children. Since his grandfather's death in the bullring,
the normally shy boy had become secretive and solemn. He was
ashamed of needing a night light to keep at bay the bad dreams that
plagued him, and in order to balance this perceived weakness and
maintain his status as hereditary leader of the children (as his grandmother never wearied of telling him he must be), he had developed
a peremptory and arbitrary manner in his dealings with his sister
Cecilia, with Ana-Maria Gomez, and with the Alvarez brood.

Maria-Elena Alvarez, a darkly pretty, frail child, had learned to
worship Roberto's slender, blond good looks. As the only daughter in
a family with three sons, she had learned to accept male dominance

324

without question. Ramon, Carlos, and Ernesto Alvarez, any one of whom could have physically dominated Roberto Marburg y Santana, had been cowed by their parents' deference to Doña Maria Santana, who was, after all, a gentlewoman born and a relative of the Bishop of Liencres.

Cecilia Marburg, a child with the sunny disposition of a born conformist, followed her brother's lead in all things as a matter of course. Roberto was the heir, the Patron-to-be of the wonderful sunny lands in California, where one day the family would live like princes in a fairy tale beside the great Ocean-Sea.

Only Ana-Maria Gomez, *peon*-born and peasant-practical, argued with Roberto about his often rash projects. She adored him, had done so ever since she could remember, and would continue to do so for as long as she lived. But it fell to her to be the voice of reason whenever Roberto undertook to do something foolish or dangerous. She was, after all, his *nana*'s daughter, and her duty, as her mother's was, was to guard and protect the young Patron.

Now, with the children gathered in the tackroom at Miraflores, she voiced her opinion with the bluntness she was born to display.

"I do not see why you can't wait until we all go home, Roberto," she said firmly. "It will only be another day and a half."

"I am not asking anyone to go with me," Roberto said loftily. "I am only asking you not to tell Doña Maria until I have gone. I do not *wish* to wait another day. My *brother* is at Santanilla, Anita."

"How do you know that?" Ana-Maria demanded. "It was only a shepherd who said he was. Shepherds," she added knowingly, "sometimes make things up."

"Your father was a shepherd," Maria-Elena Alvarez said primly. She seldom lost an opportunity to remind Ana-Maria Gomez of the vast social gulf that separated her from Roberto Marburg and, of course, herself.

"My father is not a shepherd now," Ana-Maria said, her dark eyes glittering angrily. She understood exactly what Maria-Elena was attempting to do and she accepted her right to do it. But from time to time she longed to remind the daughter of the Alvarez family that they themselves were new to Miraflores and not true gentry, as Don Roberto was. "My father is now a *mozo,* and besides, I don't see what that has to do with anything." She said to Roberto, "Doña Maria and my mother will be furious if you ride off by yourself. It is thirty kilometers, Roberto. It will take you *hours* and *hours.*"

"I think he should go," said Ramon Alvarez, a chubby, red-faced boy of twelve. "Suppose it really is his brother who is visiting Santanilla? Suppose he leaves before you get back? He was a soldier in the American war, wasn't he?"

"Yes," Roberto said proudly. "He commanded a regiment."

"Of cavalry?" Carlos, the youngest Alvarez, wanted to know.

"Of infantry. But he was wounded and decorated," Roberto said. He swallowed the lump that formed instantly in his throat when he thought of his grandfather. "My *abuelo* told me he was a hero in battle."

"That is all very well," Ana-Maria said. "And maybe the shepherd didn't make up a story. But I still think you should wait until Doña Maria is ready to return home. She will be very angry if you go off by yourself, Roberto."

"You should not argue with the Patron, Anita," Maria-Elena said. "It is not your place to do so."

"I argue with him all the time," Ana-Maria said positively. "It is my right. He is my *padrino.* Roberto, are you *certain* Don Aaron has come back?"

"The shepherd said that all the Santanilla herdsmen are talking about it," Roberto said.

Ana-Maria drew a deep sigh. "Well, if you really must do this, then I shall go with you."

Now Roberto was concerned. It rather spoiled his cavalier image of himself galloping into the courtyard at Santanilla on his new gelding (which had recently replaced the aged Blanco as his regular mount) to greet his mysterious brother Aaron.

"I don't know about that, Anita," he said. "Tomasa won't like it."

"Bother 'Tomasa won't like it,' Roberto. She will worry less when they tell her I am with you."

"I'll tell her, Roberto," Ernesto Alvarez said. Ernesto, eleven years old and a second son, had the gift of acquiescence.

"It will be dark on the way," Maria-Elena said, wide-eyed. "Won't you be frightened? Won't you get lost?"

"Frightened? Why should I be frightened? I know all the hill paths. Besides, there will be a moon tonight," Roberto said positively.

"Well," said Ana-Maria, "I am going with you. Trueno can carry the two of us easily." Roberto had rather grandly named his gelding Thunder. It was perhaps too fearsome a name for a ten-year-old docile saddle hack, but it pleased Roberto to think of the sweet-tempered beast as a war-horse.

"Very well, Anita," he said. He knew it was useless to reason with his goddaughter once she was resolved. Even his loftiest *caballero* manner failed to move her. "We will go right after *cena.*" To the others he said, "When we have been gone two hours, you may tell the grown-ups. They won't follow us then. Ramon, you saddle Trueno for me directly after dinner. Elena, you bring us some bread in case we get hungry along the way." He stood up to indicate that the secret meeting was at an end. "We'll be at Santanilla before morning."

"Roberto," Cecilia said tentatively. "What can *I* do?"

Roberto roughed her straight, dark hair and said, "You, little sister? All right, you be the one to tell the *abuela.* She won't be angry with you."

Roberto and Ana-Maria had been riding for three hours when the moon rose and flooded the landscape with light. "You see, Anita," Roberto said. "It's not so dark now."

Ana-Maria, riding pillion behind him, loosened her grip on his belt and squirmed. Her back and buttocks were already very sore and tired, and they still had a long way to go. She wondered if her *padrino* had really been as unafraid as he had seemed to be when they led Trueno out of the gate at Miraflores. He had certainly *seemed* unafraid, but she knew that the dark frightened him, and had ever since Don Alvaro died. The cattle frightened Roberto too, though he would have died rather than admit it. Perhaps it was really braver to face what made one afraid than simply to be without fear. Bulls were usually without fear, and people like Don Julio called that bravery, but to Ana-Maria it seemed more like stupidity. In any case, her *padrino* had great courage. Of that she was certain. She rested her forehead on his back and dozed as Trueno picked his way along the moonlit track toward Santanilla.

Roberto Marburg shifted his weight in the saddle and wondered if by now Doña Maria, angry and concerned, might not have sent a galloper after them. There were plenty of vaqueros at Miraflores for the task. But he doubted it. She would send one at morning with a message to Mama that he must be punished for slipping away to ride home alone and in the dark. The *abuela* did not understand that a man must have adventures, and that if the shepherds' talk was true and his brother truly was at Santanilla, it was important that he should know his younger half-brother was man enough, at least, for a journey between haciendas on his own.

When he was younger, only a child, Roberto thought, he had so often dreamed that Don Aaron would appear and whisk him away to America or New Spain or some other marvelous and exciting place where, Marburgs together, they could share exciting adventures. But the years had passed and Aaron had not come. Surely he *would* have come back, Roberto thought, if he had realized how his brother longed to know him.

And now, if the shepherds were right, Aaron *had* come home to Santanilla. Bright new possibilities opened up when Roberto thought about that. Not that life at Santanilla was so dull, though it was, or so bleak, though it was that too, from time to time. But Aaron, or rather his image of Aaron, had been Roberto's window on the wide world for as long as he could remember. Mama and the *abuela* spoke of the time when they would all live in California, but that was only a promise. He had been hearing about the New Santanilla all his life, it seemed, and the actual change seemed as distant as ever. If the shepherds spoke the truth, Aaron was here in Spain *now.*

He hoped that what he was feeling was not disloyal to Mama and Tomasa and Doña Maria. But since that terrible day in the bullring it seemed that he was always surrounded by women, and only women. Julio had moved down to the *finca,* and Mama had forbidden Roberto to go there. Even the gypsy boys avoided him. Sometimes he wondered if it was because of what had happened in the ring when El Patron was gored to death.

Nodding with fatigue, he rode through the warmth of the late summer night. Trueno had an easy gait, but nevertheless Roberto was growing weary. The moon rose and crossed the zenith and began its descent into the west.

Ana-Maria, asleep with her thin arms around Roberto, sighed and half-woke to murmur, "Will we be home soon, Roberto?"

"Pretty soon now, Anita," he said.

Owls stirred and fluttered in the sparse stands of oaks as they passed. Trueno's hoofbeats were muffled by the dry, powdery earth. Sleeping herds made patches of white in the fields. Occasionally a lamb would awaken to bleat at its mother. The stars were faint in the moon-misted night sky, but Robert could make out the great Northern Cross of the constellation Cygnus, the Swan, overhead. The *abuelo* used to teach him to read the stars, and Chole did too, though she claimed gypsies could see the future up there. He wondered how that could be. The gypsies seemed to have so many ways of knowing the future—the Tarot, the leaves in teacups, the lines in the palm of a hand—and yet they were almost all very poor. Surely, if they had such wonderful knowledge, they would all be rich? He must remember to ask brother Aaron if what the gypsies said was true. He would surely know.

He wondered what brother Aaron would think of his being promised in marriage to Maria-Elena Alvarez. Of course he would understand that it was customary in Old Castile to make such arrangements while the people involved were still children—not that he, Roberto Alvaro de Avila Marburg y Santana, was a *child,* far from it. Eleven, or as near to it as made no difference, might seem a childish age to some people, but Aaron would understand that it was quite old enough for a young man to begin to accept his responsibilities.

The betrothal might make a difference to Aaron, though, when it came to taking his younger brother along to share whatever new adventure he might now be planning. One hoped not, but one must also be prepared for a disappointment. Still, one could never be certain what the future would bring. Why, Aaron might have decided to stay at Santanilla. That would be a fine thing to have happen, though it was not a likely one.

But in eight or nine years, after he and Elena were finally married, there would be time for many wonderful things, and some of them Aaron might want to share. Like the prospect of traveling far across the sea to California to build another Santanilla in a place the *abuela* said was rich and marvelous. Yes, Brother Aaron might just want to do that. Making a new hacienda could absolutely be considered an adventure worthy of two Marburg men.

Roberto shifted in the saddle, carefully so as not to disturb Ana-Maria. His back ached terribly. It was a very long ride all the way from Miraflores to Santanilla, but the ability to stay all night in the saddle was the mark of the caballero. Everyone knew that.

He should have made Ana-Maria stay at Miraflores. This ride was very long for a girl. Elena would never have insisted on coming along the way Anita had done. She was too frightened of the Republican bandits people said plagued the roads and trails. Roberto had never seen any bandits on the roads, Republican or otherwise, but if they did appear he was positive that Trueno, even carrying double, could outdistance them. Trueno had Arab blood, and Arabs were called "drinkers of the wind" because they could outlast almost any other horse in the world. Uncle Julio had told him that a long time ago before it became a bad thing to visit him and Señora Segre and little Paco at the *finca.*

Actually, he thought, if it were only up to him he would prefer to marry Ana-Maria rather than Elena. That was not possible, of course, because Ana-Maria was his *nana*'s daughter. A long time ago, when he was very young, he had said to Tomasa that if he had to take a wife he thought he would take Anita. She had been most upset and had asked him very seriously if he and Anita had been doing things they ought not. He knew even then exactly what she meant. A boy raised on a stock ranch like Santanilla knew what the animals did and understood that men and women did it, too. Although they ought do it only if they were married; otherwise it was shameful and a terrible sin. He hoped he had put his *nana*'s mind at rest when he told her that he would never do anything dishonorable with Anita. Or, for that matter, with anyone else. Privately, the thought of doing it with Maria-Elena was terribly embarrassing. Though he supposed that by the time he was old enough to be married he would feel differently. At least so the *mozo de quadra* had told him one day when he happened to see Espada trying to mount Estrella in one of the pastures.

His head was nodding and it was difficult to keep his grainy eyes open, but they were near enough now to Santanilla that Trueno could find his own way if his rider should fall asleep.

Another hour passed, and they found themselves on the road south of Santanilla, a straight wagon track lined with very tall, dark cypress trees. Mourning doves perched for the night heard the children on horseback passing and gurgled their displeasure at being disturbed so early in the morning.

"Are we almost there, Roberto?" Ana-Maria murmured sleepily.

"Be patient, Anita," he said, "We'll be there soon now."

She rubbed her face against his back and he thought again about Espada and Estrella. The animals had not embarrassed him, but the *mozo* had, with his smirky way of talking. What had made it worse was that he had seen this same *mozo* in the feed barn with one of the *criadas* before they all got sent away. The girl had her skirts hoisted to her waist and the *mozo*, trousers down his knees and buttocks exposed, had been lying between her legs and pumping, just as Espada did. The man and woman had been laughing and whispering and sweating on a bed of loose hay. Roberto and Anita had been up in the loft trapping mice when the *mozo* and *criada* sneaked in and began to half undress. Ana-Maria had hushed Roberto until the two below were done and gone. "Mama and Doña Maria would want to know what *we* were doing in the loft," Anita said practically. And Roberto had remembered his talk with Tomasa and agreed it was best to let the matter drop. But he had never again been able to see either of the servants without remembering those white buttocks pumping away between the girl's fat legs.

Perhaps, he thought, it would all be clear and less distasteful when he grew older. Anita, who was in so many ways more mature than he, assured him that it was. "Mama and Papa do it all the time," she said matter-of-factly.

Roberto had concluded that if solemn old Raoul Gomez and Tomasa did it, it was because it was not sinful between man and wife. One could not expect Ana-Maria to make such fine distinctions. She was, after all, a *peon* and a girl.

The Northern Cross had swung round to the west when Trueno, with the two children on his back, ambled under the stone gateway to Santanilla. The moon, nearly full, hung low in the sky, sending long night shadows ahead of the riders. Roberto tried to estimate the time. Near to five in the morning, he guessed. If Doña Maria had not sent a galloper, the house would be silent, with everyone asleep. They could creep into his own room and sleep until the sun rose and then he could burst in on Aaron (if he really was, as all the shepherds said, truly there). He would confess to Aaron what he had done and why, and of course Aaron, being a man, would understand.

Trueno, smelling his home stable, began to jog and Roberto quieted him with horseman's hands. He whispered to Ana-Maria to wake up and she did so, murmuring, "Roberto, I'm so tired."

"We are home now," he said, sitting tall in the saddle and refusing to succumb to the aches in his legs, back, and buttocks.

He rode Trueno into the horsebarn and heard Espada and Estrella snuffling and whickering a greeting. There was a strange horse in the stable. Aaron *must* be here, Roberto thought. He let Ana-Maria slide to the ground and then dismounted himself. While Anita waited sleepily, he unsaddled Trueno, filled his waterbucket and manger, and put him in his loosebox.

"Now, Anita," he whispered. "Be *quiet.*"

The children crossed the compound to the kitchen wing of La Casa. They crept past Felicia's room. The early morning was fresh, but the air was warm. The wind had not begun to blow; it seldom did before sunrise. Feli slept with her windows open. Through the *rejas* they could hear her softly snoring. Ana-Maria giggled and Roberto hushed her, and they entered the gallery to the family wing.

At the glass doors that connected his mother's room to the gallery and the garden, Roberto paused to listen. He could hear nothing. Cautiously he pushed the glazed door ajar and peered inside.

His mother's great bed, white in the moonlight, was unrumpled, the counterpane stretched taut. The room was empty. Roberto was nonplussed. He whispered, "Mama?"

"Where could she be, Roberto?" Anita asked.

"Hush, Anita," he whispered. He felt uneasy, oddly disoriented. He had no answer for Ana-Maria, but where *was* she?

The children returned to the gallery and crept across the arches of moonlight spilling on the flagstones. Somewhere a mourning dove made a cooing sound in the night.

"Listen." Ana-Maria held him back.

He could hear murmuring voices, a man's and a woman's. His mother's voice.

He moved down the gallery toward the great windows of Don Alvaro's room. The room that was kept exactly as it had always been when El Patron was alive. To Roberto it was a frightening and holy place.

He could hear his mother's voice more clearly now. He could not make out the words but the tone it was soft, tender, filled with emotion and sadness.

He reached the *reja* and looked through the bars, past the open window and the casement. The moonlight, slanting low, filled the room.

He heard Ana-Maria's indrawn breath and felt his own. The great bed was disarrayed, the bedclothes thrown back. His mother and a man were making love. The cold light glistened on their nakedness, on her silvery golden hair.

Roberto stood transfixed. Suddenly his stomach heaved and he thought he might be sick. Ana-Maria pulled him back silently. He felt himself trembling. Aaron. *Aaron.*

His legs felt like wood as he walked stiffly back down the gallery. *Aaron.*

He began to weep and broke into a run for the horsebarn. Ana-Maria followed him. When he reached Trueno's stall, he did not bother to saddle him. His hands were shaking so that he had trouble putting on the bridle, but Ana-Maria helped him. *Aaron.*

He pulled himself to Trueno's back and wrenched his head toward the door. Anita said, "Roberto! Don't leave me!"

Without a word he pulled her up behind him and dug his heels into the horse's flanks.

Soon they were galloping up the trail behind La Casa that led to their favorite ridge. Roberto's eyes were so blurred with tears that he could not see, but the horse knew the way and took it.

When they reached the crest of the ridge, Trueno was lathered and breathing hard. Roberto reined him to a walk. Even now he could not bring himself to abuse an animal. Ana-Maria clung to him from behind, silent and frightened.

The first light of dawn was in the eastern sky when they reached the second ridge behind La Casa. Here Roberto dropped the reins and let Trueno come to a halt. He slid from the animal's back and crouched on the ground, wracked with sobbing. Ana-Maria squatted beside him, her dark eyes filled with concern.

Presently Roberto lifted his head and stared down at the distant hacienda. For the better part of an hour he sat so, unmoving.

As the sky grew light there was activity in the compound of La Casa. The children on the second high ridge could see that a *mozo* had saddled the strange horse and stood waiting in the dawn light.

After a time a man and woman appeared. The children knew who they were. Roberto saw them embrace before the man mounted. For a time he sat on the rangy horse, looking down at the woman. Then he wheeled his mount and galloped down the road to the stone gate and the road to Santander.

Roberto gripped Ana-Maria's thin shoulders with all his strength. "Anita," he said, "Promise me. You must never tell what we saw. Never."

"I promise, Robert," she said, and embraced him, kissing his wet cheeks.

"If you do, Anita," he said brokenly, "I will die of shame."

The cathedral on the Plaza Constitución was filled to capacity with the people of Tihuacan. Outside the day was gray and overcast, with a hint of rain in the air. But inside the old Spanish church, the warmth of a thousand candles and half again that many people kept the cold at bay.

Aaron Marburg stood, flanked by Dr. Amaya-Ruiz and Juan Ortega (almost beside himself with pride at the honor), at the opening in the altar rail. The odor of candlewax and incense lay heavy in the air. The Bishop of Sinaloa, resplendent in jeweled surplice and miter, stood waiting. The stained-glass windows near the beamed ceiling glowed with the silvery brilliance of the winter day.

For Aaron and his intimates, this was the second religious ceremony in as many weeks. Fourteen days ago he had stood at the font of the tiny village church of La Cruz, seat of the *criollo* Arsellos—relations of Don Marcello's long-dead wife. There, with Juan Amaya-Ruiz and

334

Don Marcello standing as sponsors, Aaron Marburg had been baptized and accepted into the community of the Holy Roman and Apostolic Church by young Father Bernal, a Jesuit, and the most liberal priest in western Sinaloa state.

Aaron looked out over the sea of faces. These were the people among whom he would now spend the rest of his life. They had come, some of them, out of friendship for him and Julia. Others had come as a tribute to Don Marcello, who had fought his way back to a semblance of health, some said, just to see his daughter and heiress married. The old man hobbled about with the help of a cane, his face was alive only on one side, but Amaya said that his obvious joy and satisfaction were better than any specific he could prescribe.

There was no organ in the church, but a choir of dark-faced *mestizo* boys in the loft filled the building with sweet, melodious chanting. Aaron studied the faces of the saints in their niches. Saint Teresa, Saint Claire, Saint John, and Saint Thomas. More grandly displayed was the Holy Virgin in her aspect of Guadalupe, her blue robe studded with stars of gold. Above the altar, on a cross of solid silver, hung the Christ, His hands pierced with golden nails, a crown of golden thorns on His brow. Everywhere in the cathedral was the glitter of gold and silver. The bishopric of Sinaloa was rich with the precious metals generations of *indios* had labored to dig from the mines of the Sierra Morenas.

Aaron half-closed his eyes and remembered the forgiving Christ over the altar of Sebastio's tiny church at Santanilla. Was He still so forgiving, locked in his dark and empty chapel below La Casa? Did He look down upon His new communicant with contempt? "We are all sinners, Don Aaron," the young priest at La Cruz had murmured through the grille at Aaron's first confession. *"Ego te absolvo, filius."* Was it really as simple as that? Aaron wondered. What would Adriana say to him now? Where was she, this day, this minute? What was she feeling? What was she remembering?

All of that is ended, he told himself. In time the pain will grow less. Like the Santanas, I will endure. And there will come a time when I scarcely remember her, please God. He looked again at the figure on the great crucifix. I have taken Your hand, he thought. You are right to doubt my faith, but I have given all that I have, all that I love. Let it be enough.

The crowd murmured approvingly as the bridal party appeared. Julia's hand rested on her father's arm as he limped slowly toward the altar. Behind Julia came the bridesmaids, twenty of them, each on the arm of a *novio*.

Aaron watched Julia as she came nearer. She wore a white dress of lace and taffeta that had belonged to her mother and her mother's mother. Her only jewelry was the golden coin of Iturbide, her father's talisman. Aaron could see the joy on Don Marcello's twisted face. He could not see Julia's eyes because her face was hidden behind a *mantilla* of white lace, but she was looking at him. He could feel her happiness, her trust.

When she reached his side she raised the veil and he saw that her eyes, green as the sea, were brimming with tears. Her lips were slightly parted, her cheeks flushed. Aaron felt a surging warmth of affection for her. I promise you, he told her silently, that I will never give you cause to regret this day. She smiled at him, and he at her. Then they turned to face the priest at the altar.

After the High Nuptial Mass there was a reception at Don Marcello's Italian *palazzo,* and the workmen from the Trituradora-Fénix were given a special *fiesta de boda* of their own in the gardens of the house on the Olas Altas. The sky cleared as night fell and the songs of the *mariachis* were sung under a ringed full moon.

All three newspapers in Tihuacan reported the wedding extensively. The radical *La Prensa* described the bride as beautiful, and noted that she was well known for her work among the poor. *El Diario,* scorning flowery compliments, wrote that the gentry of Tihuacan "without exception" attended the nuptial Mass and reception. And *El Observador,* seeking an international nuance, reminded its readers that Don Aaron Marburg was "a hero" of the North American Civil War. The article erroneously identified him as having served with the Army of the Confederacy, but the mistake was little noticed. Many Tihuacantecos had never bothered to distinguish one side from the other in the War Between the States anyway.

All three of the journals took special notice of the fact that though still at odds with the government in Mexico City (and therefore technically a rebel), General Porfirio Díaz sent a representative to the wedding, a full colonel of infantry bearing an enormous silver service as a wedding gift.

Machinery from Germany had been arriving at the port for some weeks now, and the work of rebuilding the Trituradora-Fénix had begun. The local bankers had become uneasy when Don Marcello fell ill, but the situation had been swiftly rectified when Aaron had appeared to take command of both his own business enterprises and Don Marcello's.

His appearance at *el Jefe*'s wedding had served notice that Juan Ortega, now *gerente,* manager, of the Trituradora-Fénix, had been elevated socially to the tiny but growing middle class of Tihuacan. He was now put in temporary command of the Trituradora-Fénix while Aaron and his new bride took their wedding trip to the United States.

In Tihuacan, this was an unbreakable tradition. Newlyweds of means *always* honeymooned in California, unless they were willing to devote six months or more to a Grand Tour of Europe. Few were. Travel was too difficult and California was too convenient. Aaron and Julia traveled by ship to Los Angeles.

The trip went well. Julia enjoyed herself extravagantly. And if, from time to time, she detected a sadness in Aaron, she did not ask questions. She allowed herself to believe that his brief stay in Germany with his family was the source of his melancholy. Julia Marburg, married fewer than three weeks, was already acquiring what her *criada* and *nana* Eufemia called *saber,* that wisdom without which no marriage can survive.

If there was something else in her husband's past, something that had ended and whose ending gave him pain, Julia had no wish to know of it. She loved Aaron fiercely, and she was resolved that nothing would ever change that.

By the time Julia and Aaron returned to Tihuacan, she was pregnant. Her life as Doña Julia Marburg stretched out before her into the years ahead. She was content.

Westward: 1879

For Adriana Marburg, the years
that passed between her last view of Aaron vanishing down the road
toward Santander and her first sight of the land left to the Santanas in
California by Don Esteban were a test of her determination and courage. She had promised herself and her family that the Marburgs would
begin again in a new country, and the doubts that plagued her nights
were firmly suppressed.

Suppressed, too, were the memories of Aaron. She was a Santana
and she lived by the family motto: *Yo perduro.*

In the spring of the year in which Roberto Alvaro de Avila Marburg y Santana reached the age of eighteen, he was married in the
cathedral of Santander to Maria-Elena Alvarez, who was one week past
her seventeenth birthday. Adriana would have preferred to wait
longer, but the poverty of Santanilla was beyond bearing.

For these newlyweds there was no Grand Tour, no honeymoon.

340

On the day following the nuptial Mass celebrated by the recently elevated Archbishop of Liencres, the entire population of Santanilla—even including Julio Santana and Soledad Segre—were dragooned into a flurry of packing and planning for the move by Adriana and her people to the property she had already, in her mind, named Nueva Santanilla.

All that had not been sold for ready money, all that remained at Santanilla was packed into trunks and crates: furniture, crockery, paintings, silver, crystal, linens, books, papers, heirlooms, *all.* For Chole Segre, Adriana left only the bare house, and that grudgingly. Before the summer winds began to blow across the dry hills of Old Castile, the Marburgs were on the move.

For weeks the drays, hauled by oxen, traveled the roads between Santander and the hacienda, moving Adriana's chattels to the quayside. With Raoul Gomez driving the wagon, Adriana made the journey daily, dealing with the new American consul, with shipping agents, with warehousemen and bankers. Through the long days she worked tirelessly, caught up in a furious determination.

During this period her son Roberto was useless to her. He was totally devoted to soothing his young wife's fears. Maria-Elena, who had been a frail child, had grown into a frail woman. She was frightened by the activity around her and by the thought that soon she would be leaving Spain for an unknown place.

To Ana-Maria Gomez fell the task of comforting her mother, Tomasa, and soothing the *abuela,* Doña Maria. As the time for actual departure approached, Tomasa was swept by storms of weeping. Doña Maria grew stiffer and more irascible. Tomasa needed to be assured again and again that the Catholic Church had, in fact, reached as far as California and that there would be priests of God there to celebrate the Mass. Doña Maria took to spending silent hours alone in the bare observatory with its memories of Don Alvaro Santana. Adriana refused to know that her mother was filled with the grief of an old woman about to be torn from her roots, but Anita understood it and took care to show Doña Maria that all of Don Alvaro's personal belongings were being packed to make the long journey to California.

So shaken was Doña Maria by what was taking place around her that she even managed, after many years of angry disdain, to be civil to Chole Segre and Julio. This civility took the form of acknowledging, at long last, her own blood ties to their children—now three in number.

On the last night she was to sleep at Santanilla, Doña Maria spent three solitary hours on her knees at the sealed door of the mausoleum containing the crypts of her mother- and father-in-law, her husband, her son-in-law, three of her sons, and her chaplain-confessor of sixty years.

When she returned to the stripped house she dispatched Raoul Gomez to summon Julio and Soledad into her presence. They came, as disturbed and weary as everyone else on the estate, Julio apprehensive, Soledad wary. Doña Maria said, "It is unlikely that after tomorrow I shall ever again see either of you again in this life. Marry. Do so as soon as you can decently arrange it. It is unworthy of the blood they bear that Paco, Clara, and Caridad go through life as bastards. That is all I have to say to you." She removed the wedding band she had worn for more than half a century. It came easily from her thin, bony finger. She handed the ring to Soledad. "Use it. Honor it," she said. "And now good-bye."

The next morning the family climbed into the landau and, followed by the last dray loaded with steamer trunks, began the final journey to Santander. Adriana's eyes filled with unwilling tears as she saw her mother lift her chin and refuse to look back at the home to which she had come as a girl.

Adriana brushed the tears away angrily. Already, with the pilgrimage barely begun, she was trembling with fatigue. Nor had she permitted herself to admit how much she too loved Santanilla. She was like the beleaguered general of a sorely tried army, and there was still half a world to cross. Her son could devote himself to comforting his sobbing wife and his lamenting *nana*. Her mother could play the defeated duelist departing the field of honor, not by choice but by bitter necessity. But Adriana allowed herself no such indulgences. We have a very long way to journey before *I* can weep, she told herself.

The family remained at Santander for a further two weeks before they and all their belongings could be loaded aboard an old paddle-wheel steamer bound for New York. It was not until the coast of Spain had sunk below the eastern horizon, and mother, son, daughter-in-law, and servants were settled in their cramped cabins, that Adriana could rest.

She did not rest long. The sea was rough and Tomasa grew hysterical. Doña Maria slapped her out of it and then retired to her cabin to read the Bible and pray. Roberto and Ana-Maria might have enjoyed the crossing but for Elena, who suffered from seasickness and complained jealously whenever Roberto was not at her side. Raoul Gomez made common cause with the deck crew, sitting in the forecastle playing melancholy Castilian airs on his guitar.

New York was a wonder—and a nightmare. Adriana, who had seen Berlin and Paris and Rome, was stunned by the size and squalor of the great city. She refused to acknowledge her disgust. She also refused to listen to complaints from any of her people.

It took eighteen days to get the Marburgs' belongings off the ship and moved across a brackish, oily river to a railroad yard in a place known as New Jersey. Meanwhile, Roberto was deputized to keep the family together in the grimy hotel they had unwisely chosen.

Another week passed before Adriana could arrange passage for all by rail to California. Crates and trunks were lost, found, lost again. A box of lace given at birth to Adriana by her *Abuela* Borjas was never seen again. Tomasa hid in her room, terrified by the clangor of horsecars, refusing to move until it was time actually to board the train.

It was now midsummer in New York, and the air seemed to sweat. Elena announced that if the weather did not cool she would surely die.

Then began a rail journey of unbelievable length across America.

Adriana saw a procession of towns, each separated from the next by mile upon mile of farmland, then of empty prairie. At first the land was green and the towns and cities made of red brick. But soon the towns were of wood, with strange fronts on the stores like free-standing walls behind which the buildings hid—long boxes with metal roofs rusting in the glare of a merciless sun.

The larger cities, with names like Dayton, Cincinnati (Adriana remembered with a swift, silent pang that Aaron had once sent a letter to her from this strange place), St. Louis—these the travelers saw in their worst possible aspects, from sidings and switching yards. Everything seemed new, and swiftly deteriorating. The Marburgs watched the harsh country pass slowly by the windows of the creeping train.

Beyond Wichita were more and vaster grasslands. Heat shimmered in the air as the train rolled slowly westward. Ragged Indians stood silently by the right of way. Men in old black hats and blankets. Women with children like tiny mummies on their backs. Strange names and tiny towns, some only a wooden fort and a single store. Alva, Woodward, Pampa. From noon until dark the sun burned into the coaches like the hot eye of God. Elena grew faint and vomited each morning. Adriana suppressed a furious desire to tell her daughter-in-law that it was almost indecent to become pregnant under such conditions as these. Doña Maria's black eyes glittered angrily as she looked at the endless, featureless plains. Adriana could read her thoughts: Was it for land like this that we left Santanilla?

Gross and uncouth men wearing revolvers on their belts and carrying enormous rifles got drunk on cheap whisky and wantonly murdered the stupid bison who loped innocently along beside the track.

In the foothills of the Rocky Mountains, Doña Maria's peppery bad temper abated slightly at the sight of rising grasslands and pastures filled with cattle and sheep. Raoul Gomez's guitar melodies grew less sad. Yipping cowboys chased the train, firing their pistols in the air. Adriana was reminded of the vaqueros they had left behind. The movement of the train as it climbed toward the mountains made Elena complain. Tomasa combed her hair and wiped her narrow brow with handkerchiefs dampened with precious water. Roberto and Ana-Marie hung from the open windows, watching the panorama of range and stream, high prairie and granite bluff. The train labored higher, pulled by double engines. It was midsummer now, but the high mountains touched the travelers with their icy, ancient breath as the tracks climbed almost to the snow line before once again descending.

The Nevada Basin terrified them. The other passengers on the train were loudly willing to tell this odd gaggle of foreigners that this was where the *real* West began. Adriana looked in horror at the endless miles of rock, sand, and alkali sink. Once again the heat made the images of the land waver and shimmer like some underwater desert.

Then, with dramatic suddenness, there were more great mountains. Their Spanish name was oddly comforting. Sierra Nevada. The Snowy Mountains. Far vaster than the Cantabricas, they seemed to make a wall of sheer gray rock through which there could be no passage. But the train crept westward still, clinging to granite cliffs above rushing white mountain rivers. "In winter," their fellow passengers told the Spaniards, "no trains can negotiate the passes. Twenty years ago, wagon trains were lost in these mountains and men ate one another." Tomasa shut her eyes so as not to see the sheer dropoffs, and Elena whimpered and shivered in the cold. All of Adriana's army shivered, wrapped in thin blankets, in the badly heated coach.

Then once again there was a swift, almost theatrical change of scenery. The train descended through the great granite scarps into a valley of land so rich and black that Raoul Gomez could not take his eyes from it. "Doña Ana," he said, "will Nueva Santanilla be like this? One could grow anything in such earth."

And Adriana, achingly weary but still resolute, replied, "Yes, Raoul. It will be like this."

Oakland, a flat city by a great bay, lay under a thick blanket of cloud. The summer sun glistened on fog banks for days on end. Adriana moved her people into a hotel and set about once again to hire coaches and drays. There were days of unloading and repacking. There were visits to the handsome city on the western shore of the bay for shopping, for finding difficult supplies, or simply to look at the narrow entrance to the bay that the inhabitants of San Francisco called the Golden Gate.

Then the whole traveling enterprise had to be put once again in motion. We are like gypsies, Adriana thought; how Julio's woman would laugh to see us now. Next came more long, dusty miles across the valley south of the bay, out of the gray summer and back into heated air untouched by the summer winds of the baylands. They crossed the Santa Clara Valley and the thickly forested Santa Cruz range. There were redwood trees here, which none of them had ever seen. Conifers as tall as cathedral towers with thick, grainy red trunks. "If there are tree gods," Raoul Gomez whispered to his wife, "they live here." Tomasa hushed him and crossed herself, hoping that no one but she had heard.

The caravan of wagons descended to the town of Santa Cruz on the northern rim of the bay of Monterey, where Spanish galleasses had once dropped their great anchors. And finally the Marburgs came to Monterey, where Adriana, like any good general, bivouacked her troops and went forth with Roberto and Raoul, on rented horses, to reconnoiter the last leg of their journey.

What she saw lifted her heart. There was grass here, and water, and pastures rising steeply to the mountains called Santa Lucia. She found a high knoll above a ridge overlooking steep drops to a rocky coastline of rugged beauty.

Adriana sat on her horse between Raoul and her wide-eyed son. "Yes," she said. "This is our land."

They returned to Monterey and set about recruiting workmen from among the Mexicans who had lived by the bay since the days when the state was a part of New Spain.

And the day when the first spadeful of earth was to be turned for the new house, Adriana declared a *special* day, because her spirits were high.

From the vast clutter of possessions they had cached in their hotel rooms and in warehouses in the town, Adriana had Roberto find Don Alvaro's sword, the Toledo blade he had carried against the Carlists. Raoul was given the old Patron's revolver to carry.

That day, Adriana ordered tents taken so that the entire family could spend their first night on the land. When they reached the knoll —Adriana in the lead, followed by Raoul and Roberto and then the buggy with Ana-Maria, Elena, and Doña Maria, and after that the first of the loaded wagons and a dray with a dozen Mexican workmen—

Adriana took a book of her father's from her saddlebag and began to read out the instructions for claiming a territory. "There must be a cross," she read, "and there should be a Mass. Then guns should be fired. The captain-general must draw his sword and say that the land is now taken. He must perform symbolic acts of ownership, the throwing of stones or the hacking of trees. And then water taken from a spring or a river must be poured on the earth. That is how it is done."

Anita clapped her hands with delight as Adriana indicated to Roberto that he should bare his grandfather's sword. Elena looked at her mother-in-law as though she thought her demented, perhaps by the terrible journey. But Adriana was smiling and so, amazingly, was Doña Maria, whose bright dark eyes seemed filled with tears of pride.

The wind blew fresh from the sea. Adriana loosened her hair and let it fly like a golden pennant. She looked at Raoul and instructed him to take the pistol, load it, and hold it high. Tomasa she told to lift the crucifix from her bosom and raise it so that all could plainly see the holy cross.

Adriana closed the old book and replaced it carefully in her saddlebag. Then she took from the bag a small leather flask filled with water from the first spring they had passed on the way to this place.

The workmen, on their feet on the dray, watched in fascination.

"Now, Roberto," Adriana said, and Roberto, grinning with delight at his mother's glorious madness, galloped to the nearest tree and struck it with his grandfather's sword.

"Now, Raoul," Adriana said, and Raoul Gomez fired six shots at the sky.

"And I," she said, and emptied the leather flask onto the ground.

The Mexican workmen all applauded and shouted. They were awed and enchanted by the slender, beautiful woman with the yellow hair who spoke to them in the elegant Spanish of Old Castile.

Adriana's voice was firm and clear. "I say that by God's grace the name of this place is Nueva Santanilla, and that it is ours until God chooses otherwise."

For the rest of their lives, all who were there that day remembered how Doña Adriana Ana-Maria de Marburg y Santana brought her family to put down their roots in the new land.

TWO

1881

At his mother's insistence, and in spite of considerations of convenience and ease of construction, the main house of Nueva Santanilla Ranch had been built on a high hilltop overlooking the sea. Roberto Marburg had never regretted it, and never less than on this day—the day, Dr. Harrison assured him, on which Roberto's son would be born.

The house was filled with women and excitement, with everyone waiting for the event. Elena had been in labor since early morning and Harrison was professionally certain that the child would be born before nightfall. Doña Maria, his mother, Tomasa, two young *criadas,* and Ana-Maria all seemed to have some function to perform, while he had none. "You have done your work, *mi macho,*" Tomasa had said. "Now stay out of the way until we call for you."

And so Roberto had walked up the rocky spine of the mountain toward its highest point, from where he could keep watch on the ranch house and still see both the east pastures, where the new herd of white-faced cattle grazed, and the series of lower hills dropping swiftly to the sheer bluffs and the Pacific.

It was a day of breathtaking beauty and clarity. The oaks growing in the steep draws and ravines were thick and green, the hills to the north, toward Monterey Bay, were turning summer-brown, and the higher mountains of the Santa Lucias showed a lavender shade mottled with green at this time of day. The sun was still high enough to make a dazzling path on the vast sea to the west, and the horizon was a sharp, clean line in the clear, sparkling air. The sky was like blue crystal, without suggestion of cloud or mist. Red-tailed hawks rode the rising currents of air along the ridgeline. Roberto had absolutely forbidden Raoul Gomez or any of the vaqueros to shoot at them. Even if they did occasionally take a lamb—which Roberto doubted—the soaring mountain birds were far too beautiful to be killed.

He sat in the dry grasses at the base of a tree, smoking and chewing on a stem of wild oat and wondering when the women would call him to come look at his newborn child.

He did not *feel* very fatherly. At least not yet. But that was to be expected. Roger Harrison, not yet thirty himself, had been stunned to be presented with a husband and wife so young. Roberto smiled wryly at the memory. Elena, already showing her pregnancy but looking for all the world like a convent schoolgirl, must have shocked his Yankee Protestant sense of propriety. Americans seemed to have difficulty grasping the fact of Spanish dynastic marriages. Forty years ago in this land, Roberto thought, it would have been the youthful *gringo* physician who was the anomaly.

He looked down at the ranch house—people seldom used the term hacienda in California now. It was still unfinished. Work on the wing where he and Elena and their children would live had been stopped in expectation of Elena's confinement. But soon the massive framework would be swarming with workmen again, local Mexicans and some *yanquis,* who worked at a pace that dismayed Raoul Gomez, a man whose very blood flowed to the tempo of Old Castile.

Nueva Santanilla had been planned to resemble the original and it did, somewhat. The layout of the residence was much the same, though smaller and better organized. The white plaster walls, the arches of the galleries, and the dull red roof tiles were pure Castilian. But there were differences. The walls were of adobe; there was little native stone in the Santa Lucia foothills. The barns and outbuildings were of wood, and so were the paddock fences. The range (to a horseman's despair) was fenced with barbed wire. Far down the slope, near the dirt road that ran between Monterey and Big Sur, a gateway had been built that almost exactly duplicated the gate of the old Santanilla, complete with the wrought-iron device hanging from the adobe keystone. The letter M had been interwoven with the Santana S. The same device was branded on the rumps of the cattle in the pastures.

So far there were only two hundred head of beef on the land, and a small breeding flock of sheep. Adriana spoke of buying more land before adding to the livestock. She spoke, too, of buying a proper Arab or thoroughbred stud to breed to the four saddle mares she had purchased from Senator Stanford's stock farm in the north.

All of this cost an enormous amount of money, Roberto knew. Every *peseta* of Elena's dowry and all the money Adriana had been able to husband those last years at old Santanilla had been poured unstintingly into the new.

Doña Maria, the *abuela,* sometimes appeared to be uneasy about the way Adriana spent, but she had never gone so far as to suggest caution. Nor would she. The old lady was still the stiff-backed Spanish patrician she had always been, convinced in her heart of hearts that money existed only to be spent on the land or given to the Church. A substantial sum had been made over as Cecilia's dowry when she began her novitiate at the convent of Santa Clara last winter. Three years ago there had been talk of leaving Cecilia at the convent of Santa Teresa of Avila, but Adriana would have none of it, insisting on an American convent.

Roberto, as the man of the house—the only man, in fact, in a household of women—was the nominal proprietor of Nueva Santanilla. And he did oversee and control the activities on the ranch, tasks that came naturally to him and for which he had been schooled since birth. But all the financial affairs of Nueva Santanilla were conducted by his mother. It was Adriana who handled the money, who paid the hands, who journeyed when necessary to San Francisco to deal with the bankers.

Sitting alone on this special day, Roberto Marburg considered his mother. He hoped that he had grown dispassionate, but he doubted that he was. There were still memories—one in particular—that knotted his belly with shame and anger. He had suppressed that early morning at Santanilla so savagely that it had grown dreamlike. Sometimes he wondered if it were the same for Ana-Maria. But he had never spoken to her of it, nor she to him. She was his goddaughter, and the injunction he had put upon her was lifelong.

Adriana Marburg was forty-one this year. To a young man of twenty that should seem very old indeed. But his mother had never grown old in his sight, not as other women seemed to do. Dear Tomasa was now heavy and slow moving, with gray in her dark hair, and she was younger than Adriana by almost a half-dozen years. Yet this very morning, as Adriana moved about the house preparing to help Dr. Harrison and welcome her grandchild into the world of Nueva Santanilla (a world of her making, Roberto reminded himself), she looked like a girl. Her body was firm and still slender. Her face was as unlined and beautiful as it had ever been. It wasn't witchcraft, Roberto thought wryly. It was the way he saw her. The goddess queen of the Santanas.

He picked up a twig and dug at the earth with it. One did not *love* a goddess, he thought. One might worship or adore her, but love was too frail and fallible an emotion. A part of his relationship with his mother had been determined by the peculiar way in which children of his race and class were reared. All the physical comforts he had ever known as a child had come not from Adriana but from Tomasa, at whose breasts he had suckled, whose large peasant hands had healed his hurts and tended his needs.

Of course, Adriana had always been there. But to be worshipped, not loved. He had come to realize that he could have forgiven Tomasa that terrible moment at Santanilla. But how did one forgive a goddess? How did one even presume to think one should? If Jesus had fled from the garden of Gethsemane, how would the apostles have dealt with His betrayal? Would they have dared judge Him?

He threw the stick away and stood; the wind from the sea ruffled his silver blond hair. He had become a masculine version of his mother, though he seldom realized it. He had the same narrow brows, the same sea blue eyes, the same way of looking thoughtfully at the distant horizon. Sometimes he wondered if there was anything at all in him of his father, whom he remembered only as a man wasting away in a sickbed.

He had been in California only a short time, but he had fallen in love with the new land. On the higher slopes of the Santa Lucia range were meadows that turned green in the mild winter rains and brown as early as April. The very seasons were different here, and gentler. Yet the Pacific storms, when they came up out of the southwest, could drench the land and fill the steep ravines with plunging, frothing torrents. And even from Nueva Santanilla, four miles as the crow flies from the ocean cliffs, one could see the breakers storming against the rocky shoreline, crashing against the land in huge explosions of spume and spindrift.

In the spring and fall the weather tended to turn almost unbelievably beneficent, with sparkling clear days of sea winds gentled by the sun. On such days the ocean's surface would be patterned by the prevailing northwesterlies; the ocean itself would display an astonishing variety of colors, from a pale turquoise green near the shore to a deep purple blue where the continental shelf began its plunge into the abyss.

Before her pregnancy had become too far advanced to allow it, Elena accompanied him down to the beaches where the basaltic spines of the mountains had been upthrust in some millennial upheaval to form chains and peninsulas of dark rock to challenge the sea. There the tidepools teemed with life and the muted colors of the temperate sea. And in the vast kelp beds just offshore, the sea otters would play, mocking the seals basking on the myriad rocky islets over which the waves rolled and broke into showers of diamond droplets in the sun.

This was a kinder land than the coast of Old Castile, but there were elements of strangeness, too. In summer the fogs covered this coast with a thick blanket of mist, causing the steamers and lumber schooners that passed to seek a course far offshore, away from the sawtooth reefs in the near sea. And there was a life deep in the earth that could frighten the unprepared. Miles to the east, in the Salinas Valley, the great San Andreas fault occasionally shifted and sent tremors through hundreds of miles of California. The first time a small earthquake had set the wrought-iron chandelier in the *sala mayor* to swaying, Elena and Tomasa had dissolved into terrified weeping. But Roger Harrison said that one became accustomed to such things here, and that they were more frightening than destructive.

Roberto looked down toward the ranch house. His mother and Dr. Harrison stood in the gallery talking. Roberto waited to see if either of them would look up toward the hill and signal him to come down, but neither did.

He wondered if he should be worried about Elena. Everyone had assured him that Elena would be fine, though the confinement and her labor might be long because she was small and this was her first child. Still, it troubled him that she had seemed so weary when he allowed himself to be driven from the house by the bustling women.

Maria-Elena Marburg was only eighteen, after all. Hardly more than a child. He thought of her dark, trusting eyes and her elfin face. It seemed that he had known her all of his life, though this was not quite true. He remembered the first time she and her brothers had come to Santanilla.

He had always been grateful that his mother and grandmother had planned and arranged his marriage to Elena long ago. He could not imagine, even now, how he would have faced the ordeal of having to find a wife for himself. Except for Ana-Maria, he had never really known a girl of his own age.

And Elena suited. She could be demanding. But how many other young women, he wondered, would have acquiesced in a marriage that meant an immediate separation from home and family? The move to California had been put in train within weeks of the grand wedding in Santander.

From time to time Elena had shown her jealousy of Ana-Maria. Which was natural enough, Roberto thought. After all, Anita was almost like a blood relation to him. The ties that bound him to her were deep and unbreakable. But Elena understood well enough that the differences of birth between herself and Tomasa Gomez's daughter were so enormous that it would be unworthy of Doña Maria-Elena de Marburg y Alvarez to think of Anita as a rival.

In time the long-standing plans for Ana-Maria's future—marriage to a good and suitable man with the approval of the family—would (with appropriate modifications due to the change of scene from Spain to California) be put into effect. Then, thought Roberto, his son would be godfather to her child, and the immemorial pattern would be continued.

From down the ridge he heard the sound of the steel triangle that was used to call men in from the field. His mother was calling to him to come down.

He broke into an eager run, anxious to see Elena and the new baby.

But when he reached the house he was greeted by his mother and Dr. Harrison with somber faces and he felt a griping thrust of apprehension.

"What is it?" he demanded. "What's gone wrong?"

Harrison, bearded (to hide his youthfulness) and balding (which belied it), spoke soothingly. "Now, go slowly, Robert. There is nothing *wrong,* exactly. It is only that this may take longer than we thought." His school-taught Spanish was slow but precise.

Roberto turned to Adriana questioningly. Her clear blue eyes, so like his own, were veiled. She said, "Elena has been in labor for eleven hours. That is not unusual for a first child, Roberto."

355

"The problem," Harrison said, "is that she is a very small woman. In the pelvis, that is. And the baby's head is large and well developed." Harrison belonged to a new school of physicians who believed that their art should be demystified for the layman. He had not yet practiced long enough to realize that frankness could, to some, be quite terrifying.

Roberto's voice went suddenly thin with strain. "Is she in danger?" He still had difficulty thinking in English.

Roger Harrison was the next thing to a man friend Roberto Marburg had in the county. They rode and hunted together and shared an occasional evening of cards. But at this moment the physician was poignantly aware of the difference in their ages. Roberto needed gentle handling right now because he was suddenly frightened. He wondered if Doña Adriana understood this. She could project such an aura of strength that those around her must have long ago learned to lean heavily on her for courage.

"She is young and healthy, Roberto," Harrison said. "A bit tired right now, and no wonder. But she still has a few hours of labor before her. There is no way in which I can spare her that."

"Oh, God," Roberto breathed.

"A drink wouldn't hurt you, Roberto," Roger Harrison said. "We may all be in for a long evening."

Adriana went to a door and clapped for a *criada*. Dolores Morales, the daughter of a Monterey fisherman whom Adriana had paid for his daughter's service for one year, appeared and bobbed at La Patrona. "Whisky for Don Roberto," Adriana said. Clearly she did not approve of Roberto needing a drink. Roberto caught her meaning instantly, from long practice.

"Never mind, Dolores," he said. "Thank you just the same."

Adriana said, "It must be a son, *hijo*. Elena will carry it off well. You will see."

Harrison said, "I can't promise a son, Roberto. But your mother is quite right. Doña Elena will be fine. Now I had better get back to her."

He disappeared into the family wing and Adriana slipped her arm through her son's. "Women bear children every day, Roberto. There is no need to be afraid."

Roberto disengaged himself and said, "I am not afraid, Mama."

"Come inside then. You had better eat something."

He followed her into the *sala mayor*. Doña Maria was there, working fretfully at a frame of needlework. It seemed to Roberto that whenever there was trouble on the ranch, or any cause for concern, Doña Maria Santana always picked up her needlework. It was always the same work, and it never seemed even to approach completion. She had taken it up since moving to California. He could not remember ever having seen a needle in her hand at old Santanilla.

"Where is Anita, Mama?" Adriana asked.

"She is with Elena. She won't leave her," the old woman said. "Tomasa is there with her too."

"Will you eat something?" Adriana asked Roberto.

He shook his head. "Not now," he said.

Doña Maria, seated, as always, on the edge of her chair, said, "*Nieto,* now promise me you won't worry. Elena is a fine girl. She will do her duty."

Why, Roberto wondered with sudden exasperation, was everyone so concerned about *him?* It was Elena who lay in the great bed trying to bring forth a new Marburg.

At that moment a muffled cry rang through the house. The sound of Elena's voice made cold sweat start on Roberto's back. My *God,* what was happening in there?

Doña Maria said, "All women cry out in childbirth, Roberto. You shouldn't even be here to listen."

"I want to see her," Roberto said.

"It would be better if you did not," Adriana said. "She would not want you to see her as she is now."

Roberto walked to the window and stood there so that the women could not see the naked fear in his face. Why was it like this? he wondered. What code said that childbirth was the sole province of women, that men were to be excluded and shielded from the realities? Did all people do this? It seemed to him that the birth of a child was something that should be shared between the man who made the child and the woman who bore it. It was not *hers* or *his,* but *theirs.* What savages we are, he thought, with our customs and mysteries that came to us from the time when men and women worshipped different gods.

Since coming to Nueva Santanilla he had been reading old Don Alvaro's books. There were hundreds of them on the shelves in the study where Adriana did her accounts. She had brought them from Spain in crates in what Roberto was certain was an attempt to recreate the atmosphere of the observatory at old Santanilla.

In one volume on ancient Hispanic customs, he had read that the whole of the relationship between the sexes among Spaniards was still strongly affected by the customs of the Roman Republic. And it might well be true, he thought. A Spanish gentlewoman resembled nothing more than a Roman matron of the old regime, steeped in *gravitas.*

But sweet Virgin Mary, not little Elena. That was not the secret worship of Bona Dea going on in the confinement room, but the birth of a child. *His* child.

He turned to face his mother and said, "I want to see my wife. Now, Mama."

Adriana Marburg understood rebellion. When Roberto showed these occasional flashes of willfulness he was most her son—and Aaron's brother. She wished he could show his strength more often. "Go to her, Roberto," she said.

Roberto strode swiftly out of the room and down the gallery to the closed door of Elena's room. Here he hesitated for a moment, but only for a moment. He pushed the door open and entered.

Tomasa, sitting at the head of the bed and wiping Elena's face with a damp cloth, looked scandalized. Anita looked up and then returned to her task of gathering stained towels. Roger Harrison, listening through Elena's sweat-soaked nightdress to her heartbeat, took the stethoscope from his ears and said, "Roberto is here, Doña Elena."

Elena's pale lips parted and she said, "Roberto."

He took the wet cloths from Tomasa and sat down on a chair at the head of the bed. Elena looked so worn and tired that tears came to his eyes. He took her limp hand and kissed the palm.

"I am sorry to be so long," Elena whispered.

Roberto shook his head, unable to reply.

Harrison looked at his watch and said, "Another hour or two, I'm afraid."

Roberto wiped the sweat from his wife's brow. She reached for his free hand and gripped it. He had not imagined that she could grasp anything so tightly.

She arched her back and some color came into her face. She resisted crying out as long as she could, but finally succumbed. The cry tore into Roberto's heart.

Ana-Maria was at his side. "Are you all right?" she asked.

He nodded savagely, "Yes, yes." He said to Roger Harrison. *"Do* something for her. Give her something. She's in pain."

"Of course she's in pain, you foolish man," Harrison said in sudden anger. "How did you think human beings get born? With music and dancing? If you can't take it, get out and let us get on with it."

Roberto held Elena's hand to his lips and said, "I'm sorry."

"Stay, Roberto," Elena whispered.

"*Sí, querida.*"

The light had faded from the windows and outside it was deep night. Roberto did not know how long he had sat there holding Elena's hand and wiping the perspiration from her brow. The room had a hot, bloody smell. Each time Elena strained in labor, Ana-Maria reached under the bedclothes to change the stained towels under her. Harrison, in damp shirtsleeves, felt Elena's mounded belly and said, "Now. It has to be now. Elena, can you hear me? Push. *Push,* girl."

Elena, livid with fatigue, seemed now almost unable to cry out as she moaned softly.

"Bear down, girl. *Bear down,* I say!"

Harrison stripped away the bedclothes and bent over Elena. His hands were bloody. Roberto was gripped by fear and shame for what he had brought Elena to this night.

"Good," Harrison said. "Good, good, *push,* girl."

Elena's lips parted and she managed a single sobbing cry.

"*Brava, brava.* You've done it," Harrison said, almost shouting.

He busied himself between Elena's knees for a moment and held out his hand for the instrument Ana-Maria handed him by obvious prearrangement.

He cut and tied the birth cord and then lifted the blood-streaked creature by the ankles and slapped it across the buttocks. The baby gasped with outrage and began to cry.

Tomasa hurried with dry towels. Ana-Maria clapped her hands delightedly. Elena gave a long, shuddering sigh and held her husband's hand.

Tomasa, after swaddling the baby in soft towels, presented it to Roger Harrison, who carried to Elena. She looked at it with barely open eyes.

To Roberto, Harrison said, "Don Roberto Marburg, may I present the cause of all this day's fuss and bother."

At the open door stood Adriana and Doña Maria. "Tell me, Roberto," Adriana said.

"I have a daughter, Mama," he said with a catch in his throat. "A beautiful Marburg daughter."

By one-thirty in the afternoon all the small shops that had arisen around the Trituradora-Fénix were closed for siesta, their galvanized iron shutters lowered. In the heat of the day the street lay empty, save for an occasional stray dog or a tardy merchant hurrying home to take the midday meal.

At the Trituradora, however, the roar of the expellers was never silent, and the workmen tending the machines, stripped to the waist and gleaming with sweat, continued to shovel copra onto the conveyor belts.

Aaron Marburg closed his rolltop desk and called for the foreman to alert Pancho, the *mozo de quadra,* to bring the buggy around to the front of the building to take the *Jefe* home for lunch.

Aaron donned his linen coat and took the white panama hat from the rack near the door. With a last look to see that all was in order in his office, he walked out into the factory to give the *capataz* of the day shift the signature that would allow the drays to load the barrels of oil awaiting transport to the harbor. That done, Aaron stepped out into the blaze of sun in the dusty street.

In the eight years since the Trituradora-Fénix had been rebuilt, the district had become far more populous. In the once-empty field across from the factory the Jaboneria Fénix now stood, built over the grave of that nearly forgotten arsonist executed by Díaz's soldiers on the night of the fire. It was a substantial building containing the vats and caustic chemical storages needed to produce *Jabón Fénix,* a newly popular household soap, and a number of industrial cleaners. The *jaboneria* employed fifty men under the supervision of Juan Ortega, who had recently completed his fifteenth year as Aaron's employee.

The street, in both directions now, was a thriving avenue of small shops and enterprises, including, of course, a cantina catering to the workers at both the Trituradora-Fénix and the soap factory.

The buggy appeared from behind the factory and Aaron climbed aboard and took the reins from the *mozo.* He flicked the horse with the buggy whip and moved off in the direction of the residential district of Tihuacan.

The first term of President Porfirio Díaz had come to an end in 1880. There had been many Tihuacantecos who had been certain that he would ignore the new constitution (which he himself had instituted) and stand for reelection. There had been as many others who were sure that he would install a puppet president to continue the reforms he had set in motion. But Díaz had done neither of those things. He had quietly stepped aside for the new president, another former general, Manuel Gonzales, accepting for a time a post in the government as head of the Department of Development, and later as governor of his native state of Oaxaca.

It was true, the people of Tihuacan all agreed, that Gonzales owed his advancement to Díaz (they were old military comrades), but only the most anti-Porfiristas claimed that Gonzales was the former president's puppet.

The election that Díaz had lost to Juárez while Aaron was in Europe had not discredited Don Porfirio. Quite the contrary. Even his rebellion and abortive attempt at a coup against Juárez had found some popular support because Juárez had been defying the Constitution of 1857, which prohibited consecutive terms for a president of the republic.

The Revolt of La Noria had been in complete disarray in 1872 when Juárez had suffered a coronary seizure and died. Sebastian Lerdo de Tejada, Díaz's prime rival, had acted swiftly. As chief of the Supreme Court he had become acting president, and immediately scheduled elections for that October. Díaz, his reputation in shreds because of his revolt against the beloved Juárez, had been forced to stand for election against Lerdo, who defeated him easily.

Those had been difficult days for Aaron and Don Marcello, who had, so the gossips said, backed the wrong horse.

But when Lerdo repeated the mistake that Juárez had made—seeking a second consecutive term in office—Díaz had been ready. Backed by a large consortium of businessmen (of whom Aaron had been one), he had issued the Plan de Tuxtepec, charging Lerdo with a number of political sins and malfeasances, the most important of which was that old Mexican obsession, seeking to perpetuate himself in office.

The so-called Revolution of Tuxtepec was decided in one sharp engagement. Old soldiers from all over Mexico had flocked to Díaz's banner and on November 16, 1876, they easily defeated the Lerdistas and occupied Mexico City. Sebastian Lerdo fled to Acapulco, there to board a steamer waiting to carry him into exile in the United States.

It had been at Tecoac, in the state of Tlaxcala, that Manuel Gonzales had distinguished himself and, in effect, won Díaz's friendship.

Now Gonzales was president, and Díaz, widowed and remarried to a girl of good family, Carmen Romero Rubio (who was, incidentally, thirty-three years his junior), was touring the United States on his honeymoon.

There would be another election in 1884, only three years hence, and Aaron did not doubt for one moment that Díaz fully intended to return and stand again for the presidency. He had not actually told Aaron so during his last visit to Tihuacan, but Aaron had learned that Porfirio Díaz, having had a great deal of power, would never be content now with none.

As he drove through the silent, sleepy streets, Aaron found himself remembering his return from Europe. He could not recall a time when he had been so lost and empty. That dawn when he left Adriana standing in the courtyard of Santanilla remained, to this day, the most melancholy memory of his life.

He hoped that Julia had been too excited and happy with his return to sense the inner sadness he had brought with him from Spain. He thought that he had managed to keep that from her. But the sense of loss he felt that morning at Santanilla had never left him. It was with him still, as familiar now as the beat of his heart.

The *caudillo*'s term as president had been spotted with insurrections and rebellions. Typically, Latin-American insurgencies had appeared to resist each reform dictated from Mexico City.

Even presidential appointments to positions within the state governments had been met with riot and armed protest. Here in Sinaloa, a general of the local militia, Diego Alvarez, had tested Díaz's resolution by refusing an order to resign, organizing instead a sharp, bitter, and bloody revolt that needed to be put down by a brigade of Federales.

It was characteristic of Díaz that he reacted to violence with superior violence. When Governor Luis Mier y Terán asked for instructions concerning captured rebels in Vera Cruz, President Díaz telegraphed him: *"Mátalos en caliente."* Kill them on the spot.

The turbulence of the last few years had served to distract Aaron from the plague of memory. Díaz made those who associated with him conduct their affairs with great skill and care. Aaron was convinced that the man presently honeymooning with an eighteen-year-old bride in the United States would not long remain away from the land that had given him wealth and a sense of his own destiny.

Aaron drove slowly through the center of Tihuacan, past the Plaza Constitución and the old Spanish cathedral church with its twin bell towers. It was in that church that he had been married, and he never passed it without recalling how Julia had looked on that silvery morning almost ten years ago. Julia was not a great beauty, but she had been beautiful that day in the cathedral, her green eyes brilliant under the white *mantilla,* her mother's wedding dress clinging to her lovely figure. It made him feel guilty even now that on that special day, *her* special day, he had been remembering Adriana.

Aaron had not, like many *conversos,* become a religious man. He was as devout as he could conveniently be, and left it at that. But sometimes he wondered if God—always assuming that He actually existed and interested Himself in the doings of men and women—kept some sort of a balance sheet. It had once seemed that Uncle Isaac (dead and buried these five years past) had believed that. And if it were so, had God chosen to punish Aaron Marburg for his undoubted (and unconfessed) sins by taking the son who would have borne his grandfather's name?

Nine months and twenty days after that vast wedding in the cathedral of Tihuacan, Marina Julia Marburg had been born without trouble and with much happiness. She was now eight years old and the image of her mother, green-eyed and raven-haired. But two years later had come Miguel. The thought made Aaron's eyes grow hot with tears. The boy had lived four months. Diphtheria killed him, in spite of all Juan Amaya-Ruiz could do. The small white coffin had rested in the transept of Tihuacan Cathedral and was consigned to the earth, at the special request of the Arsellos family, by Father Bernal of La Cruz.

If it was punishment for my sins, Aaron thought, so be it. But what sort of God destroyed children so uncaringly?

Julia had grieved until Aaron despaired for her. His own sorrow was largely lost in her deeper pain.

And then, only three years ago, had come Caridad, a fat, healthy, laughing child who banished grief. A beautiful girl, with her father's copper-colored hair (*"Mi rubia! Mi linda rubia!"* old Maria Marcías said, taking over the ask of *nana* despite all Julia could do) and her mother's green eyes.

But no son for Aaron Marburg, he told himself. Well, perhaps it was as well. Marburg men have not distinguished themselves in bringing happiness to others.

At Don Marcello's insistence, Aaron and Julia had moved into the Italian palazzo on the Olas Altas. The house was more than large enough to hold them and Don Marcello's establishment as well. In fact, the old man seldom left his room now, or the garden facing it. He had suffered a series of small strokes, surviving them all tenaciously, but retreating slowly into a wheelchair. He still enjoyed giving advice to Aaron, though he willingly admitted that Aaron needed none. He spent his waking hours playing with his granddaughters or at the chessboard with Amaya-Ruiz (when he felt the need for competition) or with Aaron (when he wanted an easy victory).

The household on the Olas Altas was now the Marburg establishment, where the *abuelo* was content to live near his daughter and son-in-law and their children.

Life, for Aaron and Julia, had settled into a familiar and pleasant routine. The Trituradora, the Jaboneria Fénix, and Don Marcello's store and other enterprises had been gathered into the Sociedad Anónima Fénix under Aaron's guidance, and they prospered.

What news Aaron had of Adriana came from an unexpected source. Since his trip to Europe, Aaron had become the regular recipient of letters (and often requests for small sums of money) from Julio Santana. It was Julio who wrote to tell him that he was, at long last, hacendado of Santanilla—and could he spare the sum of one thousand pesetas for the repair of the sheep-shearing barn? Almost in passing, he said that Adriana, Doña Maria, and Roberto and his "child-bride" were now in California, "on the land you found for them, *gracias a Dios.*"

From time to time there would be a letter—laboriously written in a childish scrawl, with many misspellings—from Chole. It was she who informed Aaron that after Clara and Caridad had joined young Paco in their brood, Julio had stopped resisting the idea of marrying a gypsy and that she was now (and Aaron could almost hear her raucous laughter) Doña Soledad de Santana y Segre, mistress of Santanilla.

Aaron had received this news just four months after Caridad Marburg had been christened by Father Bernal at La Cruz (where, it now seemed, all Marburgs accepted that sacrament). So his own sweet Cari now shared a Christian name with a cousin by marriage. There was a certain wry humor in that. He had sent money to Chole for all the children, warning her to put it by and hide it from Julio.

Aaron had wondered what Doña Maria Isabella de Santana y Borjas thought about having three lusty half-gypsy grandchildren now. Well, she had loved her half-Jewish grandson well enough, so perhaps the old woman was growing mellow in the temperate California climate.

From there only one letter had come. Not even a letter, actually, but the announcement of the birth, to Don Roberto and Doña Maria-Elena Marburg, of a daughter, Marianna Isabella Adriana Santana Marburg y Alvarez.

He had thought, as he stood with the engraved card in his hands, how like Adriana it was to burden a child with such a name, with such a weight of ancestry. But it was so typical an action, a gesture so prideful and patrician, that it was almost as though he held in his hand a private letter from Adriana.

Of course, he thought as he drove through the quiet streets of Tihuacan, little Marianna Marburg would grow up to resemble her beautiful grandmother. How could she dare do otherwise? With a sad smile he thought: Ana, Ana, my love. A grandmother at forty-one. Only you could carry it off with panache.

Eufemia met him at the door to take his hat. *"La señora* is in the garden with Doctor Amaya, Patron. *Almuerzo* will be ready in an hour."

Aaron walked through the great, cool house to the inner patio garden. Julia, in white linen, sat with Juan Amaya-Ruiz amid a blaze of hibiscus and bougainvillea.

Amaya rose to greet him. *"Holá, Jefe. Que tal?"*

The doctor now affected one of the drooping military moustaches made popular by Díaz and Gonzales. He was still regarded as one of the most eligible bachelors in Tihuacan.

Aaron stooped to kiss Julia and lowered himself into a chair. She poured a glass of *limonada* for him from a frosty pitcher. In Tihuacan ice was a rare and valuable commodity, which had to be purchased from the passing refrigerator ships carrying fruit from the Isthmus. Aaron and Don Marcello were planning to build an ice plant in the Fénix complex. A North American engineer had been hired to design it.

Little Marina came running to greet her father, her green eyes sparkling, her hair shiny black as a raven's wing. She climbed into his lap and said, "Caridad has another tooth, Papa. She bit me with it."

"I shall have to speak to her," Aaron said.

"It didn't hurt."

"She is going to be a beauty, this *morenita,*" Juan Amaya-Ruiz said. "A breaker of hearts."

"How is Marcello?" Aaron asked.

"Remarkably well, considering," Amaya said.

Amaya-Ruiz made a practice of dropping in to examine Don Marcello at least once each week.

"Will you stay for lunch, Juan?"

Julia said, "I asked him. He says he must go on about his rounds."

"Summer is a busy time for me," Amaya said.

That was no more than the simple truth. The summer heat brought a variety of illnesses to Tihuacan. Typhoid fever and malaria were common. There was always the threat of an epidemic.

"I spoke to Don Mauricio as you asked me to do," Aaron said. "He claims there is no money for 'public works.' " Mauricio Perez de Lebron was now the *alcalde* of Tihuacan, and Amaya-Ruiz had asked Aaron to intercede with him, requesting that something be done about the open sewers in the poorer *barrios.*

"The man is an idiot," Amaya said.

"It is worse than that, Juan," Julia said. It was common knowledge that Don Mauricio, who came from an impoverished *criollo* family, was swiftly repairing the clan fortunes by stealing public money. Such things were so common in Mexico that they were hardly worthy of comment. Díaz, and now Gonzales, had little time to punish corruption. They were concerned with larger things, such as increasing the miles of track being laid for the *Ferrocarriles Nacionales* and encouraging foreign investment in Mexican industry. *La mordida* had been a way of life in Latin America since time out of mind. It had come to these shores with the *conquistadores*. But public grafting still outraged Julia, who worked charitably among the *peones* and knew their needs.

"We will have to call on the merchants," Aaron said. "We can convince most of them, I think, that an epidemic is bad for business."

Amaya drained his glass of *limonada* and stood. "What would Tihuacan do without its captains of industry? We would be ankle-deep in *mierda*. Forgive me, Julia." He lifted her hand, kissed it. "You will be careful now. Understood?"

Aaron, on his feet to show Amaya from the house, said, "Careful? Are you ill, *vieja?*"

"Does she look ill?" Amaya asked.

"Julia?" Aaron regarded his wife in perplexity. She not only did not look ill, she looked radiant.

"I will leave you to share those sweet intimacies which no *soltero* can ever know." Amaya bowed to Julia. "I will find my own lonely way out. *Jefe,*" he said to Aaron. "Julia has something to tell you."

When Amaya was gone, Aaron said, "Julia? Are you pregnant again?"

"Yes. Are you pleased?"

Aaron caught her hands and held them. "I am very pleased, *querida*. Are you?"

"Oh, yes, *yes.*"

He knew what she was thinking. A son. A son to take the place intended for poor, tiny Miguel, who had lived less than a year. He sat down on the iron settee beside his wife and embraced her.

"This one won't die," Julia said, her eyes suddenly filled with tears. "I won't let this one die, Aaron."

"Oh, my dear Julia," Aaron said, the words thick in his throat. "You have nothing to blame yourself for. Nothing at all."

Julia brushed the tears from her cheeks and smiled at Aaron. "It *will* be a son. I promise you."

"When?"

"Juan says late November or early December."

"So soon?"

"I didn't want to tell you until I was absolutely certain."

Aaron placed his hands on her belly. Another life, he thought, another human being. There were times when the mystery was so overwhelming, and so beautiful, that a man could believe there *was* a God.

Though Aaron had never spoken to Julia of Adriana, he had often told her about Don Alvaro and about Don Alvaro's tales about his father. "If it is a boy—and it *will be* a boy," Julia said, "we will call him Alejandro, after your friend's father. *Está bien?* Is it well?"

Aaron thought of El Patron, who for too short a time was the nearest thing to a true father he had ever known. Don Alvaro would have been pleased. Alejandro. Alex.

"Yes, Julia," he said. Yes, you generous heart. *"Está bien."*

1888

40

"Carnal sins," Doña Maria said
severely, "are always with us, placing our souls in mortal danger."

Marianna regarded her great-grandmother with interest. The
bisabuela told the most amazing and entertaining stories. One had only
to mention her native Spain to get her started. It impressed the *criadas*
at Nueva Santanilla that Doña Maria had been the hacendada of the
family's original estate in Spain and that one of her cousins had died
an archbishop and a prince of the Church. Marianna was not exactly
certain what an archbishop was. A priest, to be sure, like those at the
mission in Monterey, but some very special sort of priest, probably with
the authority to perform miracles. Tomasa said this, and so Marianna
felt compelled to believe it.

The *bisabuela*, who was nearly eighty years old, had seen many
miracles. That was one of the things that made her stories so entertaining.

They sat together on the wide verandah of the ranch house, on the landward side where there was a lovely view of the mountains. It was Doña Maria's favorite spot. She said it reminded her of home. She had lived at Nueva Santanilla since before Marianna was born, but she still called the old Santanilla her home. She had resolutely refused to learn to speak English, and though this presented no problem on the ranch, it caused her no end of inconvenience when she left it. Consequently she left it as seldom as possible, only to go to Mass in Carmel.

"You have been out with the stock again, girl," Doña Maria said abruptly. "Look at your knees."

Marianna covered her skinned knees with her skirt and sat very quietly. She was a fair-skinned child, although burned and freckled by the sun (to her great-grandmother's dismay). Her eyes were the same clear blue of her father's, and her hair, tightly curled, was golden brown. She sat as primly as she could manage, waiting with increasing impatience for the *bisabuela* to go on with the story that she was surely about to tell, or had been, before the scabs on Marianna's knees had distracted her.

"Did the cousin archbishop teach you about carnal sins, *bisabuelita?*" Marianna prompted.

The ghost of a smile showed through the stern expression on Doña Maria's face. It was a very old face, Marianna thought, but not at all ugly. Doña Maria's features were thin and sharply defined and the skin stretched over them like fine parchment. She was a small woman. Marianna was only eight, but the *bisabuela* was not very much taller than she. Her hands were tiny and wrinkled, but still strong and capable of delivering a considerable blow, as Marianna had discovered more than once to her cost. Doña Maria said she did not know what the world was coming to, with girls almost women being allowed to roam about the ranch like the vaqueros and shepherds. That was what came of living in the United States, she said, an uncivilized land where no one really knew his place.

But from time to time the *bisabuela* would quite suddenly reach out and stroke Marianna's curly hair and say something very nice. It was the uncertainty that made being with the great-grandmother such a challenge, Marianna thought.

"No Spanish gentlewoman needs to be taught about carnal sin," Doña Maria said firmly. "We are all born knowing."

"Was I, *bisabuela?*"

"Even you, child."

"I shall try very hard not to be sinful," Marianna said helpfully.

Far off, on the rising flank of the Santa Lucias, Marianna could see her father and the vaqueros rounding up cattle. Inside the house, her mother was resting. Ana-Maria and the servants were all busy in the kitchen, preparing the midday meal. And grandmother Adriana was away in San Francisco, on business. Marianna sighed. If the *bisabuela* did not go on with her story soon, it was going to be a very dull afternoon.

Doña Maria laughed suddenly, a short, barking sound. She did that from time to time. Mama said that it was because she was very old and was remembering things from long ago that were amusing.

"I remember one Holy Week in Seville," Doña Maria said abruptly. "El Patron and I had been married only a year and I was pregnant with Alfredo, your great-uncle, who died when he was a little boy. There was a great procession with the images of the Virgin and Saint John the Baptist being carried through the streets." She smiled and rocked to and fro. "Oh, how well I remember that. As though it were yesterday."

Marianna, pleased that the great-grandmother had begun her tale, hugged her knees and shrugged her shoulders. She did so love Doña Maria's funny stories. No one else said the things the *bisabuela* did, not even Papa.

"It began to rain," Doña Maria said. "A terrible rainstorm. And the images had been dressed for Holy Week in their finest clothes. So they were put in the cathedral to wait for the rain to stop. But it did not stop. It rained even harder. And finally it was decided that the images would have to remain in the cathedral overnight." She closed her brilliant black eyes, the better to see that procession in the streets of Seville more than fifty years ago. "Now the problem arose: could the statues of San Juan Bautista and la Virgen Maria be left alone in the cathedral *all night?* Was it proper? So the canons were sent for and the situation considered. They discussed the possible impropriety for a long time. Oh, I remember how my beloved Alvaro laughed. But the canons were quite serious. 'Anyone,' they said, 'is in danger of temptation by the devil. Didn't he tempt Our Lord Himself in the wilderness?' So finally it was decided that they must send to the captain-general of Seville for a guard. And so they did. A guard came with torches and kept watch on Saint John and the Virgin until morning." The old lady's thin shoulders shook with remembered delight.

Marianna frowned and asked, "But, *bisabuela.* What did they think the statues might do?"

Doña Maria regarded her great-granddaughter with those bright, piercing eyes. "I said all Spanish women were born knowing. But perhaps not. Perhaps being born in this land of the rootless makes a difference." She cupped Marianna's small head in her bony hands. "Well, never mind, *pequeña.* You'll know soon enough."

The relationship between the old *hidalga* and her great-granddaughter was a source of constant amusement to everyone at Nueva Santanilla. Marianna's developing mind was as quick and deft as Adriana's and she burned with a restless energy that simply disregarded the strictures put upon her as the daughter of the house. She had already, with help from her father and grandmother, taught herself to read both Spanish and English; she was more familiar than any other member of the household with the books of Don Alvaro's library. She rode astride (to the horror of Doña Maria and all the female servants) and spent hours trailing after her father and the vaqueros when they worked with the stock.

Doña Maria complained often to Roberto and Elena that it was past time to send Marianna off to the convent so that she could begin her education as a gentlewoman. But the money for this was not available, and even if it had been, Roberto would have resisted his grandmother's suggestion. Roberto loved his daughter extravagantly and wished to keep her at Nueva Santanilla. He had been educated (rather spottily, he admitted) by tutors. He saw no reason why Marianna should not be educated in the same fashion.

Actually, Doña Maria's complaints were largely pro forma. No one on the ranch would have been lonelier if Marianna had been sent away to school. The old woman and the child were a familiar sight at Nueva Santanilla: sitting or walking together hand in hand and seeming always to be in deep conversation. Marianna was insatiably curious about her *bisabuela*'s life in far-off, mysterious Spain. And now that her distant memories had become far sharper and clearer than more recent ones, Doña Maria was delighted to have so appreciative an audience for her reminiscences.

And so Marianna Marburg listened avidly to tales of great balls at Santanilla and the neighboring haciendas, of handsome young men playing, with horse and lance, at *rejoneador,* of *paso dobles* and glittering quadrillas in the great bullrings of Madrid and Seville and Barcelona, of being presented to the queen, of honeymooning on a Grand Tour of Europe, of all the things Doña Maria now remembered so clearly of that other life with her beloved Alvaro now vanished into time.

From her *bisabuela* Marianna learned that men were, under a thin veneer of civilization, wild creatures who needed to be tamed by strong women. Not tamed too much, though, lest they become like the geldings on the ranch, good for docile labor and not much else. Doña Maria had fallen into the habit of speaking to her small great-granddaughter the way that, earlier in life, she might have spoken to her own daughter, had not Don Alvaro's dangerous ideas kept Adriana from her. Often she forgot that she was speaking to a child. "People say, Marianna, that Spanish culture is patriarchal. We allow them to believe that. But it is the women who rule. We wear velvet gloves, but the lives of our men are in our hands. Do not ever forget that."

When the *bisabuela* said such things, Marianna remained thoughtfully silent and listened with care. She did not know precisely what her great-grandmother meant, but already she had some glimmerings. She had always before her the example of her handsome, gentle father surrounded by his nest of women.

Marianna knew about the family feuds, though not their causes. She had been told by Felicia, her grandmother's maid, that she had a great-uncle Alfonso in the Spanish Foreign Legion—sent to Africa in disgrace for some terrible sin. She knew that another great-uncle was now hacendado of the original Santanilla in Spain, but that he too was in disgrace for some unspecified reason; Felicia believed it was for having married a gypsy. And she was told, again by the servants, Tomasa and Raoul and Felicia, that she had a half-uncle named Aaron, who was rich and handsome and lived in Mexico surrounded with Aztec gold. Though when, thinking that it would be exciting to visit Uncle Aaron, she mentioned his name to Ana-Maria or her father, she was met with a cold and sudden silence. So quite probably there was some family feud concerning him, too. It was a great pity, she thought, because her grandmother and great-grandmother spoke of him with affection. He had two daughters and a son who were Marianna's cousins and near to her age, and it would have been pleasant to know them. After all, they were Marburgs too, though not Santanas. But probably she would never know her cousins or her remarkable Uncle Aaron, so she dismissed them from her mind.

For her mother, Elena, Marianna felt a dispassionate affection. It was hard for so active a child to love the frail and demanding Elena. Not that Elena was different from the other grown women in the family in any important way. Elena Marburg held firmly to all the dicta Marianna received from the *bisabuela*. From time to time she was unkind to Ana-Maria Gomez, but that was because Ana-Maria was the daughter of a *peon*—a beloved *peon*, to be sure, but still a *peon*. Ana-Maria was like a sister to her father, Marianna knew, but not *exactly* like a sister.

She was his goddaughter, and so she existed in a kind of limbo between the status of a blood relation and a servant. She knew that there had been a great deal of discussion among the grown-ups concerning a suitable match for Ana-Maria among the many Mexican immigrants who manned the fishing boats in Monterey or worked in the fields of the Salinas ranchers.

Tomasa and Doña Ana said that it was past time for Ana-Maria to be married. Marianna's father said that there was no rush to find Ana-Maria a husband, that she should be allowed to choose one for herself, and that there was no reason at all why she should not, when she chose, decide to marry an American. There were merchants and Yankee cowboys who came to Nueva Santanilla often, and many of them had showed an interest in Ana-Maria, who might not be beautiful but was certainly womanly.

But Doña Ana, and even Doña Maria (who did not often interest herself in such matters) said that at twenty-seven, if Ana-Maria was not married soon she never would be.

In all this talk, Marianna noticed, no one ever bothered to ask Ana-Maria Gomez what *she* wanted to do.

Marianna resolved that she, Marianna Marburg, would marry young and that it would be a man of her own choice. She would never choose to be a *solterona* with others mapping out her life for her.

41

Elena Marburg stood before the pier glass in her bedroom and regarded herself with mingled happiness and apprehension. The dress she had chosen for the day could not be buttoned over her breasts. For the fifth time in eight years, she was undoubtedly pregnant. This time, she was reasonably certain, she could risk telling Roberto. She hoped that he would be pleased, though she was far from certain that he would be.

After the birth of Marianna, Roberto had shown a definite reluctance to risk another pregnancy for her. He had become a far from diligent lover. But no man of his blood could remain celibate for long, and within a year she had become pregnant again. She had miscarried in her third month, and had made the mistake of allowing Roberto to know it. There had followed a full seven months of abstention and a cold bed. Elena had suffered badly from attacks of jealousy that she had forced herself to suppress. It was totally unlike

Roberto to seek another woman, and he would have been shocked to know that Elena had dreams of him making love to, of all people, Anita Gomez. Elena had been jealous of Roberto's goddaughter ever since they were children.

Elena Marburg was not a strongly sexed woman. Church and family had developed in her a sense of what was right and proper in marriage, and for these reasons she had submitted herself to her husband's attentions with resignation. But the suspicion that Ana-Maria might be Roberto's mistress lit an unaccustomed fire in Elena's blood. She set herself to seduce her husband with emotional scenes and tears and bedroom behavior that was, by any standard with which she was familiar, wanton. It had shocked Roberto, but it had the effect she desired.

Over the course of the next five years she had become pregnant —and had miscarried—four more times. But she had never again made the mistake of allowing Roberto to know.

The last time had been painful and horrifying to her, but fortunately Roberto had been away visiting his sister Cecilia at Santa Clara. Felicia, Doña Adriana's maid, had helped her to clean up the blood and dispose of the tiny white fetus of a mere eight weeks, and Elena had waited with apprehension for the woman-to-woman talk that was surely to come with Doña Adriana. But when it did come, Adriana had only asked her if this had happened before, and Elena had lied to her and said that it had not. Roberto had not been informed. Matters such as these were women's business, and men were seldom consulted or even told of them.

But now she had held the baby into the fourth month, and with great care, she was reasonably certain she could carry the child for the full term. Elena was resolved to give Roberto what no one else could —a legitimate son, to make up for what she had always suspected (without reason or cause) was his disappointment that Marianna had not been a boy.

Over time she had seen how Roberto loved his daughter, and she was grateful that he did, but she was convinced that he—like any Spanish head of a family—wanted above all things to have sons.

She was still standing before the mirror when Ana-Maria came in to summon her to the midday meal. Anita, dark and broad-faced at twenty-seven, had the voluptuous figure of her Iberian ancestors. Her skin was the color of coffee with milk, smooth as velvet to the touch. Her eyes were black under heavy brows and her hair gleamed like a cap of sable. Elena still could not look at her without wondering if she was her husband's mistress. Such things were far from unknown between *padrinos* and goddaughters.

Anita said, *"Las chichis han crecido,* Elena." She was looking at Elena's chest with interest.

"Don't be vulgar, Anita," Elena said sharply. "Find me another dress to wear."

She hated Ana-Maria's easy familial manner. She had hated it since they were children. But that was not all she disliked. She had never felt at home here in the United States. Superficially Nueva Santanilla resembled the old, but *only* superficially. She had been uprooted from what was familiar and set down in an alien land where the pace of life was too swift, the people unmannerly, and even the weather perverse. Who could be at home in a place where winter brought green to the pastures and everything began to go sere before summer began? The growing seasons were all akilter, the rains were too warm, the nearby ocean too immense.

Toward Anita she felt a curious mix of emotions. Love, because she was familiar and unfailingly good-natured. Contempt, because she was of low birth. Jealousy, because she was bound to Roberto with ties that Elena could never loosen.

Ana-Maria took a calico dress from the wardrobe and held it up for Elena's inspection. "Will this do, Elena?"

"Yes," Elena said and stripped off the tight-bodiced frock she had on. Ana-Maria studied her as though she were livestock.

"Caray, Lena. You are *embarazada!"* she said. "Does Roberto know?"

"You are imagining things, Anita," Elena said.

Ana-Maria smiled so warmly that despite her feelings toward the girl, Elena could not help but respond. "Well, perhaps I am. And no, I have not told Roberto yet. I don't want him to worry."

Ana-Maria clapped her hands with childish delight, *"Que maravilla!* Oh, how I envy you, Elena. After all this time!"

Elena felt a stab of jealous anger. What did she mean by "After all this time"? Was she hinting that she thought her barren? And was she implying that she envied Elena because she had Roberto's child in her belly? Hot tears sprang into Elena's eyes.

"Elena, don't *cry.* It is wonderful. Everyone will be so *pleased."* Ana-Maria put her arms around Elena's bare shoulders and held her.

"It is only for Don Roberto to be pleased," Elena said stiffly, moving away from Ana-Maria. "Help me dress."

When Ana-Maria finished buttoning the back of the calico, she said critically. "Even this is much too tight for you. You will have to go to Monterey for material for the dressmaker. Or maybe Roberto will take you to San Francisco. That would be grand, Lena."

"Don't call me Lena. I have never liked it."

Ana-Maria made a humorous curtsy. *"Si, señora. A sus ordenes."*

Elena sighed tremulously. It was so *difficult* to stay angry with Ana-Maria. She remembered the peasants of Old Castile as being a sullen, often rebellious lot. But Ana-Maria had never been like that. She had always been so certain that she was loved. It made her maddeningly sweet tempered.

"I don't want to go to San Francisco. The train frightens me." She had never forgotten the long, dreadful train ride across the United States, with terrible men shooting at the buffalo from the train windows and drinking whisky all through the long, hot days.

Like Doña Maria, Elena had never learned to speak English—at least not well—and getting about in San Francisco, Monterey, or even Carmel was tedious and unpleasant. It secretly irritated her that Anita had learned to speak a *kind* of English well enough to converse with the merchants in Monterey and the few *yanqui* cowhands who drifted, from time to time, into Roberto's employ.

Ana-Maria, on the other hand, longed to be taken to San Francisco on the newly built railway from Monterey. She remembered the journey across the vast plains of America as an exciting adventure.

"Where is Marianna?" Elena asked. "She is not off with the vaqueros again, I hope." She regarded it as Ana-Maria Gomez's special task to keep track of Marianna, who was, it seemed to Elena, growing up wild in this uncivilized place.

"She is with Doña Maria," Ana-Maria said. "La Patrona is telling her stories."

"Filling her head with fairy tales," Elena said. To Doña Maria's face she would have never uttered a word of such criticism. But with Ana-Maria she could be frank. The old *bisabuela* could be very difficult.

Ana-Maria sat on the edge of the bed and hugged herself. "What shall it be, Elena? What do you want it to be? A boy or a girl?"

"Madre de Dios, Anita. What a question. It shall be a boy, of course."

"Roberto would be as pleased with another daughter," Ana-Maria said.

"What do you know about what pleases my husband?" Elena said crossly.

"I just know, Elena. Roberto is a very gentle man."

Elena turned away from Ana-Maria in frustration. What she said was true, of course. No one in all the world knew Roberto so well as did Ana-Maria.

"A boy, then," Ana-Maria said. "What will you call him?"

"Why, Silvio, after my father," Elena said firmly.

Ana-Maria did not reply. Elena was not an easy person to be with. She remembered that this had been true even when they were children. She did not use the word *arriviste,* but she knew its meaning. She had heard Doña Maria use it more than once when speaking of Elena's family, the Alvarezes. She understood that because Elena's family had bought their Spanish estate rather than inherited it, they had taught their daughter to be prickly and demanding about what was due her.

All of that seemed far less important here in California than it had been in Spain, but evidently it still was important to Elena.

"Silvio is a handsome name," she said. "And Silvio will be a handsome boy, an American caballero."

"There is no such thing as an American caballero," Elena said. "Here everyone is low-born."

Ana-Maria felt the barb, and from long experience ignored it. A part of being what Doña Maria said Elena was caused her to be insensitive to the feelings of lesser folk. No Santana had ever said anything like that in her hearing.

"I think Dr. Harrison is a caballero," Ana-Maria said quietly.

"Well, perhaps," Elena said, softening, aware that she had hurt Ana-Maria's feelings.

She sat on the bed beside Ana-Maria and took her hand. "Do you like *el doctor?"*

Ana-Maria's sparkling white smile appeared. "Are you asking me if I *love* Doctor Harrison, Elena?" She burst into delighted laughter. "What an idea, Lena! Of course I do not love *el doctor* Harrison."

Elena, stung, took away her hand. "Well it is time you were married, Anita. Time you had children of your own."

Ana-Maria stood and kissed the top of Elena's dark head. "I don't need children of my own. I shall spend my life looking after yours." She went to the door and said, "Now come along and eat. You have to take care of yourself now—for Don Silvio's sake."

R oberto Marburg, guiding his
horse easily with his knees, cracked the long whip over the head of the
yearling cow he was forcing back to the herd, and the animal wheeled
and galloped clumsily toward the othes. One of the vaqueros uttered
a shrieking, hooting yell and started the mass of cattle up the long slope
toward the high pastures.

Roberto reined in his mount and sat for a moment watching the
men and dogs work the herd. This was a good year at Nueva Santanilla
ranch. The grass was rich and the animals were thriving. As soon as the
ruddy-bodied white-faced cattle were safely in the high grass country,
the shepherds could bring the sheep down to crop what the cattle left
of the wild oats and barley.

He snapped the long whip at a patch of thistle, cutting the just-
open purple flowers off at the stem. His uncle Julio had taught him
the use of the Spanish whip long ago, and he had never lost his skill
with it.

For Roberto Marburg the years since the birth of his daughter Marianna seemed to have passed with astonishing swiftness. His love for the California land had grown into a passion. He seldom thought of the old Santanilla; the memories of that place, while not forgotten, were blessedly indistinct now.

Of all who lived on the ranch, only Ana-Maria understood fully his love of California. If anyone were ever to become a true American, he often thought, it must surely be Anita. Marianna too, of course, but for her it would be easy. It was her birthright, after all.

Elena would never be completely happy here, he knew. He was sorry for this, but there was no help for it. And his grandmother now seemed to live almost totally in the past, though in truth her criticisms of the new land seemed largely a matter of form. To a Spanish patrician, California would always be a part of New Spain, and as such hopelessly colonial.

And then there was his mother. It had always been difficult for Roberto to read his mother's thoughts and feelings. It had been, after all, her iron determination that had brought them all here. Yet it was impossible to know whether, having accomplished what she set out to do, she was happy with her success. She guided the business affairs of the ranch with as much concentration as she had ever shown in the old country, where she had milked the old Santanilla—and the Alvarez family—of enough money to make all of this possible. But Roberto did not know whether or not she was satisfied with what she had done. Doña Adriana remained the golden goddess of the Santanas, and one did not probe deeply into the soul of such exalted beings. One revered them, to be sure, but from a distance. And one learned to accept the pain they inflicted, all unknowingly, upon those who *wished* to love them, because they left no other option.

Roberto had learned to devote himself to the land and to the creatures who lived on it and the things that grew in it. Such concerns were far simpler and more rewarding than attempting to understand and control the human beings around him. Though she seldom said so, he knew that his mother would have preferred him to be stronger and more assertive. She spoke so admiringly of her father and her husband that Roberto often wondered if any men could have been such commanding personalities—and if they had, how she could have done the thing he remembered her doing when he was a child.

Yet over time he had learned to accept his own failings and devote himself to what he could do well. It was a vastly different thing to be a rancher in California than a hacendado in Old Castile. He felt that he had at least accomplished that transformation well. The men on the ranch respected him and worked willingly under his supervision. They had begun with only Raoul and the few Mexican immigrants they could find. Many of the vaqueros had now been with Nueva Santanilla for seven years or more and knew the land and the stock as well as he did. There were always transients on the ranch, American drifters out of the cattle states of the Southwest who had reached the sea in their wanderings and still owned nothing but their saddles and the pistols they loved to wear on their thighs. Some of these were unsatisfactory and were swiftly sent on their way north, or south toward Mexico. But others settled in to live and work as Nueva Santanilla's token *yanquis.*

One such was Charlie Greer, a tall, pale-eyed Texan of indeterminate age who had arrived at Nueva Santanilla just after the New Year. He was a man who made few friends, seldom spent his free time with the Mexican vaqueros, and seemed always to be on the verge of insolence. Yet he worked as hard or harder than any of the hands, and he was good with the stock. Of all the family, Greer spoke by choice only to Roberto and Ana-Maria, who had elicited from him the only twisted smile Roberto had ever seen on his always sunburned, never quite clean face.

Roberto watched him now, galloping across the range behind the herd to head off a wandering calf, lashing at his pony with the rawhide lariat end he always carried. Raoul Gomez disliked him, but that could have been because he thought Greer's attentions to Anita were inappropriate, or it could have been simple ethnic prejudice. Raoul's position among the hands was special. He was the only old Santanilleño, and he was the father of the *Jefe*'s goddaughter. These things gave him status, but Charlie Greer seemed unaware of it. He did not appear to know or care about the difference between Spaniards and Mexicans, and he was forever making disparaging remarks about the Spanish practice of running both sheep and cattle on the same ranges—which apparently no Texan would tolerate.

On a number of occasions Roberto had been close to firing Charlie Greer, but he had not done so because he himself rather disliked the man, and he considered it beneath a Santana-Marburg to discharge a man who did good work simply for personal or capricious reasons.

He tapped his pony's ribs with his boot heels and jogged easily after the moving herd and yipping vaqueros in the direction of the high pastures.

The air was fresh and tinged with the smell of the sea. A bank of fog lay close to the rocky coastline. The sun shone on the wispy top of it for as far as the eye could see. Ahead of the herd, on the steepening slope of the Santa Lucias, the conifers stood like black sentinels on the ridgelines. The sky was dappled with ragged clouds moving swiftly inland, driven by the prevailing northwesterly winds. Seagulls soared and wheeled overhead, riding the rising air currents over the steeper pitches. Roberto could hear water tumbling down the narrow ravines, fed by the myriad springs in the mountainsides.

As he rode, Roberto found himself wondering if one reason he had not got rid of Charlie Greer was that he felt a certain guilt at having dominated Ana-Maria's life so completely. It was not, strictly speaking, by Roberto's choice that Anita had been uprooted from her Spanish home and brought to the new land. But it had been a decision in which neither Ana-Maria nor her parents had been given the opportunity to participate, and to that extent Roberto, as a Marburg, shared in the blame—if, in fact, blame there was. Anita gave no indication of unhappiness with her present circumstances. Still, had the family remained at the old Santanilla, she would have been married at seventeen or eighteen, and by now she would have a brood of children. Instead, she had been brought to California, where suitable husbands were rare, and she was now twenty-seven and still a *solterona.*

Roberto did not approve of Charlie Greer's attentions to Ana-Maria. The man had no prospects, no manners, no family, and no future. But did anyone have the right to deny Anita such pleasure as she might derive from having an admirer no matter how unsuitable? Roberto thought not, and so took no action. For several years at the back of his mind, he had held the slight hope that Roger Harrison might eventually ask for Anita. That would be a far more attractive prospect. Roberto liked Harrison and approved of his profession. What point was there in Ana-Maria coming to the United States if she could not eventually improve her station in life? Wasn't that one of the golden promises of the new country?

Roberto suspected that his grandmother would have been scandalized at the notion that any Santana retainer should even *wish* to improve his or her status. To the *abuela* the social structure was a fixed pattern, as immutable as the stars in the sky. Roberto was not aware of it, but what he discerned about his grandmother's attitudes was only the continuation of a battle Doña Maria had fought with all comers (including her beloved Don Alvaro) for most of her long life.

Doña Maria would have been equally distressed at the inner changes that had taken place in Roberto Marburg over the last eight years. He did not flaunt them, but they were there. Other members of the family, notably his mother, could not but be aware of his gradual Americanization. Roberto had begun to believe that he was no longer a prisoner of Spanish traditions and mores. By nature cautious and disliking conflict, he made no open effort to challenge his mother's and grandmother's values. But he held within him a slowly growing assurance that life could be, and should be, freer in the new land. Ana-Maria *could,* if she chose, marry a professional man. Adriana herself could and did travel with only a maid to San Francisco and there conduct the financial affairs of the ranch with as much assurance as any man. And even a Charlie Greer could, in his clumsy and crude manner, pay court to the goddaughter of the owner of Nueva Santanilla.

Not all these freedoms were safe or attractive, but they were real, rooted in the young traditions of America. One could not pretend, as Doña Maria and Elena did, that they did not exist.

Even the manner of rearing children was different here, Roberto thought with a wry smile. Marianna had not been raised as she would have been in Spain, far from it. At the old Santanilla she would never have been allowed to roam so freely over the land, or follow the working hands so curiously. She would have been kept close by a true *nana,* brushed and preened and suffocated by an excess of women's learning and religion until she was ready to be surrendered to some peacock caballero in a dynastic marriage.

Adriana had escaped that sort of life because, Roberto understood, his grandfather had been an unusual sort of man—according to the *abuela,* a rebel against the social order.

Marianna had no such rebel to free her. But the journey from the old world to the new had accomplished what Roberto Marburg, left in Spain, could never have done.

It was a grand thing that Marianna had been born an American. The structures of everyday life that surrounded her resembled those that had formed Roberto's character, but the resemblance was only superficial. Beyond the gate of Nueva Santanilla lay an American world, free and open and often unruly and confusing, but filled with possibilities.

Somehow, Roberto had resolved, he would find the money to send Marianna to an American school. A church school, certainly. His resolution did not run as far as outright challenging the women who surrounded him. But Marianna would be educated as an American, and not as a brood mare for some landowner's heir.

The child was a source of never-ending delight to him. Already he could see signs of his mother's strength and intelligence in her, but leavened by a carefree happiness he doubted his mother had ever truly known.

He sensed in his daughter his own love of the land and the creatures who lived on it. Marianna adopted orphaned lambs and gathered stray cats. She rode like a centaur (sidesaddle when her *bisabuela* was watching, astride and bareback in her father's company). She had the gift of a sparkling curiosity that never failed to delight him, and she never seemed to forget anything she was told. Only this morning, after speaking for hours with her great-grandmother, she had asked him: "Has the *abuela* gone to San Francisco to see Queen Frances?" When he had explained that Mrs. Grover Cleveland was not known as Queen Frances, but only as the First Lady, she had replied thoughtfully that perhaps it was for the best, because queens seemed to make a very great deal of trouble. Plainly, Doña Maria had been telling her tales of the scrambled intrigues of the Spanish court. "Though if Mrs. Cleveland *were* queen," she said seriously, "probably the *abuela* and the *bisabuela* could teach her not to behave badly."

What a curious and delightful thing the mind of a child was, Roberto thought. A clean, fresh personality open to all the wonders of life.

He saw that he had fallen far behind the herd and the vaqueros, and filled with a momentary joy and freedom, he urged his horse into a run and galloped after the cattle yipping and calling into the soft, moist wind from the sea.

Sean Dundalk, for the last five years a city supervisor and adviser to the mayor of San Francisco, stepped out of the arcade of the Palace Hotel into the huge glass- and steel-covered court that opened onto Market Street. The circular drive was crowded with carriages and foot traffic at this hour of the late afternoon, and a cool wind swirled through the stacked galleries under the broad skylights.

Dundalk liked the new hotel. It had style and grace, and the food and drink were excellent. He lived in a suite of rooms on the fifth floor that cost him almost nothing. Politicians seldom were asked to pay for anything in San Francisco, the most open town, Dundalk was certain, in all of the western United States.

His companion, a thin stick of a man in black broadcloth, was the chief teller of the Crocker Bank, a Phineas O'Connell, who on his own time and for his own reasons acted as financial adviser to a number of city politicians. Dundalk did not particularly enjoy O'Connell's company. He was an Orangeman born, and though he had not set foot in Ireland these thirty years past, he still dealt with a true Irishman as though the Battle of the Boyne had been fought and won last year. His financial guidance, however, was peerless because his information was invariably accurate. He had been recommended by the mayor himself, and Sean Dundalk had profited handsomely from the association.

Though Sean Dundalk's Celtic enthusiasms had caused him to run through several fortunes, he had, at fifty-three, become slightly more provident, and by making the best of the many opportunities presented to a city supervisor, he was now, as Phineas O'Connell insisted on putting it, "comfortably situated." Dundalk disliked the phrase. It made him think of a fat old man seated on a plush cushion, and that was not the picture Dundalk had of himself. He had led an adventurous life, and though he had slowed down a trifle, he still liked to think of himself as a vigorous man in the prime of life.

"There are two things you must bear in mind, Colonel Dundalk," O'Connell said. "Last year's drought in Texas and Oklahoma will be forcing many ranchers into bankruptcy this year. If you have disposable funds available you will be able to buy a great deal of land very cheaply. Or if you prefer not to tie up your capital in land, I suggest you consider buying as much California beef as you can find. The price is rising and will rise much more before the southwestern producers can restock their herds."

Sean Dundalk, who from time to time remembered that he was born an Irish aristocrat and that he had not once but several times been a soldier and a gentlemen (though not always both together), disliked being advised to act the pawnbroker and profit from the misfortunes of ranchers he had never known. Yet one did what one must, and it was very difficult to *live* like an Irish nobleman's son or a former gallant soldier without money. So he would very likely take O'Connell's advice. His old commander, General Frémont, would have been contemptuous. But his other old commander, Porfirio Díaz, who was now completing his second term as president of Mexico, would have understood perfectly. Sean Dundalk often toyed with the idea of journeying to Mexico and attempting to make his peace with Don Porfirio. After all, his had been a very small dereliction of duty, when all was said and done. But Porfirio Díaz had a very long memory, and his experiences in three armies had taught Sean Dundalk never to press one's luck.

"I will see what I can manage, Phineas," Dundalk said.

"Look. There's Mr. Braden," O'Connell said. Samuel Braden was the vice-president and chief loan officer of the Crocker Bank, a dour New Englander of astonishing rectitude for San Francisco.

Dundalk's attention was attracted immediately by the handsome woman being assisted to step from a carriage by the banker. She was slender, elegantly dressed, with hair of an almost silvery blondness, and beautiful, clear features. Thirty, perhaps, or thirty-five. No more than that, surely. Instead of a hat she wore a black *mantilla* held in place by a high Spanish comb.

"Who is that with him?" Dundalk asked.

"That is the widow Marburg from Monterey," O'Connell said. "I believe she owns a ranch near Point Sur."

"Marburg?"

"Yes. Santana-Marburg, actually. The land is an old royal grant. She hasn't much money, Colonel. In fact, she owes the bank a rather large amount."

"I must meet her," Dundalk said.

O'Connell regarded Dundalk with prim disapproval. "I scarcely think she is your sort of person, Colonel."

Dundalk squeezed the teller's arm painfully and said, "She is exactly my sort of person, Phineas. I am not always a disreputable politician, laddie. I want an introduction."

"Very well," O'Connell said. He loathed being called "laddie" by this great red Irish lout whose political position made him valuable to the bank.

They approached Braden's carriage and O'Connell lifted his derby. "Good afternoon, Mr. Braden, Mrs. Marburg."

"Mr. O'Connell. Good afternoon."

"May I present Supervisor Dundalk, sir and madame?" With a touch of malice, he added, "Colonel Dundalk was most anxious to meet you, Mrs. Marburg."

Adriana's brows arched gently. Great God, Dundalk thought, what an absolute beauty. Older than he had at first thought, perhaps, but not by much.

"Forgive me, madame," he said in his most courtly manner. "Phineas mentioned your name. I have a friend named Marburg. Aaron Marburg. I knew him in the army and later in Mexico. Is it possible that you are related?"

A slow smile brightened her face. "It is possible," she said in accented English. "Aaron is my stepson."

"I would have thought your older brother, perhaps. Or even your husband," Dundalk said with a flourish.

"And have you seen Aaron recently?" she asked. Dundalk wondered why it was that he felt she was keeping her voice steady with some difficulty. She gave no sign of it, and yet he could sense that something he had said had touched her on a vulnerable spot. Holy Mary, was this the woman young Aaron had been so hopelessly in love with during the war? Well it might be. She was beauty enough to make any man remember her every living day, that was certain.

"Ah, the shame of it," Dundalk said. "I've not seen the laddie these ten years past. But we exchange a letter now and again as old comrades should. Do you see him, madame?"

"No," Adriana said.

Braden and O'Connell seemed restless and Dundalk said, "Would it be improper to ask that you join me for a glass of wine or some milder refreshment while we speak of Aaron Marburg? We are almost old friends—by proxy, to be sure—but still—" As he spoke his brogue became broader, his speech more lilting. It was Dundalk's natural reaction to the presence of an attractive woman.

Adriana turned to Braden and said, "Thank you for everything, Mr. Braden. I will come to the bank at eleven tomorrow to sign the papers."

Braden, with rare gallantry for so dour a man, lifted Adriana's gloved hand and kissed it. "Until tomorrow, *señora*," he said. "Everything will be ready for you."

He snapped his fingers at his driver, who helped a dark-skinned girl of perhaps fifteen down to the pavement. It was the first time Dundalk had noticed her presence.

"Mela," Adriana said in Spanish. "You can go to the suite and order yourself some supper now."

"*Sí, señora*," the girl said, and hurried away.

Adriana said with a smile, "Carmela is my *dueña*. She takes her duties very seriously."

When Braden and O'Connell had gone, Dundalk escorted Adriana into the Palace restaurant. It was already alight in the fading afternoon, glittering with crystal gaslights, and silver and white napery. The maître d'hôtel greeted Dundalk by name and led them to a private booth.

Dundalk, feeling expansive in the company of so beautiful a woman, ordered champagne.

"You said you do not see Aaron, *señora*," Dundalk said. "That's a great pity."

"Families disperse, *coronel*," Adriana said. "It happens."

"Indeed, *señora*. That is unfortunate, but true. It has been many years since I have seen my own people in Ireland." Dundalk smiled winningly. "Of course, I'd be less than honest if I said they would have it any other way. When I was young they paid me to stay away. Now I pay them not to trouble me."

Adriana laughed easily. "I have never before met a remittance man, Coronel Dundalk."

"I see that does not shock you, *señora*," Dundalk said eyeing her intently. Sweet Virgin Mary, she was a lovely woman, he thought, and not shy, not a bit of it.

The waiter brought their champagne and opened it. Dundalk went through the ritual of smelling the cork and tasting it. The wine was poured and Dundalk raised his glass. "To absent friends," he said.

"Absent friends," Adriana Marburg said, and tasted the wine.

"Mr. O'Connell tells me you have a ranch in Monterey County," he said.

"Yes."

"A Spanish grant?"

"To an ancestor of mine." Again that dazzling smile. "A remittance man in his time, *coronel*," she said.

"Ah, well," Dundalk said delightedly. "Then there is rebel blood in both of us."

"Perhaps there is," Adriana said. "But tell me about Aaron. You knew him in the army, you said?"

"In the United States Army," Dundalk said. "I served in three, as it happens. As a boy I was a subaltern in the Irish Guards, in my thirties I was one of General Frémont's staff officers, and in my forties I was an aide to Porfirio Díaz. I met Aaron when he was fresh from Europe, just a boy, really. When Frémont's foreign legion was dispersed, it was I who sent Aaron off to the real war.

"I met him again in Mexico in 'seventy." Dundalk refilled the glasses. "I owe the laddie my life, and that's the simple truth. There was a misunderstanding with General Díaz and I had to run for it. 'Twas Aaron Marburg who helped me to do it. When did you last see him, *señora*?"

"I have not seen Aaron for many years, *coronel*." Adriana said.

"He's growing rich, you know, in Tihuacan."

"I am happy for him."

"And, of course, he is married."

"That I knew."

"Three children. Two girls and a boy."

"Yes, we received announcements of the births," Adriana said.

Dundalk studied the calm, beautiful face. "And you, *señora*. Have you never thought of remarrying?"

"Never, *coronel*."

"I have never taken a wife," Dundalk said. "Which is a very great pity. I have always thought that I would be an excellent husband for the right woman."

"It has been my experience, *coronel*," Adriana said, "that men who cannot find suitable wives are often content with their sorrow." Her smile took the edge off the comment.

"You tease me, *señora*," Dundalk said. "Well, so you should. I tend to say foolish things sometimes. The truth is that I am a foolish man. Not all the time, but often enough to make life interesting." He lifted his glass and looked at the bubbles rising in the wine. "And lucky. I have always been lucky. That is an Irish trait."

"The Spanish understand fortune, *coronel*," Adriana said. "But one cannot rely on it."

"Very true, *señora*. I know that. But when one is lucky in his friends it makes all things possible. I remember that the last thing Aaron Marburg said to me as we parted was that he would like to have shot me dead. Instead he saved my life."

Adriana lifted a brow quizzically. Dundalk sensed that to speak to her of her stepson was a swift way to capture her interest. "I cost Aaron a great deal of money, *señora*. It all came out well in the end, but we did not know that at the time. I will not trouble you with all the details, but you may believe me that without his help I most certainly would have been stood against the nearest wall and shot by General Díaz's soldiers. Aaron had every right to be annoyed with me, but instead of using his pistol on this poor son of Erin, he smuggled me aboard a ship that got me safely out of Mexico."

"It sounds a fascinating story, *coronel*," Adriana said.

" 'Tis Aaron Marburg's part in it that makes the best listening, *señora*. The laddie behaved with disgusting generosity. He placed me forever in his debt."

"Aaron Marburg is an honorable man," Adriana said quietly.

Dundalk regarded her with interest. Somehow he had touched her. He refilled her glass. "Will you be staying long in San Francisco?" he asked.

"No," she said. "My business here is all but finished for now."

"It is unusual, if I may say so, to find a gentlewoman dealing with bankers and such."

"You find it so, *coronel?* Why?"

The directness of the question took Dundalk aback. "Most women abhor business, *señora.*"

"Or is it that most men prefer women to be helpless?" She was looking at him with the merest ghost of a smile on her lips.

"It is not my preference, Doña Adriana," Dundalk said. "It is the way of the world."

"Now that *is* a foolish thing to say, *coronel.*"

"My God, it is, isn't it," Dundalk said. "I should apologize."

"For yourself, *coronel?* Or for 'the way of the world?' "

"You confuse me, Doña Adriana. I am not accustomed to beautiful women who can deal with bankers. They are a great mystery."

"Women, *coronel?* Or bankers?"

"I surrender, *señora.* I am in full retreat."

She smiled at him. "My husband was a banker. When he died the family became my concern. There was no one else. One does what one must."

Adriana sipped her wine. She glanced at the bronze figured clock on the restaurant wall. Dundalk spoke swiftly, not wanting this marvel of a woman to escape from him too soon. "If you would honor me by having dinner in my suite, I could tell you wonderful stories about Aaron Marburg's adventures in General Frémont's headquarters. They would amuse you, I am certain. All my friends say I am a born raconteur. It is the principal talent of the Irish."

"I would be pleased to have dinner with you, Colonel Dundalk," Adriana said. "But here in this restaurant will do very nicely."

The rebuff was gentle but firm. Dundalk accepted it with good grace. To have such a woman as a mistress would be heavenly, but to have her as a friend might be even better over time. Sean Dundalk had reached an age when he could make such reasoned judgments.

He managed a roguish smile. "I don't suppose I could prevail upon you to marry me tonight—or tomorrow, perhaps? I am on excellent terms with the Fathers at Mission Dolores."

"I think not not tonight," Adriana said, laughing. "And tomorrow I must see both Señor Braden and my dressmaker."

"I am the prisoner of my destiny," Sean Dundalk said in his rusty Spanish.

"My father used to say something like that often," Adriana said, her eyes curiously bright. "The Fates command us."

Lightly, he said, "We have much in common, the Irish and the Spanish. The Armada, perhaps?"

"That might explain it," Adriana said.

Dundalk saw that she was ready to go. "Dinner, then? Here, at eight? Or is that too early? I remember we never dined before nine or ten in Mexico."

"At eight, *coronel*. We are Americans now."

He watched her go, slender, erect, and proud. What an incredible woman, he thought. How easy it would be to fall in love with her. As young Aaron Marburg had done. He was sure of it.

A brilliant March sun burned down on the gardens and battlements of Chapultepec Castle. Julia Marburg, reading diligently from the government guidebook, stood on the heights above the pillared monument to *Los Niños Héroes*. "On the morning of September 7, 1848," she read, "the North American General Scott's cavalry charged the Mexican positions at Molina del Rey, followed by infantry. In the battle, two thousand Mexicans gave their lives. Seven hundred North Americans also died. When the position fell, there was only one fortified bastion remaining in the capital—Chapultepec Castle. A furious artillery barrage failed to dislodge the gallant Mexican defenders and, on the morning of the thirteenth, General Scott ordered a frontal assault with overwhelming numbers. The last defenders of the position were the cadets of the Military Academy, who fought the invaders to the bitter end. The monument at the base of the hill glorifies the heroism of those Mexican youths, and most particularly of Cadet Juan Escutia, who wrapped himself in our sacred flag and leaped to his death from the heights rather than surrender."

Eufemia, brought along to help keep the children in order, raised her hands in a gesture of astonished grief and said, *"Ay. Dios mio!* Children! So brave!"

Caridad Marburg, at nine slender as a thoroughbred filly, had not been listening to her mother read from the guidebook. Instead she leaned across the battlements to peer down at the carriages and horsemen passing on the Paseo de la Reforma.

Eufemia, overweight and out of breath in the capital's thin air, hurried to draw Caridad back from the edge. "Not so close, not so close my angel!" This day, and the days of travel preceding it, had been exhausting for the ancient *mestiza.* It seemed to her that Don Aaron and Doña Julia simply let the children run as they pleased in this strange, foreign city. She knew, of course, that Ciudad Mexico was not truly foreign—that it was, indeed, the jewel in Mexico's crown, a European-style city built on the same filled-in lake where Tenochtitlan had been. But it felt foreign to Eufemia. It was too big, too noisy, too filled with ornate buildings and monuments, and the altitude made one pant after the slightest exertion. Eufemia longed for the familiar peace of Tihuacan, and she would be happy when this journey could be ended.

At the battlements fifteen-year-old Marina stood holding her brother Alex's hand. Both children were fair-skinned, with hair so black it shone with blue overtones.

"Right here," Marina said. "This must be the very place where Juan Escutia wrapped himself in the flag and jumped."

Alex Marburg, his seven-year-old face stern, turned to his mother. "Does Papa know what the *gringos* did here, Mama?"

Julia, her face shaded by her broad hat in the white sunlight, suppressed a smile. "I am certain that he does, Alex," she said seriously.

"And he is not angry?" the boy demanded.

"Well, it all happened a very long time ago. Papa was only a little boy then, in Europe."

"Still," Alex said, knitting his dark brows. "I am very surprised at Papa."

"Papa fought with the *yanquis* in their Civil War," Caridad said. "He does not dislike them, and you should not call them *gringos.* It is very bad manners."

"If Papa likes them now," Alex said stoutly, "then they must have learned how to behave better than when they came here to kill *Los Niños Héroes.*"

"Well, I suppose they must have done," Marina said. "We do a great deal of business with them." Business fascinated Marina, to the despair of the nuns of the girls' school in Tihuacan. She was truly, Aaron Marburg often said, Don Marcello's granddaughter.

Eufemia, breathless, sank down on the stones of the parapet. "Ay, Doña Julia. It is so hard to breathe in this place. My feet ache, and so does my poor back."

"You are only homesick, Femia," Julia said.

"*Estoy fatigada,* Doña Julia," the old *nana* protested. "And I do not like this city. It is filled with strangers."

Julia kissed her *nana* on the cheek and said, "When we return to the hotel you shall take a long nap. And maybe a tiny taste of *aguardiente* in coffee. You like that, *viejita.*"

"*Ay,* Doña Julia! You know I never drink," Eufemia said.

"I know nothing of the sort," Julia said dryly. She clapped her hands and called, "All right, children. Come along back to the carriage."

Alex, his blue eyes alert and interested, asked, "May we go to Teotihuacan this afternoon, Mama? I want to see where the Aztec priests cut out the hearts."

Caridad made a retching sound. "With a stone knife," she said, and mimicked opening her own chest to expose its contents. "How awful! How *cruel!*"

"They didn't think they were being cruel," Alex said reasonably. "They thought the gods liked them to do it. They thought the world would end if the gods didn't have hearts to eat."

"*Ay, Dios mio!*" Eufemia said. "Is that what your tutors are teaching you, Alejandro?"

"Of course," Alex said. "It is history." He addressed his mother. "I want to climb the pyramid of the Sun. May we go, Mama, please?"

"Your father will take you tomorrow, Alex," Julia said. "Now we must return to the hotel so that I can begin to get ready for the *baile* tonight."

"Will it take you all afternoon, Mama?" Alex asked.

"Yes. All afternoon. It is a very grand occasion. The birthday of Benito Juárez and the Day of the Indian Child. Your father and I shall be guests of the president," Julia said. "Now come along, all of you."

"Marina," Eufemia called. "Put your parasol up. Don't let the sun shine on your face."

"Oh, Femia," Marina said.

"Doña Julia," Eufemia said. "Tell her to mind me and open her parasol. The sun is very bright. It will turn her skin brown."

"Do as Femia says," Julia commanded.

The four women started up the gravel walk toward the central courtyard of the castle, where their carriage waited. Alex, in his short-trousered sailor suit, ran on ahead.

At the ornate entrance to the vehicle park he stopped, dropped to one knee, and aimed an imaginary rifle at his mother and sisters. "Pam! Pam! Pam! I am a *Niño Héroe* and you are *yanqui* soldiers!"

"Oh, Mama," Caridad said tolerantly. "Why are boys so silly?"

Eufemia, panting for breath as she walked, said, *"Linda,* if your mother knew that she would have the secret of life."

The aide, a dark and slender young man in an ornate uniform of dark blue decorated with an extravagance of gold bullion, marched across the broad expanse of parquet and presented himself to Aaron Marburg. *"El presidente"* will see you now, Señor Marburg," he said.

The anteroom of Porfirio Díaz's office in the National Palace was crowded with waiting petitioners, many of whom had arrived long before Aaron. They watched him follow the military aide with expressions of mixed resentment and respect.

The National Palace was originally built by Hernando Cortes on the site of Montezuma II's "New Palace." Over the intervening years it had been enlarged and rebuilt many times, so that it now covered the entire long block between Calle Moneda and the Avenida Corregidora facing the Plaza de la Constitución, the vast square more commonly called the Zócalo. The square, one of the largest in the world, had earned its familiar name from the Spanish word for pedestal, for the many empty pedestals that had, over time, stood in the plaza awaiting statutes that often did not appear. Statutes took time to complete, and political changes, at least until now, had been swift in Mexico.

Diagonally across the Zócalo from the National Palace stood the cathedral, built on a part of the old Aztec temple precinct once occupied by the Tzompantli, the Wall of Skulls. It was an immense baroque structure that had taken two hundred and fifty years to complete and so consisted of a multitude of architectural styles, all of which, quite fortuitously, had resulted in an impressive, and peculiarly Mexican, edifice.

Aaron caught glimpses of the cathedral and the smaller, appended Sagrario Metropolitano (a parish church not connected with the great cathedral and used by thousands of the city's inhabitants for customary prayers) as he passed by tall windows facing the Zócalo. But soon he was deep inside the *palacio* and the windows opened onto inner courtyards and gardens. There were seventeen of these inner patios. Most of them were never seen by anyone except those who worked within the huge building.

Aaron followed the aide down a long corridor, past the gold decorated portals to the president's formal suite of offices, toward a slightly less imposing room where Díaz preferred to do business.

The outer room was used by secretaries, all of them men, and by a half-company of the Presidential Guard, a praetorian force recruited by Díaz personally from the Rurales (whose numbers Díaz had nearly doubled since moving permanently into the presidency).

The young aide rapped once on a closed door and then opened it, military fashion. Porfirio Díaz, growing portly now, and dressed in a civilian suit instead of the uniform he still sometimes affected, rose from behind his enormous desk to greet Aaron with an *abrazo*.

"*Bienvenido a mi capital,* Aaron," he said. "Welcome to Ciudad Mexico."

"Don Porfirio." Aaron acknowledged the greeting formally. Despite his seeming ease of manner, Porfirio Díaz had always retained the *mestizo*'s powerful sense of the fitness of things, and he *was* the president of Mexico. One forgot that at one's peril, most particularly now that it was plain at last that, the Constitution notwithstanding, he intended to remain president until it suited him not to be. Aaron had often thought of the discussion he had had with this intense ruthless man about the realities of power in this land. Nothing Díaz had done in the intervening years was inconsistent with the ideas he had expressed over brandy in Don Marcello's lamplit *corredor*.

Aaron's business ventures had prospered over the years and in a small way they had contributed to Porfirio Díaz's personal fortune. Diaz had never been an intrusive or greedy partner, and the knowledge that the *caudillo* was "interested" had smoothed over many of the difficulties inherent in doing business in Mexico. For that Aaron felt a genuine gratitude. He realized that his ventures were small compared with many of the vast projects being undertaken across the length and breadth of Mexico: railroads, water conservation dams, harbors. Díaz had opened Mexico wide to foreign investment and industrial activity on a scale that dwarfed the Trituradora-Fénix Enterprises. But Aaron and Don Marcello had been among the first to back Díaz, and Don Porfirio was a man with a long memory.

"Sit, sit," Díaz indicated a settee against the wall of the long, high-ceilinged room. From the look of it, Aaron guessed that it was European and old, probably brought here by poor Empress Carlotta. On a table stood a crystal decanter of Díaz's favorite bourbon whisky.

"And how is Doña Julia? We will see her, of course, at the ball tonight?" Díaz poured two glasses and sat. "Doña Carmen longs to sit and gossip."

"Julia is well, Don Porfirio," Aaron said. "She has taken the children to Chapultepec today."

Díaz lifted his glass and studied the deep amber liquid for a moment before murmuring, *"Salud,"* and drinking it down. He still took liquor like the revolutionary soldier he was at heart, neat and quickly, without ceremony. Aaron lifted his own glass and drank.

"Chapultepec, yes," Diaz said. "I remember well the first time I saw it. I was fresh from a farm in Oaxaca, dust between my bare toes. I thought I had never seen anything so grand. The house of an emperor, no less." His smile was white, but the dark unblinking eyes remained alert, wary. Aaron had never seen Porfirio Díaz completely at rest. It was more than possible that he never *was* at rest, unguarded. Now, as a dictator, Aaron thought, he never could be.

"You don't come to the capital often enough, Aaron," Díaz said. "You are wasted in the provinces. I could use you here."

"I'm a simple man of business, Don Porfirio," Aaron said. "I would make a bad bureaucrat."

"I doubt that, but let it go. Still, you should have a place here. There are opportunities you should not be missing." He studied the younger man speculatively. "Would Doña Julia object to living here in the capital?"

"I think so. She loves Tihuacan. As do I," Aaron said.

"Well, then, perhaps not permanently. There is a small estate in Tacubaya owned by a friend of mine. He wishes to sell it. I would regard it as a great favor to me if you would look it over. You should at least have a home here in Ciudad Mexico. Here is where all the important decisions will be made in the future. Think about it, Aaron."

Actually, Aaron thought, the idea of buying a house in Mexico City had already occurred to him more than once. It would be pleasant to live here during the hot season on the coast. And the advantages were obvious.

"I will send you one of my secretaries in a day or two. He can show you the property," Díaz said. "You are at the Régis? You always stay there, I think."

It was typical of the man, Aaron thought, that he had such a minor bit of information at his fingertips. Don Porfirio's police intelligence gatherers were legendary—both for their efficiency and their severity. Díaz had come to the presidency promising Mexico stability and order.

The almost indigenous insurrections that had plagued Mexico since the days of the Spanish were put down coldly and without mercy, but there was less bloodshed now than before.

"Tell me of Don Marcello," Díaz said.

"Surviving, Don Porfirio. He takes no part in business, of course. But he is a man of great determination. He says he will see his grandson grown and his granddaughters married before he dies. He may just do that."

"The Genoese *tigre*," Díaz said approvingly. "May he outlive us all. How old is your son now?"

"Seven. And a great handful," Aaron said proudly.

"Shall I appoint him to the Military Academy? He could enter at sixteen."

Aaron raised a hand and shook his head. "Thank you, no, Don Porfirio. On the day I was carried out of the Wilderness by two Quakers, I promised myself no son of mine would ever be a soldier."

"There are worse careers, my friend."

"That's as may be, Don Porfirio. But no, I shall send him off to the United States for his education. Julia will be unhappy, but I think it for the best."

Díaz refilled their glasses. "Well, you may be right. The *yanquis* have much to teach us, and there is no reason why we should not send our sons to them to be schooled. I have a reputation as a lover of the United States. Some even say I am selling Mexico to the *gringos*, but I know what I am about. We need their science and their industry. If we wait until our own people are ready to make a modern state, we will be living on tortillas and beans until the year two thousand. I don't love the Americans, Aaron, but I admire their energy. If we can partake of that without allowing them to influence our institutions, all will be well. What they really want from us is profits, and there is plenty for all. One day we will have to throw them all out of the country, of course, but that won't be for many years yet." He drank his whisky and said, "That is one reason I should like you to spend at least part of every year here in the capital. You know the Americans. You can help us deal with them."

"I cannot really claim to know the Americans, Don Porfirio," Aaron said.

Díaz smiled again. The unlined face could become a mask when he did so. "You fought for them. You are, in fact, a citizen of the United States."

"The second statement is true because of the first, Don Porfirio,"

Aaron said. "My father-in-law often suggests that I renounce my American citizenship and become a naturalized Mexican."

Díaz shook his head. "No, I do not recommend that. I should like you to remain as you are. It may be of some advantage to us in the future." He took a gold watch from his waistcoat pocket and looked at it. "Lo siento, Aaron. We will speak again after you have seen the Tacubaya property. And of course we will see you and Doña Julia here tonight."

The two men rose. Díaz once again embraced Aaron and the same military aide appeared to escort him from the private presidential suite.

In the open carriage returning to the hotel from the Zócalo, Aaron found himself remembering the first time he had come to this city to search the records on behalf of the Santanas. That event now seemed immensely distant in time, part of another man's life.

In the clear spring air he caught occasional glimpses of the distant fire mountains, the great volcanoes the Aztec rulers of this place had regarded as images of the gods. Popocatepetl, the Smoking Mountain, and Iztaccihuatl, the Sleeping Woman. They dominated the mountain ranges ringing the valley in which the city had grown from Aztec capital to European metropolis. On his first visit he had engaged a guide and horses to climb those slopes as far as the snow line.

He had been a young man then, still in pain from his half-healed wounds, still angry with Micah and the world. What a great pity it was, he thought, that the young are so lacking in understanding of the real world.

Had he known even then how, and how much, he loved Adriana? He must have done, yet how hard he had fought to remain ignorant. One was reminded of a child, denied something desired, and so refusing even to admit the desire is real.

He rested his head on the leather cushions and looked up at the clear, empty sky. Adriana, he thought. Did she know, wherever she was at this very moment, that no day went by that he did not think of her?

He remembered the look of her, the taste and feel of her, as though it were yesterday. We are growing old, my love, he thought. The years pass swiftly, we live our separate lives, and yet, somehow, we do not grow apart. The memory of her standing in the intimate dusk of Don Alvaro's room at Santanilla was as sharp and clear in his mind as the day around him. The curve of her cheek, the soft angle of her naked shoulders, her breasts firm and hot under his hands, the taste of her mouth and the smell of her silky, silver gold hair, the strength of her arms about him—he remembered it all with an aching longing.

He allowed himself a wry, sad smile. It was said that one grew intolerant as one grew older. At least, so said the young. He remembered thinking so himself, long ago. And yet it was not true. Age might not always bring wisdom, but it did bring self-realization, and that, in the final analysis, was what made memory bearable. One learned by experience that there were many kinds of love: as many, perhaps, as there were people upon whom to bestow it.

If, to my surprise, he told himself, we all meet someday in that afterlife Father Sebastio was forever promising, I shall tell Julia, and Adriana, and Don Alvaro, and Micah this thing it has taken me forty-five years of living to discover.

The ballroom of the Palacio Nacional glittered with crystal and gaslight. Two hundred couples whirled about the great room in the waltz —women in silk and taffeta and jewels, men in black and white formal attire and gold-bullioned uniforms.

In a space left in the center of the room, Porfirio Díaz and his lady, Doña Carmen, danced as grandly and formally as Maximilian and Carlotta had ever done.

Aaron stood with the American ambassador and watched Julia whirl by in the arms of the British military attaché, a colonel of the Life Guards. She smiled at Aaron as she passed, her broad skirt swinging.

"Don Porfirio has performed miracles," the American said. "When I think of what this country was in Lerdo's time, it is truly astonishing." The Americans, Aaron knew, regarded Díaz with an almost proprietary friendliness. It was during his first term as president that the United States had fully recognized the government in Mexico City as the legal and legitimate rulers of the republic.

"We are progressing," Aaron said. "It takes time."

The ambassador, a tall New Englander with muttonchop whiskers and only the most rudimentary grasp of the Spanish language, reminded Aaron of Simon Pauley. Aaron spoke in English to him, and the diplomat seemed grateful. He was a political appointee of President Grover Cleveland's and he was uncertain whether or not, after the November elections in the United States, he would still have his post in Mexico City.

"Of course, there have been incidents along the border," the ambassador said. "One supposes that is inevitable, given the nature of these people."

Aaron was aware of the incidents, though they were not being reported in the Mexican journals. Diehard supporters of the exiled Lerdo de Tejada had attempted to raise a populist rebellion in eastern Chihuahua state and, with a fine revolutionary disregard for national borders, had raided Texas ranches near Eagle Pass. To Díaz that was the ultimate sin. It was absolutely vital to his plans for the development of Mexico that the nation be seen to be orderly and at peace. A large force of Rurales had met the Lerdistas on their return to Mexico and slaughtered them in a short, vicious battle. The leaders of the Lerdista field force had either been killed in battle or executed out of hand.

"I am not quite certain what you mean by 'the nature of these people,' Mr. Ambassador," Aaron said.

"Oh, I think you do, Don Aaron," the American said. "Mexico is a rich and beautiful country. But we can't ignore the fact that since Independence the presidency has changed hands seventy-five times."

Aaron looked through the crowd of dancers to where the president and his wife whirled to the music of a Strauss waltz and said drily, "I don't think it is apt to change hands again soon. Do you?"

The ambassador chuckled. "No. You are quite right about that. Don Porfirio has a strong and steady hand. Exactly what this country needs."

"He studied for the priesthood before joining the army," Aaron said. "Did you know that, Mr. Ambassador?"

"No, I did not know," the ambassador said. "One would not ordinarily think of Don Porfirio as suited to the religious life."

"In Mexico one takes education where it can be found," Aaron said. "Díaz is trying to change that by building public schools. But there is resistance to the idea from both the church and the people."

Julia had circled the ballroom again, and as she passed by with her red-coated Briton, she lifted her fan and made a pouting face to indicate that her partner was a poor dancer.

"Señora Marburg is lovely," the ambassador said. "Is she of *criollo* descent?"

"On her mother's side," Aaron replied, watching Julia with a smile of commiseration. "Her father is Italian by birth."

"That explains her vivid coloring," the American said. The ambassador was well known in the capital for his enormous appreciation of feminine beauty. Only last year he had been saved from a challenge by his diplomatic status. What would the dour and strait-laced Simon Pauley have made of such a representative of the United States, Aaron wondered.

One had better distract the American from Julia, thought Aaron.

It would embarrass Don Porfirio if the envoy of the United States should be challenged still again, and this time by a personal friend of the president of the republic.

When one needed to distract an American, one need only speak of politics. Americans were mesmerized with the process of electing their leaders. It sometimes seemed to Aaron that elections were continuous in the United States. Or perhaps they only seemed so to a European.

"Will President Cleveland be returned to office in November, Mr. Ambassador?" Aaron asked.

"I think there is no doubt of it, Señor Marburg. The Republicans have no candidate who can effectively challenge him. Except, perhaps, Benjamin Harrison. His only claim to the office is that he is the grandson of William Henry Harrison, our ninth president."

"The way in which Americans elect their presidents has always fascinated me," Aaron said. "If you will forgive my saying so, it appears that a man need not be wise, but only popular, to find himself in the White House."

"That is the essence of democracy, Señor Marburg. For one hundred and twelve years it has worked very well for us."

Aaron found the reply rather fatuous, but not surprising. He wondered if Americans would be quite so self-satisfied if they had not found themselves, by the purest accident of geography, isolated from the more covetous (and more sophisticated) powers of Europe by two vast oceans.

Don Porfirio and Doña Carmen had stopped dancing, and by so doing had stopped the music in mid-phrase. The room now hummed with conversation and laughter. Díaz, resplendent in the uniform of a full general, circulated through the crowd of guests. Aaron looked for Julia and her scarlet-clad escort.

Still in her mid-twenties, Doña Carmen was a handsome, if not strikingly beautiful, woman of the *criollo* class with dark hair, dark eyes, and an olive complexion. She wore a French ball gown and a sparkling assortment of jewels. Aaron bowed formally over her hand as they were joined by Julia and the British colonel. Julia curtsied deeply. The two women were close acquaintances, but on occasions such as this formality was the fashion.

"*Señor Embajador,*" Díaz said. "*Bienvenido en mi casa.*" To the British attaché he gave a regal nod of his head. *El presidente,* Aaron thought, had come a long way from the family farm in Oaxaca.

Julia linked her arm with Aaron's and stood silently as Díaz exchanged small talk with the British colonel.

Aaron's attention wandered. He was thinking of the children back at the Régis, and guessing that they were bullying poor Eufemia in the unmerciful way of Mexican children with their *nanas.*

A slight movement behind one of the marble pillars of the colonnaded room caught his attention. One of the many *mozos* stood there, strangely unoccupied for the moment and looking in the direction of the president with an expression of mingled fear and hatred. The tension in the man was unmistakable. He had the look of a soldier nerving himself to charge a daunting enemy.

Aaron glanced swiftly about the room to locate the nearest member of the Presidential Guard. There was none in sight. The crowd of richly dressed guests swirled and flowed about Díaz like sparkling water about a stone in a stream. He could half-hear Doña Carmen telling the British attaché the meaning of the Day of the Indian Child, and how her husband had decided to celebrate as a national holiday the birthday of Benito Juárez.

The man behind the pillar reached into his white cotton jacket. Aaron waited no longer. He took a half-dozen swift steps to the man's side. As the pistol appeared, Aaron seized the thin, dark wrist and smashed it against the pillar. The pistol clattered to the floor. A woman guest uttered a small shriek. Aaron held the *mozo* against the pillar. He heard him say, almost weeping, *"Hijo de puta! Quiero matarlo!"*

Suddenly Aaron found himself surrounded by Presidential Guardsmen. They clustered around the *mozo* like wasps. The man appeared to vanish among them and they rushed him out of the ballroom. Only a very few of the guests were even aware of what had happened. Aaron heard the *mozo* try to shout, *"Viva Lerdo!"* But the cry was swiftly muffled as the would-be assassin was rushed into the bowels of the building.

Julia, her face white, caught Aaron's arm and held it. The American ambassador and the British colonel looked flustered. Doña Carmen had already turned and signaled to the musicians to begin once again to play. Díaz, his face an Indian mask, handed the fallen pistol to a frightened Presidential Guardsman. He regarded Aaron with a slow, death's-head smile. "Once again, Don Aaron, I am in your debt."

He stepped forward, bowed to Julia and said, "Honor me with a dance, Doña Julia."

Within a minute, the dancers were once again circling the ballroom floor.

"Good God," said the American.

"I say," the British colonel said. "That was bloody fine work, sir. Bloody fine."

A mozo appeared with three glasses of *aguardiente* on a tray. "With the compliments of Doña Carmen, *señores,*" he said.

Aaron and the others took the glasses, and as the president of Mexico danced by with Julia Marburg in his arms, Aaron lifted his *aguardiente* in salute and then drank it gratefully down in a single swallow.

At five in the morning Aaron stood on the balcony of his hotel room overlooking the Paseo de la Reforma. There was little traffic on the broad avenue at this hour. The city lay sleeping. He could see the church towers, dozens of them, rising above the roofs in the gray light.

He fumbled in the pocket of his dressing gown for a *cigarillo* and a light. The smoke rose straight up in the still morning quiet. He turned to look through the French doors into the room. In the great *leto matrimonial* Julia seemed at last to be asleep. From the adjacent balcony belonging to the room where the children and Eufemia slept, there was no sound.

Aaron and Julia had left the presidential ball at two, their carriage escorted all the way back to the Régis by a mounted and armed cavalryman. The ride had been silent and tense. Julia had said almost nothing about the night's events and when he had taken her hand she had snatched it from him without explanation. He drew smoke into his lungs and thought that there was no accounting for the strange behavior of women.

He remembered now the smell of the frail man with the pistol. It was the acrid odor of fear. Once, long ago, in the Wilderness, he had smelled the same odor on himself and his men. The stink of a man terrified for his life.

He heard movement behind him. Julia appeared in the doorway. Her breasts, barely covered by her silk nightdress, rose and fell swiftly. Her eyes were shadowed. She walked barefooted out onto the balcony. Aaron said, "Did you sleep at all?"

She did not reply. Instead she stood before him, stiff and angry. "What is it, *querida?*" he asked.

She clenched her fists and struck him on the chest. Once, twice, then again and again. *"Don't—you—ever—do—anything—like—that— again!"* He put his arms around her and held her. She struggled to keep on striking him. Then quite suddenly she stopped, drew a deep, shuddering breath, and began to weep silently, great wracking sobs that shook her entire body. Her arms went about his neck and held him with astonishing strength. "Don't you know what you mean to me?" she asked. "Don't you know that if anything should happen to you I would surely die?"

Aaron held his wife close to him, feeling the warmth of her body and the strength of her love as the daylight grew in the eastern sky.

45

Adriana Marburg stood at the window of the ranch office at the end of the west gallery. Through the broad arch she could see the sloping ground with the new paddocks and the stud barn. The two thoroughbred mares most recently purchased from Senator Stanford were in fine fettle, pacing nervously about their paddocks, tails held high. They could smell Conquistador, the bay Arab stud newly arrived from the Hacienda Nuevo Leon in northern Mexico. Conquistador had cost one thousand dollars, and she had had to go more deeply in debt to buy him, but Adriana was certain that the investment would be a profitable one. The ranchers around Monterey wanted to improve their riding stock, and an Arab's get from the thoroughbred mares at Nueva Santanilla could be sold at an excellent profit.

It pleased Adriana that now in addition to the sheep and white-faced cattle on her range she could now begin to breed good saddle horses. Her father had tried for years to make a horse herd earn out at the old Santanilla. He had never quite managed it, but he would have been proud of what his daughter was accomplishing in the new country, on land given his ancestor by the Spanish king.

Adriana was dressed for riding in boots, leather chaps, and fringed jacket. Since coming to California she had taken to riding astride. A half-smile touched her lips as she considered what Don Alvaro would think of that. His liberal ways had never extended to approving of women on men's saddles. He would have thought it indecent, as Doña Maria never lost an opportunity to remind her daughter. But now it was only at the periodic fiestas in Monterey, where the local ranchers displayed their best riding stock, that Adriana still used a sidesaddle. New ways for a new land, she thought, and opened the window to let the sea wind enter the room.

Roberto had been alone in the Santa Lucias while she had been in San Francisco. She disliked it when he rode off by himself into the high country. South of Nueva Santanilla the mountains were wild, not high by comparison with the Sierra Nevadas or the Rockies, but steep, isolated, and often dangerous. Some of the acres left the family by Don Esteban lay near Mt. Carmel and were the home of deer, puma, and wild pig. From time to time Roberto would take Raoul or one of the other hands with him and they would return with a Pacific muletail over a packsaddle or a boar on a *travois* (since the horses often rebelled at having to carry one of the ugly beasts).

But Roberto was not a hunter by nature. He was a first-rate tracker, but he disliked killing animals. He almost never wore, as the vaqueros did, a pistol on his belt. They claimed to go armed for protection from vermin. But Roberto seldom killed even snakes, preferring to avoid them instead. When forced to kill, he used the long Spanish whip instead of a firearm.

Adriana awaited him restlessly. She had sent Felicia to summon him to ride with his mother. Adriana had found that it was simpler and more pleasant to deal with her son while they rode the mountain trails or along the beaches at the base of the cliffs than here in the ranch office. Roberto disliked paperwork and offices. She sighed at the thought and admitted that it was not, after all, his fault. He had not been reared to be a businessman. The Santana women had seen to that.

Roberto was nothing if not conscientious, however. At this moment he was probably paying his duty call to Elena, who had taken to her room (and for some days to her bed) in anticipation of her second confinement.

Adriana knew that she should not be impatient with her daughter-in-law, but the fact was that Elena had been less than a total success as a rancher's wife. She was too frail of body and too trivial of mind to be a proper mate for Roberto Marburg. In fairness, Adriana had to admit that it had been she, with Dona Maria's encouragement, who had as much as commanded Roberto's and Elena's marriage. And Adriana was too honest to deny to herself that Elena's dowry had figured large in her calculations. Without the parvenu Alvarez's money, it would have been impossible to move the family from Spain to California. To whom could she have turned for help? She thought now of Aaron, as she often did. He would have helped, if asked, even though in those years he had not been rich—as he now apparently had become, according to Sean Dundalk.

Adriana had never regretted her affair with Aaron. It remained a warm and treasured memory. But even without that memory it would have been impossible for her to ask him for money. The idea was unthinkable. And so the Alvarez marriage had been the only other available alternative. It would have been far better if Maria-Elena had been something other than what she was. But as Don Alvaro said, *Las Parcas nos mandan.* One had to accept what fate sent one's way. And what they had sent Adriana was a soft-willed, unintelligent girl given to troubles in childbearing and fits of jealousy. A less tolerant husband than Roberto would have taken to mistreating her long ago.

Pray God, Adriana thought, that this time Elena bears a son so that the worrisome cycle of pregnancies and miscarriages could come to an end. Despite her antipathy, Adriana was genuinely concerned about Elena's health. The mistress of Nueva Santanilla remembered only too well the protracted labor when Marianna was born.

Adriana opened the door to the arched gallery, so reminiscent of the Spanish Santanilla, and stepped outside. The mares were racing about, whickering and breaking wind with excitement. She looked at them and smiled ruefully. We females, she thought. We live, despite all our claims of independence, to be brought to life by males. She seldom thought about Miguel these days, but she did so now, remembering his fine features, his smooth olive skin, his shining cap of dark hair. And when her concentration wavered for a moment and the colors changed, it was Aaron standing there in her memory.

She heard the click of boot heels on the tiles and Roberto turned the corner of the building. His almost white-blond hair curled out from under his flat vaquero's hat. His skin, darkened by constant exposure to the sun, made his eyes look as blue as sapphires. He might not be

411

the most forceful of men, my son, Adriana thought, lifting her cheek to be kissed, but like his father he must surely be one of the most handsome.

As they rode out of the home pasture, Roberto on his tall chestnut gelding Rojo and she on the white-blazed bay mare she had, for sentimental reasons, named Estrella, they caught sight of Marianna trying to carry a litter of six adolescent cats from the stable to the house. The cats were squirming out of her grasp and jumping to the grass, making it necessary for her to recapture them over and over again. One of the old sheep dogs, too old to work the flocks, had attached himself to the child and followed her wherever she went. He stood now, tongue lolling, regarding the cats with yearning, yet too intelligent to risk Marianna's displeasure by chasing them.

"We shall have to do something about engaging a tutor for Marianna soon," Adriana said.

"I want her to go to an American school, Mama," Robert said. "The public school in Carmel to begin with."

Adriana regarded her son intently. The flat brim of her hat hid the arching of her brow. "Oh? And have you discussed this with Elena?"

Roberto allowed Rojo to pick his way along the path toward the sea cliffs on a loose rein. "She is against it, of course."

"Why 'of course'? "

Roberto favored his mother with a rueful smile. "Because she thinks no Spanish gentlewoman could possibly learn anything from *yanqui* Protestant schoolmasters."

"And you disagree, Roberto?"

"I do," he said.

Adriana rode in silence for a short time. Presently she said, "I stopped to see your sister Cecilia at Santa Clara. She will take her final vows in June. She says that with two years of tutoring, Marianna could enter the convent school whenever we choose."

"And that is what you would like, Mama?"

Adriana tried to keep the impatience out of her voice. "It is what *you* would like that matters, Roberto."

Roberto set Rojo's way down the steepening path toward the coast road. "I rather thought it was what Marianna wanted that should be important, Mama," he said.

"She is seven years old, *Madre de Dios,*" Adriana said. "You must decide. You and Maria-Elena, of course."

"Elena tries to live too much in the past," Roberto said. "I find that strange in a woman still in her twenties."

"This is not Miraflores," Adriana said. "We are not Alvarezes."

"I think the notion of Marianna coming home after a day in an American school, jabbering like a *yanqui,* rather frightens Elena."

"It would frighten Elena less if *she* learned to speak English," Adriana said dryly.

They rode in silence for a time, along the rutted tracks of the narrow wagon path the district ranchers deigned to call "the highway south." There was talk of completing the road, and surfacing it with gravel, as far as San Luis Obispo. That talk had been common since Junipero Serra blazed the mission trail from Nuestra Señora de los Angeles to San Francisco. Someday it would be done, the Marburgs knew, but for their lifetimes it seemed likely that "the highway" would remain a trail, suitable only for men on horseback. Travel between Monterey and San Luis Obispo was by rail or coach through the Salinas Valley. The Santa Lucia Mountain coast remained difficult and isolated, if spectacularly beautiful. A wagon, if skillfully handled, could reach Point Sur, but not much farther south.

"How is Elena this morning?" Adriana asked. She did not want to say that she disliked listening to Elena's complaints and had, for that reason, failed to call upon her. She did not want to say it, but she was very much afraid her son knew exactly how she felt. She genuinely regretted this, remembering how tediously her own mother had behaved toward Miguel Marburg when he had first come as a bridegroom to old Santanilla.

"She seems all right," Roberto said dubiously. "She worries me, though. The baby seems very large already, and you remember how she suffered with Marianna."

"Your grandmother would say that is her Alvarez blood," Adriana said with a smile. Doña Maria was convinced that peasant mothers deliberately bore large infants to make up for their poverty. Nothing anyone could say would convince her that this notion was nonsense.

There seemed little to say between mother and son about Maria-Elena. Each was fully aware of the other's attitude on the subject.

"Do you want Marianna to attend the convent school, Mama?" Roberto asked.

"Dios mio, Roberto. She is *your* daughter."

Roberto looked at his mother steadily. "She might as easily have been yours, Mama."

Adriana returned his gaze unflinchingly until he turned away, ostensibly to watch the trail. As they had ten thousand times in these long years, thoughts of Aaron troubled Adriana. Sometimes it seemed to her that Roberto could see straight into her soul and see his half-brother there. It was impossible, of course, but there were times when his sapphire-colored eyes were incredibly wise and very, very sad.

They had reached an overlook above the shore. By unspoken consent they stopped and let the horses graze on the fresh young grass underfoot. From where they sat, a sheer drop of two hundred feet leveled out onto a tiny beach and a shallow indentation of the coastline forming the suggestion of a bay. At either cusp of the crescent of sand, dark rocks extended out into the deeper water. They were being laved gently by a falling tide now, but both mother and son had seen waves crashing against the rocky spears of land with enormous power, exploding spume dozens of feet into the air. Inside the sketch of a bay, the sea otters romped like unruly children in the tangle of kelp. The sun, high in a cloudless sky, burned down into the green shallows and farther offshore into a deep of cobalt blue.

Adriana pushed the hat from her bright head and looked up at the gulls soaring on the thermals. "How very beautiful it is," she said.

Roberto looked at his mother and then at the sea. "I thought I would hate it while we were traveling," he said. "I thought nothing in the world could be worth that journey."

Adriana laughed freely. "It was bad, *hijo.* Yes, it was like a walk through hell."

"Do you know who was always on your side, Mama? Who always took your part, no matter how you dragooned us?" Roberto asked.

Adriana replied without turning to look at him. "Anita, of course." She smiled suddenly, looking like a young girl. "Ana-Maria was Sancho Panza to my Don Quixote. Without her with us, the windmills would have defeated us utterly."

"But you never had a doubt," Roberto said.

"I had many doubts, *hijo,*" Adriana said. "But what becomes of us if we allow doubts to overcome us? Life is to be grasped and shaped. That is what your grandfather used to say. We must take what the fates send—but we need not take it *as* the fates send it. God knows that he never did."

"I wish I were like Don Alvaro."

Adriana regarded her son with troubled affection. It saddened her that she had often felt the same wish. "You are Miguel's son."

"But not like Don Miguel either, am I?"

No, she thought. It is Aaron who is that. It was a thing she would die rather than say. "You are Roberto Marburg. That is enough to be."

Roberto looked down at the sea and did not make a reply. She wondered what he was thinking. Adriana could easily plumb the inner thoughts of most men. But not Roberto's.

He indicated the trail down to the beach. "Shall we go down?"

"You've been there before?"

"Often. With Anita."

Adriana suppressed the questions that came immediately to her lips. No, not with Ana-Maria. God knew the girl would be willing enough. If Roberto asked it, she would launch herself from these cliffs expecting to fly. She worshipped him. But to Roberto it would be the grossest abuse of honor even to look at Ana-Maria Gomez as a woman. Adriana realized, and not for the first time, that though her son was only indifferently religious, he had a well-developed sense of sin.

"Yes," she said. "Show me the way down to the beach."

The trial was steep and treacherous, but both mother and son had spent too many years in the saddle to be troubled by it. Roberto led the way down until Rojo reached the white sand beach. There he waited for Adriana and Estrella.

At the base of the sea cliffs the air was tangy with salt. Adriana sat for a time breathing in the ocean smells and listening to the sound of the waves. "We could have our own anchorage down here in this cove," she said.

"It is not well enough protected," Roberto said. "When the wind is from the south, the waves can reach almost to the foot of the bluffs."

"A pity," Adriana said. "It is a beautiful spot." She urged Estrella into motion toward the water. As the sand grew damper and firmer underfoot, she touched the mare with her crop and set her first into a canter and then into a full gallop in the shallows. Roberto followed her and they raced the length of the crescent beach, their horses' hooves raising bursts of spray.

When they reached the rock barrier at the southern limit of the cove, Adriana reined Estrella to a halt and waited for Roberto to catch up. She was laughing, her face flushed, her hair damp with spray, her eyes bright. Roberto thought, She must have looked like that when she first knew my father, when they rode together across the hills of old Santanilla.

Adriana walked Estrella up the beach and dismounted, looping the reins over a driftwood log. Roberto joined her, took a *bota* from his saddlebag, and offered it to her. "Do you remember how to drink from one of these?" he asked.

Adriana's smile flashed. "No Spaniard ever forgets that, *hijito,*" she said, and lifted the wineskin and poured a thin stream into her mouth.

"Raoul would be proud of you, Mama," Roberto said, taking the *bota.*

For a time they sat in silence on the driftwood log, Adriana watching the sea and Roberto watching his mother. How seldom he saw her in this mood, he thought. It was as though she had shed years from her age. And then he thought, she was a child when she married, not yet thirty when she was widowed. For more than twenty years she had carried the burden of the Marburg family on her slender shoulders. What right had anyone to judge her?

"Mama," he said, "I love you very much," and kissed her cheek.

She regarded him with an expression of pleased surprise. "What a sweet, gentle man you are, *hijito,*" she said.

She looked again at the breaking waves and then got to her feet and walked slowly to the water's edge.

He had meant to please her, and he had done so. And yet his spontaneous gesture of affection seemed to have changed her mood again. The laughing girl had gone as suddenly as she had appeared, and once again she was the Patrona of the Marburg y Santana family.

He stood and joined her and they walked slowly along the beach, leaving shallow bootprints in the wet sand.

"Marianna must have the best education we can afford for her," Adriana said suddenly.

"Of course, Mama," Roberto said.

"She can attend the school in Carmel for a year or two, but then it must be the convent school. And then, perhaps, even university."

"University?" The idea shocked him. No woman of his acquaintance had ever had a university education. It was unheard of.

"This is not Spain," Adriana said firmly. "Women have a place here."

"Of course, Mama. But—"

She put a hand on his arm. "Yes, I know, I know." She smiled faintly. "Your grandfather would have been scandalized."

"I was not thinking of grandfather," he said. After all, Don Alvaro was safely dead among the ancestors in the dark paintings in the *sala mayor.* "I was thinking of the *abuela.*"

"And Elena."

"That too," Roberto said.

"Elena will do as you say. You are the man," Adriana said firmly. Roberto was struck by an impulse to laugh aloud at the inconsistency.

416

Adriana Marburg, he thought, was a woman struggling between two traditions. But a lesser woman would not, could not, even make the effort.

"Well, when the time comes we will do what is right for Marianna," Adriana said. "But I want you to think about it. Nueva Santanilla will need what she can bring to it."

Despite everything, Roberto thought, my mother *is* Spanish. Her vision of freedom is the freedom to accept one's duty, to endure.

"Yes, Patrona," he said. His use of the ancient honorific was unthinking and totally appropriate. "I will do as you say."

Ana-Maria Gomez, her black hair blowing in the wind, stretched to put the last of the newly washed bedding on the line strung between posts in the kitchen courtyard behind the ranch house.

Despite the wind, the sun was hot and her cotton dress stuck damply to her body. She had kicked off her *huaraches,* as she often did, because she liked the feel of grass on her naked feet. Her arms were bare and brown, as were her sturdy legs. Strands of hair blew across her face and she brushed them away as she worked.

Though this sort of thing was accounted servant's work and was usually given to one of the Mexican girls on the ranch, Anita was perfectly willing to do it herself. All of her life among the Marburgs she had filled the peculiar niche created for her between servant and family member. As the Patron's goddaughter, she was obeyed instantly by any of the household staff, but as the blood daughter of Raoul and Tomasa Gomez, former tenants on the old Santanilla estate, she knew precisely the limits of her authority.

As she stretched to lift the heavy quilted cotton counterpane, she felt the wind lift her broad skirt almost to her hips, exposing her muscular thighs and buttocks. She pushed the skirt down with one hand, still holding the quilt on the line. She fastened it with the last of the wooden pins she held in her teeth and turned to look back at the house. Tomasa was not watching, for which small mercy Anita gave thanks. Her mother was very likely with Doña Elena, who was near to her time with Roberto's second child.

Down in the pasture, Marianna played with her cats, waving a clump of wild oatgrass over their heads and making them leap and strike at it joyously.

"Ain't you going to do any more lifting?" Charlie Greer, the *yanqui* vaquero, leaned on the rail fence, watching her. "I do appreciate it when you lift up high, Miss Annie."

417

Ana-Maria flushed and held her blowing skirt. "What are you doing up here at the house?" she asked in English.

"Your pappy sent me up for the hands' coffee tub." He half-turned toward the distant bunkhouse where the vaqueros not actually working were gathering to eat the noon meal.

"Then you had better go to the kitchen and ask for it," Ana-Maria said.

Greer made no move to leave. He hooked a high boot heel over the lowest rail of the fence and pushed his hat from his spiky sand-colored head. He wore grimy chaps and a dark woolen shirt that Ana-Maria could smell even at a distance. The enormous Navy Colt he always carried hung low on his thigh.

"He sure does play good on that git-tar," he said. "Listen to him pluckin' away."

Ana-Maria had been half-listening to her father's guitar while hanging out the wash. He had been playing some of his old and favorite *jotas*. Many years ago, as a boy, he had served with the *tercio* that followed Don Alvaro Santana against the Carlists. He had learned to play after winning the guitar from another soldier in a card game.

"Sure I can't help you, Miss Annie?" Greer had a way of looking at her that made her feel naked. She would never have said such a thing to anyone, least of all to Roberto. Perhaps if Charlie were cleaner, or less obviously a drifter, she might have been willing to accept his attention as a compliment. But he was as he was, of indeterminate age, not personally fastidious (well, that was to be expected in an itinerant cowboy), always unshaved and uncombed—and always watching her with those cold, blue eyes.

"I have work to do, and so do you," Ana-Maria said.

Charlie Greer made a show of looking about him. "I sure don't see the big *Jefe* anywhere around, do you?" He had a way of speaking of Roberto that infuriated Ana-Maria. Always on the edge of insolence, voice tinged with contempt.

Ana-Maria picked up the two heavy galvanized tubs she had used to bring the washing down from the house. Charlie Greer was through the fence and at her side in a stride. He took the tubs from her. "These're too heavy for a girl like you, Miss Annie. You just let me carry them."

Ana-Maria was tempted to argue the point, but she would have felt ridiculous tugging and pulling at the tubs to take them from Charlie Greer.

"There's a fiesta in Monterey soon, you heard?" he said.

418

"Of course I have heard," Ana-Maria said.

"Sure. Whatever. Big Mex doings. Will I see you there?"

"No," Ana-Maria said curtly. She disliked even having Charlie Greer, a Protestant if he was anything at all, making fun of the Catholic Mexicans in Monterey. Besides, she had hoped that Roberto would take her to the fiesta, as he would certainly do if Elena delivered before then.

"You'll be with El Grande Patrono, I guess," he said.

Ana-Maria said, "You shouldn't use Spanish words if you can't pronounce them properly." It was the only thing she could think of to say to him to blunt his familiarity.

To her disappointment, he only laughed. "You Mexican girls have lots of *frijoles,* you do indeed."

"I am not Mexican," Ana-Maria said. "I am Spanish."

"Same thing where I come from."

Ana-Maria's eyes glittered with anger. "Is it being from Texas that makes you ignorant, then?" she snapped.

He laughed familiarly. "You never known a real Texan, Miss Annie. You ought to try one. You'd never be satisfied with anything less."

Instinctively, Ana-Maria swung her open palm at his face but he dropped one of the tubs and caught her wrist and held it. "Nice Mex girls don't hit men in Texas," he said, grinning.

"If I told El Patron what you said, he would have you run off Nueva Santanilla," she whispered furiously.

"You wouldn't do that, though. You wouldn't take a man's job and keep just because of a little Texas teasing."

Ana-Maria pulled her hand free and said, "Get back to work, vaquero."

"Why, sure. Whatever you say, Miss Annie." He dropped the other iron tub at her feet. "Say, I been meanin' to ask you for a long time. How come Don Roberto he goes to all those Pope Catholic doings in town? He ain't Spanish."

"Of course he is Spanish," Anita snapped.

Charlie Greer shook his head and grinned slowly, "Now that's funny. Marburg. Ain't that kind of a Jew name?"

Ana-Maria, trembling with anger, picked up her tubs and began to march toward the house.

"Hey," Greer called. "You forgot these." He held her *huaraches* in the air. "Can I keep 'em? I'll put 'em under my pillow so I can dream about the wind blowin'."

Anita dropped the tubs and strode back to Greer to snatch the *huaraches* from his hand. "You be careful, vaquero," she said furiously.

Greer regarded her with cold eyes. "No, girlie. *You* be careful, hear?"

Ana-Maria almost ran to the house. When she entered the kitchen she could smell the bitter tang of boiling coffee. Tomasa stood near the window, hands on ample hips. "Anita. You should stay away from the vaqueros. You know El Patron doesn't like to see you flirting with them."

Ana-Maria bit back a hot retort. Through the window she could see the Texan ambling, with the sinuous gait of the horseman afoot, toward the house.

She glared at her mother, put on her *huaraches,* and walked out of the kitchen seeking the sanctuary of her own room.

To Aaron Marburg's astonishment, on his return to Tihuacan from Mexico City, among his accumulated correspondence he found a letter from Cousin Rachel.

He did not immediately recognize the source of the letter from Frankfurt because it was inscribed on the flap with the unfamiliar name of "Rahel Sharon." But the spiky, defiant handwriting plucked the strings of memory. In addition to the letter, the stamp-crowded envelope contained a pamphlet in German entitled *Der Judenstadt,* by Theodor Herzl. The name meant nothing to Aaron.

He put the pamphlet aside and turned to the letter. Though it had been sixteen years since he had had any contact with his cousin, he recognized the hectoring style immediately.

"Dear Cousin Aaron," Rachel wrote.

You will see by the change of my name that I am married. No doubt that surprises you. My husband is a Russian Jew, a learned man and a hard worker. He is more secular than I could wish, but he is a good person and devoted to the welfare of our people.

I write "our people" advisedly in dealing with you. Uncle Isaac, before he died, told me that you had become a Roman Catholic and married your shiksa. He also said that it was the last time he would, in this life, speak your name. To my certain knowledge, that is a vow he kept.

Aaron, sitting at his desk in the office of the Trituradora-Fénix, could not entirely suppress a sigh. Terrible Rachel, who had badgered him as a child and who, at their last meeting, had symbolically excommunicated him from the family, had not changed one iota. Nor had age improved her disposition. He found himself pitying the redoubtable Herr Sharon. Proper Jew he might be, but he had a cross of Christian proportions to carry.

Rachel's letter continued:

You have no interest in the state of the family in Germany, so I will not trouble you with news of your relations. I only mention Uncle Isaac because you should be made aware of how deeply you and Cousin Micah Marburg disappointed him. It is no more than just that you should be told.

Ah, Rachel, Aaron thought. If there were an *auto-da-fé* and I were bound to the stake, you would light the faggots yourself, all in the interests of justice.

He read on.

My husband Avraham, I am proud to declare, was one of the early members of Chibath Zion in Pinsk. That will mean nothing to you, but to those of us who have not abandoned our heritage it is a mark of honor and courage. Even in the gentile press of Catholic Mexico, accounts must have appeared of the terrible pogroms that have swept Russia since the terrorist assassination of Tsar Alexander II. Alexander II was a tyrant whose kindness to the Jews consisted of forcing them to serve in his army for a mere twenty-five years. Among Russians, this was considered enlightened. His son, Alexander III, has dealt with our people more simply. He allows his Cossacks to kill Jews for sport.

I do not write this to engage your sympathy, for I am sure you feel none, but rather to tell you of Avraham and the reason for his leaving Russia.

We now work together for the Colonization Society (to which, I am sure you know, Uncle Isaac left his entire estate). The work is difficult, because buying land in Palestine is a highly complicated business, requiring endless negotiation with the Arabs who live there and with the Turkish officials who must be bribed at every level of government.

The Society, however, and all of us who work for Eretz Yisroel have been immensely encouraged by the appearance of the enclosed booklet. Herr Chaim Weizmann, one of the intellectual leaders of what we now call the Zionist Movement, feels that Herzl's book is, as the French say, simpliste, *and that it puts forth a program that depends too much on the charity of rich Jewish magnates. He is probably correct. Zionism cannot wait for the eventual conversion of such as the Rothschilds. But the book is well worth the reading, despite the fact that Herr Herzl is apparently unacquainted with the Jewish patriots who have preceded him in the field of Zionism, with Chibath Zion, or even with Nathan Birnbaum—a Viennese like himself—who invented the word by which our Movement is known. Herzl does not mention Palestine, preferring to make his Jewish State into a purely theoretical, and therefore righteous and unthreatening, construct.*

Nevertheless, as I say, the book is worthy, and for that reason I send it to you. A theoretical Zion may be more to your Roman Catholic tastes than a real one, but I recall that for all your faults, you were always a man of intellect.

Avraham and I shall continue to work here in Germany until we are able to accumulate sufficient funds (fifteen thousand Deutschmarks would suffice) to pay for our passage to Palestine and there to purchase a few hectares of land on which to live. Avraham was injured by a Cossack's horse and has a chronically bad back, but he assures me that his disability would be no bar to the establishment of a small citrus farm in Palestine when, and if, we are able by dint of hard labor and frugality to acquire the small sum of money that would make our dream possible.

May the God of Israel soften your heart.

Your cousin, Rahel.

Ah, Rachel, Aaron thought almost with affection. Who but she could spend three pages berating him for his failings, only to finish with so transparent a request for money? Request? No, Rachel probably had never *requested* anything in her life. When they were children, Micah used to say with what seemed to Aaron excessive tolerance: "What is hers is hers. What is yours is negotiable."

Aaron leaned back in his swivel chair and stared out of the window at the facade of the Jabonería Fénix across the street. The Sphinx trademark painted on the blue-plastered wall gleamed yellow and black in the semitropical sun. He closed his eyes and imagined Rachel and the virtuous Avraham Sharon at work in some dingy back-street office in Frankfurt, now transformed into a Zionist cell by the enthusiasms of Theodor Herzl, Chaim Weizmann, and Herr Nathan Birnbaum—whoever they might be.

He had read some sketchy accounts in copies of the European newspapers, months out of date, of course, of Jewish settlements on land purchased from Palestinian Arabs. Apparently they were communal farms of some sort, vaguely Marxist in organization, with the land owned by the colonists collectively.

Firebrand Zionist Cousin Rachel might have become. But not Zionist enough to give up the bourgeois notion of private ownership.

Well, Rahel Sharon, Aaron thought, I cannot quarrel with that— even thought I could probably quarrel with you about almost anything else under the sun.

He rang the bell on his desk and Juan Ortega appeared. He was accoutred in a blue and white striped shirt, celluloid collar and cuffs, blue sleeve garters, and white silk necktie—the very model of a member of the new managerial middle class of Tihuacan, Aaron thought amusedly.

"Juan," he said. "I want you to go to the Banco del Pacifico for me. See Carlos Largo, the foreign exchange clerk, and find out the rate of exchange of pesos to dollars and dollars to Deutschmarks. Ask the bank to make up a letter of credit on the Rothschild bank in Frankfurt for fifteen thousand marks. Get the best rate you can. Here is the name." He wrote Cousin Rachel's name on a slip of paper and handed it to Ortega.

"*Sí, Jefe,*" Ortega said, accepting the paper. Juan loved dealing with the bank. Twenty years ago, as a barefoot *peon,* he would have been afraid to enter a bank or speak to men like Largo. Now he was a respected member of the mercantile community of Tihuacan and he and his wife and children lived in a fine new house on Cabo Sur with a view of the harbor. Don Aaron had made it all possible.

Though the day was warm, Juan returned to his office and donned his linen suit coat.

"Don't accept the official rate, Juan," Aaron called through the connecting door.

"Certainly not, Patron," Juan said, and hurried out through the factory to the street.

Aaron leaned back and leafed through the slim volume Rachel had sent him. It was a scholarly treatise on the absolute need for a Jewish state written in high academic German—a language Aaron had allowed to grow rusty from disuse. It was also surpassingly dull. He closed the book and dropped it into a drawer in his desk. There, Rachel, he thought dryly. You have succeeded in making me feel guilty, unworthy of claiming any credit for having performed a generous act.

Somehow, he was certain she would be pleased.

At midnight Maria-Elena Marburg experienced the first labor pains preceding the birth of her second child. Raoul Gomez was dispatched immediately to Monterey to fetch Dr. Harrison to Nueva Santanilla.

Ten hours later, midmorning on the first day of April, Elena was delivered of a nine-pound girl destined to be named Consuelo Maria Isabella Marburg y Alvarez, after her maternal grandmother and Doña Maria Santana.

The birth was relatively easy, which was attributed to Consuelo's being Elena's second delivery. Roger Harrison remained at Nueva Santanilla for a day in order to assure himself of the condition of mother and child. Before he departed, he informed Roberto Marburg and his mother and grandmother that the state of Doña Elena's health and that of the child was excellent, but that Doña Elena was deeply depressed because for the second time she had failed to provide Roberto with a male heir. "However," he said, *"post-partum triste* is not uncommon in these cases. Affection and care will soon set things to rights."

Doña Maria's opinion of this prognosis was testy. "Latin phrases do not impress me, Ana," she said to her daughter. "The girl is weak in the blood. We made a mistake in breeding her to Roberto." Adriana was grateful that neither Roberto nor Elena were within earshot when the old lady delivered herself of that opinion.

Roberto devoted what time he could take from the ranch to Elena's comfort. He was extravagant in his praise of the child, who was as dark as her mother and calmly self-possessed as she suckled from the Mexican girl, newly delivered of her own dark and strapping boy, whom Adriana had employed to be wet nurse.

Marianna accepted the arrival of a sister with skeptical approval. As soon as Consuelito was big enough to get about the ranch and play with the animals, she informed Anita, would be time enough to decide whether or not she liked her. To Marianna, the baby's appearance was no more remarkable than that of a new lamb, kitten, or foal. Time, said Marianna sagely, would tell.

But Elena's depression did not lift as Roger Harrison promised. In tears, she apologized again and again to Roberto for having borne another daughter. He could not calm her.

Then four days after the birth, Elena grew restless and feverish. When questioned by Adriana, she admitted that she had some pain. Examined by Tomasa and Doña Maria, Elena writhed at their touch. Doña Maria, frowning, examined the towels used to absorb Elena's *post-partum* discharges and wrinkled her nose. The women of the house conferred. Dr. Harrison was summoned back to Nueva Santanilla. When he arrived, he was informed that in their opinion Elena was in the early stages of childbed fever.

A swift examination confirmed their suspicions. Elena was ill, and growing more so by the hour. By nightfall, her temperature stood at 102°, and her pain was intensifying.

To a pale and concerned Roberto fell the task of reassuring Elena. The girl was badly frightened. It showed in her eyes. She begged him to send for a priest.

Raoul Gomez was dispatched to Carmel and near midnight returned with Father Clarence, an Irish Franciscan who now served as Doña Maria's confessor. But Roberto refused to allow him to do more than sit with Elena and pray with her. Roberto had no wish to have Elena frightened still more by having Father Clarence administer extreme unction.

By noon of the following day, Elena had begin to produce a profuse lochia, stringy with clotted blood and foul-smelling. The odor of death moved into the room.

Roger Harrison, consumed with guilt at his failure to have prevented Elena's puerperal sepsis, remained at Nueva Santanilla in close attendance. To Roberto, he said apologetically, "We know what it is. We know how it begins. But we have nothing in the pharmacopoeia to stop it."

Roberto nodded bleakly and said, "Then it is in Father Clarence's dominion," and called the priest to do what he had not allowed him to do before.

When they were alone, Ana-Maria asked Harrison, "Will she die?"

The doctor's ruddy face showed his fatigue and despair. "I don't know, Anita." Then he asked, "What will *he* do if she doesn't make it?"

Ana-Maria ran her hand over the letters carved into the hearth of the *sala mayor*. They were the same as the letters carved into the stone at old Santanilla. *Yo perduro.*

"This," she said.

For three more days Elena's fever hovered between 102° and 104°. Her frail constitution spent itself in battle against the raging infection. She drifted in and out of coma.

On the fifth day, her legs suddenly began to swell with phlebitis. Anita, Adriana, and Tomasa worked in relays to keep then covered with cool cloths. The household chores were left to Felicia and the other *criadas* while the women hovered protectively over Elena. Her belly grew swollen and discolored. Her discharges became more profuse and bloodier. Her skin was flushed, stretched over the facial bones like a mask. Roberto could scarcely bear to look at her, but he did not leave her side. He even slept on a pallet in the corner of the room. Roger Harrison watched his patient helplessly while Father Clarence prayed.

On the morning of the last day, Elena arched her back and gasped, a sudden sharp pain piercing the cottony armor of her feverish stupor. Harrison rushed to her side and placed his ear against her laboring chest.

She was having great difficulty breathing. She made hacking, coughing noises as the pulmonary embolism choked off her life. She gripped Roberto's hands with unbelievable strength, looking at him with wide, terror-stricken eyes, eyes that slowly glazed.

Roger Harrison straightened and looked at Roberto, defeated.

Anita whispered an *Ave.* She and Adriana made the sign of the cross on their breasts.

Roberto slowly knelt at his wife's side. Adriana, aching to comfort him, thought: I know his mind now. She could feel his grief and regret. Grief for a girl dead at twenty-five. Regret for not having loved her more.

Anita said softly, "Shall I call Father Clarence?"

Roberto shook his head. "Leave me with her," he said.

Harrison, exhausted from his long vigil, and the two women sat in the *sala mayor.* Anita, her eyes closed, began to tell her rosary. Harrison could hear the soft click of beads in the gray silence of early morning. Somewhere outside a sheepdog howled. There is no God, the doctor thought bitterly. There never has been.

Adriana Marburg sat silently erect, her face pale but composed. What sort of woman was she, Harrison wondered, without tears for a dead girl?

He looked at the Santana motto carved into the hearth and wondered if he was too modern a man to understand its true meaning.

A spring rain was falling on the ridge overlooking the sea and the south pastures of Nueva Santanilla as the Marburgs buried Maria-Elena. Roberto watched remotely as Father Clarence consecrated the grave. Over his wife's narrow coffin Roberto looked at the women: his mother, his grandmother, a weeping Tomasa, Anita, and holding Anita's hand, his daughter Marianna. In a wide, silent semicircle stood the vaqueros and the household servants. The Mexicans stood with heads deeply bowed; Charlie Greer stared blankly at the grave.

How ironic it was, Roberto thought, that Elena—who had never learned to love Nueva Santanilla—should be the first of the family to find a final resting place in the California earth. The grief that he felt was like a stillness within him. We Marburgs brought her here, he thought, and she died trying to give us a Marburg heir. It seemed to him that God, or the fates of whom his grandfather used to speak so familiarly, had taken a moment from His eternity to punish the sin of family pride. Roberto studied his mother's somber face and wondered what she would say to such a notion.

Father Clarence stepped aside and Roberto, with Raoul Gomez and two of the Mexican vaqueros, lowered the light coffin into the grave. Father Clarence read the service for the dead, his Latin strangely accented to Roberto's Spanish ears.

Roberto took up a spade of earth and dropped it on the coffin. His mother and grandmother did the same. And then two vaqueros set about closing the grave. There was a temporary wooden marker put in place. It would be replaced when a proper granite slab, carved by the stonecutters of Colma, arrived.

Slowly the mourners dispersed, each of the vaqueros and *criadas* pausing to murmur a condolence to Roberto and his family.

The *velada,* the wake, had been a private affair, with only Roger Harrison and Father Clarence from outside the family present. It had struck Roberto then, as it did again now, how isolated from their neighbors the Marburgs of Nueva Santanilla were. There had been no one, among the ranchers of the district, whom he had thought it needful to invite.

He looked at Marianna, walking down the slope toward the house with Anita, and resolved that she would not live in such isolation.

Before turning away with Doña Maria, his mother searched Roberto's face and seemed about to speak. But he was still held by his inner solitude and she sensed it, as she always seemed able to do, and so turned without speaking.

When all had gone, Roberto stood in the rain by the grave, watching the newly turned earth darken. Forgive me, Elena, he thought, for leaving you in this lonely place. In time, others will come to lie beside you. You are only the first.

The family remained in deep mourning, as was proper, through all that spring and summer. The business affairs of the ranch prospered, the horse herd increased, young Consuelo (now almost exclusively in the care of Tomasa and Dolores, the wet nurse) throve. And Adriana Marburg watched her son with silent concern. She knew that Roberto and Elena had not been deeply in love. Given the circumstances of their marriage, that could not have been expected. But Elena was a part of Roberto's past, of his childhood, and—always generous with his affection—he had been fond of her.

What most troubled Adriana was her suspicion that Roberto

blamed himself for Elena's death. He went through the motions of living his ordinary life, but the sense of remoteness that she had first sensed at Elena's funeral was not dispelled by time, as she had expected it to be. Instead it seemed to grow more profound. Roberto had always been an introspective person. Now he seemed totally absorbed in making inward judgments upon himself that Adriana could not fathom.

She considered discussing this with Father Clarence or Roger Harrison, but decided against it. What, after all, could she say to either man? That she was unable to penetrate her only son's reserve sufficiently to comfort him? Her Santana pride bridled at such an admission.

Roger Harrison was often at Nueva Santanilla that summer. At first he had appeared tentatively, unsure of his welcome, wary that Roberto might in some way hold him responsible for Elena's death. But it was soon apparent that Roberto did not, in fact, blame the physician. Though he remained as distant from Harrison as from anyone else, he accepted and even encouraged his frequent presence.

It was plain to everyone on the ranch that it was Anita Gomez Roger Harrison came to see. Tomasa, doubtful of the suitability of a match between her daughter and an American doctor, was torn between ethnic prejudice and pleasure at the thought of Anita as a professional man's wife. Raoul Gomez, though seldom consulted, encouraged Anita to be civil to Doctor Roger. Raoul had by now been long enough in America to understand that an improvement of the condition into which one was born was possible here. Any question of marriage, of course, would have to be decided by Don Roberto. As Ana-Maria's *padrino,* he was ultimately responsible.

Adriana, made restless and uneasy by Roberto's detachment, resolved that what was now troubling him was the emptiness in his life as a widower. Doña Maria instantly (and surprisingly) agreed with her daughter's diagnosis.

"Is there no one suitable in the district whom Roberto can marry?" she asked Adriana.

"I think it far too soon to think about marriage," Adriana said, certain that thus far, at least, she knew her son's mind.

"Then tell him to find recreation," Doña Maria said.

When pressed for an explanation of what she meant, the old lady said impatiently that any grown woman should know exactly what she meant by recreation. *"Parranda!"* she exclaimed testily. "He needs to remember he is a man, *por Dios!"*

Adriana considered this for a time. Such matters were not easily discussed with Roberto, in whom Adriana had more than once detected a streak of prudery. Eventually she asked him if he did not wish to go off to San Francisco for some few days "to get away from the ranch." But he showed no interest whatever in her suggestion, no matter in which thinly veiled form it was made.

In despair, Adriana invited Sean Dundalk to visit Nueva Santanilla. The company of an older man of Roberto's own class, one with whom he could speak freely, might do him good.

Roberto accepted her decision with the same distant, thoughtful disinterest he had shown toward everything since Elena's death.

When Sean arrived, bright-eyed and hopeful that his invitation indicated some interest in him on the part of Adriana, Roberto acted the perfect Spanish host. But it was obvious to Adriana that her son and the ruddy, extroverted Sean Dundalk were never destined to be more than acquaintances.

Roberto, a Sharps carbine held across his saddlebow, led Rojo around the top of the brushy draw. Behind him, mounted on one of the Nueva Santanilla geldings, came Colonel Dundalk, a double-barreled British Purdy shotgun held at the ready.

At the bottom of the draw, Raoul Gomez and one of the vaqueros began noisily to climb the gut of the narrow ravine on their cattle ponies.

The morning was sharp and clear and the air held promise of the heat of late summer. Through gaps in the thickets of mesquite and chaparral could be seen the glint of the distant Pacific, like a slab of blue steel under the high sun.

"Get ready, Colonel," Roberto said. "He'll be coming up the draw fast."

Far below, Raoul and his companion beat at the brush with their long Spanish whips.

"Shouldn't we dismount?" Dundalk asked, dry-mouthed. He had never before hunted wild pig, but he had heard impressive tales of the animal's ferocity.

"No, Colonel. Your mount is trained to stand for a shot. It is better that way. Listen. He's coming."

Deep in the brushy draw there were crashing noises. The men at the top could see the mesquite swaying and breaking.

"Take him, Colonel. *Now!*"

A scruffy brown boar of four hundred pounds broke from cover, snuffling and grunting. Tiny red eyes gleamed furiously over a long face armed with nine-inch tusks.

Dundalk leveled the Purdy and fired one barrel. The pig had taken him by surprise. He had no idea the things could move so swiftly. His shot was a clean miss.

The boar, further infuriated by the noise of the Purdy, swung his head and galloped at Rojo's feet. Roberto expertly backed his mount in a half circle to clear Dundalk's field of fire for a second shot. He did not level the old Sharps he carried.

"Again," he called to Dundalk. *"Shoot!"*

Dundalk fired the second barrel and the heavy buckshot struck the pig just behind the shoulder. He staggered, but did not fall. Instead he whirled once again and crashed back into the brush.

Roberto Marburg dismounted and called down to Raoul to stand fast and beware the wounded boar.

"We shall have to go in after him, Colonel," he said.

"On foot now?"

"Yes. We can't risk the horses."

Sean Dundalk dismounted and reloaded the Purdy. He had done a great deal of hunting in his time, but he had yet to see an animal so daunting as that red-eyed boar. "I'm sorry I didn't stop him, Roberto," the Irishman said. "I thought I made a good shot."

"Buckshot doesn't always bring them down," Roberto said shortly. He disliked hunting, but as the Patron of Nueva Santanilla it was his duty to entertain his mother's guest, who had specifically asked to be taken out for wild pig.

"Stay behind me and three paces to my left," he said, and started into the brush.

Dundalk's tailored Savile Row breeches and polished huntboots were not the ideal clothing to wear tramping one's way through mesquite, but he had declined Robert's offer of leather chaps. He regretted it now, as the sharp spines pierced the English whipcord as though it were gauze.

Ahead, a few yards down the draw, Dundalk could hear grunting and snuffling and short, barking roars. The sound was chilling. Roberto held up his hand and they halted. Roberto turned and handed the Sharps to Dundalk, then pulled a Colt Peacemaker from his belt. The brush was a tangled thicket ahead.

"You aren't going in there after him?" Dundalk asked, appalled.

"Wounded animal, Colonel," Roberto said and dropped to his hands and knees. With gloved fingers he carefully separated the matted, thorny brush. There were splashes of bright red blood on the leaves and branches.

Roberto moved forward cautiously, the heavy revolver held ready. There was a thrashing and a thick grunt. Dundalk caught sight of an open, tusked mouth. The Colt fired once.

Roberto backed out of the thicket and called for Raoul to ride up with his lariat. He stood and thrust the pistol back into his belt. "All right now, Colonel." He held the branches back so that Dundalk could see the dead pig.

"Holy Mary. What a beast," the Irishman said. "I would have picked up a Rebel mine sooner than crawl in there after him."

"There are thousands in these mountains," Robert. said. "They descend from wild peccaries and domestic sows from the haciendas. Sometimes they get half again as big as this one."

"Mother of God, I had no idea."

Raoul arrived and dismounted. He wound the lariat around the pig's forelegs and threw the bitter end to the vaquero, who made a half-hitch around the broad pommel of his Mexican stock saddle and backed his horse up the hill, pulling the pig after him.

Rojo and the other horses whickered.

"They don't like his smell," Roberto explained.

"But mine stood while I shot," Dundalk said. Shot badly, he added silently.

"They are trained to do that. Hunting pig on foot isn't safe," Roberto said. He took a *bota* from Rojo's saddle and passed it around. He squinted at the sky. "Raoul will make a *travois* and bring him along. We had better get back to the house, Colonel. Grandmother dislikes being made to wait for *almuerzo.*"

The midday meal at the ranch house was, mainly because of Sean Dundalk's presence as a guest, a mildly festive occasion. The family remained in mourning for Elena, but Adriana had made the decision that it was time to begin to put the tragedy of her death behind them. Roberto had displayed no displeasure at inviting Dundalk and none at his presence at Nueva Santanilla. Adriana took satisfaction in that. The girl was, after all, dead. She had been given the full rites of the church and the respect due her as the wife of the master of Nueva Santanilla. Her family in Spain had been notified and Masses sung both there and in California for the repose of her soul. It was time, Adriana felt, for Roberto to get on with his life.

Consuelo Marburg seemed well on the way to becoming a healthy, happy child and it was obvious that Roberto loved her well. To Adriana it appeared that a sad episode had come to an end.

On this late summer day Dr. Harrison had come to pay his sedate respects to Ana-Maria, who seemed (as far as Adriana could tell from her actions) well disposed toward him. She sat now, dressed in her best, at the huge oak table in the *comedor,* flanked by Roger Harrison and Doña Maria and across the table from Colonel Dundalk. Roberto sat at the head of the board, Adriana at the foot.

At Nueva Santanilla, the midday meal was the largest of the day and there had been *paella* and *sopa* and *ensalada* with a crystal carafe of California wine for each diner. Felicia and three *criadas* were in the process of clearing the table for a serving of *pan dulce* as Colonel Dundalk entertained his hosts with tales of San Francisco politics.

"I have heard that you might run for Congress, Sean," Adriana said. "Is that true?"

Dundalk regarded her with open admiration. She was dressed all in black still, but he wondered if it were a mark of mourning, or was it because she looked so spectacularly beautiful in that somber shade. It heightened the creamy pallor of her skin and made her pale hair gleam.

"I have been asked to consider it, dear lady," he said. "But the thought of spending much time in Washington City is not appealing. It's a place where the air freezes in winter and sweats in summer. Only expatriate Englishmen could have built a city in a river bottom like that." He turned to Roger Harrison and Robert. "What California needs is young men in politics. Have either of you laddies ever given any thought to that?"

"Not I, Colonel," Harrison said. "I have no taste for politics." He glanced at Anita. "Nor any desire to leave Monterey County."

Adriana examined him critically. Roger Harrison was not exactly a "laddie," though a man Sean Dundalk's age might choose so to consider him. The doctor was ten years older than Roberto, a mature man approaching forty. And rather obviously searching now for a wife.

Adriana turned her attention to Ana-Maria Gomez. She did not always take her meals with the family, but Roger Harrison's presence required her appearance at table. She had grown into a handsome woman, Adriana concluded. She had the sturdy figure and broad face of her Iberian ancestors. And, Adriana suspected, she would probably grow plump after bearing children. But on the positive side there was her sweet and willing disposition, her large and expressive eyes, beautiful hair, voluptuous hips and breasts, and skin like *café-au-lait* velvet. Perhaps it was time seriously to consider her marriage. In Spain she would have been wed long ago.

But Ana-Maria showed no anxiety about her unmarried state. She doted on Roberto's daughters, and Nueva Santanilla would be a less happy place without her.

"What do you say, Doña Adriana?" Sean Dundalk asked.

"I am sorry. What did you ask me?" Adriana said.

"I was suggesting that Roberto might think about a political career, dear lady."

Roberto, rolling the stem of his crystal wineglass between his fingers, said idly, "And I told the colonel that you would make a better legislator than anyone in the district."

"What a revolting idea, Roberto," Doña Maria said snappishly. "Women know nothing of politics. Nor should they."

"I don't agree, Mama," Adriana said. "I think it is past time for women to take a hand in the way we are governed." She lifted an eyebrow at Sean Dundalk. "Of course we must have the vote before anything sensible can be done."

"Oh, I say," Roger Harrison murmured. "What an idea. I think I agree with you, Doña Maria. Women should not concern themselves with something so unsavory as politics. Your pardon, Colonel."

"It isn't the colonel's pardon you should ask," Adriana said. "But women have too much good sense to expect men to have open minds. Even my father never went so far as to suggest that women should be allowed to vote, did he, Mama?" She smiled at Doña Maria.

"Don't you bait me, Ana," the old lady said fiercely. "Don Alvaro —may God keep him always at His side—was a dangerous man. I loved him in spite of his absurd liberal ideas, but truth is truth."

Adriana put a hand on Doña Maria's wrinkled, sticklike wrist and said, "Please take note, Sean, of the way Mama pronounces the word *liberal*. As though it stings her tongue. Doña Maria is a royalist."

"What else should I be?" Doña Maria said firmly. "What else, when the ground under our feet is a gift from a Spanish king?"

Roberto said to Dundalk, "Don Esteban Santana used his grant only as a pig-hunting preserve, Colonel."

Dundalk lifted his hands in disclaimer. "Ah, laddie. The less said about pig hunting today, the better."

Felicia and the maids brought in the *pan dulce* and small cups of bitter Moorish coffee.

"You are very silent today, Miss Annie," Roger Harrison said.

"One learns by being silent and listening, Don Roger," Ana-Maria said.

"Anita has the gift of inner peace, Roger," Roberto said quietly.

Adriana watched as Ana-Maria looked at him with adoration in her eyes. Yes, it was past time she was married and embarked on a life of her own.

Felicia appeared, running into the *comedor,* distraught.

"Ay, Doña Ana! There has been an accident. Raoul has taken a fall from his horse and hurt his leg. The vaquero says Don Roberto should come at once."

Roberto was on his feet instantly, as was Roger Harrison. The two men rushed out into the gallery, followed by Adriana and the others.

The vaquero who had been in the draw earlier with Raoul stood hat in hand. "It is Gomez, Don Roberto. His horse shied from the pig you killed. He fell. I think his leg is broken, Patron."

Roberto shouted for two horses to be saddled. "Where is he?"

"I made him comfortable, Patron. Up near the rock ridge," the vaquero said, naming a landmark four miles from the ranch house and high in the steepest part of the near mountains.

"Anita," Roberto said. "Go tell Greer to hitch up the buckboard and take it up to the spring. Roger, come with me." He ran off in the direction of the stable.

Sean Dundalk said, "Can I help, Adriana?"

"I think not, Sean. Roberto and Roger know what to do. I suggest we retire to the *sala mayor* and wait."

Tomasa Gomez appeared from the kitchen, wringing her hands under her apron. *"Ay, Dona Ana! Que hago?"*

"Make Raoul's bed ready for him. Have hot water and clean cloths in case the doctor needs them. And stay calm, *vieja.* Raoul is not a frail reed."

Tomasa hurried off to do as she was told. Roberto and Roger galloped out of the stable, the doctor's bag bouncing on the crupper of one of the geldings as they raced for the hills.

Sean Dundalk shook his head ruefully, "Ah, Doña Adriana, I am beginning to think I am bad luck to the Marburg family."

Adriana drew a deep, calming breath and turned to her guest. "Come inside to the *sala* and finish your coffee, Sean."

"I feel I ought to be doing something more useful than that," Dundalk said as the buckboard rattled across the courtyard, Charlie Greer and Ana-Maria on the seat.

"Come," Adriana said, and guided Dundalk into the *sala mayor.* She went to a massive table and poured a drink from a cut-crystal decanter. "To calm your nerves," she said with a wry smile.

Dundalk accepted the neat whisky gratefully.

"It should not surprise me at all," Dundalk said, "if the moment I appear at a Marburg establishment I were to be shown the door. It's bad luck I am, Doña Ana. Bad, rotten, luck."

"Surely not, Sean," Adriana said.

"Ah, you don't know. I never told you the full, disgraceful tale of what I did in Mexico," Dundalk said.

"With Aaron?" Adriana asked.

"'Twould be more accurate to say *to* Aaron," Dundalk said mournfully. He finished his whiskey and held the glass invitingly. Adriana indicated that he should again visit the decanter.

Dundalk poured and returned to stand by the hearth. "I was aide to General Díaz at the time, him that's president of Mexico now and looks to be *El Supremo* forever." He sighed heavily and sipped at the whisky. "Drink, dear Adriana, that's what it was cost me my post down there. The Irish sin, love of the grain." He finished the liquor in his glass and stared at it dramatically. "Díaz was only beginning then, but he had a fine start, I must declare. We rode into Tihuacan with a full brigade of picked troops ready to lick their weight in wildcats or Lerdistas, take your choice. The truth is that Don Porfirio was planning not to wait for an election. What he had in mind was a *coup,* and we sashayed into Tihuacan to pick up a shipment of weapons from a boat in the harbor." He walked to the window and looked out. "Can they get the buckboard all the way to the ridge? The country seemed rough to me."

"They will take the buckboard as far as the springs and wait there for Roberto and the others to bring Raoul down from the ridge. If he can't ride, then they'll put him on a *travois,*" Adriana said.

"Ah, yes. Well. Where was I? Oh, the weapons. Don Porfirio's farm implements, we called them. Rakes and hoes. A hundred or so cases of repeating rifles and ammunition for them. Fresh from Díaz's backers here in the States." Dundalk paused. The memory was oddly exciting, pleasing. Perhaps it was because it had all been part of a great adventure in Mexico, and at a time when the years had not yet begun to weigh heavily on him. "Yes. Well, Aaron was summoned to a dinner with the great man and asked to store the weapons in his copra warehouse. I don't know why I didn't warn him. Ah yes, I do. Why deny it? I was Díaz's man, and it's God's truth I didn't think any harm would come to Aaron. You see, there was no way he could refuse Díaz's request, now, could he? So the soldiers unloaded the weapons and stacked them all, neat as you please, in Aaron's warehouse. Ah, the poor laddie. He was just starting out, and that warehouse and oil factory were all in the world he owned. He got out of the Union army with five hundred dollars and a bad arm, you know, and not one thing more." He studied Adriana shrewdly. "It's a strange thing. When I knew him in General Frémont's headquarters I somehow thought of him as well off. But it seems that he was not. He worked hard to own that factory and warehouse, and here came General Díaz and Aaron's old comrade-in-arms to pack it to the rafters with weapons and ammunition."

Dundalk went to the window again.

"They won't be back for hours, Sean," Adriana said. "Finish your story."

"I don't bore you with my old soldier's talk, then."

"No, Sean."

Dundalk shrugged. "Well, the rest of it is not so neat nor so lovely, dear lady. I was left with a detachment to guard the weapons. It was Cinco de Mayo, *El Supremo*'s own celebration of his defense of Puebla. And, incidentally, the anniversary of the battle of the Wilderness, where Aaron was wounded—though I never heard him mention that to a soul."

"No, Aaron wouldn't," Adriana said softly.

"Anyway, there it is." Dundalk lifted his empty glass as though it were a piece of evidence in a courtroom. "The drink, you see. *La borrachera*. My Spanish isn't what it was, but I know how to pronounce that word well enough. The general spirit of the fiesta infiltrated my lines. Not to put too fine a point on it, my men got drunk and so did I. We had no idea there were any insurgents within a hundred miles of us. And it's very wrong we—I—was. At the height of the celebration a hundred—well, perhaps not quite so many—a dozen *campesinos* in white pajamas came running through the warehouse with dynamite. The whole thing went up like a torch, guns, factory, and all."

He shrugged again and smiled at Adriana. "I had to ask Aaron to help me get aboard a ship and out that very night. Díaz would have had me against a wall before morning, and I do believe Aaron would have liked to have been put in command of the firing party. But instead of that, he helped me get away."

Adriana smiled distantly. How very like Aaron that he had never told her of this, had never spoken of it at all, even though he had come to her bed still bearing the scars of the fire.

"A remarkable man, your stepson," Dundalk said, regarding Adriana intently.

"Very," she said, returning his gaze evenly.

"Yes. Well, there you see how the Marburg luck runs when Dundalk heaves over the horizon."

"He has done well," Adriana said with a thin smile. "In spite of the Dundalk curse, I think."

"Aaron? Well, *I* think Aaron was destined to be a rich man. Perhaps what happened was for the best. It wasn't Díaz's time quite yet. And the fire left Díaz in Aaron's debt, and that is a thing *El Supremo* never forgets."

"I know very little about Mexico," Adriana said. Then she asked, "Did you know the woman Aaron married?"

"Not well. But what I do know of her is all good. Her name was Julia Marini, *criollo* and Italian, bright and charming."

Adriana was surprised at the swift pang of jealousy that knifed through her. After so long one would have thought it no longer mattered who shared Aaron's life and his bed. But it did. "Is she—beautiful, Sean?" she asked quietly.

Dundalk studied Adriana's face. "Not nearly so beautiful as you," he said.

Adriana stood and laid a hand on Dundalk's arm. "I thank you for that, Sean. You are a kind man." She paused and then added, "And too perceptive for anyone's good. I think this particular conversation is at an end. We won't repeat it. Now help yourself to whisky, Sean. I must go help Tomasa and Doña Maria get ready for Raoul."

"A minute more, Adriana," Dundalk said. "May I ask you something?"

"One can always ask, Sean."

He looked steadily at her finely made face and wide, clear eyes, thinking: A woman of her age has no right to be so beautiful.

"Well, Sean?"

"Why did you ask me to come to Nueva Santanilla?"

"Ah, I see," Adriana murmured. She went to the window and stood there, slender and erect against the light. "I asked you as a friend, Sean. Did you misunderstand me?"

Dundalk thrust his hands into his whipcord coat pockets and thought carefully before speaking. "No, dear lady. I may have had hopes, but no more than that."

"I asked you," Adriana said, turning so that her face was in shadow, "because I thought your company would be good for my son."

"I understand."

"I hope you do, Sean. Roberto is—" She shrugged suddenly,

impatiently. "I don't know what he is. I do not always understand him. Sometimes I think he is too gentle a man to survive in this world."

"There is nothing soft about him, Adriana," Dundalk said.

"I said gentle, Sean. Not soft. No Santana is soft. Nor any Marburg, either." She turned again to face the light. "When Roberto was born it was a different world. His father doted on him; we all did. He was a beautiful child. Miguel gave him a kind of love he never gave Aaron. I don't know why."

Dundalk joined her at the window. "Perhaps it was because he loved you and never loved Aaron's mother. Men are like that, you know."

"Roberto was raised in a house of women," Adriana said. "I would never allow him to grow close to my brother Julio. Aaron was away. All Roberto had was my father. And he saw Don Alvaro killed. Roberto was caping a young bull and my father thought he was in danger. Roberto saw the bull kill him. A terrible thing for a child to see."

"He feels responsible for that? Surely not," Dundalk said.

"He never speaks of it. But it is there, inside him. Death is a Spanish obsession, Sean."

"And an Irish one," Dundalk said. He said thoughtfully, "He has no fear of death. That I can attest to personally."

"Of course not. He is a Santana."

"And a Marburg," Dundalk said.

"There is a difference, Sean. To a German-Jew death is an adversary. To a Spaniard it is an old and terrible friend."

Sean Dundalk felt an involuntary shudder along his spine. This woman, as beautiful as a Toledo blade, was a Spaniard too. When she spoke of love and death it was with an intensity unfamiliar to one such as himself, who had spent his life running from the obligations of birth, race, and honor. If I were made of the same stuff as she, he thought, I would be shivering now in the ruins of Castle Dundalk among my family's starving tenants, helping them to bear the burdens of poverty and famine. For the first time in many years he saw himself clearly as a frivolous man and was saddened. The very idea of loving a woman like this one grew daunting.

"I should make ready to go, Adriana," he said.

She had sensed his mood. "Stay a while, Sean," she said. "I asked you here for Roberto's sake, but I enjoy your company."

I am a distraction for her, he thought. I will never be more. But already he could deny her nothing.

He wrapped himself in his Irish charm and said, "Ah, well, dear lady. I will stay as long as I am welcome." Then he very formally lifted her hand to his lips and kissed it.

Raoul Gomez came down from
the high country by *travois* and buckboard, a broken femur splinted and
wrapped with belts, his grizzled head cradled in his daughter's lap while
Charlie Greer drove the wagon.

Raoul was in pain, but his worst injury (he muttered to Anita) was
that sustained by his pride. That a man who had followed the sheep in
the Cantabricas and the cattle in the Santa Lucias with never a mishap
should now have fallen from his pony and snapped a thigh bone was
a humiliation.

Once at the ranch house, Roger Harrison had placed the leg in a
foot-to-hip cast, ordered Raoul to bed forthwith, and informed Roberto
that his foreman would be incapacitated for at least two months, possibly as long as three.

"Fortunately," the physician said, "the break is clean and the
vaquero who was with him had sense enough not to rough him about.

But Raoul won't heal like a boy. He's already complaining. Tell Tomasa to keep him quiet."

To Roberto, Raoul apologized profusely. "Patron, I was careless. My pony smelled the pig and got his legs tangled in the *travois*. I am ashamed, Patron."

Raoul was a difficult patient. Within a week he was begging Dr. Harrison to remove the cast. Within two weeks he had made himself a crutch and was actually getting about from place to place, attempting to oversee the shepherds in the lamb sheds and the groom assigned to care for Conquistador. Tomasa and Anita appealed to Adriana to order that Raoul follow Roger Harrison's instructions exactly.

An uneasy truce descended on the Gomez family. Raoul still clumped about the ranch on cast and crutch, but never in Doña Ana's sight. He could be seen at any hour of the day, swinging the heavy plaster-of-Paris cast about the paddocks, usually with Marianna and the retired sheepdog following after. Mornings he would sit in the sun and play melancholy *coplas,* the spontaneous musical improvisations used by the Spanish to express every contingency from a celebration of birth to a lament for the dead. The theme most often heard was in a minor key and had been entitled (by Anita) *The Copla of the Broken Thighbone.*

Sean Dundalk stayed on at Nueva Santanilla, his protracted visit quite in keeping with the tradition of Spanish hospitality. It was plain to Dundalk that Roberto considered him a special guest of Adriana's, but he, too, appeared to take some pleasure in Dundalk's company.

One bright morning a week before Dundalk's long-delayed return to San Francisco, the Irishman arose rather later than usual and was told that Don Roberto had ridden away from the ranch house at dawn. Dundalk, not wishing to disturb the workings of the household by rattling about at loose ends, saddled his mount and rode south to the ridge alone.

As he reached the first rocky upthrusts of the low range above the house he caught sight of Roberto's Rojo standing, loose-reined, beneath a clump of scrubby oaks. Dundalk paused and searched for Roberto. He found him standing alone and silent on the bluff where his wife lay buried.

He did not intrude. Instead he turned his mount along the ridge-line until Roberto was out of sight. Then he dismounted, lit a cheroot, and surveyed the panorama of pasture, mountain, and distant sea.

Returning to the house later in the morning, he detoured out onto the burial bluff and dismounted at Maria-Elena Marburg's grave.

He looked thoughtfully at the granite slab that had been carved with a cross and the name of the girl who lay beneath the stone and the dates of her birth and death, 1863 to 1888. Not long for a life, Dundalk thought. But who could say what God intended? It had been a very long time since Sean Dundalk had attended Mass. When Adriana and Doña Maria and the other women took the buggy into Carmel of a Sunday, Dundalk always managed to be otherwise engaged. But now he dropped to his knees in the dry earth by the grave and said an *Ave Maria.* He told himself that he did it because he pitied the girl in the earth under the granite marker. She had married a Marburg, and she had been consumed.

Sometimes it seemed to Charlie Greer that a fire lay banked in his belly, a smoldering anger that had been ignited by the old man who had raised him with fist and rawhide strap. Greer had not made any claim to being his father. Charlie had no memory of either father or mother. He had been sold or used to pay a gambling debt when he was barely old enough to walk, or at least that was what old Greer had always told him.

Ezekiel Greer had hacked out a small spread in the Texas panhandle, stocking it with stray longhorns and whatever else he could steal. But the place never provided a living even for one, let alone two. Charlie's memories were of hunger, of freezing winters and sweltering summers, of endless days in the saddle looking to take other people's stock, and of nights he preferred not to remember at all, in the stinking soddie with the old man humping him from behind, rank with years-old sweat and sour-mouthed from Mex *mescal.* Charlie could not remember a day when he was not struck in the face or whipped.

When Charlie was (as near as he could figure it) about thirteen, he stole three dollars from Zeke, the only hard money the old man had seen in years, and Zeke went crazy and came after him with a bowie knife. The banked fires in Charlie's belly flared suddenly and he snatched Zeke's buffalo gun and fired a one-inch slug through the old man's scrawny chest.

The war was on then, and Charlie set fire to the soddie so that any passersby would think the Indians had been raiding, and headed for Kansas. He spent the next four years riding with Quantrill, whom some people called a butcher and others called a Confederate patriot. Whichever he was, his methods suited Charlie Greer just fine.

But when it began to look as though the war was lost, Charlie was shrewd enough to guess that Quantrill's Guerrillas had a damned good

446

chance of being hanged as war criminals. He deserted and began wandering. From Kansas to Wyoming Territory to Oklahoma to Texas again, to Arizona, and finally to California. He was thirty-seven when he reached Nueva Santanilla, and the anger still burned in his belly.

He rode now, down the trail from the mountain pasture to which he had delivered a half-dozen white-faced heifers, through the chill of a summer fog.

He had never become accustomed to the strangeness of the weather on the California coast. In spring and fall, the days were sparkling clear and mild, but in summer the whiteness would often drift in from the sea, muffling the trees like a shroud, giving them strange, misty shapes that Charlie found oddly disturbing. For years Charlie had been plagued with dreams of the old man and of the things he had done while riding with Quantrill. He always kept a bottle near at hand. Whisky made all the world seem warmer, more inviting.

He was half-drunk now, cradling the pint against his chest as his scrub mustang picked his way unguided down the trail toward the ranch. Charlie's mind had a way of skipping from subject to subject when liquor blurred the edges of perception. He was thinking that the Mex vaqueros must have cheated him in last night's bunkhouse poker game. How else could he have managed to lose a month's pay? He had been drinking, of course, but that wasn't the answer. No goddamned Mexican was smart enough to take Charlie Greer at five-card draw, so plainly they had robbed him. He would have challenged them, but they were too many, and like all greasers they stuck together against a white man. So now there was no money for the whores in Monterey. That made Charlie angry. Not that the women in town were worth what they charged, God knew. Not one of them really earned her fifty cents, and if a man hit one to express his outrage, some lousy pimp with a nickel-plated revolver was there in two minutes to turn you out and tell you not to come back.

All his adult life Charlie had looked at more settled men with longing and envy. He often tried to imagine what it would be like to have a woman of his own, one that you didn't have to pay and didn't have to share. A woman and a piece of land. Land like this, with grass and water, land a man could live on and hold.

The thought turned sour. It seemed that all the land in the world worth owning was already in the hands of people like the high-and-mighty Don Roberto. And all the women, too.

Sometimes he found himself looking at Doña Adriana from a

distance and wondering what it would be like to have her. Each time he did, he felt a twisting fear inside, deep in his groin. A woman like that was so far above him that even the thought was difficult to encompass. Of course, he told himself, she was old. Almost fifty. But a man could still look at her and wonder.

Anita, now. That was a different thing entirely. She wasn't so very different from the whores he had known all his life, was she? Young, lusty—she must be that. All greaser women were hot. It was in their blood. He thought carefully about Anita as he rode. No, she wasn't like the whores. Only a damned fool would make that mistake. A man could make a life for himself with a woman like Anita and a few acres of land. A man could amount to something.

He wondered what she would say if one of these days he just said to her that he was tired of drifting, that he wanted to put down some roots, maybe even get married. He couldn't remember ever thinking of marriage before. Swaying in the saddle, he half-closed his eyes and tried to think soberly about it. The trouble was that all he could think about was Anita naked, under him, those brown legs wrapped around him. His penis engorged and thrust achingly against his tight-fitting Levis.

A bitterness rose in his throat and he had to hawk and spit. The image in his mind had shifted, changed, and now it wasn't himself he saw with Anita Gomez, it was Roberto Marburg. The thought fed the anger that was never completely still in Charlie Greer.

Sullen with fury, he dug his roweled spurs into his pony's flanks and hauled back on the curb at the same time. The small horse jolted forward, stopped in pained confusion, bucked sideways trying to avoid the sudden punishment. He cuffed the animal across the ears with a clenched fist. "Goddamn stupid shit," he said aloud.

He drew a deep breath and relaxed the tight reins. The pony looked back at him, white-eyed. There was blood on the soft lips.

Charlie drained the last of the whisky from the pint and threw it away. Now he had no more until next payday, and all because the Mex vaqueros had cheated him at cards.

He slumped against the cantle and let the pony start again down the trail that ran between clumps of chaparral and through stands of darkly green oaks. The fog seemed thinner, the daylight more silvery. Somewhere nearby he could hear a covey of quail clicking in the underbrush.

He thought about Roberto Marburg, savoring his resentment. He had told Anita that Marburg was a Jew name, and the more he thought

448

about it the more likely it seemed. Old Zeke used to talk about Jews from time to time. He used to say that nine-tenths of the world's problems came from Jews. Dirty kikes, he called them. Next to the Jews Zeke hated Pope Catholics most. Charlie Greer burned with the injustice of it all. Land like this, all owned by Jews and Pope Catholics. Where was the fairness in that?

This morning, after giving the hands their orders for the day, the high-and-mighty Jew-Catholic Don Roberto had gone off to Monterey with Doña Adriana and their big, red-faced guest, who called himself *Colonel* Dundalk. To do what? Charlie wondered. To do whatever people like that did, with all the world's money in their pockets.

He swayed again in the saddle and almost fell. He topped a ridge and there was bright sunlight, with the fog layered in below, pressed against the mountainside below the treeline. The sky was a hard, pale blue without clouds. He halted the pony and sat looking down at the sweep of the land falling away toward the bluffs overlooking the sea.

Anita sat in the grass far below, her head resting against a rock outcropping. Her calico dress was a spot of color against the thin brown of the last summer grasses. As Charlie watched, she stretched her legs and drew her skirt above her knees to feel the sun.

Charlie Greer knew that she often climbed to this place alone. Once he had followed her for half the distance before bearing away toward the trees where he could watch her unseen.

What did she think about, he wondered, alone with the sweep of the land and the sky and the distant sea? Today all of her attention seemed to be on the flat expanse of the fog bank below, a white ocean of cloud breaking high against the steep face of the mountains to the south and completely covering the ranch to the north. It was as though in all the world there were only two human beings, Anita Gomez and Charlie Greer.

Charlie nudged the pony into a walk, down the slope toward where the girl sat dreaming and plucking idly at the grass.

She heard him approaching and turned. He swung out of the saddle and stood at the pony's head. "Hello, Miss Annie," he said.

She scrambled to her feet, poised, it seemed to him, for flight. She hesitated and said, "I didn't see you coming."

He dropped the pony's reins and took a tentative step forward. "I was up at the high pasture," he said, groping for something to say that would keep her here. The wind blew her black hair and pressed her skirt against her thighs. How would it be, he wondered, to have a

449

woman like this for his own? To see a look of kindness in her face when he rode in at night?

"Don't be scared, Miss Annie," he mumbled. "I mean no harm."

Her black eyes were wary, but she didn't bolt. That was something.

"Ah—how's Raoul this morning?" Charlie asked, searching. "He's going to be all right, ain't he?"

"Yes," Anita said.

Charlie squatted on his heels and plucked at the grass. "That's good. That's real good." He looked beyond her at the sea of clouds along the shore. "Pretty up here," he said.

Ana-Maria nodded.

"Lonely, though."

"I don't get lonely," she said.

The touch of defiance in her tone flicked his inner anger. "No. I just guess you don't, do you." He was unsteady in his squatting position. He wished quite suddenly that he had not had so much to drink on the ride down from the high range. It was hard enough to talk to her without having the whisky tangling his tongue.

"I saw you from way up there," he said, gesturing vaguely at the ridge above them. "I could tell it was you."

"Are you drunk, Charlie?" she asked. She didn't say it angrily. That was something, he thought.

"No, I ain't drunk," he said, standing up.

She took a step backward, away from him, and the bitter taste was back in his throat. It's like I smelled bad or something, he thought.

He moved forward and she seemed about to step around him and run. "For *Chrissake,*" he said. "I won't bite you. Look—" he extended his open hands at his sides. "See? I just want to talk—"

She seemed to relax slightly. "About what, Charlie?"

"Hell, I don't know. Anything. Anything you say."

"I don't think so, Charlie," she said.

The anger smoldered inside him. Who was she to be so high and mighty? "Why won't you never talk to me?"

"I don't like the things you say."

"I don't mean no harm. You know that."

"No, I don't know that. You frighten me, Charlie."

Excitement surged in him. In Charlie Greer's life there had been only two kinds of people. There were those whom he feared, like old Ezekiel and Major Quantrill, and there were those who feared him. He felt strong when he made someone afraid.

The wind pressed the calico against her legs, showing their shape. He looked at the gold crucifix that rested between the swell of her breasts. He had heard her tell Carmela that it had been a saint's-day gift from Don Roberto when they were children.

It was a funny thing between the rancher and Anita. Charlie Greer didn't understand it. But he had been told by some of the vaqueros that when Anita married, Don Roberto would give her money and some land. Vague, unformed ideas jostled about in Charlie's mind, unruly as cattle in a chute.

Something in his pale eyes tipped the balance and Anita darted to one side, ready to run. His hand snapped out and caught her arm. "Wait, *wait!*"

"Let go of me, Charlie!" She tried to pull free and nearly managed it. He caught her again by the sleeve and tore her dress. She began fighting him, clawing his face and kicking.

He hit her on the side of the head and she staggered. He hooked the neck of her dress and pulled the buttons free. Her soft, full breasts swayed nakedly, nipples dark against the pale coffee-colored skin.

Charlie Greer felt a flood of emotions. Sexual arousal, anger, and suddenly, fear. It had finally happened. He had gone too far, too far to explain his behavior to Don Roberto or the girl's father. Too far to stop now.

He hooked a boot behind her leg and threw her heavily to the grass. She struggled like a puma, kicking and biting, but he had her and that was all in the world that mattered now. He had tried to treat her right, tried to talk sweet to her, but she didn't want to listen, so now it had come to this. He pulled her skirt up to her waist and with his free hand hit her again to keep her quiet. He could see the tiny dark veins of the inside surfaces of her thighs, the black bush of her pubis, the deep indentation of her navel. He rubbed his beard on her breasts as she fought and tried to roll free of him. He could hear her crying out in Spanish, but her voice seemed to come from far off. The sound of his own panting exertions blanketed all others. He unfastened his chaps and Levis. There were already deep scratches across the girl's belly from the sharp-edged buckles.

She arched her back and almost dislodged him, but he laid his forearm across her throat and cut off her breathing until she lay still. Then he released her and took his penis in his hand. He guided it into her, shoving with all his weight and strength and hearing, at last, the wail of mourning as her hymen tore.

He pumped at her furiously, maddened by her shut, dry aridity, by her agonized rejection. He felt himself spurt and lurched backward, looking with shock and a sudden terror at his own blood-smeared flesh.

Anita lay as though dead, her eyes closed, her breath coming in deep wracking sobs.

My God, Charlie Greer thought wildly. They'll *kill* me. Old Raoul, the vaqueros, Don Roberto—they'll kill me or geld me for what I've done.

Fumbling at his clothes, he went at a hobbling run to his pony. The animal sensed his panic and shied, but Charlie brought the beast under control and swung himself into the saddle. He looked down the slope in the direction of the ranch and saw, with a shock, one of the Mexican hands riding up out of the fog, leading a packhorse loaded with supplies for the men at the high pastures.

For just a moment Charlie thought of going back to the bunkhouse to retrieve his few belongings, his Winchester and bedroll, his extra shirt. Then the absurdity of it struck him. What damned fool would risk his life for such a handful of junk? He had the clothes on his back, his Navy Colt, a box of ammunition. What more did he need? Hell, he had come to Nueva Santanilla with no more. His heart was pounding. It felt like it was trying to jump out of his chest.

He glanced back at Anita. She was on her hands and knees, vomiting into the grass. Damn her. See what the bitch had brought him to.

He whirled his pony and hit him hard with the spurs, galloping back onto the ridge. To the south lay the Santa Lucias, and almost trackless wilderness between here and San Luis Obispo. A man could lose himself in those mountains. There was water and game. Don Roberto would probably take the time to get a posse together from Monterey. By the time he did that, a man could have covered miles. By the time they come for me, he thought, it will be too late. But as he galloped toward the south his chest was thick with fear. Vigilantes hanged men for what he had done. Somewhere, he thought, Old Zeke must be laughing.

His face a mask of shock, Raoul Gomez stood unsteadily in the corner of Ana-Maria's room watching the women gathered about his daughter. Tomasa had stopped her wailing, but she still sobbed as she bathed Anita's battered face with cool water. He could hear Don Roberto and Colonel Dundalk talking in low tones out in the gallery.

Vasquez, one of the hands, had brought Anita in on his pony. The man's face had been pale with dismay. He had been torn between the need to bring Anita down to the house at once, and his desire to go after Charlie Greer, whom he had seen vanishing into the brushy country of the high ridges. In the end there had been no choice, of course. He had put Anita on his pony and carried her home.

Raoul Gomez, nearly incapacitated with grief, had sent a galloper into Monterey for El Patron and Doña Adriana. It had been late afternoon by the time they had arrived.

Doña Maria had been at home, thank God, and she had taken command, examining Anita's injuries and ordering her put to bed at once. What could be done for the girl was being done. What remained, Raoul Gomez thought, was men's business. He hobbled out into the gallery where Don Roberto was speaking to *el coronel,* Dundalk.

"Patron," Raoul said, his voice still shaking, "may we go now?"

Don Roberto looked at him. Never had Raoul seen such an expression on the Patron's face. He looked like a man carved from stone, pale as death, and as implacable.

"Lo siento, Raoul," he said "But not you."

"Patron—" Raoul felt the tears of shame and fury in his eyes, on his cheeks.

Don Roberto put his hands on the older man's shoulders. "You have the right, Raoul. But you cannot ride. You will delay me. I am sorry, old friend."

Raoul Gomez, propped on his crutch and cast, knew that Don Roberto spoke no more than the truth. He lowered his eyes in humiliation and Don Roberto pulled him close in an *abrazo.* "Do not worry. What must be done will be done. Go tell them to saddle Rojo. I shall want water and food and the Sharps rifle. Go now, old man, and be certain."

Raoul hobbled off toward the stables, where a number of the hands stood about waiting for news of Anita.

Sean Dundalk said, "I will ride to Monterey, Roberto. To notify the sheriff we'll need a posse."

Roberto, standing in the doorway to Anita's room, seemed not to be listening.

Dundalk asked, "Do you know where he's gone to ground?"

"I will find him," Roberto said.

"A posse can be here by noon tomorrow."

"If you like." Roberto did not take his eyes from the girl on the bed.

Doña Maria came to the door and said in a low voice. "She sleeps now. I have given her laudanum." Her birdlike hand rested on her grandson's arm. "You must not blame yourself, Roberto."

Roberto's eyes seemed gray rather than blue. "I should have got rid of him before this," he said bitterly. "I knew what he was."

"Only God can see into a man's heart," Doña Maria said.

"Have you sent for Roger Harrison?" Roberto asked.

"No," said Doña Maria. "This is a family matter."

Roberto stepped into the room and went to the bedside. He

looked down at the bruises on Ana-Maria's face. He reached out and touched her hair with his fingertips. *"Lo pagará,* Anita," he whispered.

Adriana looked across the bed at her son. He straightened and their eyes met. To Dundalk it was a strange moment. Mother and son —male and female images of the same person. Adriana had once said that she did not understand her son, that there was always a barrier between them. Sean Dundalk sensed that for this moment, at least, that barrier was down. The personas of mother and son were one. Dundalk felt the exclusion of this powerful blood-sharing.

Roberto and Adriana came out into the gallery. In the cold, foggy light of the waning afternoon Dundalk was struck by how much they resembled one another, and how each resembled the subjects of the portraits in the *sala mayor.*

"Can you find him?" Adriana asked.

"Yes," Roberto replied.

"Bueno." The single word had weight. The Patrona was giving her sanction to whatever her son now chose to do.

Dundalk said, frowning, "Won't you wait for the posse, Roberto?"

A shake of the head, as though the question did not even merit a spoken answer.

A vaquero came, leading Rojo. The gelding was saddled, a rifle in its boot, a blanket roll and buckskins tied behind the broad cantle, the Spanish whip coiled over the horn.

Tomasa emerged from Anita's room. Her face was tear-streaked, gray, etched with lines of grief. Roberto embraced her and whispered something to her Dundalk could not hear.

She kissed Roberto on the lips and said, *"Vaya con Dios, mi hijito."*

Dundalk protested, "It is very late, Roberto. Wouldn't it be better if you waited until tomorrow?"

Roberto Marburg took the reins from the man holding Rojo and swung easily into the saddle. "I will leave a trail for the posse to follow, Colonel." He made the offer, Dundalk thought, with total indifference, as if a posse of *yanquis* had nothing whatever to do with him.

He wheeled Rojo and moved away with a slow, deliberate parade-ground gait. Dundalk was reminded of the cool, formal way he had gone into the brush after the wounded pig. Dundalk had the eerie feeling that the nineteenth century had suddenly been replaced by the thirteenth. There was a ritual being performed here, the meaning of which lay just beyond Sean Dundalk's understanding.

As Roberto rode past the vaqueros, none of whom had offered to accompany him, they removed their hats. Then Sean heard the music. He had heard it before, long ago, before a battle in Díaz's army. Then it had been played by a regimental band. Now it was being played on a single guitar, by Raoul Gomez, who had once been a soldier. It was a poignant, minor-key melody. The *te guelo:* the music used to warn an enemy that no quarter would be given. Roberto inclined his head to Raoul as he passed, the gesture signifying agreement.

Rojo moved into a slow canter as he left the ranch behind. Marianna, small, erect, and somber, stood among the vaqueros watching her father vanish into the fog. Neither she nor any other raised a hand or spoke a word in farewell.

They all know something that I do not, Dundalk thought. Even that child knows.

He turned to Adriana helplessly. "Why alone? The man is dangerous."

"Roberto is *el padrino,*" she replied.

When she saw that he still did not comprehend, she said by way of explanation, "If Raoul had been able, he would have gone with him. But since Raoul could not, it is for Roberto alone."

"Aren't you afraid?"

Adriana's eyes seemed to have turned as gray as her son's. "Of course," she said.

"You baffle me," Dundalk said.

"Roberto is a Santana, Sean. *She* is a Santana. What must be done will be done."

"Will he try to bring the man back? It *is* the law, Adriana."

"Come with me, Sean."

She led him down the gallery and into her own bedroom. Dundalk looked about him at the great *leto matrimonial,* the heavy, ornately carved wardrobes, the *prie-dieu.* From a table she took a book and put it into Dundalk's hands. "Is your Spanish good enough to read this, Sean?"

A faded ribbon marked a page. Dundalk held the slim leather-bound volume to the dying daylight from the widow. On the flyleaf, in ink aged to pale brown, was written: *To my beloved son Alejandro from his father Santiago Esteban Alvaro Santana y Calderon de la Barca, November 1766.*

"A birthday gift," Adriana said. "To a thirteen-year-old boy."

The book was a long poem, *El Alcalde de Zalamea,* written by Pedro Calderon de la Barca, who, to judge by the inscription, must have been related to this Don Santiago's mother.

Dundalk opened the book to the marked page. Four lines had been underscored with that same faded brown ink.

Al Rey la hacienda y la vida
Se ha de dar; pero el honor
Es patrimonio del alma
Y el alma solo es de Dios.

Dundalk looked across the shadowed room at the Patrona of Nueva Santanilla. "Now do you understand?" she asked. " 'To the King one ought pledge life and fortune; but honor is the patrimony of the soul—and the soul belongs to God alone.' "

At sunrise of the fourth day in the mountains, Charlie Greer became aware that he was being tracked. His route through the Santa Lucias had been a zigzag path, partially because he wished it so and partially because the summer fogs made direction finding difficult. He estimated that he was now somewhere south and west of Ventana Cone, a six-thousand-foot-high peak between two sparsely timbered valleys.

He had not made the progress he had hoped to the south because the country was much rougher than he had expected, with sharply defined ridges and deep draws made almost impassable by thick growth of greasewood, mesquite, and chaparral.

He was ravenously hungry as well. He had vastly overestimated his ability to kill game with only a handgun. The Navy Colt he favored for its intimidating effect in barroom brawls was nearly useless in hunting the Pacific muletail deer that either fled at his approach or, infuriatingly, stood and watched him from a distance, far out of range of the crude weapon he carried.

He had managed to kill a gray squirrel, shooting it out of a dead conifer. But the heavy bullet had almost literally exploded the small rodent into bloody shreds, and he had been forced to eat even the offal in order to assuage his hunger pangs.

Sleep had been almost impossible. Several times he had tried to lie up and rest, but his fear magnified each sound, bringing him alert, pistol in hand. At night the thrashings of the hobbled pony, as hungry as he and looking for forage, were so loud Charlie was certain they could be heard for miles.

Twice he had seen the smoke of distant campfires, which might have meant hunters or some of the local, placid Indians. But though he considered approaching them and begging—or stealing—food, his instincts warned against it. Who could tell what sort of men sat around those campfires? They could be lawmen, or people hired to hunt him down by Don Roberto.

In the gray morning of the third day, the night after having gorged himself on the nearly raw squirrel, Charlie Greer became violently ill. He vomited up bits of undigested meat and bone and as the sun topped the eastern ridges he found himself squatting and defecating a putrid-smelling gruel. He could not be certain that it was the squirrel. He had drunk deeply the night before from a nearly summer-dry creek whose water had been green with algae.

His pony was suffering. There was very little grass in the Santa Lucias at this time of year, and when decent forage was available, Charlie could not bring himself to allow the animal time to feed.

For a day he made very poor distance south, stopping every half hour to relieve himself of the aching stomach cramps by racking his by-now-empty bowels. All that he accomplished was to make himself more miserable; his bottom was raw and the movements of his horse were torture. His hunger did not diminish, but his wrenching guts made the very thought of eating unbearable.

At dawn on the fourth day he found himself on a bare ridge overlooking a barren valley separated from the coast by still another rocky ridge. As the sun rose behind him and struck the skyline across the valley, Charlie saw a flash of silver light that made the breath catch in his throat.

He sat his weary pony in a place totally without cover. And as the sun rose higher he saw the single horseman on the crest opposite. The morning light was reflecting from silver conches on the man's saddle.

Don Roberto's saddle had polished conches. Charlie, even at this distance, recognized the tall chestnut horse. It was Rojo, and the rider was Roberto Marburg.

He was looking across the valley at Charlie Greer, outlined like a target against the rising sun.

Charlie jerked at his pony's mouth and began to gallop along the ridgeline to the south. Don Roberto too moved along *his* crest, but at a walk, never taking his eyes from his quarry.

Charlie looked fearfully west as his pony ran south. His stomach cramped with mingled panic and nausea. If the man had a long gun, and he almost certainly had, he could take Charlie out of the saddle with a single shot.

Charlie reached the shoulder of the ridge and plunged down into the tangle of mesquite below, out of sight of the hunter. The undergrowth was punishing, but he spurred and whipped his pony through it and up the steep southern slope of the draw. When he could see the opposite ridge clearly, the apparition was gone.

But he was *there,* somewhere just out of sight, coming on. Hunting, hunting. Charlie Greer had been tracked before. He knew deep in his aching gut that Don Roberto was nearby.

There was blood on the pony's right foreleg. In his plunge through the mesquite a broken branch had gouged the muscle and laid back the hide. Charlie had a wild desire to beat the stupid animal, but he held himself in. He felt lightheaded from lack of food and from his rumbling belly illness. Cramps hit him again and doubled him over, but he dared not stop. He had almost nothing inside him, but what was there burned as the pony jolted up the draw and a foul smell told Charlie that he had soiled himself.

He reached a rising tableland of sparse meadow angling to the west, toward the sea. It wasn't the way he wanted to go, but it was open ground that he could cover fast. He jammed the long rowels of his spurs into the pony's ribs and slashed at him with the rein ends.

The horse responded, but sluggishly. Charlie had foundered horses before. He knew all the symptoms. The unsteady gait, the heaving, roaring breathing, the gluey slaver at mouth and nostrils. "Don't you die on me, you son of a donkey whore," he breathed. *"Run, damn you, run!"*

He looked backward and saw, with bursting heart, a horseman rising from the draw. Don Roberto's thoroughbred was walking, just walking. The tall horse was as implacable as its rider. Charlie was tempted to draw his pistol and fire back over his shoulder, but the hunter was far out of range.

Charlie's pony topped the rising ground and started down another steep draw filled with brush and fallen trees. Between the steep hillsides Charlie Greer could see the ocean, flat and glistening in the sun. Why was there no fog this morning, he wondered, cursing. No fog—and when he reached the bottom of this draw, no cover. Nothing except a sloping mile of ground between the draw and the bluffs above the sea. To the north lay Point Sur, like a hazy giant's finger pointing out into emptiness.

The pony, driven hard, tried to jump over a fallen log of gray, weathered wood. Charlie hit him hard with the spurs as he made his leap and the pain of the sharp steel rowels made him flinch away. He fell, belly on the dead tree, forelegs on one side, hind legs on the other. Trapped, the pony panicked and began to struggle. Charlie, still in the saddle, raged and ripped at the animal's sides with his Texas spurs. The pony screamed and twitched and rolled, spilling his rider into the brush.

Charlie scrambled to his feet and pulled desperately at the reins trying to free the animal. The pony's legs were twitching and kicking and blood had begun to flow over the bone-gray log. Then Charlie saw that the pony had impaled himself on a broken branch. He exploded in terrified fury, shouting obscenities at the mortally injured beast.

He turned down the slope and began to run. As he cleared the tree line he still could hear the pony screaming. Ahead of him lay open meadow, sere and dead now, falling away to he top of the sea cliffs. The only thing left to him, he thought, was to find a way down the cliffs to the rocks and the sea. There were caves all along this stretch of coast. Flight was no longer possible, and he thought now only of concealment and ambush.

He was still a thousand yards from the cliffs when he heard a single shot, the rolling crash of a Sharps carbine. The pony stopped screaming. Charlie Greer ran on, stumbling and falling in his heeled boots, toward the cliffs.

He was halfway there when he looked back and saw Don Roberto on his chestnut gelding, ride out of the treeline. The long Spanish whip was in his hand.

For four days, Roberto Marburg had ridden through the fog-shrouded mountains and across the sunlit meadows like the fourth Horseman of the Apocalypse.

He had discovered that even the most gentle man (and he knew himself to be gentle, even to his own disadvantage) has a threshold beyond which he becomes capable of unbelievable savagery.

His grandfather often had said that the fates commanded a man, hinting, in his almost secular way, that life is a matter of encountering —and surpassing—predestined challenges. Yet no Catholic was licensed to believe that. St. Thomas said that man alone, of all the earth's creatures, possessed the divine spark of free will. The ability to choose between good and evil, said the saint, was evidence of the existence of the soul. All this Roberto knew and believed, but now it lay like charred bones in the fire within him.

He had tracked Charlie Greer with the single-minded fervor of a Dominican Inquisitor resolved to commit a heretic to the flames. He had not rested. He had eaten and drunk in the saddle. He knew himself to be not quite sane. For these four days he had ridden with ghostly images of death and sin: Don Alvaro with the horn in his breast, Adriana incestuously naked in brother Aaron's arms, Maria-Elena killed by his own pallid lust, and now Anita, his other self, savaged by a brute he had known to be dangerous.

As he left the dead pony and rode out into the open ground above the cliffs, he saw Greer. His mind seemed to blaze with light. The creature he had been stalking since leaving Nueva Santanilla was *not* a brute, but a human being with the same duty to make choices God forced upon every man. Debased he might be by the life he had led, but he had chosen as a man to do as he had done, and he must pay a man's price for that choice. Roberto Marburg, who would kill an animal only with reluctance, had become an executioner, as implacable as any hooded Spanish torturer at an *auto-da-fé.*

He rode forward toward the stumbling man, the whip now held at arm's length. Charlie Greer turned and screamed with fear, tugging at his cumbersome Navy Colt.

He raised the weapon and fired at the horseman. Roberto set Rojo into a canter, as graceful as a *rejoneador.* The whip cracked over Charlie Greer's head.

Charlie fired again. Roberto felt the heavy bullet burn his cheek. He wheeled Rojo and snapped the whip forward again. The steel tip ripped open Charlie's Levis at the groin and he howled with pain and dropped the pistol into the grass.

Roberto circled him, like a lancer working a bull. The whip cracked again and straightened Charlie up. His hands went from his bloody groin to his face. The tip had snared his cheek and blood cascaded over his chest and shoulder.

Roberto guided Rojo skillfully, with the delicacy of the lifelong horseman. To the right, to the left, backing Charlie toward the cliff.

Charlie scrambled in the grass, searching for his Colt. His face was bloody, his groin naked and torn.

The whip ripped open his Levis again and he screamed and staggered to his feet holding the Colt. He fired four times wildly. A bullet shredded the buckskin fringe of Roberto's sleeve. The whip struck the pistol and jerked it from Charlie Greer's hand. Rojo bumped him, sending him reeling.

He stumbled toward the cliff, holding his bloody crotch and making bubbling sounds through his open cheek. The whip stung his buttock and he screamed again.

He tried to run, but there was nowhere to go. He stopped at the edge to beg for mercy, but there was no mercy. The tip of the whip exploded one eye to jelly. His face was on fire. Through a blinding red blur he could see the horseman looming over him and he shrieked, *"Zeke—no!"* and backed over the edge to tumble like a bundle of rags to the sea-frothed rocks a hundred fifty feet below.

Roberto dismounted and picked up the Navy Colt. He walked to the edge stiffly, like a man suddenly old. He threw the weapon over and watched it fall into the surf. Far below a broken thing rolled amid the rocks with the movement of the sea.

Slowly, with sanity returning and sick at heart, Roberto Marburg mounted Rojo and turned the animal's head to the north, back toward Nueva Santanilla.

52

Adriana Marburg sat erect and still in the *sala mayor*. In the corner Dolores, the wet nurse, suckled Consuelo, as unaware of her naked breast as a madonna. Sean Dundalk, still in travel-stained riding kit, looked self-consciously away from the girl and at Doña Adriana.

"There is precious little more I can tell you, dear lady," he said with awkward formality. "We met him about twenty miles south of here. He gave the sheriff detailed instructions on where to find Greer and said that he would await the posse here. We could tell he had been shot at. His cheek—" He shrugged. "Well, you know."

"Go on, Sean," Adriana said. Her voice was controlled. If she felt any emotion she was not showing it. She sat unmoving as a statue, all in black, her beautiful face as still and pale as a death mask. From the *comedor,* shut off now from the *sala* by the great oak double doors, came the sound of men's voices. Sheriff Delgado and Roberto had been closeted for nearly an hour.

Dundalk drank whisky from the crystal-stemmed goblet in his large hand. "We found nothing except Greer's dead pony. The buzzards showed us where to look. But if Greer went over the cliffs there, well, he's gone and there's an end to it."

Consuelo made baby sounds and Dolores closed her bodice. Adriana said, "Bring her to me, *chica.*" Dundalk had a disconnected thought that it was strange to hear Mexican colloquialisms spoken in Adriana Marburg's elegant Castilian.

The girl brought the baby to Doña Adriana. The Patrona inspected her carefully and then said, *"Bueno,* take her to Tomasa now."

"Sí, señora." Dolores padded out, he *huaraches* scuffing on the polished floor tiles. How much did she listen to, Dundalk wondered. Did she listen at all? The troubles of the house were her troubles as well, but she displayed the typically Mexican assurance that those who ruled would deal with such matters.

"Then it is finished," Adriana said.

"My dear Adriana," Dundalk said. "This is not Spain. This is not the Middle Ages. There are laws."

"We shall see," she said. "The sheriff is *criollo.*"

Dundalk helped himself to whisky from the familiar decanter. She might well be right. He found himself hoping that she was. Delgado's family, too, had once held land from the Spanish king. California, the Yankee's golden land, was veined with old Spanish families. Many were impoverished, but they remained Spanish. One tended to forget that in the Anglo society of the cities and the hustle of Yankee politics.

"Young Colton searched the rocks. He found Greer's pistol in a tide-pool," he said. "There's no doubt that Roberto was shot at. No doubt at all." The Coltons' Santa Marta Ranch bordered Nueva Santanilla to the north and east. They ran five thousand head of white-faced cattle there.

Adriana made no comment. She sat with her chin slightly lifted, listening to the murmur of voices from the *comedor.* Dundalk could not make out what was being said, but the conversation was in Spanish. It struck him that Monterey County was very nearly a Hispanic enclave in California. Here, as in some places to the south, the old language persisted.

"Is the girl all right?" he asked.

"Yes," Adriana said.

She seemed to mean, Dundalk thought, that Anita was all right *now.* But was she, he wondered? What could lie ahead for a woman so brutalized? And he remembered some of his Mexican campaigns with

465

Díaz, and what the soldiers of both sides did to helpless women, and he was ashamed of what he had seen.

The doors to the *sala* opened and Sheriff Delgado, a dark-faced man with a drooping white moustache, came into the *sala mayor* with Roberto Marburg.

Outside, in the courtyard between the house and the studbarn, the Santanilla servants were feeding the fifteen horsemen of the posse. Dundalk could hear voices and the whickering of mares and geldings made nervous by the scent of Conquistador inside the barn.

Sheriff Delgado's black eyes were unsmiling. "Very well, Don Roberto," he said in Spanish. "I think nothing more needs to be said."

Roberto, tall and pale as his mother, stood silently.

To Dundalk, Delgado said, "I thank you for your assistance, Colonel. You may be called upon to make a deposition later." He turned again to Roberto. "I will take the pistol and saddle with me to Monterey. If any relative should wish to claim them, they will be there."

He strode across the tiles, his Mexican spurs ringing, and lifted Adriana's hand to his lips. *"Con permiso, señora.* My men thank you for your hospitality."

Dundalk, limp with relief, looked at Roberto. But the younger man's face, half-concealed by the bandage on his cheek, was unreadable.

The sheriff walked out of the *sala,* straight-backed and correct. Dundalk poured a glass of whisky and carried it to Roberto. "Thank God, Roberto," he said in Spanish.

Roberto accepted the glass with a slight inclination of the head. He was looking intently at his mother.

Adriana said, "Leave us, please, Sean."

Outside, men were mounting their horses and straggling out of the compound toward the north gate, weary from days in the saddle.

Inside the *sala* a heavy silence lay between Adriana and her son.

She studied his face, so very like her own. He seemed aged. Dante Alighieri might have looked so upon his return from hell.

"Sit with me, Roberto," she said gently.

He ignored her request. He stood beside the huge, dark fireplace looking at the motto carved there: *Yo perduro.*

"What did Sheriff Delgado ask you?"

"About this," Roberto said, touching his bandaged cheek.

Adriana felt a chill, as though a polar wind had blown into the long, beamed room. An inch to the right and her son, her only son, would have died. She put the thought from her mind with a shuddering effort. "It is ended, Roberto," she said. "You did only what had to be done."

"How terrible that sounds coming from a woman," Roberto said.

"Perhaps so, but it is no more than the truth. You must try now to put it all behind you."

"Honor is satisfied," Roberto said ironically. "No, Mama. It is not merely that I have killed a man that troubles me. It is that I *enjoyed* doing it. That, surely, is a sin." His tone turned suddenly savage, as though he demanded of her that she plumb the depths of his pain. "I used the whip, Mama."

Adriana's eyes showed her pity and her anger. "Enough, Roberto. *Basta.* It is done, finished. Even the *yanqui* law does not condemn you."

Roberto smiled bitterly. "A man can still be hanged here for stealing a horse, Mama. Did you know that?"

"Think of Anita now," she said.

"I have been thinking of Anita," he said. "I have been thinking of little else." He walked to the window to look out at the last of the posse men riding away toward the north gate. Then he turned to face his mother. "I am going to marry Anita, Mama."

Adriana's expression did not change. Under tight control, she said. "When did you decide this?"

"A long time ago, Mama. Though I did not know it until two days ago."

"Have you mentioned this to Ana-Maria?"

"No, I have not yet. But she will marry me. You know that she will."

Adriana closed her eyes for a moment. "Yes, I know that." She looked steadily at her son. "Do you know what you will be facing?"

"Mama, don't tell me about my station in life and hers."

Adriana flared with quick anger. "What do you take me for, Roberto? Though God knows that there *will* be problems. Raoul and Tomasa will be distressed. But I suppose you know that."

"They will survive it," Roberto said dryly. "Better here than in Spain, I think."

"There may be problems with the Church. You are her *padrino.*"

"We are not related by blood."

Adriana regarded her son with mingled emotions. Was it possible, she thought, that as she grew older she was becoming more like Doña

467

Maria? She tried to imagine what the ancient patrician would say about her grandson marrying the daughter of a shepherd and a *criada*. With all the world trembling around the Marburgs was she, Adriana Ana-Maria Santana y Borjas, reverting to medieval type, like any feather-headed daughter of the *gentecilla?*

"We must think about this, Roberto," she said.

"I have thought about it, Mama. I shall marry Anita. If the Church objects, we shall marry in a civil ceremony."

"I do not even like to think what your grandmother will say about that," Adriana said.

"I have already spoken to the *abuela,*" Roberto said. "Everything I have said to you I have said already to her."

Adriana was stunned. What have I done, she thought, that my son should turn to others before coming to me?

"Do not ask me why I went to Doña Maria with this, Mama," Roberto said with a remoteness in his voice that Adriana had never before heard. "She approves. Or at least she does not object. Does that surprise you?"

"Yes," she said softly. "It does."

"And I have written to Cecilia, who has a right to know. I told her what I have done and what I plan to do."

"Cecilia too."

Roberto fixed his mother with a level gaze. It was the look of a man who had been tempered, a man who had gone to hell and had come back changed. "I am more like you than we knew, Patrona," he said.

"I think we are strangers," Adriana said.

"Far from it," Roberto said. "We do what we must do. And we endure. Once, a long time ago, you decided to marry a Jew. Did you ask Doña Maria and Don Alvaro? Or did you tell them, Mama? We both know the answer to that. The only real difference between us is that you were born that way and I have had to *become* so. I am not the same man who left Nueva Santanilla a week ago. I will never be again."

Adriana drew a deep breath. In spite of the aching hurt he had inflicted on her, she found a growing pride in her son. What he said was true. He was not the same soft and gentle man he had been, and she would miss that man terribly. But why should she weep for the boy, when the man now stood before her?

A man who could face a man's concerns, she thought. "Very well,

Roberto. You are the Patron. There is one thing. What if Anita is pregnant?"

Roberto's clear blue eyes were mirror images of her own.

"The child will be mine," he said.

Fin de Siècle: 1889-1899

There by the Pacific the seasons turn with an elemental simplicity. In winter the rains come and transform the mountain pastures into lush green grassland. Spring brings a few sweet days of brilliant color in the fields, but the flowered time is short because the sun of early summer dries the grasses and turns the hillsides the color of young lions. Through the months of high summer the fog nestles against that rugged coastline, pushing up the steep hillsides through the black-green conifers to shroud the land in a silver garment. Then in autumn the sky turns to brilliant blue, pale with high, thin clouds, and the sun is warm and beckoning. The sea sends long rollers against the dark red rocks and crescent beaches, and as the season ages and winter approaches again the waves grow higher, angrier, and they explode against the shore in dazzling bursts of silver droplets and white spume. In late November there are some few days that seem left behind by the bright autumn, but they do not last, and by December the skies have turned dark with storms and the rains drench the grasslands and mountains and the yearly cycle is begun again. It was like that at Nueva Santanilla, with the turning of the seasons like a slowly spinning coin to mark the passing years.

As soon as Ana-Maria was able, she and Roberto Marburg were married by Father Clarence in a family ceremony attended by two friends only, Roger Harrison (who mournfully committed himself to bachelorhood—a vow that would actually last three years) and Sean Dundalk.

In the spring of 1889, Anita bore a male child. He was small and dark and closely resembled his mother. He was christened Esteban Santana Marburg.

Tomasa Gomez oscillated between a grandmother's love for the new child and a deep Iberian depression at the sight of him.

The ranch prospered, the herds grew. A townhouse in San Francisco was purchased. Don Roberto seldom used it, but Doña Adriana used it often. She remained the business head of Nueva Santanilla. The tempering of Roberto had not improved his ability to deal with agents and bankers, and it had not diminished hers.

Raoul—now known as Don Raoul—ignored his new status. He remained foreman of the vaqueros, and the only outward sign of change were the silver conches on his saddle. He was, he said, a shepherd and vaquero. He had been such all his life. He had no intention of learning to read, of attempting social graces that were beyond him, or of behaving like a member of a class other than his own. The Mexicans on the ranch grew vastly respectful.

There was, of course, gossip in the district about Esteban. It was whispered that it was fortunate he so resembled his mother's Iberian forebears. But after the story of Charlie Greer's end became well known, no one spoke ill of the boy in Don Roberto's hearing. The master of Nueva Santanilla was now regarded with something like awe in the county.

Marianna was sprouting into early adolescence. She was slender and quick-moving. She closely resembled her grandmother Adriana except for the great mane of hair that turned, year by year, more coppery, like newly minted pennies in the sun. She attended school in Carmel with the other ranchers' children and read Don Alvaro's books avidly. An open-hearted, generous child, she loved her stepmother deeply. To Marianna, Anita's changed position in the household made no difference whatever. Anita had always been there to love and be

473

loved. That she now lived in Papa's room and was spoken of as Doña gave Marianna only pleasure.

In the late summer of 1891, a clumsily written letter arrived at Nueva Santanilla from Spain. It was from Don Julio. It opened with a rather boastful announcement of the birth of Soledad's fourth child, a third daughter. Since both Julio and Chole were now in their fifties, the child had been christened Milagro—"miracle."

Julio wrote also that he had received a letter, the first in over twenty years, from Alfonso Santana. "Our brother," he wrote Adriana,

> *has, to my deep astonishment, been a success as a soldier. He is a general of a brigade, if you please, and now it appears that his unit of the Legion Extranjera is to be transferred to Cuba. He informs me (in jest, I hope, for your sake) that since he will almost certainly end his military career in the New World, he intends to visit both you and Aaron! You, sister, might tolerate such a visit. I cannot imagine Aaron Marburg doing so. Also, you may remember that Captain Torres of the Guardia who was cashiered for killing Santiago's old mistress? He is with our military brother. As orderly. How that must rankle!*

The remainder of the letter was devoted to a complicated request for money, "because you would not wish me to sell even more of the land of our ancestors, surely?" Without comment, Roberto sent money. Without acknowledgement, it was accepted and spent. Adriana hoped that the children—Paco, Clara, Caridad, and now Milagro—at least shared in the spending.

Consuelo, at the age of three, had her mother's fragile constitution. Twice during her first three years she suffered serious illnesses. She was nursed day and night by Tomasa and Ana-Maria, and gradually grew stronger.

In the spring of 1894, Doña Maria Isabella de Santana y Borjas celebrated her eighty-fourth birthday. There was a great fiesta at Nueva Santanilla, with *piñatas* for the children of the ranchers and a formal *cena de cumpleaños* in the *sala mayor*. When Doña Maria's health was drunk by the fifty dinner guests, she announced that her Spanish chaplain, who had come to Santanilla barefoot and half-starved by the Dominicans who trained him, had reached the age of eighty. Therefore she, a Santana and a Borjas, intended to outdo him. "I often hear him summoning me to Judgment," she said, "But I will obey in my own good time, and not before Don Alvaro calls me."

Roberto arranged for his grandmother, who retired early, to be serenaded by *mariachis* from Monterey and by Don Raoul playing her favorite *coplas* outside her *reja,* so that she might remember how it was when she was a girl and beloved of Don Alvaro.

That very night (as the story was told by those who were guests at her fiesta) Don Alvaro called. Doña Maria was found by the maid Carmela dead in her bed. The former hacendada of Santanilla was buried on the bluff next to Elena Marburg with all the pomp and panoply the local church could muster. In 1895, after long consultation between Roberto and Adriana, Marianna Marburg was dispatched to the convent school of the Sisters of Santa Clara, where young ladies of the Roman Catholic faith were given the education suitable to their station in life.

Marianna loathed convent life, but endured it mainly for the sake of her stepmother Anita, who impressed upon the girl that whatever Don Roberto deemed suitable for a member of the family *was* suitable.

That same year, Ana-Maria Marburg bore a second son, a blond and smiling boy of ten pounds birth weight, who was christened by Father Clarence with the name of Miguel Alvaro Marburg. Esteban, now four years old and known to the Anglo vaqueros on the ranch as Stephen, had become his father's shadow, silently following Roberto everywhere. Adriana was touched by the boy's solemn devotion to Roberto. At times she came near to forgetting the cloud over his parentage. By the time Miguel, known as Michael, learned to walk, the brothers were known as Día y Noche, Day and Night. It was a designation that would stay with them all of their lives.

Consuelo, stronger now, began to attend the ranchers' school in Carmel. At seven she was becoming a beautiful child, frail and dark. Unfortunately, Adriana thought, she seemed to have inherited her mother's intellect as well as her constitution. Her grandmother commenced to make plans for an early marriage.

In the summer of 1897, when Marianna was sixteen, the sons of the local ranchers became aware of her. Home for the summer, she swiftly reverted to her old ways of riding astride and bareback, her hair flying in the wind. Ana-Maria could never discipline the girl, and so the task fell to Adriana. She did it with some reluctance, remembering other times when she herself had ridden the foothills of the Cantabricas in exactly the same way that Marianna now rode the ranges of Nueva Santanilla.

Johnny Colton, the eldest son of neighbor Young Colton (so called to distinguish him from Old Colton, the founder of Santa Marta Ranch) came home from the university in the East. He was twenty and a junior at Rutgers (a name Adriana Marburg found almost unpronounceable). John III was a muscular, handsome boy with far more than the ordinary amount of charm. He had known Marianna only as a gawky child. He discovered her now as a startlingly lovely young woman. He began paying court—not only to Marianna, but to her family. With the instincts of the embryonic womanizer, he knew that the way to Marianna was through her still-handsome grandmother.

Adriana found this amusing. And she was delighted by the skilled manner in which sixteen-year-old Marianna kept the smitten Johnny off balance and enthralled. Marianna, her grandmother decided, was unlikely to develop into a woman easily manipulated by men. Even those she plainly relished.

Nevertheless, Adriana was glad to see the summer come to an end and the handsome Mr. Colton return to the East.

That year Aaron Marburg celebrated his fifty-fourth birthday, Julia her forty-eighth. Their eldest daughter, Marina, was married to Juan Manuel Sebastian de Lorca y Vega, a hacendado of Sonora state who owned twenty thousand acres. Aaron regarded de Lorca as a *criollo* anachronism, but the young man was sincere (if rather dull), had been educated abroad, and appealed to both Doña Julia and Marina. Aaron, with another marriageable daughter in his house, reluctantly gave his consent to the wedding.

The nuptial Mass took place in the national cathedral in Ciudad Mexico, with the president and his lady in attendance. At Aaron's expense, the young couple were dispatched to Buenos Aires on their honeymoon trip. Buenos Aires was chosen because a substantial part of Marina's dowry was to be spent on Argentine bloodstock for La Hacienda de San Jacinto.

The following year Caridad Marburg was married to Diego Perez de Lebron, son of the former *alcalde* of Tihuacan. Diego was a young man with twice the sense and three times the ability of his father, one of the long-time fixtures of Tihuacan's power structure.

Caridad and Diego were wed in slightly less showy surroundings than were Marina and de Lorca. For them the cathedral on the Plaza Constitución served adequately. Only two hundred of Tihuacan's establishment attended, and of these only one hundred were invited to the *fiesta de boda* given at Don Aaron's house on the Olas Altas.

The newlyweds' wedding trip, however, was grander than that of Marina and Sebastian de Lorca. Diego and his bride were dispatched to Europe, specifically to Scotland, to buy new machinery and equipment for the Compañia de Navigación Fénix, specifically three Tyne-built tugs and a dozen cargo-lighters to be used to land heavy cargoes from ships in Tihuacan harbor.

When the young couple returned from their extended stay in the British islands, it was expected (by those who concerned themselves closely with other people's affairs) that they would move into the house on the Olas Altas with Don Aaron and Doña Julia. Since the death of Don Marcello and with Alex away at school in the United States, the Marburgs lived alone in the vast palazzo with a troop of servants under the command of the old *soldadera* Maria Macías. But Aaron presented his daughter and her husband with a new, modern house in Cabo Sur. Don Aaron, the gossips murmured, was getting set in his ways.

On a bright tropical morning in February, 1898, the United States battleship *Maine* exploded at anchor in Havana harbor. The warship, commanded by Captain Charles Sigsbee, had been sent to Cuba in January to protect American life and property threatened by the revolutionary turmoil there. After years of unrest and sporadic fighting between Spanish authorities and Cuban revolutionists, a degree of self-government had been offered the Cubans by the new Liberal Spanish premier, Sagasta. But the Cubans had resolved that nothing less than total independence would do. The result had been the uprisings of late 1897—which in turn had brought the U.S.S. *Maine* to Havana harbor.

The explosion and loss of the warship resulted in the death of two hundred sixty American sailors and marines. The outcry in the United States press was unanimous, inflaming public opinion against the Spaniards in Cuba. A U.S. Naval Board of Inquiry in March reported that the battleship had been sunk by a submarine mine. A Spanish naval court declared that carelessness in the forward magazine had caused the explosion. The American press lashed the public, and the slogan *Remember the Maine!* became part of the American language.

Succumbing to the force of public opinion, President William McKinley sent an ultimatum to the Spanish government demanding independence for Cuba under American protection.

At Nueva Santanilla Adriana Marburg and her son watched developments with misgivings. The new "yellow press," under the leadership of William Randolph Hearst, inflamed the nation to jingoistic fervor. Because of the heavy concentration of Americans of Hispanic origin in Monterey County, few incidents occurred there. But else-where in the country the press fanned an anti-Spanish firestorm.

On April 11, President McKinley bowed again to public pressure. He asked Congress for a resolution authorizing intervention in Cuba. By April 20, the resolution was passed and the United States was at war with Spain.

For nearly two years the romance between John Colton and Marianna had been conducted by mail. In January of 1898, the year young Colton was to have been graduated from Rutgers, some unspecified escapade resulted in his expulsion. The rumors in Monterey were that his mis-conduct involved both liquor and women. Marianna defended him fiercely.

Through the intervention of his father and a number of influential friends, it was arranged that Johnny should complete his final year at the University of Virginia.

But in May of that year Marianna received a letter from Johnny informing her that he had left school to join Colonel Roosevelt's Rough Riders for the war in Cuba.

"I do hope, dear Marianna," he wrote,

> *that you aren't in sympathy with the Spanish in Cuba, for they have been mistreating the natives terribly. And then there is their cowardly attack on the* Maine *which took so many innocent American lives.*
>
> *I am joining Roosevelt's brigade because they are all such splendid fellows. I expect adventure, of course, but it is of more importance than that. I should not like you to think me a frivolous person. I am certain that you would not wish me to remain safe at home while other fellows fight to fulfill our country's Manifest Destiny, which is to rule the Caribbean and the Pacific. We must Remember the Maine!*
>
> *Besides, dear Marianna, there will be so much riding, and the army needs horsemen! Promise me that you will wait for me no matter how long the war lasts.*

Marianna, who had remained so levelheaded through several years of Johnny Colton's courtship, was conquered by his photograph in uniform, with slouch hat and saber. She knew that he was feckless, reckless, and drank too much, but all this made him even more roman-tic. Marianna Marburg, filled with the wisdom of adolescence, was in love.

But John Colton III was not destined to be a hero. Almost immediately upon landing in Cuba he was laid low by bacillary dysentery. Shigella caused more casualties than the Spanish among the soldiers of the Expeditionary Force. Johnny Colton spent four miserable weeks in a field hospital before being shipped back to the United States. He was still under treatment in December, when the peace treaty between the United States and Spain was signed at Paris.

In January John Colton returned to Santa Marta Ranch, romantically gaunt and hollow-eyed. His father, Young Colton, had broached the subject of a marriage between John and Marianna to Roberto Marburg.

There were problems. The Coltons were Protestants. Marianna was, in her father's opinion, far too young for marriage. The notion of a university education for her—which had first shocked and then pleased Roberto—would have to be abandoned. But there were no truly insurmountable difficulties. A dispensation could be obtained. Young Colton, a secular man but nominally a High Episcopalian, had no objection to his grandchildren being raised Roman Catholics. And Roberto Marburg could deny Marianna nothing—least of all could he deny her heart's desire.

If Ana-Maria had an opinion, she did not voice it. Now plump and placid, the storms forgotten (or at least hidden away within), she lived only to support Roberto in all that he thought and did.

It was Adriana who viewed a marriage between Johnny Colton and Marianna with misgivings. Adriana had, in the beginning, been amused by her granddaughter's first romantic fancy. But now the imminent prospect of a marriage put a different complexion on matters. Johnny Colton had come home embittered and disappointed at his failure to become a war hero. His unhappiness took the form of drinking and sleeping with the low women of Monterey—and some were very low indeed.

Marianna, of course, refused to believe it. There were explosive engagements between granddaughter and grandmother.

As Adriana Marburg approached her sixtieth year, she found it bitterly ironic that she should discover herself skirmishing with a mirror image of herself as a young girl.

In the end, all that she could accomplish was delay. Roberto Marburg and Young Colton agreed that the wedding would take place in midsummer of 1900, when Marianna would be nineteen.

Marianna, condemned (as she saw it) to an eighteen-month engagement by her grandmother's interference, grew angry, headstrong, and insolent.

Adriana bore it, outwardly austere and patrician, inwardly melancholy and filled with apprehension. She was a Santana, and the Santanas endured.

THREE

1900

Roberto Marburg looked up from his work as the *mozo de quadra* rapped on the heavy oak door to the ranch office. He took the gold watch from his waistcoat pocket: exactly ten. When his mother was at Nueva Santanilla and not at the townhouse in San Francisco, this pattern never varied. At ten each Tuesday and Thursday, they rode together until noon. Long ago it had been Doña Adriana who had to be summoned from the ranch office, but now it was himself. He heard the sound of his mother's boots on the gallery tiles and stood up. He was, as always on Tuesdays and Thursdays, dressed for riding. Ana-Maria had ordered a Mexican vaquero's outfit for him, a *traje de charro* of tan suede trimmed with silver. He thought it showy, but Anita said proudly that it showed how well he had kept his figure. Should that be something to be proud of, he wondered? In less than a year he would be forty—not old, certainly, but far from young.

Since the business of Marianna's engagement to the Colton boy had come to occupy his thoughts so often, Roberto found himself remembering Maria-Elena.

Each Sunday, whether or not he attended Mass, he made it a practice to climb to the bluff and stand by the stone that covered her. Often Anita would come with him, bringing flowers. They would stand there in silence, captives of memory.

We were children together, we three, he would think. Who could have guessed that *Las Parcas*—those fates whom his grandfather had been so fond of invoking—would bring them here? Life had so many strange twists and turnings. Beside Elena lay the tiny, steely *abuela,* a woman who in her old age had survived being torn from her native soil and brought halfway across the world, to lie here overlooking an alien sea. But she had learned to love Nueva Santanilla, of that Roberto was certain. He hoped with all his being that Elena was as much at peace as the *abuela.* He prayed to God that she did not roam some gray purgatory plagued by the jealousy of Anita she had felt when they were children. I beg for forgiveness, Elena, he would think, but perhaps the Fates do command us, as Don Alvaro said. You are here, and Anita is in my bed. We shall know if what I did was right when we are all reunited—all of us who were children together at the old Santanilla: Roberto, Ana-Maria, you, Elena, and your brothers (what has become of them?), and Cecilia (who is Sister Mary Magdalen and all but gone from the world). We will speak of it then. Until that time, lie peacefully.

"Patron," the *mozo de quadra* said through the door. "Doña Adriana is waiting."

Roberto smiled in silent amusement as he opened the door and spoke to the concerned vaquero. The effect his mother still had on the hands was astonishing. When she was in residence at Nueva Santanilla it was as though royalty were present. One did not keep Doña Adriana waiting.

Adriana was already mounted on her young thoroughbred mare, Infanta, a daughter of Conquistador and one of the mares bought from Senator Stanford before he turned his farm into a college. The *mozo de quadra* had saddled Blanco for Don Roberto. Blanco was a gray half-blood Roberto rode when working the stock. Anita had named him for the pony Roberto had once owned.

"*Buenos dias,* Mama," he said.

It always astonished him to see her, nearly sixty, still slender, erect, her hair graying but streaked with gold and her skin, meshed now with fine wrinkles but firm and stretched over the fine bones of her face, so that at a distance one might take her for a woman thirty years younger.

485

She had given up riding astride two years ago, reverting to the sidesaddle as more suitable to, as she put it, "a woman of a certain age."

Her dressmaker had fitted the black riding habit perfectly. Above the waist she displayed the figure of a girl. Below, the skirt was impeccably draped. Her boots and the crop looped over her wrist showed twenty years of meticulous care, the leather worked to a softly glowing sheen. Beneath the brim of her flat, broad-brimmed Spanish hat her eyes were as clear and blue as they had been on the day they left old Santanilla.

"Good morning, Roberto," she said. "Where shall we ride today?"

Roberto could not repress a smile. For as long as he could remember his mother had approached a morning gallop with the open pleasure of a child released from confinement.

"The north range, I think, Mama," he said in English. He swung himself into the saddle and dismissed the groom. "Raoul tells me the road is in bad condition from last month's rains. I'd better have a look."

The mare went into a sidestepping dance and Adriana quieted her with a gentle touch of the curb rein. *"Ya basta, Infanta."*

It had been Consuelo, while reading to Día y Noche, the two boys, from Don Alvaro's old books, who had discovered that Infanta was the title given to Spanish princesses and therefore a perfect name for the Patrona's mare.

Side by side, mother and son rode out of the walled compound around the house. The rains had cleared the air and the sky was a pale blue filled with tumbled, towering cumulus clouds. They were driven by the onshore wind across the face of the sun so that their shadows seemed to fly silently across the land that was swiftly greening as spring deepened. Here and there were bright spots of color in the pastures as patches of purple lupin and California poppy blossomed.

The home pastures were empty now. The cattle and sheep had already been moved into the higher ranges of the northern Santa Lucias. As Roberto and Adriana walked their horses across the new grass, one of the stable cats who had been stalking a burrowing animal raised his head to regard the horses and riders reproachfully for having spoiled his hunt.

Adriana was reminded of El Cid, who had been a mighty slayer of mice at old Santanilla. Strangely, the memory brought with it a sadness to which she had not been subject for many years. Since receiving that single letter from Julio, thoughts of Spain had often come unbidden. What was Santanilla now, she wondered. A gypsy camp entirely? And yet the Segre woman had, in her peculiar way, been good for Julio. Certainly no other woman would have put up with him. Adriana sighed as she rode. Perhaps descendants of El Cid still slept on the roof tiles in the sun at old Santanilla. Gypsy women were said to be fond of cats. She hoped so.

"I spoke to Young Colton again yesterday, Mama," Roberto said.

"What an absurd name for a grown man," Adriana said.

"A little tolerance, Doña Adriana," Roberto said. "We are going to be relations."

"Much against my better judgment," Adriana said.

"*Justicia,* Mama," Roberto said.

Blanco farted noisily.

"The horse knows," Adriana said.

"Don't be vulgar, Mama. Johnny is what Marianna wants."

"*Ay,* Roberto. Don't tell me what young girls want. I remember only too well."

Roberto rode in silence. His mother regarded him with a slightly raised eyebrow. "Thank you for that, Roberto."

"For what, Mama?"

"For making no comment. You have become very tolerant. I suppose I must believe that is good. But I would almost rather you say to me what is in your mind, if it meant you would deal with Marianna more firmly."

"It pains me to see you so at odds with the girl, Mama," Roberto said.

"It will pass, Roberto," Adriana said. "When I see that I have been mistaken about John Colton, I will say so. To you *and* to her."

"I must be satisfied with that, I suppose," Roberto said.

"Yes, *hijo.* So you must." She tapped Infanta with her crop and cantered on ahead. Roberto followed with a wry smile. It was uncanny how similar were the responses of his mother and daughter when they were balked or criticized in any way. The chin rose, the eyes narrowed, the lips set, and ahorse or afoot, they cantered away.

He flicked Blanco with the rein ends and uttered a yipping vaquero's cry. At a dead gallop he overtook his mother and passed her. Why was it, he wondered, that we are never so close as when we are behaving like children? He put Blanco at the low log fence separating the pasture from the open range and cleared it easily. He turned to see his mother's mare take the same obstacle as though she were winged.

He reined in and waited while the Patrona cantered up and circled him, her cheeks flushed with pleasure. "You always know how to distract me," she said. *"Sin verguenzo . . .* you are shameless."

"I plead guilty," Roberto said, smiling.

She placed her mount beside his and they moved on, down the slope toward the road from the gate. "I don't wish to be difficult, Roberto. It is that I am worried about this marriage. Johnny is not a man. He is a boy—a spoiled one. And there are other things."

"I have heard the stories, Mama."

"Do you believe them?"

"I don't know," Roberto said. "They may be true."

"Then?"

"She is in love, Patrona," Roberto said, looking at his mother steadily. "Have *you* never been in love?"

Adriana reined in and stopped. She returned her son's gaze unflinchingly. "You know that I have, Roberto. Do you want me to tell you how often, when, and with whom? I am old enough to do that, you know, if you wish it."

Ah, thought Roberto bleakly, there's the Santana in her. The old memories rose in his mind like a tide that could engulf a man's hard-won peace of mind. No, dear God, the last thing he wanted was to dredge up the past. "I do not wish it, Patrona," he said distinctly. "I only want your blessing for Marianna, who loves you very much."

"My love has always been hers, and always will be," Adriana said. Her face was somber. Then it lighted with a smile and she lifted her slender shoulders in a very Hispanic shrug. "She is my younger self, Roberto. Do you imagine I do not know that she will have what she will have? With or without my blessing, your blessing, or God's?"

She set Infanta in motion again, this time at a walk. Over her shoulder she said, "Oh, come along, Roberto. It is too fine a day to quarrel. And summer is still far, far away."

The sound was like that made by firecrackers when the railroad coolies celebrated their lunar new year, a rolling, popping racket that echoed across the sparsely timbered grassland near the adobe gate.

Adriana reined to a stop. *"Por Dios,* what is that?"

Roberto halted Blanco, who snorted nervously and twitched his ears at the sound. The noise continued. It seemed to originate somewhere on the county road to the north.

"It sounds like a motorcar," Roberto said. "But it couldn't be. Not out here."

"An *automobile?"* Adriana's voice betrayed her disdain. There were no more than three automobiles in all of Monterey County, and they *never* strayed far from the grimy, oily mechanics' shops where they could be repaired.

But through the stand of pines down near the county road there was movement: a machine that appeared to be a horseless buggy, followed by a cloud of blue smoke, rolled noisily up the track, approaching the adobe arch from which depended the S / M iron symbol.

Infanta rolled her eyes and cantered in place. Blanco flattened his ears and snorted at the popping invader.

The automobile consisted of a flat platform with what looked like an oversized bicycle wheel at each corner. A metal box without sides contained the engine and a maze of polished brass and copper piping. At the rear, three spare wheels were stacked and strapped to a rack. Between wheels and the motorcar's pilot were stowed a heavy canvas sack, an axe, a shovel, a neat coil of heavy rope, and a mud-spattered leather suitcase.

At the helm sat a figure in a once-white long duster, sporting cap turned front to back, and goggles. On the running board visible to the Marburgs was fixed a steel bracket containing three metal cans, one red, one white, one blue. On the curve of the cowling that provided the only protection for the driver was fixed a nickel-plated strip announcing in bold cursives that this was a Locomobile. The information was repeated in painted letters across the copper radiator between the two large brass acetylene headlamps.

Blanco backed away from the machine suspiciously. Infanta whickered and had to be calmed.

The motorcar rolled to a stop under the adobe arch. The cloud of exhaust smoke overtook it and then dissipated in the damp spring air. The clattering engine fell silent and the driver dismounted, tall and leggy, and looked up at the wrought-iron device hanging in the arch. Then he began to march purposefully across the field toward Adriana and Roberto.

Under the open, flapping duster he wore boots, whipcord trousers, a Norfolk jacket, and a heavy roll-neck sweater. As he approached he removed elbow-length gauntlets and his back-to-front tweed cap. For all the world, Adriana thought, like a knight removing his armor after an engagement. Dark, curly hair had been plastered down by the cap, and the young man ran his fingers through it. He pulled the goggles down so that they hung at his throat. A cloud shadow passed and a beam of bright sunlight illuminated the youthful face.

Adriana gasped. There, striding across the muddy field toward her, was Aaron Marburg. No, of course that could not be, and the young man's coloring was not the same. But the features—the high broad forehead, the slightly aquiline nose, the generous mouth, and the brilliant blue eyes were Aaron's. The resemblance was unmistakable. Adriana wondered if Roberto could see it as clearly as she.

The young man stopped a dozen yards away and displayed a flashing white smile. In English he asked, "Is this the Marburg ranch Nueva Santanilla?"

"It is," Roberto said neutrally.

The visitor examined Adriana with frank and open admiration. He changed from unaccented English to fluent Mexican Spanish. "Then you, Patrona, must be Señora Adriana Marburg. I am your grandson Alex."

54

There was a fire burning in the great heart of the *sala mayor.* It took some of the chill from the air of the damp spring morning. Alex Marburg, a tiny cup of bitter Moorish coffee in his hand, paced the large room energetically, examining the dark Santana portraits on the walls.

"This is really marvelous, *abuela,*" he said to Adriana, who watched him bemused. "It is like discovering a whole new family." He gave her an open smile. "Of course, I am not a Santana, but we are all related one way or another, aren't we?"

"One way or another," Adriana agreed. It touched her heart to see the boy's enthusiasm. Aaron might have been like this, she thought, if life had dealt with him differently.

Alex looked at Roberto, who stood, still in riding kit, spraddle-legged before the fire. "You have no portrait of grandfather Michael? Of Don Miguel?"

"None was ever painted," Roberto said.

"Well, I guess that sort of thing isn't done much anymore, is it, Uncle Roberto? But it's rather a shame, I think. A family is such a wonderful thing to have. Sisters and brothers, cousins, aunts and uncles. I have sisters, but you are my only uncle. My mother was an only child. That's rare in Mexico. But you know all about that. I shouldn't be running on so, but this is an occasion for me."

"And for us," Roberto said wryly. Adriana gave him a chiding look.

Outside, beyond the arched gallery in the courtyard, Día y Noche were climbing all over Alex's motorcar. Esteban sat at the controls wearing Alex's cap and goggles while Miguel made motor noises.

Ana-Maria, peering through the window, said, "Can they damage anything, Alejandro?"

"Oh, no, Tía Ana-Maria. Not after what El Loco has been through. Let them play with him." Alex had been warmed immediately by the welcome he had received from Doña Anita.

"Tell us of your journey," Roberto said. "From Oakland, you said?"

"Yes, uncle. I'm in my last year at St. Mary's College. The school of banking." He made a slight face and a shrug. "I don't know if you know where that is. It is on Broadway, just on the outskirts of the town. A Jesuit school, of course. Well, since it is my last year and I shall be going home in June, I decided to stay north over the Easter holiday." He grinned sheepishly. "I have been planning this trip all year, actually. Ever since I met Assemblyman Dundalk." Alex glanced at Adriana with that same flashing smile. "He is a great admirer of yours, Doña Ana. I must say I can see why."

Felicia came into the room and said, "Patrona, Don Alejandro's things have been taken to the guest wing. What hour shall you want *almuerzo?*"

"Are you hungry, Alex?" Adriana asked.

"Starved, Patrona. I left Salinas at five this morning."

"At noon, Feli," Adriana said to the now-portly Felicia. "And send someone to Santa Marta to collect Consuelo and Marianna. Tell them a cousin has come to call." The girls had ridden off to the Colton ranch early in the day to visit the still convalescing Johnny.

"You were in Salinas at five?" Roberto asked. "How fast does that infernal machine travel?"

"Oh, it can make fifty miles an hour on a good road, Uncle Roberto. Last year a Panhard won a race in France averaging sixty-eight

492

miles an hour. I think a Locomobile could do better if it were specially prepared," Alex said proudly.

"That is more than a mile a minute, *Dios mio,*" Ana-Maria said, aghast. "How can one breathe at such velocity?"

"Forgive me, Tía Anita," Alex said, "but that sort of worry is quite without foundation. The English proved it long ago when they built their very first railroad."

"Still," Roberto said, "from Salinas here in a morning."

"I did rather make good time," Alex admitted proudly. "Of course, I was lucky. They have just put new gravel on the corduroy sections of road. You know, between the logs. And I didn't have a flat. It was different between Oakland and Salinas. That took me two full days. And two punctures. Repairing inner tubes is very time-consuming. Still, two and a half days all told isn't bad at all."

"By train you can go to San Francisco in a day," Adriana said.

"Yes, of course. But it isn't the same, is it. I mean, by automobile one does it oneself."

"That sounds like Aaron," Adriana said softly. Roberto gave her a quick glance.

"Papa doesn't know yet about El Loco," Alex said sheepishly. "I spent nearly my whole year's allowance on him. But it will be all right when he sees him. I'm taking him back to Tihuacan with me, of course."

"Him?"

"Silly, isn't it? I suppose one shouldn't personalize machines that way," Alex said.

"He is a horse—of sorts," Adriana said. "Could you teach an old woman to drive him, Alex?"

Ana-Maria threw her hands up. *"Ay, Doña Ana, por Dios, no."*

"Mama," Roberto said. "You hate motorcars."

"Only when they frighten the horses," Adriana said. "Well, Alejandro?"

Alex regarded her with shining devotion. "I couldn't teach an old woman, *abuela.* But I can teach you."

Roberto slapped his leg with his riding crop and said, "I have things to attend to before lunch. I had better get about them."

Ana-Maria watched him leave the room. Surely, she thought, he does not hold the sins of the father against this handsome boy? Her Roberto could not be so cruel.

Alex stood now before another of the portraits. "This is your grandfather, *abuela?"*

Adriana joined him before the painting. "Yes," she said. "Can you make this out?" In the lower right-hand corner, a replica of the Santana arms had been painted in miniature, together with the name of the subject.

"This is Don Alejandro, then," Alex said delightedly. "I was named for him, *abuela.* My mother chose the name because it belonged to the father of your father, Don Alvaro, whom my father loved very much. He still speaks of him."

Adriana felt a warm dampness in her eyes. Old people, she thought, cry so easily. "Yes, I thought as much when we received the announcement of your birth, Alex. Don Alvaro was more father to Aaron than Miguel ever was."

The boy turned and looked down into her face and she had the wrenching feeling that Aaron stood beside her, regarding her with love.

She turned swiftly away and refilled the tiny porcelain cups with coffee from the brass urn on the spirit lamp. Alex took his and said, "I am so glad I've come, *abuela.*"

Ana-Maria watched with sad, dark eyes, remembering. I was only a child, she thought, but I can still recall how she grieved after Aaron rode away so long ago. She never said a word, but I sensed how deep was her pain—and perhaps her guilt, for having loved the father, and then the son. And now here was Alex come to torment her in her old age.

"Anita," Doña Adriana said sharply. "Why did you let Marianna run off to Santa Marta today? It is not fitting that she should spend so much time with Johnny."

Ana-Maria, taken aback, protested, "They are engaged, Patrona."

Alex looked from one woman to the other in perplexity.

Adriana said, "Anita will show you your room, Alex," and left the *sala,* her boot heels rapping sharply on the tiles.

"Is something wrong, *tía?*" Alex asked. "Did I say something to make the *abuela* angry?"

Anita gave him a quick *abrazo.* "No, of course not, Alejandro. It is that you remind her so of—of someone else."

"Do I look like my grandfather?"

"Yes," Anita said. But far more like your father, she thought.

"I'd hate to think I did wrong by coming here without so much as a note by way of warning," Alex confided. "My father says I am impulsive."

"And what young *macho* is not?" Anita asked soothingly. "No,

Alejandro. You are certainly welcome here." Let the past stay buried, she thought. There is pain enough in the world day by day. "Now come along with me and I will show you to your room. Don Roberto will want to show you Nueva Santanilla after lunch. Have you riding clothes?"

"What I have on, *tía,*" Alex said.

"Then I will bring you something of Roberto's. Come."

The noon meal was laid on the long oak table in the *comedor.* To Alex, accustomed to the hurly-burly of a college refectory, it seemed remarkably formal for an everyday *almuerzo.*

His uncle Roberto sat at the head of the table, flanked by Aunt Anita on one side and Doña Tomasa on the other. Doña Adriana sat at the foot of the table with the two boys, Esteban and Miguel, on either side of her. Alex was impressed with their decorum. Mexican children would have been fed away from the adults, where their lack of meal-time discipline would disturb no one but their long-suffering *nanas.*

Across from Tía Anita sat Don Raoul, a thick-set man with the blunt hands of a laborer and dark eyes under a thatch of white hair. Next to him sat Cousin Consuelo, an adolescent girl of twelve who showed signs of becoming a beauty. Her wide eyes had become fixed on Alex. She was fascinated by her Mexican cousin.

Across the table from Consuelo and next to Alex was an empty place. Cousin Marianna had sent word by her sister that she would be along from Santa Marta Ranch later in the afternoon. Alex had not missed the displeasure in his *abuela* 's manner when Consuelo delivered that message.

"Tell us all about Don Aaron," Tomasa Gomez said warmly. "Is he doing well, Alejandro?"

"Quite well, Doña Tomasa," Alex said. "The Sociedad Fénix seems to keep growing. Papa is a formidable businessman."

"And you, Alex?" Don Roberto asked.

Alex shrugged expressively. "I don't know, *tío.* Not yet. All I know is what can be taught from books."

Don Raoul, with the heavy concentration of a man searching for words, asked, "Have you land in Tihuacan?"

"Property, Don Raoul," Alex said. "But not land. Not like this." He indicated their surroundings.

"No cattle, no horses?"

"No, Don Raoul. We are merchants, mostly. We make and sell. Coconut oil, soap, ice, things of that sort. My grandfather, Don Marcello Marini, founded a store in Tihuacan, and that has been enlarged as part of the Fénix enterprises. And there are the tugboats and cargo-lighters. Papa and some friends have started a bank, the Banco Comercial. I suppose that is where I shall end up. But no cattle, no sheep." He smiled deprecatingly. "Of course my sister Marina is married to a hacendado in Sonora state. Plenty of livestock there." He was tempted to add that the hacendados of Mexico with whom he was acquainted all tended to treat their people less well than their cattle, and that his brother-in-law Sebastian de Lorca was no exception. But that would been disloyal.

"There have been uprisings in Sonora, I understand," Roberto said.

"Yes, *tío.* So there have been." He did not add that one of them had taken place on the Hacienda de San Jacinto and had been put down by the Rurales with great ferocity. It troubled Alex that his family was so closely tied to the government of Porfirio Díaz, who had ruled Mexico with an iron hand for twenty years. The Jesuits at Saint Mary's College were divided in their opinions of the Porfiriato. Those of Hispanic or Latin descent seemed to approve, while the Anglos spoke of the Mexican president as a tyrant who would one day be overthrown. It all seemed very far away when one lived in the United States. It never failed to astonish Alex that Americans knew so little about their near neighbor to the south.

Consuelo, who had been fiddling with her food and not eating it, cast her great dark eyes on her cousin and asked, "How long can you stay with us, Cousin Alex?"

"Only a day or two, I'm afraid."

"You will stay until Easter," Adriana said.

"I should like to, *abuela.* But it will take me two days to get El Loco back to Oakland," Alex said.

"Then until Good Friday."

"*A sus ordenes, Doña Adriana.*" Alex could not imagine contradicting the queenly patrician enthroned at the foot of the great table.

Consuelo smiled her pleasure. "Have you horses at home, *primo hermano?* She used the form of the Spanish phrase for cousin, one limited to *first* cousins. She seemed to be establishing a personal claim, and Alex was amused by it.

"In Tihuacan we keep carriage horses, *prima.* In Tacubaya I have a very elderly pony who is now retired from service."

Doña Tomasa asked, "Tacubaya? Where is that, Alejandro?"

"It is a district of Cuidad Mexico, *tía,*" Alex said. "We spent the *tiempo de calor* there. Tihuacan can be very hot in midsummer."

496

"Oh, I should like to see Mexico City," Consuelo said excitedly.

"Then visit us, cousin," Alex said. "My mother would be pleased if you would." He looked around the table and added, "All of you, at any time. There is plenty of room, and I think you would like Mexico City. Tihuacan can be pleasant in season, too."

Consuelo said, "Oh, Papa, could we do that?"

"Not all at once," Don Roberto said dryly. "Alejandro is being polite, *hija,* not invoking an invasion."

"I am quite serious, Tío Roberto. Doña Julia would love to know the American branch of the family."

Roberto looked down the length of the table at his mother. Alex sensed the flash of tension between them.

Doña Adriana said, "One day, perhaps, Alex."

"I am badly out of practice, uncle," Alex said. "I haven't ridden for three years and Don Porfirio used to say I'd never make a cavalryman."

"Relámpago is tolerant," Roberto replied. Raoul had mounted the boy on the oldest and most docile gelding on the ranch, a thoughtful beast with the glaringly inappropriate name of Lightning Flash.

With Consuelo mounted on her small bay Arab mare, Roberto had given Alex an hour's tour of the land immediately surrounding the home pastures of Nueva Santanilla.

The day had remained chilly, but bright with spring sun. The sky was cloudless in the vernal light. The conifers were dark green, the grasses a lighter green dotted with wildflowers. From the ridge the house and barns were starkly white, with the deep red of the roof tiles glowing with a light of their own in the high sun. To the west could be seen the ocean, patterned with wind and current. Far from the shore a lumber schooner ran south on a broad reach, surrounded by questing flights of gulls.

"Nueva Santanilla is beautiful, Tío Roberto," Alex said. "Was the old Hacienda Santanilla anything like this?"

"Different," Roberto said, remembering. "But beautiful, too, in its way."

"I want to see Spain before I settle down to work," Alex said. "I want to see France and Germany, too. And Italy, where the Marinis came from."

"All that may take some time," Roberto said. "I should imagine that since you have been away from home for three years, Aaron is anxious to have you back."

Alex sighed. "Well, yes. I suppose so. But there is so much to see, uncle, to *know—*"

"So there is a streak of the adventurer in you," Roberto said, letting Blanco lower his head to graze on the still-fresh grass.

"My father says all Marburgs have it," Alex said.

"I think it is marvelous to want to see the world," Consuelo said.

Roberto sat Blanco quietly, looking out at the sea. Presently he said, "You probably know I have not seen my half-brother for a very long time."

"I think that is a great pity, *tío*," Alex said.

"Yes. Well, we do not always control the events in our lives, young Alex. I was still a child when your father left Santanilla to come to America."

"Uncle Aaron was a hero of the Civil War, wasn't he, Alex?" Consuelo said breathlessly.

"Well, he was in it," Alex said. "And he was wounded. Actually, he seldom speaks of it. I think the wound was quite serious. He came here after the war for a short time. Did you know that, *tío?*"

"Yes," Roberto said shortly. "He saw this land before we did."

"I didn't realize that, *tío*," Alex said. "He has never mentioned it to me."

"Well, that was all a very long time ago. Years before we emigrated."

Alex looked about him and said, "I don't know how he could have left, once having seen Nueva Santanilla."

Roberto made no reply. He said abruptly, "It is time to go back now."

"Oh, Papa," Consuelo protested. "Not yet. Alex wants to see more. Don't you, Alex?"

"Then show him," Roberto said. "But don't stay out too late." He clucked to Blanco and set off down the hill at a canter.

"Papa is very annoyed with my sister Marianna. I told her he would be, but no one can really tell *her* anything," Consuelo said.

Alex could think of no appropriate reply.

Consuelo said, "Come on, I'll show you where the *bisabuela* and my mother are buried." She turned her slim mare and galloped off. Alex followed at a slower pace on the reluctant Relámpago.

On a high bluff overlooking the land that fell away to the sea, Consuelo stopped and dismounted before two granite stones lying flat in the earth. Alex joined her.

"That is great-grandmother, Doña Maria Santana," she said.

"*Que tristeza*," Alex said. "My father told me of her. She was a formidable person."

"Yes. I was only four years old when she died," Consuelo said, "But I remember her very well. And there is my mother, Doña Elena. I don't remember her at all. She died when I was born. It was Anita who raised Marianna and me, actually. *She* was my father's *ahijada,* but she married him when Doña Elena died. It is all very complicated, isn't it?"

Before Alex could reply, he heard a galloping horse approaching. He turned to see a girl riding up the hill at a breakneck pace. It was as though something had struck him a thudding blow on the heart.

He had an impression of a mane of red-brown hair flying in the wind, a flashing smile, a beautiful face, and eyes as bright as sapphires in the sun.

Consuelo said sulkily, "Oh, here *she* comes. Just because she is nineteen and engaged, she thinks she can do as she pleases."

The girl halted her horse and dropped lightly to the ground. Alex Marburg was certain he had never before seen a girl so striking.

"This," Consuelo said reluctantly, "is our cousin, Alejandro." To Alex she said, "This wild person is my sister Marianna."

Roberto Marburg stood in the archway of the gallery, his attention fixed on the distant figures of his daughters and their unexpected cousin Alex. He could see them clearly on the bluff, manikins made tiny by distance.

For the first time since Alex's sudden arrival at Nueva Santanilla he now took time to examine his own feelings, and he was distressed by the dark anger he discovered in himself. It was an emotion that defied all reason, but it was there—he could not deny it.

Why, he wondered, after all these years was he suddenly to be plagued by Aaron's son, by Aaron's proxy? The boy was likable, certainly. Well-mannered and intelligent, all that one could desire in a young man. But he was Aaron's child. He brought, all unwitting, memories Roberto had spent a lifetime seeking to suppress. By his mere presence Alex damaged connections between Roberto and his mother that had been years in the rebuilding.

"Roberto."

He turned to see Ana-Maria standing behind him, a troubled expression on her broad face. She knew. She could feel it. Anita had always been able to read his mind. My other self, he thought.

This was the first opportunity he had had to be alone with Anita since Alex's arrival. It did not surprise him that she should seek him out. Anita, of all the people in the world, had to know what the appearance of Aaron's son at Nueva Santanilla meant to him.

499

"Can we speak, Roberto?" she asked.

"I was not prepared for this," Roberto said bitterly. "I should have been, God knows. But I was not."

She slipped an arm around his waist and rested her dark head against his shoulder. "He is only a boy, Roberto. The past has nothing to do with him or he with the past."

In all the years since he had stood in the Spanish dawn with Anita outside his mother's room at old Santanilla, they had never spoken of what they saw. He could not speak of it now. All that he could say was, "The past is all that we are, Anita. We bury it, but it is always there. And here," he struck himself on the chest with a fist, an angry gesture. "If I am to forget all that has gone before, then why am I here? Why did she make me into the man I am now?"

"Doña Ana is a great lady, Roberto," Anita said. "But she is not perfection. No one is. Only God."

"I wish God had seen fit to keep Aaron away from here," Roberto said heavily.

"That is *Alejandro*, Robert. It is *not* Aaron Marburg." She gripped his arm for emphasis.

"I see Aaron each time he moves. I hear Aaron each time he speaks. And so does *she*. Can't you see how she looks at him?"

Anita said softly, "We were children, Roberto. What did we know? How could we understand?"

Roberto shook his head. "I want him gone, Anita. Gone from here, gone from our lives."

"I have never said this to you, Roberto," Ana-Maria said, "And it is something that perhaps I should have said long ago. Who are we to judge Doña Ana?"

"Don't talk like a *peon*," Robert said harshly.

Ana-Maria regarded him calmly. Her manner was composed. "I am a *peon*, Don Roberto. How else am I to speak?"

"Forgive me, Anita," he said, contrite. "I spoke in anger."

"There is nothing to forgive," Ana-Maria said. "I know why you married me, Roberto. I know that you did it out of love. That is why I say that we have no right to judge Doña Ana—*or* Don Aaron. If they loved one another, let God be their judge. Surely they have paid for their sin, if it was a sin? I know I would die if I were separated from you. Think of how long the years have been for them."

"You shame me, Anita," Roberto said. "Because my heart is not so generous as yours." He kissed her on the crown of the head. "I apologize for speaking to you as I did. It was not right."

Ana-Maria Marburg regarded her husband soberly. How very strict were his notions of right and wrong. She pitied him. Of what use would it be to this thirteenth-century man to tell him that tolerance was a part of love? He would not hear it. He was, after all, a Santana. But he had always lacked the Santana willfulness that broke for others the ancient patterns. He had been reared mostly by Doña Maria, fenced round with medieval concepts of duty and honor. Who knew it better than Ana-Maria de Marburg y Gomez? Had he not killed a man to satisfy the code of blood and family?

It grieved her that Alejandro's appearance had awakened the old memories. But given the man Roberto was, how could it be otherwise? In his deepest heart Roberto would always believe that the family was diminished by the taint Aaron and Adriana had laid upon it. And even though her own standards were less severe, she must stand with him, his partisan in all things. That, after all, had been her life. To Ana-Maria, Roberto would always be *el caballero dorado*—the golden horseman whom she had loved since childhood.

"The boy will soon be gone," she said.

"*Dios perdóneme,*" Roberto said. "It cannot be soon enough for me."

55

For Alex Marburg, his few days at Nueva Santanilla were a mingled joy and sorrow. The appearance of his cousin Marianna had been like a flash of heat lightning in a summer sky.

He had never thought of himself as a romantic person. He was to be a banker, and bankers were quite the reverse: practical, competent, pragmatic. He had never allowed himself to be unsettled by flights of fancy.

Yet the first sight of his cousin had left him shaken. She was beautiful, but Alex had met pretty girls before. He had not spent a full day in her company before he began to think of her as the most engaging, exasperating, and outrageously provocative girl he had ever known. She made the eligible girls of Tihuacan seem vapid with their preoccupation with gossip, religion, and self-adornment. Marianna needed no adornment. Dressed in denim trousers, boots, and a man's shirt (as she often was, to Doña Tomasa's evident distress), she was, quite simply, spectacular. Her red-brown hair held glints of sunlight. She had the body of a young goddess, Alex thought appreciatively, an Artemis. Her eyes were blue as the deep sea—as blue, in fact, as Alex's own. Her smile was quick and generous, bright as a ray of sun on white clouds.

The sorrow was that she was engaged, promised to another, whom Uncle Roberto, Alex suspected, liked better than he liked his unexpected nephew.

Marianna, who had seldom been curbed, could bestow praise and punishment with equal candor. Alex, accustomed to the giggling girls of Tihuacan and Ciudad Mexico, found this fascinating.

Within an hour of their meeting on the bluff, she told him frankly that he sat a horse like a sack of potatoes, that she found his combination of dark hair and blue eyes very agreeable, and that she was willingly giving up a promised university education in order to marry a hero of the Spanish-American War. From that moment Alex decided retroactively that he loathed the currently popular song *When Johnny Comes Marching Home Again.*

"I want you to know my Johnny Colton, cousin," she said. "The *abuela* does not like him, but he is a wonderful man. If you are going to be my friend, you must like him, too."

Alex silently aligned himself with Doña Adriana and said that he would be delighted to meet a bona-fide hero of the war in Cuba. "At home people tend to take a different view of the American adventure," he said in a noncommittal voice.

Marianna shrugged as though the opinions of people in far-off Mexico were unimportant. Plainly, whatever the rest of the Marburgs felt, Marianna was totally an American.

She arranged a typical Monterey County entertainment for her exotic new cousin—an abalone hunt on the beach below Nueva Santanilla.

John Colton arrived mounted on a beautiful horse that seemed to have been molded of pure gold, a palomino. Quite gratuitously (Alex thought) he put the spirited animal through a number of parade gaits, caracoles, and rearings to display the beast's qualities to Marianna and the family. The vaqueros, recognizing young Colton's obvious skill, gave him grudging applause. Alex watched the performance grimly.

John Colton III was twenty-three, not quite so tall as Alex, but muscular and given to swaggering. There were shadows under his brown eyes that Alex recognized instantly as the marks of considerable dissipation. Marianna seemed to find them romantic.

When Alex complimented Colton on the beauty of his horse, Johnny airily mentioned that he had another, a young mare, that he was schooling as a wedding gift for his Marburg bride come summer.

The day was spent on the beach in company with all the Marburg children, including the boys Día y Noche and Consuelo. A kitchen *criada* was sent along, together with a vaquero to care for the horses and gather driftwood for the fire.

Alex, descending the steep trail on Relámpago, was aware that he was cutting a somewhat less than heroic figure on the ancient gelding.

The change to swimming apparel was accomplished in a deep cave in the cliffs. First Marianna and Consuelo, and then Alex and Colton. Esteban and Miguel changed unself-consciously on the beach.

It seemed to Alex that young Colton made an unnecessary display of his muscles as he clambered into the knee-and-elbow-length bathing suit, but by now Alex understood that nothing Colton could do would be pleasing to a rival. Alex thought of himself that way, and it was obvious that Johnny Colton did also.

The day was not an unqualified success for Alex. The girls, hampered by their layered swimming dresses, could not actually seek the abalone, which affixed themselves to the rocks at depths of from five to thirty feet. But Alex was armed with a knife and given intense instructions by Consuelo on the art of prying the tasty mollusks from the rocks. John Colton plunged into the cold Pacific water without a backward glance.

Having been raised in a seaport with some of the best beaches in the western hemisphere, Alex was an accomplished swimmer. But the knack of diving down to pull abalone from the rocks was not to be acquired in a day. While Alex struggled to capture one abalone, Johnny Colton collected a dozen—enough to feed everyone on the beach. The *criada* and vaquero had taken the meat from the shells and were busily pounding it to tenderness by the time Alex, scraped and breathless, waded from the sea.

Warming themselves by the roaring driftwood blaze, the picnickers ate as the sun, bloated and red with atmospheric diffraction, sank into the Pacific.

Alex watched Colton and Marianna through the flames. Colton was drinking from a silver cup and flask. Earlier he had offered Alex a drink and Alex had accepted, expecting brandy. But the contents of the bottle had been whisky, which Alex disliked, and he had accepted no more.

Marianna put her head close to Colton's and said something. Colton shook his head. Marianna reached for the silver cup and Colton knocked her hand away. Alex felt a surge of anger, but his cousin said nothing, did nothing more.

The sparks rose in a rushing column into the starry, moonless night. Consuelo said, "Do you like it here, Cousin Alex?"

His smaller cousins, Día y Noche, sitting sleepily at his feet waited for his verdict.

"It is—" He paused and looked down into the upturned faces. "Rather cold."

"No, Primo Alejandro," Esteban protested. "This isn't cold."

"You should be here in winter," Miguel said. "The water is *freezing.*"

Alex tousled their already salt-spiked hair. "I come from a warm country where the Indians used to run about in feathers."

"And eat hearts. I read about that," Esteban said.

"Some of them ate hearts. Sometimes. On special days," Alex said.

Across the fire Marianna and Johnny Colton were whispering. Alex felt despair. He said, "If you would all like, tomorrow we can go sailing." He had noticed, at a stop in Monterey, that there were small fishing sloops available for charter. He was a skilled sailor. He looked through the flames at Colton. He didn't look like a sailor. Perhaps he would opt for staying away. "Do you sail, John?" he asked.

"I have. In the East. Many times," Colton said.

Instinct told Alex young Colton was lying. He seemed the sort of person who could never admit to inexperience of any sort.

"Good, then," Alex said. "I'll take El Loco to Monterey and charter a boat for the day. The rest of you can come along in a wagon and I will meet you there on the pier."

"May we go with you in El Loco? Please?" It was Esteban who spoke, but both of the boys were asking eagerly.

Consuelo said, "Doña Anita won't let you go. She hates boats."

"I'll speak to her," Marianna said. "I would like to go sailing on the bay. I have never been. Is it difficult, Cousin Alex?"

"No," Alex said, looking at Colton. "Two men can sail one of those little sloops easily. Even one can do it in a pinch. Right, John?"

"Of course," Colton said, and emptied his silver cup.

Of course, thought Alex. Tomorrow we balance the scales. There was nothing in the world, Alex had long ago discovered, that could so set down a braggart as a day on a sailboat.

That night he slept the sleep of the blessed. He even dreamed kindly of Relámpago.

It was a source of wry, self-deprecating amusement to Adriana that she was disappointed when all the younger Marburgs and John Colton rushed from the house, looking forward to spending a day on the water under the captaincy of young Alex. It was quite out of the question that she should have been asked to go along, and if she had been she would, of course, have refused. The very idea of a sixty-year-old woman clinging to the gunwales of a sloop in a twenty-degree heel was ludicrous. Roberto, like all ranchers, thought that boats served one purpose only, and that was to take fishermen to the place where they could coax from the deep sufficient fish to be eaten one day each week (and no more). To use a boat for pleasure was a thing that would never have occurred to him. He had, in fact, been highly dubious of Alex's outing.

The children had returned to Nueva Santanilla after the hour of *cena* sunburned, damp with salt spray, and tired. Día y Noche had had a splendid time. Consuelo seemed to be laughing behind her fingers at her sister. And Marianna was plainly annoyed with her cousin Alex. Whatever had transpired on the whitecapped waters of Monterey Bay had not pleased her overmuch.

The following morning was the time allotted by the well-organized Alex to a motor trip in El Loco for the *abuela,* and Adriana (behaving, she thought, like a woman one-third her age) had presented herself at the stables, where the Locomobile had found temporary shelter, at seven in the morning.

Alex was already on hand, wiping the oilier surfaces of his machine, priming the carburetor, and lubricating the triple-strand link chain that drove the rear wheels. Día y Noche were with him, serving as apprentice mechanics, handing him rags and spout cans of benzine and oil. Marianna was nowhere to be seen, and Adriana assumed that her day on the water had tired her and she was sleeping late. But it was not like Marianna to lie abed when something of interest was taking place. Adriana suspected that at some point during her driving lesson, Alex might confide in her that his sailing day had not turned out exactly as planned.

"Good morning, Alejandro," she said. "As you see, I am ready." She wore, for lack of anything more suitable, an old whipcord split riding shirt and a buckskin jacket. Her gold-streaked white hair was fixed in a tight knot at the back of her narrow, well-shaped head. A small hat shaded her eyes. Out of long habit, she carried a riding crop, which made her small grandsons shout with laughter.

"Look, Alex," Esteban called delightedly, "The *abuela* is going to beat El Loco if he doesn't behave!"

"This is for mechanicians," she said in Spanish. "To be used when they make fun of old ladies."

"*Abuela,*" Miguel said, hugging her thigh, "I am not afraid."

"I should think not," Adriana said. She looked at Alex. "Did all go well yesterday, Alejandro?"

Alex wiped his hands on a bit of cotton cloth. He said, "Well, ah, yes, Patrona. Fairly well."

Esteban, his dark eyes intense, said, "Oh, you should have seen Johnny, *abuela.* He was so funny."

"He dropped the anchor over the side by mistake," Miguel said. "Alex had to pay the man who owned the boat for it."

Adriana looked inquiringly at Alex, who busied himself intently with something under the raised bonnet.

Esteban, Noche, said seriously, "You know, *abuela,* Marianna behaved quite badly. After all, it was not Alex's fault Johnny got sick and threw up."

"It appears to have been an eventful day," Adrianna murmured.

"All right, all right, all right," Alex said heartily. "Who is going to help push El Loco outside now? Let's pay attention to business."

Adriana watched the Locomobile rolled out into the sunlight, her brows arched. The story of the day's sailing should be instructive, she thought with an inward smile.

"Can I crank, Cousin Alex?" shouted Esteban.

"No, I'll do that. *Abuela?*" He had taken a white duck duster from a compartment in the rear of the car. He helped Adriana put it on over her clothes. "Now the goggles, and you had better take this hat." He waited while she removed her own and replaced it with the tweed cap he had been wearing when he arrived. "Now will you please step up?" He helped her into the passenger seat, a metal bucket upholstered in black leather.

He leaned in and made some adjustments on the dashboard. "Now you, Noche. Sit here. When I tell you, turn the magneto on."

Esteban bustled into the seat beside Adriana. "This is the magneto, *abuela,*" he said. "And this is the choke. And this is the spark. And down there is the gas pedal. And over there is the handbrake—"

"And these three cans on the running board are for gas, oil, and

507

water," piped Miguel. "See, red for gasoline, blue for oil, and white for water. The water goes in that thing in the front."

"If El Loco grows thirsty," Adriana said.

"Oh, *abuela*," Esteban said. "That is the *radiator*."

"I see," Adriana said attentively.

"Cousin Alex told Marianna he would teach her to drive, but she says she doesn't like motorcars at all. She was very rude," Miguel said.

"Was she," Adriana murmured again. "Was this before or after Johnny Colton lost the anchor and threw up?"

"Oh, after," Miguel said. "Marianna wouldn't ride back in El Loco. She took the buggy and dropped Johnny off at Santa Marta. She is going to take his horse back today."

Adriana looked amusedly at Alex, who quickly ducked his head behind the radiator to insert the crank.

"You really won't need the stick, *abuela*," Miguel said politely. "May I take it for you?"

Adriana surrendered the riding crop.

Alex stood up and said, "All right. Ready?"

"Ready!" shouted Esteban.

"What shall *I* do, Alex?" demanded Miguel.

"Well, let's see. You hold on to the spares so the car won't move while I crank it."

"All right, I'll hold on tight." Miguel stationed himself at the rear of the car, his small, oil-stained hands gripping the spare tires, white-knuckled.

"Now here we go," Alex said. "Two turns to prime the cylinders."

"El Loco has three cylinders, *abuela*," Esteban explained seriously.

"Pay attention now, Noche."

"I'm ready, Alex!"

"Turn the magneto switch to on."

"Magneto on, Alex."

"Are you holding the car, Día?"

"I've got it, Cousin Alex," Miguel shouted excitedly.

"All right. *Now*." Alex spun the crank and the engine came to life with a rattling roar, a cloud of blue oil-smoke and a smell of raw gasoline. El Loco vibrated busily. Adriana held firmly to the cowling. Esteban climbed up and kissed her on the cheek. "Don't be afraid now, *abuela*."

"I won't be. Now stay well out of the way, Día y Noche," she shouted to make herself heard over the clatter.

"El Loco won't kick us!" Miguel shouted back, laughing.

Alex climbed in behind the tiller. He looked over at his grandmother. "Ready? Here we go."

El Loco trundled down the road between the pastures with a metallic thrashing of chains, popping exhaust, and blue smoke.

Alex said, *"Abuela,* you had better put the goggles on. I won't go faster than forty but the wind can injure your eyes."

Adriana did as she was bid. Forty miles an hour, she thought. Far faster than a horse could run. What other wonders did the new century hold in store? The wind felt fresh on her face. It was rather frightening to sit on this peculiar machine and travel at such velocity, but it was exhilarating too.

Alex drove under the adobe archway and onto the county road. From time to time he would take his eyes from the path ahead to look at his grandmother. She was holding onto the sides of the seat, but she was smiling. Lord, Alex thought, she must have been a beauty when she was Marianna's age. Even now she retained so much of what made a woman good to look at: the fine, regular features, the elegant bearing, the lean, straight body. If she looked like this at sixty, what must she have been at twenty? His father spoke of her seldom, but when he did it was with a reminiscent tenderness that Alex had never before understood. Once, mellow with drink, his father had called her "a brave spirit." Having known her for only a few days, Alex Marburg thought that perhaps he understood some part of what his father meant.

"How fast are we traveling now, Alejandro?" Adriana made herself heard against the noise of the motor and the rush of wind.

"Twenty miles an hour, *abuela,"* Alex shouted back.

"Que maravilla!"

"We could go faster, but the road is too rough."

"Go as fast as you wish," Adriana said. "I am quite comfortable."

The Locomobile clattered along the narrow gravel-surfaced track toward Carmel, under stands of dark evergreens and through rolling, open pastures. Horses snorted and ran at the motorcar's approach.

Alex slowed and pulled onto the verge to stop. "Would you like to drive, *abuela?"*

"Very much," Adriana said. "You will instruct me."

They exchanged seats and Adriana grasped the tiller in her gloved hands. Alex explained the operation of the dog-clutch, brake, and throttle. He had to raise his voice to make himself heard over the clattering of the three-cylinder engine. They sat in a haze of thin smoke, and Adriana listened attentively.

Alex, poised to take emergency action, said, "Are you ready, *abuela?*"

"I am ready."

"All right. Advance the throttle slightly. *Slightly, abuela!* There, that's right. Now release the handbrake. Good. You are doing fine. Now release the clutch."

"This?"

"Yes, that's it. Very gently. And be prepared to steer now."

Adriana followed instructions, and El Loco jerked into motion. She guided the car onto the road with a delighted smile.

"Good, *abuela.* Marvelous. Just keep us on the road."

The Locomobile rolled down the slight incline toward Monastery Beach.

"May we go faster now?" Adriana asked.

"A little bit. Advance the throttle further." Alex made adjustments to the spark. "Good. There."

"How fast are we going now?"

"Fifteen. Maybe a bit more."

Adriana hunched over the tiller, her head thrust forward, her eyes bright behind the round goggles. The car reached the bottom of the grade and sped along the road, followed by a cloud of dust and exhaust smoke.

A pair of horsemen appeared ahead. Adriana recognized Young Colton and one of his vaqueros. She did not diminish speed but signaled them with her free hand to get out of the way. Colton, a heavy man on a cobby gelding, galloped away from the road shouting angrily. The vaquero's mount, wanting no part of the approaching apparition, bolted across the landward field toward the trees.

The car sped past Colton on his rearing horse and Adriana inclined her head to him in a regal gesture. Then he was swallowed in the cloud of dust and smoke behind the Locomobile. Alex looked back to see the big man fighting his frightened horse to a standstill, then El Loco topped another rise and he could see no more.

"Abuela," he said, "usually we slow down when passing horsemen."

"Yes, I can see that would be best," Adriana said, still intent on the road ahead.

The shallow climb had overheated the engine. Alex said, "We had better stop up there on the bluff so I can put more water in the radiator."

Adriana guided the car once again onto the road verge and reversed the process of setting the machine in motion. Alex flipped the magneto switch and El Loco fell silent except for the creakings and tickings of cooling metal. *"Abuela,* I am impressed. You learn so quickly."

"Some things," Adriana said, with a satisfied smile.

"You are absolutely marvelous."

"I did do well, didn't I, Alex?"

Alex dismounted, unstrapped the white can and added water to the radiator. Adriana had climbed down to watch.

"I rather think I should like to have one of these machines," she said. "They will never replace the horse, of course, but in time they might become popular."

Alex replaced the water can and fumbled for a *cigarillo. "Permiso, abuela?"*

"Of course," Adriana said, and walked to the edge of the bluff to look back at Monastery Beach and the shallow cove. Colton and his vaquero were nowhere to be seen. The morning sun was pleasantly warm and a fresh breeze was blowing off the ocean. Adriana removed Alex's cap and goggles. There were smudges on her cheeks.

She spread her riding skirt and sank down on the grassy ground near the edge. The surf broke against the rocks fifty feet below. She patted the earth beside her. "Sit with me, Alejandro."

Alex did as he was told.

"Now," she said. "Tell me about your excursion yesterday."

"Ah, well. That," Alex said.

"I should like to hear. Did Marianna have a good time?"

"Oh, yes. I think so, *abuela.* For most of the day. It was only later that she—" He shrugged. "Well, I think she became angry when I lost my temper. I shouldn't have done that. I should have known John Colton was no sailor. But on the beach he said he had sailed often on the east coast. So when he failed to secure the rode—"

"Rode? I don't understand you."

"The rope that holds the anchor. It is called the rode, *abuela."*

"Is it. How interesting."

"We had come inshore to anchor and eat lunch, you see. The wind was northwesterly. It usually is on this coast. And the bay was a bit rough, so I took us into the lee of Santa Cruz to drop the hook—the anchor, that is. Well, I told Johnny to go forward and drop the anchor—which he did. But he had neglected to secure the rode to the bitts—"

"Bitts?"

"The posts in the deck you use to secure the rode."

"Ah."

"Well, *abuela,* when you anchor a boat you have to have the anchor attached to the boat or the whole evolution is not—well, not successful."

"And Johnny failed to do that."

"I'm afraid so. The bitter end of the rode was free, so when the anchor went down, the rode ran out and over the side. I shouldn't have yelled at John, but I did. I was really quite annoyed. We lost the hook and two hundred feet of good hemp rode. Anchors and line are expensive."

Adriana looked at the distant horizon to hide a smile.

"Día y Noche thought it was very funny, and so did Consuelo," Alex said. "John doesn't like it much when people laugh at him. Noche said it was like hitching a horse to a loose branch. But with a horse, he'll come back when he gets hungry. An anchor in eighty feet of water is gone." He inhaled deeply from his *cigarillo* and then flipped it arching into the sea far below. "John offered to pay, of course, but I couldn't allow that. It was my party, after all."

"Of course," Adriana said.

"So we had to eat lunch out on the bay. In about eighteen knots of wind and a heavy swell. A small sloop's motion when you heave to—"

"Heave to?"

"Set the sails and tiller against each other so that the boat makes no headway."

"Yes, I see."

"A small sloop's motion under sea conditions like that can be rather violent. It didn't bother anyone else, but John had been nipping at his flask. I warned him it wasn't a good idea, but he told me to stop playing at being captain, so I did. We ate the sandwiches Doña Tomasa made for us and John got sick. Marianna got very angry."

"With Johnny? That would be unkind."

"Oh, no. Not with Johnny, *abuela.* With me. She said I deliberately took us out on a rough day to show how much better a sailor I was than John, and that I *wanted* him to get sick." Alex stared moodily at the empty sea and said, "I admit I might have wanted to show off a little, *abuela.* We sail a great deal in Tihuacan and it is something I do well. Far better than I ride a horse. But nobody wants a passenger on a small boat to throw up, *abuela,* believe me. Most particularly if he doesn't make it over the side. It can be very unpleasant for everyone on board."

"I can well imagine," Adriana said wryly.

"So when we reached the pier, Marianna told me she did not care to ride back to Nueva Santanilla with me in El Loco. She took the buggy and drove John back to Santa Marta." Alex sighed. "What I did was wrong, I suppose. I had a feeling he wasn't telling the truth when he said he was an experienced sailor. I guess I wanted to look better than he."

"For Marianna?"

"Yes, *abuela.*"

"She is engaged, betrothed, Alex. The marriage contracts are signed," she said gently. 'Didn't you know that?"

"Not about the contracts," Alex said. "I didn't know people still did that."

"Some do, Alejandro."

Alex looked at her intensely. "I don't like the way he treats her, *abuela,*" he said. "I don't like *him.*"

Adriana placed a hand on his. "Alex. You have known Marianna for three days. Do you really think you know what is best for her?"

"Yes. No—I don't know, Patrona," he said miserably. "I am making a fool of myself."

"A thing no Marburg suffers willingly," she said with a smile.

"She doesn't love him."

"Oh? You know that? On the basis of a three-day acquaintance?"

"He is not right for her, *abuela.*"

"Alex, you are very young."

"I am nineteen, *abuela.*"

"That is young, Alejandro."

He stood and walked to the edge of the bluff. "When is the wedding to be?" he asked.

"In early July," Adriana said.

"There is still time, then."

"Alejandro. She is your cousin."

"In Mexico cousins marry all the time, *abuela.* Besides, she is only the daughter of my father's half-brother." He turned to look at Adriana with an expression of troubled affection. "I call you grandmother, Patrona. But you are not really my grandmother. Except by marriage —not by blood. Perhaps I have no right to speak of you as *abuela.*"

"It gives me pleasure, Alex," Adriana said. "More than you can know."

A shining smile overcame the concern in his manner. "I am very glad of that, *abuela,*" he said.

"Now help me up," Adriana said. "It's time we returned to Nueva Santanilla."

Alex raised her to her feet. "You won't speak to Marianna of what I said?"

Adriana shook her head. "No, Alex. I will not."

He bent and kissed her on the cheek. "Thank you, Patrona. I know how young I am. But thank you for not calling me foolish."

Adriana looked up into the young man's face, so familiar, so evocative of so many memories. "Oh, my dear," she said. "Never that. Never, never that."

Alex Marburg departed from
Nueva Santanilla on the Saturday between Good Friday and Easter. He
attended church with the family and took Communion from Father
Clarence before the bare altar.

Marianna's pique with him remained, but seemed (to his relief)
somewhat less vigorous. He managed, with great skill and tact, to
promote an evening ride through the hills with her, free (for once) of
his by-now almost constant convoy of two small boys and a twelve-year-
old sister. Later, when he had gone, Día y Noche had admitted to
having been bribed with the promise of a long motor trip in El Loco
on the occasion of Alex's next visit to Nueva Santanilla. When such a
visit might take place, however, was unspecified.

The Patrona watched Marianna carefully, wondering if Alex's
presence at the ranch was missed. It was difficult to say. It seemed to
Adriana that her granddaughter was quieter, more introspective than

was her wont. This could well have been because of some unsanctioned declaration by Alex on his last evening. But it might equally be caused by the slow but inexorable acceleration of the juggernaut of a Nueva Santanilla wedding.

Adriana had told Alex that marriage contracts had been signed by Roberto and Young Colton. This was true, and as a result of this legal agreement there appeared, the week after Easter, a team of surveyors along the boundary line between Nueva Santanilla and Santa Marta Ranch. The land measurers were set to the task of defining the boundaries of a new ranch, to be formed by acreage donated by both families and another substantial plot of five hundred acres of highland meadow to be leased from the federal government in the name of the new holding.

An architect from San Francisco and his helpers set about with pegs and string outlining the shape of the new house to be built for the newlyweds. This part of the work progressed so swiftly that by the end of April Santanilla laborers were already at work making adobe bricks.

As the preparations for the wedding progressed, Adriana's misgivings grew. There seemed no obvious change in Marianna's attitude toward Johnny Colton. In fact, she seemed even more solicitous of him than before Alex Marburg's visit. It made Adriana uneasy, but every effort to win Marianna's confidence seemed to fail. It appeared that because the *abuela* had voiced objections to the marriage early on, she was to be punished for disloyalty. Adriana would have found it amusing if it had not troubled her so. Marianna was reluctant even to discuss the two-week stay at the San Francisco townhouse planned for late May, during which time the Patrona's dressmakers would be making the bride's trousseau.

With all of the family above the age of twelve increasingly engrossed in the nuptial preparation, Adriana fell back into her old solitary ways. Ever since her girlhood in Spain, a troubled mind had caused her to mount a horse and ride long hours alone with her thoughts. Don Alvaro, she remembered, had done the same before he had found such solace in burying himself for days on end in the observatory.

She was quite alone on a windy spring day when, unwisely for a woman of her age riding sidesaddle, she had urged Infanta to attempt a four-barred gate and took a nasty fall.

She landed hard, striking her abdomen on the edge of a culvert hidden in the new grass.

The grass saved her from broken bones, but not from considerable pain and, as she saw when she had recovered both Infanta and her horsewoman's pride and returned home, some deep bruises.

She told no one of her misadventure. She could not imagine herself fighting off the family's solicitude for having been so clumsy as to fall off her horse.

But the bruises were slow in healing, and she hurt badly inside. So badly that she wondered if she had perhaps broken a bone or injured something vital.

A week after her fall, she called for the buggy and a vaquero to drive her into Monterey. If the household had not been in turmoil with preparations for the wedding and the festivities to follow (very nearly every rancher family in the county would be invited), Tomasa or Anita would have remarked on what was, for Adriana, a stodgy choice of transport. Adriana's old maid, Felicia, had seen the bruises but had been warned to keep silent. Adriana intended to have no one fussing over her and asking questions as to how the injuries came about.

In Monterey she attended Roger Harrison's surgery, and to him she gave a straightforward account of both accident and injuries.

The afternoon light, softened by drawn shades, made the surgery pleasantly dim. Roger Harrison, the father of two boys and a daughter now, sat behind his desk—a plump, prosperous, balding man who had never lost, in Adriana's eyes, the unformed look of his young manhood.

"You had better examine me, Roger," she said. "I dislike being handled, but if someone must do it I should prefer it to be you."

Roger Harrison assumed his tutorial manner and said, "Doña Adriana, why have you waited a week to see me? Why didn't you send someone to fetch me the day of your fall? A woman of your age—"

"Bother a woman of my age," Adriana said tartly. "I came to have you examine my bruises, not my judgment."

"Just as you say, Doña Adriana," he said, rising from behind his desk. "If you will go into the examination room, the nurse will assist you to disrobe." Ofttimes it was better not to bandy words with the Patrona of Nueva Santanilla.

Adriana stood. "There is something you should probably know. I have had bleeding."

Roger Harrison felt a twinge of apprehension, but he was too professional to allow it to be seen by the patient. "Many women have irregular bleeding, Doña Adriana. It is quite probably nothing to be concerned about."

"Don't take me for a fool, Roger," Adriana said, her still clear eyes steady on him. "I am sixty years old, and I have lived every one of those years as a woman. It is highly unlikely that I have begun to menstruate again. What it is, and how serious, is for you to say. But I expect it to be said frankly and honestly, Roger. Do you understand me?"

Dr. Harrison bowed his head before superior force. "Of course, Doña Adriana. It shall be as you wish."

"Thank you, Roger. You are a good boy," she said, and swept through the door into the examination room.

The pendulum clock atop the bookcase of medical volumes ticked loudly in the afternoon quiet. There were patients waiting in Dr. Harrison's anteroom, but they would have to wait longer. Roger sat behind his desk, mentally composing the letter he intended to send to Dr. Weisskopf in San Francisco if he could persuade Doña Adriana to see him.

Carefully, and unemotionally as possible, he reviewed the findings of his examination of the lady of Nueva Santanilla. They were familiar to any practitioner who, like himself, did a great deal of obstetrical work. But in the case of Doña Adriana his personal feelings were involved and, he fervently hoped, might be clouding his objectivity.

He stood as the door of the examination room opened and Adriana Marburg returned to the office. What an amazing woman she was, Roger Harrison thought. And what a woman she must have been thirty years ago, when she had taken her family in charge and moved them, lock, stock, and barrel from Spain to California. Time had worn her, but it had tempered her, as well. She was like a Spanish sword, strong, flexible, and ageless.

"Please sit down, Doña Adriana," he said, indicating a chair at the side of his desk.

Adriana sat, back straight, shoulders square. How many years of training, how many generations of breeding, Roger wondered, to make a woman sit in quite that way? She wore no jewelry. She never had, in all the years that he had known her. Only a wedding band and a small golden crucifix at her throat.

"Well, young Roger," she said. "You were certainly thorough. I am excruciatingly uncomfortable."

Roger Harrison ventured a smile. I am ten years older than her son and she still calls me young Roger. He seated himself, taking refuge behind the desk. It held the familiar things of his everyday life: the rather stiffly posed photograph of his wife and children, his leather desk set, appointment book, a small nautilus shell found by his eldest son, pens, pencils, notepaper, ashtray, humidor, all the ordinary objects a man in general practice collected over time. He regarded Doña Adriana over these trivial battlements and wished himself a wiser man, a better physician, a worker of miracles—knowing that he was none of these things.

"You had a bad fall, Doña Adriana," he said. "But your injuries are, fortunately, quite superficial."

Adriana Marburg waited, composed and still. Dr. Harrison's manner told her plainly that there was more to come.

"I am concerned, however, about the vaginal bleeding you describe. It could indicate something more serious."

"Such as?"

"I would prefer not to make guesses, Doña Adriana. I am only a general practitioner—a country doctor, if you will—and I think it imperative that we should obtain a second opinion. From a specialist, Patrona."

"I see." The lovely face remained composed. For Roger Harrison the worst moment was over. Oftentimes patients slipped into panic when it was suggested to them that something was seriously awry. But he had not expected any such reaction from Doña Adriana. It would be a denial of everything he knew to be true of her. The woman had proved her courage many times.

"I want you to see a Dr. Arnheim Weisskopf in San Francisco, Patrona. Gynecology is a new specialty and he is the best man in the field west of Chicago."

"As bad as that, young Roger," Adriana Marburg said.

"Not at all, Doña Adriana." Harrison's protest carried all of his hopes and professional conviction. "It is simply that your symptoms may be indications of a number of possible complaints. Frankly, I would like you to avail yourself of the very best diagnostic talent. As I say, I am only a country doctor. Dr. Weisskopf is a wonder in cases where the symptoms are ambiguous."

"I asked you to speak frankly, Roger. Do not disguise your suspicions with medical euphemisms. What is it you fear?"

Roger Harrison sighed. He should have known better than to play word games with Adriana Marburg.

"Very well, Patrona," he said. "My examination suggests that you *may* have cancer. Not as a result of your fall, but of long standing. It is possible—and I emphasize the word possible—that the fall has aggravated a condition already present. I cannot be certain this is the case, or even if a carcinoma is present. Dr. Weisskopf is skilled in early diagnosis, and that is why I want you to see him."

Adriana sat, unmoving. The ticking of the pendulum clock was the only sound in the room. Presently she said, "I thank you for being honest, Roger."

"When can you see him?" Harrison asked quietly.

"I shall be taking Marianna to San Francisco in approximately a fortnight. You may arrange an appointment for me then."

"I would prefer that you see him sooner, Patrona."

"That is not possible, Roger. There is too much to be done at Nueva Santanilla."

"Yes, of course. The wedding."

Adriana said, "Under no circumstances are you to mention this to Roberto or to anyone at Nueva Santanilla." She favored him with a bleak smile. "Tomasa and Anita are both *scandalosas*. Do you know the word?"

"I think so, Doña Adriana. It means excitable, doesn't it?"

"More or less," said Adriana.

"I will write to Weisskopf and ask that he see you on the morning of the twenty-first. Will that be satisfactory?"

"It will do," Adriana said. She stood and looked about the room as though she were seeing it for the first time. It was a reaction Roger Harrison had seen many times. To be told that one had a possibly life-threatening illness alerted the mind, sharpened the perceptions.

Roger rose and walked with Adriana to the door. "Try not to think on it, Patrona. I may have alarmed you for nothing."

"We shall see, young Roger," she said. He watched her straight back as she walked through the reception room and out into the late afternoon.

The light was failing. An early summer fog was rolling in from the bay. Roger returned to his seat, took a sheet of paper from his desk and began to write his letter to Weisskopf.

He longed for the comforting domesticity of his home, for the shouts of his children at play, for the affectionate nagging of Elizabeth, his wife, and for the fortifying effect of a good stiff drink of straight whisky. This had been an afternoon he would too long remember.

57

The late spring night in Tihuacan was warm and the air was heavy with the scent of the night-blooming jasmine in the garden of the palazzo on the Olas Altas. A nearly full moon, low in the west, made a shimmering path of light on the dark sea beyond the Malecón.

Julia Marburg and Aaron escorted their guests through the gallery to their waiting carriages. It had been a small and intimate gathering assembled to bid farewell to Julia, who in two days' time would be on her way north to Hacienda de San Jacinto so that she could be present at the birth of Marina's first child.

Aaron walked with an arm about Caridad's slim shoulders and a hand on Diego Perez's arm. He was fonder of Diego than he would ever be of the rather arrogant hacendado Marina had married, but on balance he was satisfied with both his sons-in-law. Diego was displaying energy and a good head for business, and Sebastian de Lorca, while subject to all the defects of his class, was at least a good husband to Marina. Aaron was of an age now to appreciate the fact that there are limits to the blessings one can expect in life.

Julia walked to the *porte-cochère* arm in arm with Juan Amaya-Ruiz. "Don't concern yourself too much about Marina, Julia," Amaya said. "She is a healthy girl and should have no trouble whatever presenting you with a strapping grandson."

"Or granddaughter," Julia said. "Which is what Aaron prefers."

"Will you stay long at Hacienda San Jacinto?"

"Until the end of July. Then I shall meet Aaron in Tacubaya. Alejandro will be home by then."

"You will be glad to have the boy home, I think."

"I have missed him."

The *mozo* appeared, leading Dr. Amaya-Ruiz's horse and buggy. "Ah, Julia. I remember when I used to dash about like a cavalryman. Those days are gone, thanks be to God." The doctor patted his small paunch. "Thank you for a delightful evening, *señora*. And have a fine journey to Sonora."

Julia presented her cheek to be kissed and stood back as the doctor climbed into his buggy.

"Good night, Doctor," Caridad called.

"*Buenas noches, linda,*" Amaya-Ruiz said. "And to you, Diego." Everyone was fond of Diego Perez de Lebrun. He was far better liked than his elder brother Jorge, now a senator from Sinaloa and busily enriching himself at public expense as a loyal Porfirista.

Aaron stood beside the buggy to bid his old friend good night. Amaya asked, "When do you leave for *la capital?*"

"As soon as Julia is off to Sonora," Aaron said.

"Will you see Don Porfirio?"

"Very likely," said Aaron.

"Give him my thanks for cleaning up the water supply. And tell him there are about twenty more public health concerns which need attention here."

"I will tell him you said so."

"*Caray, hombre,*" Amaya said. "I am getting weary. I think I shall retire soon."

"You? Never," Aaron said.

"I can, you know. Thanks to you and the Sociedad Fénix." Over the years Aaron had encouraged the doctor to invest in the various Fénix enterprises. Amaya-Ruiz had become a rich man.

"Well, perhaps I am not quite ready for retirement. But I think I fancy a trip to Paris to renew old friendships."

"Once an *imperialista,* always an *imperialista,*" Aaron said. *"Vaya con Dios,* Juan."

The doctor waved and touched the reins to his horse's rump. The buggy clattered out into the dark Malecón.

The *mozos* brought the Perez de Lebruns' carriage. Caridad kissed her father and climbed into the vehicle. Diego made his farewells to Julia and climbed in after his wife.

Caridad said, "Papa, we will expect you for dinner on the fourteenth before you leave for Tacubaya."

Aaron nodded his agreement and with his arm about Julia watched his daughter and son-in-law depart for their house in Cabo Sur.

"Peace at last," Aaron said as they walked slowly back through the *corredor.* The first weeks in May were hectic times for the Marburgs. There was always a spate of Cinco de Mayo fiestas among the *gentecilla* of Tihuacan, and as Aaron's success in business grew, so did his social obligations. Then there were the fiestas given for the employees of the various Fénix enterprises. For many of them, a mere appearance by *el Jefe* sufficed. Juan Ortega could handle the position of host, since he was now an executive officer of the Sociedad Anónima Fénix. But the fiesta given for the workers of the Trituradora was a special event and Aaron could not delegate the role of host. All of that was now behind him, for the year 1900, at least.

"Are you sleepy, *vieja?*" he asked Julia. It was near to midnight, but the air was still warm and the night was redolent of flowers.

"I will send for chocolate," Julia said. Never a drinker, in recent years she had developed a taste for bitter chocolate with a dash of *aguardiente.*

They sat at a wicker table in the *corredor.* It was the same table, Aaron remembered, where he had sat down so long ago with Don Marcello and General Díaz. He was reminded of the French proverb that said: The more things change, the more they remain the same.

Julia rang the silver bell that stood on the table and Maria Macías shuffled out of the darkness of the house. "Tell Guillermina to bring us coffee and chocolate, Maria. And then get yourself off to bed. There's no need for you to wait up longer."

"If you drink too much chocolate, Doña Julia," the old *soldadera* said, "you are going to get fat. I know what I'm talking about." She put her hands on her own large buttocks before disappearing in the direction of the kitchen. Julia looked after her with tolerant amusement.

"She will never learn manners, that one."

"I wouldn't know her if she did," Aaron said.

"She was good to me when Eufemia died," Julia said. "That gives her privileges in this house." Julia's *nana,* Eufemia, had died in her sleep the year Marina was married, and Julia still grieved for her. Her new personal *criada* was a girl of seventeen who eyed Alejandro hungrily each time he came home on holiday.

Aaron took Julia's hand. "I shall miss you, *vieja.*"

"Two whole months," Julia said.

"For Marina," Aaron said.

Julia regarded her husband in the dim light reflected from the gas lamps on the garden walls. It pleased her that he had remained a handsome man. His hair was thinner, his forehead higher, and there were deep lines in his narrow face. But he was erect and slender still, and his eyes were as clear and beautiful as they had been on that day, so long ago now, when she had first seen him—the stranger come to Tihuacan to change her life.

"I had a letter from Alex today," he said.

Julia waited. If a letter had come, it was unusual that her husband had not shown it to her immediately. It was unlike him to be inconsiderate, so there must be another reason he had withheld it. "There is nothing wrong, I hope?" she asked.

"No, of course not," Aaron said. "He asked for money, of course."

"Of course."

"It seems he owns a motorcar."

"Dios mio. Those devices are dangerous, *viejo.*"

"More costly than dangerous, I think," Aaron said wryly. "He spent his entire year's allowance on it."

Julia waited again. Aaron's manner seemed constrained. Presently he said, "He has discovered the Santanas."

"The Santanas?"

"Well, the Marburg-Santanas. My half-brother Roberto's family."

"I see. Does that distress you?"

"No, of course not, Julia," Aaron said. "I never liked Roberto as a boy, but that was more my failing than his. He was only a child when I left Spain for America. I have not set eyes on him in years."

Julia was silent for a long, thoughtful moment. Then she said, "And you didn't see him, did you, when you visited Spain to call on your stepmother?"

"No," Aaron said shortly. "He was away."

"What else did Alejandro say?"

Aaron drew a deep breath. "He has met his cousin Marianna Marburg. He does not say so in exactly so many words, but I rather got the feeling that the girl has made quite an impression on him."

"An impression? Has Alex fallen in love?"

Aaron fumbled irritably for his cigar case and matches. He puffed a Havana alight. "Why is that the first thing women think of to ask? The girl is his first cousin."

"Yes. Through Don Miguel. But you and Roberto are only half-brothers. Cousins have been known to fall in love before."

"You make too much of it, *vieja.*"

"*I* do? I haven't even seen the letter," Julia said.

"It came to the office. I forgot to bring it home." Aaron looked over his shoulder and shouted for the *criada.* "Where is that stupid girl with the chocolate?"

"She will come when it is ready," Julia said. "What else did Alex say about Roberto's family?"

"He said, for one thing, that Marianna Marburg is engaged to be married."

"And?"

"That Nueva Santanilla Ranch is thriving."

"That's good news certainly?"

"Of course. Roberto and Ana-Maria's boys are growing."

"Boys do," Julia said. "Girls too, with time."

Guillermina hurried into the *corredor* with a tray. Julia served Aaron a cup of bitter, syrupy coffee and a tiny cup of chocolate for herself. She waited while he added a touch of *aguardiente* to each cup. "Go to bed now, Guillermina," she said. "Rosa will get these things in the morning."

When the girl had gone, Aaron said, "I suppose what disturbed me was that I was taken unaware. I should have realized that with Alex at school at St. Mary's, it was probable he would see that—that branch of the family."

"It was more than probable, Aaron. It was inevitable. I wondered that you didn't suggest it to him when he first went north. They are of his blood, after all. What reason could there be for any estrangement? You say yourself that Roberto was only a baby when you last saw him. I know Don Miguel favored him over you. But that is hardly his fault, is it?"

Aaron smiled grimly into the darkness. "How many years have you wanted to say that to me, *vieja?*"

"It was for you to do as you thought best," Julia said. "But Alex and Marianna and Roberto's other children—they are another generation."

"Of course," Aaron said. "I never really intended there to be any bad feeling between me and my brother. It is simply that we do not know one another."

"Then that should be remedied," Julia said. "You are both Marburgs. From what you tell me of your family in Germany, perhaps the only Marburgs, except for your children and his, that there ever will be."

Aaron squeezed her hand and said, "You are right, of course. You usually are, *vieja.*"

"And did Alex meet Doña Adriana? He must have."

"Yes," Aaron said.

"That is all? Just 'yes'?"

Aaron gave a short, rueful laugh. "He rather seems to have fallen in love with *her.*"

"Ah," Julia said.

Aaron looked at his wife and said, "That is all? Just 'ah'?"

Julia held his hand tightly, and when she spoke there was pity in her voice. "Oh, my dear. Did you love her so very much?"

Aaron looked at his wife in astonishment.

"Did you really think I didn't know, Aaron? Are you still that innocent about women?"

"Julia, Adriana is my *stepmother*—"

Julia touched his lips with her fingertips. "A very long time ago, *querido,* long before we were married, before you had ever touched me, even before I began to love you—I knew there was someone else."

"Julia—"

"Hush, now. Let me say this. I knew. I have always known." Dare she tell him, she thought, of the hundreds of nights when she wished Adriana Santana dead, or old and ugly? Of the nights she had lain in his arms wondering if it were truly she he made love to, or another? No, there was a limit to frankness between men and women. With love and years came deep affection and honesty, but there were still things better left unsaid. Most particularly now, years after the battle was won and the victory assured. She said, "I knew you loved another, and I knew it must be she. But you married *me,* Aaron. *I* bore your children and shared your life. It has been a fine life, *viejo.* Should I accuse you now? Of what? Of marrying me when you loved her? Of giving me the life you might have given her? It has been a marvelous life, and I am grateful for it. I pity her, dear one.

She will never know what I have known. What more needs to be said between you and me?"

Aaron sat in absolute silence, holding onto Julia's hand as a man in the sea might hold to his rescuer. Presently he stood and pulled her to her feet. He held her and softly kissed her lips. "It is late, *vieja,*" he said gently. "Let's go to bed."

She felt his arm, strong now after so many years, around her as they walked through the dark *corredor* toward their room.

How I love him, she thought. And then, with a deep sadness she thought: Yes, it has been a fine life—yet how much finer it would have been if he had loved me the way he loves her still.

58

The Marburg townhouse was a tall, wooden Victorian structure on the northern slope of Russian Hill. To Marianna it had always been a magic palace, a labyrinth of high-ceilinged rooms lit by stained-glass windows, dark halls and narrow stairways, shingled towers and peaked roofs. The exterior was decorated with wooden scrolls and gingerbread and the interior cornices with plaster angels and rosettes.

It had been built in 1880 by a clipper captain in the China service and the site had been chosen specifically for its splendid view of the Golden Gate, and between the Marin headlands and Fort Point, a narrower view of the Gulf of the Farallones. There was a widow's walk on the north façade of the third floor, a place where the master's wife could survey the strait, watching for the return of his tall ship.

The captain, a New Englander, had retired from the sea in 1892, and with his dour wife had returned to his native Massachusetts.

Adriana had bought the house and staffed it with a Chinese cook and a Mexican housekeeper. There was a small stable at the bottom of the steep garden where a landau and two horses were kept. When the house was to be used by the family, Adriana would dispatch a vaquero and two *criadas* to lend assistance in the house and to the groom-gardener, who lived in quarters above the stable.

Russian Hill was less fashionable than Nob Hill (or Nabob Hill), it being the "bohemian" section of the city where artists, painters, and writers were said to congregate. But in actual fact few such individuals could afford the price of Russian Hill real estate, and those who could tended to be as sedate and proper as ordinary citizens.

From the widow's walk above Filbert Street could be seen the truly bohemian section of the city, the district still known as the Barbary Coast, where whores and gamblers and crimps abounded. Marianna could remember as a child standing on the walk in the dark summer nights and listening to the distant sounds of revelry and who knew what delicious debaucheries. To Marianna, San Francisco had always been a fascinating wonderland. "Yes," the *bisabuela* had once said to her drily, "like Sodom and Gomorrah, the Cities of the Plain." Her great-grand-mother had always been certain that one day God would punish San Francisco not only for its sinfulness but for its smugness.

But in Marianna's opinion, San Francisco had a very great deal to be smug about. It was a beautiful city, situated at the tip of a vast peninsula and overlooking both the Pacific and one of the world's great bays. To stand at a window on a clear summer day and observe the ships in the harbor—square-riggers, sloops, lumber schooners, hay barges, side-wheelers, tugs, paddle-wheelers from the San Joaquin and Sacramento rivers, great steamers, tiny tugs, and ferryboats—was a childish pleasure Marianna had never outgrown. Ranch-born and ranch-bred, she could not imagine ever living in a city. But as a place to visit for excitement and adventure, San Francisco did nicely.

The first pair of days of her two-week stay were anything but adventurous for Marianna, however. Her grandmother had left her in the hands of old Felicia while she rode off in the landau on some unspecified errand, and Madame Colbert and her trio of twittering assistants had arrived to begin the tedious business of measuring Marianna for a new clothier's dummy. The old one no longer matched her measurements.

Madame Colbert (as far as Marianna knew she had no other name) was a Frenchwoman of indeterminate age and a vast capacity for gossipy chatter. She had been Adriana's dressmaker for fifteen years and had a Gallic flair for style and design. Her assistants, Irish girls Marianna's age and younger, partook of Madame's energy. Marianna had the distinct impression that had they not done so they would have found themselves rapidly unemployed. Madame Colbert's panache cloaked a very French frugality in the running of her boutique.

Marianna stood impatiently in bare feet and shift while Madame explored her with tape measure and notepad. She had rather hoped that she would see yardage and samples on the first day, but she did not. She saw only Madame and her ruddy-faced assistants working under Felicia's supervision. Doña Adriana did not return until dinnertime, and when she did she was uncommonly silent and seemed quite tired out.

On the second day, Doña Adriana once again vanished, but this time she returned before Madame Colbert's arrival, and so was on hand to give her opinions on the mountains of samples that now seemed to overflow the upstairs parlor where the dressmaking and measuring was taking place.

The lavishness of the planned trousseau quite astonished Marianna. She had been to the city on shopping expeditions before, but now she was being outfitted on an unprecedented scale. When the discussion turned to the selection of nightdresses and negligées, she found herself becoming distinctly uncomfortable.

Like any ranch-bred girl, Marianna had few illusions about sex and the meaning of marriage. But she had never before been forced to think, in such specific terms, of what being married to Johnny Colton was likely to mean.

The early ardor of a fifteen-year-old girl had been replaced now with the more considered view of a woman approaching twenty. It was far easier to be romantic about Johnny at a distance than nearby. Marianna had come to realize that her fiancé was given to making headstrong—and not always attractive—gestures. That had been painfully obvious on the dreadful day with Cousin Alex on Monterey bay.

She was still furious with Alex, and she planned never to forgive him. But it was a fact that he had warned Johnny about drinking too much in that miserable little boat. And John had immediately taken the warning as a challenge. For a young man to accept a challenge from another was perfectly reasonable behavior, Marianna thought, *if* one had some hope of success. Even gallant failure was acceptable (though Marianna doubted she could love it for long). But John had deliberately and stubbornly put himself in a position that made indignity inevitable. That was the act of a stupid man, or an arrogant one. Marianna found neither characteristic attractive.

Alex Marburg, now, had quite surprised her. When she thought of him sitting on swaybacked old Relámpago like a dustman on a mule, she really had to smile. Whatever else her handsome cousin might be, he was no horseman. He was as proud as Johnny, and perhaps with more reason. Without a word of complaint he had done his best with the old gelding, and with the abalone as well, coming out of the sea blue with cold and scraped and battered by the rocks and the surf, holding his ridiculous single "ab." *Yo perduro.* He was no Santana, but he had performed quite admirably. Of course, all the time he had been *planning.*

He had shown one swift flash of anger that evening on the beach. He had seen John knock her hand away from his cup—an act that had infuriated her, the more so because she felt she could not show it. Would Alex have fought Johnny on her account? Did he remain silent out of consideration for her?

She had to admit that she would really like to see him again. To have such feelings now, so near to her wedding, was probably shameful. But he was her *cousin,* after all. Her first cousin. Despite the fact that she intended never to forgive him for the boat business, she did rather like him. If that was improper, there it was. It was how she felt —and there was precious little time left to her to act as she chose. The preparations for the marriage, the contracts, the new house abuilding, the talk of land and cattle and money, and now this—Madame Colbert and her hive of workers cutting and stitching to make the finery an heiress of Nueva Santanilla required when she became a bride of Santa Marta. Not for the first time, cold chills ran down her narrow back.

She tried to imagine sleeping with Johnny Colton. He was physically attractive enough as a man. But would he come to her bed drunk? She despised him when he drank too much. And it did not make her sympathetic when he mumbled, as he often did, his excuses.

He will stop after we are married, she told herself. He will have no reason to drink too much when we are alone together.

She caught sight of herself in a pier-glass mirror, a tall and slender girl with firm, high breasts and long, well-shaped legs. She imagined Johnny lifting her shift, touching her there, and there, and *here.* She shivered violently.

"Are you cold, Mam'selle Marianna?" Madame Colbert, on her knees and with pins between her teeth, managed to ask.

"No, Madame," Marianna said. "I am quite comfortable."

One of the Irish girls giggled and said, "A ghost stepped on her grave, Madame."

"Mon Dieu!," Madame Colbert said reprovingly. "That is nothing

531

to make the joke about, you foolish girl. Not six weeks before a wedding."

Six weeks. To hear it said gave Marianna a tiny flutter of panic. How very quickly the days slipped away.

Doña Adriana appeared in the doorway to the room. She was dressed, as she often was, in black silk. The darkness heightened her pallor. There were pinched lines around her mouth. *Pobrecita abuela,* Marianna thought. Was she still so silently set against the match? The Patrona was growing old.

"Marianna," she said, "we have a visitor."

"A visitor, *abuela?*" Surely not, Marianna thought. The idea of Johnny Colton appearing suddenly to surprise her was oddly distressing.

"Ah, Madame Marburg," said the dressmaker, "we are finished for this day." She stood and began gathering her things.

"Who is it, Patrona?" Marianna asked.

"Get dressed quickly, *corazón,*" Doña Adriana said. "Your cousin Alex is here."

They stood on the sidewalk before the Grand Opera House amid the theater crowd pouring out of the auditorium onto gas-lit Mission Street. Marianna hugged herself, laughing with delight. "Oh, I enjoyed that so, Alex. It was such great fun."

They had seen a performance of what the broadsides all over the city proclaimed as the Great Extravaganza—a pageant entitled *1492.*

"I'm sorry we didn't have better seats, cousin," Alex said, "but I only managed to get what we had at the last minute. The show is very popular."

"I can see why," Marianna said breathlessly. "It was so grand, Alex. Columbus and the Indians and Queen Isabella—you know, that is one of my Christian names—and why do you suppose the queen was played by a man? Well he was very good, even so. I did enjoy it, Alex. It was so sweet of you to take me."

"Are you cold, Marianna?"

The night was overcast with San Francisco's famous summer fogs. The lights of the city turned the mist amber and made it appear to be a ceiling just above the tops of the tall eight- and ten-story buildings along Mission Street.

"I arranged for supper at the Palace Hotel," Alex said. "We can walk there, but if you are cold I will call a hack."

"Oh, no. Let's walk," Marianna said. "I want to look at things."

Alex offered his arm and they made their way through the murmuring, dispersing crowd of men in top hats and bowlers, women in
crinolines and fur wraps.

"You have been to the city before, cousin," Alex said.

"But not like this," Marianna said. She looked about her delightedly. "Never unchaperoned."

"We are cousins," Alex said.

"Of course we are," Marianna said, holding his arm. "The *abuela*
would never have agreed otherwise, would she?"

"I wouldn't think so," Alex said.

"Of course," Marianna said. "She likes you."

"I should hope that she does," Alex said stoutly. "Is there any
reason why she shouldn't?"

"There is plenty of reason why *I* shouldn't," Marianna said.

They walked through the fresh dampness of the night along Third
Street toward Market. In the distance Marianna could hear the rumble
of the cable cars, the clopping noise of horses on paving stones, the
clanging of trolley bells. So much activity so late at night. It had to be
well past eleven, but there were probably hundreds of people just out
walking on the streets under the gaslights.

"You mean the day on Monterey Bay," Alex said.

Marianna said, "You were really unforgivable."

"I may have been at that," Alex said. "Particularly when your *novio*
dropped the anchor into the bay."

Marianna's shoulders shook with laughter. "That *was* rather
funny, you know."

"Expensive, too," Alex said.

"He offered to pay," Marianna protested.

"Yes, he did. But there are misdeeds, Cousin Marianna, which
cannot be paid for in mere coin."

"I think we had better change the subject, or I shall grow angry
with you all over again," Marianna said.

"I wouldn't like that," Alex said. "I have just now elected you to
be my favorite cousin."

"Consuelo will be terribly hurt. She rather fancies you, you
know."

"It is part of my plan," Alex said.

"What plan is that?"

"To win the Santana-Marburgs over one by one."

"You have succeeded admirably with grandmother."

"What a fine lady she is," Alex said with feeling.

"She can be very difficult," Marianna said.

"Of course. She's like a queen."

"You should have known the *bisabuela*. If Doña Adriana is like a queen, Doña Maria was an empress. She used to tell me such wonderful stories about Spain and about Don Alvaro."

Market Street was so brightly lit it seemed like midday to Marianna. She had never seen the street late at night. A cable car rolled along the tracks in the center of the broad avenue, its seat filled with people. Marianna found the cable cars fascinating: they looked so strange, moving so swiftly without so much as a single horse pulling. What a wonderful thing it was to be young and alive at the beginning of the twentieth century! The buildings, some of them more than ten stories high, had electric lights in them. Ahead of the strolling couple, the Palace Hotel was ablaze with the new lights. It glittered with them.

The restaurant at the Palace was filled with late diners. Marianna watched wide-eyed as the maître d'hôtel greeted Alex and guided them to a small table in a booth surrounded by mirrors that reflected and amplified the lights hidden in the crystal chandeliers.

"Do they know you here, Alejandro?" she asked.

"I would like to impress you by saying yes, cousin," Alex said. "But no. I stopped by here earlier today to reserve a table. Sometimes, after a ball game with St. Ignatius, some of the fellows stop here for supper. But only on very special occasions."

Marianna looked across the table at her cousin and smiled at him. "Thank you, Alex."

"For what, Marianna?"

"For telling me that this is a special occasion. I should not allow myself to be pleased, but I am pleased just the same."

Alex ordered sand dabs, salad, and a bottle of French Chablis, explaining ruefully, "It is Friday. The Jesuits never let one forget."

Over salad Marianna asked, "How did you know we were here in the city?"

"The *abuela* said you would be—when I was at Nueva Santanilla, that is. Last week I started coming here every other day. Not to call, just to watch. Until you arrived."

Marianna felt as though a hand had gently squeezed her heart. "Oh, Alex, you shouldn't."

He regarded her with a burning intensity. "You aren't married yet, Marianna," he said.

Marianna flushed and looked away. "I can't listen to such things, Alex."

534

"Then I won't say them. Jut look at me, dear Marianna."

"Oh, I see you clearly."

"I know you do. I can feel it. And so can you."

"In six weeks I shall be married to John Colton," Marianna said.

"We shall see."

"Alex—!"

"Drink your wine Marianna. It is very good."

Marianna did as she was bid. In spite of the turmoil within her, she could not help smiling at her mad cousin. Because he must be quite mad. One did not say such things to a betrothed woman. Of course she had a certain warmth of feeling for him. He was her cousin, after all, a Marburg. That was what she felt, and what he felt as well. Given the strictness of their upbringing, what else could it be? The excitement of being alone together in the city, the newness of the world around them —no more than that.

"Now," Alex said. "Tomorrow."

"Tomorrow?"

"I thought we might take a picnic to Golden Gate Park if the day is fine. Perhaps the *abuela* would like to go. And then in the evening a play at the Tivoli, if I can arrange tickets. Or perhaps not. Maybe a ride across the bay on a ferryboat. They are great fun and the view of the city is marvelous from the water. And then the day following, a motorcar trip into the Berkeley hills in El Loco—"

"*Alex.*"

He leaned across the table and took both her hands in his. "I am your *cousin,* cousin. Family." His bantering tone changed and he regarded her with total seriousness. "You have ten days before going back to Monterey County, Marianna. The *abuela* told me. I want them, cousin. Give them to me. There will be empty days after."

Please sit down, Mrs. Marburg," Dr.
Weisskopf said, indicating a leather chair in the center of his consulting
room.

Even under less trying circumstances, Arnheim Weisskopf would
have been difficult to like. He was a small man, three inches shorter
than Adriana, with the roosterish demeanor often displayed by small
men. His head was shiny-bald, the fringe trimmed to the skin in the
Teutonic manner. His face was pinched, dominated by close-set eyes
of watery brown behind thick lenses. He affected a fringe beard that
left his upper lip naked over a small, prim mouth.

But the eyes held an inquiring light and the almost feminine hands,
now at rest on a file of closely written pages, had been sure and imper-
sonal. This was a man, Adriana thought, who dealt with human beings
as objects, a physician of the new sort, more interested in the disease
than in the patient, a man skilled in the ability to remove himself from

human contact. Weisskopf was a man who would speak the truth without the slightest compunction. Of that, at least, Adriana was glad.

In his manner of speech he fell easily into the European idiom, complete with Viennese locutions. His age Adriana guessed was somewhere between thirty-five and forty-five, not older. His manner was what Miguel would have described as rabbinical.

"Now, madame," he said. "We have performed all of the usual tests and some others of my own devising. Are you prepared to hear the results of my examination, or would you prefer that I simply forward them to Dr. Harrison? You might wish to have them explained by your own physician."

Adriana was conscious of the heavy beating of her heart. For the first time in many years she was fully aware of herself as a human body, a creature of blood and bone and sinew. Ever since her examination by Roger Harrison she had been dreading this moment, but it was only now that she could sense the workings of her body as a machine, one that could simply cease to function. How fragile we are, she thought, how mortal.

"Please go on, Doctor," she said.

"Very well, madame. These are my findings. Please ask for clarification if I use terms you do not understand."

Adriana suppressed a flicker of irritation at the pedantic manner. She managed a nod.

"My preliminary examination confirmed Dr. Harrison's gross diagnosis in part, madame. Your physician suspected adenocarcinoma of the cervix in the intraepithelial layers, or to state it more simply, preinvasive cancer. Had this been the case in toto, I should have recommended immediate surgery." He paused. Like a schoolmaster, Adriana thought, with a map and pointer and a backward pupil. "However. Dr. Harrison's diagnosis, while thoroughly professional, was incomplete. I have at my disposal more modern methods and facilities. The Roentgen machine, for example." He opened a folder on his desk and extracted a photographic plate which he held to the light of the windows. "These devices are not yet in general use within the profession, madame, but they will be within a very few years. The photographs are as yet indistinct, but they give the physician strong indications and are an invaluable diagnostic tool."

God in heaven, Adriana thought. He is going to lecture me on X-rays. She had a clear flash of memory: Dr. Danton sitting in the *sala mayor* at Santanilla discoursing on the unsuitability of treating Miguel with nitroglycerin. What was there about men that made them so eager to lecture women? Why did they assume that the female mind was incapable of understanding equal to their own?

"Are you all right, madame? Do you wish a glass of water?"

"Thank you, no, Doctor."

"Well, madame. The Roentgen plates would, of course, be meaningless to a layman." He returned the glass carefully to its folder. "But suffice it to say that in your case they show clearly that your carcinoma is well past the preinvasive state. It was not caused by your fall, by the way. It is a condition of long standing. Therefore the prognosis is guarded."

"Please be more precise, Dr. Weisskopf," Adriana said.

"Very well, madame. I believe your cancer to be inoperable. Of course, exploratory surgery is not totally contraindicated, but—" He tapped his mouth with his fingertips in a peculiarly nervous mannerism. "I must say frankly that the trauma in a woman of your age would be considerable."

"I see." How slowly one learned of one's fate, Adriana thought. Sentence by sentence, word by word.

"I can give you an estimate of the course of the disease. A fairly accurate one. You are in some pain now, I believe?"

"Yes," Adriana said.

"There will be more. It will have to be controlled with laudanum."

Adriana shivered.

"Adenocarcinoma metastasizes, usually to the lymphatic system, in seventy percent of the cases," Weisskopf said. "You will grow anaemic and quite weak. The weakness, however, may mitigate the pain."

"How fortunate," Adriana said faintly.

"You will find it so, madame," Weisskopf said.

"How long, Doctor?"

"Ah, madame. That is the question. Please understand that it is extremely difficult to predict. The human body is not a mechanical device, after all. Each patient reacts differently. However." Again the tapping of the lips with the fingertips. Was that this pedantic little man's device for reminding himself to remain aloof from the dying? Adriana wondered. "However. I believe you can be certain of six to eight months of relatively normal living. With care, of course. And many patients in your condition live a year or even eighteen months."

Adriana closed her eyes. I don't believe this now, she thought. But it will come to me. Each time I see clouds on a summer day. When I see my grandchildren playing. When Infanta nuzzles me for a bit of sugar. When the sunset turns the Pacific golden. When I remember

Miguel, and my father, and poor foolish Jean-Claude, and Aaron. Each one of those things and a thousand thousand more will say to me: *Never again, Adriana.*

"I am truly sorry, madame," the little man said. "It is never pleasant to say such things to a patient."

"You make the matter very clear, Doctor. I thank you for that." Adriana felt a sudden need to stand on the soil of Nueva Santanilla again, to feel the sea wind blowing against her face, to see Roberto and dear Ana-Maria and Tomasa and old Raoul. She longed to go home.

"I shall write to Dr. Harrison in detail, madame, outlining a suggested course of treatment."

"Yes, of course, Doctor."

Adriana stood erect, and the doctor, unexpectedly impressed by her carriage and bearing, came around his desk to escort her to the door. It was not his habit, and when she was gone from the consulting room he told himself that he had just passed sentence on an uncommon woman, and he was sorry for it.

"Alex, I don't *know* why she decided to return home tomorrow. I thought we had two more days." The last was said with with wrenching sorrow. Marianna stared down at the water splashing off the paddle-wheels, concentrating on the way it cascaded through the lights and down into the darkness. She did not want Alex to see that she was near to weeping.

They stood on the deck of the *Queen Charlotte,* a walking-beam side-wheel ferryboat that plied the water between San Francisco and Sausalito. They had come on board at four in the afternoon and this was their third round trip. Suddenly it seemed their only place of refuge.

Alex's face was made ruddy by the sun setting. The evening was clear, with a brisk westerly wind blowing across the waters of the bay. On the Marin shore Yellow Bluff was already in deep shadow. The *Queen Charlotte,* laden with persons who lived in Marin County and worked in the city, drove stolidly through the whitecapped chop of the strait toward Richardson's Bay. Alex and Marianna huddled together at the boat-deck rail, chilled by the wind and filled with despair.

"Marianna, do you want something hot to drink?" Alex asked.

"No," Marianna said miserably.

He removed his coat and put it over her shoulders.

"You'll freeze, Alex," she said.

"Don't go, Marianna," he said.

The girl shook her head. Her reddish hair whipped in the wind, lashing her cheeks. She brushed it back, brushed her eyes as well.

"You can't marry him," Alex said stubbornly.

"Alex, stop this. You'll make me cry." Marianna glanced at the strolling passengers. Incurious people, she thought, they don't know or care what we feel. They only look and turn away.

Alex put his arm around her and they pressed against the rail, not looking at one another but only at the sun, half sunken into the distant horizon. Gulls still flew over the *Queen Charlotte,* cawing and begging for tidbits. Some children raced by on the deck, laughing and shouting.

Alex said, "I love you, Marianna."

"Don't, Alex. Don't, don't, *don't.*"

"Let me speak to Uncle Roberto. Let me do that, at least."

"Please, please, Alex. I asked you not to say such things. It's too late for all that."

"Why, damn it, why?" His lips felt wooden from the cold. "This isn't Spain, Marianna. We don't have to live like that."

"I am promised, Alex. *Promised.* Don't you understand what that means? Oh, God, I shouldn't even be here with you. The *abuela* will be furious."

"How can you marry Colton when you love me?"

Marianna glanced again at a passing couple. "Alex, people will hear you."

"Let them. Let them hear me. Answer me, Marianna. How can you marry him when you love me?"

"I do *not* love you, Alex," Marianna said desperately.

"Look at me and say that."

A fat woman and a disheveled boy holding a piece of bread appeared to stand at the rail only feet from Marianna and Alex. The boy began to throw bits of bread into the air for the shrieking gulls.

"Let's go inside," Marianna said. "What time is it?"

"Seven o'clock."

"Oh God, the Patrona will be so angry, Alex."

"I will talk to her."

"You will *not,*" Marianna said. "Here." She took his coat from her shoulders and handed it back to him. She walked toward the door to the salon and he followed her, carrying the coat.

"Put it on," she said. "You mustn't get cold. Dear Alex." She stepped quickly over the coaming and into the steamy interior of the cabin.

The seats here were like church pews. Through the steel deck could be felt the thrumming of the steam engine deep in the bowels of the ferry.

Marianna sat down and said, "I think I would like some hot coffee now."

"I'll get it," Alex said. He went to the counter and ordered two coffees from the steward. They were served in thick white mugs bearing the device of the Southern Pacific Railroad. He paid and carried them back to Marianna.

"It is almost June. How can it be so cold?" Marianna said, shivering. She sipped at the steaming, bitter coffee.

The ferry turned toward the headland and made its way into the slip, an open V of planks and pilings. The passengers stood and began to file down the broad stairway to the main deck. Alex and Marianna remained alone in the large, low-ceilinged salon. The steamy air smelled of food and salt water.

"We have to go back," Marianna said.

"All right," Alex said.

Passengers for the return journey to San Francisco began coming into the salon. Alex glared at them when they seemed about to sit nearby.

"Please. Don't, Alex."

"We have to talk, Marianna."

"There is nothing to talk about. In a month you will have forgotten all the things we have said that we should not have said."

"Never. Not in a month, not in a dozen years. I love you. I have never loved anyone else. I *will never*—"

"Hush. Please." She touched his lips with her fingertips. He held them and kissed them. Her eyes filled with tears and she looked away. A man in a bowler hat looked at them disapprovingly. Marianna said, "Oh, I'd rather be cold. Let's go outside again."

They went out onto the deck. It was darker now and there were lights reflecting on the water. Below, on the main deck, the deckhands closed the barrier and the steam whistle blew. The mournful noise echoed off the wooded Sausalito hillsides. The ferry began to move again, out into the bay, and the wind grew colder. Overhead a thin crescent of moon hung in a dusky blue sky. Most of the gulls had perched on the pilings now and they bobbed their heads and watched the *Queen Charlotte* get once more under weigh.

They were alone on the boat deck now. The evening had grown even colder. The windows of the salon had fogged over with moisture.

They could see the other passengers moving indistinctly behind the misted glass.

Alex put his hand beneath Marianna's chin and lifted her face. Her cheeks were wet. He kissed her, long and gently.

"Oh, no, Alex. Please."

"I shall always love you."

She shook her head.

"I don't care about marriage contracts or houses or palomino horses or Santana honor. I will fight for you until the minute the priest says you are married. I can't help it, Marianna."

She rested her forehead against his chest and wept. "I will never forget you, cousin," she murmured.

"Because you love me. You don't love *him*."

"Please, dear Alex. No more. No *more*."

Alex unfastened his stiff collar and took a golden chain from his neck. From the links depended a polished coin.

He placed the chain over Marianna's head. "My mother gave me this," he said. "She had it from her father. It isn't Marburg and it isn't Santana. I want you to have it." He kissed the coin and let it fall between her breasts. "It isn't over, Marianna," he said. "When he comes to claim you, I'll be there. Yes, I will be there, and you can still change your mind." He held her, warming her by putting himself back to the wind. He could feel the slender firmness of her body, he could smell the fresh clean scent of her hair. I'll never give her up, he thought. If I am damned for it, so be it. Let the Marburgs and the Santanas and the Coltons rage, let the world crack. She belongs to me and I will never let her go. Never. Never. *Never.*

W hat was it, Adriana asked herself, that brought her now to this bluff overlooking the sea? It was here that Doña Maria lay beside poor Maria-Elena, two women under their great flat stones. But surely it was not morbidity that drew her to this place? She had never feared death—there had been no time in her life for such things. Yet the proximity of the dead gave her comfort. When I am here beneath my own slab of gray granite, I will not be alone, she thought. Perhaps that was why this high promontory, which she had always thought beautiful, attracted her so.

Behind her, Infanta snuffled softly as she grazed on the drying grasses. The ugly Viennese had been correct. There would be more pain. She felt it now each time she got into the saddle. What a bitter thing it was that her joy in riding free across the Marburg lands would be one of the first things to go. In just two weeks it had become difficult to ride. But she persisted. Each morning she would mount and ride as far as the bluff. There she would stop, set Infanta to grazing, and sit on the grass looking out over the empty sea.

Since her return from the city she had been almost totally self-absorbed. She realized this and felt a certain guilt for not taking a greater part in the bustle of preparations for the wedding that now occupied everyone else on Nueva Santanilla. Ana-Maria and Tomasa seemed concerned, but it would never have occurred to them to question her behavior. She was the Patrona and they were, despite all that had taken place, who they were born. How our bloodlines guide us, Adriana thought, generation after generation.

She smiled faintly. Don Alvaro, the self-taught liberal, would have frowned at such a thought. But Doña Maria, secure under a stone that bore the Santana coat of arms as well as the holy cross, must be smiling.

For a moment she was consumed with jealousy of her parents. How much easier it would be, she thought, to meet death as Don Alvaro had met it, violently, completely, and suddenly. Or as had Doña Maria, quietly and peacefully, full of years and waiting impatiently for the call to join her beloved Alvaro.

The jealousy swiftly dissipated. *Las Parcas nos mandan.* It was their fate to die as they had done. Her own fate was harsher, but it was her own.

She had not gone to see Roger Harrison after her return from San Francisco, and when it had become apparent to him that she did not intend to do so, he made an excuse to come to Nueva Santanilla to speak with her. "We will take it as it comes, young Roger," she told him. "When I need you I will send for you. But before that time you will speak to no one."

She thought frequently of Miguel now. His had been still another way of dying, slowly, so slowly. At least, she thought, I shall be spared that.

And she thought of religion.

For all the years of her life she had thought herself a conscientious, if not absolutely devout, Catholic. She had practiced the rituals and performed her genuflections. She had touched holy water to brow and breast and eaten the bread and drunk the wine that were the Body and Blood of Our Lord. As a girl she now remembered an unquestioning faith, a faith that had eroded slowly through the years until little save the rituals remained. She would have imagined that now was the time she would rush to return fully to the faith she had once known, but it had not happened that way. She found comfort in the candlelit stillness of the church, in the majestic beauty of the Mass, but she had no sudden urge to bury her face in the folds of the Virgin's garment, and that surprised her.

She, Adriana Marburg y Santana, who had given a daughter of her body to Holy Mother Church, stood curiously apart from all religion. How that would have distressed poor Father Sebastio. She raised her face to the sky. The summery day was clear; a great towering cumulus of fair weather hung motionless in the heights.

She said aloud, *"Orate pro nobis nunc et in hora mortis nostrae."* Pray for us now and in the hour of our death. She was tempted to ask: "Are You there? Are You *really* there?" And was there a purgatory where her soul must wait? A heaven and a hell? She found within herself no deep desire for reassurance from Father Clarence. What he knew to be *so* was the product of his own personal faith, and faith was not something transferable. It had surprised Adriana to discover that she was a doubter. Not that she was without hope. Never that. Our Lord on the Cross had said to Saint Dismas, "Today you shall be with me in Paradise." How very lovely it will be, she thought, if He spoke the truth. And if He did, what shall I say to Miguel and Don Alvaro and Doña Maria when I see them? Shall I say I was a sinner? Of course, she thought. But most of those sins I do not regret. I have no regret for having loved two men, though that might be thought a great sin indeed. She smiled thoughtfully. Jean-Claude was a very small sin. Yet even that I don't regret. So shall I go into the earth unrepentant, still filled with Santana pride?

She looked out over the empty ocean, at the twisted cypress and pines on the wooded slopes of Nueva Santanilla. She smelled the earth and the growing things in it. She looked across the hills at the sheep grazing peacefully in the home pastures. She listened to Infanta's hooves pawing at the ground, impatient for a gallop across the open fields. She saw the silver surf breaking on the distant rocky coast. She looked down at Nueva Santanilla's red-tiled roofs.

What I do regret, she thought, is that I shall soon experience all of this for the last time. Her eyes filled with unwanted tears, and she thought of Aaron. No, that was too hard to bear. I loved Miguel when I was a girl, she thought. Would he forgive me for loving Aaron when I became a woman? Time and fate would tell. But to die without ever seeing her last and true love again, *that* was bitter.

The memory of Aaron brought thoughts of young Alex. And Marianna. The girl seemed troubled and unhappy, not at all what a woman should be in anticipation of her wedding day. When Johnny Colton had come to inspect the new house with her, she had been distant, preoccupied. She had seemed unwilling to let him touch her. Had she fallen in love with Alex? Adriana wondered. In my own preoccupation, did I allow them too much freedom to be together? Or was it precisely this I intended? Have I grown foolish and meddlesome and romantic in my old age? Was something left undone here? Something brought into being by my own longing after a remembered love?

The wedding gifts were arriving. The invitations to the ceremony had long ago been sent. There were fiestas given for John and Marianna almost every night now by their friends. The banns had been published. That was what the girl had wanted since she was fifteen, wasn't it?

What I most desire now, Adriana thought, is her happiness. Perhaps it was foolish to see another as oneself reborn, and yet she had always felt so about Marianna. She is my heiress, Adriana thought, to some of my money and all of my heart.

She moved, and deep inside her a hot wire of pain pulled tight. She clenched her fists and closed her eyes until the spasm had passed.

Then she stood, gathered up Infanta's reins, and mounted to ride slowly back down the hill toward the ranch house.

Adriana awoke from fitful sleep aware that someone was whispering her name.

"Doña Ana, Doña Ana. *Por favor. Dispierta.*"

It was Felicia asking her to wake up.

Adriana, who had not fallen asleep until well after midnight, sat up in the vast bed and strove to organize her mind. The room was dark and cold. The fire on the hearth had burned down to embers. Felicia, looking disheveled in her nightdress and robe, had placed an oil lamp on the nightstand. She held the little *criada* Carmela by the arm as though the girl might bolt.

It did, in fact, look very much as though Carmela would do exactly that. She was fully dressed and badly frightened of Felicia, who looked both outraged and apprehensive in the Patrona's presence.

"Yes, Feli," Adriana said thickly. "What is it? What time is it?"

"It is after two, Doña Ana," Felicia said. She shook Carmela by the arm. "Now tell her, girl. Speak. Tell her what you told me!"

"Señora Felicia—" The girl was in tears. She whined as Felicia shook her again. "It's not my fault, *señora.* It isn't!"

"*Madre de Dios,* you stupid girl. Tell the Patrona what you told me. Tell her at once!"

"Let go of her, Feli. You are frightening her," Adriana said.

Felicia released her hold on Carmela's arm and the girl fell to her knees at Adriana's bedside. *"Por Dios,* Patrona. It is not my fault. I swear by the Blessed Virgin."

"What is not your fault, girl?" Adriana demanded. She placed a hand on the girl's head. "Now tell me what is troubling you."

The *criada* snatched at Adriana's hand and held it against her cheek. "I swear to you, Patrona. I begged her not to."

"You begged who? Not to do what?"

"Tell her, you wicked girl!" Felicia hissed. "Tell her at once."

"I have been Doña Marianna's maid, Patrona—since she came back from San Francisco."

"Yes," Adriana said evenly. "Go on."

"Ay, Patrona," the girl sobbed. "How can I tell you?"

Adriana suppressed a surge of impatience and apprehension. She spoke carefully and reassuringly. "Just tell me, Mela. You won't be punished."

Felicia made the sounds of reproval. Adriana silenced her with a look.

"Doña Marianna, Patrona, she has been going out late at night to meet a man." Carmela buried her face in the bedclothes as though she expected a rain of blows.

"Are you certain of this, Carmela?" Adriana asked.

"Oh, yes, Patrona. I have been keeping watch for her in her room."

"Hiding in her bed, Patrona," Felicia said, scandalized. "In case some one of us should look in. Foolish, stupid girl!"

"How many times have you done this?" Adriana asked.

"Three times, Patrona. Four, counting tonight," the girl said faintly.

"Tonight? Where is Marianna now? Has she left the ranch?"

"I don't think so, Patrona, not yet. She must still be in the stable saddling her horse."

"Feli," Adriana snapped. "Go to the stables at once. If she is there, tell her to stay where she is until I get there."

"Sí, Patrona. Shall I wake Don Roberto?"

"Certainly not. Now *go.* She is not to move until I come. Is that understood?"

"Sí, Patrona," Felicia hurried from the room. Adriana turned her attention to the whimpering Carmela. "Who has she been meeting late at night?"

"Oh, Patrona, I don't know—"

"Don't lie to me, Carmela. Is it John Colton?" The moment the words were spoken she knew that Marianna would never do this for a stolen hour with the Colton boy. "It is her cousin Alejandro, isn't it?"

Carmela, sobbing, nodded her head.

"Stop whimpering, girl. You are not to blame. You were doing only what Doña Marianna ordered you to do. Now get up and bring me my clothes. Riding clothes, girl. Hurry."

As she dressed she imagined the scene: Carmela hiding in Marianna's bed, Felicia looking into the room and finding her there—God knew how, but Feli was given to prying so it was hardly a surprise that the childish plot should be uncovered.

"Be still now, Carmela," she said. "I don't want the whole house awakened." She finished buttoning her buckskin riding jacket. "Now go to Don Raoul's room and awaken him. *Only* him, if you can. Tell him I need him in the stable. Tell him—" She cast about for a suitable tale. "Tell him Infanta is not well and I am with her. Doña Tomasa is not needed. Be certain to tell him that."

"*Sí,* Patrona."

"Go now. Swiftly and *quietly.*"

The girl vanished into the dark gallery and Adriana poured water from a pitcher into a basin and splashed her face. Then she went to her dressing table and overturned a jewel box. There were three one-hundred-dollar gold pieces there. She swept them into her palm and pocketed them, suddenly thinking of the new golden pendant Marianna was wearing. An Iturbide Mexican gold coin. A gift from her cousin, she had said. A wedding gift. Good God, Adriana thought. I have been such a fool.

She walked swiftly down the gallery and across the dark courtyard toward the stable. A single light was burning there. She could hear the horses, made restless by the presence of people at an unaccustomed hour.

She glanced at the sky. The night was dark, overcast and starless.

Felicia, fat and formidable, stood in the doorway to the tack room. Marianna's horse, one of the smaller geldings, stood in his stall, saddled. There were saddlebags on his crupper. Whatever this was, it was no silly night prank. Wherever Marianna had been going, this time she intended to stay.

"She is here, Patrona," Felicia said, still guarding the door to the tack room. She stepped aside and Adriana entered.

Marianna stood, dressed for riding, her hands white-knuckled on her crop, her face furious and tear-streaked.

"Go wait for Raoul, Feli," Adriana said. "When he comes, tell him to saddle Infanta."

"*Sí,* Patrona," Felicia said, looking at Marianna reproachfully.

When the *criada* had gone, Adriana faced her granddaughter. "Tell me why, Marianna," she said.

Marianna seemed about to speak in frustrated anger, but quite suddenly her expression changed to one of abject misery. "I cannot marry Johnny, *abuela.* I can't *do* it."

Adriana went to her and put her arms about her. "Why, dear one? It is what you have wanted since you were fifteen. When I said I thought it was not a good match, you fought me. Even your father had doubts, but it was what you demanded. What has changed?"

"Alex," Marianna said tearfully. "Alex has changed everything."

"I see."

"Do you really see, *abuela?* Have you ever loved a man?"

Adriana closed her eyes for a moment. "Yes, *corazón,* I have. As difficult as that may be for you to believe."

"Oh, Patrona. I didn't mean that the way it sounded. It is only that Alex and I love each other. I tried not to love him, *abuela,* truly I did. But I cannot bear it any longer. I was going to meet him tonight and we were to be married—" She gave Adriana a hunted look of despair. "Now, I don't know what I shall do. I *cannot* marry Johnny. I know how terrible that is to say, but I cannot do it. Oh, God, what will Papa say?"

Roberto would say that he and the family had been disgraced. God help him, Adriana thought, given the way we raised him, Doña Maria and I, what else could he say. He would stop the wedding—*that* he would do. But he would never give his sanction to a marriage between Marianna and her cousin—Aaron's son. On that point he would remain obdurate, even if it condemned his daughter to a life of misery. The man who killed Charlie Greer could never give his daughter to the son of the brother who had, in his eyes, abandoned the family.

Adriana felt the three gold coins in her pocket. If she had intended to take no part in this save stopping Marianna from ruining her reputation, then why had she taken the coins from the jewel box? I am too near my end to lie to myself, she thought.

Raoul Gomez peered into the tack room, his face confused and puffy with sleep. "Doña Ana? The girl said something was wrong with Infanta."

"There is nothing wrong with Infanta, Raoul. Saddle her," Adriana said.

"At this hour, Patrona?"

"Now, Raoul. Do it yourself. I don't want the *mozos* awakened."

"Patrona, I don't understand."

"Just do as I say, Raoul. You will oblige me."

"*Sí,* Patrona," the old Spaniard said, and withdrew, shaking his head.

"Where is Alex?" she asked.

"*Abuela—*" Marianna protested.

"Speak now, girl. Where is he?"

"At the junction of the Carmel road, *abuela.*"

"With that machine of his, of course?"

"Yes, Doña Ana."

"And where did you plan to go?"

"We could be in Salinas by morning, we thought. And then— anywhere Papa could not find us."

My poor Roberto, Adriana thought.

"What are you going to do, *abuela?*"

"*We* are going to speak to Alex tonight, at once. Then we shall see."

Adriana stepped out into the stable. Raoul had finished saddling Infanta and he stood at her head, his face a mirror of his worried perplexity. "You should not be riding alone at this time of night, Patrona. Wherever you are going, let me come with you."

"No, old friend. Not this time."

She indicated that Marianna should mount her gelding. To Raoul she said, "Help me up."

The pain snatched at her as she mounted Infanta. A cold sheen of sweat beaded her brow. She sat still until the pain subsided. Then she said, "Wait for me here, Raoul. The rest of you go to bed. I don't want anyone else disturbed this night."

She turned Infanta into the darkness. "Come, Marianna. Quietly."

They walked their horses until they were away from the house. There was a full moon now above the overcast that turned the cloud ceiling silvery. The road was a dim ribbon in the darkness. Adriana touched Infanta with the crop and the two women, grandmother and granddaughter, cantered through the night toward the Carmel road.

Alex Marburg, leaning on the fender of El Loco, heard the two horses approaching. It took him a moment to realize that there *were* two, and that Marianna had not come alone. He braced himself for whatever might come. His heart was pounding with excitement. If this meant a fight, if they had been discovered and the horsemen were Colton and Uncle Robert, then so be it. There was no turning back now. He had even written to his father, but he had so timed the letter that whatever his father chose to do would be too late.

He stood in the road in the dim light of the lowered acetylene headlamps and waited.

His heart gave a great leap when he recognized Marianna. And then he saw that the second rider was Doña Adriana. For a moment he faltered. The *abuela* could be a far more formidable obstacle than either Uncle Roberto or Colton.

The women dismounted and Marianna held the horses. Doña Adriana looked at Alex and said, "This is how you honor your family, Alejandro."

She could have said nothing more calculated to reduce him to shame. But he and Marianna had decided. They would live their own lives at any cost. He had hoped that what they had chosen to do could be done honorably, but even honor was not too great a price for Marianna. He would pay it if he must.

He tried to speak formally, but his voice sounded thin and without substance. "*Abuela,* I am sorry for the way this must be. I know how distressed you and Uncle Roberto will be. I did not—" He began again. "I never intended to bring trouble to the family. But how can I explain to you what has happened to me—to us? We love each other, Patrona. Give us your blessing."

"What an arrogant young man you are, Alejandro Marburg," Adriana said. "You ask my blessing, but you intend to do as you please with my blessing or without it."

Alex looked pleadingly at Adriana. Despair plucked at him. And then quite suddenly he realized that if the *abuela* had intended to stop them from eloping, she would never have brought Marianna with her. She would have come with Uncle Roberto, or even with a pair of vaqueros to enforce her commands.

Marianna had tethered the horses and she came to stand at his side. "*Abuelita,*" she said, "if you love us, help us."

"How very unfair are the young," Adriana said.

"We do not mean to be, Patrona," Alex said. "But we are fighting for our lives."

Adriana drew a deep sigh. "Where will you go?" she asked. "No. Don't tell me that. You, Alex, what will you tell your father?"

"What I can tell him, *abuela,* I already have. I wrote to him before I came back to Monterey. I told him what I intended to do. God help me, I took advantage of him. There has been an uprising of the *peones* on a hacienda near Hacienda San Jacinto. He must already be on the

551

way there to collect Doña Julia and my sister Marina and her new baby to take them to Mexico City. By the time he knows what I have done, he will be able to do nothing about it."

"Ah," Adriana said dryly. "Aaron will like that, won't he?"

"He will be very angry, *abuela*. I am sorry for that."

"You are sorry for a great deal, it seems, Alex Marburg," Adriana said sternly.

"I truly am," Alex said. "But not for this." He put his arm protectively around Marianna. "By tomorrow we shall be married."

"In a civil ceremony," Adriana said. "Hardly a marriage at all."

"The rest can come later. Please, *abuela*. Give us your blessing."

Adriana opened her arms and held them both. Do not deny it, she told herself. This is what you intended from the moment he first spoke to you about Marianna.

She kissed each one. "Now go. Go quickly and go far." She took the three gold pieces from her pocket and placed them in Marianna's hand. "Your dowry, God help us all."

The girl held Adriana in a long embrace.

"Go, *go*," Adriana said. Marianna broke away and retrieved her saddlebags. Alex sprang to crank the motorcar into life. He turned up the lights, flooding the road with a yellow glow and making shadows leap among the dark trees. This, then, is what romance will be in the twentieth century, Adriana thought ruefully. Noise and smoke and the stink of gasoline.

Over the clatter of El Loco could be heard the sound of a galloping horse. Someone was coming from Nueva Santanilla.

Alex put his arms around her and kissed her. "Thank you, *abuela*. God keep you."

Adriana said hurriedly, "I shall write to my bankers in San Francisco. If you need anything, make contact with them. Marianna will tell you who they are."

Alex clambered into the driving seat of the Locomobile. He gave a great, happy shout. "I have everything I need, Patrona! Everything!"

The car jerked into motion and rolled swiftly away, a traveling island of smoky light and noise in the pine and cypress forest. Adriana turned to meet the approaching horseman. It was Raoul Gomez.

"Patrona, what is happening? Who was that? Where is Doña Marianna? You told me to wait for you, but I could not obey you."

Adriana watched the glow of the motorcar's headlamps finally vanish in the distance.

Raoul had dismounted and was standing in the dark beside her. "What has happened, Doña Ana?"

"My granddaughter has eloped with her cousin Alejandro, old man. What do you say to that?"

"Is it what you wish, Patrona?"

Adriana placed a hand on Raoul's arm. "Yes, Raoul. It is what I wish."

"Then," the old Spaniard said firmly, "it is well."

The elopement of Marianna and Alex Marburg struck Nueva Santanilla like a clap of thunder. Roberto's first reaction was to enlist the services of the county sheriff to corral the lovers and return them for punishment. Adriana stopped any such move on the first day. Roberto was gray-faced with fury, but he had been ruled by women too long to defy his mother, even under such provocation as this.

Adriana had returned to Nueva Santanilla, dispatched Raoul to his bed (though not to sleep), and waited for the morning. When Nueva Santanilla began to stir, she went herself to the *alcoba* where Roberto and Ana-Maria slept and informed her son, in the simplest and most straightforward words, that he had better notify Young Colton that the engagement of Marianna Marburg and John Colton III was now at an end.

Roberto, fogged with sleep, listened with growing amazement and anger.

"You did this, Mama? You?"

"They did this, Roberto. I simply approved it," Adriana said. Ana-Maria, still huddled in the *leto matrimonial* in her wrinkled night-dress, listened wide-eyed.

"*Damn that boy,*" Roberto shouted. "I knew he was trouble the day he walked into this house."

Adriana regarded her son calmly. "John Colton was wrong for her, *hijo*. I told you so from the beginning."

Roberto went to the wardrobe and began dressing furiously, his mind a confused tangle of frustrations and prohibitions. The complications and ill-feelings that this would cause between Nueva Santanilla and Santa Marta were incalculable. But it was his mother's complicity that angered him most.

"Where are they?" he demanded. "Where have they gone?"

"Too far to recall now," Adriana said, with that maddening calm.

Roberto put his head through the open doorway and shouted for Raoul. He turned to his mother and said, "I'll have the sheriff find them. I'll have them brought back here. *Hijo de puta,* I'll kill that boy."

"You will do no such thing, Roberto," Adriana said. "And he is as well born as you are. So stop raging like a bull and accept it. They fell in love and they ran away to be married. There's an end to it. Now send a galloper to Santa Marta for Young Colton. We must put a stop to the preparations at once."

Roberto stood before Adriana, his face livid. "You favored Alex because he is Aaron's son. That's it, isn't it? Well, damn him. Damn Aaron. And God damn you, Mother."

"*Roberto!*" Ana-Maria, shocked, leaped from the bed and pushed her way between mother and son.

Adriana's blue eyes were steady, but they were filmed with tears. "Have no fear, Roberto," she said. "God already has."

"Doña Ana," Anita cried, "Roberto does not mean what he says."

Adriana turned and left the *alcoba* without looking back. Ana-Maria clutched her husband by the sleeves and shook him. "How dare you speak to her that way? What were you thinking of?"

Roberto pushed his wife away. "Leave me alone, Anita. For God's sake, let me be."

"She is the Patrona," Ana-Maria whispered.

"She is God's curse on me," Roberto said.

Ana-Maria crossed herself.

The house was stirring now. Roberto and Ana-Maria heard Infanta clattering out of the courtyard.

"Go after her, Roberto," Ana-Maria said.

Roberto sat down on the rumpled bed and shook his head. "I can't."

"You must."

"No, Anita. Let me be."

Ana-Maria Marburg sat beside her husband and pulled his head onto her breast. She knew him so well. She understood his deepest thoughts and shared his oldest memories. Would it never burst, she wondered, that hidden pocket of poison that tainted his kinship to the person he loved most in all the world?

Presently she said gently, "Don Raoul is coming, *viejo*. You will have to send him to Santa Marta with the news."

To dismantle all the preparations for a full Spanish *boda* due to take place in three days' time was a traumatic experience for everyone involved. There was the church to be notified, wedding gifts to be returned, decorations to be taken down.

Young Colton's anger had been only barely restrained short of insult. To have his son's fiancée snatched from under his long Colton nose by a Mexican stranger was a family humiliation that would plague relations between Nueva Santanilla and Santa Marta for generations. To this was added the older Colton's disappointment of the secret hope that Marianna would change Johnny Colton's dissolute ways.

The marriage contracts were destroyed, the agreements relating to land, stock, and water rights were declared null and void. The nearly completed house on the borderland between the ranches stood as an embarrassment to both families, empty and serving no purpose but to stand as a monument to scandal.

Johnny, drunk in a Monterey whorehouse, was heard to say that it was just as well it had happened this way, since he had been having many second thoughts about marrying a Jew.

The children of Nueva Santanilla, Día y Noche, told the vaqueros that *they* were delighted with Marianna's change of mind. Alex Marburg owned a motorcar and could sail a boat and would take them off one day to adventure in Mexico, where the Indians wore feathers and ate hearts. Johnny Colton could never have offered anything to equal that. Girls usually didn't show very good sense, they said, but this time Marianna had grown clever just in the nick of time.

Consuelo was of two minds about her sister's elopement. She was consumed with jealousy because she had planned to have Cousin Alejandro for herself as soon as she was old enough. But since that was now impossible, she intended to accept him as a brother-in-law with ladylike grace. Who could tell what romantic possibilities were contained in a relationship with the mysterious Mexican Marburgs?

Between Roberto and Adriana the tension remained electric. They saw one another only at mealtimes. Roberto set about burying himself in the business of running the ranch, while the Patrona spent more and more time away in the hills, riding on Infanta.

It seemed to Tomasa and Anita that Doña Ana grew frailer day by day. They attributed this to the state of affairs between the Patrona and Don Roberto.

And so the uneasy days slipped by at Nueva Santanilla. The date of the canceled wedding passed and the summer deepened, with the seasonal fogs climbing the wooded hills and shrouding the land.

Adriana was on the bluff, wrapped against the misty cold, when she saw a horseman, made small by distance, dismount before the ranch house.

It seemed to her in these dwindling days that her senses were sharper and more receptive than she ever remembered them being. The scent of a flower, the distant cry of a bird, the feel of the breeze upon her cheek seemed pure, each sensation worthy of noting and remembering. She found that she could recall times and events she had almost certainly forgotten until now. The odd twist of a fallen oak on the slope behind Don Alvaro's observatory, the musty smell of the holy water in the font of the cathedral in Santander, the droning Latin of Father Sebastio's rendering of the liturgy. All these things and more came into her mind and were there illuminated by an inner light, like the golden sun of a shortening day.

Sight, sound, taste, and touch, all took on a crisp identity reminiscent of childhood. The feel of a cat's fur under a stroking hand, the sharp and bitter tang of freshly brewed coffee on a chill morning, the melancholy grandeur of the *jotas* and *Malagueñas* played by old Raoul on his ancient guitar, the silvery sound of her grandchildren's laughter. These things, too, were made more beautiful and more poignant for being numbered.

Her estrangement from Roberto saddened her, but she found that she did not any longer have the strength to batter down the walls he erected between them. Time would reconcile him with Marianna. He loved the girl too much to remain obdurate. The longer future was now beyond Adriana's purview. Time and the fates had very nearly done with her, she knew. The darkness was falling, and it took all of her failing energy to remain unafraid.

When the horseman came, she stood and looked at the distant figure and thought: *Aaron.*

Infanta was restless and Adriana had difficulty mounting her without assistance. But she managed it and climbed into the saddle, ignoring the pain.

She touched the mare with her crop and set off down the slope from the bluff at a gallop, her hat on her back, the wind snatching at her hair. It did not for a moment occur to her that she might be mistaken. With her new clarity of perception she had recognized Aaron. There could be no doubt whatever that it was he.

She galloped Infanta straight into the horsebarn with an abandon she had not indulged since she was a girl in the Cantabricas. She called for a *mozo,* tossed him her reins and slipped to the ground. Her heart was beating swiftly. Raoul appeared at a run.

"Patrona! Don Aaron is here, *here, now!*"

"I know, old man, I saw him from the bluff. Where is he?"

"In the *sala mayor,* Patrona. With Don Roberto," Raoul said breathlessly. "They are arguing."

As she hurried along the gallery toward the *sala,* Adriana could hear angry voices. One, unmistakably Aaron Marburg's, was shouting: "What have you done to my son? Where is he?"

Roberto's voice trembled with fury. "What have *I* done with your son? God curse you and damn you. He came here like a thief in the night and stole my daughter—!"

Adriana stood in the doorway to the *sala,* riding crop in hand. Aaron, graying now and with his face deeply lined, stood face to face with his brother.

Adriana struck the wall with her crop. The crack of the leather against the adobe was like a pistol shot. Ana-Maria, who stood fearfully watching the two angry men, gave a sharp gasp.

Adriana said, "You have not seen one another for forty years and this is the way you speak to one another? *You are brothers!*"

The two Marburgs turned, startled.

Aaron met her eyes. "Ana," he said. *"Ana."*

He strode across the room to stand before her, his anger forgotten in the rush of other emotions. He reached out to touch her cheek with his fingertips. "My dear, dear Ana. How I have longed for this moment."

"And I," Adriana said. She could feel the flush in her cheeks, the surging rush of memory. *"Corazón,"* she said, uncaring.

"Stop this. Damn you both, stop this!" Roberto's protest was a cry of anguish.

Ana-Maria rushed across the room and clung to him as he glared wild-eyed at his mother and half-brother.

Adriana looked away from Aaron to Roberto. The momentary joy in her face was gone, replaced with a sad, deeply troubled look. "Roberto," she said, gently. "Look at us, *hijo*. We are old. Be kind, Roberto. I beg you."

Roberto's face was drawn, the skin pulled tight across the bones. "Must I be kind to your lover? Holy Mary, how can you ask such a thing?"

Ana-Maria turned to Adriana in tears. "Patrona, forgive him. He does not mean what he says."

Roberto said, "I mean it, Anita. You know that I do. You were there. You remember. You saw them together. Damn you, damn you both."

Aaron stood staring at his younger brother with eyes as hard as iron. "How dare you, Roberto," he said coldly. "How dare you speak to her that way? Who gave you the right to judge her? Damn me all you choose, but speak to her that way once more, and I swear to God I will kill you."

Adriana said, "Aaron, no."

"Let me speak, Ana. It is long past time someone did." He placed himself squarely before his brother. "Look at me, Roberto. Yes, *look* at me. What do you see?"

"I see my mother's lover who was her stepson, and it sickens me."

"Then look again, little brother," Aaron said. "Let *me* tell you what you see. You see a man who has loved Adriana Santana all of his life, and who is prouder of that than of anything he has ever done. Now let me tell you what *I* see. I see the brother who was loved and cared for from his first hour. By that woman who stands there. I see a house and land, a whole life here, that you owe to her." He drew a deep breath and slowly his tone became less angry. "How dare you make judgments on her, Roberto! What did she do that was so wrong? She took me for her lover —and why not? She was a free woman. Our father had been dead for years. What did you expect of her? She was married when she was a girl. She was widowed before she was thirty. What would you have had her do? Join a nunnery? She loved me. I thank God for it. We were of an age. We were not related by blood. By God, we could have gone off together and made a life, and who had the right to say no to us? You? The ghosts we live with? If she had given me one indication, one hope, I would have turned my life upside down to stay with her. Damn you, boy, don't you realize what she did for all of you? Don't you realize how hard she worked to build all this? For you, Roberto. For you and your children.

559

And you dare to judge her? What a fool you are." He regarded his brother's stricken face with an expression almost of compassion. "Oh, I know. You are what they made you, all of them. They did it out of love, but God help them, they made you into an intolerant man." A bleak smile touched his lips. "I suppose it is the most natural thing in the world that you and I should dislike one another. You may not remember, but I do. Micah never loved me. He tried, but he couldn't manage it. He loved you. Everyone loved the golden child. By the time I was old enough and had seen enough not to hate you for it, it was too late. And I loved your mother, Roberto. I loved her from the first moment I knew her. So there was no way for you and me to be brothers. So don't ever again speak to her as you just did."

He blew his breath out and ran a hand across his stubbled cheek, his anger spent. "There. That was years in the making." He took Anita by the hand. "I want no family quarrel here, Anita. I only came to find my foolish son. And it seems I have come too late for that. Well, Roberto?" He extended his hand. "We may never be friends. But can we be brothers now?"

Roberto sat down on a couch and buried his face in his hands. Ana-Maria said softly, "Leave me alone with him, Don Aaron. Please."

Aaron nodded and walked across the room to put his arm around Adriana's shoulders and guide her out into the gallery.

"My gallant knight," she said ironically.

"We were born four hundred years too late, you and I," he said with a wry smile. "Did he hear anything I said, Ana? Did he listen?"

"Who knows? You may be right. We tried too hard to make him a Santana, we women. We should have remembered that he is first a Marburg." She walked slowly at Aaron's side, loving the touch of his arm across her slender shoulders. "My dear," she said, "ten years ago I would have taken you straight to my bed and let the world go hang."

Aaron's pleased smile took years from his face. "You said we are old. Not you, Ana. Not ever."

She thought of Doña Maria and Father Sebastio. There were worse things than to live long and die full of years. But she shook off the darkening mood.

Aaron asked, "Tell me frankly. What did you think of my son? I always hoped you would approve of him."

"Having him near me was like seeing you again. He is no boy, Aaron. He is a man, and he knows what he wants."

"And takes it," Aaron said. "What is Marianna like? Is she the same?"

"I fear so. They may be too much alike to have a peaceful life. But they love one another, of that I am certain. Be good to them, Aaron."

"I assume I will hear from Alex eventually," Aaron said.

"You are closer to him than I."

"I doubt that. You have always known the Marburg men better than they know themselves."

"Do you think so?"

"Believe it, Patrona."

They had reached the end of the gallery. Aaron's hired nag stood patiently at the hitching rail.

Aaron said, "Tonight a ship will be calling at Monterey for me, Ana. I must be in Tihuacan in three days and in Sonora in four more. There is trouble there. There will be a revolution in Mexico soon. It's in the air."

Adriana placed a hand on his arm. "We will make the best of what time we have," she said.

"I am sorry. I didn't mean to rush into your life again for an hour or two. I always hoped that we would have some time for one another."

"Las Parcas, corazón," Adriana said with a sad smile. "We have until nightfall. Be grateful."

She guided him up to the bluff in the deep afternoon. While their horses grazed, she showed him where Doña Maria lay beneath her great granite stone. He knelt and crossed himself in the Mexican manner, brow and breast. So he has some religion after all, Adriana thought. That is a good thing. It will sustain him as he grows old.

Aaron regarded the Santana arms on the marker. With a finger he traced the incised letters. *"Yo perduro,"* he said. "You do that, you Santanas."

"It is in the blood," Adriana said.

"Don Alvaro said something like that to me years ago." He stood and said, "I still remember him so clearly, Ana."

"He thought well of you."

"I am glad of that," Aaron said. "And the old Patrona—did she ever learn tolerance?"

"A little," Adriana said. "A very little."

"How she disapproved of me."

"She was sorry when you went away."

Aaron looked across Doña Maria's marker. "And that is Roberto's Alvarez bride," he said somberly. "Twenty-five years old. What a pity."

561

"Ana-Maria has been a good wife to Roberto," Adriana said.

"New ways for a new country?"

"They have loved one another since they were children. What else really matters?"

"If love were all that mattered," he said, looking at her. "Our lives would have been different."

"We do what we must, *corazón.*"

He placed his hands on her shoulders. "You have always been the Patrona."

"How very stern you make me seem," Adriana said.

He half-smiled at her. "Not stern, Ana. Noble, perhaps. But that is in the blood too. Someone must lead us lesser mortals. Who better than the lady of Santanilla?"

"Oh, my dear love," Adriana murmured. "We are all mortal."

The westering sun had burned away the bank of summer fog except for small patches of mist clinging to the forested slopes below. There was a sunpath of golden coins on the sea.

Aaron and Adriana walked slowly up the slope to a place where the grass held the last of its vernal green.

Aaron regarded her searchingly. "Are you well, Ana? You seem frail."

"Santanas are never frail," Adriana said firmly. "Ribby, sometime, like cattle on poor grass. But never frail."

He laughed and kissed her on the lips.

She pressed her cheek against his chest so that he could not see the tears that sprang to her eyes. She could hear the beating of his heart.

The sunpath broadened on the Pacific. Two hawks soared on the currents of air rising from the warm ocean. Adriana spread her skirt and sat on the grass. Aaron said, "Not a day goes by in my life, Ana, that I do not think of you." And he remembered Santanilla, the old hacienda, in this same ruddy sunset light.

She touched her fingertips to his lips.

Presently he said, "Tell me something."

"What thing, my love?"

"Micah. Why did you ever marry him? He was old."

"Old? He was forty when we met." She seemed amused.

Aaron was forced to smile. "He seemed old to me."

"But handsome," she said firmly. "All the Marburg men are handsome."

"You loved him? You truly loved him? I could never bring myself to believe it."

"Oh, my dear," Adriana said gently. "Love is many things. We know that, you and I. You love your Julia. I should be sorry if you didn't."

"Ana," he said. "You are a woman of quality."

She looked out over the land to the gilded sea with an enigmatic smile.

He stood and helped her to her feet. The movement gave her pain, but she did not show it.

"It is late," he said.

"Yes. Very late."

"I will go down and try to make peace with Roberto. Will you come?"

She sighed. "No. I leave that to you."

He took her hands. He was filled with a sense of urgency he could not define. "I will come back, Ana. I give you my promise."

"Corazón," she said, her eyes shining. "You will find me right here."

He took her in his arms and kissed her and she thought: This is the last time, the very last.

She watched him mount his rangy horse and canter slowly down the slope in the lengthening shadows. He turned in the saddle to look back.

When she could see Aaron no longer, Adriana looked seaward. The sky was ruddy and the sun touched the horizon. The day was nearly ended now.

Noble, he said. She smiled. Well, I am hardly that. I have lived as I was born to live. Without regrets. And I would do it all again, if God permitted. Pride, she thought, it was always my surpassing sin.

El Patron was right. The Fates do command us—even at the end, into the dark. But when one is loved—oh, when one is truly loved—one does not go into the night alone.